THE CHIVALRY OF CRIME

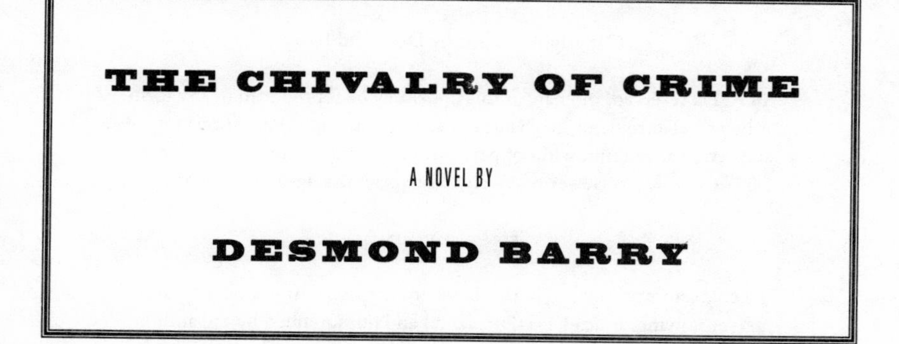

THE CHIVALRY OF CRIME

A NOVEL BY

DESMOND BARRY

LITTLE, BROWN AND COMPANY

BOSTON NEW YORK LONDON

FIRST EDITION

The characters and events in this book are fictitious. Any similarity to real persons, living or dead, is coincidental and not intended by the author.

LIBRARY OF CONGRESS CATALOGING-IN-PUBLICATION DATA
Barry, Desmond.
The chivalry of crime : a novel / by Desmond Barry. — 1st ed.
p. cm.
ISBN 0-316-12038-3
1. James, Jesse, 1847–1882 Fiction. 2. Ford, Robert, 1862–1892 Fiction. I. Title.
PR6052.A7274C48 2000
823'.914 — dc21 99-21443

10 9 8 7 6 5 4 3 2 1
MV-NY
Printed in the United States of America

No one should know more about Jesse James than I do, for our men have tracked him from one end of the country to the other. His gang killed two of our detectives, who tracked them down, and I consider Jesse James the worst man, without exception, in America. He is utterly devoid of fear, and has no more compunction about cold-blooded murder than he has about eating his breakfast.

Robert A. Pinkerton, *Richmond Democrat*, November 21, 1879

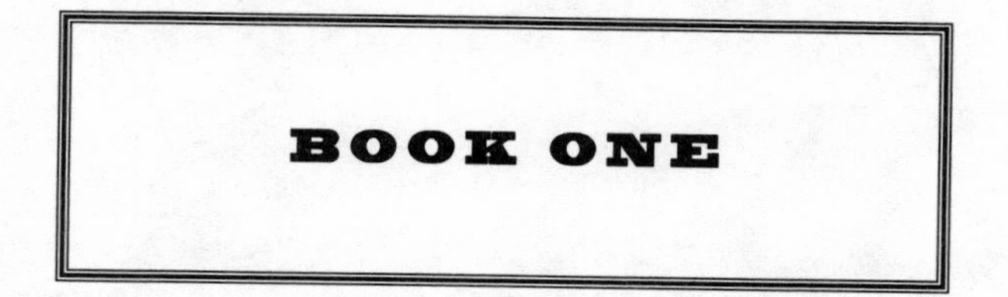

BOOK ONE

1

JOSHUA BEYNON WAS A WOULD-BE SHOOTIST WHO OWNED NO GUN. He was fifteen, big-boned, limbs all angles, back bowed as he leaned over the leather-bound ledger that was set square on the blotter of his rolltop desk. He breathed in the musty scent of dust, the sweet odor of bone meal glue, and faint traces of his mother's perfume. The ledger was fat and stiff with the clippings and pictures fixed onto its pages. He settled his shiny-peaked conductor's cap onto the back of his head and pushed his glasses tight to the bridge of his nose. Yellow light from the kerosene lamp flashed upon the lenses. He turned to the next empty page in the ledger and smoothed it down with a well-scrubbed hand. The ink bottle stood next to the brass writing set. He eased the cork out of it, careful not to stain his fingers. He laid the cork down next to the bottle, took his wooden-shafted pen, dipped the nib into the liquid, leaned over the ledger, and wrote in perfect copperplate across the lines and columns of the numbered page.

Friday, May 13, 1892

I did an extra few hours at Frazee's today, for he received a delivery of pickles from Denver, and he wanted me to unload the barrels. My clothes stink of brine, but I did earn an extra ten cents. I was in the store when a gambler from Kansas City came in. He sold to Frazee a Colt .45 caliber Peacemaker revolver. It is a similar model to the pistol once carried by Jesse James, but it takes bullets instead of cap and ball. Frazee allowed me to hold the gun. It is perfectly balanced from front *sight to polished walnut grip. The pistol comes in a somewhat battered wooden box that is lined with red velvet — unfortunately a little oil-stained. Frazee has given the gun pride of place in the glass-topped cabinet next to his cash register. I am sure he will sell it quickly, for he is asking but $5.75.*

Joshua laid his pen down on the groove of the writing set. He pushed his glasses back up onto the bridge of his nose again. From the bottom right-hand drawer of his desk, he took out a prettily painted porcelain pig that had once belonged to his sister. He stood the pig behind the blotter and the ink pot. Pink china tinkled as he dropped a new dime into the slot in its back. A pleasant sound, certainly, but not nearly pleasant enough. He was far short of $5.75. He turned to the last pages of the ledger. The glue had come unstuck on the corner of a small advertisement for an Iver Johnson .38 caliber revolver that Joshua had clipped from the Sears Roebuck Catalogue. He smoothed down the corner of the illustration. He knew the text by heart. The gun was nickel plated, fully automatic, and available for the price of $3.37, plus seventeen cents postage. Until that afternoon, Joshua had thought the Iver Johnson revolver a practical gun — certainly affordable — quite adequate. But there was no comparison with a Colt .45.

Joshua took his pen and once more dipped it into the ink bottle. He added .10 to the column of figures to the right of the advertisement, drew a short line beneath it, and recorded the new total: $2.64. He was pitifully short of the amount he needed. His plan would have to work perfectly. Right now, his father would be leaning on the bar of Soapy Smith's Orleans Club, on Amethyst Street. Within an hour, the old man would return home drunk and generous to the point of folly. Joshua could get the money out of his father as long as he timed the request perfectly. He had successfully done so in the past for smaller amounts, so why not now, with the beautiful Colt at stake? No matter what time his father came home, Joshua would be awake. He had often waited up for his da in the empty house. The time when his da came home from the bar seemed to be the only occasion that Joshua saw him these days. Certainly the only time when his father was happy. Joshua had to stay awake.

He turned the stiff pages of the ledger and stopped a third of the way through the book at his latest acquisition, a daguerreotype of Clell Miller, once a member of the James Gang. The black eyes were wide open, the skin pocked by buckshot, and an autopsy scar made a ragged line on the dead bandit's upper chest. The daguerreotype had been made right after the Northfield, Minnesota, raid. Joshua had fixed Miller's image onto the page next to a true prize: a picture of Jesse James himself, bearded, head askew, eyes closed, as he lay in his coffin. He had bought the prints through the mail from advertisements in the *Police Gazette*. Morbid, his father had called them. But Joshua was obsessed by the reality of them. And what was more real than a man in a coffin?

Joshua was sick of dreams. It was a dream of quick riches that had dragged his father across the ocean and half a continent, family in tow, from Wales to this mining valley in Colorado. But what had they found? Pneumonia had killed his mam, his younger sister, Elsa, and his baby brother, Ewan, and left his da bitter and Godless when once the family had been devout. Day and night, as Mam lay in a fever, Joshua and his da had been on their knees praying to an indifferent God, a God who had let Mam die, drowned by the fluids in her lungs. God, in His infinite cruelty, had destroyed her. Was there a way to wreak vengeance upon God? The preachers said that God was wounded by every sin of man. Joshua had resolved that he would wound Him, then, by breaking His commandments. On the Sunday after Mam's death, Da had not risen for chapel and Joshua rejoiced in the transgression; neither of the surviving Beynons had heard hymn nor homily since.

God's greatest power lay in the taking of life, as he had taken Mam away. If Joshua was to oppose God, he needed to understand that mystery. And who could know death more intimately than a murderer? As far as Joshua was concerned, the best thing about living in Weaver, Colorado, was that he lived in the same town as Robert Ford, who had made a corpse of Jesse James. The same corpse in the daguerreotype upon which Joshua now laid his fingertips.

The chair scraped against the pine floor as Joshua stood up. He crossed the room to where his pea coat hung on the back of the bedroom door and slid a folded magazine from his coat pocket. It was the latest issue of the *Log Cabin Library*. The magazine had come into Frazee's store that very day. Joshua couldn't resist buying it even if it meant having ten cents less to put toward the cost of the gun. Without taking his boots off, he lay down on his bed, careful not to dirty the red-and-blue patchwork quilt that his mother had made not a month before she died.

JESSE JAMES'S HUNT TO THE DEATH was the magazine's banner headline. Below it, in an etching, the bearded Jesse James pointed a six-gun at two Mexicans. Next to the hero stood a dark-haired woman with a knife. If this story couldn't keep him from sleep, nothing could. Joshua opened the magazine and began to read from where he'd left off at Frazee's:

After Frank and Jesse walked about the premises for a while, a little old Mexican with a face of parchment and a mouth that had not seen a tooth for twenty years mumbled out something to the effect that the proprietor of the ranch, the Señor Manuel, was ill and could not take part in the coming festivities.

"I wonder," said Frank to Jesse, "if he is the Manuel who supported Vasquez in the flat, who was plugged in the arm by a shot from your pistol?"

"I don't know," returned Jesse, "but I tell you what, Frank, I am going to find out."

The words on the paper began to blur. Joshua found himself full of thoughts of the Colt and Frazee's voice and columns of figures that didn't add up and the rocking motion of a clipper ship.

It was the clatter of china that woke him up. The kerosene lamp sputtered on the desk. Gray dawn light paled the window.

–Dammit!

The magazine had fallen to the floor. Had his father just come in? Had he slept? It must be around five A.M. If his da was in the kitchen now, he would already be preparing to go to work, still drunk. Joshua rolled out of bed. He opened his bedroom door and descended the dark and narrow stairs. The kitchen was in gray shadow, unlit. His father sat bent over the kitchen table, the heavy shoulders hunched, the wiry dark hair sticking up in tufts. All he could see of his father's face was the line of the thick eyebrows. A cup lay on its side in a saucer. Pale brown tea pooled on the red-and-white checked oilcloth. His father didn't look up at him but dipped a finger into the liquid and traced savage zigzag patterns over the tabletop. Joshua sat down at the table.

–Want another cup of tea, Da?

His father lifted his head. The bleary eyes were sunk into dark hollows. He was unshaven. The big nose was just like Joshua's own, though no spectacles hung upon them. Dried spittle whitened the corners of his wide mouth. Joshua knew that he should keep his own mouth shut. The reek of alcohol and tobacco was stale. The taut and creased gray skin of his father's face was evidence of a foul hangover. But when would there be another secondhand Colt .45 caliber Peacemaker revolver sitting beside Frazee's cash register? Frazee would sell the pistol that very day.

–Da, there's a fine pistol at Frazee's. It's only five seventy-five.

The right side of his father's wide lip curled to reveal yellow-stained teeth. His face seemed to grow larger and nearer.

–Are you going to war, boy?

Joshua's face grew hot from his neck to the tips of his ears. He stayed silent.

–A noonday showdown, I shouldn't wonder.

His father winced and put a hand to his forehead.

–Frazee would give it to me for five and a quarter, Da.

–You will strut down the street with your pretty little gun and be shot like a dog by the first drunken hothead who is spoiling for a fight. A fine end it will make for you.

Joshua knew that he needn't panic. He just needed a cold, hard reason that his father would have to at least consider.

–Weaver is full of thieves, Da. You know that. You heard about Mr. Atkins being robbed. He said to me, Joshua, if I'd had a gun, I would have shot the swine as he came through the window.

His father licked at cracked lips.

–There's nothing in this house to steal.

–What about your cash box?

–What bloody cash box?

Joshua couldn't believe the pathetic pretense.

–The one you're always digging into, before you go out drinking. The one that you keep in the bottom of your wardrobe.

A muscle in his father's cheek began to flutter slightly.

–Don't you touch a penny of that, do you hear me? If you touch a bloody penny of that, I'll flay you, I swear it. Now, you watch your lip, boy.

–I've got two sixty-four, Da. I'll pay you back.

–You wish to spend two days' pay for a working man on a broken-down, secondhand pistolero's pistol. Have you no sense?

His father swept his hand across the table but missed the crockery. Stooped over, he stumbled toward the kitchen sink. Joshua was sure the old bastard was about to throw up. There was a hiss as his da sucked air between his teeth and brought himself under control. Joshua didn't look at him but sat bent over in his chair, hands dangling between his knees. His father crossed the flagstoned kitchen and scooped up his caped topcoat and tall beaver hat from the floor next to the kitchen door.

–I am going to work, now, to earn the money to feed you. And you, you can cut firewood and stoke the stove. Then you may go to your job at Frazee's to earn yourself a bit of pocket money, but don't think about any gun, anymore. Understand me?

Joshua didn't answer. He looked down at the crumbs that littered the floor directly beneath the table. The kitchen door opened, and his father stepped out onto the gravel. Stone crunched, crunched ever quieter as the footsteps receded down the path.

Joshua straightened up and walked over to the potbellied stove. He grabbed the poker and drew it back as if he would slam it against the black cast iron. Then he spun and threw the poker across the table, where it shattered the overturned tea cup. Shards and poker clattered on the flagstoned floor.

–You bloody drunkard! he yelled. Keep your bloody money.

Tears formed behind the thick lenses of his glasses.

–Bugger you. I'll get it without you, you skinflint, drunken bastard.

He bumped his shoulder on the lintel of the door as he made for the stairs.

–I don't care a damn.

The money in the porcelain pig was enough to make a down payment. Frazee would accept it, he was sure.

II

JOSHUA LOCKED THE WEATHERED DOOR AND SLIPPED THE COLD iron key into his pea coat pocket. A gust of wind battered against him. He pushed his glasses up tight to his forehead and pulled his lapels shut over the porcelain pig that nestled, bulky and hard, next to his chest. Tugging down the peak of his conductor's cap, he set off down the steep path toward the town. Below him, the tumbledown buildings of Weaver were crammed into the cranny of West Willow Creek Canyon. The white spire of the post office clock tower rose above the roofs of the shacks and the flop hotels and the white canvas ridges of the tent stores. The hands on the clock read ten minutes past eight. He was certain that the Colt Peacemaker could not have been sold. He would arrive at Frazee's store a few minutes late, after its opening, certainly, but before any significant number of customers had come to buy.

Where Joshua's side of the valley doglegged to the north, a shaft of light broke through the pearl gray cumulus and lit up Bulldog Mountain, turning its crags a fierce red. Below the mountain's rocky dome, dark green pines swept down toward the southern rim of the canyon, but the trees stopped abruptly some fifty yards higher than the canyon's edge. A broad swath of destruction had been cut across the slopes by ax and saw. Among the clear-cut stumps and slash, smoke rose from the stacks of three log-built engine houses that housed the gear for the cages and the crushers and — most important of all — the cableway. It was Da who had convinced the owners of the Amethyst Mining Company that they should invest in it. A line of rusty buckets made jerky and squeaky progress from the Amethyst Mine's spindly tower and across the huge outpouring of shattered rock that cascaded from canyon rim to valley floor, the tailings disgorged from the ore sorters. The rattle and clatter of stone on metal echoed down the valley as the buckets emptied into the chute of the turn station — a ramshackle shed on stilts that squatted above the tram track — and into a waiting ore wagon below it. The empty buckets swung out of the shed and rose on the cable, back toward the mine where his da — nursing his headache, no doubt — was in one of the buildings that teetered on the edge of the canyon's rim. His da, who would take a belt to him for sure should he ever find out that Joshua intended to defy him and buy the Colt Peacemaker that awaited in Frazee's store.

But you will never see that gun, Joshua thought.

His broken boots ground the gravel of the path down to town. He would need to hide the pistol. Across the valley, the red rock outcrops and pine-covered slopes of Campbell Mountain rose to over eleven thousand feet. There were plenty of places over there where he could hide a gun. Equally, he could wrap the pistol in oilcloth and hide it among the pines on the hillside behind his house. But he would prefer to keep it close to hand. If in his bedroom, perhaps he might hide it behind the books on his bookshelf. Or pry up a floorboard.

A serried rank of rotted planks bridged the feeder creek that cut the hillside and formed the narrow gulch below him that was filled with the stilted stores and tent platforms of Weaver's Amethyst Street. Twenty yards downstream, among the broken rocks, a blue-gray coon hound sniffed and skipped and snapped at the foam that splashed over the sandstone blocks.

–Get on Carys, you bitch, Joshua called to the dog. Ca-rys! Ca-rys!

The hound splashed across the churning waters of the creek and dashed up the bank and onto the path. She shook, spraying him with water.

–Damn you, Carys! he yelled.

Joshua picked up a stone and threw it ahead of them, where it skipped and bounced into the noisome pile of garbage that marked the beginning of Amethyst Street. Carys ran nose down after the stone, her paws scrabbling at the ashes and vegetable peelings, shattered plaster, and broken lath on the pile. The path turned to mud as it entered the top end of the street. The narrow thoroughfare was cut up with hoofprints, marked with wagon tracks, and scattered with yellow manure, though not a horse or a mule was in sight. The tent stores, rough pine shacks, and jerry-built hotels that led down the hill toward Main Street were coming alive for Saturday morning business.

On the left-hand side of the street, in the window of Chang Jen Wa's laundry, a wizened old pigtailed Chinaman was bent over a board. His elbow swung back and forth, back and forth, the hot iron in his fist flattening down the creases on a pair of trousers. What dream had drawn him across the Pacific? Hour after hour, day after day, that Chink would work his futile way toward death in this narrow rock canyon thousands of miles from his birthplace.

Next to the laundry, built on a stilted platform, was Bob Starks's mining supply store. Starks — a beanpole of a man with a full beard that reached to his chest — was already hanging pans and sieves and shovels onto the outside walls of the store. Equipment for the pursuit of more foolish dreams.

Joshua crossed through the mud and onto the boardwalk that led to Greene's Assay Office. The stink of horse piss rose pungent and stale as the walking boards bounced under his soles. Greene's shiny-paned bay window seemed out of place on this rundown side street. Joshua tilted his head in front of the flawed glass panes, and his bespectacled face stretched and melted like pale pulled taffy. He did not look like a shootist. Not like Mr. Ford. Or Jesse James. Joshua thought he looked more like a gangly sailor, perhaps, in his pea coat and peaked cap. But a gun would not be out of place in a sailor's hand. He imagined the heft of the revolver and the desire for it drew him away from his distorted reflection and he hurried toward Frazee's once more.

He crossed the alley between the Orleans Club and Tilly's hard goods store, where the mud was ankle deep. Water seeped into Joshua's split boots until he reached the decently built boardwalk outside the Orleans Club. He scraped his boots against the doorstep. The double front doors were shut at this time of day and the brown-stained curtains drawn. The girls who worked the four-bed crib attached to the building were no doubt asleep. Joshua shifted the porcelain pig beneath the lapel of his pea coat. Here was another mystery in his life that he wished to unravel. He desired to lose his virginity in the same way he desired to possess the gun. The loss of one and the acquisition of the other could be accomplished by the same means. In Weaver, all things were possible with money. The women of the Orleans Club sold their bodies for money. But when he thought of gratifying his desire with a fallen woman, an unnameable dread gnawed within him, clawing its way up his back like a physical creature. He had no misgiving about defying the Commandments, but such fornication would somehow be a betrayal of his mam. He feared that his da had already done such a thing, and even the thought of it angered him, fueled his rage against his father, and increased his desire for the gun.

Rain began to spit. Joshua rushed down the plank decking. He ran toward the junction of Amethyst and Main Streets, boots thumping on the boards. Four pear-shaped Polish women came out of the front door of Frazee's General Store and opened up their red, green, yellow, and blue umbrellas. The wind filled the colored canvas, twisting the umbrellas in the women's grips. Still running full tilt, Joshua bumped among the broad-beamed women, the umbrella spokes clawing at his shoulders as he hurried by.

–Sorry! Sorry! he yelled.

The women cursed him roundly in their incomprehensible gutturals. These great fat women who opened their white thighs for their miner husbands were as untouchable to him in his lust as the virginal girls down in Creede, where he went to school. Joshua rattled through Frazee's front door and swung it shut behind him. He twisted back and caught the handle just in time to stop it banging.

–What the hell's your hurry, boy?

It was Frazee who had addressed him, but four other men stood in front of the long wooden counter, while Frazee was behind it. Frazee was an inordinately tall man whose gray mustache and thick head of gray hair made him look older than his actual years. His hands were tucked in behind the bib of his gray apron. Above him towered shelves that were loaded with cans and sacks and dark brown bottles. On the counter in front of him was an open wooden case with a red oil-stained velvet lining. It was empty. Every muscle in Joshua's long body contracted. The shelves full of cans and biscuit boxes seemed to lean inward as if they would bury him.

Soapy Smith stood to the left of the cash register. The beautiful Colt revolver lay on the flat of his palms. It looked as natural in his hands as it might in those of Jesse James or Robert Ford, for Soapy was the town's potentate of vice: a gambler, a whore-master, an employer of con men, bouncers, card dealers, and faro wheel operators. He was named Soapy for the slippery cons upon which he had founded his empire. A smile lifted his bristling mustache and his heavy cleanshaven jowls as he examined the gun. He was immaculately dressed in a yellow brocade vest and a camel-hair suit with a matching peaked cap. A gold watch chain dangled over his portly belly. At his shoulders stood his bodyguards, Clarence Thompson and Mickey James. Opposite him was Ed O'Kelley, one of his lesser minions.

–This is a nice old pistol, Frazee, Smith said.

–It ain't pricey, neither, Frazee said.

Joshua shifted the pig under his coat.

–I want that pistol, he said.

Smith's bodyguards regarded Joshua with malicious curiosity. They towered on either side of Soapy Smith. Mickey was a dull ape of a man with a thick browridge and stubble that shadowed his face from high on his heavy cheekbones down to the tight collar of his shirt. Thompson was halfway handsome, with a square chin and tanned skin shaved clean. His dark eyes were lively and spiteful. Both bodyguards held cudgels. Their tweed jackets bulged at the hip where they carried guns. Opposite them, Ed O'Kelley was scrawny and disheveled in a crumpled suit and battered derby hat. A heavy mustache almost curtained his mouth. The collar of his shirt was grimed by dirt and sweat and specked with dry blood. He, too, regarded Joshua with a malevolent eye. A sour smell filled the store. It might have originated with O'Kelley or with the barrel of oysters in brine that stood just behind him.

–You're Aaron Beynon's boy, ain't you? asked Smith.

–That's right, said O'Kelley.

Joshua shot a furious glance at Smith's henchman and then back at the Colt in Smith's hands. What the hell did his da have to do with anything?

–Aaron ain't never carried a gun, far as I can recall, said Smith, and I see him 'most every night down at the Orleans Club.

–The gun's not for my father, said Joshua.

–Well, ho! The boy needs a gun, said O'Kelley.

Smith grinned and nodded to Frazee.

–Maybe he wants to build a rep, said Frazee, have a showdown with Bob Ford, himself.

At that, the bodyguards and O'Kelley broke into laughter.

–I wouldn't mind if the boy shot that son of a bitch, Smith said.

The shopkeeper smiled paternally at Joshua.

–Mr. Smith wants to buy the gun, Josh, Frazee said.

–I ain't said that, said Smith. Not yet, I ain't.

Frazee seemed angry at being contradicted, but then he commenced to smile again. Joshua's coat was tight over the porcelain pig. He didn't want to reach up and undo a button. The straw from the grain sacks was making his nose itch. He was afraid that his voice would crack and squeak.

–I'd like to buy the gun, Joshua said.

He said it even and calm.

Soapy Smith's smile was like a spill of axle grease. He raised the pistol toward Joshua and nodded.

–This young man has made up his mind before me. I believe he has beaten me to the draw.

Frazee smiled again, inclined his head slightly toward him. Joshua fixed his eyes on the pistol. He couldn't believe that Soapy Smith had given it up to him. He stepped forward to take it from Smith's hands, but Smith turned away and laid the gun back in its soiled velvet case.

–Thank you, Mr. Smith, Joshua said.

Smith nodded and hitched his thumbs into the pockets of his vest. Clarence Thompson slapped his cudgel against his palm.

–Well, Josh. That's five dollars and seventy-five cents, said Frazee.

Frazee tapped a finger nervously on the counter.

–Pay the man his due, Smith said.

Joshua would have to show them the pig.

–I don't have all the money . . .

Smith and Frazee glanced at each other for a second, and then back at him. O'Kelley hawked something out of his throat and spat it into the sawdust on the floor.

– . . . here, I mean. But I got most of it.

–Oh well, said Soapy Smith.

He turned smartly toward the box on the counter again.

–Wait! Joshua yelled.

He fumbled at the buttons of his pea coat. He dug inside the open flap and brought out the pig, which rattled in his hands. The pig had an inane and innocent smile. Joshua was acutely aware of the tiny purple peonies around the coin slot. Soapy Smith and O'Kelley and Thompson and James began to guffaw like a small herd of tubercular donkeys. Joshua felt as if the tips of his ears would burn off. Even Frazee couldn't keep back a broad smirk.

–There's two dollars and sixty-four cents in here, Joshua said.

He walked past Smith and his men and held the pig out toward Frazee. Frazee kept his hands behind the bib of his apron.

–By my reckoning that's three dollars and eleven cents short, said Frazee.

Soapy Smith tilted his cap back on his head and rubbed the heel of his palm against his eyes in order to wipe away the tears.

–That ain't even half, said Smith. Nope.

–I can get it, said Joshua.

He just needed time. Frazee had to understand.

–I'm sorry, Josh. I think Mr. Smith wants this gun.

–He said I could have it, Joshua said.

–Hold on, Frazee, said Smith. I am a sporting man and I have a proposition to make to this gentleman here.

Joshua held the pig to his chest, his hands bent over it like a stick insect's claws. He blinked behind his lenses.

–What I propose is this, Mr. Frazee, said Soapy. If this young man comes up with three dollars and eleven cents by next Saturday, he can buy the gun and I will personally give him five dollars and seventy-five cents on top. If, on the other hand, he cannot raise the money, I will buy this pistol from you and the boy here will give me that pretty little piggy bank and all the money inside of it.

–I can't let you do that, said Frazee.

Joshua shot a glance at him and then looked Soapy Smith full in the face.

–I'll do it. I'll get the money all right.

Frazee turned to Joshua.

–Where you going to get more than three dollars? Frazee said.

Before Joshua could open his mouth and stutter an answer, Smith butted in.

–That's his problem, Frazee. He ain't a boy. He's responsible for his own goddamn self. Don't tell me you ain't gambled none.

Frazee drew the wooden box back across the counter and closed it on the Colt. He latched the brass clasps and slid the box under the counter and out of sight.

–Give me the stakes, said Frazee.

Smith pulled a tan tooled leather wallet from the pocket of his camel-hair trousers. He drew out six crisp dollar bills and laid them on the counter. Joshua placed the porcelain pig on top of the green bills. Emptiness yawed in the pit of his gut. Where would he find three dollars and eleven cents in a week? Frazee paid him fifty cents for a Saturday and his da took twenty-five cents of that for the household expenses. He hoped that his da wouldn't ask him where his savings were. He hoped that Soapy or O'Kelley or Clarence or Mickey wouldn't boast to his father about the bet and that Frazee wouldn't tell his father about it, either. There was a film of sweat on Joshua's palms. His cold fingers tingled. He would earn fifty cents today, twenty-five of which he could keep for the gun. That would leave him two dollars and eighty-six cents short. He could lose the gun and all his money if he didn't come up with the balance. His idea of a theft to get the rest of the money was just that. An idea. He had not planned beyond buying the gun. Now theft had to be an option. Perhaps his only option, if time grew short.

–He'll owe me a quarter, said Soapy Smith. If'n he chances to win, that is.

III

LIGHT SEEPED THROUGH THE CHINKS IN THE SPLINTERED DOOR where Bob Ford's hard-brimmed homburg hung upon a peg. Rain rattled against the tin roof and the wooden walls of the outhouse. Bob rested his elbow on his bare and hairy knee and let the Remington .44 swivel on the trigger guard and dangle in his fingers. There was no place he wanted to set the gun down. He breathed slow and shallow so that he would not have to endure the stink of ordure that arose from the pit below him. The May morning cold made him shiver. The darkness drew him into himself. Bob squeezed his eyes shut and water seeped from the corners. He wished his brother Charley was still alive. All week long he hadn't been able to get Charley out of his head. Charley had killed himself. Eight years and one week ago. In the blackness, the void that sucked at Bob, he could see his brother's corpse. He could see it as if the suicide had happened yesterday: dead on the bed, cheeks sunken and gray behind the heavy mustache, eyes wide, glazed, lifeless. Laid out in a fine brown suit, with powder burns on his blood-soaked worsted vest. Charley had shot his self clean through the heart. Soaked the goddamn mattress, too. And Bob had killed him, as surely as if he had pulled the trigger himself.

How did you do it, Charley? he thought. God damn.

The first time Bob had a woman, it was Charley who took him to a whore in Kansas City. Charley couldn't even get it up his own self because of the morphine. First time Bob ever stole anything as a kid, it was Charley who put him up to it. It was Charley who got him into the James Gang and Charley who stood behind him when he shot Jesse James. And if he hadn't shot Jesse James, Charley would still be alive.

I killed my own goddamn brother, thought Bob. I made him famous from Kansas City to New York, and he couldn't take it. So he's dead and I'm here sitting in a shithouse in southwest Colorado feeling sorry for myself. His throat was choked. He didn't approve of this kind of sadness. He thumbed the hammer back on the Remington. Click. He flipped his wrist inward and poked the pistol beneath his chin. The gun felt heavy. If he pulled the trigger now, he would never, no more, have to remember Charley's face; or the bearded face of Jesse James as it had appeared in his coffin, garishly rouged by the undertaker, lip and cheek, with that incruent hole in the side of the head that he, Bob Ford, had put there. One squeeze and he would never have to listen to some total stranger call him a coward or challenge him to fight for being the famous Slayer of Jesse James.

But now Bob couldn't get out of his tormented mind's eye the face of a failed suicide in a bar in Jimtown: the jaw bent at an impossible, inhuman angle; the nose like a balloon attached to a mess of scar ridges; the eyes set one almost above the other. With his thumb pressed down on the hammer again, he squeezed the trigger and lowered the hammer slowly.

–Damn me, he said. I am Bob Ford, the Slayer of Jesse James. I am Bob goddamn Ford.

It was a role he had played even on the Broadway stage in faraway New York City. He stood up in the rattling, stinking darkness and pulled up his pants. The tears at the corners of his eyes he pressed away with his thumb.

–Goddamn it. I ain't doing this. This ain't me.

He tucked the Remington into his waistband. The .44 dug into his belly. He should have worn a holster for the gun but that would have ruined the fall of his jacket. Bob had paid a Jimtown Chinaman fifty dollars for that fine gray suit and he was determined to have it look its best. Such a man as he should always look dressed. He took the homburg from the peg, ran his hand through his fair hair, and settled the hat at an angle on his head. He held his body stiff and straight and pushed open the door of the outhouse. He blinked as he stepped out into the backyard of the Brainard and Beebee Hotel.

–Goddamn dump.

The red brick edifice rose out of the pitted and muddy waste in front of him. Steady rain made circular patterns on the puddles of the backyard, where three fat and piebald pigs rooted through the kitchen garbage. Mud oozed around the soles of his shiny, polished boots as he crossed the yard. At his approach, the pigs scuttled away, grunting, trotters splattering through the yard's vegetable and animal filth. Bob was going back to Weaver to start his new business. The women were waiting for him on the wagon in front of the hotel.

Hell, they can wait, too, he thought.

The women had blamed each other for forgetting the letter that he had reminded them to take from the vanity drawer. When he realized that neither one of them had it, the black came over him in a nauseating rise from the pit of his gut. He had jumped down off the wagon and left them bitches whining and complaining and blaming one another for leaving behind the letter that was their very ticket back to a life of independent business. Bob had tried not to seem panicked. He had told the women that he was going to the jakes, then to get the letter. Them harlots were probably soaked through if they hadn't had the good sense to shelter while they waited for him, and madder than forty furies by now. Probably blamed him for the rain, too.

The hotel's back door was ajar. As he entered the rear stairwell, a sweet and heavy stink of boiling cabbage came from the kitchen down the corridor. Bob's boots clumped on the bare treads. The cabbage smell stayed with him as far as the next landing. His legs were still shaky on the next flight of stairs. He climbed toward the dim light above him. The thought that someone might already have thrown out his letter gave him the butterflies. He knew it wasn't rational, but he was convinced that if the letter was in his pocket when he reached Weaver, it would ensure his protection. It was his talisman of safe passage. His attachment to that piece of paper made him feel stupid and all the more determined to get it.

On the third-floor landing, the window at the end of the corridor was so grimy that it provided little more than a pale gray glow. A rattle of raindrops tattooed the cracked glass, pocking and streaking its grime.

I'm getting out of this rotten goddamn hotel once and for all, he thought.

Bob crept down the murky landing. Barely visible on the low ceiling, four dull copper-green candelabra hung from a crumbling plaster medallion, their curves strung with dusty cobwebs. The ceiling and wallpaper were a pale sepia in the murk. On each side of the corridor were two doors. The bare floorboards creaked with every step. At the door to his old room, Bob took off his homburg and laid his ear to the wood paneling. He could hear no sound.

Bob coughed and rapped on the door.

–What the hell you want? It was a woman's voice.

–It's Bob Ford, he said. This was my room until this morning. My wife left something in the vanity.

–Well, come in and get it! she yelled.

Bob turned the cold brass knob and leaned against the door.

–Hold up there, can't you?

That was a man's voice. The door stuck momentarily, swollen from the damp, creaked, then shuddered open. Bob gaped at the fat bulk of Jimtown's leading citizen, Dr. Henry Harding, as he squirmed desperately and pulled closed his long underwear at the same time he yanked up his brown pinstriped suit pants.

–A little house visit, Henry? asked Bob.

Catching Henry like that lightened Bob's demeanor considerably.

–By God, Henry, put that thing away, said Bob, you're holding up my whole family's travel plans.

The whore on the rumpled bed had one hand to her mouth as she hooted and shook, her dark ringlets awry, one skinny breast bare, fallen out of her white linen nightdress. Bob thought she looked hardly more than fourteen.

The florid moon of Henry's face swayed above his jerking shoulders.

–Couldn't you wait a moment until I'd rearranged myself?

Henry blustered and tugged ferociously at his waistband. He fumbled with his buttons. His breath came in gasps.

–Easy, Henry, or you'll be in need of your own services there. I just got to get something I left in a drawer.

Bob slipped past Henry. He saw that the vanity drawer was open.

–Damn.

The vanity top was cluttered. The girl's pots and jars and round tins for rouge and creams and kohl were all reflected in the right wing of the mirror. A dozen red roses tilted and bent in a glass vase. The dark-lipped petals peeled away from the drooping red heads. Dot had left them there. Old Brainard hadn't wasted any time letting their old room. The girl's purple silk scarf hung out of the open drawer. Bob lifted the scarf gingerly. He relaxed into a smile when he saw that the wrinkled brown envelope was still there. He took the letter out just to make sure it was safe:

Dear Mr. Robert Ford,
With regard to your inquiry of the 7th Inst., the Town of Weaver's Vigilance Committee herewith permits you to return to the aforesaid Town with the proviso that you not engage in any further public gun-play and live Peaceable with Citizens herein. And Yes, you may open a tent saloon on the East Meadow below Amethyst.
Signed,
The Committee of Twenty.

Bob glanced in the mirror, moved his head around his collar like a turtle, and tried to see what Henry was doing. The good doctor was stuffing his shirt into his pants with a fury, and the girl giggled at his contortions.

–Henry, honey, don't be shy, she said. Come on back for another, once he's gone.

A lamp with a sooty glass chimney stood on a spindle-legged bedside table. The light gave the girl a jaundiced look and the room a sickly yellow glow. The girl on the bed smiled at Bob.

–You come and see me on your own sometime, why don't you?

–This is it, ma'am, Bob said.

He turned to the doctor.

–I thank you, Henry, for your indulgence.

–Close the goddamn door on your way out, huffed Henry.

Bob slipped the envelope into his pocket, smiled at the girl on the bed, and nodded to Henry, who stood with one hand on the brass rail. His fly was bunched, for he had misbuttoned himself.

–I'll leave you to finish your business, Henry.

Bob swung the door shut behind him. It stuck without latching. He touched his jacket above the precious envelope.

Now for them hopped-up hussies, he thought. If they ain't so doped up that they fall off the wagon, we'll all be in Weaver by four this afternoon.

IV

A BEAM OF SUNLIGHT BROKE THROUGH THE CLEARING CLOUDS AND came down directly between the canyon walls. It lit up the red rocks and the pines and flashed on the foaming and roiling of West Willow Creek. The morning's storm had turned the creek into a river that roared around boulders, rolled its way down the canyon, undercut the already eroded banks, and threatened to wash out the road where Bob Ford's four-muled wagon eked and moaned around the switchbacks on its way toward Weaver. The mules strained in their traces. Under the soaked, roped-down tarp were twelve hogsheads of beer, eighteen cases of whiskey, a ten-foot carved mahogany bar, six tea chests of straw-packed glassware, a Schulz player-piano, a Louisiana-made Duchamp faro wheel, two green baize-covered gaming tables, four box mattresses, a trunk full of linen, four wash basins and jugs, and four porcelain chamber pots — everything that Bob Ford needed to set up his new business. Bob, reins in hand, sat, damp, between his plump wife and his skinny mistress. A purple-bonneted head rested its weight on his left shoulder and a blue-bonneted head on his right. He wished that the sun would shed more warmth, but what little heat he felt was still better than driving through the rainstorm that had hammered down upon them from Jimtown all the way through Creede and halfway to Weaver. Bob's sharply cut three-piece suit was sodden, his stiff-brimmed, homburg was rain-stained, and the pool of water by his feet had darkened and tide-rimed the soft leather of his gray tooled boots. He was chilled to the marrow of his bones, and his collar had rubbed his neck raw. But Bob was happy. He could have sung over the thunderous roar of the water if he hadn't been concerned about waking the women. He belonged in Weaver. It was going to be Bob Ford's mountain kingdom once more. Those miners would flock to his card tables and his faro wheel. He planned on having a stable of girls a man would kill for. All the other card sharps, con men, saloon keepers, whores, and thieves in Weaver's boomtown population might have the same idea he did, but Bob Ford was a match for them all. The thought of getting his hands on those miners' cash had him squirming on the wagon seat like a half-grown boy with a boner.

The purple bonnet on his left shoulder lifted and Ella, his mistress, blinked up at him like a marmot unused to the light of day. A few tendrils of red ringlets lay against the white of her neck. Her eyes were bloodshot from sleep. She smiled a wide red smile, coquettish and guilty, feral, a little unhinged. She scared him.

–Where are we, Bob? she asked.

–Ain't far now, he said.

Dot was still asleep on his other shoulder.

Ella reached down between her feet and rummaged in her macramé drawstring bag. She came up with a slim mahogany case. She thumbed open the clasp and eased up the lid. Nestled in the red velvet was a glass cylinder fitted with a long steel needle. The shiny instrument had curved brass finger loops and a brass plunger. It looked like a jeweled insect.

–Goddamn it, Ella, you can't do that now. I ain't stopping.

–I ain't asked you to stop, said Ella.

Dot's head slowly rose off his right shoulder.

–Where the hell are we? asked Dot.

She rubbed her plump little hands. The cold and damp had turned them red. Dot craned her disheveled head around Bob's shoulder to peer into his face. Her face was framed by the bonnet. The kohl around her eyes had streaked. Rain had trickled through her pancake makeup, all the way down to the neck of her dress. Blue satin clung to her plump frame like a rag with no hope of drying. She had that needy, jealous look in her big blue eyes, as if she was about to burst into tears. Well, he guessed, the peaceful ride up the mountain was about to unravel.

–Honeybob, asked Dot, would you have any tabacca?

Bob glanced at Ella. She jostled him as she struggled with the cork stopper of a squat brown bottle. Bob shifted the reins from his right hand to his left, leaned toward Ella, and dug into the pocket of his pants for his tobacco pouch. Ella screeched in his ear.

–Watch what you're doing, why can't you?

Ella had the bottle open. She held it away from her body, balanced on her fingertips so that the liquid inside would not spill.

–Keep them animals steady, Ella said.

Bob handed Dot his tobacco pouch, and she dug into the muslin bag.

–Them animals is steadier than any one or all three of us, Bob said.

Ella glared at him. She plucked the syringe from the velvet lining of the box, put the needle into the bottle, and drew up on the plunger so that the solution rose into the glass cylinder. At that precise moment, the load swayed behind them and the wagon seat tilted. Dot squealed as she tipped the tobacco and cigarette papers fluttered down over the mules like little white butterflies. Bob sawed at the reins, but the mules just kept on going.

–Goddamn it, yelled Ella, I done spilled some on my dress.

Dot giggled.

–We must of hit a rock, she said.

–It was a rut, Bob said.

–Don't you even know how to drive a goddamn wagon? yelled Ella.

Bob had half a mind to toss the reins into her lap and jump off the wagon, but it would have done no good other than to leave him afoot, for he had borrowed the wagon and team from Missouri Bill McCall and the mules knew the road so well that they would have hauled the outfit into Weaver without ever faltering a step, driver or no driver. These mules even kept to the outside of each bend as they rounded the switchbacks. Bob spat over the haunches of the outside wheeler. At least with the reins in his hands, he was under the illusion that he controlled his own destiny.

Ella laid the syringe on the box in her lap and recorked the bottle. She dug into her bag again and came up with a pale yellow length of rubber tubing. She stretched her left arm out. Above her delicate wrist was a crisscross pattern of purple and red lines. They matched her organza dress. She slipped the length of rubber around her arm, just above her elbow, tied it off, and she tapped to raise a vein. She held the syringe up to check for air bubbles. The brass and glass glinted in the sunlight. Bob gripped the reins tighter and stared at her.

–You be careful how you do that, he said.

–You wanna stop the wagon?

–I ain't stopping the wagon.

–Well, I ain't gonna kill myself, she said. I ain't like your brother.

–Goddamnit! hollered Bob. You leave Charley out of this.

Ella smiled up at him, a hideous, mirthless smile, and pressed the needle against her forearm. There was something about the brass syringe and the pressure on the flesh and the way the needle popped into her blue vein that made Bob want to lay her down and poke her every time he watched her take a shot. And she knew it. She drew the plunger up a little and a thin stem of blood grew into the glass cylinder and bloomed in the solution.

–Oh honey, she said, her voice all husky.

And she pushed the plunger down. All that juice flowed right on into her. Ella leaned over her arm and gripped the rubber tube in her teeth. She pulled her head back and the tourniquet uncoiled like a pale yellow worm. With the unruly tube dangling from her mouth, she slid the needle out. A bead of blood arose on her forearm. Quickly, she laid the syringe on the red velvet and pressed a lace-bordered handkerchief to her arm.

–Oh yes, she breathed.

–Put that kit away now, Ella, said Bob.

–Oh yes, she said.

She moved slow and deliberate. Her fingers were narrow and bony. She closed the lid on the syringe, fixed the clasp carefully, leaned over and dropped the mahogany case back into her drawstring bag. Her head turned and she smiled up at him from under her long dark eyelashes. Her eyes were glazed, the pupils like pinpoints. She had him angry and horny and feeling like she had stripped him naked in public, all at the same time. And she knew it. Her head rolled back against the tarp beside him. She was still functional. Just like Charley after a shot. He was so used to the morphine that he could regulate just how far he wanted to go. And Ella was the same.

The wagon rounded another switchback and rose into a thick stand of pines. The air was cold in the shadows. The wind wafted up the scent of resin and rotting needles.

–Needle never killed Charley, said Dot. Charley killed hisself with a gun.

Bob twisted in his seat.

–Yeah? he said. Well, I know that Charley killed a whore in Jefferson City by filling her full of morphine, 'cause I was the one who had to dump her body in the alley.

–Charley never meant to kill that girl, drawled Ella.

–That's exactly my goddamn point, said Bob.

–This whole goddamn affair is suicide, Ella said.

–What you talking about?

–Taking us back to Weaver to cut in on Soapy Smith's trade. He won't take kindly to that.

–I ain't got no beef with Soapy Smith, said Bob.

–Well, he got a beef with you, said Dot, 'cause Soapy Smith would burn down a outhouse with his grandma inside if he thought she'd be cutting in on his business. And you aim to cut in on his business.

–Can you shut up about Soapy Smith? I can handle Soapy Smith.

–He's got friends in that town, Ella said.

–So have I, Bob said.

–Who you counting on? Ella said.

– Dick Liddil and Silas Strickland, Bob said.

Dick had always been handy in a scrape.

–Goddamn, Ella said. A broken-down jockey and beat-up old nigger.

–Strick's a goddamn prizefighter.

–They both seen better days, Ella said.

Bob nodded at her pale face with the pinpoint pupils and the drawn cheeks.

–Ain't we all, he said.

It was ten years since Bob and Liddil had ridden with the James Gang.

–Well, just you watch out, sniffed Dot at his shoulder.

–Bob'll watch out, said Ella.

And I ain't dead yet, thought Bob.

The wagon came out of the pine stand. Over the clamor of the stream came the rattle of drive belts and the long high whine of a circular saw. They approached a lumber mill that stood on the opposite bank of the roaring creek. It marked the beginning of Weaver. A ten-foot-diameter paddle wheel churned in the water. Beside the stone gear house, stout pine pillars supported a low-rake shake roof. On the torn pine slopes above it were scattered dilapidated shacks that had once belonged to the canyon's original prospectors. A smudge of smoke rose and curled up to the canyon's rim. Probably some squatter up there with no money to stay in town.

The mules picked up and hauled the rattling wagon past the sawmill. Up here, between Bulldog Mountain on one side and Campbell Mountain on the other, the high walls of the canyon were closer together. A tumbled juxtaposition of tin roofs and canvas tents rose one above the other through the ramshackle town's Main Street.

–Weaver, Colorado, said Bob. We're back in business, Dot.

Dot's small mouth twisted in a sneer.

–Flatbacking for horny gold diggers again, she said.

Bob didn't relish the thought of Dot taking up her old profession, either; but she'd been gainfully employed in it since he'd first met her.

–Damn, said Ella, they don't even wash the dirt off.

–We'll find a few girls down in Jimtown, said Bob, and get them to come up here. They'll come for the money.

–Well, said Dot, I don't want to be responsible for all the female side of the business.

The mules pulled on into Main Street. Buildings of clapboard and rough pine, store facades and painted signs lined the street ahead of them: Dave's Place, the Last Chance Restaurant, Jordan's Paints and Oils. The road was just wide enough for two wagons to pass by each other, which was fortunate because a huge ore wagon hauled by a six-mule team was barreling down the hill toward them. Roughlocks clanked on the ore wagon's wheels but did nothing to slow the wagon. The driver, Missouri Bill McCall, was hunched over in his seat, reins in his fist, the brim of his hat turned back from his broadly mustachioed face like a mule skinner hell-born, whip raised above his head as if the mere threat of it kept the mules running.

–Get that goddamn wagon over, yelled McCall.

McCall's wagon slewed and bounced toward them, spilling ore.

–Jesus, he's gonna hit us, Dot squealed.

McCall's lead mules raced by Bob's team, missing them by inches.

The mule skinner grinned at the ladies, grunted cordially as his wagon rattled level, then he was gone. The narrow street stank with the rank miasma of mule piss.

–Goddamn that son of a bitch, said Dot.

–Hell, Dot, he knew what he was doing, Bob said.

–He could of killed us.

–He's the best mule skinner in the canyon.

–And the biggest goddamn liar, too.

–Aw, come on, Dot. Bill's always been a good buddy to me.

–He ain't worth a shit, said Ella.

–He'll be at the new saloon spending his money more than anyone, said Bob.

–And reporting everything we do to Soapy Smith, said Dot.

–Bill's his own man, Bob said.

–But he's got a big mouth, said Ella.

–I don't give a shit about him nor Soapy Smith, Bob said.

–If he stays away from us, I'll be all the happier, said Dot.

Bob sucked in air and let her have the last word.

On the boardwalks to their right and left, all the loafers and miners and matronly miners' wives who stood in front of the stores had turned to stare at them and their heavy wagon that labored on up Main Street. Every one of them knew him, the Slayer of Jesse James. He gave the town character. The vigilance committee had run him out not two months ago for firing off his pistol one night on a drunk, although he had never killed a soul in Weaver. And now he was a man of property, fully intending to take his place in the business community, albeit on its seamier side. But some folks in the town wanted competition for Soapy Smith, even if they would not admit it directly.

Bob reached down behind his feet for a leather-handled whip. The lash was stiff and wet. Red, white, and blue ribbons were braided into the black tip. Dot moved to give him room. Bob swung the whip up and cracked the colored poppers between the flanks of the lead mules, more for the onlookers than for the mules. Outside Jordan's Paints and Oils, a bearded Polish hulk and his round-bellied wife stood stock still and ogled them from under the wooden awning. Bob dropped the whip between his feet and reached into his pocket. He brought out a silver flask, unstoppered it, saluted the two Hunkies on the boardwalk, and took a good swallow of brandy. It burned down into his stomach. He handed the flask to Dot.

–Come on, he said. We're back in Weaver. It's time to celebrate.

–So where's the goddamn bunting and the brass band? said Dot.

She took a good slug at the brandy.

–We'll have ourselves a party, said Bob. Just you wait till we get to the new cabin.

The mules pulled onward, hooves sunk to the fetlocks, and the wheels of the wagon churned the red mud of the street. Some thirty yards ahead, on the right side of the street, was a newly built building with a sign hanging outside. It read POST OFFICE.

–Look at that, said Ella.

Her voice was full of awe and reverence.

The white walls stood out sharply from among the seedy storefronts around it. The building's sash windows were framed by pastel blue shutters and shallow planters. The boxes had sprouted a sparse growth of plants — chrysanthemums, Bob thought — as yet, all leaf and no flower. The post office's crowning glory was a clock tower with a corrugated tin roof. The roof pointed its small, sharp pyramid skyward between the red rock walls of the canyon. The pointers on the clock's black metal hands looked as neat as a pair of aces, both of them spades.

–It's as beautiful as church, Ella said.

–Ain't that the truth, sneered Dot.

–Never thought so many people could sign their names up here, said Bob, let alone compose letters.

–Seven minutes past four, said Ella.

Seven minutes past four when a scrawny, mustachioed man stepped from the alley opposite the post office and walked foot by deliberate foot into the middle of the street. He was clothed in a suit of dirty tweeds and wore a derby hat. He held a pistol in his grip, down by his right side, as if position alone would conceal it.

–You think that's a welcoming committee? whispered Bob.

–Ain't that Ed O'Kelley? said Dot.

The gunman stood in the middle of the street. The mules pulled toward him. He was not twenty yards in front of the lead mules. O'Kelley lifted his pistol, arm straight out, level with his shoulder. The gun pointed straight at them.

–Oh Jesus, said Dot. Shoot the bastard, Bob. Shoot him, for God's sake.

Bob's hand slid toward the Remington tucked in his belt. O'Kelley's arm wavered. He looked puzzled as if he saw them now for the first time.

–Jesus, he's drunk, said Bob.

–Well, shoot the son of a bitch, anyway, whispered Dot.

Bob eased his pistol from his belt. His left hand, still with the reins, felt for the letter under his jacket. No gunplay it said. It was his talisman. His lucky charm.

–To hell with you all, shouted O'Kelley.

O'Kelley swung his gun up high. A shot cracked out, and echoed around the canyon walls. Dot screamed. Bob instinctively threw himself right and found his head in his wife's wet lap. He glanced over the heads of the mules. O'Kelley fired four more shots into the air as he spun in the street. Bob heard a spang! spang! He heard screams, squeals, and doors slamming on the boardwalks. Ella curled slowly over Bob's back, her body no longer supported by his shoulder, and began to giggle.

–He shot the goddamn clock, she said.

–He's just drunk, said Bob. He wasn't aiming to do no harm.

Bob straightened up, lifting Ella up with him.

–Two bullets in the damned clock face, laughed Ella.

–One left in the gun, said Bob.

The mules marched steadily forward, drawing the creaky wagon ever closer to O'Kelley. Bob kept his eyes on O'Kelley's gun hand. The wagon drew level with the post office on one side and Happy's Grog Shop on the other. Main Street was too damn narrow. Bob felt awfully close to the pistol-waving drunk.

–Don't you shoot no more, now.

Just as the lead mules drew within five feet of him, Ed O'Kelley fell to his knees. His left hand sank to the wrist in red mud, but his pistol hand was still raised, his head skewed skyward.

–Don't shoot, now, you hear?

O'Kelley's face showed no sign that his senses registered either sight or sound. The drunk's left arm bent as he failed to support the weight of his own body, and he sank head down into the clinging red muck. Bob marveled that habit or instinct led the man to tilt his gun barrel upward and out of the ruinous mire so that the forty-four appeared shining in a shaft of sunlight like a frontier Excalibur.

Bob looked up at the clock. Two black bullet holes bisected the angle of the clock hands. The hands on all four faces would never move again.

–Too bad about that clock, said Bob.

–We almost got killed, said Dot. Why didn't you shoot him?

–He was drunk, for Chrissakes. You can't kill a man for being drunk. Look at him.

Bob pointed the Remington at the prone figure in the mud as the wheel mules pulled past him.

–I sure would like a smoke, said Bob.

–There ain't no tabacca, said Ella.

Dot stayed silent.

Ella scowled at the half-buried drunk as the front wheels drew level with him, then she coughed and spat on the back of O'Kelley's head as he lay face down in the muddy red furrows of the road. Bob cracked the poppers again and they left O'Kelley behind them — an insignificant muddy heap in the middle of the street. And fifty yards farther on, as the wagon approached the junction of Main and Amethyst Streets, a gangly bespectacled boy of about fifteen stepped off the boardwalk from in front of Frazee's General Store. A blue-gray coon hound twisted and squirmed around the boy's legs. The boy stopped, just as O'Kelley had, in the middle of the street. The coon hound rushed snapping and yapping toward the lead mules. The boy tipped back a shiny peaked cap, pulled back his pea coat, and hitched his thumbs in the loops of his pants.

–Now what the hell? said Bob.

–Goddamn it, said Dot. I feel like a target in a goddamn shooting gallery.

–It's all right. He ain't armed, said Bob. He's just funnin'.

–That ain't funny, whined Dot.

–Mr. Ford! Mr. Ford! the boy called.

Bob recognized the kid. It was Aaron Beynon's boy. He'd been a problem to Aaron since the mother died.

–Welcome back to Weaver, Mr. Ford, he called.

–Thank ye, boy, thank ye, said Bob.

The boy had a big grin across his face. The kid was a goddamn idiot. Bob stared at the big-boned son of a bitch until the wagon was past him.

–That boy could of got hisself killed pulling a stunt like that, said Dot.

–This town always was a goddamn madhouse, said Bob.

–That's Weaver, Ella said. And you ain't even tangled with Soapy Smith yet.

–Looks like you are about to, said Dot.

She pointed across Bob's body. Bob looked to his left, up Amethyst Street. They must have been watching for the wagon, for coming down the boardwalk from the direction of the Orleans Club was Soapy Smith with two broad-shouldered henchmen behind him. They were still a good forty yards away. The two bodyguards wore flat tweed caps as if in uniform, and they swung cudgels across their bodies like a pair of drum majors. There were bulges at the waists of their jackets. Between them, Soapy Smith was lit up like a kerosene lamp in his pale camel-hair suit and yellow silk waistcoat. He swung his arms loosely like a man out for a casual stroll.

–The hell with this, said Bob.

Bob reached down for the whip and cracked the poppers between the ears of the lead mules. They picked up their pace and hauled on toward the end of Main Street.

–Well, ladies, Bob said. If Soapy wants to face me down, he can walk all the way to the goddamn cabin through a quarter mile of red mud and mule shit. Bob Ford takes his next greeting in the comfort of his own home.

The mules hauled on past the livery stable. Across the meadow and just beyond the cemetery was his new log cabin. And beside it was the platform upon which he would set up his new tent saloon. Bob Ford was back for business.

▼

IF JOSHUA HAD ALREADY BOUGHT THE COLT .45, HE COULD HAVE shot Ed O'Kelley and claimed that he had prevented a murder. He played the possible scene over and over in his mind: drawing the revolver from his belt, cocking the hammer, raising the heavy pistol and bringing the foresight in line with the middle of O'Kelley's swaying, drunken body, squeezing the trigger, hearing the bang, feeling the kick, and seeing O'Kelley punched off his feet by the bullet's impact. And Robert Ford, the Slayer of Jesse James, would have been eternally grateful to him. But Joshua had no Colt. He was a helpless boy, standing weaponless outside Frazee's store, and Soapy Smith, Clarence Thompson, and Mickey James were marching down the boardwalk on the other side of the street. They reached the junction of Amethyst and Main. Joshua didn't want them to see him. He stood back tight to the doorway of Frazee's store, tilted to his right, and clamped his hand around Carys's muzzle so that she wouldn't yap.

Clarence Thompson, the handsome member of Soapy's bodyguard, pointed up Main Street at Mr. Ford's rocking wagon. It had just passed the livery stable.

–We'll never catch Ford before he gets to his cabin, Thompson said.

–Are we going after him, boss? asked Mickey James.

Soapy Smith looked on Mickey with contempt.

–You have a prior appointment? Soapy asked.

The browridge that shadowed Mickey's eyes twisted into knots under the skin as if the simian Irishman sought an answer to Smith. But no words came out of Mickey's mouth.

–Then let's make a social call on Mr. Ford, Soapy said.

Clarence grinned, his white teeth a sharp contrast to his tanned skin.

–Don't worry none, Mickey, he said.

The two bodyguards stayed close to Soapy's shoulders as they set off up Main Street. Joshua let them gain a good thirty yards on him, then followed. Carys, tongue lolling, stayed at his heel.

Soapy Smith controlled all of Weaver's gambling and prostitution, and Mr. Ford, everyone knew, was coming to town to set up a new gambling saloon and a crib for sporting women. Everyone expected a confrontation. Joshua had not imagined one so immediate.

Three men against one, Joshua thought. Not good odds.

But there was a coldness about Mr. Ford that Smith and his bodyguards did not possess. A darkness, as if a shadowy angel stood at his shoulder. Set him apart from other men. Made him more than other men. If the confrontation came to a shooting, Mr. Ford would prevail. And if Mr. Ford shot Soapy Smith, the Colt Peacemaker was as good as Joshua's. He would have no need to worry about working to raise the money for it or about planning any theft. He hoped that it came to a killing. He hoped that he would witness it.

Beyond the livery stable, the canyon floor flattened out and widened. The road forked. The right-hand fork led down to the creek, where smoke rose from the chimneys of the houses and the tents of the miners and the carpenters and the mule skinners who lived down close to the bank. Soapy and his men had taken the upper fork. It led across the wide meadow below the cemetery and from thence the path led up to Mr. Ford's cabin. A sudden chill crept through the marrow and the joints of Joshua's big bones as he came within sight of the grave markers on the hill, among which lay the corpses of his mother and brother and sister. He wrapped his arms around himself to stop his shaking and stumbled on beneath the empty sky and the red rock canyon walls toward Mr. Ford's cabin.

Buckets from the Amethyst Mine were still coming down the cableway and into the turn station, where they dropped their loads to clatter down the chute and into waiting tram trucks. The narrow-gauge tram line passed not twenty feet from the log cabin's front door. Mr. Ford's loaded wagon — the mules still in the traces — was just off the trail and in front of the cabin. The two women stood on the short green slope between the wagon and the cabin's front door. Mr. Ford leaned against the tailgate of the wagon, one hand on the tarp, the other resting on the pistol at his waist. Soapy and his men were not thirty yards from him. The wind blew up dust off the side of the trail, and Joshua screwed up his eyes against the airborne grit that blew behind his lenses. Carys began to bark and yelp. She must have caught scent of the mules again. She raced up the road and passed by Soapy and his men. Soapy glanced back over his shoulder.

–You got no business here, boy, called Soapy.

–Come back here, Carys! Joshua shouted.

He ran up the road toward her. His body still shook as if some force within him sought to unhinge his every joint.

–Get the hell out of here, kid, said Soapy.

–Leave the boy alone, said Mr. Ford.

Joshua ran by Soapy and his men. He was out of breath when he reached Mr. Ford. Running had quieted the violence of the tremors, though his hands still shook. Mr. Ford didn't even glance at him. He had his homburg tilted back. He kept his eyes on Soapy and crew, who stood not five yards away from him. Mr. Ford's finger was curled loosely around the trigger of his pistol. The pistol was cocked. Joshua raised a hand in greeting as he passed Mr. Ford. Carys was snapping at the heels of the right-side wheel mule. Joshua pulled a soft cotton rope from his pocket. The two lead mules stood quiet as could be in their traces, but the wheelers shifted their shoulders and bounced their heads toward one another, then away outward. Carys was almost under the belly of one. It kicked out and Carys yelped. Joshua grabbed her. He looped the rope over the hound's head. Right away, she began howling again.

–Boy, you should train that dog for coons, said Mr. Ford. He ain't never gonna tree no mule.

Mr. Ford had his back to Joshua. His eyes were still on Soapy. Joshua's face turned a bright red under his peaked cap. The damned dog kept howling.

–Get that hound out of here before I have to shoot it, said Clarence Thompson.

–Boy's a friend of mine, Clarence, said Mr. Ford. And I don't appreciate you telling him to go 'way, nor threatening the life of his dog.

Joshua knelt down and clamped his hand around Carys's muzzle. Her howl turned into a muffled whine. Soapy nodded and pursed his lips.

–Take it easy, Clarence, he said. I don't mean to sour the atmosphere here. See, Bob, I just come to make you a business proposition.

Mr. Ford nodded.

–Take the dog and tie her up to that post up there, said Mr. Ford.

He gestured with his chin but didn't take his eyes off Soapy. Joshua's breath came shallow in his chest. He feared to cross the narrow gap between Mr. Ford and Soapy, but he did as he was told.

–Yessir, said Joshua.

Joshua dragged Carys up the slope to the wooden platform, where heavy tarred piles had been driven into the sodden earth. Four six-by-twelve solid chestnut beams were nailed down in a frame upon them. Broad pine boards formed a sizable floor around which had been built an eighteen-inch knee wall. Carys struggled against the rope, but Joshua pulled her toward the platform. Two string lines to lay out a stair had been stretched from the platform and fixed by stakes close to the roadside. Joshua tied Carys to one of the stakes.

–Hush, girl. Be quiet, now, he said.

He squatted beside his dog and put his arm around her.

Up on the slope, the two women stood bedraggled and blue-lipped, watching Joshua, watching Ford and Soapy Smith. The women looked a little ridiculous in their bonnets. Joshua knew that Dot Ford was the plump one in the blue dress and the other was Ella Mae Waterson. Joshua had once heard his da tell his friend Mr. Atkins that the women were both whores and Bob Ford was nothing but a cheap pimp.

–State your business, Jefferson, said Mr. Ford.

–Well, said Soapy, seeing how you ain't got much to start with, I got an offer. I want to buy this lot off of you. I'll build you a dance hall on it. I'll bring in girls to work it. And Ella and Dot don't need to do more than they care to. And you can be the manager, Bob, for a fair wage. How about it?

–I don't work so well for other folks, Jefferson, said Mr. Ford.

–Think of the ladies, Bob, said Soapy.

–This is a prime piece of real estate we come into, Bob, said Mrs. Ford. Sure would be a shame to lose it.

She planted her fists on her hips. The other woman looked sick. She kept her fingers laced in front of her, and her wide red mouth was a tight line. Soapy grinned at Mrs. Ford. His two pig eyes leered at her. He twisted his knobbed fingers over the head of the cudgel.

–Aw, Dot, said Soapy. You enjoy your work too much to give it up?

He slapped his cudgel onto the palm of his left hand. He slid the shaft up and down, up and down, through his closed fist.

–What you say, Dot? said Soapy. When Bob gets set up, maybe I'll come and avail myself of your services. Bring a few of the boys along, too.

Mrs. Ford reached up to tuck a loose hair into her bonnet.

–I choose who I fuck, Soapy. And it won't be you. Or any of your boys.

Joshua glanced at her. He had never heard such foul words from the mouth of a woman.

Soapy turned back to Mr. Ford.

–Most people in this town are happy to work for me, Bob.

–I work for myself.

–I respect that a man of your reputation finds it difficult to work for others, Soapy said. But I have a genuine concern for you and your family, and I would sincerely like to do business with you. Hear me out. You have just acquired some valuable property in a town that I care about. I want to extend to you an opportunity that I only offer to my closest business associates. I have set up a life and property insurance company and I can offer you full coverage for any loss that might occur through accident or act of God.

Carys wriggled in Joshua's arms but he held her tight to him. He shook his head. What high and mighty opinion of himself did Soapy Smith have if he would insure a man against an act of God? He thought Mr. Ford ought to take him up on his offer.

–Jefferson, Mr. Ford said, right now, I don't have any beef with you nor anyone else. I don't need no insurance policy.

Soapy Smith shook his head, stared at the ground, and shifted a twig with the toe of his boot. He looked up again.

–You know, Bob, said Soapy. I thought I could offer you my protection. There's lots of young yahoos around here would like to build a big rep. The way you flaunt yours, it might only be a matter of time before someone calls you out.

–I ain't met one yet who succeeded in that enterprise, Jefferson, said Mr. Ford. And I ain't got no price on my head to worry about.

–Not put there by no sheriff or governor maybe, said Soapy. But what about a sporting man, Bob?

–You always was a sporting man, Jefferson, said Mr. Ford.

–I won't deny that, said Soapy.

–I guess I am, too, said Mr. Ford.

Mr. Ford spoke directly to the goons.

–I'll take my chances, gentlemen. What about you?

Clarence and Mickey nodded. They were nervous.

There would be no bloody killing this evening.

It requires darkness, Joshua thought. Silence. An alleyway.

Soapy looked up at Joshua.

–You should keep your nose out of other people's affairs, boy. You understand me? There's some things it's better not to see. Believe me. Come on, boys, he said.

Soapy turned around, and without a word he pushed between Clarence and Mickey. The goons looked confused. Clarence jerked his head at Mickey and they followed after Soapy.

The left-side wheel mule released a copious cascade of piss that splattered on the mud and soured the evening air. Joshua watched the men's progress down the road toward the livery.

–I'm going inside, said Mrs. Ford. It's too damn cold out here.

She rubbed her upper arms, shuffled woodenly up to the cabin door, and disappeared inside.

–I'm going over to Chang Jen Wa's before it gets dark, said the sick woman. I got a yen.

–Jesus Christ, Ella, cain't you slow down none? said Mr. Ford.

The woman didn't answer him. She went down off the slope and headed back toward town, but she did not follow Soapy Smith. She stumbled down the road toward the fork that led to the creek side.

Mr. Ford turned toward Joshua.

–If you'd like to earn a dollar, Mr. Ford said, you might take some of that lumber for kindling and light the stove inside the cabin.

Joshua looked down at him. A dollar? Just to light a fire? A miner had to work half a shift to earn a dollar.

–Yes, sir, surely, sir. Right away, he said.

Joshua got up from beside Carys and scurried to where scraps of lumber had been thrown on a pile near a pair of sawhorses.

Damp sawdust and wood shavings lay in heaps on the churned earth. He scuttled about in the lumber pile for short and narrow lengths that would fit into a woodstove. A dollar for this. He stole a look after Soapy Smith, but Soapy and his henchmen had disappeared behind the livery stable.

–Goddamn it, boy, hurry up, up there.

Joshua snatched at more kindling. The shift whistle blew up at Amethyst. Evening sun rays from behind the mountains lit up the fringe of pines on the canyon rim, gold and orange. Above the cabin, he could hear the engine of the day's last ore shipment from the cableway's turn station. The engine hissed and shuffed and rattled and creaked as it started down the narrow-gauge railroad track.

–Boy, Mr. Ford called out. If I ever see you pull a stunt in the street like you done this afternoon, I will shoot you dead. Do you understand me?

Joshua lost his grip on the kindling in his arms and a few sticks spilled onto the ground. Mr. Ford was annoyed with him.

–What's your name, boy?

–Joshua Beynon, sir, he said.

–Pleased to meet you, Joshua, said Mr. Ford. Now pick up the goddamn lumber you dropped and get that fire lit inside, for I'm freezing my balls off out here. I got to get these mules down to the stable before dark, so you get the stove lit before I come back.

Joshua's muscles cramped with the cold. He ground his teeth to stop them chattering. Soapy Smith and his men might be waiting for Mr. Ford near the livery stable. He didn't want Mr. Ford to be killed. Not now that he had just met him. Mr. Ford might not want to work for Soapy Smith, but Joshua would happily work for the Slayer of Jesse James.

Harness rattled and jingled, hooves slapped in mud. Mr. Ford had the mules unhitched from the wagon. They were still in their traces, two by two. In his homburg and well-cut suit, Joshua's benefactor looked too much the dandy to be a mule skinner. With a flick of the whip in his right hand, Mr. Ford neatly turned the lead mules in the road and the wheelers followed them around until the whole team faced the town. He was leaning back with the reins wrapped around his left fist, and he walked the mules past the wagon and down toward the livery.

Joshua gathered up the sticks again. Was Mr. Ford serious about the dollar? Or was he just kidding him? Mr. Ford was a con man, just like Soapy Smith. Would he just come back and laugh at him? It was worth the risk. All Joshua had to do was to light a fire. With such pay Joshua might have the Colt Peacemaker in no time. And Soapy Smith's money from the wager, too.

VI

THE FRONT DOOR OF THE CABIN WAS AJAR. JOSHUA LOOKED through the gap. The floor was made of wide pine boards with hardly a scuff mark on them, even at the threshold. A large rag rug covered the middle of the floor, and a long table was set upon it, with eight chairs arranged around the table. The walls beyond the table were of narrow, tongue-in-groove oak. Mr. Ford must have paid a lot of money to have that milled. A framed picture — a hart in a thicket — hung between the two doors on the wall opposite Joshua. The doors, Joshua thought, must lead to bedrooms. The stove was to his right at the far end of the room. The colored rug stopped a foot short of its slate base. A small table cluttered with bottles and ladles and empty jars stood against the wall to the left of the stove and a glass-fronted sideboard was at the right. Joshua hugged the bundle of kindling and turned sideways to enter the cabin. Carys stopped at the threshold and whimpered.

–Why, what a fine young man you are, said Mr. Ford's wife.

Joshua looked back. She had not been visible from the doorway. She sat in a rocking chair, off to Joshua's left, at the far end of the room. A brass lantern stood on the windowsill next to her. The wick must have been slightly uneven, for it caused the flame to flare and gutter and dance upon her fleshy cheeks and chin. The rain had made a mess of her powder and paint, but her small plum mouth was creased in a smile. She had removed her bonnet and her blond hair was awry. He could smell her sweet perfume over the scent of the damp lumber in his arms. She pulled the shawl back from her shoulders and bent forward in the chair. Joshua looked directly at the globes of her breasts as they pushed against damp blue satin. His face flushed. She licked her lips. He gnawed at the inside of his cheeks.

–I'll be so pleased when you've got that fire lit, honey, she said. I'm about froze half to death. I need a little warming.

–Quick as a flash, Joshua said. I'll have this lit in no time.

He kept looking back at her as he crossed the room to the potbellied stove. He let the kindling fall and clatter on the slate. He squinted back at Mrs. Ford.

–I got soaked through on the way up here, she said.

Joshua nodded and turned back to the stove. He opened the top hatch and peered inside. Despite the shadows, he could see well enough that the stove didn't need cleaning. Beside the stove was a box of dry straw to be used for tinder. He took a handful and stuffed it into the firebox. The rocker squeaked behind him. He kept his back to the woman. Perhaps he should ask her something. Did you have a nice ride up the valley? Stupid. It had rained. She said she'd been soaked. He picked at the kindling and poked it through the stove door. Carys whimpered at the doorway. The nails on her paws clicked as she scratched the floorboards just inside the door. Damn dog was embarrassing him. He took a fat log from a black metal hod and maneuvered it into the stove.

–Your daddy is Aaron Beynon, ain't that right?

–Yes, miss.

Her voice continued behind him.

–He's a good man, and he's made a mighty fine boy, I'd say. We used to see Aaron a lot at Bob's old saloon before it got burnt down. 'Specially after your good mama died.

Joshua jerked his hand back and skinned his knuckles on the stove door. He looked down at his smudged fingers. Was she saying that his father had gone with her? In a crib? The fine hairs on his back prickled all the way up to his neck. He squinted into the crisscross wood patterns in the stove. He slammed the stove door shut.

–That's kind of you to lay the fire, she said.

I'm doing it for money, he thought.

Like she did other things for money. With his da?

–You'll be old enough to come visit us, wouldn't you? she asked.

He turned to face her. Was she trying to sell herself to him? Suddenly he wanted the fire lit and to be out of this woman's house.

–Miss, would you happen to have a match? he asked.

–Look in the drawer of the cabinet, she said.

The glass-fronted sideboard was stocked with preserve jars and small sacks of dry goods.

–By the way, my name's Dot.

He grabbed for the drawer, pulled at the round knobs until it squeaked open. There was a big bowie knife in there, turned aslant over the rest of the contents. A dozen .45 caliber bullets were scattered about the front of the drawer. There was some kind of rubber bag with a long tube and a big wooden matchbox that nestled among the loops of a tangled ball of string. Joshua let go of the knobs and the front of the drawer dropped. He grabbed for it and caught it just in time to stop everything from falling out onto the floor. He lifted the bowie knife aside to get at the matches, jiggled the drawer shut, and turned back to the stove. His hand was shaking. He was certain that his father had been with her.

–Do you have a sweetheart, honey? Dot asked.

Why didn't she just shut up? Joshua reached up to open the damper in the chimney. He wanted to say yes. But it would be a stupid lie. He knelt to open the door to the lower grate. He snapped the match lit — it wavered in his fingers — and poked it under the grate to light the straw. Smoke and yellow flames curled up into the stove. The kindling began to crackle and spark.

–Well, do you? she said.

–Uh . . . no. Not at the moment, he said.

She laughed.

–Boy your age needs a little female company, she said.

Carys barked outside and then Mr. Ford appeared in the doorway.

–Goddamn, ain't you got that fire going yet? he said.

Mr. Ford looked dapper in his homburg and his three-piece suit. He didn't look at all ferocious. He slammed the door shut and the snowshoes hanging on the back of it rattled.

–It's all ready, Mr. Ford, Joshua piped.

His voice came out in an ingratiating whine. This whole thing was fast becoming just one embarrassment after another. Mr. Ford eased the Remington out of his waistband and laid it on the table beside the woman. He dipped his hand into his trouser pocket and flipped a coin toward Joshua. Joshua grabbed at it, but the coin hit the heel of his hand. It clattered on the pine boards and rolled under the kitchen cabinet.

–Snap up your hand, boy, and trust your eyes, said Mr. Ford. Even if you do wear peepers.

Joshua's ears burned. He nodded.

–That's the only dollar I got, said Mr. Ford.

He straddled the chair next to Dot and rested his arms on the back of it. They were both looking at him, she with the streaked makeup and leaning forward to show her breasts; he with the smooth-faced smirk under his homburg.

–I don't need any dollar, Mr. Ford, said Joshua. But let me get it for you anyway.

–You earned it. What you talking about?

Joshua couldn't tell him. It was so complicated. His father. The woman, Dot. His mother. Joshua couldn't take the money because it would connect him to them. But he wanted to be connected to him. To Mr. Ford. To them. To her and what she did with men, but he was afraid. That was it. More than anything else he was afraid, and he was ashamed of being afraid.

–You get it, it's yours, said Mr. Ford.

–No sir, really, said Joshua. I'll get it for you.

Joshua got down on his hands and knees. He slid his hand beneath the cabinet among the dust balls, the clinging spider webs, and the greasy boards. His fingertips brushed against the coin. He brought it out from under the cabinet and stood up, unfolding himself to his full height. His cheeks were so hot he felt like a beacon.

–Here's the dollar, Mr. Ford.

Joshua held the big coin out toward Dot and Mr. Ford. The killer was smirking at him.

–Keep it. You can earn a lot more if you'll come and help me unload that wagon tomorrow morning.

This was a simple calculation. If he kept the money, Joshua was a dollar and eighty-six cents away from buying the Colt. If Mr. Ford had given him a dollar to light a fire in the stove, how much more would he give him to unload a wagon? He pocketed the coin and looked across at Mr. and Mrs. Ford. At the thin-faced convicted killer who had escaped the noose and at his coquettish wife, her cheeks streaked with kohl and rouge run, who sold her body to men other than her husband.

–I'll see you in the morning, Joshua said.

VII

THE TOP EDGE OF A TEN-DAY-OLD MOON NUDGED OVER THE RIM of the canyon and spread its white light like a frost over the town. The puddles on Amethyst Street glistened with it. And it was reflected in the windowpanes of Frazee's store that were otherwise in darkness. Joshua kept to the shadows as he walked up the boardwalk toward his own house on the hill. He would help Mr. Ford in the morning, even if it meant making a damn fool of himself in front of Bob and Dot Ford again. He needed the money. Up the street, lights were on in the Orleans Club, though the sign above it was in darkness. The voices inside were already loud and would get louder as Saturday night progressed. A fiddle sawed a muffled jig. Perhaps his da was already in there. Joshua hurried past the double doors that were closed against the evening cold. Beyond the Orleans Club, warm yellow lamplight glowed in Tilly's Hard Goods, one of the few stores left open on the street. Mr. Tilly was at the cash drawer counting the day's takings. A shotgun rested on the counter. How easy would it be to walk in with a pistol and demand money? Jesse James had robbed banks and trains. Mr. Ford had done the same. Could he, Joshua, ever do the same? It was unimaginable. He passed Greene's Assay Office and Chang Jen Wa's laundry and reached the pathway to his house.

Up on the hillside, the Beynon house was lightless. Joshua hurried over the plank bridge across the creek. It was cold up here in the mountains. He would be glad to be home. As he approached the saltbox house, Carys commenced to bark. She had run on ahead of him, hungry, no doubt, after her day of chasing mules and wagons. She stayed close to him only when she had a mind to, and Joshua considered that Carys's mind was not the dog's strong suit. She would be at her bowl under the kitchen porch.

Joshua turned the key in the heavy lock on the front door and slipped it back into his pea coat pocket.

The living room air was damp. Joshua felt for the matches that he knew were on the lamp stand. He found them and struck one. He lifted the glass chimney and touched flame to the black wick.

Light bloomed and revealed the sacrilege of neglect in this cold shrine to his mother's memory: the curtains drawn, as always; wisps of cobweb hanging across the pastel patterns stenciled around the walls; and, on the backs of the green armchairs and the settee, delicate chenille covers gray with dust. Joshua's lamplight was reflected in the varnish of the four Margolis chairs and on the surface and the legs of the table. It shone in the panels of the Steinway upright piano. Not a note had been struck at the keyboard since his mother's death.

Joshua crossed to the empty fireplace. His breath was visible around him. He set the lamp on the mantel and looked into the oval mirror. His eyes were magnified into two blue marbles by his crystal-lensed glasses.

–I am giving up my job at Frazee's, Mam.

The room remained silent, but he knew that his mother's spirit was listening.

–I'm going to work for Mr. Robert Ford now. Mr. Ford is opening a new saloon, you know. Perhaps I can become his accountant.

That was a lie, of course. The old man would think him a fool for talking his thoughts out loud like this, but Joshua didn't think that his mother could read his mind. Even so, he knew that she did not approve of his plans.

–Nothing to worry about, Mam.

Joshua leaned back from the mantel, pulled back the pea coat, and stuffed his hands into his trouser pockets. The dollar coin that Ford had flipped to him was in the left-hand pocket. Two quarters from Frazee in the right. He would earn more the next day. The Colt .45 was almost his.

–It's Da that I'm worried about, Mam. He's drinking terrible, he said.

He wanted to tell her about Dot and his father — how he suspected that his da had been with her in a crib — but he couldn't bring himself to do that. And he couldn't tell her that Dot had practically offered herself even to him. Or how much he wanted to buy Dot's services.

–Mam, I don't know what to do, Joshua said to the glass.

But it was his own bespectacled face that stared back at him, not his mother's. He rubbed at the soft fuzz on his cheek. It became more visible when he turned his head toward the yellow lantern light. Small chance of growing a beard for at least a year or more. Even a year was optimistic. Mr. Ford didn't have a beard. That didn't stop women from liking him. Dot Ford had practically invited Joshua to buy her. Had he imagined it? Whether that hint was real or imagined, his hips eased forward and his peter hardened. He blushed. Joshua didn't want to be in this room any longer with the invisible eye of his mother fixed upon him. He picked up the lamp. The glass chimney wobbled as he went through into the kitchen. He pulled the door shut behind him to keep his mother's spirit in the living room. He set the lamp down on the table. Shards of china still littered the flagstoned floor. Joshua took the corn broom from its place beside the back door and with short, sharp jerks swept the broken pieces of crockery over to the potbellied stove. He could clean out the china with the ashes.

Joshua dug into his pocket for a precious twenty-five-cent coin and placed it on the table for his drunken, stupid father. He didn't want the old sot to come yelling up the stairs in search of his money. Leaving the door to the kitchen unlocked, he went up the narrow stairs to his bedroom.

He slung his pea coat and conductor's cap onto the quilt on his bed and crossed the room to his desk. The pine chair creaked as he sat in it. He pulled his ledger from between *The Complete Works of William Shakespeare* and *Evangeline* and opened it to the record of his savings. He uncorked his ink, dipped the steel-nibbed pen in it, and added $1.25 to the column of figures. Carefully, he blotted the numbers dry. He was only one dollar and eighty-six cents short of $5.75, and he had six whole days left to find the rest of the money.

Joshua turned the pages of the ledger and stopped at the place where he had pasted in a letter. It was in his Aunt Sharon's hand. That damned letter that she had written to his mother just over three years ago.

You would not believe all the economic opportunities that Jack and I have encountered, in a land where the resources are abundant and the people to exploit them so few.

He had read and reread that one line a thousand times since his mother's death. That one line was the cause of all that had happened to the Beynon family. Joshua took off his conductor's cap and set it on the desk. He leaned his elbows on the blotter. The letter triggered the unstoppable litany that came to torture him again. What if his mother had not received that small inheritance in 1888? What if his aunt Sharon had not married Jack Ammonds? What if Sharon and Jack had not emigrated to America? What if his mother and father had simply refused Sharon's cajoling them to join her? So what if the Amethyst Mine did need a good accountant? Joshua's da had had a steady job in Wales. He had been the accountant at Deep Navigation Colliery for eleven years. Why should he go halfway across the world to do the same thing? Uncle Jack wrote that he had convinced the Amethyst Mine owner that Da was the man for the job. It had tempted his father. And his mam couldn't wait to see Auntie Sharon.

–We're going to leave behind these black slag heaps and give you children a new life, his mam had said.

That was at his twelfth birthday party, just before she had given him the diary. Three months later they were in Weaver. They had moved into their new home a month before Christmas. Everything had been perfect up to that point, and even a little beyond. The epidemic broke out in February. Elsa was the first to have the sickness. Mam nursed her day and night, but she died after a week of fevers and horrible ceaseless coughing. Ten days later, he saw the flush on his mother's own face. Ewan, the baby, was already a screaming little ball of pain and coughs and wheezes. Joshua had boiled water and carried it in a copper pan up to his mam's bedroom. He thought he would steam the rattling fluid out of her lungs. Ewan died that day. They didn't tell his mam but wrapped the blue-faced body in Aunt Sharon's quilt and put it in the front room on the piano stool. Joshua and his da prayed all night that his mam might be spared. Hour after hour, they knelt in the bedroom. His mother's face was drawn and flushed. She gulped for air and shuddered. She followed the baby into death not two days later. They laid the bodies next to Elsa's in the cemetery's overburdened communal vault. They had to wait for spring sun to thaw the ground before they could bury them all.

That was when Da started drinking, first up at Robert Ford's first saloon — the one that had burned down — and later at Soapy Smith's. Then Da argued with Uncle Jack and Auntie Sharon and refused to let them into the house. Joshua didn't mind. He went to school down in Creede during the week and to Frazee's on Saturdays. And he saw less and less of his father. There was always food in the house and wood for the fire, but Da always had work to do. Or he had to drink. And lately he didn't come home at all. He slept with the whores. He slept with the bloody whores. Like Dot Ford. How could Mr. Ford allow his wife to go with other men? How much money would a whore charge? Always money. Money for work. Money for a gun. Money for a woman. Would a whore take on a fifteen-year-old boy? She probably would for the money. Always the money. What would Dot look like naked?

He imagined the globes of her breasts, and his buttocks clenched. His peter pressed against his trousers. He closed the ledger. He would like to see her naked. He would like to know what it was like to be between her legs. He blushed. Strained to hear if anyone approached the house. The canyon was silent beyond his bedroom window.

Joshua reached down under the curved base of the mahogany bookshelf and he recovered a dusty brown envelope. A narrow red string, wound around two leather tabs, held the flap closed. He unwound the string and slid out six *cartes de visite* that he had purchased from the drunken degenerate Ed O'Kelley for the sum of one dollar. Joshua arranged the cards on the blotter. Each stiff card was edged with gold around a black-and-white daguerreotype of a woman in a state of undress: skirts lifted to the waist; unlaced bodices baring breasts; one woman wearing nothing more than a satin carnival mask. He decided that Dot would look like the plumpest of the women. The one reclining on a divan, with nothing to cover herself but a hand fan of peacock feathers. Yes, she was a plump one, that Dot. Joshua unbuttoned his trousers. He would pay her with the money that he'd win from Soapy Smith.

VIII

ELLA'S BONNET SCRAPED AGAINST HER EARS. SHE YANKED AT THE ribbon under her chin, tugged it off, and tossed it away from her. She stumbled through the grass and mud on numb feet. The dark rock walls of the canyon rose above her. Her arms itched. And the skin on her ribs. And the cold skin of her thighs. Watery mucus trickled down and tickled her upper lip. She sniffed it back. The salty snot triggered a spasm in her intestines. A wave of nausea rolled up into her throat. She retched up bile, and spat it, bitter, into the grass. She shivered, hugged herself tight, rubbed the prickly goose flesh of her upper arms, and stumbled on. Fifty yards away, a fire sparkled in the encampment of the Chinese. Pines formed a dark green curtain above the tents. Wet gunny-sacks and scraps of sodden newspaper lay in the brown puddles through which she picked her way. She shivered as if her bones wanted to shake themselves apart. The Chinamen at the camp looked so goddamn warm, all bundled up in their padded cotton jackets. Over the flames of their campfire, a blackened kettle hung from a chain fixed to a wrought-iron tripod. Seven of Chang Jen Wa's road crew squatted around the blaze as if waiting for steam to curl from the kettle's spout. Four of the men had their backs to Ella, each with a long black braid resting between his shoulder blades.

Help me, goddamn you, she thought.

She said nothing. Her bones grated. Ankles and knees ground in their sockets. Tiny, busy hooks and claws scraped away at her marrow. The hurt would not stop until she got something into her. The morphine and her syringe were back at the cabin. Too far to return now. How could the ache get so bad on such a short walk? It was as if someone had opened a faucet and drained her of her afternoon shot. A few pipes of opium would set her right. A sudden cramp crushed her belly in a vise. She doubled over. She was dizzy, in a cold sweat. She stumbled toward the fire.

Dear God, I gotta stop it.

Tears were on her cheeks. She had never, ever, wanted to stop before.

Only one of the Chinamen raised his head at her approach. The brim of his battered felt hat was turned up at the front over his broad, flat forehead. His face was green in the firelight, the cheekbones sharp to the point of starvation. His eyes were a soft brown. So soft. She wanted to cry.

–You want Chang Jen Wa? the man asked.

She nodded. The road gang was silent for a moment. A young man with a sparse beard glanced at her and then turned back to stare at the kettle again. Another tugged at his pin-striped railroad engineer's cap and spat into the fire. The oldest Chinaman grinned at her. He had four teeth in his head. Out of the dark red hole of his ruined mouth came garbled sound. The only Chinee she could understand was chippy jargon, and she knew that well enough. She heard "*fan qui*" and "*yen*" but nothing else she recognized. All the other men laughed. All except the soft-eyed man in the turned-up hat.

–Is he here? she asked.

The wave passed. She was almost normal. Only slightly nauseous. The soft-eyed one stood up. Ella followed him. He walked between the two lines of tents. A wave of prickly cold crawled across her skin. Chang Jen Wa had always frightened her. Whenever she saw him she was weak like this. She breathed deeply through her nostrils. Breathed out. Looked up. Chang Jen Wa's house was a witch's cottage from a fairy story. Like the houses in the stories that Ella's mama had read to her when she was a baby. The gingerbread house. A Chinaman in a German's house. The German was dead now. Died of the pneumonia. Chang Jen Wa had snapped up his property. Chang Jen Wa would snap up the world. Snap up Ella. Eat her alive in the gingerbread house. Her guide rapped at the solid oak door. The window cut into it was shaped like an ace of clubs. Lamp glow shone yellow. Ella folded her arms across her belly. The door swung open. A Celestial girl held up the light. From neck to ankle she was draped in black-and-gold brocade. Her face was flat and smooth, the long sweep of her eyes kohled. Such a small nose and lips. Part of her black hair swept up to a topknot, and the rest of its abundance cascaded over her shoulders and down almost to her waist.

–I want to see Chang Jen Wa, said Ella.

The girl nodded and stepped back, tottering as if her feet were sticks. Ella stepped over the threshold, one hand on the lintel to steady herself. The ceiling of the small hallway pressed down to suffocate her. The Celestial's shifting lamp made shadowy insects scurry in sickening waves across the walls. There were more doors on either side of Ella. The girl opened one on the right. Ella followed her into a tiny room. Heavy drapes blocked out all light from outside. A fire blazed in the soot-blackened hearth. Its flames lit up the scroll paintings on the walls that depicted a heathen pageant. Demons with rolling eyes and bared fangs sat horses or stood astride tigers. The demons gripped swords and lances and bows. Others held dripping hearts and entrails to their ravenous mouths. Ugly sons of bitches. Why the hell would anyone want to hang them up in their house? Ella bent her bony body, squatted over a low divan, and let herself fall onto it. She needed to be warm again, but the heat of the fire would not penetrate her icy skin. Her nails clawed into the flesh of her arms. Chang Jen Wa was not here. He would punish her with time. Torture her. Make each minute an hour. Time had to stop. A steel band tightened across Ella's forehead. Sharp pain behind her eyes. Her body shook. If that Chink bastard didn't come in directly, she would fix herself a pipe. The Celestial girl had tottered away. Left her with only the firelight. She breathed deep against the nausea. The door opened and Chang Jen Wa waddled toward the fireplace. The light of the fire shimmered on the green brocade tunic stretched tight across his belly. He was the bringer of bounty.

–Oh . . . , he said.

His fat hands with their short fingers fluttered up to his chin, stroked his thin mustache. The eyes sparkled. He had bags under his eyes, a double chin, the skin yellow and smooth like a child's.

. . . you don't look well.

She didn't look well? Of course she didn't look well. If she had a knife she could stab him.

–Wait, he said and turned and went out again.

Wait? Dear God.

A bell tinkled. She would get down on her knees to him if she had to. Chang Jen Wa reappeared.

–The boy is coming, he said.

A small Celestial slipped past him into the room, a pigtailed boy in white cotton pajamas carrying a red lacquer casket. The boy knelt at the table to the right of the fireplace and flipped up the casket's lid.

Behind him, Chang Jen Wa slid his hand inside his silk tunic and brought out a gold fob watch. He clicked open the lid, studied it, snapped it shut and repocketed it without comment on the hour, as if he were impatient that the face of the watch did not reveal something else to him other than the time of day. Was he mocking her impatience?

The small Celestial took a *yen poon* from the red casket and laid it on the table. He began to fill the little compartments in the black lacquer tray with hooks and knives and merciful needles. Then he set up a *yen gah* rack with enough holes in its flat top for five bowls. Oh yes, she would need more than one pipe. Into the holes he laid the round brass *ows*, not ornate, but rather like enclosed tobacco bowls with a narrow hole in the center. Ella didn't need prettiness. And then he took a plain wooden box from the red lacquer casket. He laid five long bamboo *yen tsiang* on the right of the tray. The pipe barrels had beautiful flower-shaped brass collars whereon to fit the bowls. What a dear child. He was so speedy with the instruments. Next he placed a small wooden block down on the tray and laid a long needle on it. The point of the needle was brown with hop stain. It was coming now. His delicate fingers placed the thin curved blade of a *yen shee gow* next to the needle, where he would have it ready to scrape the spent bowls. There was time enough for that, why didn't he get on with it? The Chinese boy took out a small, round red lacquer cylinder. His deft fingers unscrewed the top. This was it. He dipped the needle in and twirled it. On the point of the needle was a dark brown sticky pill of opium. A glistening ball of pure *li yuen*, the best of the best opium. She didn't need to taste it to know. She dug her nails into her palms to control her impatience. The boy prepared the pill and pressed it onto the brass *ow*, close to the small hole in the center of the bowl. He fitted the *ow* onto a thick bamboo pipe. Ella smoothed and smoothed her purple organza dress. He came toward her, cradling the pipe on his palms, and she snatched it from him. The boy turned back to the table and picked up a taper. With a sweep and dip of his wrist, he lit the taper from the fire and Chang Jen Wa held up his hand.

Chang Jen Wa took three long joss sticks from a box that stood on the mantelpiece beneath a picture of a heathen demon. The Chinaman's pudgy little fingers held the ends of the joss sticks in the flame of the boy's taper. Ella was holding a cold, dry pipe. The heathen son of a bitch, what the hell was he playing at? She needed a lamp. Chang Jen Wa shook out the flame and the ends of the sticks glowed red as streams of perfumed smoke spiraled into the air. He turned to the left-hand side of the fireplace. Another table. Upon it sat a jade idol. Its smooth, serene features mocked her. Chang Jen Wa put the joss sticks in a conical brass censer that stood in front of the idol. At last, the boy lit the *yen dong*. He brought the lamp toward her divan. She leaned forward and the child stopped, confused. She brought the pipe close to the lamp in his hand. He didn't need to put the lamp down. Her mouth was tight around the pipe and she sucked greedily. He could hold it for her. The smoke was in her throat. She swallowed and swallowed, filled her lungs with the tearing smoke, bit into her lower lip so that she would not cough and lose any.

Chang Jen Wa motioned to the boy. The child set the lamp down on the flat wooden arm of Ella's divan and turned back to the table. The dear little child was already preparing a second pipe. She was still shaking. The pain in her head was monstrous, but the smoke was already soothing its way along the spiderous tracks of her nerves. Two more pipes and everything would be fine. She thanked Chang Jen Wa's heathen gods for smiling on her. The glaring demons on the wall were there to protect her now.

–There, said Chang Jen Wa, that's better, isn't it?

He had only the trace of an accent.

Ella handed the spent pipe to the boy. He gave her another loaded one and she leaned over to light it. She took a deep drag on it. She sucked at the second pipe and stretched out on the divan.

–Dear God, I thought I was dying.

–Yen sick only.

–You don't use it?

–I once use it. But no more.

Ella nodded. Chang Jen Wa ran a road crew and a laundry and

he sold opium to whites. He wouldn't allow his own people to use it. It made good sense. Who the hell could dig a road or wash laundry if they were doped up or sick?

–Now you just sell it.

–I am a sinful man.

Ella leaned toward the lamp. She puffed on the pipe and got the opium to bubble. Her bones had melted into a warm and bendable heap. Her head fell back against her pillow. She gestured at the serene jade idol.

–You a religious man? she asked him.

–I am a sinful man, he said again.

–Is that your God? she asked.

–There is no God, said Chang Jen Wa. All gods and demons are dreams. Heaven and Hell are just dreams. All this . . .

He gestured around the room.

–. . . is just a dream.

He smirked at her. The lips curled up and she saw two gold teeth. Chang Jen Wa was playing with her mind. He wasn't no religious type. Not even a heathen one. He pressed his fat fingertips together. One of his eyebrows had twisted down over the eye. He had a little crease above his nose. His lips pressed into a purse.

–Why don't you come and work for me, Ella? he said. Then you can have all the hop you want.

What? What was he talking about?

She smiled. He wanted her to service his Chinamen.

Maybe they would be cleaner than whites. Had to be cleaner than miners. She could get morphine and opium most anywhere, but it might be less arduous if she were so close to the source of it all.

–What would Bob Ford do? she said.

He shrugged. His slanty little eyes flashed at her.

–He wouldn't stop you.

–He's just getting set up again, Ella said. He wouldn't appreciate me branching out on my ownsome. He needs all the help he can get.

–I don't mean that you will work in Weaver, Chang Jen Wa said. Maybe you get away from here. Colorado will soon be no good for Chinese. Most white men want to drive us out. I am getting my crew out before it is too late. Very soon. I think San Francisco will be better for me. I know many people there. I would take you with me. Only work for high class. My colleagues. They pay you big money. Not like miners or even roadworkers.

Ella nodded. She had never been with a Chinaman or a nigger. If Chang Jen Wa wanted her to go with men like himself who controlled labor and owned laundries and opium dens, life might not be so bad. But if they gave her enough hop she would do anything for anybody.

–So you'd take me with you to San Francisco? she teased.

She gave her voice that flirty little come-on that would stiffen his pecker. Maybe Chang Jen Wa just wanted to do it with her tonight and was setting her up.

–Sure, he said.

She passed the spent pipe to the boy. Watched him scrape off the hard residue into a little *yen shee hop* box. She felt sleepy. Laid her head down. Closed her eyes.

–Yes, she said, take me with you.

Yes, she would. San Francisco. It had to be better than Weaver. Chang Jen Wa's voice soothed her. He took her hand. He helped her up off the divan. He led her into a courtyard. It must be evening. The light was golden. Golden, like the pillars all around them. And the steps that led up through the pillared doors and into the bare temple. Only the fat green idol, gigantic, sat on a gilded altar.

–This way, said Chang Jen Wa.

He led her past the smiling idol and down a stone corridor. A narrow door opened onto a vast and crowded saloon room, full of men and smoke and crib girls. And, God damn, Bob Ford, in his fine gray suit, sat at a table playing cards. God damn. With Jesse James. Jesse when she first met him. When he was young. Sixteen. His square jaw was smooth. His hair long to the shoulders of his heavy duster that reached his busted boots. It was just a dream. God damn. And there was that kid with the glasses and the peaked cap standing behind Bob. What the hell was he doing there? Ella giggled. Dot had her hands on the kid's shoulder. The gangly kid was dressed in one of Bob's brown suits.

The Golden Palace Saloon, thought Ella.

–Is this San Francisco? she said.

–This way, said Chang Jen Wa.

They stopped at Bob and Jesse's table. She heard the sharp crack, crack, crack of a hammer. Through a huge window on the right-hand wall, Caleb Barebones, the town carpenter, was building a gallows. The framing hammer in his fist rose and fell, rose and fell, like a steam-driven piston. The hammering and the buzz of voices in her ears and the laughter all confused her.

–Take me out of here, she said.

Jesse blocked her way. His eye sockets were empty of eyeballs. Just two dark holes. And another dark hole in the side of his head.

–You owe me, Ella, he said.

–Take me out of here! she screamed.

She jerked upright on the divan. Chang Jen Wa had gone. The fire blazed bright. The joss before the idol had burned out. The little Chinese boy sat next to the table. She was cold. Another pipe would settle things down more. This was good dope. She had to take some back to Bob and Dot. A peace offering. How could she tell them that she was leaving for San Francisco with Chang Jen Wa? Bob would try to stop her. Dot too. But she would take them the opium. Maybe in the morning.

IX

EARLY NEXT DAY, JOSHUA STOOD ON THE EMPTY SUNDAY-MORNING boardwalk. He lifted his face to the sun and let its heat penetrate him as if he were a savage who worshipped the planets. The pure light lit him up as it did the red walls of the canyon and the white tents and the offices and stores of Weaver.

His father had still not come home. No doubt the old man was drunk somewhere, which was not unusual for a Saturday night. But Joshua did not want his father to turn up on the road and catch him unloading Ford's wagon. His father hated Bob Ford, but Joshua had money to earn and he didn't need his father to jeopardize that.

Carys zigzagged across Amethyst Street until she reached the horseless hitching post in front of the Last Chance Restaurant. She squatted down and pissed beside it. She stood again and busied herself by sniffing at a pile of rotten foodstuff just inside the restaurant's alley. Her tail thumped from side to side. Why it was that such foul matter could make a dog so happy, he failed to understand. He could smell the rot from all the way across the street. The businesses of Weaver were closed for the Sabbath, but such was the lack of piety in this part of town that only one family of Hunkies passed him on their way down toward the Resurrection House of Prayer and Blessed Salvation. A crocodile of five children followed their broad-arsed parents past Chang Jen Wa's laundry. Down here on Amethyst Street, all the thieves and whores and gamblers were asleep at this early hour. Joshua walked on.

A raggedy Ed O'Kelley sat hunched over on the steps outside the Orleans Club. His derby hat hung precariously from the back of his tousled and greasy red hair. He turned his face to look at Joshua. One of his eyes was hidden behind the slit of a garish and puffy bruise that mottled the left side of his face. The other one, bloodshot, had evil life within it that examined Joshua warily. The sunken cheeks were stubbled red, and the big red mustache was crusted with food matter, undoubtedly regurgitated. O'Kelley's arms were crossed over one knee. He rested a hobnail boot on the bottom step. The other was deep in mud.

–Have you seen my father? Joshua asked.

–That damn dog o' yours don't care where it piss, do it? said O'Kelley.

A sour stench as of rotten apples and stale tobacco wafted up from the disheveled drunkard. It turned Joshua's stomach.

–He didn't come home last night. I wondered if you might have seen him.

–Yep. I seen him.

The head turned down. O'Kelley spat into a puddle.

Down on Main Street, the post office clock tower read seven minutes past four. Joshua judged the time to be around eight o'clock.

–Would you know where he is now, Ed?

Joshua shifted his weight. He hated having to ask information of O'Kelley.

–Fur as I remember, he got in a wagon with Stumpy Stokes last night and they headed down to Jimtown. They was looking to go to Dave Sponsilier's dance hall. If they ain't in a ditch or drowned in the creek, I'd say they'd be in some whore's crib in Jimtown.

Joshua chewed at the inside of his cheek. He pressed his lips together.

–Son of a bitch.

–Man's got to have his pleasures, boy. Reckon you know that by now.

Joshua turned red. Ed was just reminding him about the *cartes de visite*.

–Didn't anyone think to arrest you for shooting up the damn clock, Ed?

O'Kelley's single visible eye rolled in Joshua's direction again. It made Joshua want to poke it with a stick.

–They come for me, jailed me, and Soapy bailed me out all within a hour, he said.

–I . . . I thought, uh, you were about to shoot Mr. Ford yesterday.

O'Kelley hawked in his throat and spat into the street.

–If I was going to shoot Bob Ford, I would of shot him directly. Not the damn clock.

Joshua wanted to rile the man.

–Mr. Ford drew his gun, you know. You were lucky.

O'Kelley's mouth twisted under the mustache.

–He drew his gun on me?

Joshua flushed again. He had expected O'Kelley to act scared, but the man was either still too drunk or too stupid to feel that he had been in any danger.

–You can't blame him, said Joshua. You had your gun out, too. It looked like you might want to kill him.

–The son of a bitch pulled his gun on me, you say. Old Soapy don't like his sort. If Bob Ford pulled a gun in this town, he's looking to get killed. And I ain't afraid of him, neither. I don't give a shit who he shot. Fur as I know, he ain't shot no one since.

The conversation seemed to go off at the wrong tangent whatever Joshua said. He wished that he had kept his mouth shut, but that smelly man on the step below him would be a fool to force Bob Ford into a duel.

–I wouldn't tangle with him, Joshua said.

–You wouldn't tangle with him. The man's a goddamn coward. He shot Jesse James in the back or he wouldn't have shot him at all. He got a big rep for killing a big man. Just the same as a kid like you could get famous easy by shooting Bob Ford. Even if he is a damn coward.

–I don't believe Mr. Ford's a coward.

–You best keep away from scum like that, said O'Kelley. Soapy told your pa he seen you up at Bob Ford's house.

Joshua felt the skin on his neck go tight.

–What did my father say?

–Said he'd take a strap to you when he got home. Seen as he ain't got home, I'd say you got that to look forward to.

–If that drunken son of a bitch takes a strap to me, I swear to God I'll kill him this time.

–Then he got that to look forward to, ain't he?

O'Kelley jerked his head down in a sharp nod. His body was suddenly wracked by a spasm of coughing. He shook as he hacked, and the holster of his pistol bumped back against the step he sat on. He held his rancid jacket under the armpits and retched over his knees. Joshua swallowed some saliva and sucked air through his teeth.

If the old man already knew that he had been at Bob Ford's house, then if he saw him there today it made no difference. The punishment was coming just the same.

–I'm going, Ed. Thanks for the information.

Joshua headed up the boardwalk in the direction of the canyon head. The drunkard called out.

–You'd do well to stay away from Bob Ford, boy. He's got something coming to him, believe me.

Bob Ford is better than any of these bastards, Joshua thought. He'd shoot them all, I bet. And my da has to get himself involved with Soapy Smith and his stinking minions, the son of a bitch.

Carys the coon hound dashed down Amethyst Street after Joshua and fell in step behind his stamping heels. Joshua turned onto Main Street and marched up past the livery stable and the cemetery toward Mr. Ford's cabin. Beyond it, the lines of buckets on the cableway from the mine hung unmoving over the canyon. A hundred feet below the turn station end of the cableway, the unhitched wagon stood on the road in front of Mr. Ford's cabin. Mr. Ford and a Negro leaned against the tailgate. They were smoking. On the slope between the wagon and the house, a third man, blond and wiry and short, was seated on the folded tarp that had been pulled from the wagon load. He was reading what appeared to be a magazine.

Stacked on the bed of the wagon was a pile of barrels, boxes, mattresses, and furniture. The top of a wheel painted with colored numbers arched over the load like the sign for a carnival.

–Well, here he is, called Mr. Ford.

–Ready and willing, said Joshua.

Joshua kept his head down and looked up at the men from under the peak of his cap. Mr. Ford was not in his smart suit. He had on blue bib overalls and a red-checked shirt. His smooth face was tight, jaws clenched against the morning cold. The most striking thing about the Negro beside him was the whiteness of the man's hair. Joshua had not seen many black men in his life. The Negro had a heavy ridge over his eyes topped by white eyebrows. His nose was flat. The lips were big. He had the look of a fairground prizefighter. The black man's barn jacket pulled tight across his chest and his round belly. Joshua didn't trust Negroes. And the man eyed Joshua as if he were an opponent in the ring.

–'Bout time you turned up, the Negro said, I'm getting too old to be doing this kinda fatigue. 'Specially of a Sunday morning.

–Niggers are supposed to work, said the blond man up the slope.

He had a mustache like a cavalier and long hair that came to his shoulders. He was reading the same copy of the *Log Cabin Library* that Joshua had bought not two days before, *Jesse James's Hunt to the Death*.

–Only if you pay 'em, the Negro said. We been free nigh on thirty years.

–Twenty-seven, the blond man said.

–Time enough, the Negro said.

–You gonna work or you gonna talk? the blond man said. Niggers these days always gotta have the last goddamn word.

–You ain't done a honest day's work in your life.

–I'm retired, get that boy working.

–Joshua's a strapping young man, said Mr. Ford.

Mr. Ford and the Negro flipped away their cigarettes at exactly the same moment, though in opposite directions.

–He's a man full-growed, said the Negro. Put him to work.

Every word sounded as if the black man was clearing his throat. The Negro was talking about him as if he weren't there. He had no right. This Negro was almost ordering him around.

–This here is Silas Strickland, said Mr. Ford.

Silas Strickland held out a hand the width of a cast-iron skillet. The palm was pale. Joshua hesitated, then offered his own hand. The black man crushed it in his grip. The Negro's eyes seemed yellowed, but Joshua felt that this Silas Strickland saw well enough. His big white-haired head nodded slowly.

–Must be Joshua, I guess, he said.

–Yessir, Joshua said, and wondered if he should have used "sir" to a Negro.

Strickland grinned at him.

–Well, don't be taking no example from Dick Liddil up there. We got work to do, boy, and Liddil is the laziest son of a bitch this side of the Mississippi.

Dick Liddil? Joshua thought. Dick Liddil had been one of the James Gang who had robbed the Glendale train. Joshua had read about it in Buel's book *The Border Outlaws.* Liddil had testified against Frank James in a deal with the law. Joshua was standing among living legends.

–I *am* working up here, said Liddil. Just using my *brain* is all.

–Reading that crock of shit supposed to be about Jesse James, said Mr. Ford.

–Well, it is a crock of shit, said Liddil. I'll give you that.

Liddil would know. According to what Joshua had read, Liddil knew Jesse James as well as, if not better than, Mr. Ford did. Being among living legends had made Joshua forget that he should tell Mr. Ford about his conversation with Ed O'Kelley. And O'Kelley's threat. Now the timing didn't seem right to tell him. Joshua judged that he should wait until after the wagon was unloaded.

–What do we have to do? Joshua said.

Strickland ambled over to the back of the wagon, flipped out the iron pins, and dropped the tailgate. The chains rattled against the woodwork. His white-haired head was hunched between his broad shoulders, his big arms swung easy. Joshua sniffed the air, curious as to whether a black man might have a different scent than a white. Mr Ford climbed up onto the tailgate.

–Get on up here, Josh, said Mr. Ford. Let's get this thing started.

Joshua pulled himself up onto the tailgate beside Mr. Ford. He lifted a green baize-covered table and swung it down to Strickland, who gripped it in his thick-fingered hands and laid it against the wagon wheel. There would be four card sharps around that table soon enough. Mr. Ford handed down the second table, and Joshua gripped a pair of chairs that had been tied together, seat to seat. Dick Liddil sat up the slope and did not once glance up from his magazine. When the chairs were all set down on the roadside by Strickland, Mr. Ford nodded toward a gigantic canvas bundle about six feet long and four feet wide.

–Tent, said Mr. Ford.

Joshua slid his fingers under the scratchy hemp. This was going to be heavy. The life of the saloon would take place beneath that canvas awning. Loose tongues, loose women, loose wallets, fistfights, knifefights, and gunfights. All orchestrated by the Slayer of Jesse James. And Joshua would be there to see it. In Mr. Ford's employ.

–Ready?

Joshua nodded. The cord cut into his fingers and the muscles in his back tightened under the strain. He was determined not to show any discomfort, though Mr. Ford grimaced and blew opposite him. They swung the bundle onto the edge of the tailgate.

–Let it drop, said Strickland.

Mr. Ford jerked his chin at Joshua and together they tilted the bundle. It slid off the wagon and thudded onto the ground.

–Give us a hand here, Dick, said Strickland.

Liddil raised one eyebrow, shook his head, and recommenced reading.

–You lazy son of a bitch, said Mr. Ford.

He said it with a voice full of venom and affection.

Liddil leaned over and spat.

–He ain't never done a day's work in his life, said Strickland.
–Don't expect me to start now, Liddil said.

By seven minutes past four in the afternoon, the white canvas of the great tent rippled in the wind. Inside that tent, which Joshua had helped to set up, were the ten-foot carved mahogany bar, the Louisiana-made Duchamp faro wheel, seven barrels of beer, two green baize–covered gaming tables, and sixteen chairs. The mattresses, box springs, linens, wash basins, jugs, and piss pots that had also been on the wagon had all been carried into the house by Joshua and Silas Strickland under the direction of Mr. Robert Ford. Dick Liddil had not lifted a finger to help but had read his magazine and brought a tray of coffee from the cabin and once relieved himself, pissing copiously into the sawdust shavings by the side of the tent platform. When the afternoon had cooled, he had gone inside the cabin and had not reappeared.

With the most of the wagon load gone, the Schulz player piano stood revealed in all its glory. Joshua leaned on the wagon's tailgate. He tilted his conductor's cap onto the crown of his head and pushed his glasses back against the bridge of his nose. His eyes blinked behind the lenses. It was a fine piano. Cherrywood gleamed in the early afternoon sunlight. Delicate beading framed the wood panels. Some kind of lever-and-box mechanism was fixed in front of the keyboard, and instead of normal piano pedals it had two enormous foot treadles. With all the music-making mechanisms inside that upright frame, the piano was going to be monstrously heavy.

–Come on up, Strick, called Mr. Ford.

Strickland passed Joshua, his white woolly head hunched between his shoulders as he bounced up the board ramp.

–Stay down there, Josh, said Mr. Ford.

Strickland and Mr. Ford laid their weight against the piano. Strickland swung around his side of the instrument, and its little brass wheels squeaked and rumbled across the back of the wagon. Strickland was close to the board ramp at the tailgate. Joshua hopped from foot to foot. There was no room for three people to be on the floor of the wagon. Strickland lifted his end of the piano. The cords on his thick neck stood out. His lips were turned down. He stepped back onto the plank ramp and let the little brass wheels come to rest on the top of it. Mr. Ford eased the piano forward. The ramp bowed under the weight of Strickland and piano. The piano tilted. Strickland got in a squat, his chest pressed up against the end of the piano. His left hand clawed for purchase on the smooth rear of it. The piano swayed. Joshua waved his arms in a mime of pushing the instrument upright again. If it fell, it would crush him like an insect.

–Hold the goddamn thing, Strick, called Mr. Ford.

Mr. Ford's already pale face turned a chalky white. Only his bent fingertips held the piano's bulk in balance.

–Oh my goddamn blasted ribs, said Mr. Ford.

–Ease it down now, ease it down, said Strickland.

The Negro backed down the ramp. The cherrywood bulk gleamed in the sunshine. The little brass wheels squeaked again.

–What can I do? called Joshua.

He danced next to the wagon wheel, dodged forward toward the ramp.

–Stay out of the goddamn way, spat Mr. Ford.

There was no need for that. He had only wanted to help.

–Goddamn, I am ruined for life, swore Mr. Ford.

Strickland had the bulky instrument in a tight embrace. His black cheek was pressed to the side of it like a lover's. Mr. Ford's fingers pressed down on the top of the piano until it came off the ramp and to a rest on the muddy road with Strickland's bull-like body still wrapped around it. Strickland unwound himself. He blew.

–Let me take over now, said Joshua.

–Rest up a second, boy, said Mr. Ford.

Mr. Ford's feet were still on the ramp. He leaned against the cherrywood, bent over his right side and clutching his ribs. He eased himself down off the ramp and walked across to the grassy slope below the tent. He lowered himself to the ground, panting, one hand clutching his ribs. Strickland ambled across to Mr. Ford and dropped his bulk onto the grass beside him.

–Rest up, boy, Strickland growled to Joshua.

Joshua wished Mr. Ford would tell the damn Negro to stop ordering him around. He had no choice but to obey. He squatted down next to Strickland. Mr. Ford winced as he lifted his hand and dipped into the pocket of his overalls for his tobacco pouch. He pulled out the makings and tossed the pouch to Strickland. Joshua almost wished that he smoked so that he could partake in their ritual of companionship. And it was a pity that Dick Liddil was not there with them. Mr Ford scratched a match into life. It flared in the cup of his hands, and he leaned toward Strickland for the Negro to light up. The stink of phosphorous and tobacco smoke drifted by.

–Goddamn it, I am ruined for life, said Mr. Ford.

He sighed out smoke. He waved one hand in the air painfully. He sucked in air through his teeth.

–What about this goddamn piano? asked Strickland.

–Whyn't we get the damn thing into the cabin, said Mr. Ford. Then we can have us some music tonight.

These men certainly use terrible language, thought Joshua.

–By God, Mr. Bob, that sounds like a fine idea.

And now, Mr. Ford had invited the Negro into his house for a party.

–Come on, boy, Strickland said. We got work to do.

Joshua got up. He looked at the slope. The cabin door was a lot farther to haul the piano than getting it into the tent. Strickland strolled over to the tent platform. A pile of lumber stood between the platform and the cabin. Strickland chose two wide and stout ten-foot boards, shouldered them, and hauled them back to where the piano stood behind the wagon, where he threw them down. He took one of the boards, dragged it to the front of the piano, and slid it up close to the brass wheels.

–Lift the goddamn thing, Strickland said.

Joshua bit his lower lip. The damn Nigger was pushing these orders too far. Joshua strode over to the piano and with one heave lifted the end onto the plank.

–Good kid, said Mr. Ford.

He was not a kid, but he was pleased at Mr. Ford's compliment. Joshua had the front end square on the board. He stood on the keyboard side of the instrument. Strickland wrapped his bulk around the back end of the piano and bulled it forward along the plank. The cherrywood monster creaked past Joshua and almost off the end of the board. Mr. Ford, still bent over his injured ribs, pulled the other plank head-to-head with the first. Joshua went to the front of the piano and lifted it forward again. On the flat, he and Strickland proceeded quickly, but on the slope, the piano wanted to slide off the skids or tilt over, and they fought to keep it upright. The big Negro kept grinning at him. Joshua's mouth was a hard line. He was not going to show the slightest strain or aggravation. Mr. Ford laid the board for the final ten feet that would bring the piano to the cabin door. Strickland gave a great heave, and Joshua guided the wheels straight and true to the threshold.

–Finally! Joshua yelled.

–What the hell you doing hauling that thing in here?

Mrs. Ford blocked the doorway. Her plump face was puffy and she had no makeup on. Her breasts jiggled against her red silk robe, and Joshua's flag was suddenly at full staff. He wondered if she had been dallying with Dick Liddil while Mr. Ford had been hard at work.

–Mr. Bob be planning a party, Miss Dot, Strickland said.

He laid one hand flat on top of the piano and unbuttoned his barn jacket with the other. His legs were spread wide. He pursed his lips.

Mrs. Ford smiled at Joshua. She clutched the robe to herself and tilted her blond head.

–Well, get that thing in here and bring up a case of whiskey, she said. As soon as I get my dress on, I'll be ready to get drunk.

Joshua was ready, too. He had never been drunk in his life before. This seemed like a good place to begin. In the company of Silas Strickland, Negro; Mrs. Dot Ford, whore; Dick Liddil, train robber; and Mr. Bob Ford, the Slayer of Jesse James.

Mrs. Ford was seated at the beautiful cherrywood musical contraption, clothed once more in her blue satin dress. The dress was somewhat wrinkled and still crusted with red mud at the hem. Mrs. Ford had the aspect of what Joshua imagined as a painted goddess in ancient Greece. She had kohled her eyes and rouged her cheeks, and her little plump lips were red and smiling. Her hands adjusted levers, this way and that, at the keyboard of the player-piano. Her feet worked the treadles. She was playing a march. Joshua sat at the table, in the chair closest to her.

Strickland took the seat to his right and Mr. Ford the far end of the table. Three bottles of whiskey and five clean tumblers stood on the table, and Dick Liddil, sitting opposite Joshua, filled the tumblers, one and all. Joshua picked up a tumbler and gulleted the drink. It burned into his throat and down into his stomach. He screwed his face up with the shock.

–Easy there, boy, said Liddil.

But he refilled the glass right away.

Joshua sniffed deeply. Mrs. Ford's dress held the sour smell of her body, as well as vestiges of some kind of perfume. Her scent and the whiskey, aided and abetted by the tinklings of the player piano, created a divine intoxication in his skull. The golden glow surrounding Mrs. Ford was marginally paler than the whiskey in his glass. Smoke wraiths from the cigarettes rolled by Mr. Ford and Dick Liddil and Strickland curled in a flat stratum over the table and stung Joshua's eyes. He had drunk whiskey on a few occasions previously and had not enjoyed the taste, but he resolved to persist until he was used to it. The second tumbler was somewhat easier to stomach than the first. His body was full of a warmth that eased the work pain from his muscles and bones.

–What do you reckon for the grand opening, Dick? Mr. Ford said.

Liddil twirled up the ends of his cavalier's blond mustache.

–While you sons of bitches was busting a gut, Liddil said, I was using my brain. I know a couple of sporting events would surely draw the crowds. A horse race. And a prizefight.

–Leave me out of this, Liddil, Strickland said. I'm too goddamn old to get in a ring no more.

–Strick, Liddil said, Strick. I would not have you hurt. I have searched this canyon from Weaver all the way down to Jimtown to find a man who looks like a monster but with a jaw of glass. And I have at least three candidates already. And I, as promoter, and as your dearest friend, will allow you to choose the opponent you want.

–How come you don't never fight these sons of bitches your own self? Strickland said.

–My skills, Strick, Liddil said, are strictly in the equestrian field and in the field of finance. Have I not always looked after your best interests?

–Well, I wanna see any son of a bitch you pick before I get in any ring again.

–You have my word, Mr. Strickland. And rest assured, I will do my part by riding in the horse race.

Joshua nodded. Liddil was in fact the ideal build for a jockey: short and wiry and muscular, although he could be a mite overweight.

–Where's the course going to be? Joshua said.

–Start at the livery, up to the cemetery gates and across the meadow, and the finishing line will be right outside Bob Ford's new tent saloon. Soapy Smith will be furious.

The piano lost tempo and went slightly off key as Mrs. Ford looked back over her shoulder, a look of anguish on her plump face, but Mr. Ford just smiled. The lantern light lit on the pale stubble of his cheeks and around his mouth.

–Well, growled Strickland to Mr. Ford, how you off with old Soapy these days?

Joshua glanced toward the end of the table to catch Mr. Ford's reaction. Mr Ford pursed his lips. His smooth face looked a little drawn. A flock of fair hair dropped over his forehead.

–Yesterday he just about told me that he put a bounty on my head.

–How so? Liddil said.

–Form of a bet, Mr. Ford said. He bet, I don't know how much, that a man couldn't kill me.

–In a duel? Liddil said.

–Didn't specify, Mr. Ford said. Young Josh was there. What you think, boy?

Joshua pressed his fingertips around the tumbler. He was not used to being included in conversations with famous killers concerning duels.

–I'm not sure, Mr. Ford.

–Bob, said Mr. Ford.

–I'm not sure, but I seen O'Kelley this morning. He said about Soapy not liking you.

Mr. Ford's shoulders straightened.

–What'd O'Kelley say? asked Mr. Ford.

Joshua was not sure that he ought to answer. But he did.

–Just that Soapy said you got it coming.

–Yeah? Well, I know that. What else he say about yesterday? About what happened in the street?

–He said that he never meant to shoot at you. He said that if he was to shoot you, he'd do it directly.

Strickland burst into a gravelly laugh and drank a long pull on his whiskey. Dick Liddil's lips pursed in a silent whistle.

Mrs. Ford worked nervously at the levers of the player piano. She glanced back again, her teeth worrying her plump little lower lip. The piano had begun to play *Dixie*, and it seemed as if she could not stop her feet from pumping the pedals.

–That all? asked Bob.

Then Joshua said something. He knew before he said it that he shouldn't have said it, but he needed to say something, and what he said was the only thing he could think of to say.

–I told him he was lucky, because you drew your gun and could have shot him dead, right there, if he tried to kill you.

–You told him I drew on him?

Joshua nodded and flushed beet red. He wished that Mrs. Ford would stop pumping at that player piano.

–Then what he say? insisted Bob.

–He said you were looking to get killed if you pulled a gun on him.

Bob rested his elbows on the table and leaned his chin on top of his interlocked fingers. Joshua realized that he was unwise to have had such a conversation with Ed O'Kelley; that he should not have told the man that Bob Ford had drawn a weapon; that he should not have volunteered a report of his conversation with O'Kelley; and that he was in danger of losing this amicable contact on account of his stupid mouth.

–Let's settle our accounts, said Bob.

–Fine by me, said Strickland.

Bob pulled his money pouch from the breast pocket of his bib overalls. He took two silver coins from the pouch.

–Strick, here's two dollars on account of you being an experienced hand.

–That'll do it, said Strickland.

–I reckon Josh here deserves close to the same. How's a buck fifty?

Joshua's knee started bouncing under the table. A dollar fifty was close enough, even if he had hoped for two.

–That's fine, Mr. Ford, he said.

Bob took a silver dollar and two quarters from his pouch and slapped them on the table in front of Josh.

–Where's mine? said Liddil.

–You didn't do shit, said Mr. Ford.

Before Liddil could protest, the front door swung open and banged against the wall. Joshua twisted in his chair and stared at the apparition framed by the lintel.

Ella Mae Waterson's hair was a crown of stiff copper ropes that coiled down to the elbows of her purple organza dress. Her face was as white and waxy as a spermaceti candle. Her thin nose hooked over the red slash of her mouth, her lips slightly parted to reveal the yellow of her teeth. Her dress hung on her like a shroud. Her arms were bare, and the purple crisscross marks like tattooed serpents writhed up her left forearm. She dangled a muslin bag from her fingers.

–By Christ, Ella, what the hell have you been doing? said Mr. Ford.

–I brought you all a present, she said.

Joshua took another slug at the whiskey, then glanced down at the money and back at Ella. She stepped away from the door. A little Chinese boy with a pigtail and wearing a white cotton tunic entered the cabin. He was like her spirit familiar. He had a red lacquer casket that he carried in front of his chest. Joshua knew that it was something exotic and oriental. He imagined the present to be a vase or a tea pot. Mrs. Ford continued to pump the treadles, but she had let go of the levers and the timing of the music became erratic and jerky. She waved a tumbler with a nervous wiggle.

Ella looked down at the Chinese boy.

–Put that casket on the table, Ella said.

–She brought us a little Chinaman, said Mr. Ford.

–She brought us a piece of opium, giggled Mrs. Ford.

Joshua slid the coins off the table and pocketed them. Being around Bob Ford was like being in a theater. And he was even getting paid to watch the show. The maddening plunk of the player piano mechanically filled the room as Dot's knees rose and fell. Ella stalked across to the stove trailing purple organza and spun around to face them again like a pantomime witch, like a Medusa. Her long bony fingers waved in front of her face, and she pointed toward the bedroom.

–If all our beds are in place, I think we should retire for a little recreation, she said.

Joshua sat back in his chair. Now what? Was he invited, too? Nobody had told him to go home. The whole room hummed behind the tinkling music. He wanted to see what would happen next. Ella had marched into a bedroom, the Chinese boy at her heels like a little acolyte. Well, he had got drunk all right. Maybe now there was going to be some whoring. Joshua stood up, grinned sheepishly at Mr. Ford, and followed Ella into the bedroom.

X

THE INSIDE OF JOSHUA'S HEAD WAS A SOUNDLESS EMPTY DOME. Thoughts rose like bubbles in the emptiness and burst before he connected the words of them. He was on the bed. He craned his neck back as if that would enable his eyeballs to swivel around and look into the empty space of his skull. Not just broken words rose into that void, but images. The visions were clearer than thought: his father, hung over, black lines creasing the face, the bags under the bloodshot eyes. Mrs. Ford's face coming between Joshua and his father. Her shoulders bare. Her breasts like globes that swung over him. Her lips descending to kiss him. Then Frazee the storekeeper pushed her aside. Frazee was smiling down over the beautiful Colt Peacemaker nestled in its red velvet. Joshua could see the Colt clearly, but it was just a dream picture. To buy the pistol, he would have to come out of the soft golden darkness. He didn't want to come out. He had lain here for hours, beyond all harm or trouble. But the Colt. He could see it in all its perfection. It wasn't real in here, where he lay in his warm pool of visions. The real Colt was in Frazee's store, and he knew that he had to get it. Now. Joshua was rising. He was a hooked and sluggish fish being pulled from a muddy pool. His limbs were light but impossible to lift. If he were to lift an eyelid, he would see into the room. Light refracted through the crystal lenses and the net of his lashes. The straight lines of the ceiling rafters came into focus. A cloying sweetness hung in the air, though he could not remember when the last pipe had been lit. He turned his head. Silas Strickland lay on the pallet opposite him. His prizefighter face was in repose. His mouth gaped open so that the pink tongue was visible in the black face. The eyes were closed. His white hair was like crinkled wire. A warmth that he could only name as love filled Joshua's chest and seeped into his loose limbs and neck. He dug his elbow into the rough shuck mattress that whispered and crackled beneath him and he raised his shoulders to look for the others.

No one had moved much. Mr. Ford, asleep, was blocked up against the wall by his wife's bulk. His right arm was curved over her blue satin belly. Her head was propped up on the pillow. Her straggly blond hair hung off the side of the bed. Saliva had trickled from the corner of her mouth and made a large damp patch on the pillow. At the window above the bedded couple, a strip of pale light glimmered at the bottom of the drapes and fell upon the little Chinaman who was curled in a fetal position on the cold hard floor. Next to him stood the table upon which pipes, hooks, scraping knives, and needles lay scattered. Only one lamp was lit. Joshua tilted his head toward the fourth bed. Two glazed and saucer-like eyes stared back at him from behind Dick Liddil's prone and unconscious body. Ella's pale face was like a paper etching among the twisted copper snakes of her hair. The yellow lantern light cast shadows on the triangles of her collarbone. Her skinny breasts curved within her purple organza dress.

–I have to get home now, Joshua said to her.

–Git on home then, Ella said.

Ella's head eased back against her pillow. Her eyelids dipped, her slack chin rested on the bony breastbone.

Joshua swung his booted feet off the edge of the shifting mattress, and his head spun pleasantly as he sat up. He was in a room of the dead. The room itself breathed the bodies of those on the beds. Joshua used both hands to push himself to his feet, and he was surprised at how poised, how balanced, he felt standing. His cap and pea coat were at the foot of the bed. He didn't remember taking them off. The coat was heavy. He slid his arms into it, shrugged it up onto his shoulders. He fitted his cap on his head. Strickland's eyelids rose momentarily, his gaze out of focus, and then he drifted back into sleep.

–I'm going now, Joshua said.

But no one answered him. The door handle sank down under his hand. He pulled the door toward him and lurched into the living room. His legs were like thick sticks threaded together at hip and knee with weak catgut. A laugh rattled up out of his chest. It frightened him. He stumbled toward the front door. Ford's snowshoes hung there. The curved frames and webbing appeared to be in motion — like dancing nets. He opened the door onto the jagged canyon and the brightness of the light struck him full in the eyes. Why was it so bright when a lid of gray clouds fit tightly on the rim of the canyon, pressed down over the town of Weaver? Joshua stepped forward into the outside world. How long had he been in Mr. Ford's house? He couldn't pin down the day. A muffled rattle came from the turn station where the cableway buckets emptied the ore from the Amethyst Mine. It was not Sunday, then. He could remember the wagon, and the raising of the tent and the furnishing of the saloon. He could remember the whiskey and Dot at the piano. But the opium had taken him into a world where all these images that swirled in his memory had taken on a life of their own and combined and recombined into new stories, some of which seemed to play out for entire days and were as real as the world he stumbled through now. And then the visions had disappeared into deep periods of sweet darkness whose duration he could only guess at. A few hours was equally as possible as a few days.

Where was Carys? A cold rush of goose pimples spread from his buttocks to his shoulders and over his scalp. The way his limbs moved was hideous and unnatural. Every step needed to be measured before he put his wooden foot down. He didn't want to walk down to Main Street and up Amethyst Street to his house. He didn't want to see any people. He had to buy the Colt now. If he had another thirty-six cents, he could buy the Colt.

He decided to cut across the hillside toward the creek. Past the cemetery. His ankles wobbled on the uneven tussocks of grass as he climbed across the hillside toward the cemetery gates. Beyond the fence, weather-rotted boards and stones and tilted crosses marked the earth-mounded beds of the dead. Among those dark memorials were three slate markers carved with the names of his mother, his sister, and his brother. He did not feel that their spirits were loose on that hillside but rather that they lay and dreamed like those in the room he had just quit.

The split-rail fence that marked the border of the land of the living from the land of the dead ran along the bottom of the cemetery's slope and reached a stand of pines. Joshua followed it until dark-needled branches began to poke at him. He pressed close to the fence but would not cross it. He forced his way forward against the clutching pines. His legs moved but the branches dragged him back and scratched at his face. It took forever to get through the copse, but finally he broke free and the creek was running beside him like a cascade of broken glass. Down below were the roofs and tents of Amethyst Street. He crossed the plank bridge over the creek and there was nothing between him and his dark-stained house. At least his father would be at work. The old man wouldn't see him in this state.

Joshua followed the gravel path up to the weathered wooden door. He slid his hand into the pocket of his pea coat. The cold iron key was safe. He could lock the door behind him. He should have been at school down in Creede. Miss Murphy would ask him where he had been. What business was it of hers? A man full-growed, Strickland had called him. Miss Murphy could go to hell. His father would ask him, too. How could he have slept so long?

Joshua did not light the lantern in the damp front room. He did not want to face his dead mother's lurking presence. He went straight through to the kitchen. The stove was cold. If he borrowed the money from his father's cash box, the Colt would be his and he would be richer by five dollars and seventy-five cents — before his father even came home from work. Joshua started up the stairs. He knew where his father hid the key. All that he was doing was taking a loan for an hour or so. When he came back from Frazee's with the Colt, he could even increase the money in the box. His father's room smelled of sour sweat and stale tobacco. The only reminder of his mother was the big brass-railed double bed and the walnut wardrobe in the corner.

The wardrobe door creaked open at his touch. Not a stitch of her clothing was left in there. Nor much of the old man's, either. Just the Sunday suit that his da had not worn since she had died and next to it a greatcoat that hung in the naphtha-odored gloom. Joshua lifted the soiled towels that lay in a bundle on the bottom of the wardrobe. The cash box was little more than a pathetic piece of tin with a shiny handle folded into the lid. He knelt down and lifted it out onto the pine floorboards. It was locked with a ten-cent padlock. At least that looked robust. Joshua reached behind the curved leg of the wardrobe. The key hung on a small nail that was fixed into a batten board on the bottom of the wardrobe. Joshua unlocked the box.

There was hardly more than sixty cents in it. No wonder his father had no fear of burglars. Joshua plucked out three dimes, one nickel, and a penny. He would put back at least a dollar more than he had taken out. It was time to get the Colt.

He had wanted to run all the way from his house to Frazee's but all he could manage was a few lurching, languid lopes and then he had to walk again. Everything about the canyon was fake. The rock walls and pines of Campbell Mountain and Bulldog Mountain had been painted onto a flat blue board that was the sky. The houses and stores were little more than flimsy boxes that would blow away in the next gust of wind. As he came into town, he didn't look at anyone. All the Hunkies and matrons and hotel bums were looking at him. Where was his dog, goddamn it? He passed Soapy Smith's Orleans Club and Tilly's Hard Goods. He slowed down in front of Frazee's. The windowpanes in the front door gleamed in the late morning sunshine. Joshua leaned into his bespectacled reflection in the glass and peered into the store. Frazee was behind the counter. He had that What-the-hell-you-doin', boy? look on his face. Must be easier to see out than in.

There was no one else in the store. Joshua could buy his gun without any complicated questions from friends of his father's or nosy old ladies. The door rattled as he went in.

–What the hell you doin', boy?

Joshua nodded to Frazee. This was going to be a straightforward purchase and sale. A wind roared in Joshua's ears. Frazee's mustache was mobile over his mouth, his eyes widened and narrowed behind the half-moon glasses.

–You look like you took sick with the typhoid, said Frazee.

–Has my da been around?

–Do you need me to git the doctor?

–I've come for the Colt, said Joshua.

Joshua breathed in deep, and the warmth came into his bones, and the wind roared louder in his ears. He was Leviathan risen from the deep. He would swallow Frazee whole. The pink pig was standing on the shelf behind Frazee. The edges of Soapy Smith's six dollar bills curled up around the pig's short legs. Joshua would have that money. Frazee rubbed his hands against his stained apron as if he wished to clean them of the butter that he had been cutting.

–You want the Colt? he said.

Joshua took the money from his pocket and laid down $3.11 on the polished wooden counter, coin by coin.

–By God, said Frazee. Where'd you get all that money in only two days?

–It's all there, said Joshua.

There was no room for argument now. Frazee had to hand over the gun.

–You didn't steal this nowhere, did you?

Frazee was becoming more than irritating. He had no right to be demanding answers when all he was or could hope to be was a damned shopkeeper with biscuits and briny oysters to sell. And by some quirk of his sorry fate, a Colt .45 Peacemaker revolver.

–Give me the damned gun, said Joshua. I worked for my money, Mr. Frazee. I worked two days for Mr. Robert Ford, and you don't have any right to accuse me of theft.

He had only borrowed the money from his father, and it was going back right away as soon as he collected his winnings.

–Does your father know about this?

–This is my money, Mr. Frazee, not my father's . . .

His voice boomed in the empty store. Frazee scowled and began to dig into his armpit as if he had fleas in there. The god-damn shopkeeper was nervous.

–. . . and the rest of the money is in the pig.

Frazee's head rolled around as if it was too heavy to keep straight on his neck. Joshua stared him straight in the eye. He had Frazee squirming. Frazee reached up and grabbed the pig. He placed it on the counter in front of Joshua. That pig's days were over. To the right of his money box, Joshua saw a brightly varnished mallet that Frazee used to hammer spigots into vinegar barrels. Joshua picked up the mallet and swung it up over his shoulder. He whacked it down on the pig. Pink porcelain shattered all over the counter. Shards scattered onto the floor. Coins clattered on the countertop.

–Goddamn, said Frazee.

He must have jumped back a foot.

Joshua didn't see what the man had to swear about.

–You can clean that mess up, boy, Frazee squeaked.

Joshua tapped the hammer against the counter. He was not going to push a broom or a pen for this damn shopkeeper any more. He wanted his gun. With his left hand he began to stack the small coins.

–Five, six, seven, eight, nine, ten dimes makes another dollar . . .

He would get plenty of work from Mr. Ford.

–. . . one, two, three, four quarters makes another . . .

Joshua was man enough to make his own decisions. His father could say and do what he wanted, and drink himself to death if need be, but Joshua would not work another minute for Frazee. He set up the last of the coins, lifted his chin, and squared his shoulders.

–. . . plus the two quarters here makes up fifty; one dime makes sixty, and four pennies makes sixty-four; which, added to the three dollars and eleven cents, makes five seventy-five, which is the exact amount for the gun that I believe is sitting under the counter.

Joshua grinned as Frazee bent down and retrieved the mahogany box, his shopkeeper instincts and Joshua's determination controlling him like a marionette. Joshua slid the piles of dimes, quarters, pennies, and dollars to his left. He swept the embarrassing porcelain shards to his right in order to make room on the counter for the gun case.

–You are gitting too big for your britches, boy.

Joshua tightened his grip on the mallet and stared at Frazee. The shopkeeper was scared. Frazee set the box down. Joshua wanted to flip up the top of the gun case to see the Colt, but he wouldn't play the eager kid for Frazee.

–And if you would pass me five of those dollar bills on the shelf, Mr. Frazee, I'll take three quarters out of this pile and you and I and Soapy Smith will be all square.

–You can't take that money without Soapy here to see you won it.

–He'll trust your word, Mr. Frazee, I'm sure.

–I can't give it to you.

Joshua owed his father's cash box thirty-six cents, and whatever Frazee dealt out to him would be infinitely less painful than facing his father's retribution over a perceived theft. Joshua leaned his gangly body forward and set the mallet down on the counter. He slid the gun case toward him and tucked it under his left arm. Then he swept the five dollars and seventy-five cents in coins into his left hand and allowed all the coins but a quarter to slip into the pocket of his trousers. He laid that quarter back on the counter.

–That's for a box of shells, and the broken pig is all the proof that Soapy needs that I won the wager, fair and square.

All the varnished fronts of the shelves gleamed at him. Frazee looked as confused and flustered as a beaten bantam at a cockfight.

–I'll have your hide, boy, he croaked.

–I won't be working here any more, Mr. Frazee. You don't pay enough and you keep bad company.

Joshua's head was as light as air. He turned on his heel and sauntered over to the side room. There was a shelf just inside the entrance where Frazee kept boxes of ammunition. He picked up a box of .45 caliber pistol shells and made for the front door. He glanced back, afraid for a moment that Frazee had come out of his stupor and would try to stop his escape, but the man's mouth was open and the eyes behind the half-moon glasses were almost as glazed as Ella Mae Waterson's back up in Mr. Ford's cabin.

–Proof's right there, Mr. Frazee. One broken pig.

And he slammed the door behind him before Frazee could move or say another word.

Joshua marched through the town. He nodded to all the bustled and bonneted ladies on the boardwalk. His shoulders were broad and wide, his pocket full of coin, and his pistol by his side. The ore buckets above him swung magnificently on their spidery lines.

When he reached home, he ran straight up to his bedroom. He laid the mahogany case on the bed and opened the clasp. He lifted the lid to view the gleaming hard reality of the Colt. He took the precious weapon into his hands and — as if he had been used to doing so all his life — deftly slipped a shiny new .45 caliber bullet into each chamber and snapped the gate shut. He pointed the gun at the brass pen set on his rolltop desk. With his eye in a fixed squint along the barrel to the foresight, he swung the gun and drew a bead on the lantern. He swung the gun down to the desktop and aimed at the etching of Jesse James on the cover of the *Log Cabin Library* dime magazine.

–Drop the gun, Jesse, and get your hands in the air.

Joshua brought his thumb up to the hammer. It was stiff. Hard to pull back. Maybe the pistol needed oiling. He should take it apart and clean it before firing a shot. He used the heel of his left hand to push back the hammer until it clicked. The gun was cocked. He kept his finger loosely on the trigger.

–Pow! he said, and Jesse bit the imaginary dust.

He should go up into the trees on Campbell Mountain. Just behind Chang Jen Wa's camp there was a clearing. No one would see him. Shots on the mountainside were common to hear. Everybody did target practice from time to time.

But first things first. He needed to put back the thirty-six cents that he had borrowed from the cash box. He put the Colt down on the red velvet lining. It was still cocked. That was fine. Maybe he could take a shot out of the back window of his father's bedroom even before he cleaned it, as long as no one was around. Joshua dug into his pockets, pulled out a silver dollar, and laid it beside the Colt. Interest for his da on the borrowed money. Then he brought out a handful of change and picked out thirty-six cents. He took the money and the Colt and crossed the passageway and went into his father's bedroom. The wardrobe was still open. The lid of the cash box was raised, just as he had left it. Downstairs, he heard the door of the kitchen scrape open. God damn.

–Joshua!

He had to reply. How could he not?

–I'll be down in a minute, Da.

–What the hell are you doing up there?

He had that empty feeling in his head.

–Just putting something away.

Footsteps banged on the stairs. Joshua rushed over to the cash box.

He laid the Colt down next to it and tried to let the coins fall from his palm as quietly as he could let them into the cash box. They rattled on the tin.

–What the bloody hell?

His father was in the room. Joshua turned his head. His father was stooped over. One hand gripped the lintel above his head. The left hand was stretched out in front pointing at Joshua. His face was all dark furrows and shadows, eyes and cheeks and jowls all moving against each other like a dark sea in motion.

–I'm putting it back, Da. I just borrowed it, see? And a dollar interest for you, look.

–You are stealing, boy.

–No, Da. I'm putting it back. Really.

His father's bulk grew. Joshua sat back and lifted his arms above his head. He waved the silver dollar.

–And I've got more where this came from, Da. Look!

Joshua went to his pocket. His da had stopped in the middle of the floor. The mouth was open, the eyebrows squeezed together, the eyes dull.

–And what is that behind you? said his father.

Joshua glanced back. It was the Colt that he meant. Joshua reached for it.

–Don't you touch that bloody gun.

Joshua's hand jerked back as if the pistol might be red hot. Then he reached out again and took it in his grip. He wasn't looking at his father but at the slim barrel of the gun.

–It's mine, Da. I bought it fair and square.

–Put it down, I say.

–It's mine.

All unconnected arms and legs, Joshua lurched to his feet. He was bent over the Colt as if to protect it from harm, from his father's malevolence.

–Give it to me, his da said.

Joshua kept his back turned. He leaned against the wall. He was still folded over the Colt. His father hadn't gone for the belt yet. Joshua was not going to give him the gun. His father could beat him all he wanted. He would protect it until he was beaten senseless if he had to. Fingers dug into his neck. His collar twisted and tightened and he squawked against the choking. He tried to stay bent over, but he was jerked upward by the collar. He almost lost his feet. A fist slammed into his right shoulder blade, jolted his every bone, sent a tingling numbness down his arm. He kept a tight grip on the Colt. With the next blow bright light flashed and his empty skull banged against the wall. His cap came off and his glasses dangled. His right ear rang and burned. Joshua swung his left arm up and across his face to protect his head, and the next blow caught against his wrist without causing much hurt.

–Give it to me, you little bastard, cried his father.

He would not. Never. It was his. He had bought it with his own money. Another blow landed between his shoulders, and Joshua slid into the corner of the room. His father kicked at his shins. Joshua felt hardly any pain, but he lost balance and went down on one knee. He managed to get his glasses back in place. He could feel his father over him. Hear the rasping of his breath. His collar tightened again and his father reached in and grabbed his right wrist. Fingers dug into his forearm. The old man pulled at him, and he couldn't match his father's strength. Joshua's upper arm twisted and the muscle tore and burned. His father yanked hard and pulled his right hand free. The Colt waved heavy in his grip. He tried to pull the gun back under his body again, but his father had grabbed at his fist with both hands. His upper arm burned and ached, but Joshua jerked backward to get free, and the gun went off with a bang.

His father screamed, hopped around the room holding his thigh, dancing like a drunkard who clowned an Indian war dance.

It was comical for a second, the old man whooping and bouncing on one foot, his hands clutching his thigh. Then thick red liquid oozed out from between his da's fingers and began to spatter onto the wood floor. The blood pumped out from under his hands and gouted in great splats onto the floor. There was a stink of cordite in the air, and greasy white smoke hung between Joshua and his father. His ears rang from the bang and his father's blow.

–Oh, son, his father said.

His da wasn't angry any more. His face was pale. The skin had smoothed out, the lips were dry and open, his eyes were clear, calm, and afraid. The gun dangled in Joshua's fingers.

Stop it now, Joshua thought. Enough's enough.

His father fell back onto the floor. He sat there in the middle of the bedroom, slightly bent forward over his straight legs. The blood spread in a red pool between them. His da's fingers clutched to the wound did nothing to stop the flow.

Joshua thought, Oh God, Da, my arm is aching.

–It won't stop, son.

–I'll get the doctor.

–Don't leave me, son.

–You're hurt, Da.

–Get a bandage.

His father heaved and brown watery vomit splashed into the red pool. He was crying real tears. The blood had spread to his feet and out from under his thighs. His crotch was soaked with it. Joshua looked at the Colt. Should he put it on the floor while he got the bandage or take it with him? He didn't think they had any bandages. He laid the Colt on the bed. His arm was aching terribly.

–Hold on, Da, he said.

His father nodded.

Out in the passage, Joshua looked down the stairs and at the door to his room. They didn't have any bandages. He turned back into his father's room. His father's breath came in shallow rasps.

The towels, he thought.

He crossed over to the wardrobe again. One of the towels seemed almost clean. He picked it up.

–I feel faint, his father said.

Joshua knelt beside him, twisting the towel in his hands.

–Lift your leg up, Da.

Sticky blood soaked into the knees of Joshua's trousers.

–Oh Jesus God, Joshua said.

Da's mouth was open and slack. The sight and smell of the blood and vomit made Joshua suddenly gag and retch. He breathed through his mouth to get himself under control. His arm ached and he blinked away tears.

–Come on, Da.

His father was breathing fast and shallow.

–I can't see right, son. Help me up.

His father still clutched his leg, but his body swayed to one side as he tried to get up. Joshua laid the towel over his father's hands. His da let go of the leg and planted his palms in the spreading red pool. He tried to raise himself again and Joshua pushed the towel beneath his father's thigh and twisted it around the leg to make a tourniquet. His da slumped over and away from him. Joshua's eyes were burning. Tears made everything blur. He blinked them away. He tried to pull his father back to a sitting position, but the old man was too heavy. His da lay on his side. The head lifted an inch and dropped back heavily on the wooden boards. The breath rasped and crackled in his da's throat.

–Jesus, no. Oh Jesus, Da.

The room felt so terribly empty. Silent. Da's face was ashen and blood-smeared and the eyes glassy, and shadows marked every crease and wrinkle. All around, the blood. The sticky-sweet, darkening blood. He twisted the lapels of his da's jacket in his bony fingers and pulled the dead body up toward him as if he could will it back to life. The muscles had relaxed, and Joshua could see his own features there on the dead face in front of him, what he would become as time etched its course into his own flesh, when his own last breath rattled out and no other breath was drawn in. A loud mewling noise originated in some atavistic darkness and it came out through Joshua's open mouth and filled the emptiness of the room.

XI

THE ROOF OF BOB'S MOUTH WAS SCALY AND SALTY. HIS TONGUE was likewise coated and his nose so blocked that if he did not keep his jaw wide to breathe, he was going to gag. Dot lay deep asleep beside him. Her familiar scent, the sweet perfume and stale sweat, and the fleshy bulk of her warmed his body. Her broad behind pressed against his early-morning hard-on, but he needed coffee more than the aggravation of waking her up and getting her horny, too. Liddil and Ella were both in a stupor, the low snores of Strickland rising and falling, providing a bass rythmn. The bed opposite Strickland was empty. The boy must have gone home. Bob slid down toward the foot of the bed from between Dot and the wall. The room wobbled and then settled into solidity. Not an unpleasant sensation, but it made him conscious that something was missing. That deep distance from the world's myriad annoyances, from the saloon, from Soapy Smith. Another pipe would augment that well-being. Maybe later.

The stove in the living room was still warm. The iron scraped along the flagstone. He pulled open the firebox. A few embers glowed in the darkness. Joshua had cut such a stack of kindling that there was hardly room to get past it to the sideboard. He snapped a few sticks and eased them down into the stove.

Behind him came a soft knock on the front door. He brought the coffeepot with him to answer it. The rain barrel was outside anyways. He pulled the door open.

–Jesus Christ, Josh, you been cut, boy?

Tears ran down behind Joshua's thick glasses and made wet lines through the dried blood on his cheeks. His hair was clumped and stiff with blood. The boy's shirt stuck to his side with blood still wet, the knees of his pants were black with it. He held a pistol in his right hand, and both hands were brown where blood had dried on them.

–I killed him.

He meant Aaron, Bob knew. The boy must have butchered his own father with a carving knife, there was so much blood on him.

Aaron must have got in a few cuts his own self. Bob laid a hand on the boy's bony shoulder and steered him into the cabin.

–Are you hurt?

–I didn't mean it, Joshua said. He tried to take the gun off me and it just went off.

The boy stumbled toward a rocking chair.

–It was a accident?

–He tried . . . and then the gun . . .

–Are you cut somewheres?

Joshua looked directly into Bob's eyes. He was bewildered. He looked down at himself, and shook his head.

–He just wouldn't stop bleeding, he said.

A sudden high whimper and then a keening sound came out of Joshua's open mouth. Bob reached out and wrapped an arm around Joshua's shoulder. In his other hand, the lid of the coffeepot clanked. Such grief and abject sorrow in that bony and blood-stained frame was a shock. It reminded him of Charley. The boy sobbed and shuddered. The blood had a sweet stink to it. His voice was squeaky. No real words. Just crying like a baby. Bob took the pistol from Joshua's fingers. He guided the boy to the rocker and helped him to sit. Joshua rested his elbows on the dark, stained knobs of his knees, dropped his heavy square head into his hands, and sobbed, his whole body in shudders. Bob laid the heavy Colt and the coffeepot down on the table. The gun was sticky with blood. Behind him, the bedroom door creaked.

–Sweet Jesus Christ.

Dot, hung-over, bedraggled and wrinkled, her eyes wide in her puffy face, shambled across the room from the bedroom doorway.

–He's been cut, she said. Look at him, Bob.

Bob had never known Aaron to carry knife or gun, but he was unsure if the boy was hurt or not. Joshua blinked away tears and looked up at Dot like a stray calf searching for a mother.

–One bullet hit him in the leg, Joshua said, then the blood wouldn't stop. I tried to stanch it, but he just kept bleeding. He bled to death.

–Let me see you, Bob said.

He pulled at the boy's shirt to loosen it where it stuck to his side. No cuts or holes in the shirt at least. Aaron's blood, then.

Strickland came into the room, stuffing his plaid work shirt into his bib overalls.

–Oh my Lord. What the hell going on, Bob?

–Boy's father got shot, Dot said.

–Who the hell shot him?

Bob lifted his chin toward Joshua.

–We got to get the sheriff, he said.

The look that Dot gave him would have frozen a hogshead. The sheriff was no friend of the Fords. But what choice did they have? Accessory to murder? Joshua looked up. The glasses dug into his wide nose. His lips were pressed tight together. He said nothing. He was so desolate, Bob wanted to put him on a wagon and take him away to somewhere quiet and peaceful, but he knew of no such place in the world or he would have gone there himself, long ago. The world was made up of cow towns and mining camps and cities full of thieves and con men. Then there was the law. No avoiding that.

–Sheriff? Damn, Strickland said.

–Let's go to the house first, Dot said. See if Aaron's still . . .

–Ain't the case, Bob said.

He leaned against the table, one hand close to the sticky Colt.

–Listen, Josh. The sheriff'll bring the doctor to look at what happened. They'll see it was a accident and that's it. You understand?

Joshua nodded and Bob turned to Strickland.

–Help Ella straighten herself out back there and get the little Chinaman out of here. Ain't no cause to complicate matters any further than they already are. Neither one of them will be much good as witnesses. Wake up Dick and have him help you with Ella.

Strickland rubbed the back of his broad neck and his white hair. Dot gripped Bob's arm and walked with him to the door.

–Take care of this, Bob, she said.

–You stay here with Dot, boy, Bob said. Everything's going to be fine.

All the opium gone out of him, and death's enormity unavoidable. Not even another pipe would fix it. The boy's killing his father was a disruption of normal habit from which it was impossible to escape.

* * *

Aaron Beynon's room was a goddamn mess, the wardrobe door ajar, a cash box lying on the floor open and — as far as Bob could tell — almost empty. Blank-faced, bled-out, a saturated towel around the upper thigh, the corpse lay in a pool of congealing blood that was thick and nasty and had already stained the pine boards brown. Bob rolled a cigarette, and when he lit it, the acrid tobacco smoke mixed with the sweet fetor that rose from the floor so that he felt as if he had inhaled disgust itself. None of this scene of carnage looked good for the boy.

Sheriff Mort Gardner thumbed back the brim of his black hat and pursed his lips. Deep lines ran from beside his wide nostrils to his jaw line. His steel gray mustache and heavy brown cheekbones gave him the look of a one-time range hand who had never gone soft. His black frock coat and round-brimmed hat gave him a graveyard air. Bob couldn't help thinking that if Gardner had made one mistake in his life, it was to marry Soapy Smith's sister. He might have an air of rugged independence, but Bob knew that Soapy controlled Gardner through that nagging bitch of a wife and doubtless the odd cash gratuity. Deputy Fat Wallace, who stood behind the sheriff, aped his boss's style of dress but resembled an overstuffed scarecrow in Gardner's castoffs. The gut for which Wallace was so aptly named hung over the black leather of his gun belt. His collarless, once-white shirt was grubby and stained with gravy.

–Looks like a robbery, said Wallace.

–Looks like a shooting to me, said Gardner.

–Boy said it was a accident, said Bob.

Gardner inclined a thumb toward the cash box.

–What you make of that?

It looked as if the boy had raided the cash box.

Bob shrugged. No point in making anything easier for Gardner.

–Thieving little bastard shot his own pa, Wallace said.

–Innocent until proven guilty, Bob said.

–Get the coroner, Gardner said.

Bob followed Wallace down the stairs, through the kitchen,

and outside. He leaned against the wall and watched the fat deputy waddle down the path toward town. Beyond the graveyard, the white canvas of Bob's tent saloon was rippling in the afternoon wind. Smoke rose from his cabin, where the boy was waiting. He would be in a cell soon. Just like he, Bob Ford, and brother Charley had been all those years ago, waiting to be tried for the murder of Jesse James. Bob leaned back against the windowsill of the house and smoked four cigarettes before Wallace and Dr. Abrahams came panting up the path from town, each one as fat as the other, but Abrahams better dressed, silver-haired and clean-shaven. He swung his little black bag in a red and pudgy hand. Bob smoked one more cigarette before Gardner, Wallace, and Abrahams came downstairs again and Abrahams declared that Aaron Beynon had bled to death. The cause of death would have to wait until after the trial.

Bob flicked away his stub.

–Have the undertaker get the body, Abrahams, Gardner said.

They started down the hill for the boy.

Bob pushed through the door of the cabin, and Gardner and Wallace followed him. Joshua was in the rocker by the table with his hands clasped between his knees. The big eyes, wide open and frightened, stared out from behind the round-rimmed glasses. He was poised on the points of his toes as if he would bolt. He was still dirty with blood.

–It's just us, Josh, Bob said.

His words had a sick and empty feel to them.

Dot sat slumped by the stove and picked at the cording of her chair.

–Poor boy hardly stopped crying, she said.

–God forgive me, Joshua said.

–By God, boy, Gardner said. You look like you done butchered a hog.

Everything was getting worse by the second. Why hadn't Dot had the boy clean up? She seemed as stunned as Joshua was. If Bob had been in the same mess, he would have wished better from her. She knew the law. Strick and Liddil must have got Ella and the little Chinaman over to Chang Jen Wa's. Right this minute, they were all probably lying on a divan without a care in the world. He wouldn't have minded smoking a pipe of opium for himself. Just one, to relax. Or a strong drink.

–Would you have any tabacca, Bob? Dot said.

Bob slid his hand into the pocket of his wrinkled jacket and pulled out a new sack of baccy. He tossed it into her lap.

–It was a accident, Dot said.

–I'm taking the boy in, Miz Ford, Gardner said. It don't look good in that house. Aaron's lying dead in his own room with the cash box 'bout empty.

–I was putting it back, said Joshua.

–Looks to me like he was robbing it, said Fat Wallace.

Goddamn that fat son of a bitch.

–Aaron was shot in the leg, said Bob. Bullet must have hit a artery, he's bled out blue.

The boy began to whimper in the rocking chair. It creaked. He twisted to his left as if searching for something in the far corner of the room.

–That the gun? asked Gardner.

Bob nodded. The Colt was still on the table, the walnut grip and some of the steel dull where the blood had dried. He wanted to believe that the whole business was an accident, but he knew that when a boy had a gun in his hand, one way or another, it would probably go off. Aaron Beynon was a drunk. And he had treated that boy miserably. Joshua could have shot him out of fear or sheer hatred, and who could have blamed him for it? Aaron's death was little loss to the world, except perhaps a loss of business for the tent saloon.

–That boy wouldn't harm a fly, Bob said.

–If Aaron was shot in the leg, you can see it was a accident, Dot said.

Her fingers shook as she pulled out a paper to roll a smoke. She dragged at the strands of shag in the sack.

Gardner picked up the Colt and examined the chamber.

–One shell used, he said.

–Joshua don't have it in him to kill no one, Dot said.

She overwet the edge of her cigarette paper and curled it clumsily so that the smoke turned out baggy and misshapen. Bob slipped a matchbox from his pocket and snapped a match alight for her. The cigarette burned unevenly down one side, but she sucked smoke into her lungs and then blew out a long gray plume. Bob flicked the spent match onto the flagstone under the stove.

–Aaron's dead and the cash box is empty, Gardner said.

–I was putting it back! Joshua cried. Ask Frazee, ask Soapy.

–Get this over with, Gardner, Bob said.

–Stand up, son.

The big-boned boy came unsteadily to his feet, and the chair rocked back behind him. He was shaking. He leaned over to his right as if he had no bones on that side.

–What you got in your pockets, boy? Gardner asked.

Joshua slid his hands into his pants.

–Put it on the table, said Gardner.

The coins clattered down beside the Colt.

–Jeez, there's more than five dollars there, said Fat Wallace.

–Two fifty of that, I give him, said Bob.

–That's right, said Dot. He earned it working for us.

–Where you get the gun, boy?

–Bought it at Frazee's.

–Ain't cheap to buy a Colt, said Wallace.

–You got a lot of money for a kid, said Gardner.

–Yessir, said Joshua.

–Ain't a crime to have money, Bob said. 'Specially when you earn it.

–You was putting it back? Gardner said.

–Nossir, not this. I won it from Soapy Smith.

Fat Wallace grinned.

–You a card sharp too, boy? he said.

Gardner's eyes narrowed in contempt.

–Tell the truth now, Josh, Dot said.

The boy was all hunched over and moving from foot to foot like he badly needed to piss.

–Ask Frazee. Ask Soapy, Joshua said. I won it.

–Won what? asked Gardner.

–I bet Soapy that I could raise the money, Joshua said, to buy the Colt before Saturday, and he bet the price of the Colt that I couldn't. Frazee held the stakes.

That's one sharp young son of a bitch, Bob thought. And I gone and helped him win the bet. Why the hell didn't he ask me for the rest of the money instead of looting his daddy's cash box? The story gave the boy a chance. Half a chance. Aaron was still dead.

–We can ask Frazee 'bout that, said Gardner. Soapy, too.

Gardner picked up the Colt and the coins next to it. He let the coins fall into the left pocket of his frock coat and tucked the Colt into the waistband of his gun belt.

–Let's go down to the jailhouse, boy. Then I'll go ask Frazee a few questions. I got to hold you for this killing until we get it all straightened out.

–Yessir, was all Joshua said.

–I'll come with you, Bob said.

–Me, too.

Dot crossed the room and put her arm around Joshua.

–Let me get him washed up and a change of clothes, Mort, she said. He can't go nowhere all messed up like this.

Gardner nodded.

–Just put the clothes in a sack and give them to Wallace here. I might need them for evidence. Then we'll go down to the jailhouse.

–What do you say we go down to Frazee's first and straighten some of this out? Bob said.

–We can do that, said Gardner. But leastways, I got a dead man, a empty cash box, and a shooter, so, whatever Frazee says and the way I see it, we going to have us a trial for murder.

XII

HEAVY CLOUDS HUNG ON THE UPPER SLOPES OF CAMPBELL MOUNTAIN. Wet wisps dipped down toward the rim of the canyon and were whipped away by the gusty wind. Behind Bob, Sheriff Gardner, and Deputy Fat Wallace, the canvas of the newly erected tent rippled in the evening chill. Dot would soon have Joshua cleaned up, and then they would take him down to the jail. The boy's dog lay under the corner of the tent platform with her head between her paws. Her blue-rimmed eyes stared up toward the cabin door. Bob shivered. He should have put on a jacket over his plaid shirt and bib overalls. The aftereffects of the opium had left an itch on his skin that no bath could wash away. Side by side, each man rolled himself a cigarette. The leather quirt that dangled from Gardner's wrist tap-tap-tapped against the calf of Bob's boot and irritated his nerves. Bob licked his cigarette paper and rolled it up tight, too tight. When he tried to light up, the cigarette wouldn't draw, and he had to flick it away and roll another. He lit up the second cigarette and the smoke bit against his throat and lungs and calmed his frayed nerves.

With Aaron dead, the poor kid had no one. Bob felt moved to help Joshua, but he had met the kid only two days before, and he needed to see what advantage could be gained from being involved in a murder trial. He had to figure the right angle from which to view the situation. In any situation, there had to be a way to turn a profit. Bob dragged on his cigarette and mulled it over.

Aaron Beynon had owned a fine saltbox house, probably full of furniture, and he might have had some money in the bank in Jimtown. The kid was now an orphan. Therefore all of the Beynons' property belonged to him. If the boy sold the property, he would have a sizable capital sum which he could invest in Bob Ford's saloon enterprise. With such an injection of capital, Bob could build a new dance hall and a ten-bed crib next to it. Far better than a tent. The boy would be thrilled to be part of such a business venture. As soon as he got over his daddy's death. Such an investment would secure a future for him, all alone in the world as he was. Yessir. The grand opening of the tent saloon would have to wait a few days. Bob needed to set the boy straight. Get him a lawyer of his own personal recommendation. He turned to Sheriff Gardner.

–You think he done it deliberate, Mort? Bob said.

–Looks that way to me, said Deputy Wallace.

–He didn't ask you, drawled Mort Gardner.

–I thought you thought that way, too, said Wallace.

–How the hell you know what I thought?

–You arresting him, ain't you?

–There's probable cause, said Gardner.

Bob drew on his cigarette again and blew smoke from his nose and mouth together. He flicked the ash with his middle finger. The tremor in his hands was not so noticeable.

–Then he didn't do it, Mort? asked Wallace.

Sheriff Gardner pulled down the brim of his black hat.

–Goddamn it, Wallace, hush your fat mouth and let the damn judge decide.

The deputy colored up and looked at the hot end of his cupped cigarette. Bob expected a retort but none came. It was shameful to let a man speak to you like that. He would never have allowed it himself.

The cabin door opened, and Dot, blond hair bedraggled and blue dress rumpled, ushered Joshua forward. She had dressed him in an old brown three-piece suit and a collarless pin-striped shirt that belonged to Bob. The clothes fit the boy remarkably well. He might have been a son to him. When the dog saw Joshua, she bounded up the grassy slope toward him, yipping and baying. The boy gave the dog a wan smile and stroked her head, and the dog, tail wagging, tongue lolling, circled around Dot and Joshua.

–Let's get to it, said Sheriff Gardner.

He got up off the steps and set off down the hill without a glance backward. The sheriff had the air of a man taking a pet goose to slaughter, sad to lose it, but hungry, too. Wallace scooted after him, his fat bulk straining against the seams of his black suit, following at Gardner's heels like a faithful hound.

–You all right, boy? called Bob.

Joshua waved his hand, looked at Dot, looked at the ground.

–Don't worry none, Honeyjosh, Dot said.

Mother Goose, thought Bob.

He settled the Remington more comfortably in his waistband and set off after Gardner and Wallace. Dot could take care of the boy. The funereal procession came onto Main Street. Bob flicked the butt of his cigarette in a long arc out into the wagon ruts of the muddy street. He did not look up at the clucking matrons or the curious children with their high-pitched voices or at the muttering loafers on the patios of the flophouses. Word of Aaron Beynon's killing had already spread, and Soapy Smith, flanked by his goons Clarence Thompson and Mickey James, stood outside Frazee's General Store, waiting for them it seemed. Ed O'Kelley leaned back against the bar of a hitching rail.

–This is your fault, Ford, called Soapy. You led the damn kid astray.

Sheriff Gardner was still between Bob and the goons, but he seemed to shrivel inside his black frock coat in front of Soapy Smith.

–Watch your goddamn mouth, Bob said.

He felt awfully short of temper. Enough to bring the tremors back.

–Jefferson, I'd like a word, said Gardner to Soapy. Would you come on into Frazee's with us?

–Stay here, boys, said Soapy to the goons.

Soapy opened the door to Frazee's and stepped back in a parody of courtesy. His flat cap was tilted over one eye. Bob pushed past him. Behind the counter, Frazee's gray eyebrows and gray mustache twitched in agitation. He ran his hands up and down his grubby apron as if he could brush the dirt off it. Bob walked over to the window and sat on the sill so that he would be able to keep Soapy in plain view. Dot, her arm around Joshua, guided the boy into the store. Joshua kept his head down. He dragged his broken boots forward as if they were loaded with iron and it was all he could do to lift them. Soapy followed them all in and leaned against the doorjamb.

–Don't you fret none, Josh, said Dot. We'll clear this all up, right now.

The boy's face was drained. The heavy glasses hung off his nose as if they were about to fall. Dot had an innocent smile on her pouty little lips. She stood with her hands clasped in front of her, shoulder to shoulder with the boy. Fat Wallace placed his ugly bulk against the door.

–What's going on here? What's going on? Frazee pleaded, his voice cracked and high.

–Boy says he bought a Colt in here, said Sheriff Gardner.

–Damn near stole it, said Frazee. He come in here and put a handful of coins on the counter and asked to see the Colt. I told him he couldn't have it, but I didn't see no harm in him looking at it. He grabbed the Colt and the money both and lit off with it.

–How come you didn't report any theft, if he didn't pay for the pistol? asked Gardner.

–There was the matter of Mr. Smith's money, said Frazee. And

I thought that we could talk to the boy's father, God rest his soul, and straighten it all out without getting the law involved.

–What's this about Jefferson's money? Gardner said.

Soapy grinned at Bob from across the room, as if he were just about to reveal four of a kind to Bob's full house. He straightened up off the doorjamb. Bob mirrored him and got up from the sill.

–That was just a prank we was playing on the kid, said Soapy. I told Frazee that if the kid could get the money by Saturday, I'd let him buy the gun. I knew the kid couldn't get that kind of money, so I paid Frazee for it in advance and told him I'd take the gun off of him when the kid give up on it. Seems the prank got out of hand. Ain't that right, Frazee?

Frazee's head dipped in agreement.

–What the hell? said Dot.

The boy was still silent beside her. Frazee was blushing. Bob stared hard at him, but the shopkeeper had turned toward Soapy like a puppy dog begging for his master's favor. Then Frazee spoke to Sheriff Gardner.

–I thought that I could clear this all up with Aaron, Mort. Joshua is just a kid.

–I would have helped Aaron whip his ass, said Soapy.

–I can see it would take the two of you, said Bob.

–They're lying, cried the boy.

Gardner's reply was little more than a croak.

–So now we have theft of the gun, theft of money from his pa's cashbox. And the murder.

–He wouldn't do that! screeched Dot. He's just a boy.

–Now hold on here, Mort, said Bob.

Gardner and Soapy seemed determined to see this kid swing. Joshua stared at Soapy. The boy's mouth was a hard line. His hands were balled into fists. Dot stood in front of Joshua. Her arms were folded over her big breasts, her blond hair awry, her eyes wide, lips twisted, as if she dared anyone to lay a finger on her charge.

–Tell them, Bob, she said.

This was not a situation that called for hasty action. Bob rubbed his jaw. He needed a shave. He needed a bath and to set himself to rights after the opium. The trouble was, the way he saw it, there wasn't much anyone could do for the boy at this point. The whole damn mess was going to trial, that was sure.

–I'll get the kid a lawyer from Denver, said Bob.

Soapy grinned.

Bob probably wouldn't have to worry about getting shot in the back by Soapy Smith for a while. Soapy was having too much fun torturing him by getting his protégé hanged.

–Wallace, said Sheriff Gardner, take the boy down.

XIII

IRON GRATED AS FAT WALLACE UNLOCKED THE CAGE. A SHAFT OF light from the dying sun cut through the barred window to give the cell a red glow. A steel shadow grid lay across the floor and across Joshua's borrowed trousers. Mr. Ford's trousers. Joshua sat slumped on the very edge of the cot, then glanced up. Beside the disheveled Wallace, Mr. Ford was impeccable once more. There was something absurd about the face smooth from the razor, the gray suit without a wrinkle. Death was an enormity. In the face of it, everything else seemed so trivial.

–You came to see me, Joshua said.

–Yeah, Mr. Ford said.

Mr. Ford glanced toward the corner, where a stained bucket stood on the discolored floor boards. An odor of stale piss hung in the cold evening air, the effluvium of shame.

–Good thing it ain't Saturday night, said Wallace, else the kid would have some pretty unsavory company.

Wallace was unsavory. What could be worse? He talked about Joshua as if he were no more than a shadow, and indeed Joshua felt that his hold upon the world was tenuous, as if he were as dead as Da, was beckoned and drawn closer to the world of shades.

–Saturday night is a long way off, Mr. Ford said.

–His daddy spent one or two nights in here, I can tell you, said Wallace.

The mention of his father stung. Now that his father was present only as a loss, he could think of a thousand things he would be able to say to him if only Da had come to the cell instead of Mr. Ford.

–Thank you, Wallace, said Mr. Ford.

The fat deputy did not even lock the cell door and likewise left the outer door of the jailhouse ajar. That tantalizing vision of freedom was worse than hearing the lock grate shut.

–Come and get me in the office when you're done talkin', Bob, Wallace said.

Mr. Ford turned to Joshua.

–How you doing, Josh?

Joshua had no answer. He was in hell. But there were no flames. God's joke upon him. To make room for Mr. Ford, he slid himself sideways toward the black-and-white ticking pillow, his arms and legs all in motion against each other, awkward until he finally settled his limbs into a geometric stillness, elbows on knobbed knees, fingers steepled before his pursed lips. Mr. Ford plucked at the knees of his pants and sat at the foot of the cot. He smoothed his waistcoat down and moved his shoulders to settle his jacket comfortably. He made a motion as if to put his arm around Joshua's shoulder.

Joshua shrank back. No touch. He couldn't stand the idea. Mr. Ford raised his hand as if in apology and lowered his head. If only he could let Mr. Ford comfort him, but it was impossible, for this pit of loss was deeper and more isolated than any cell had made him. When he spoke, it was as if his voice came out of a well.

–Who's going to bury my father?

–I'll take care of the funeral arrangements. Ed Becket's down in Jimtown. He'll be back tomorrow. He's got your pa on ice in the mortuary.

Joshua could not shut out the image of Da, cold and stiff among the ice blocks.

–Can I go to the funeral?

–Of course you can.

–Where's Carys?

–Dot's got your hound tied up out front of the cabin. She'll be fine.

What does he hope to accomplish by coming here? Joshua wondered. A part of him was glad to see Mr. Ford and another part was equally disgusted. Every emotion was accompanied by its opposite in a hideous dualism.

–I killed my da.

Mr. Ford nodded.

–Why didn't Soapy tell the truth about the bet? Joshua said.

–Soapy Smith's word ain't worth a shit, Josh, you know that, but you can let Mr. Pearl, the lawyer, deal with him.

–Frazee, too?

Mr. Ford regarded the cell floor between the toes of his boots.

–Frazee, said Bob, is a gutless bastard who has to pay Soapy Smith protection money to stay in business, so don't expect nothing from him. Abe Pearl is the best lawyer in the territory. He has to convince the district judge, not lead-brained Mort Gardner. You understand?

Joshua understood. Soapy Smith was using Da's death like a puppeteer jerking the strings, with Frazee and the sheriff and Mr. Ford his puppets, to show the rest of the town that it was Soapy Smith who controlled Weaver, who held power even over life and death. Like the vicious God who had taken away his father.

–I'm going to kill Soapy Smith when I get out, Joshua said. It's his fault I'm in here.

Every muscle in Mr. Ford's body tightened up. Suddenly he was an inch from the lenses of Joshua's glasses, staring in his face. He hissed.

–Now listen, boy, don't you mess this all up for me. One crime at a time, you hear? You'll get yourself hung if you don't keep that damn trap shut.

Joshua's eyes blinked rapidly. So Mr. Ford doubted him, too. Soapy had him convinced. What a fool.

–Do you think that I wanted to kill my own father? Joshua said.

–Don't matter what I think, said Mr. Ford.

–You believe Soapy, don't you, Joshua said.

His cheeks began to burn with rage. Why was everyone being so stupid? Tears welled up and filled his eyes. Mr. Ford looked down between his feet again.

–Look, it was a accident, said Mr. Ford.

Joshua clenched his teeth. What a pathetic pretense. Did he expect him to believe such a lame statement?

–I'm going to kill that bastard Soapy for doing this to me, said Joshua.

Mr. Ford gripped Joshua's upper arm, pulled Joshua to his face again.

–Keep your goddamn mouth shut, boy, he said.

Mr. Ford's fingertips dug into the muscle that Da had wrenched so horribly, reviving the pain that had made Joshua pull back and set off the gun. Joshua's lip quivered. He pried Mr. Ford's fingers from his arm.

–Don't touch me, Joshua said.

Mr. Ford was on his feet suddenly. His hands were visibly trembling. He narrowed his pale gray eyes.

–Your daddy's dead and gone, boy, said Mr. Ford. And nothing going to bring him back or change that.

The rage that flooded Joshua seemed to light up the bars and the floor and the walls of the cell and Mr. Ford standing in front of him.

–Yes, Joshua said. I killed my da and I'm going to kill Soapy Smith.

Mr. Ford's face turned a reddish gray in his fury.

–You got to get out of here first, he said. So get shut of any idea what you gonna do to Soapy Smith or they will hang you for your daddy's killing. Do you understand?

Joshua understood perfectly. The whole town was against him, and Mr. Ford doubted him as much as any man. Joshua looked up at Mr. Ford.

–You will help me kill him, won't you? Or are you a coward?

Mr. Ford flushed and balled his fists.

–Do you know who you are talking to, boy? You are just a child whose toy gun popped at the wrong time and your daddy is dead. That does not make you anything. It was Jesse James I killed, boy. Not some goddamn drunk in a barroom fight.

Joshua kept his hands steepled in front of his tight-lipped mouth. He stared at Mr. Ford with all the malice in his being.

–So how did it feel? Joshua said. When you killed Jesse James? To put the gun to his head like that and pull the trigger? I always wanted to know.

Mr. Ford leaned over him.

–You want to know what it felt like. I'll tell you, boy. Nobody shows me contempt. Jesse James took off his gun belt and put it on the cot that I slept in. He did it to show me contempt. He knew that I planned to turn him in to the law. And I knew the son of a bitch planned to shoot me the first chance he got. But he couldn't do it in his own home in front of his wife and kids. So I snatched the only chance I'd ever have. He reached up to straighten a picture on the wall and — Pow! I put a bullet in him.

Mr. Ford jabbed a finger at him and Joshua jerked his head back. Mr. Ford stared down at him. Joshua had provoked him. Now a calm came into Mr. Ford's face.

–Then it was the damnedest thing. When I seen him lying on the carpet like that — dead — with the blood spouting out of his head, I commenced to laugh and I couldn't stop till Jesse's wife came in screaming bloody murder.

–You know what? Joshua whispered. I laughed when I saw my father hopping around like that. Before the blood came. And I was glad the gun went off. I was glad.

Joshua's face twisted up and tears squeezed out from between his eyelids. His shoulders humped up as he fought against the spasms in his throat. He wanted to say something more, but he couldn't talk without breaking down and making a spectacle of himself. He fought with muffled whimpers to hold the grief inside his contorting body. His hands clutched his upper arms, his head bobbed until the wave subsided.

Mr. Ford paced over to the piss bucket and back to the open cell door. He leaned back against the bars of the cell and put his hands in his pockets.

–You scared, Josh? Mr. Ford said.

Joshua shook his head. If he admitted that he was scared, a huge gulf would open up beneath him. He would fall once more into a fit of sobbing. A madness that would send the cell spinning around him again.

–We all get scared, said Mr. Ford.

–I bet Jesse James was never scared in his life, Joshua said.

Mr. Ford laughed. Joshua forced a snot-smeared, twisted smile.

–Everybody gets scared, Josh, Mr. Ford said. But you got to tough it out. You understand me, boy?

Joshua nodded.

–I feel like I'm in a nightmare and I can't wake up.

–I'll get you out of here.

–I just wanted to buy the gun, said Joshua. If he had just left me alone to buy the gun, I wouldn't have killed him.

The shadows in the cell had deepened. Soon they would need a candle or a lantern to see one another.

–Sometimes things just get out of hand, said Mr. Ford. You see a gun in Frazee's store. It seems simple enough to buy it. Then a whole chain of events is set into motion that you ain't got no control over. It's just cause and effect, boy. But there don't seem to be much sense to it. Sometimes, some causes, you just can't predict the effect.

Joshua nodded. Cause and effect. Yes, Mr. Ford would know all about that. He could not have predicted what had happened to him following the killing of Jesse James or he might never have done it. And if Mr. Ford had not killed Jesse James, he would never have been in Weaver at the same time as Joshua. And if Mr. Ford had never been in Weaver at the same time as Joshua, Da would still be alive.

–How ever did you get to know Jesse James? Joshua said.

Mr. Ford sat down again. He dug into his jacket pocket for his tobacco pouch and plumped tobacco onto his cigarette paper, licked the edge, and rolled it up. He held the cigarette between his fingers, unlit.

–I guess everybody always asks you about him, Joshua said.

–Yep.

–I'm sorry.

–It don't matter. I told ever'one else.

He looked down at the cigarette but he still didn't light it.

–I come from Ray County, he said, and all my people were Confederates. And when Jesse James was on the run, my folks give him shelter. The Confederacy lost the war, but all my mama and papa wanted to remember was those who stood up against the Union. And Jesse stood against the Union all his life. When he was sixteen years old, he took off from home to ride with Bill Anderson's guerrilla band. But Jesse never stopped fighting when the war was over. All the stories I heard growing up was about

Quantrill's Raiders, Bill Anderson's band, and Jesse James; a lot of them I heard from my folks, but most of them I heard from Jesse himself.

There was a pride in Mr. Ford's voice. Joshua was silent. He interlocked his fingers and squeezed his hands between his knees but Mr. Ford seemed lost in his own grief. He shook his head.

–I never wanted to, God knows, but I ended up killing that son of a bitch.

Mr. Ford lit his cigarette and blew his smoke into the blank dusk of the cell. Then he began to talk. As he spoke, he paid less and less attention to Joshua, but his smoky words took him and Joshua step-by-step into the world of dream, of myth, Mr. Ford like a preacher upon the pulpit becoming touched by the spirit, at first quietly and then possessed by the ritual reenactment of the life that he, Mr. Ford, had destroyed, the life that now overshadowed Mr. Ford's own so completely and would continue to overshadow it unto death, even as the killing had ensured his immortality in the world's eyes in the opprobrious role of a Brutus or a Judas Iscariot. Mr. Ford's words were as a balm to Joshua's sorrow or a lifeline as he dangled over the pit of grief that threatened to swallow him up. Joshua didn't want Mr. Ford to have to stop in the telling of his tale, and with all the desperation of the will of the condemned, he sought to seal the entrance to his cell against the sheriff's or Wallace's trespass.

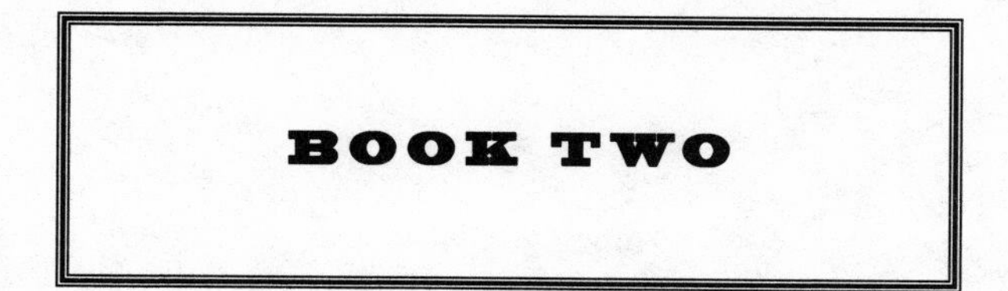
BOOK TWO

XIV

A METALLIC CRACK SPLIT THE HOT JULY AIR. THE NOISE OF THE shot echoed off the domed hillsides that surrounded the fields of golden grass. Jesse James stopped his scythe in mid-swing. Tall grass, in a slow topple, fell at Jesse's feet. He ran a hand through his long brown hair that was wet with his sweat. He listened. Silence but for the whisper of grass that swept toward him in waist-high waves whipped by the wind. He swung the scythe behind him again, then swept the crescent blade forward to carve a new swath through the stalks.

Down the stubbled slope to his right, two black men, shirtless, stood on the floor of a hay wagon. Two other slaves approached the tailgate. They carried great hay sheaves — long stalks, the heads of them heavy with seed — that bobbed upon the Negroes' shoulders. Behind the wagon, at field's edge, the silver leaves of a row of cottonwoods glinted and shimmered under a light touch of wind. Jesse swung the curved blade back. The scythe hissed and pinged as it toppled more grass. Jesse was ready for war, for the war that had ebbed and flowed north and south for the past two years and that he had seen none of, though news and rumors of war had swirled around the peaceful farmstead. Jesse envied his elder brother, Frank, a veteran already of battles at Prairie Grove and Pea Ridge and Osceola and the sack of Lawrence. Frank was in the thick of it, while he, Jesse, now sixteen, still followed the rhythms of the farming year.

He swept the scythe through the grass. He knew that the Lord chose each man's time to be His instrument. Jesse willed his time to be near.

He heard shouts in the distance. He didn't recognize the voices. Gruff shouts. From the farmyard? A big brown barn stood between the field that he was mowing and the yard. He heard a scream, then his mother's high screech that pierced the hot air and caused the sweat on Jesse's face and neck and back to chill so that he shivered. Yonder, behind the slaves on the hay wagon, four riders in dark blue uniforms, rifles in hand, on big bay cavalry horses weaved through the cottonwood trees. He held the scythe above his shoulder and raced across the field toward the gate, toward the barn and the farmyard and away from the soldiers and the Negroes. The gate was closed. He flung the scythe away so that he could vault it. The scythe handle clattered behind him and the vibrating blade buzzed. His palms hit the top bar of the gate and he sailed over. Paddock boots hammered upon the dry ground. Another scream from his mother beyond the barn. A bearded face appeared out of the wide-arched shadow of the barn's rear door. The soldier held a carbine across his chest.

–Hey, boy!

Jesse veered around to the side of the barn. He ran toward the white-walled house. The soldier was behind him, boots pounding on the hard earth. Jesse's hard breath rasped in his chest. Blood pulsed in his ears. He flung himself into the farmyard, bumped into the rump of a spinning horse, stumbled into a dust cloud, felt the flank and harness of another mount smack into his cheekbone. He fell into a whirl of stamping hooves. He was winded.

–What have we here?

There was grit on Jesse's tongue and teeth. Grit in his eyes. He sucked in dust in great whooping gasps as he struggled to his feet. Through the tears that had flooded into his eyes, his stepfather appeared blurred. Pa Samuels dangled from the branch of the elm tree that grew beside the porch. Samuels's feet kicked in free space. His tongue protruded, his face a reddish black, fingers clawing frantically at the rope around his neck. Then a soldier put his horse forward and loosed the rope. There was the whir of hemp over bark, and Jesse's stepfather dropped heavily to the yard.

The flat of a saber smacked against the side of Jesse's head and he found himself face down in the dust, stunned.

–Read it out, sergeant.

Jesse's head was all pressure and pain. The sergeant's voice rasped and grated in his ears.

–Brigadier General Thomas Ewing, Jr., Commander of the District of the Border has issued this order, being Union Order Number Eleven:

Such officers will arrest, and send to the district provost marshal for punishment all men — and women not heads of families — who willfully aid and encourage guerrillas, with a written statement of the names and residences of such persons and the proofs against them. If they fail to remove promptly, they will be sent by such officers under escort to Kansas City for shipment south, with their clothes and such necessary household furniture and provision as may be worth removing.

Jesse lifted his head. His left ear hissed. Through the legs of the horses, Jesse could see the Union officer. He was an absurd caricature of military elegance. The blue uniform was creaseless, from gold epaulets down to his red gaiters. A red plume curved over the wide brim of his black hat. His beard was trimmed close to his sharp jawline. He was mounted on a pale gray Arab stallion. Though Jesse's mother sobbed, and his stepfather choked, Jesse beheld the Arabian with a shocked awe. It was a beautiful horse: perfectly muscled, a short head, an upward curve to the nose.

–Let me go, Mama screamed.

She was on the porch, behind the officer on the horse. The swarthy, unshaven soldier on her left was at least a foot taller than she. He was stooped across her back, holding her forearm and her collar. The soldier on her right was fat and florid, with a thick blond handlebar mustache. He was struggling to keep her wrist in his grip. Mama's brown hair had come loose and hung down over her white blouse. Her wire-rimmed glasses dangled from one ear. Jesse wanted to reach out across the farmyard and save the glasses from falling.

–We know that Frank is with the guerrillas. And you willfully aid and encourage him. Therefore, you will remove yourselves from this farm and report to the district provost marshal.

The officer's voice was calm, matter-of-fact, as if manhandling a boy's mother was the same as harnessing a mule.

–We don't know where he is, she cried. Frank's been gone three years, for God's sake, please (she was sobbing now), he might be dead for all we know.

–The son of a bitch is not dead, ma'am, said the officer.

Jesse raised himself onto his hands and knees in the dirt. The horses, the soldiers, his mother, the slumped body of his stepfather, hoofbeat and dust swirl, seemed cut into stark relief by bright white sunlight. The officer ran a finger under his jaw. He leaned over his pommel to speak to Mama.

–We know he's with Bill Anderson's guerrilla band. We'd just like to know where Mr. Anderson is.

–Please, we don't know. How would we know? I don't understand.

Jesse was on his feet. The pain and pressure in his head threw him off balance. His knees would not support his weight. He staggered toward the beautiful horse. He heard hiss. He breathed dust. About twenty yards away, to his right, Pa Samuels crawled in the dust, his plaid jacket twisted over his shoulders, his head hanging down, the bald pate shiny with sweat. A length of rope ran up from his neck to the branch of the elm. Pa Samuels coughed and made choking noises. His mouth opened and shut like a fish on hot sand. The soldier, with the rope about his saddle horn, spurred his skittish roan forward; and once again, Pa Samuels hung in the air, legs kicking, hands gripping the taut noose.

–Leave him be, yelled Jesse.

The stock of a carbine cracked against the right side of Jesse's head. The dusty ground hit the left side of his face.

–Another little rebel, the officer's voice said. You people don't know when to stop, do you? Grab that boy, sergeant! Tie the little bastard to the wagon wheel.

His mother was screaming.

–Please, God. Please stop.

Fingers dug into Jesse's armpits; his eyes stung with sweat and dust and something was sticky and wet about his right ear. Jesse wanted his pistol, the one Frank had given to him. He was being dragged along in a solid current, the sights and sounds of which were beyond his control. He was somehow detached from his senses, as if he floated along both inside and outside his head. Rough hemp twisted around his wrists, pressed the skin above his veins against the hot metal of the wheel rim. Jesse yelled out, and craned his head back to look at his stepfather.

–Let him down.

The officer guided the Arab toward Jesse.

–Your boys, said the officer, think that a few back-trail killings and Kansas farm burnings will keep your sacred Cause alive. But you see, ma'am, we got Lee whipped and Hood whipped, and soon we'll have Forrest whipped. And after him, Sterling Price. And right now, I am going to whip this little rebel son of a bitch to within an inch of his life.

The officer had a smug grin on his face.

Jesse twisted against the hemp. It scraped and burned his wrists. His mama was crying.

–Leave my boy alone, please, she cried.

–Don't beg him, Mama, don't beg him, Jesse called.

Pa Samuels was choking. Jesse wanted to beat the officer's brains out with a stone. He should have held on to the scythe.

–Ma'am, you could save that young chap a lot of pain if you would just cooperate a little. All I need to know is the whereabouts of one Franklin James and William Anderson.

–They're in the bush, she screeched, you'll never find them!

–We don't know nothing! Jesse shouted.

Jesse felt a knife slit the fabric of his sweaty shirt and the cloth being torn from his back, but his eyes were fixed on his stepfather.

–Cut him down! Jesse yelled.

His voice was hoarse with fear and dry dust. From the periphery of his vision, Jesse saw the hairy, muscled arm of a soldier rise and swing. A burning trench of pain cut across his shoulders. He screamed, saw the arm swing back again, and heard the whistle of the switch, felt his own taut skin split and the fiery parting of the flesh beneath.

–Where's Frank? the voice said. Where's Frank?

The air in front of his eyes was a blinding white. The pain burned up his breath, and his whole being, so that there was nothing else in the world but pain, in his head, in his back, in his arms, down his legs; and repeated pain, and his head spun and the voice echoed. Then darkness.

XV

HOOVES STEPPED ON PEBBLE WITH THE SHIFT AND GRIND OF ROUND stone upon round stone. He twisted beneath the warmth of the blanket and came up onto his knees behind his saddle. Small stones dug into his knees. His back ached. The dressing picked at his skin and the healing wounds itched. His pistol was under the saddle but he did not reach for it. He was in guerrilla country. Anderson's band was known to be in the area, and he wanted to meet up with them. He peered into the warm August fog that hung and twisted on the river. It was shot through with the first golden light of dawn, making silhouettes of the four big willows that hung their slender branches over the twelve-foot-wide stream. Branch tips trailed in the murmuring shallows. Behind him, tied to a beech tree, his horse snorted. Jesse's muscles tightened. If the rider had heard that, Jesse would soon be staring at the muzzle of gun. He shivered. He kept his fingers spread on the seat of the saddle. His feet tingled without circulation, his toes cold in his boots.

A long chestnut head appeared, stretched forward between the two umbrella-like trees on the opposite bank. The rider was a hunched shadow over the neck of it. More horses took form downstream from the chestnut. Damp riders in long linen dusters appeared out of the bush. Their hat brims were wilted over matted hair and coarse beards. The horsemen let their mounts come to water.

The leader guided his chestnut to the bank directly opposite where Jesse knelt. From under the shadow of his hat brim, the horseman regarded him out of one pale and bright eye. Where the other eye ought to have been was a red and welted slit. The creases on the rider's face were thin shadows on the pale complexion. The other men slouched around him on their mounts, eyeing Jesse at his leather pew. More men kept arriving behind them. Jesse's glance flitted from man to man. His teeth were clenched to stop them chattering. It hurt the muscles of his jaw. His feet were getting numb. He felt a chill in his stomach when he saw that some of the men wore blue uniforms and others gray.

–Oh dear Lord, he thought, this is just another band of Union Jayhawkers in Confederate uniforms.

–You saying your prayers, boy? said one of the horsemen.

The leader of the riders cocked his head, and commenced to laugh — a neighing sound — and the other riders joined in as if yanked on a chain: guffaws, coughs and hacks, and an odd high twitter. Horses wheeled and the animals' long heads jerked upward. The men's dusters fell open, showing heavy pistols tucked in broad leather belts.

The one eye swiveled around in its socket.

–Where you from, boy? asked the leader.

–Clay County, Missouri.

–Good stock.

Jesse thought, They got to be Confederates.

He relaxed his shoulders, raised his head slightly, and smiled. The leader sat still, hunched over, while his horse drank leisurely. Jesse let his hands slide back on the saddle leather. Dragoon pistols suddenly appeared, big and heavy, one in each of the leader's fists. Jesse's nails dug into the saddle seat.

–Keep those damned hands in sight.

Jesse closed his eyes, half expected the explosion. He heard a snort. Then quiet. He squeezed against the loosening of his bowels. His bladder was too tight and painful in this cold morning.

–Hey, George, that's my goddamn cousin.

Jesse opened his eyes. A rider eased his horse from the rear of the company and through the ranks. He was dressed in Confederate gray, with a battered gray cavalry hat jammed down over his long fair hair and a passably thick fair beard that made him look older than his years, but Wood Hite was certainly a cousin.

–What you want here, Jesse?

–I'm looking for Frank.

The stones were beginning to dig into Jesse's knees intolerably. He stopped the muscles of his face from twisting into a grimace.

The one-eyed leader turned to Wood.

–Frank who?

–Frank James, Wood said.

–By God, we got us another young rebel, boys.

Again the laughter of the company, like a mechanical beast.

The leader crossed his wrists over the pommel of his saddle, let the pistols dangle.

–Stand up, boy, the leader said. Frank's with Bill Anderson's company. I reckon we should meet up with them in a few days' time.

Jesse pushed against the horseless saddle and stood. His muscles were cramped and his feet numb from kneeling in the cold. His back still ached from the whip. He stood crooked.

–What the hell you doing out here in the bush? Wood said.

–I come to join up, Jesse said.

–Join up? said the one-eyed commander. How old are you?

–Be seventeen, a month from now.

–You armed?

–Yessir.

–What kind of ordnance you got?

–Colt Dragoon. Frank give it to me. It belonged to a Union officer he shot at Prairie Grove, when he was with Shelby's command.

–Old Jo Shelby is a great man, but he's hamstrung trying to fight these murdering sons of bitches like a gentleman, you understand me, boy?

Jesse nodded but he was not sure that he did understand.

–I'm George Shepherd. You want to find Frank, you saddle your mount and fall in.

Shepherd tucked his pistols back into his belt.

–Thank you, thank you, Jesse said.

–Get your horse, Wood called.

Jesse nodded to his cousin. He gripped the pommel of his saddle and swung it up from the ground and onto his hip. He tried not to stumble as he struggled back to where his horse was tethered in a beech copse away from the streamside. He slung the saddle onto the roan's back and cinched the girth tight around its belly. At that instant the landscape was transformed as if the world had become entirely other as the sun blazed down through the dissolving gold-flecked fog and refracted on the bubbling river and on copper beech leaves shimmering and shadows fell a deeper black behind every granite pebble and mottled branch. Across the stream, the riders kicked their horses into motion. Jesse pulled himself up into the saddle. Every tugging ache in his back and the sharp pain in his knees and the painful return of sensation in his cramped toes were a relief and a pleasure. He urged his horse toward the stream bank. The horse shied momentarily, then stepped into the stream and crossed to join the ragged company. His cousin Wood waited for him and fell in alongside him.

–How's your mama and Samuels doing?

–Militia come and run 'em off the farm. They'll be in Nebraska by now.

–Son of a bitch. They burn the farm?

–Mama locked it up. Ain't no telling it'll stay locked up. Militia been looting all over.

–We're all kin here, Wood said. This ain't war, it's family business.

Jesse fell silent and Wood let him be.

Like a pair of watchdogs, two heavily armed guerrillas sat their mounts on each side of the path, and Jesse and Wood filed between them onto the trail that passed under golden-leafed scrub oak and twisted-limbed locust trees. Other riders closed in behind them, and the trail climbed slowly through a forest of elm, oak, and maple. Bare green domes of hilltops rose out of the woods. Blue jays nodded on the high branches above them. The twitter and flutter of finches animated the undergrowth of mulberry. Cardinals and orioles flashed red and orange. It might have been paradise had not the whine and pick and itch of mosquitoes irritated his face and arms and neck. His shirt stuck to the dressing on his back. As they rode through the morning, the August heat and the damp of cloud banks fell heavy upon the hills. Horse rumps and saddlebags, dusters over cruppers, swayed in front of Jesse as the company wound northward over the backwoods trails, and he found himself sleepy from the swaying rhythm and the close heat.

Soon after noon they came upon a shack in the woods. A small clearing had been made all around it, and on both sides and out back of it, beanpoles were hung lush with tendrils, broad green pointed leaves, and long pods. Yellow squash bent fat and bulbous above the mounded earth. There were thick clumps of cabbage and rows of potato plants with their purple-and-white flowers. Jesse's belly rumbled. He had not eaten since dawn. The riders of the company broke ranks and crowded the space in front of the shack. He was separated from Wood now by a small knot of five riders that pushed forward between them from the rear of the column. He suddenly felt terribly alone.

George Shepherd called out.

–Hello in there!

A gangly homesteader appeared in the rough-framed doorway. His gnarled hands twisted big and broad, over and around each other in a continuous nervous motion before the crotch of his ragged overalls. He had no shirt. His skin was streaked with dirt and sweat. The man's hair was plastered to his big skull above the jug-handle ears. Shepherd leaned over his pommel.

–You got anything to be afraid of?

–Don't guess.

–You got a woman in there?

–Nossir.

–You mind stepping out here where we can see you?

–Nossir.

The man came across the tilted porch in a series of twists, head lolling, the hands working against each other relentlessly. Jesse wondered if he was some kind of retarded mountain man or had some form of crippling disease, but when he reached Shepherd's mount he stood straight enough and looked right up at him.

–Where you live before you set up this shack here? Shepherd said.

–Come aways from Kansas.

–Whereabouts in Kansas? I got people up that way.

–Just about Lawrence.

Shepherd nodded.

–I lived in Lawrence myself for a spell. You grow that garden back there?

–Yessir.

–Would you mind if my men helped theyselves to a few roots and vegetables?

–Don't guess I got much choice.

–Don't guess you have. You're a smart man, Mr. Kansas. Would you mind fetching me a spade?

–Nossir.

Shepherd nodded.

–Well, step to it, then.

The homesteader turned toward the house. Time began to flow like molasses. In one fluid movement synchronized with the homesteader's turning body, Shepherd's right hand dropped a slack rein, glided back to his belt, and swung the big pistol out from his body, barrel pointed at the back of the homesteader's head, and bang — the pistol bucked and the homesteader dropped beneath a wreath of smoke and a spray of blood drops. The roan shied and whinnied. Jesse reined him back under control by instinct. Of the other riders' mounts, a few jerked up their heads. The homesteader's body was sprawled, arms in the dirt, the gnarled and broad hands flat on the edge of the porch, and blood pulsed into a pool between the man's naked arms. Jesse felt his own knees and ankles shaking. His hands shook. He gripped too tight against the leather of the reins. The only thought in his head was Oh dear Lord. Oh dear Lord. And the dread in the realization that the act was irreversible. Definitively irreversible.

–We're in a war, friend. You just kill 'em and move on. Or they kill you and move on. Or a dirt farmer like this one sets you up to get kilt by the next passing Union patrol. You cain't trust no one from Kansas, you hear?

Jesse turned to look at the guerrilla behind him. The horseman's cheeks were smooth and rosy, as if he was in his early twenties, but his beard was surprisingly full and long and had been combed out on the chest of his gray tunic. His eyes were soft and alive.

–They's fresh food back there, Wood, Shepherd said.

Jesse turned to look forward again at George Shepherd and his cousin Wood Hite.

–Take four men and load a couple mules.

Wood was up ahead leading the panniered mules. The vegetables in the baskets were probably worth no more than a couple of dollars on a good market day in Kansas City. There was enough to feed maybe forty grown men, but Jesse had no appetite all of a sudden.

–I sneaked past that garden about a week ago, said the young guerrilla behind him. But there weren't nothing ripe then. I'm sick of beans and grits.

–That old boy never seen it coming, did he? Jesse said.

–He's eating his grits in Hell now.

Jesse kept his silence, his head bowed so that no one would tempt him to talk. He kept his place in the line and followed the company over a heavily timbered pass in the hills. They guided their mounts downward. The gentle slopes on either side of them were dense with sycamore, maple, and linwood. It was late afternoon. The trail followed a rill that ran downhill and northward toward the Missouri River.

A meadow opened before them and the guerrilla band spread out, their horses breaking into a trot. The small stream continued along the edge of the clearing, which was bordered by locusts. The stream disappeared into the woods below the meadow. Serried campaign tents surrounded the clearing, though there was but one campfire and not five men visible in the entire meadow. Jesse dismounted numbly. He led the roan toward a picket line where four other horses were tethered. The animals cropped at the bunch grass in front of their feet. He unfastened the roan's halter and tethered him with a slip rope. He uncinched the saddle and relieved the roan of its weight and that of the saddlebags. He took a rag from a saddlebag and rubbed the horse down with short, hard sweeps. Then he fed him with fresh oats that he found in a bucket by the picketstake.

–Ain't your fault, Jesse said to the horse.

Shepherd had ridden to the far northern edge of the camp and picketed his horse there. Wood had led the panniered mules to a wagon, where a bandy-legged old curmudgeon in a Confederate uniform inspected the vegetables. The young guerrilla with the flowing beard was at the first campfire. He filled a tin mug from a coffee pot. Jesse hauled his saddle and saddlebags onto his shoulder and made for the bearded man's fire. He dropped his tack and slumped down among the group of men, who had begun to unpack pots and dry goods for the evening's meal.

–Name's Ol Shepherd, said the young guerrilla, George's brother.

Jesse felt a revulsion that twisted his whole body back against the saddle. All these men were tied together.

–This is Frank James's brother, said Ol Shepherd to the others.

At least three men greeted him, but Jesse didn't look up.

–You ain't seen a man kilt before, said Ol Shepherd.

–Nope.

–Happens all the time around here.

The others laughed. He looked up. All the men around the fire looked to be in their twenties. They had scrubby beards and long hair. No two uniforms matched. The lankiest had on a brown homespun shirt embroidered with roses and hearts. Two of the others wore military dress — one Confederate gray with yellow facings, the other a Union army blue coat that barely buttoned around his belly.

–Don't get yourself kilt now, said the fat man.

Jesse nodded.

–Drew Corbett's the name. You hungry?

Jesse was but he shook his head.

–Here comes the quartermaster, said Corbett.

A gnarled curmudgeon approached the bivouac. He had the bulbous nose of a committed drunk. His cheeks were flushed. He came on through the pungent smoke that billowed from the campfire's blaze. Now that it was dusk, the trunks and branches of the trees at the edge of the clearing wove a pattern like a spider web in front of which the quartermaster scuttled, stained mouth and ruddy cheeks working around his chaw. In his blunt hands, he held out a bundle as if it were a harvest offering at a Baptist church.

–Chow down, boys, he said.

He dropped the raw potatoes and squashes in front of Ol Shepherd and stamped off bow-legged back to the mules. Wood was distributing more vegetables to other men's campfires.

–I ain't eating that, Jesse said.

–Why? Ol Shepherd said.

–It ain't right what he done. Your brother.

–I'm gonna cook it anyways, Ol said.

Jesse squatted by the crackling fire. The soldiers commenced to poke the potatoes under the embers at the edge of the fire. Ol filled a pot from a pail next to the fire and set it over the blaze. He dropped the yellow squashes, whole, into the water.

Jesse plucked a blade of grass and chewed the end of it. The juices in his stomach began to gnaw at him. Across the clearing, Wood squatted next to George Shepherd and along with four other men passed around an earthenware jug. Each man took a liberal swig. Another fire had been started by the others in the company. But even so, there were far too many tents for so few people.

–Where is everybody? asked Jesse.

Ol cut himself a wad of chaw.

–Bill Anderson and his brother and your brother and a bunch of others all gone on a raid, he said. We just here to look after the campsite.

–When'll they be back?

–Two, maybe three, days.

Over the clearing, the sky had turned a deeper blue and the air had turned cool in the evening shade. Venus sparkled just above the treetops. Mosquitoes bobbed and floated around the fire. Jesse looked over the men around him. Each soldier was armed with two pistols worn in heavy holsters. Bowie knives hung from their belts.

–Yea, child, these men are Angels of Destruction, said Ol as if he read Jesse's thoughts.

Ol spat a brown squirt into the dirt. The chaw was balled in his cheek.

–Yea, said Jesse, He sent out his arrows and scattered them; and He shot out lightnings and discomfited them.

Ol laughed.

–Your daddy was a preacher, he said.

Jesse turned red.

–How'd you know?

–Your brother Frank told me. Told me old Mr. James died in California. Preaching to miners. Looking for gold his own self.

–Consumption got him. That's how come Mama married Samuels.

–How's old Samuels doing?

How did Ol know Samuels? Jesse picked at the grass between his legs. Everyone talked family business. He didn't want to talk about family business. The militia hadn't killed Samuels, but he hadn't been right since they'd strung him up. Samuels could hardly speak. Hardly walk.

–He's fine, I guess, Jesse said.

–You guess?

Jesse arms curled around his knees, and his body withdrew against the saddle at his back. This Ol was being more friendly to him than his cousin Wood, who was drinking a jug with the one-eyed George Shepherd.

–You lost your voice? Ol asked Jesse.

–No, I ain't.

–You just stick here with me, Ol said. Frank should be back soon.

Ol dipped his knife into the fire and drew a potato out of the embers. The skin was black and it smoked. Ol flicked up his knife and the potato flew toward Jesse. It landed next to his knee. The roasted skin split and the aroma made him ravenous. Jesse dug his clasp knife from his pants pocket and picked up the potato, using the cuff of his sleeve so as not to burn his hands. He cut back the burnt skin. Unholy communion.

–Oh dear Lord, Jesse said.

His teeth sank into the white flesh.

XVI

GRAY CLOUDS PRESSED DOWN HEAVILY OVER THE CLEARING AND A low thunder rumbled around the shrouded hills. Every breath that Jesse took was drawn as if through damp cotton. Despite the muggy heat, he sat close to the embers of Ol Shepherd's campfire for the comfort of the coals' red glow. He pulled at the neck of his undershirt. It was damp with sweat and tended to tug at the clean dressing on his back. War was an indolent business. The men of the camp did little else but lie in their tents and doze. He picked up a cottonwood wand, ran the blade of his clasp knife around it, and curled off a spiral of bark. He and Frank had made arrows like this when they played together as little boys. Frank would remember if he saw one. With the knife point, Jesse cut out little triangles to create an Indian pattern.

From the trailhead came hoofbeat and the chankle of harness. Two men rode into the clearing. He could tell they were men by the beards on their faces and the cigars that jutted, smoking, from their mouths, but they were dressed in women's bonnets and long dresses. They held rifles upright on their skirted thighs. Their horses' pink mouths foamed over the bridle bits; the mounts' breastplates and cinches were lathered and rimed. Behind these riders appeared an Indian, hair braided with feathers, face half blue and half white, as if the flesh were cracked and rotten. He wore a Union tunic. In his hand was a war lance from which dangled matted clumps of hair.

–Oh dear Lord, said Jesse.

Men in dirty butternut shirts came off the trail two by two behind the Indian. Their exhausted horses pranced and stumbled around the tents. The guerrillas wore dusters, stained brown with dry blood. Their faces were streaked with greasy powder, cheeks barred with dark gray that looked like dull heathen war paint. Their hands were blackened. All lolled in their saddles as if exhausted. Jesse ran toward the trailhead, skipping out of the way of a rider who was dressed entirely in black: black frock coat, black hat, long black hair and curly beard. He sat upright and stiff on a black mount. The horse was in a strut, red eyes rolling. On each side of the bridle hung clumps of matted hair of the same kind that decorated the Indian's war lance. The rider's eyes were fixed, unblinking. That gaze chilled him. Fascinated him. The rider rode on into the clearing.

Fires blazed and crackled, started by the quartermaster's four helpers. The painted Indian squatted by a blaze and swigged at a whiskey jug. He commenced to sing a rhythmic song in his barbaric language. The men in women's bonnets and lace shawls whooped and danced and swooped around the flames, twirling their skirts. Riderless horses neighed and whinnied and kicked and plunged, ran to the little brook to drink. A soldier in a torn gray tunic appeared. A burlap sack lay across his saddle horn. He led in a string of heavily laden pack horses. He yelled high and long at the center of the clearing. Eyes mad and rolling, whiskey-drunk, arms flailing. He flung down his sack. Silver plates and tableware clanked and tinkled and rattled as they spilled over the ground. The men who were dressed as women grabbed trident candlesticks and waved them in the air. Their knees lifted in a wild jig.

Now his brother's centaur form appeared at the trail head. The head of his sorrel horse had dropped with exhaustion. Frank's arms were spread in triumph. In the right hand, he hefted an earthenware whiskey jug, in the left, a Sharp's carbine. The horse's legs strutted stiffly, as if the beast was close to its end. Jesse ran toward him. Frank's slouch hat was jammed down low and his big ears bent forward under the brim. His unshaven jaw jutted out over the upturned collar of his duster. As he caught sight of Jesse, his eyes lit up and his lips pulled back from his teeth in a clenched grin.

–What the hell you doing here, Jess?

Frank swung down from the saddle of the sorrel, staggered backward, flailing the carbine and the whiskey jug.

–Hey, big brother, Jesse said.

He gripped the lapels of Frank's duster to pull him into an embrace and Frank flung his laden arms about him. The whiskey jug thudded against Jesse's dressing. Pain seared through the whip wounds. He sucked in breath. He rubbed his smooth cheek against Frank's stubbled one. His smile stretched his face taut. Frank wrestled him off the trail, and they fell heavily against the roots of an oak. He felt the dressing tear from his wound and bit his lower lip so as not to cry out. Dear Lord, it hurt.

–Oh Jesse, Jesse.

Frank's breath was hot and stinking with whiskey.

–Where the heck you been? Jesse demanded.

Frank lay back limply. Jesse pulled Frank's weighted arms off his shoulders. He feared that his back was bleeding under the dressing.

–Been to hell and back.

–Dod dingus, Frank, you're drunker than a skunk.

–By God, Jesse, we gave them Federals something to remember us by. There ain't a telegraph line standing between Huntsville and Fredericksburg, and we strung up every son-of-a-bitch Union man we laid hands on.

–I'm just glad you're alive, Jesse said.

He could feel tears well from his eyes and run hot on his cheeks.

–What you blubbering for? said Frank.

And then it came out of him, a river of words over which he had no control, and he told Frank of the Arab horse and the prancing officer upon it. And he told of their mother's screams. And Pa Samuels with his black face, and his tongue protruding. And how Samuels couldn't eat right, or stand right, or talk right anymore. And he told Frank about the beating he took, the pain of which burned in his back this instant, and how he was glad of the pain because it made him ache for revenge all the more.

–I want to search out that officer and gut him, Jesse said.

Frank tilted his head. His face, which had been flushed with drink, now had a sweaty pallor.

–Mama? asked Frank.

–They never hurt Mama. When I told her that I wanted to fight the Federals, she said I should go on and find you.

–They burn the goddamn farm?

–Not the house. But the crop. Mama said that she and Samuels would be safer in Nebraska.

–By God, someone's going to pay for this, Frank said.

Jesse came up on one knee, pressed against the ground with the back of his hand, and pushed himself to his feet. Frank used the tree trunk to steady himself as he rose, laden as he was with jug and carbine.

–Come on, Frank said. Come with me.

Frank gripped Jesse's upper arm, fingers digging into the muscle. They stumbled forward together. The clearing was a chaos of men and horses. The mess hands had cauldrons on tripods suspended over fires. Frank guided Jesse toward the man in the black frock coat, who sat in front of a campaign tent.

The commander's black eyes bore into them as they approached. His head was tilted like a fighting cock's. His hands rested on the hilt of the saber that was planted between his feet. The buckskin gloves were bloodstiff and powder-streaked. An unknown anxiety gnawed in Jesse's gut and constricted his throat.

–Bill Anderson, this is my brother, Jesse, said Frank.

–Do you want to fight, boy? Anderson asked.

The eyes glared at him. Anderson's voice had a reedy, piping sound.

Jesse nodded.

–You will ride with me, Anderson said. You hear? Do you want to know what it is to fight, boy? Let me tell you. No quarter. Give none and ask none. Do you understand me?

Jesse nodded again.

Anderson bobbed his head as if in approval.

–Come here, boy, he said.

The hem of Anderson's frock coat dropped off one knee. Jesse smelled blood, burnt powder, gun oil, and the sulphurous smell of cordite. Anderson reached under his coat and pulled from his holster a heavy Navy Colt pistol. He held it toward Jesse, butt first.

–It's loaded, he said.

Jesse took the worn wooden grip, held the gun, barrel downward, his left palm supporting it under the chamber. Felt its weight. A ship design, for which the gun was named, had been cast into the metal. It was old and much used, and the certainty that Anderson had killed with it thrilled him. Killed men like the Union officer on the farm, like the two rough soldiers who had manhandled his mother, like the trooper who had spurred his horse forward to drag Jesse's stepfather into the air by a rope.

–It's yours, said Anderson.

Joy filled Jesse's chest. He had come here for this. For less than this, even.

Blessed be the Lord my strength, which teacheth my hands to war and my fingers to fight.

–I'll ride with you, Mr. Anderson, Jesse said.

The point of Anderson's beard lifted as he pursed his mouth.

–Then you're mine, boy, he said. You're mine.

Anderson swayed in his chair, rocked the saber under his palms. He nodded once. Sharp. Like a black cockerel pecking up a single grain.

XVII

THE HOOVES OF JESSE'S ROAN AND OF THE HORSES IN FRONT OF him and behind him fell muffled upon mud-soiled clothes and among scattered boots and women's shoes and between two broken valises that lay on the road like the detritus of a flash flood. In the roadside ditch was a china doll with the painted face cracked away from a shock of abundant yellow hair. There was no sign of the wagons from which the jetsam had been cast. The road ran north between dry stone walls beyond which were fields of bent and dry brown stalks, stripped of corn, whose leaves lifted and rattled beneath the iron-gray sky. Though it was still August, the morning air was frigid, as if the season was in revolt, wet and chill, fall's harbinger. Five pairs of men were in front of Jesse, and beyond them was their commander, Bill Anderson. There were six pairs of men behind Jesse, and his brother rode by his side. Frank's square face stared ahead at the dark blue backs of the men in front of him as if he was in a trance, his mind in some other world.

A sudden gust of wind took the company broadside, and rain struck hard on Jesse's numb cheek and his cold ear. He welcomed the sting of it, for it spread a crystal coldness through his veins and sharpened senses dulled by the long ride. He reached up to fasten the brass collar button of his Union Army tunic, the uniform of the enemy that would bring him close to the enemy. He turned to his brother, whose reverie the rain squall had broken.

–You know where we at? Jesse said. I lost all sense of direction.

Frank nodded under the shadow of his hat brim.

–'Bout thirty miles north of the Missouri River, I reckon. I'd put us in Carrollton County. Close to where Bill was born.

The wind whipped another squall of swirling rain across the road. It rattled on Jesse's cavalry hat. The roan shied across the road toward Frank's sorrel. Jesse pulled the horse back toward the center of the trail.

–Kind of far east, ain't we? said Jesse.

–In the thick of trouble soon. Bill's got Archie Clements out looking for it.

Jesse nodded. He wanted to be blooded.

–And he's looking for trouble to attract more trouble, Frank said. If we draw the Federals north, there'll be less of them to fight Sterling Price coming up from Texas.

They rode into the bottom and over an unsigned crossroads. The rain spat only desultorily after the squalling shower. A mass of circling swifts rose up from the thick wood of elm and ash and oak that covered the hillside beyond the fields. The birds shape-shifted above the company, a fluttering funnel that was drawn away south like iron filings to an invisible lodestone. The company's road ascended into the woods on the hillside that the swifts had quit. Once among the trees, a shimmering green canopy with luminous shocks of red and orange where the maples had already begun to turn, they were sheltered from the wind that gusted in the branches above and scattered a living confetti of leaves into the lane where they rode to swish and rattle beneath the horses' hooves as the company ascended through the woods. A rider appeared over the brow of the hill and galloped like a jockey toward them.

–There's Clements, Jesse said.

–Just you watch out for yourself when the shooting starts, Frank said. Stick close by me if you can.

Anderson raised his hand to call the company to a halt. Clements reined his sorrel horse in close to Anderson. The sorrel shook its bridle as if it wished to be free of the bit. Clements brought the horse's nose down with a sharp tug on the reins. The scout was a small man. He had cinched up his stirrups high to his saddle so that his knees almost reached the pommel. His polished cavalry boots gleamed in the stirrups. His uniform was almost comical. He had turned back the sleeves of his Union lieutenant's tunic, and the yellow piped epaulets drooped off his shoulders. Only the hat fit, shading his weasel-thin face. Clements's narrow mustache curled up as he spoke to Bill Anderson in a voice loud enough to be heard by all.

–There's a Union column moving east on the road to Rocheport, he said. Just on the other side of these woods. They ain't but a quarter mile away. Must be a good fifty of 'em, mostly infantry. They got two scouts, with one mounted officer and six wagons.

–These woods cover us to the road? Anderson asked.

–I reckon, said Archie. And there's a logging trail just over the brow ahead that'll bring us onto a ridge. It's right above the road where that column is marching.

Bill Anderson put his black horse forward.

–Move out, Anderson called.

The commander's buckskin gauntlet lifted and dropped forward. Jesse put heel to the roan. The troopers ahead of Jesse spurred their horses after Anderson. Jesse tried to feel himself as a moving cog in an engine of war, but he felt more like a rabbit among a pack of dogs. No one seemed to mind that they were outnumbered nearly two to one. Frank commenced to whistle "John Brown's Body." The sound scraped across Jesse's suddenly raw nerves. The company was moving forward at a trot. The backs of the men in front of Jesse swayed on their mounts. He had a thousand questions but he was loath to ask Frank in case sheer nonsense tumbled from his mouth. What did he have to do? Would it be a charge? And they were dressed in the same uniforms as the Union. He didn't know all these men in front of him or behind him, and he feared he would shoot one of them.

–Prepare your weapons, boys, called Bill Anderson.

A knot twisted in Jesse's gut. He couldn't reach for his gun. His fingers were frozen from the rain. The company was still on the trail with a ditch and a dry stone wall on either side and closely packed trees beyond that. At a gap in the stone wall, Clements turned off the road. Anderson led the men onto the logging trail. Frank wheeled off the trail beside Jesse with his pistol drawn already. Jesse drew the Navy Colt that Anderson had given to him. The gun was heavy in his hand. He tried to keep it steady, but it waved around as his horse moved through the trees. They passed among gnarled-bark maples and copper-leafed beech. George Shepherd, cheeks hollow, one eye sharp, the other an empty slit, was not five yards to Jesse's left. George had a long staff across the saddle horn of his mount and he tugged at the ties around it and pulled away the leather cover to reveal a tightly furled flag. Jesse eased the roan closer to Frank. Tree trunks, bark patched darkly by the rain, floated by. The sharply outlined trees grew sparser. Jesse felt the nearness of battle in the contraction of his every muscle, with the crack of every twig beneath his horse's hooves, with every flutter of leaf. Between the tree trunks he could see that the guerrillas were above an open hillside that sloped down onto rolling, pale yellow prairie. The rain had ceased, but the wind was as gusty as ever.

On the road below, a column of marching infantry and six supply wagons moved eastward. Three mounted men, one an officer, were in the van. Beyond the column, and parallel to the road, a river cut into the prairie. A solitary oak, massive and ancient, stood by the river bank like an outcast from the woods in which Jesse and the guerrillas hid. And beyond the great oak, a wide and featureless grassland stretched away north. The blue-coated guerrillas ahead of Jesse broke from the cover of the woods as if they had heard a command from Anderson that Jesse had not.

–Come on, Jesse, said Frank.

Frank put the sorrel out into the open. Jesse brought the roan out beside his brother. Ol Shepherd came up on Jesse's right. Down below, two mounted Union troopers pulled off the road to face them. Anderson sat his black stallion in front of the guerrilla line. He turned to George Shepherd and nodded. George unfurled his flag. The Stars and Stripes of the Union fluttered brightly in the easterly breeze. On the road below, a few soldiers in the marching column began to wave.

Jesse had always imagined that he would ride into action beneath the Stars and Bars and that he would be dressed in gray, but here he was in the uniform of the enemy. He gripped his reins in his left hand and the Navy Colt in his right.

The Lord works in mysterious ways.

Then the east wind sent a shiver through the damp yellow bunch grass as if the hand of the Lord itself had passed over the prairie and swept away Jesse's fear. An icy confidence spread along his every nerve.

Thou art my staff and my rod.

He drew a deep breath into his lungs. A cog slipped into place in the clockwork of his mind and turned wheels and axles and ratchets previously unfelt by him. Through the pinions of his senses, he was connected with the Lord's own engine, the engine that drove the streams and rivers and winds and guided the movement of men and horses upon the grasses of this prairie, where his roan stood still among the horses of the company.

The clouds broke open above them, and shafts of sunlight, the Lord's myriad eyes, fell upon the country to light up their enemies, who marched, still unsuspecting, in the valley below. All around Jesse, not one man among the company, he was sure, shared this revelation, for they sat slumped in their saddles. They looked disheveled in the rumpled uniforms of their enemies. Their long greasy locks hung over bearded faces that were ravaged by drink and dulled with fatigue but possessed by a cruel hunger.

–Praise the Lord, Frank, Jesse said.

His brother glanced at him, cocked his head, the hard square face under the cavalry hat quizzical.

–Amen, Frank said and cracked a smile that turned up his stubbled cheeks.

–You all right? Frank said.

–I'm fine, Jesse said.

Jesse reached out across the two feet of space between their mounts and laid a hand on Frank's shoulder, and his brother reached up and squeezed his forearm. Jesse held the roan steady.

Below him, two Union vedettes broke from the marching column in the valley. Their mounts approached at a canter but slowed down as they drew nearer and then pulled their horses to a stop. Jesse knew that some scout's sixth sense had warned these men that something was wrong, radically wrong, about the horsemen strung out along the hill. The Union vedettes turned their horses and raced back down the slope. Anderson's order came to Jesse as little more than a flat and quiet request.

–Start on down, boys. They know who we are.

George Shepherd speared the Stars and Stripes into the sod of the ridge and eased his horse down the slope. Jesse touched the roan with his heels, and the horse sprang forward out of the line. He pulled the horse back under control, and Frank came up on his left again and Ol Shepherd on his right. They moved slowly down the hill, and Jesse stroked the roan's neck and told him to be easy. In the valley below, a Union officer, all red plumes and gold epaulets, sat astride a dark roan. The Union troops ran off the road and into battle formation, a long line of blue coats and muskets.

–Stay calm, Frank said.

Jesse was calm.

The Union officer shouted.

–Fix bayonets!

Now the clatter of metal on metal.

–Ready your weapons! called the Union officer.

Jesse held the roan back on a tight rein. Blue-coated infantry men were not sixty yards away from him. The barrels of their muskets waved, a line of bristling steel. Now every hair on Jesse's body prickled.

Anderson shrieked.

–Charge!

A high and wordless berserker screech split the air, and the men kicked their mounts forward. Jesse screamed out into the storm of hoof rumble and waving pistols and yelling men. Muzzles flashed along the Union lines, crackled and growled. Invisible balls whirred and whizzed over his head. He heard screams and the whinnies of horses. A cloud of white smoke floated in front of the blue-uniformed line and lifted away. And Jesse was upon them. His first shot exploded from the muzzle of the Navy pistol. No one went down. The roan dashed across the road beyond the Union lines, and Jesse was on the open prairie with the Union wagons behind him and the river not fifty yards in front. He pulled the roan around to face the road again. Five frightened Union soldiers fled through the bunch grass toward the river. George Shepherd and Frank, the only other guerrillas who had broken through the Union line as Jesse had, pulled their horses around and took off in pursuit of them. On the road, the Negro wagon drivers lashed their teams, and the mules bolted onto the prairie, moving diagonally northeast between Jesse and the road. The wagons rattled and swayed across the open ground toward the river, leaving the Union troopers behind them where the dashing Union officer waved his saber to rally his men.

Jesse leveled his pistol. He sighted on the officer's narrow back. He squeezed the trigger. The pistol bucked in his hand. Still the officer waved his sword. The militiamen struggled to reload their muskets, ramrods waving above their heads, yelling encouragement to one another. Beyond them, Anderson had rallied the guerrilla horsemen upon the slopes. It would have been easy to shoot at the militiamen's backs, but Jesse made the roan prance in place as he cocked his pistol again.

Anderson's horsemen on the hillside fired a pistol volley and charged down upon the militia's ranks. More muzzle flash and smoke as they hit the line and the Union soldiers scattered onto the prairie, the guerrilla horsemen among them in pursuit.

–Now, thought Jesse, now.

He held the roan's head close on the rein. A young militiaman ran toward him. The soldier flung away his useless musket. His hands were shaped into claws and drawn up near where his brown leather cross-belts came over his epaulets. Ammunition pouches slapped against his hips as he ran. His lips were pulled back from his clenched teeth. The kepi bounced off the soldier's head. His short dark hair was plastered down with sweat. Jesse raised his pistol. The boy soldier glanced up. He kept on coming. Fifteen yards. He was so close that Jesse saw a red flush spread in a band below the boy's teary eyes and across his beak-like nose. The pistol bucked in Jesse's fist. The soldier was flung back on the ground as if suddenly hit by a massive weight. Jesse cocked the pistol again. He charged past the writhing boy and rode straight toward the road. Anderson's rebel yell split the air not twenty yards away. Anderson rode his horse in circles around a militiaman, who jabbed upward with his bayonet. Jesse drove the roan straight at the militiaman and fired his pistol. The bullet knocked the soldier forward beneath the hooves of Anderson's mount. Anderson's horse spun away. Jesse reined in close to the militiaman's feet. The soldier twisted onto his back, and his boots scraped against the grass as if he would raise himself from the ground, but now his trunk was as still as if it lay under a massive and invisible stone, the arms twitching by his side. Blood bubbled out of the soldier's open mouth over his thick dark mustache and ran into his nose, so that Jesse thought he might drown on it. Blood trickled down over the pale, clean-shaven cheeks. The man's wide eyes bulged as if the fear behind them would pop them out. He was like a crushed insect in its last agony. Anderson guided his black horse up close until its hooves were just behind the dying soldier's head. He waved his hands from side to side as if he conducted a cacophonous orchestra of pistol shot, battle cry, groan, and scream.

–By God, boy, you've no beard, but you know how to fight, said Anderson. No quarter, boy. No quarter.

Under the brim of his cavalry hat, Anderson looked down upon the dying soldier. The commander's dark hair fell down about his beard. Then in all his magnificent madness, Anderson looked back up at Jesse.

–And so? he said.

Jesse looked at him, puzzled.

So what? he thought.

–Finish the job, boy, said Anderson.

The pistol trembled in Jesse's fist. He lifted it and fired three deliberate shots into the prone body of the soldier. The bullets ripped and twisted the torso, then the soldier lay still. A white cloud of powder smoke drifted away toward Anderson. A smile curled Anderson's mustaches upward. The commander slid down off his mount and knelt beside the corpse as if he might pray for the dead man's soul, but he drew a thin-bladed skinning knife from a belt-sheath, grabbed a handful of the dead man's lank hair, and yanked the head up. The keen blade scored a red line across the pale forehead. The point of the knife slid down above the ear. The commander tugged at the boy's hair, and it lifted up from the glistening red skull. He slid the blade around the nape of the neck and the scalp tore free, greasy and bloody in his hand, while the bared skull tipped back onto the ground. Anderson held up his limp and matted trophy. He winked at Jesse again. Jesse struggled to keep the roan under control as the horse tossed its head and shied. Anderson knew war.

–Come with me, boy, he said.

Anderson remounted and Jesse brought the roan up beside his horse and they rode together across the battlefield. Knots of men skirmished about them. All around the crack and pop of ordnance, the slaughter of fleeing Union soldiers who scattered all over the prairie. Jesse scanned the detritus of battle on the prairie: blue-coated bodies, muskets, a single glittering saber. Each breath he took was the Will, each creak of harness, each twist in the saddle, each puff of dust raised by hoof-fall, and the warmth of the setting sun upon his back and the ache in his back.

Down by the river, the wagons had stopped. The mules were dead in their traces. The six Negro drivers stood at gunpoint, their hands tied behind them. Heads bowed. Not one of them tried to run or cry out or protest his fate. Frank flung a rope over one branch of the solitary oak. The noose hung empty. George

Shepherd secured a second rope. Jesse knew that all of these men were caught in a gyre of Will given only to the anointed to fathom. And not even Frank with all his years in the bush, nor Bill Anderson, who was the honed edge of the Lord's instrument of vengeance, understood His Will as in that moment Jesse did.

The exaltation remained upon him even when he left the field of battle and the company rode hard across the prairie, south and east. Anderson rode ahead of him, his grisly trophy hanging upon his horse's bridle, fresh and clotted among the dry. The pale dusters of the company were stained like the aprons of butchers, and Jesse was one of them. Blooded.

Light faded and the gray clouds above turned white and broke up and were driven away westward by the hard wind. The sky was clear above the chill prairie. His mouth was dry. He was hungry. The roan must feel so, too, he thought. And all the men and horses of the company. Their scout, Archie Clements, appeared on the prairie southeast of them. He pointed toward a dip on the plain and a stand of willows that arose out of a thick canebrake that formed a line across the prairie. Beside Jesse, Frank swung his sorrel toward the cluster of trees before anyone else in the column thought to break stride. Jesse spurred his roan and set off after him. His parched horse scented water and galloped hard. Among the bunch grass, he disturbed five crows that fluttered up from some unseen carrion and cawed in protest. The roan followed Frank's sorrel into the thick canebrake and past the willows and down to the bubbling creekside. Jesse slipped from his horse's back and ran upstream a short way. He leaned over the stream and gulped at the water.

–Take it easy, boy, said Frank.

–I sure am hungry, too, Jesse said.

–Be quick to eat then, Frank said. Half the Union soldiers in Missouri will be chasing us by now.

The twenty-six men and horses of the company were strung out along the gully cut by the little creek. The men, still in their blue uniforms, made little sound up and down the streamside. Even their horses' hoof-falls were muffled by the grass. The chankle of harness hardly carried through the canebrake. Jesse knelt over the stream. Faint traces of mist like wispy cerements floated up into his face off the surface of the water. He splashed his face. Beside him, the roan raised its dripping muzzle, shook its long head. Jesse raised his aching body from the streamside and stroked the horse's neck. He went to his saddlebags, where he had a nosebag full of oats for the horse and a loaf of stale bread for himself. He dipped the dry bread in the stream and had gnawed at it for only a few minutes when Anderson called out the order.

–Mount up.

Jesse grabbed the pommel of the roan's saddle, but before he could remount, Frank drew him aside.

–Wait a second, Frank said.

Jesse, puzzled, stood by the roan. The other men downstream were already mounting, and Jesse feared Bill Anderson's impatience.

Frank took a coil of rope from the saddlebag on the sorrel. He cut two lengths of rope off the coil and handed one of them to Jesse. He fastened his saddlebag, hitched one end of the rope around his saddle horn, and cinched it tight. Jesse tied a similar knot on his own saddle.

Frank mounted the sorrel and Jesse pulled himself into the roan's saddle. Frank looped the rope around his waist and tied a knot close to his belt buckle, then he passed the rope behind him again and tied a knot behind his back. He passed the loose end of the rope through two brass rings stitched into the cantle of his saddle. He secured the rope at his waist again so that he was in a web fastened in front and behind himself. Jesse knotted and threaded his own rope at pommel and cantle and shifted his hips one way and then another to test the tension of the ropes within which he was cradled.

–Now if you fall asleep, you won't fall out of the saddle, Frank said.

Jesse nodded.

–Move out, called Anderson.

Frank rode into line and Jesse followed him. Once more they rode out onto the prairie. Night deepened above and around them, moonless, shot with stars that wheeled above them. And the grasses whispered and wheeled below the hooves of their horses. The riders rolled around Jesse as if they were drunk in the saddle.

As the night advanced, Jesse dropped into fits of ragged sleep and the web at his waist held him secure on the horse's back so that he let himself pass into that place of near delirium between sleep and dream where great hypnagogic pillars appeared beside the column. And the shapes of trees where there were none seemed to crowd among the riders. And he heard voices like the calls of his mother when he was a child, and shouts of the dying, screams, the hooves of the horses like a charge of cavalry. And someone — a man's voice, he thought — called his name and caused him to start awake in the voiceless night. He fought off consciousness.

His head fell back and the Milky Way spiraled bright above him and took on a writhing life of its own — he didn't know if his eyes were open or closed — and its light blurred until Jesse saw the whole constellation twist and coil, writhe in angry knots as if it were a snake that would shed its skin, and the buzz in his ears was its furious rattle. The sound and vision just as suddenly disappeared as he jerked forward in his saddle, and the sky was once more black and star-shot. Jesse shivered, then flushed, as the blood flooded his head and the night turned red before his open or closed eyes, and he was suddenly lucid and sharp; but he heard his father's voice, his father's preaching voice say: Now's the very witching time of night when churchyards yawn and hell itself breathes out contagion to this world. Words like Pa Samuels read to him. From the Bible. And Shakespeare. And he saw Pa Samuels hauled up into the elm tree, and he shook fully awake of a sudden.

The rope cut into his waist. His bladder was full and his kidneys ached. He unbuttoned himself and twisted his body to make water. He pissed from the rocking saddle. Drops of water fell warm on his thigh. He closed his pants. And drifted off again. And he saw the image of a china doll with the face cracked at the hairline and the Jayhawker captain on a white Arabian and his mother between two soldiers on the porch and the blood that bubbled from his victim's mouth. He was awake again, and he sensed the column of horsemen around him, the column that flowed through the relentless night. They were a wind over the dark sea of prairie. And vengeance would open its baleful eye upon the enemy when morning came once more for they were a host. A plague. A deluge. A fire. Glorious. Oh glorious war.

XVIII

DAWN'S RED EYE LIKE THAT OF THE GREAT DECEIVER HIMSELF rose over the bristling black stubble of the flat and scorched wheatfields and as it rose Jesse felt the exaltation drain out of him as a tide sucked out by the moon and he was left an empty shell, bereft of the presence of the Spirit that had buoyed him for nigh on thirteen days. He glanced from left to right as if he would see a tangible sign of what had left him, but all he saw was signs of the torch, the split-log fences that were charred and broken, their posts like a line of rotten and twisted teeth. In front of him and behind him, all the men of the company — even his brother, Frank, and his commander, Bill Anderson — were suddenly strangers to him, alien faces ravaged by fatigue, angled by hunger, eyes burning in the brazen and sickly light of morning. Jesse scanned the country for sign of pursuit or ambush, and seeing none, he slumped over his pommel as if the tendons of his muscles had been cut, and he let the roan carry him down the trail and into a desolate farmyard.

Bent and blackly scaled columns of burned-out buildings leaned one against another in a series of contorted triangles where barns and outbuildings had once stood. Wisps of smoke rose from the charred beams, and the beds of embers beneath those ruined supports glowed red as the light breeze fanned the coals. The farmhouse itself remained untouched by the fires and stood unreal in that blackened landscape as if some deranged artist had painted its squat stone shape onto the wrong canvas. A chimney rose above the low shake roof, but no benevolent stove smoke curled skyward. A small window breached the wall on either side of the pale door. Jesse pulled the roan to a halt beside Bill Anderson and Frank.

–Come on out, called Bill to the farmhouse.

A high keening split the air. The howl came not from behind the door or windows, but from the chimney side of the house, and the cries and wails of children joined in sudden counterpoint, an infernal caterwaul. Bill guided his black horse leftward, and Jesse followed close behind him. Jesse's hands were shaking. He dreaded the vision that might await them around the corner of the house, but when he saw it, all that appalled him was that it caused a rise in his pants.

A woman in a blue gingham dress knelt close by the granite-stone chimney stack. Wisps of strawberry-blond hair hung down in the woman's face. Her shoulders were broad. A small boy clung to her left arm. She cradled a waiflike girlchild in her right, pressing the child to her breast. On the ground in front of the mother and children were the bodies of two grown-up boys. The bodies lay one across the legs of the other. The elder boy seemed to have been about seventeen, the other some four years younger. Both had the same shock of red hair and long nose, with a mask of freckles across their faces. Perhaps they were Irish. Both had been shot in the back. Their plaid shirts were powder-burned and bloodstained. The hoofprints of a great many horses had churned up the mud where they lay.

The devil's got inside me, Jesse thought.

He twitched at the roan's reins. The horse bobbed its head and shivered as if it would be rid of him.

The woman's eyes were wide and tear-filled. Her mouth twisted and bared her teeth on one side. Then she squealed. Jesse never heard such a sound come out of a human before. It sounded like a hog in its last agony, the throat cut and the struggle gone out of it, and the cry fell dead in the dead fields.

–Ain't you people done enough to us? she asked.

–Who done this? Bill asked.

–Militia, she said. Ain't you militia?

–We ain't militia, Bill said.

–They didn't want my boys joining the guerrillas, they said.

–They left an easy trail to follow, Bill said.

–You ain't militia?

–They won't come back, Bill said.

He spurred his black mount and set off in the tracks that led eastward, away from the ruined buildings and around a stagnant pond. Jesse put heel to the roan and the whole company was in a canter after Bill, leaving the sorry family behind them.

From a brake of huckleberry bushes, a cluster of hogs fled squealing in all directions across the burned wheat fields. The company rode for an hour straight with no sight of men or mounts but only the tracks that they left on the ground.

On the border of Carrollton and Ray Counties they rode along a lane with thick woods on either side of them. In the deep of that forest of alder and walnut and sycamore, they came upon a curious specimen of humanity. Amid the clatter and clank as of tin pots and pans, a disheveled and hairy form, afoot, scuttled with no small hurry toward them. The man's back bent beneath the weight of an ungainly and amorphous burlap sack. His clothes looked rotten from long seasons' wear. The brim of his hat drooped down over beard and hair.

–Halt there, you son of a bitch! called Anderson.

Jesse pushed the roan up close to the troopers ahead to see what would happen. Anderson cocked his head, guided his black horse forward past the tinker, and turned back in the road again. The old man commenced to turn around on himself like an auger, as if he wished to spiral himself into the muddy ground.

–Goddammit. I ain't done nothing. I ain't done nothing. I'm good people.

–What news, old man? asked Anderson.

The tinker's watery eyes shifted under the battered hat brim. An arc of brown liquid squirted from the wet gap in a snuff-stained beard that was crusted with ancient food.

–You're Bill Anderson, ain't you?

–Maybe, said Anderson.

Archie Clements moved in front of the tinker, and Jesse guided the roan out to the trailside, the better to witness the exchange of Anderson and the tinker.

–Never fergit a face, said the tinker. I was in Huntsville when you and your boys rode in and tore the place up. You ain't riding fer the Union, neither. Don't matter what clothes you got on.

–There's a war going on out here, said Anderson. What brings you to this part of the country?

–Ain't but picking up a few things folks don't want no more.

–I should hang you for looting.

I'm a rebel. Only takes from the Unions and sells to the rebels. You shun't hang me.

Anderson laughed.

–You seen any Federals hereabouts? he asked.

The old man's head dipped between his shoulders. The damp sack rattled on his back as he hunched up. He looked up from under his bushy eyebrows. He spoke quietly, as if a spy might hear him out there in the woods.

–You keep heading down this road, he said, and you'll hit Wakenda. They's a whole regiment of militia down there. Camped. But I reckon they'll be on the move by now.

The tinker spat again and nodded to himself.

–Southern man, I am, he said. Reb to the core.

Anderson's hand rested on his saddle horn, close to his pistol.

–You ain't seen us, you hear?

–You can count on it, said the tinker. I'm a reb. Heart and soul.

Bill Anderson turned his black horse away from the tinker.

–Move out, he called.

Jesse squeezed the roan's flanks and the horse picked up into a canter. The smell of horse and harness, the creak of leather and fall of hoof, the stillness of leaf and branch, the rub of rein between his fingers, even the salty dryness of his tongue, now sparked his spirit in anticipation of renewed action. Jesse breathed deep, as if filling his lungs would dispel the last trace of clinging anxiety, but he found no such anticipated relief, for even here in the woods, the late morning's sun had heated the still air and sapped it of its freshness. It felt stifling, rather. Even pestilent. His spirit sank once more.

–Arm yourselves, but hold them low, Anderson called.

Jesse drew his Navy Colt, cocked the hammer, and held the pistol close beside the roan's neck. They broke free of the woods. Down below them, by the side of a stream, over the far bank of which arched four willows, was a company of Missouri militia preparing to resume march or patrol. Troopers were leading their horses from picket lines toward the road. The brazen sun glinted on the instruments of bandsmen who were climbing aboard a wagon.

Ahead of Jesse, Bill did not slow his mount's canter, and the company poured along the trail toward the unorganized militiamen. A pair of sentries had been posted on the trail some fifty yards from the camp, and on seeing Bill's column approach, the two men swung their muskets from their shoulders and held them at port arms. In the camp itself, the half-clad militiamen turned to look in the direction of the blue-uniformed Confederate guerrillas, but none of the Union troops revealed sign of alarm.

–Halt and identify, one of the sentries called.

–Sixteenth Regiment, Kansas Cavalry, Bill shouted.

He rode hard at them, and in their confusion the sentries leaped aside and the guerrilla company drove between them toward the still-forming militia column and were suddenly among the enemy. Jesse's pistol roared and a militiaman dropped. Screams and gruff shouts and the whinny of horses sounded all around Jesse as he raced the roan into camp. Blast and flash and smoke of shot raged and flickered in the still, hot air. He whirled the roan and cocked the Colt within the same motion. Aimed at another fleeing trooper and fired. Missed. The cacophony of battle drove out thought. He was machine. As if cog and spring coiled and unwound to lift his limbs, align his eye and foresight, and finger-squeeze the trigger. He was pistol buck and powder roar and muzzle flash and drifting smoke. No quarter. Then silence fell upon the field.

Frank was not thirty yards away. His brother sat his sorrel behind fat Drew Corbett and his fat gray mare. The two of them were in front of the Union bandwagon, where the musicians stood as if upon a stage. Jesse touched his heels to the roan and the horse pranced toward Frank. Corbett called out to the bandsmen.

–Come on down off of that wagon, boys. Ain't no one gonna shoot no trumpet-playing son of a bitch.

Ol and George Shepherd walked their horses toward the wagon. On it, the bandsmen stood in a tight and frightened cluster of white faces, blue uniforms, and brass instruments. The peaks of their kepis shone, and their tunics were piped with yellow and red as if to brighten the dullness of the day. They clustered around the great tuba, with their trumpets and cornets and trombones and a black serpent.

–Get down, boys, called Drew Corbett. You can give us all a tune.

The trembling began in Jesse's hands again.

–Dear Lord, he thought. Don't forsake me now.

The drummer boy on the wagon reached down behind him.

Jesse thought that he was reaching for his drumsticks, but the drummer boy came up with a pistol.

Dang, thought Jesse, put that thing down, now.

Corbett's eyes widened. His mouth turned down sadly, not frightened, but more disappointed. The drummer boy leveled the pistol.

–Hey, boy, shouted Frank.

The shot knocked Corbett backward off the gray and the fat man writhed in the bunch grass and his horse bolted away.

–God damn! yelled Frank, why in the hell you do that?

He's dead, thought Jesse.

The drummer boy jumped down from the wagon. Ol Shepherd and Frank opened fire. The boy jerked like a puppet as the bullets ripped his body. Thirteen pistols in the hands of seven men swung back to point at the band.

–Bastards, spat one-eyed George.

He fired, and his shot triggered volley after volley from the guerrillas, who gathered like ravenous dogs upon fallen prey. Brass spanged. Bandsmen screamed and lurched as if trying to keep their feet, then pitched from the wagon-bed and into the grass below. Jesse's pistol bucked and kicked in his grip. The bodies spun as his bullets hit home. The Colt was empty. It seemed to take but seconds. On the wagon, not one of the corpses of the bandsmen twitched. They were dead. The absurd bell of the tuba was a pocked and obscene brass standard around which the musicians had fallen. Tangled in the pile of bodies shone trumpets and trombone slides, the black coils of the serpent. The white skin of the bass drum was bullet-torn and ragged.

Corbett's body lay close to the front wheel of the bandwagon. A large stain darkened the dark blue of his tunic that had ridden up off his flabby, ginger-haired gut. The pig eyes, glazed and unseeing, were turned toward Jesse. And the wet mouth was open as if Corbett were in a normal drunken stupor. His pistols were still in his fists.

A hand pressed warmly between Jesse's shoulder blades. He twisted in his saddle, and looked into the crazed black eyes of Bill Anderson.

–They ain't one worth sparing, said Anderson. They are all scum.

Jesse heard a flat pop. Something slammed into his chest and

Anderson disappeared from sight. Blue sky. Jesse hit the ground. His throat made a hooping noise. A sharp pain lanced through his ribs with each shallow gulp of breath that he tried to take.

–Over there.

Whose voice was that? George's?

–Sniper by the goddamn river.

George Shepherd.

Jesse twisted on the bunch grass, tried to get up. Frank's big-eared face appeared above him. The eyes in the stubbled face were bright and tender.

–Easy Jesse, lay still, he said.

–Frank, Jesse said.

Something terrible had happened.

–Am I going to die, Frank?

Frank was silent.

Mama. Oh Mama, he thought.

–Lie still, Frank said. You just gone and took a goddamn bullet.

Jesse's breath came in shallow sips as Frank was at the buttons of his tunic. His brother tore at the red cotton undershirt sticky with blood. A light charge. It must have been a light charge. Too light to drive bullet through bone. It had hit him like a hammer. He was nauseous and he feared the cloying air would not penetrate his lungs.

–I can get the ball out, Frank said. I can see it.

Ol Shepherd's bearded face appeared upside down over Jesse's own. Ol's heavy hands pressed down on his shoulders. And Jesse did not complain. Someone had hold of his legs, pressing down on them. Frank had a bowie knife in his hand. Jesse's teeth ground together. He moaned. Worse than the pain, was the knifepoint scraping against bone and cartilage. Then the ball popped free. It was as if a stone fell from his chest. He began to shake. Blood welled up from the wound and tickled the prickly gooseflesh of his chest. The misshapen face of the quartermaster hovered above him, all bulbous nose and gnarly chin and puffed eyes. He pressed a soft cotton pad against Jesse's chest. A sharp, lancing pain penetrated him to the lungs as they lifted him to a sitting position. The sky above the swimming faces of Frank and Ol and the quartermaster was a steel blue or gray, he couldn't tell which. George Shepherd and Wood Hite laid a stretcher beside him.

–Ease over onto the stretcher and we'll get you into an ambulance, Frank said.

–What ambulance? Jesse said. We ain't got no ambulance.

–There's an ambulance belonged to the militia, Anderson's voice said.

Jesse shivered.

–I want to ride, Frank, said Jesse.

Frank settled his hat back on his head.

–We'll take you where you can rest up a while, Frank said.

–Rest up awhile?

–At the Rudd farm.

–You're leaving me behind.

Frank bowed his head.

–Bill won't risk the company for someone can't pull his weight.

Can't pull his weight?

–I can ride, Jesse said.

–You can't walk, Jess.

–You're not leaving me behind, Frank.

– We'll reach the Rudd farm by midnight.

–You'll stay with me.

–Ain't the case. Buck up, now.

–I ain't gonna get in no wagon unless you take care of me. I don't want to be with no strangers.

–The war ain't over, Jess.

Jesse turned his head left and right. The whole of the mounted company was looking at him. Every eye upon him. Waiting for him to get onto the stretcher. Listening to him beg for his brother's succor. Like a child. Frank put an arm around his shoulder. He shook it off and a sharp pain buckled him. He bent over helplessly. Ol Shepherd slid his hands under Jesse's armpits, Wood lifted his knees, and when Frank lifted him under the hips and laid him on the stretcher, a darkness flooded Jesse's vision and pain deprived him of breath. He lay back and bright balls burst behind his eyelids as he was lifted and moved through space with a nauseating swaying motion. The bearers laid the head end of the stretcher onto solid support. Jesse opened his eyes. The stretcher slid backward over the tailgate of the ambulance, and he was in renewed darkness. His own brother lifted up the creaky tailgate and shut him up in the shadow.

XIX

THE NICKERING OF THE ROAN AWOKE HIM. IN THE DARKNESS, HIS head and shoulders instinctively shifted off the pillow toward the dull clump of footsteps on the boards above his head. He recognized the slow rhythm. It was old man Rudd. Jesse raised himself on his elbows. In the total dark, the crackling of his straw mattress was the sound of a sudden rain shower, but no moisture fell upon his face. Air hardly entered his lungs. His heart pounded loud in his ears.

Wait. Wait, he thought.

His nails dug into the boards above him. Rudd was at the hay sheaves now, dragging them back from the trap door above. Thin slits of light cut the black and laid bright pinstripes down the length of Jesse's long underwear. Motes of dust and wisps of hay drifted down through the chinks in the floorboards. A crack like a shot as Rudd snapped the bolt back. The iron hinges creaked, and old man Rudd's wrinkled and bearded face peered in at him, the long gray hair haloed by a shaft of sunlight that lit it up from behind. Jesse lunged toward the light, grabbed the edge of the opening as a drowning man would clutch at a raft.

–Come on out of there, boy, Rudd said.

The great beamed arches of the barn curved above him. Rudd's rough hands brushed down Jesse's long, skinny body. Rudd was a good six inches shorter than Jesse, and his back was bent like an old wrangler's after he was thrown down and stamped upon by a score of unbroken horses. The muscles under the old man's calico shirt and blue overalls were as hard and tight as fence wire. His fingers raked at Jesse's body.

–Militia passed by about a hour ago, Rudd said. Thought it best to wait before I roused ye. They headed north toward Gallatin.

–North?

–Yep. Opposite direction to where Anderson's at.

Jesse backed away from the old man's fussing.

–Bill still down around Fayette?

–Last I heard.

–That's where I'm headed, then.

–I put a change of clothes for ye on the trunk by the barn door, Rudd said. Ye can get washed up and dressed and come into the kitchen for breakfast.

Jesse nodded. Rudd and his wife had treated him well for a month, but the fever had passed and the pain in his chest was bearable and Jesse was ready to leave.

–Yessir, he said. I thank you kindly.

The old man walked stiffly through the broad barn doors and out into the warm September morning.

Jesse ran his fingers through his long brown hair and walked over to the roan's stall. The horse lifted its nose over the half door, and Jesse stroked down its blaze from ears to muzzle, where a few oats were stuck around the pink mouth.

–Today's the day, boy, Jesse said. We ain't skulking and hiding no more.

He rode all day, east, over a pale and golden sea of grassland. He was a mote adrift under God's blue canopy. The fall wind had a chill in it, so he wore his duster buttoned up over his new, clean clothes. He stayed away from roads and houses. He built no fire that night but camped in a stand of cottonwood and ate the bread and a tough and stringy chicken leg that Mrs. Rudd had packed for him. He lay beside a fallen tree, leeward of the wind, and slept lightly. He awoke as the stars faded and Venus still sparkled on the western horizon. He saddled the roan and set off riding toward the lapis dawn, with the quiet prairie still in shadow and wisps of wind that rose from time to time to chill the flat, pale grassland. He rode for a good hour before he came upon a stand of elm. The few leaves left upon the trees were dry and brown. As he approached, he heard a high crying. A Negro woman sat cradled in the roots of a stout trunk. She sang to herself, her head shaking. The bodies of three Negro men hung from a branch above her.

A father and two sons, he thought.

The eyes were still wide and protruding from the sockets. The woman looked up at him and began a high unearthly wail. The tracks of horses that had beaten down the grass and the wide swath led out across open prairie. About as many horses as would be ridden by Anderson's company. He followed those tracks and left the woman and the bodies behind. The hanging Negroes looked like Anderson's work, too.

The sun was hard in his eyes, and his shadow long behind him when the silhouette of a rider ghosted above a rise in the undulating plain and disappeared. Jesse reined in. There was no cover but the shallow dips in the prairie. Whoever was out there had seen him, and he saw no point in trying to sneak by them.

–That you, Jesse?

It was his cousin Wood Hite's voice. It came from his left.

–It's me, Jesse called.

–Come on in, yelled Wood.

Jesse urged the roan forward. The horse's ears flattened. The tail flicked. The roan snorted, tossed his head. Jesse spoke to him softly and guided him over the rise. Four riders sat their horses close to a smoldering campfire. Behind them, a riderless horse, pale gray, jerked its head against the rope that held it tied to the broken stump of a blasted tree. The three white men held carbines across the pommels of their saddles. They wore pale canvas dusters over their blue uniforms. Bill Anderson's brother, Jim, sat his horse next to Wood Hite. One boy, who looked younger than himself, Jesse did not recognize. The boy's beardless face was pale, the wide eyes dull and cruel. The Osage scout, his face once more painted half blue, half white, feathers twisted in his long black hair, flanked Wood on the left. The Indian held a bow in his right hand. The horsemen stared up at him as if he had just emerged through a rupture in time and was a vision unwanted by them.

–Jesse, said Wood.

His voice was flat.

–Wood.

–We seen you coming, said Wood. With the spyglass.

He waved the brass cylinder around. At the hooves of Jim's horse lay a trussed bundle clad in a blue uniform. Something was wrong with the posture. Jesse stared at it, trying to assemble the incongruous parts into a whole. He licked his dry lips. The hands and feet of the body had been roped together behind the waist. The dead man's head had been forced into the crook of his left arm. The stump of neck between the epaulets on the shoulders was ragged and bloody.

–He kindly stumbled upon us, said the boy. Didn't want him reporting nothing to his unit.

–You looking for us? asked Jim.

–Bill, Jesse said. And Frank.

–They're yonder, Wood said. Some two miles northeast of here. Gone toward Fayette. More then two hundred men. Quantrill was with them. Him and Bill fought cat and dog last night. You should have seen them go at it. The militia in Fayette is holed up in a stockade. Quantrill didn't want to attack it, so Bill called Quantrill a goddamn coward. Then Quantrill told Bill he had no intention of committing suicide and took his men back toward Lexington way. Now Bill's got to attack the goddamn stockade just to prove he's got more sand than Quantrill.

–That's right, Jim said.

–Can I catch up to him? Jesse said.

–I reckon, Wood said.

The face of the dead Union soldier gazed blankly at Jesse. The soul that once lit up those eyes was beyond the mercy of humanity, a mercy that might yet be found somewhere in the world but not on these plains. Jesse turned his knee into the roan's shoulder and guided the horse away from the hollow. He flicked the roan's rump, once, with the end of his rein, and the horse leaped into a gallop. He had seen many a sight of death and of mutilation, but he could not help but think that this one was ill-omened.

He rode onto Main Street, Fayette, a long, straight, hoof-marked dirt road flanked by storefronts and houses and boardwalks. The street rose toward a green hill at the end of town. Every building and boardwalk was devoid of life. Not even a dog stirred. Not a horse or wagon in sight. If the citizens were hiding in their homes, the only thing that could protect them would be Bill Anderson's lack of interest. Jesse rode hard to the end of Main Street and turned the horse into a meadow. Some two hundred men had deployed into battle lines at the foot of a low green hill, as if they were preparing for a parade review. Off to Jesse's left, another group of some fifty horsemen had lined up in reserve. No sign of Frank. Bill Anderson sat his big black horse out in front of the double ranks of horsemen. He had waxed his black mustaches and curled up the point of his beard. He gripped two big pistols in his fists.

–Arm yourselves, he called.

The clicking as of a half-thousand metallic insects swept down the line. Then a strange silence settled upon the company. Jesse pulled the roan into the second rank of the battle line, between Archie Clements and Ol Shepherd. Clements and Shepherd saw him but they did not so much as nod. Jesse drew his pistols. Cocked them.

The hill that rose above them would have been a pleasant sight in peacetime, for the green slope was dotted with clumps of low, gnarled locust trees. A gravel pathway led in a long sweep up past a red brick house and ended at the gate of a makeshift stockade that had been built on the top of the hill. The redoubt appeared to be constructed out of railroad ties, which gave the ten-foot-high walls a formidable flat and featureless aspect broken by the small square apertures from which protruded the barrels of muskets.

Beside Jesse, Ol Shepherd's cheek twitched, and that involuntary tic lifted his mustache and beard. He stared hard up the hill at the stockade. On their right flank, the house was garrisoned, too, and it was certain that any charge would be caught in a withering crossfire. Jesse felt conspicuous in his canvas duster among the men who wore Union blue uniforms. And it struck him. Quantrill had been right. This charge was insane.

–Trot! called Anderson.

The commander was the first horseman upon the grassy slope. Jesse put the roan forward. The horse breathed hard beneath him. The two lines of horsemen moved like a wave over the hill. He was caught in this flow toward destruction. The featureless wall in the distance.

–Canter! called Anderson.

Jesse touched heel to the roan and rolled with the horse's motion.

–Charge! yelled Anderson.

Jesse hooked the roan and the horse leaped forward. The wall of the stockade growled and flamed. A sigh swept by him. The scream and plunge of horses was all around him. Men yelled. A roar and a hiss of ball issued from the red brick house. The roan shuddered beneath him and suddenly buckled, head tossing upward, and Jesse tumbled over the horse's left shoulder. The impact jarred his wounded ribs. He twisted away from the hooves that stamped all around him. He still held his pistols. The roan was on its side. Its legs kicked beneath it as it tried to rise, head stretching vainly upward as if it could lift itself by its neck. Blood oozed from a large hole in the horse's chest. It had taken a ball in the shoulder, too.

–Oh Lord, Jesse said.

The pistols dangled in his fists.

–Get up, boy, he said.

Jesse holstered one pistol and grabbed the horse's reins. He tugged at them. Another volley erupted from the wall above and yet another from the house on their flank. Thick gouts of blood splattered up from the roan's cheeks and shoulders and into the smoke-filled air. Jesse was unhurt. The roan's muzzle lowered, chin stretched out upon the green grass, the whole head bloody, dark red. One eye rolled at him. Uncomprehending.

–Oh no, Jesse said.

He raised his pistol, pointed the muzzle between the horse's ears and squeezed the trigger. The pistol bucked. The horse shuddered once and was still. Some of the roan's blood was on his leg. Unknown men stumbled around him, bloodstained, dazed. White smoke drifted up from the front of the stockade. He drew his second pistol again. Raised both weapons. Cocked them. He fired and fired until the hammers clicked on empty chambers, and then he turned away from the splintered and unbreeched wall of the redoubt and stumbled downhill, leaving the dead horse behind him among the moans and cries of the wounded and dying. At the foot of the hill, Anderson's black horse danced amongst the chaos of men and wounded horses. Bill's glittery eye peered down upon him, devoid of reason. His beard twisted as he smiled.

–Why, Jesse, Bill said. You've come back to us.

Riderless horses whinnied and raced across the slope. The still-mounted wounded, slumped over in their saddles, struggled to keep their horses under control and guide them back to the guerrilla lines.

–They killed my horse, Bill, Jesse said. They killed my goddamn horse.

Bill swiveled on the saddle.

–Archie, he called. Bring me that chestnut quarter horse.

Bill pointed across the park toward the picket line behind the reserve troops, who still sat their horses in battle line; in front of them, the battered guerrillas who had charged the redoubt were in total disarray. Little Archie Clement turned his sorrel and cantered it through the broken lines to the picket horses. He led back a chestnut quarter horse about fifteen hands high.

–Give it to Jesse, Bill said.

–For me? Jesse said.

–You plan on walking from now on? Bill said.

It was as if the charge had never taken place. That the wounded and beaten men all around him had as much solidity as the white powder smoke that lifted and drifted over the debris of the battlefield. As if victory and defeat were the same to his commander, for Bill had found contentment in the violence of action. All that counted was abandon to the cause of violence — out beyond the mundane — where there lay some awful and fugitive Truth, a revelation of some supreme mystery that had to do with God's vengeful heart, a mystery which Jesse longed to share in. He took the chestnut by the halter and ran his hand over the stallion's nose. It was a fine horse. It looked at him with its wide, bright eye. The head was a little short, but it had a strong neck set on powerful shoulders. It had fine, muscular haunches and strong, slender legs. It might not be the roan, but this horse would do. More than do. It was his, now. A present from Bill. Just like the Navy Colt. He would follow Bill wherever he led. There was nowhere else to go in this world of mayhem and destruction.

–Mount up, Bill said. We can't do no more damage in Fayette. I reckon we'll do better in Centralia. I aim to burn it to the ground.

XX

A SWEET SMELL AS OF BARBECUED PORK FILLED HIS NOSTRILS. UP on the burning porch a body lay sprawled, the source of the unholy perfume. Flames twisted from the blackened, square holes where once were windows. Jesse's horse was skittish as it passed between the blazing houses. The heat of the flames warmed his cheek. The houses at the end of the lane were burning, too. This was Hell of their own creation. Jesse's horse dipped its head, annoyed at the bridle, frightened by the flames. He kept the rein short, twisted in his buckskin gauntlets. In front of one of the houses, a young woman held a hysterical girlchild to her bosom. Her husband, a man in a brown suit, leaned his head against the garden's cherry tree and wept. Let them weep. Let them remember Union Order Number Eleven, written in their name, that had driven Confederate families from their homes and farms that were then put to the torch in more than three counties. The house on the other side of the street was burning, too. His cousin Wood and Bill's brother, Jim, sat on the lawn in front of it and guzzled at whiskey bottles. For backrests, they leaned on carpet bags that were stuffed to bursting. Their cavalry tunics were open, hats tilted back from their lean and bearded faces. Jim Anderson waved to Jesse, staggered to his feet from their parody of a picnic, and grabbed Wood by the wrist.

–Come on, Wood, he said.

They came out through the garden gate and staggered arm in arm next to Jesse as he rode toward the railroad depot, where Bill Anderson sat his mount in the yard. A thick pall of black smoke curled into the clear blue sky. Great twists of orange flame roared from the windows of the railroad office. Blue heat flared through a gap that had burned through the south wall of the building. Such destruction brought Bill Anderson a powerful joy.

Wood handed Jesse a bottle and he tilted it up. The warm liquid swilled into his mouth and he swallowed, savoring the burning sensation in his throat, the fumes that rose into his nostrils. Jesse was in a kind of bubble. Bill Anderson and Archie Clements and Frank and Wood and Jim Anderson were all on the inside of it with him; and the citizens and the buildings and the burning were on the outside. It was like a baleful dream, brightly colored. Everything brightly colored: his uniform, the flames, the sheen on the horses of the mounted guerrillas as they pranced by him and gathered in the railroad yard for some final consummation of the destruction they had begun. Bill Anderson rode over to the water tower and pulled up his horse beside a great pile of wooden ties. Jesse dismounted beside him.

–Archie, said Bill, get some men and drag some of these ties onto the tracks.

Clements slid from his bay and hung his arm over Jesse's shoulder. He pulled Jesse's head downward in a headlock. The whiskey reek that Clements breathed upon him was hot and rancid in his face. Jesse swung a drunken arm and smacked Clements across the chest. Clements staggered backward, lost his footing, and hit the ground. Jesse spat. The reek of whiskey and Clements's horsy odor were still upon him.

–Goddamn it, Archie, that boy gonna whip you, you don't watch out, Ol Shepherd said.

The others of the company whooped and guffawed. Clements gnawed at his lip. Grinned in embarrassment. He spat.

Jesse breathed in deep. His body was growing stronger and stranger to him every day. His once gangly lack of coordination was changing into a powerful and fluid vigor capable of dominating men older and more experienced than himself. He did not need to stand back and wait to be told what to do, but even if he did have a mind of his own, he had allied himself with the company.

–Goddamn it, Jesse, Clements said. Get on over here.

Bill Anderson had a pocket watch open on his palm.

–Train's due about a quarter hour, he said.

Jesse could refuse to help Clements and push his ascendancy further, but to refuse Clements would be to refuse Anderson. And the company. Above all else, Jesse was one of the company, men who depended upon each other for a greater strength in the face of the hostile and delirious world. Each man was the others' guarantee of survival. He was not ready to defy Anderson just to best Clements in a test of will.

The whiskey that flowed in his veins had made him conscious

of every robust muscle and nerve. Jesse unbuttoned his blue tunic. He draped it over a diagonal brace that was nailed to a leg of the water tower. From the inside pocket, he retrieved the large wad of Federal bills that he had looted from the drawers of the Main Street stores and stuffed the money into the pocket of his pants. With Bill Anderson, he had everything.

He nodded to Clements and followed him over to the pile of wooden ties. Clements looked up at him from a weaselly eye, the shoulders hunched, head twisted and bowed. Their exchange was not yet over. Clements would seek to cause him anguish in front of the others at the first possible opportunity.

–Help them, Wood, called Bill Anderson. Come on, boys, help out.

A cloud of smoke from a curly cheroot curled up around Bill's hat brim. Wood Hite and Jim Anderson took off their tunics. Jesse lifted his end of the first of the heavy ties. The wiry little scout was struggling. The ties stank of creosote, were sticky with it, and it stained their hands brown. They tossed the first tie across the tracks. Clements maliciously grinned at him for every second of the ten minutes it took to heave a small mountain of wood across the tracks.

One-eyed George found a gallon jar of kerosene in the small storage shed next to the water tower. He splashed the reeking liquid onto the creosote-impregnated wood. Jesse stepped away from the tracks. George tossed on a match. Blue, yellow, and orange flame twisted up from the pyre. Clements took a whiskey bottle from Ol Shepherd and downed a deep swig.

–Just in time, boys, stated Bill Anderson.

Jesse looked back down the track as the Wabash Railroad train rounded the long curve on the wooded hillside. It came over the trestle bridge. The train slowed. Jesse pulled on his tunic. Every man of the company had a pistol in his hand. Frank passed Jesse a bottle of whiskey. He slugged at it and handed it off to Ol Shepherd. The train was gigantic. The smokestack and the big, black and shiny circle of the boiler grew before his eyes. Puffy clouds of steam and smoke arose into the air. The metal brakes groaned and squealed. The black-spoked steel wheels clattered on the rails. Below the boiler, the heavy grill of the cowcatcher rocked its point over the tracks. The train approached the blazing pyre. A loud fusillade of pistol shots exploded around Jesse. Cordite smoke drifted acrid past his face. Bullets spanged and rattled against the boiler, the smokestack, the engine cab of the train. He yelled out, sharing the collective triumph as the train squealed to a halt. Anderson rode up to the engineer's cab. His Union tunic was open, his hat cocked at a crazy angle, a pistol in his right fist.

–Get down off of there, he called.

The fat engineer and the young, big-boned stoker held their hands up, came down the engine's steps, and stopped in front of Anderson.

–Move over toward the water tower, gentlemen.

Anderson gestured with his pistol.

Flames rose higher from the burning barricade. The train hissed softly, its valves breathing steam.

–Go to it, boys, ordered Anderson.

Jesse ran down past the tender and was first up the steps of the brown-and-gold-liveried carriage and through the door. The whole carriage was filled with Union soldiers. Jesse swung up his pistol but not one of the Federals so much as raised a musket or revolver. He judged their number to be around thirty.

–Surrender, you bastards, Jesse called.

To a man, the Federals all remained in their seats and raised their hands. It surprised him. He, a boy coming into manhood, and thirty men before him in stark terror.

–Got soldiers here, Bill, Frank yelled behind Jesse.

–Get them sons of bitches out here, Bill called.

–Stand up! Stand up! Jesse said.

One soldier was on crutches. A few others had the pallor and thinness that spoke of a long bout with dysentery. Jesse jabbed the muzzle of his pistol into the blue-coated backs in front of him. Not one of them had a gun. He ushered them along the carriage and out onto the rear platform, where Bill Anderson pushed them down the carriage steps. Jesse came out of the carriage and stood on the platform beside Bill. More of the company jostled around the carriage steps. The Union soldiers fell into a gauntlet of drunken guerrillas, who waved pistols in their faces. A whiskey bottle cracked on the head of the soldier on crutches. He went down. Clements kicked at him. The company swung gun butts and gun barrels at the prisoners' heads, but no one else fell down.

No one made a sound louder than a grunt. A young Union soldier balked on the step just below Jesse.

–I ain't going down there.

–Get down, boy! bellowed Anderson.

–I ain't going down.

Anderson raised his pistol. It roared. Blood, brains, and skull shards rained across the faces of the men below. The Union soldier's body tumbled down the steps to ground level.

–Dear Lord, Jesse said.

These men were not armed. But they were the enemy. The enemy. He had to remember that. Might be in less than a week these men would be armed and hunting down the company.

–Tell them boys to strip, ordered Anderson.

Clements was down beside the tracks.

–You heard him, Clements said.

Arms and legs twisted out of stiff jackets, boots, pants, loose underwear. Hands cupped between their hairy legs. Some men shaking now.

Jesse followed Bill down the steps of the carriage. He stepped over the dead Federal. All around him a melee of naked men and the drunken leers of the company. The nakedness of the Federals in front of the heavily armed guerrillas was a vision of vulnerability so acute that he thought of them as a herd of frightened shoats being driven into an abattoir.

–March them out of the station and into the open, boys, called Anderson.

Jesse prodded at a prisoner's back. All around him the men were in a frenzy of anticipation. His pistol waved at the stooped and bony back of the Federal in front of him. He could have counted the vertebrae. They were going to kill them, he knew. He was going to kill them. There was a sense of evil about it, but he was part of the company and the whole company was howling like a pack of dogs and moved as packs of dogs did around cowed prey and he was one of those slinking shapes herding the naked boys forward. The Union boys did not look like soldiers.

The train hissed rhythmically as he passed its blackness on his right. He passed the barricade of burning ties. Bill stopped the march on the track beside the culvert. Clements hurried up behind Jesse.

–There's hair here, boy, there's hair, giggled Clements.

He had a thin-bladed skinning knife in his hand.

The guerrillas formed a half circle around the prisoners. Pistols and bottles dangled from the guerrillas' hands. Jesse could sense the fear, could smell it now. And a more obvious smell arose as somebody up the line of white and naked men lost control of his bowels, his bladder.

Clements ran his thumb across the edge of his knife.

–You ready, boy?

It was the world that had turned evil all about him, and was he not but part of that world, that war, and would not that war, that force of nature, not turn upon him and destroy him if he did not play his part as he was called to do, or worse, to play it halfheartedly? If the company let these naked men go free, they would once more don a uniform and take up arms and come down upon the company mercilessly. Anderson would not allow it, so the company could not allow it, and so he, Jesse, a part of that company, could not allow it. And he had to prove himself as part of that company, and whatever Clements did, Clements was not going to best Jesse in front of the company. Jesse pressed his lips together. He was fully aware of what he was doing now.

–I'm ready, he said.

But the pistol was heavy in his hand. It would be an effort to lift it.

Bill lit another cheroot.

–You soldier boys know that no Union man never give Bill Anderson's boys no quarter, he said. You know that?

A dark-haired boy, no more than eighteen, legs hairy, curly black beard on his jaw-line, piped up.

–Our outfit never tangled with guerrillas, he said. We always treated Confederate prisoners fair and square.

–You contradicting me, boy?

He was contradicting Bill.

–No, sir. We never harmed no prisoner.

–Boy, I believe you're contradicting me and that's aggravating.

–We never harmed —

Bill's pistol came up and the boy's mouth dropped open. Anderson fired. A fountain of blood spurted and pulsed like a horn arisen from the boy's forehead before he slid into the culvert.

–Have mercy! a soldier said.

Clements raised his pistol and shot him. Then Wood fired. And Jim Anderson fired. And all along the line the guerrillas fired as the soldiers cried out.

–Lord have mercy!

And Jesse fired.

–Dear God.

–Save us, Lord.

This was evil as the world was evil, and the company could not leave man alive to perform more evil, to kill another Confederate soldier or guerrilla or drive away others of their mothers or their sisters.

Damn them to hell, Jesse thought.

He fired again. The white bodies twisted in the ditch. Jesse pointed his Colt. He fired into the arms and legs and torsos and heads that lifted and flopped in the confines of the culvert. His bullets made red furrows in the white flesh. The stink of singed hair and cordite and greasy powder smoke drifted past Jesse. To his right, Wood Hite swung a musket by its barrel up high in the air and whacked it down against a frightened face that rose from the ditch.

This was company work. War's work of attrition.

Clements jumped down into the ditch, his thin skinning knife held out from his body. The corpse of the crippled soldier, crutches gone now, lay closest to him. Clements knelt beside the body. He carved at the skin of the head and expertly lifted the soldier's bloody hair. Clements's hands were red. Was this evil? Clements's weasel-like face squinted up at him. Challenging him. Was the weasel evil when its teeth tore open the neck of a squawking chicken in order to drink its blood? Was that not nature?

Jesse jumped down into the ditch beside Clements. Bill Anderson was right above Jesse, looking down upon him and the dark-haired soldier that Bill had shot dead. Jesse gripped a hank of the bloody matted hair and pulled the head up. The eyes were glassy. Strange how they saw nothing. Fresh blood still dripped from the nose. The mouth was slack, the teeth protruding. Jesse slid his Bowie knife from its sheath. He dug the sharp point into the skin of the forehead. It tore back some three inches toward the crown of the head.

–Damn, Jesse said.

Red bone beneath. He slid the knife point down across the forehead to get the scalping started again, but all he did was to dig a line through the skin at the hairline that was separate from the tear on the skull. He brought the knife behind his left hand, clutching the hair, and laid the point to the end of the tear on the skull and cut a circle back toward the forehead. The head dropped forward into his lap and he clutched a hank of hair with a piece of greasy skin at the bottom about the size of a silver dollar.

–You got a long way to go, boy, Clements said.

Bill Anderson had his head cocked and a wry smile twisted his beard. He shook his head and strutted back toward the train. Clements followed him. Jesse tossed the matted hair among the bodies in the culvert. He wiped his bloody hands on his pants.

The whiskey was wearing off. His mouth was dry. His head ached.

Harness creaked as he gripped the pommel of his saddle just as three scabbed and mange-ridden dogs crept from behind the pile of burning railroad ties. They slunk toward the silent culvert. Their noses lifted. Sniffed. There was a blankness, a shadow upon the face of every man in the company. The slaughter in the ditch was beyond battle. It was a greater terror visited upon the land to drive the enemy from Missouri so that the state would be left only for Southerners. It was what the Unions had done to Jesse's family. Had his mama and her babies not been forced to flee to Nebraska? There would be more slaughter to come before this war was over. Was that evil? Or just war? He kicked his horse into a gallop toward the fiery canyon of the burning town whose flames raged and waved and clutched and coiled all around him.

XXI

HE STARED DOWN AT THE CHESTNUT'S MANE, INTO THE ROUGH weave of the hair, as if he might unravel some secret there. He had, he thought, done little as yet that he could crow about as they rode along the tracks and roads to some new action, or when they rested at bivouac. While others could brag of myriad acts of outrageous violence wreaked upon their enemies, he could only envy Clements and Ol Shepherd and George Shepherd and his brother, Frank, men with reputations earned in countless battles and skirmishes. The actions that they bragged about contributed to the greater story of the company, wove into one fabric the brutal and barbarous world on which they relied for their survival, but now he had another chance to prove himself, to test himself against his comrades' feats in arms, for across the low valley, blue-coated figures scurried over the opposite hilltop.

–What the hell they doing, Jesse? Bill Anderson said.

Jesse patted the chestnut's neck and glanced up.

Anderson had his saddle pommel gripped in one hand and a canteen in the other. His eyes were bloodshot, with deep, dark diagonals beneath them. Wrinkles creased his face from the corners of his eyes to his curly black beard. He lifted the canteen and sipped small sips from it.

–Yonder, Anderson said.

Jesse nodded. He put the chestnut stallion forward, and it tapped its hoof and tossed its head. He pulled the horse to a stop. He took the brass spyglass from his saddlebag, opened it to its full length, and put it to his eye. A troop of Union mounted infantry had drawn to a halt. Below them on the hillside, a lone vedette rode uphill waving his arms in warning. Jesse could not believe the condition of the men's mounts.

–They ain't got nothing but tired old plug horses and a few starving mules to ride. And I don't know what they doing for a formation. They all dismounting.

–Lord have mercy on them, Frank said. They going to fight us on foot.

Anderson slid his canteen into a round leather satchel on his saddle, then drew his pistols.

–Let's get 'em, he called.

Jesse drew both of his own guns and kept his reins in his left hand. All along the line, the men straightened in their saddles, gripped their dragoon pistols in their fists. On the opposite hilltop, men hurried like ants into their lines. There was a thrill in watching the movement. A dark and dangerous pattern, shifting and changing upon the green grass, each element in that display armed and potentially lethal to him, a pattern of living and breathing men that they would fall upon and seek to scatter out of its temporary cohesion into chaos and then extinction.

–Walk, called Anderson.

Jesse kept the chestnut on a tight rein as they started down the hill. His body rocked in the saddle. The familiarity of the pistols in his fists and the surge of awareness of every muscle and nerve beneath his skin was heightened by the possible proximity of injury or sudden death.

–Trot, called Anderson.

Jesse loosened his rein and squeezed the stallion with both knees. The horse kept in prancing step with the advancing guerrilla line. The chestnut, too, sensed danger and had no reasoning mind with which to avoid it. He could feel the horse responding to him more willingly now. There was a trust in the animal that he had not sensed heretofore. It had abandoned its well-being to Jesse's care.

–Canter, called Anderson.

Jesse touched the stallion with his heels and rolled with the horse's fluid and half-panicked motion. All was noise now. A rolling continuous thunder of hoofbeats. He was part of a wave made up of horsemen that flowed down through the bottom of the dip in the prairie and rushed upward over the rising slope toward the line of Union riflemen.

–Charge! screamed Anderson.

Jesse kicked the stallion's flanks and it surged forward. The air split with screeches and howls over the rhythm of hoof rumble. A low growl and crackle erupted from the hilltop and the air buzzed and hummed and down the line a guerrilla dropped. Above the

Union line, a long white cloud lifted into the air. Jesse let the stallion have its head, and the horse raced out in front of the charging horsemen. In front of him, blue-coated soldiers tore at cartridges and ran long ramrods into the muzzles of their guns. And he was upon them. His pistols blazed and bucked. And he was through the line. He wheeled the stallion, the horse a sentient extension of his knees. It tossed its head and he pulled it to a halt. The mounted Union officer spun his mount to face him. Raised his saber. Charged. Jesse brought both pistols up together. Everything else but the glitter of saber and roll of dust and the growing vision of man and horse faded away from the periphery of his vision. Both foresights aligned with the widest part of the hunched and charging body. He fired. The head snapped back, the mouth gaped open, silent, arms flung back, the saber toppled and dangled, jerking on its braid cord tied to the wrist, reins free. The body dropped heavily over the bay's haunches, and the horse bolted by, its rider spreadeagled and already dead. And around Jesse all was chaos and cracks of ordnance, the orange flame of muzzle flash, white puffs of powder smoke erupting into the air and drifting languidly. The plugs and drays of the Union soldiers reared and plunged, broke loose from the hands that sought to keep them reined together in fours. The enemy soldiers were nothing but old men and boys. Some raggedy company raised in a hurry and sent off in rash pursuit of Bill Anderson's veterans. Those ill-prepared soldiers now scattered among the mounted guerrillas like so many startled prairie turkeys, elbows raised in panic, scrawny necks extended, legs pounding in futile circles. Jesse let out a ululating yell. Past his shoulders, the unseeing head of an enemy soldier waved upon the point of a bayonet.

No quarter, he thought. No quarter.

Jesse holstered his pistols. The men of the company were stripping the bodies for the uniforms, mad scavengers in this cemetery of undug graves. Wood Hite cut the braid at the officer's wrist and brandished the saber. He hacked at the officer's shoulder, the blade rising and falling as he sought to separate the arm. Clements knelt about his own bloody business. Bill Anderson guided his black horse through a slaughter that made the ground writhe.

–God damn 'em all, Bill called.

–God damn 'em, Bill, Jesse said.

–I seen you, boy. You got their goddamn officer. You're a fighter, boy. A born fighter.

Jesse nodded and grinned. Some eddy in the tides of war had swirled him in front of that officer. And he had killed him. And he knew that the killing of the officer would now be legend in the story of the company. Like that. By chance. The absurd sight of human butchery that was going on all around him touched in him a black hilarity, a kind of madness, demonic laughter in his head that seemed not part of him but some form of inner invasion. The company had waded yet deeper into sanguinary excess. If they kept up this carnage, they would draw every militia man and regular soldier in the state of Missouri away from the Confederate army of Sterling Price and into their own bloody arms. That was Bill's plan. Or, it suddenly dawned on him, Bill was committing suicide. After what they had done at Centralia and to this geriatric company of Union militia that had been foolish enough to pursue them, Federal troops would hunt them down, war or no war.

He looked up into Bill's eyes, the crinkly lines around them, the evil mirth there. Of course. Bill had no faith in Sterling Price. The Yankees had Lee pinned down outside the Confederate capital. The greater war was lost, and Bill could not live without the war, for he was so deep into furious glut that all else seemed senseless and unreal, a world of empty shadows. And he, Jesse, would ride into whatever inferno the company called down upon themselves. But he had no intention of dying under a Yankee bullet or bayonet, whatever end Bill might pursue. In that, he would surpass Bill Anderson.

–Best be moving, Bill said. Cox's regiment will be coming for us next.

Cox's men would not give themselves up to the slaughter as easily as this rustic company had done. Jesse turned the chestnut stallion to follow Bill's dark mount.

XXII

JESSE DREW THE SHOTGUN FROM HIS SADDLE SCABBARD AND leaned the butt upon his thigh. Anderson pulled back his duster and rested his hand on the pommel of his saddle.

–Hello the house, called Anderson.

Jesse was certain he smelled bacon on the wood smoke in the air, but his desperate mind could have been conjuring it. His stomach creaked and gurgled. No food for two days. Hunger and fatigue had evaporated his exaltation.

Behind the windows a lamp shone. The house was sided with a dark-stained clapboard. It had a lean-to woodshed on the east side of it and a low extension on the west. The extension had been framed and sheathed but had no siding, and a burlap sack flapped in the window opening. The farm family was sure to be awake. If they still had any cows to be brought in and milked.

–Is there anyone home? Bill called.

The front door opened a crack. Half an unshaven face became visible, gray hair tousled, the eye leery.

–Who the hell is it?

–Bill Anderson.

The man behind the door said nothing. Jesse glanced at Frank. Frank shrugged. Bill wasn't concerned to hide who they were any more. The commander pulled a cheroot from the left-hand breast pocket of his tunic and snapped a match into flame to light it. The farmer found his voice.

–What you want here?

–A little something to eat and we'll be on our way.

–I'll ask the missus if she can fix something for you.

–There's more than twenty of us, said Bill.

–She's capable.

The door closed and every one of them heard the bar fall behind it.

–Hello the house, called Bill.

But the door didn't open again. Bill pointed to Ol Shepherd and Archie Clements and motioned them to ride to the back of the house. The two guerrillas — Ol bearded and portly, Clements diminutive and dapper — guided their mounts out of the column and disappeared around the corner of the woodshed.

–Open the goddamn door, called Bill.

From behind the house, the shadow of a rider took off northwest across the flat cornfield.

Clements and Shepherd kicked their horses into pursuit.

Jesse spat. Clements and Shepherd didn't have a hope. They had all been in the saddle day and night for a week, and the horses were fit for nothing other than the knacker's yard.

A puff of smoke rose from Clements's gun, then a crack echoed across the flat field. The fleeing rider was not hit. Clements and Shepherd pulled up and fired off four more rounds to no avail. The house was still quiet. Bill pointed at the window. Jesse jumped down off his horse and ran up onto the porch. He swung the gun butt. Glass shattered and wood splintered. A woman screamed inside. Jesse stepped away from the window with the shotgun clutched to his chest. No shot from inside.

–Don't shoot, don't shoot! called the farmer.

The front door came open again, but this time the farmer stumbled out onto the porch. He was unarmed. His shirt was open and his boots were unlaced. Bill had his pistol leveled now. Jesse covered the farmer from the left.

–Who rode out there? Bill demanded.

–My son, he answered. He was scared you'd kill him.

–Why'd I want to kill your son? asked Bill.

Clements and Shepherd reappeared in the farmyard. Their mounts breathed hard.

–Son of a bitch was a militia man, said Clements.

Anderson nodded and turned back to the farmer.

–What outfit is he with?

The farmer scratched at the back of his tousled hair. His left hand rose and flopped back at his side. His face was all screwed up as if he couldn't make up his mind what to say or how to say it if he was going to say anything and he probably would rather not have said anything anyway. But he did.

–Well, he's with Major Cox, he said.

Cox, Jesse thought. It was Cox who had been hunting them for weeks.

Bill glanced across at Jesse and nodded. A curt nod, the beard dipped to the chest. He wanted the farmer dead. When Jesse didn't fire, Bill turned his black eyes on him. Quizzical. Jesse had the shotgun low across his body. He pressed it against his hip. The farmer's son was on his way to warn Cox. The farmer dropped his hands. He still faced Bill, sideways to Jesse. Jesse gripped the shotgun tight and squeezed the front trigger. The flat bang made his ears ring, and the butt of the shotgun jerked against his hip. The scattershot nearly ripped the farmer in two. It must have broken his spine for the body folded back on itself as it fell. A long and keening whine came out through the door of the house and the woman rushed out.

–You filth! she screamed at Jesse, you murdering filth!

The woman was fat and dumpy and Jesse judged her to be in her late fifties. She dropped to her knees beside the bloody body.

A shotgun makes a goddamn mess, Jesse thought.

–Mount up, Jesse, Bill said.

He flicked his smoldering cheroot in a tumbling arc away from him.

The woman had the farmer gripped by the shirt and seemed to be trying to pull the body back into some semblance of normal human posture but the torso just flopped around and bumped on the porch boards.

Jesse strode past her off the porch. She didn't even look up at him, but he couldn't avoid looking at her. Her apron was already bloody. Jesse lowered the hammer carefully on the unfired load. He would need to clean the other barrel. The cordite and powder stank. His ears still rang. What he had done was behind him. He slid the shotgun into his saddle scabbard and mounted the stallion. The sky was lighter to the east. The woman howled at the hidden dawn.

–Move out, said Anderson.

Goddamn, Jesse thought, we ain't going to eat.

Stretched out for miles to the north and south of them, stubbled cornfields lay yellow and desolate under the low, scalloped gray sky. A murder of crows flapped up from the north field, cawed to them as if in raucous mockery, and bobbed away in a black line toward the wooded ridge west of them. Jesse sat upright in his saddle through force of will, though his muscles sought to curl him into a small and inconspicuous ball on that pale and open farmland. No sign of Major Cox and his militia yet. Hunger gnawed at Jesse's belly. His head was light. All the men must feel like he did. Chilled and damp and hungry. Exposed on those open fields. The shifting of his companions in the column was as the movement of his own limbs and the stallion between his legs. The stallion smelled musty beneath him, the ribs visible through the skin. It snorted. Jesse feared that it had taken a chill, for it wheezed and stumbled. Ahead of Jesse, even Anderson's black brute seemed to labor to maintain its usual strut. Archie Clements, up beside Anderson, tilted and bobbed on the saddle of his bay as he fought off sleep. Frank bent over his pommel, his coat batwinged about him, his shadowed eyes darting glances at the empty fields as if he saw movement where there was none. The road rose before them over the ridge where the crows had gone. The ridge was cross-hatched with the branches of leafless elm, here and there patched yellow with autumn oak that fluttered and rustled under the somber clouds. The company would be invisible in those woods. Safe.

–Jesse!

Bill Anderson called on him.

–Yessir, Jesse said.

–See what's on the other side of that ridge.

–Yessir.

–And don't get yourself kilt.

–Yessir, Jesse said.

Jesse pushed the stallion past Archie Clements and Anderson and eased it into a canter toward the wooded ridge. Brackish pools stood between the muddied rows of cornstalks in the fields and reflected gray clouds. The stallion's hooves splashed in the puddles on the road. At least it wasn't raining now. Jesse looked back over his shoulder. The line of men and horses resembled a tired and ragged funerary procession as they moved along the road through the barren cornfields. Jesse turned forward again to face the ridge and the woods. The rocking motion in the saddle eased the ache in his limbs. He loosed the covers of his saddle holsters and drew one pistol as he reached the woods. The stallion's hooves stirred the leaf carpet in the lane. He slowed the horse to a walk. At each side of the road was a drainage ditch, and behind it a low stone wall — broken and moss covered. Not a bird stirred among the trees. The wind was all that rattled the branches. Jesse approached the brow of the hill. He heard hoofbeats beyond it. One rider. Jesse kicked the stallion from a walk to an instant full gallop and pointed his pistol between the horse's ears. He charged over the hill. Fifty yards away, a blue-coated militia man reined in, spun his mount, and raced back down through the woods and away from Jesse. Jesse fired. Missed. His shot would warn Bill and the company. The stallion flew down the leafy road. Six Federal foot soldiers appeared at the edge of the woods. They raised their muskets.

Jesse reined in, fired two shots, and pulled the horse around to face it back up the incline. The stallion panted and its gait was labored on the rise. Shots crackled behind him. He heard a hum and a spack as ball hit bark around him, and then he was over the crown of the hill and safe.

Bill Anderson and Archie Clements reached the tree line and started up the road toward him. Frank was close behind, with Ol Shepherd behind him, and then the rest of the men. They all had their pistols drawn, a column of shaggy barbarians, bearded, ragged, muddy. Jesse grinned. They surged up the road through the woods.

–How many you see, boy? called Bill.

–One rider and six afoot, he yelled back.

Bill Anderson pulled up. His black mount twitched and swiveled its ears; its breath steamed in the damp woods air.

–Let's hit 'em before they organize, he said.

He pushed his horse past Jesse. Archie Clements rode at his flank. Jesse pulled the stallion in beside Frank's sorrel.

–Maybe them bluecoats got something to eat, said Frank. I ain't ate in a coon's age.

–Didn't see no wagon, said Jesse.

They walked their horses over the brow of the hill. Down where the road widened and the woods gave way to field again, some seventeen men ran to form up across the road. Eight bluecoats knelt and leveled their muskets, and eight took position behind them. A metallic clatter as they fixed their bayonets. No sign of any horses. An officer in a field kepi stood to one side of the ranks. His saber waved and glinted. In the other hand he held a pistol down by his side. The road was narrow. The damp air stilled. No wind rattled or swung the bare branches of the trees around them. The stallion snorted. Leaves crackled as the horse stamped and pawed the ground. Pistols clicked.

–Let's get 'em, Bill said.

Clements let out a whoop beside Jesse. Jesse yelled high and long. They charged. The whirl of tree and branch around him. The rattle of hoof and high yells in his ears. Damp bark and leaf mold in his nostrils. His pistol heavy in his fist. The bluecoat line still and silent. The officer brought up his saber. Here it come. Steel glinted. The blade fell.

The air exploded at front, right, and left. A thousand bees hummed. He was not hit. Nor the stallion. A cloud of bitter white smoke drifted from behind the stone walls to either side and into the road's confusion of screams and neighs. Another crackle of musketry and the zing of ball. Ol Shepherd fought to keep his horse standing. Wounded horses, riderless, swirled around Jesse in the narrow lane, plunged and kicked. The stallion fought free of the melee. Jesse twisted in his saddle and fired uselessly into the woods. Frank and Bill were ahead and had their horses tight-reined and under control. Clements was down. He was pinned under his horse and trying to drag himself free. Jesse cocked his pistols again.

Bill and Frank charged down the hill. Jesse raced after them. He fired and cocked and fired again. The militiamen scattered for the roadside as the horsemen hit the line. Jesse was through their ranks. The stallion raced down the road after Bill Anderson and Frank. Bill Anderson raised his arms high in the air, pistols in his fists, his head flung back and bobbing loosely on his shoulders. He tipped from his saddle and landed in a heap on the hard road. Frank did not stop, and Jesse's stallion raced by Bill's body and after his brother. Jesse pulled the horse to a halt and spun it in the road.

More bluecoats charged into the road from the north field. Their bayonets made a bristling line of steel between Jesse and Anderson. Jesse leveled his pistols and fired into the crowd of militia. Two soldiers fell. Jesse cocked his pistols again. Frank pulled his sorrel up beside Jesse. Frank's hands and face were black with powder streaks.

Three militia men broke away from the frenzy thirty yards away and charged up the road toward them. Jesse and Frank raised their pistols as if mechanically linked, and they fired together. The middle soldier dropped to his knees. He clutched his chest. His two companions stopped running.

–Let's get Bill, yelled Jesse.

The voice from his throat was shrill like a child's.

Frank holstered a pistol and grabbed Jesse's bridle.

–Hold up, Jess.

–Bill's down there.

–Ride out, said Frank. There's too many of 'em.

–Bill's down there.

–Bill's dead.

–I didn't know, Frank, I swear to God.

–No way to know.

Frank didn't blame him. How could Bill be dead? Bill hadn't seen the militia, either.

Nobody shot at Jesse and Frank. They were away from the knot of the battle and their way was clear to escape. Ol Shepherd broke free of the crowd of bluecoats in the road and his horse leaped the fence into the south field. He fled away from the battle. Archie Clements swung onto a loose mount and broke away after Shepherd. Muskets crackled ahead of them. The air buzzed with flying ball.

–Let's go, Jesse said.

Frank spun the sorrel and put spur to him, and Jesse wheeled the stallion and followed his brother over the flat prairie and into the darkening west.

Frank wanted to find Quantrill down in Kentucky, but Jesse needed to find out about Anderson. Where they had taken the body. Where he was buried. Jesse tied up the stallion in a stand of wide-trunked, leafless ash trees a quarter mile north of the buildings of Richmond, Missouri. Frank secured the halter of the sorrel close by the chestnut, and Jesse led the way through the stones and boards of the cemetery toward the distant lights and sounds of revelry. He saw no sign of a freshly dug grave. He did not think that the Federals would leave Bill's corpse upon the field of battle. He was too big a prize.

The back of the long, high barn of the livery stable rose before them as they came from among the gravestones. They skirted the building and came out onto Fifth Street, where three saloons were ablaze with light and alive with the sound of songs and shouts and the sawing of a fiddle. The tent barracks of the militia glimmered at the end of the street, but he saw no sign of picket, patrol, or sentry, and the street was deserted but for one lone walker whose cane tapped against the boardwalk as he approached Jesse and Frank with the gait of one infirm or ancient of years.

–Howdy, Jesse said.

The head of the walker lifted and shifted to its right as if afraid and half blind. The long, bent body swayed over the cane. He was a tall old man, his gaunt, whiskered face hidden by the wide brim of his hat.

–Who's there?

The voice was broken.

–Just come into town, Frank said.

–We're with the Sixteenth Kansas, Jesse said.

–Well, Cox got Bill Anderson, the old man said.

–So we heard, Jesse said.

–They took pictures of the body outside the photographer's store, the old man said. Propped him up on the boardwalk in a chair. They had his guns tucked into his cartridge belts.

–They bury him yet? Frank said.

–I don't reckon, the old man said.

–Where they got the body? Jesse said. I'd like to see what he looked like.

The old man shook his head.

–I don't know where the body is, he said. But you go down to the militia camp and you can see his head. They nailed it by the hair to a telegraph pole. It's got his peter hanging out the mouth for a tongue.

XXIII

WHITE CANVAS RIPPLED IN THE SPRING WIND LIKE A FALSE WHITE sea upon a vast vaudeville stage. Jesse had never seen so many people gathered together in one place. Out in the fields, soldiers in gray twill trousers and sweat-stained red undershirts slouched around stands of muskets. Other men squatted and smoked near the campfires close to the road, where fat, slatternly Mexican women flapped dough between their palms and slapped flat tortillas onto iron skillets that nestled in the embers. Big-featured women in colored serapes held out to him some lumpy foodstuff wrapped in dry corn husks. Jesse kept the chestnut stallion on a tight rein and close to Ol Shepherd's bay. Wood Hite and George Shepherd rode up in front of them. Jesse's cousins Bud and Donny Pence came behind. They had picked up Bud and Donny from George Todd's band after Todd was killed outside Independence. The Pences were from Kentucky, where Frank was now if he had succeeded in locating Quantrill. But that was far away from Texas. It had taken them five months to get to Bonham, where the Confederate army wintered. They had ridden down through the Burned Lands, those Missouri border counties that the Unions had put to the torch, and from thence through the Indian Nations, keeping to territory known to be under the control of the Confederate Indian general Stand Watie, though they avoided contact with any man, keeping to back trails.

Jesse's stallion lifted his hooves, light of gait, as if the horse, too, sensed that the war was distant from them here. And the South was defeated. Rumor had it that Lee himself had surrendered to Grant. Only a few men continued to fight. Guerrillas mostly, like themselves. Jesse would go north again to Missouri, though they had heard that the Federals would not give parole to bushwhackers but only to the regulars. With Bill's death, the fight had gone out of Jesse, but he was determined that if he could get no parole, he would raise a company that would terrorize every Yankee in Missouri and states adjacent, war or no war.

Jesse unbuttoned his duster, took off his hat, and wiped the sweat from his forehead. He pushed the stallion forward to get closer to Wood and George. George's one-eyed head bobbed, the lower lip jutting out wet and stained in front of a soft brown wad of chaw. The bottom of his face was streaked with tobacco juice. His dark hair was plastered down against his stubbled cheeks. He kept his duster buttoned up to his chin. He waved a hand at the encampment beyond the fence.

–All these goddamn troops either got to muster out or follow Jo Shelby into Mexico to fight down there. Ain't no more Dixie to fight for.

–I ain't fightin' for no goddamn Messican, said Wood Hite.

George grinned a brown-stained grin.

–Only Messican I aim to fight for is a goddamn Messican whore, he said.

The men all laughed. Jesse glanced at Ol Shepherd. Ol turned up the brim of his hat. His face not covered by his huge beard was a blazing red from sunburn. He looked dour and serious. His chin was tucked in against his neck so that the brown beard had a sharp bend in it and stood out at an angle from his gray tunic.

–I heard they got houses full of whores outside Bonham, Ol said.

–Ain't that adultery? Forbidden in the Bible, said Jesse.

He said it to needle them, but he was halfway serious. At every Texas town in which they had camped for the last five months, the others had gone into town to lie with women, while Jesse had gone just once; and then he had hesitated before the woman's door and turned back to camp without consummating his lust. He had told none of them. He thought that he should save himself for a good Christian girl when at last they returned to Missouri. But as they approached Bonham, lust crept through his every nerve, and his curiosity ate at his God-given reason.

–I ain't wed, George said, so how can it be adultery if I just git my pecker wet?

–Well, then, it's fornication, said Jesse.

Was he trying to convince himself or George?

–Ain't he the preacher's son, said Ol.

George shook his head.

–Boy's right, he said. Them whores give you somethin' to make your pecker itch and shrivel till it fall off. It's the Lord's vengeance.

–I been with plentya whores, Wood said. And mine ain't fell off yet.

–Nobody'd notice if it did fall off, said George, 'cause there ain't much there to start with.

Jesse laughed with the others.

Wood turned in the saddle.

–Listen, little George, let's measure your'n aginst mine.

Then Wood was at the buttons of his duster, and he was at his trouser buttons behind the pommel of his saddle.

–Keep that thing under cover, there could be ladies around, said Ol.

–Not among these sons of bitches, George said . . .

He waved toward the encampment.

–. . . not if they got any sense, anyway.

–Women like a man in uniform, Ol said.

–And they like the smell of blood on a man, said Wood.

Wood bared his brown-stained teeth in a twisted smile. His eyes narrowed. An unholy hunger glittered in them. And Jesse feared for any woman in Wood's hands.

–Maybe young Jesse here could get hisself a little Texas rose to lift her skirts for him, said George.

Jesse pulled at the stallion's rein and the horse snorted in complaint.

–That ain't the kind of woman I want, said Jesse.

–It ain't? asked George.

–I aim to settle down with a good Christian woman.

–I ain't agin that, said George. I don't plan on marryin' no whore . . .

He spat a great gob of brown juice into the road.

–. . . just having a poke is all.

–Cain't shirk your duty, Jesse, Ol Shepherd said. We'll find you a nice young 'un.

–Where we going to bivouac? said Wood.

–In the whorehouse, said George.

Jesse laughed and spurred his horse onward toward the first buildings of Bonham. Ol Shepherd stayed close by his side. They rode past a crew of Negroes in chains. The picks of the Negroes rose and fell in a ragged wave above a roadside drainage ditch. Around the barns and feed stores on the outskirts of the town, small brown-skinned men hauled sacks and barrels and crates through the yards and loaded wagons with them. Ol Shepherd and Bud and Donny Pence were silent behind Jesse as they rode into the busy Main Street. Clothing stores and goods stores and saloons and hotels lined the narrow street. The boardwalks were packed with soldiers in gray uniforms. Women in bonnets and full-skirted dresses clutched string sacks laden with paper packets and drew along behind them curious and unruly children. Jesse was dirty, but he took comfort in the fact that George and Wood looked worse than he did, by his own judgment at least. The dust of the journey clung to their hats and dusters and shirts and boots. The men were unshaven, their hair long and greasy and unkempt. And something more than trail dirt clung to them.

–I need a drink, said George Shepherd.

Ol Shepherd and Wood let out a yell. Jesse flinched. The Lord would test him among these men. All thought of bivouac had rapidly evaporated. George guided his horse to the nearest hotel on the street. Bud and Donny Pence continued riding up the street.

–What about those two? Jesse asked.

Ol Shepherd shook his head.

–They can take care of their own selves, I reckon.

Jesse dismounted in front of a red brick building that was as a big as a palace in a storybook. Shepherd pulled his bay across to the hitching post and dismounted next to him. It was strange being in a town after so long on the prairie and in the killing. The people of the town — even the soldiers — were of a world entirely other than theirs. These townspeople were separated by a lack of knowledge of good and evil that Jesse shared with the Shepherd brothers. And with his murderous cousin Wood.

–Come on, Jess, George said.

Jesse followed George up the steps from the street and through the arched glass doors of the building. They were in a huge room that was paneled in light-stained oak. Four long, heavily gilded mirrors hung on the west and east walls of the room. They reflected the tables and chairs and the entire crowded interior that seemed to stretch to infinity within the glass. A crystal chandelier glinted and sparkled where it hung from a cast plaster ceiling. Below it, a pall of cigar smoke hung in blue and aromatic layers upon the air. A walnut bar ran along the length of the far wall and curved around to the right into another room. Jesse had never seen so many men in fine suits, brocade vests, and silk cravats, or in the dress uniforms of Confederate officers. There were no women. The smokers and drinkers sat at polished tables. Their fingers curled over fat cigars. They cradled crystal balloons of liquor. The swell officers were ogling him and Ol and George and Wood.

Jesse slapped his hat against his thighs as if to beat off the trail dust. He scraped the scuffed and busted toe of his boot across the pile of a red plush carpet. The pair of pistols that was tucked into his belt held open the flaps of his duster. The Shepherds and cousin Wood were armed to the teeth, too. The bartender shifted from foot to foot as he twisted a napkin in his fingers. His waxed mustache twitched. He lifted his chin as if he was being strangled by the starched collar of his immaculate white shirt.

–You gentlemen will be wanting a drink?

Of course they were wanting a drink.

The bartender waved a limp hand toward the glass-fronted cabinets behind him. The display of finely labeled bottles almost reached the ceiling. The man would need a ladder for the topmost bottles. One-eyed George nodded in the direction of a corpulent businessman who sat at the table to his right. The man had his bulbous red nose in a balloon-shaped glass.

–I'll take a bottle of whatever that gentleman there is drinking.

–That's a fifty-dollar bottle of brandy, sir.

Jesse was convinced the man had made a mistake. How could a bottle of liquor cost that much, even if money wasn't worth a damn anymore?

George pulled out a wad of bills.

–Confederate or Federal? he asked.

The bartender cleared his throat.

–I'll take ten dollars Federal, the barman said.

–That ain't patriotic, said George.

–You may pay how you wish, sir.

Taylor slapped a Federal ten-dollar bill on the varnished bar and a silver dollar on top of it. The bartender set up the balloon-shaped glasses. Cognac, it said on the bottle.

–To Jeff Davis, said George.

Jesse took a swallow of the liquor. It was like drinking some kind of perfume: a little sweet and smooth, but with a bite to it. The liquor was better than he expected, nothing like the rotten whiskey they had drunk in the bush. Jesse downed his drink in three gulps. He could feel the eyes of the businessmen upon the company, even though the swells had struck up conversations once more. More liquor appeared in Jesse's glass and he drank it off. They emptied the first bottle, and his cousin Wood called for another. Jesse finished the liquor in his glass as the waiter arrived with more. The room had taken on a golden glow, and the voices and the tinkle of glass and the scrape of the chairs all commenced to have a muffled and somewhat hollow sound. Taylor was laughing about being in Texas and safe instead of bushwhacking through Sni country and Jesse felt as though he were afloat on an unseen sea.

–To Bill Anderson, George said, the best goddamn commander that ever shot a pistol.

–And Anderson's boys, Ol said. The best set of fighters that ever rallied to the Southern Cause.

The glasses clinked again.

–It's the officers ain't worth a damn, Wood said. By God, with more men like Bill, we would have whipped the Federals and burned Washington long ago.

–I couldn't stand being in the regular army, Jesse said. Those good old Southern boys were just herded about like sheep being took to slaughter.

A drunken Confederate officer appeared like a long gray reed next to their table. He was hatless and blond. The line of his jawbone looked razor-burned, his flushed face smooth.

–You are not a gentleman, sir, he said.

And the next thing Jesse knew was that George fell off his stool and Wood and Ol had pistols in their fists and the bartender had his hands out begging them not to shoot anyone and then they were on the street, each man with a bottle of that perfumed liquor, and it was still daylight, though it seemed to Jesse as if they had been in the hotel for hours. Bud and Donny Pence staggered toward them down the boardwalk.

–Boys, said Donny, I heard about a capital drinking house they say is down that alley not twenty yards away.

Jesse cheered with his happy company. They all followed the Pences to where a rank odor came from between the hard-goods store and a butcher's shop. Jesse had enough wit left to step around the feces and rotting matter in the shadowy alley. Donny Pence kicked at a mange-ridden dog that worried some form of unrecognizable carrion. It yelped and slunk away.

Jesse remembered the rotten curtain over the doorway to the darkened room and the pungent oily smell as if of turpentine and the roughness of the benches and the tables. He remembered laughter and insults and singing and then he remembered nothing. There was a black space from the moment when he tossed his empty bottle of liquor to the floor of the cantina and the moment when he found himself lying against the board fence at the end of the alley. The mange-ridden cur was sniffing at his boots. The stink of creosote made him retch the moment he fully awoke.

He twisted onto his side to vomit. His skull was an overfull receptacle of such pain that he thought he had been poleaxed. He was still wrapped in his duster, and his hat was pulled down over his head. He must have removed his two pistols from his belt, for they slid heavily down the inside of his duster to the muddy ground as he lifted himself upright. He patted the inside of his jacket. His wad of money was still there. Everything that he had left from Centralia. He stood up. His tongue was swollen and dry. His bladder was bursting. He unbuttoned himself and pissed a sour and copious stream that formed a foaming orange puddle in the mud of the rank alley. Jesse lurched between the buildings toward the street. At the end of the alley, he heaved. The liquid splashed sweet and sour between the busted toes of his boots. His hat fell off. He spat.

–That was bad luck, said Donny Pence.

Donny sat on the steps of the butcher shop. His head leaned against a pillar. In his gaunt and stubbled face, his lips were blistered and cracked as if no liquid had passed them in days. His eyes were pinholes in the darkness of their sockets. The early morning sun blinded Jesse as it slanted flat and low between the buildings. The streets were deserted of Bonham's citizens.

–Where's Ol? asked Jesse.

He squinted at Donny. A pain originated in Jesse's right eye and dug a sharp and steady line through his forehead and over the top of his head to the muscles at the back of his neck.

–What the hell you want him for? Donny said.

–He's my friend, said Jesse.

–*You* know where he is, Donny said.

Donny was still drunk and so was Jesse.

–No, I don't, Jesse said.

Donny looked puzzled, as if he didn't know whether to believe Jesse or not.

Oh Lord, Jesse thought, this drink has weakened me.

Donny pulled himself to his feet. He had no duster. His shirt-front was stained with some brownish foodstuff and the armpits of his butternut shirt were dark with sweat. His serge pants were torn at the knee. But for all his tattered appearance, he had not lost his pistols.

–I'll take you, Donny said.

The heels of Jesse's boots hit the too-solid boards; the concussion jarred his entire body and pain spiked through his skull. His head spun. He could vomit at any moment. His mouth and throat were parched. He knew where Donny was leading him, and he was doing nothing to resist. What would his mama say? He could never tell her. She should never know. Donny turned the corner off Main Street, and Jesse followed him into a narrow, muddy street of broken-down houses. At the end of the short street stood a three-story mansion in a shameful state of disrepair, and it was as if this great house had spawned the handicapped and misshapen rookery of shacks around it, with their tar-paper walls and their poorly fitted tin roofs. Donny approached the mother mansion. Four pillars held up the tilted verandah. The once-red paint on the building's clapboards was blistered or completely stripped away to the bleached gray wood, and the shutters on the lower-floor windows each hung from one rusted hinge. The panes of the upper-floor windows were cracked and dusty. Two of the four steps up to the porch had rotted out. On the porch, a Negro boy in pale brown rags was curled up like a dog on the entrance mat. Donny stirred him with his toe.

–Open the door, boy, he said.

The child raised his dusky head and blinked. His glazed eyes took a moment to clear before he looked directly at Jesse and ignored Donny. Jesse blushed.

–This door ain't never closed, he said.

–Open the goddamn door, Donny said.

The Negro rose, arms and legs little more than sticks, clothes hanging off his meager frame as if he had not eaten for months.

–I'm in sore need of water, Jesse said.

The child didn't seem to hear him.

–Open the goddamn door, Donny said.

The little Negro turned the brass doorknob and slipped inside the house. Donny had an ugly grin spread across the bottom of his stubbled face. He leered at Jesse.

–Ol's in here, Donny said.

He winked.

–You ain't never seen nothing like this, boy, he said.

Jesse followed him into an empty parlor. The red plush love seats and armchairs were empty. Empty and half-empty glasses stood on the tables in front of them. Broken cigar stubs sat in porcelain trays full of ash. The stale smell of them turned Jesse's stomach again. As his eyes became used to the twilight, he saw that every flat surface in the room had upon it an animal frozen by the taxidermist's art, a veritable menagerie: twisted weasels, grinning foxes, spread-winged owls, rattlesnakes that wound about each other. Behind the animals, paintings hung upon the walls, each one with the theme of copulation: a woman being ravished by a swan; another by a minotaur; a centaur; satyrs chasing maenads.

–Upstairs is this way, said the little Negro boy.

Jesse wanted to get out of there, but he could not lose face in front of Donny. If Jesse ran out now, Donny would have something on him that would make the men guffaw every time he mentioned it. Jesse felt so nauseous that he could hardly think straight, but he knew well enough that he wanted Donny to have no advantage over him. All men wanted what Jesse wanted, did they not?

–Where's them whores? Donny asked the Negro boy.

The boy looked at Donny as if at a stupid and hungry mule who stood not a yard from a full feed box. Donny pushed his hat forward to scratch at the back of his lolling head. If he felt sick like

Jesse felt sick, he was showing no sign of it, and how could he not feel sick if he had drunk as much as Jesse had? Maybe he hadn't drunk that perfume. Maybe he was just too dumb to feel sick.

–Ain't many womens left awake, the Negro boy said.

–Well, take me to a live 'un, said Donny.

–I'm looking for Ol Shepherd, said Jesse.

–They ain't but two men left up here, said the boy, a skinny man with a big knife and another with the bushiest beard I ever seen.

–That's him, that's Shepherd, Jesse said.

–Well, I know where he at, said the boy.

He looked proud of himself. Spawn of the devil. The boy slipped through the curtain. Jesse allowed Donny to go next up the stairs. The darkness of the stairwell soothed the pain in Jesse's head. What was he doing here? He was still drunk. Was that an excuse? He followed hard on Donny's heels. The man smelled sour.

Heavy velvet curtains at the end of the hallway shut out the morning light. Lanterns still burned on the lamp holders on the wall and lit the corridor with a jaundiced glow. To Jesse's left, the carpeted stairway continued on up another flight of stairs to the next floor. Three doors stood on each side of the corridor with lamps between them. The boy stopped outside the middle door on the left. Donny leaned against the opposite wall. The air was stifling. Jesse pressed his fingertips against the faded paisley pattern on the wallpaper and took a deep breath.

–He's in here, mister, said the boy.

Jesse drew a finger and thumb down each side of his lightly stubbled chin. Maybe Shepherd would have some water in there. He knocked. No answer.

–Go on in, mister, said the boy.

Jesse turned the handle on the door and looked inside. The light from the corridor laid a pale yellow ray on the pine-board floor. A scattering of bills of various denominations covered the floor between the brass legs of the bed. Behind the shining bars of the footboard, an amorphous heap stirred under a patchwork quilt. Ol Shepherd's tousled head turned toward Jesse, eyes squinting, the big beard overflowing the sheets. A woman raised her head up to the level of Ol's shoulder. She was blond as far as Jesse could make out in the half dark. Her lip rouge had smeared. She had a dark spot on her flabby jaw.

–Goddamn, boy, how did you get in here? rasped Ol.

–Donny, Jesse said.

The woman was naked. Her heavy left breast was bare and rested like a fold upon her ribs. The dark nipple was an eye that stared at him. Her other breast was covered by the sheet. Jesse had never seen a woman naked before. His duster felt heavy on his shoulders. The two pistols weighed against his belt. Another hardness pushed against his pants. Donny, breathing hard, was at his shoulder.

–Hi Ol, Donny said.

Ol raised himself off the woman.

–I ain't finished, honey, he said to her.

–Ol, have you got any water? asked Jesse.

–What?

A crystal decanter of clear liquid stood on a sideboard. Jesse crossed the room, grabbed the decanter, and pulled the stopper. He sniffed. No odor. He up-ended the decanter and poured the water down his parched throat. It was fresh in his mouth. The liquid worked its way around his cramped intestines. He didn't want to look at the bed.

–Oh Lord, did I need that, Jesse said.

–Does he want a poke? asked the woman.

–Go find him one, honey, said Ol.

–You ain't finished yet? asked Jesse.

–I ain't.

The woman slid out of bed. She was buck naked. Jesse judged her to be around thirty years old. She had a big belly and heavy hips and thighs and her breasts hung down on her belly. He glanced at the thick thatch. He felt the blood rush to his cheeks, to his ears, to the staff between his legs.

Oh Lord, my rod and my staff, he thought.

It was a blasphemous thought. Jesse was glad of the dark.

–C'mon honey, the woman said, I know just the girl for you.

–Ol? said Jesse.

Jesse's voice was hardly more than a whisper.

–Go on, said Ol.

Ol sat up in bed, the quilt across his waist, elbows resting on his knees, bushy chin between his hands. The woman laid her hand on Jesse's cheek. It soothed him.

–Come on, honey, she said.

–Where we going? Jesse said.

She was standing pressed against him. He could smell her sweat and perfume. He couldn't help the strain in his pants.

–How about me? asked Donny.

The little boy giggled behind him.

–You wait, the woman said.

She took Jesse by the sleeve of his duster.

–Follow me, she said.

He was allowing this woman to guide him.

–Oh Lord, my head hurts, Jesse said.

He tried to ease his arm away from her, but she would not let go of his sleeve. She led him down the corridor to the next door. She did not knock, but opened it and pulled him into the room. It was dark. The posts of the bed glinted with the light from the hallway. A mound of covers stirred. He heard a high whimper. How could he be doing this?

–Ella, called the woman, wake up, honey. I brought someone to see you.

–What? Now? I don't want to, Margie.

The girl in the bed had a soft, high voice. Young.

–Come on, Ella, said the blond woman, you got to see to the young gentleman.

–Goddamn. What the hell time is it, Margie? Ella whined.

–I don't want to be no trouble, Jesse said.

He couldn't call her ma'am.

The springs of the bed creaked. Light flared as Ella struck a match. She lit the candle that stood on her bedside table. Her brass bed was identical to the one in Ol Shepherd's room. The candlelight lit up the pale skin of her face, her wide red mouth. It glinted on her copper ringlets, made shadows beneath her pretty bright eyes. She had on a white cotton nightdress. He was glad that she was not naked like the woman who held his sleeve.

–'Least you brought me a young and handsome one.

Ella smiled at Jesse.

–Put your money on the sideboard, Ella said. Then you can wash up. I like a man who's clean.

She was younger than he was, of that he was sure. And she was ordering him around like that. There was a decanter on the sideboard. And two glasses. He was parched again. But he was frozen where he stood. He could not bring himself to reach into his pocket and bring out his money. The naked blond woman was behind him. She eased the heavy duster off his shoulders. He let her do it. She folded the duster and laid it across the back of a red plush armchair. Jesse took off his hat and the blond woman took it from him and laid it on top of the duster on the back of the chair.

–I ain't never done this before, Jesse said.

–Don't worry none, honey, said the blond woman. The Lord forgives us all. Just put two dollars Federal on the sideboard.

He reached into his tunic and without bringing the roll out of his pocket, he peeled a five from it. He laid the bill down next to the decanter. The blond woman glanced across at the girl on the bed.

–I don't believe I got any change, said Ella.

Jesse shrugged at her.

–You can owe me, he said.

He drew his pistols from his belt and laid them on the sideboard, too. He turned to the naked blond woman.

–Would you mind if I had a drink? Jesse asked.

–Go ahead, the woman said.

Jesse looked at himself in the mirror over the sideboard. His lips were cracked and mottled, the cheeks thin, and his eyes sunken. He looked as bad as Donny did. He poured some water into a glass and drained it.

–I'll leave you now, said the naked woman. Your friend back in my room must be getting a mite impatient.

She closed the door behind her. Jesse was alone with the girl.

–Would you have some physick? Jesse asked her. I have a terrible pain in my head.

The bed clothes rustled. She was out of bed. She was a pretty little thing, a little on the skinny side, but he liked the way her red ringlets shook and how she didn't seem afraid of anything. She was almost as tall as he was. Her nightgown reached only to her knees. She was shameless. Her eyes were a bright green. He was sure that she was younger than he. She picked up a dark bottle that stood on the bedside table and held it out to him.

–Drink this, she said.

The elixir was thick and sweet and bitter all at once. He tried not to taste it so that he wouldn't gag.

–One more swig, she said.

He drank again, and then she took the bottle from his hands and stood the bottle between the water decanter and his guns. The elixir burned in his stomach. It was like liquor, but he had to keep it down if it was to stop the sharp pain in his head. Her hands were on his shoulders. Under the lapels of his jacket. His jacket was heavy with the wad of money. She slid off the jacket and it bumped on the floor. Her fingers were on the buttons of his shirt; now on his smooth bare chest. His hands weighed like bags of lead at his side. Gooseflesh prickled his back and his shoulders. She let his shirt fall to the floor. He looked down on the back of her head, the red hair. She worked at his belt buckle. And then at the buttons of his pants. His mother would be horrified.

–Oh my, he said.

–Oh my, she said, looky here.

He could feel the cool air on his staff. His rod. Oh Lord. Then her fingertips. He curled back the muscles of his stomach and dug his toes against the ground so that his seed would not spill upon her hand. Her shoulder blades poked against her white cotton nightgown as if she had wings that were trying to sprout. She straightened up.

–Sit down on the armchair, she said.

Jesse shuffled across the room, hobbled by his rolled-down pants that were caught in the tops of his boots. His staff pulsed and waved, bounced as he slid each foot in front of the other. She giggled. He collapsed into the armchair.

–Better get these boots off, he said.

He reached down past his red and angry stiffness and tugged at the heels of his boots. She looked down upon him, her arms folded across her chest and watched him as he slid his boots off. He pulled down his trousers. His feet were black and rancid.

–Oh my, she said.

She crossed to the curtained window. Beneath the window was

a pitcher and basin on a cast-iron stand. Naked, he followed her across the room. He scratched at his hair. Water splashed into the china bowl. He dipped his hands into the bowl and brought the water up to cool his red face.

–You can do your feet, too, she said.

She crossed to the sideboard, and picked up the bottle of physick.

Jesse sat down in the armchair and settled his feet in the bowl. Ella slugged at the bottle. Did she have a headache, too? The medicine was starting to diminish the pain in his head. The water was cool on his feet.

–Where you come from? she asked him.

–Clay County, Missouri, he said.

–You a long ways from home.

He nodded. The water around his feet had turned gray. He reached down and rubbed from his ankles to his toes. His feet were clean now. She had left a towel on the arm of the chair and he dried himself off with it.

–You in the army? she asked.

–I was with Bill Anderson's company, he said.

Her shoulders hunched for a second and her eyes flicked up at him like a frightened animal.

–Was you on that Centralia raid? she asked. It was in all the newspapers.

She took another swig at the physick bottle.

–I guess, he said.

–Folks around here don't know what to make of that raid. Some says Anderson shouldn't of done it.

–Nope.

–You think he shouldn't of done it?

–I don't know.

–Did you ever kill anyone?

–I kilt a lot of Unions and a nigger or two, he said.

He hadn't killed a nigger but he thought it would impress her.

–Come here, now, she said.

It hadn't impressed her at all.

She pulled her nightgown over her head. Her body was skinny. Her titties were like two pale little crab apples on the grid of her ribs. Her hips and shoulders were all angles. She sat on the edge of the bed. She had wispy red wire between her slender thighs. Jesse folded the towel, laid it on the arm of the chair, and stood up. The footbath had cooled him down. The medicine had calmed the pain in his head and given him a glow in his bones. He approached her. She gripped him by the hips. He laid his hands on her red hair.

–I'm gonna put a hood on that big thing of yours, she said.

A hood? She reached across to the bedside table and picked up what resembled the transparent finger of a glove. She rolled it down onto itself between her fingers and thumbs as if she were rolling a diminutive stocking, and then she brought it against the head of his staff. She smoothed it down tight over his shaft. Mighty tight. The membrane glistened.

–It's like real skin, he said.

–It's a lamb gut.

–Like a sausage?

–Like that, she said.

Such a thing, he thought.

He wondered if it was government issue.

She took his hand and pulled him over to the bed. She made him lie down upon his back and she straddled him. His hands reached up to her skinny ribs, her little breasts. His mouth was against hers. No pain in his head anymore. He felt fine after that medicine. Her tongue was suddenly wet and hot in his mouth and he thought she would choke him. The scent of her hair and her neck was in his nostrils.

She pulled at him and rolled him over so that he was on top of her.

Her tiny ribs he held like a fragile bird's between his palms. He held his weight up on his elbows. Then she reached between his legs and gripped him. Her fingers tight around the base of it. The tip of it was suddenly hot. The heat spread from the head of his staff to the middle of it. Her hands slid over his buttocks and she pulled him down into her. Enveloped by her.

–Oh Lord, he said.

This was heaven itself. Her tongue was in his ear. The hot breath and her sweet smell overwhelmed him. She rocked her body beneath him. He cried out. He shuddered. He was lost somewhere deep in the night of her body. And he knew now that he should stay in Texas forever. She curled up in his arms and stroked his face. He was exhausted after all the drink and the medicine and the pleasure. She slid away from him and he peered blearily over the top of the blanket. She was a shadow in the room's twilight. Water tinkled from decanter to glass. She was a skinny little waif of a girl. His head fell into the depth of the pillow. She seemed to be folding his clothes neatly for him. He drifted off.

He awoke to a woman screeching and suddenly Ol Shepherd was framed in the doorway. Ol was clothed but his shirt had been hurriedly stuffed into his pants and his vest and jacket and duster hung upon him loose and unbuttoned. His eyes were wide above the bushy beard.

–Let's go, Jesse, he hissed.

More screaming came from down the corridor.

Jesse whipped back the covers and the bed creaked beneath him as he scrambled out of it. He was embarrassed to be naked in front of Ol. Confused. The skinny girl wasn't in the room any more.

–What's the matter? What's happening?

–It's Wood, Ol said. He cut one of the girls. Cut her bad.

–Dear Lord, Jesse said. Let me get into my clothes.

Wood appeared at Ol's elbow. He held both pistols level at the height of his chest. He pointed the muzzles down the corridor from whence he had come.

–Come on, Jesse, Wood called. Let's get out of here.

A bright slash of sunlight penetrated the heavy velvet drapes and struck the red plush armchair whereon lay Jesse's clothes. He grabbed his uniform jacket from the armchair, dug his hand into each pocket. Just dust and lint. A pit opened in his gut. He ransacked his waistcoat and trousers. His entire roll of bills was gone.

–The little bitch robbed me, Jesse said.

–Come on, Ol said.

–I'll do for that little whore, Jesse said. Where the hell is she?

Still the woman screamed down the corridor. Wood did not turn his head, as if he had someone held at bay. Wood's pistols shook as he laughed.

–Well, Jesse, Wood said, I'll have to learn you how to treat 'em right.

Treat 'em right? He ought to whip that little bitch. What the hell was Wood talking about?

Jesse stuffed his shirt into his pants. It was all bunched as he buckled on his cartridge belt. At least she had not taken his guns. Ol stepped aside as Jesse came to the door. He glanced down the corridor. A dark-haired Mexican woman, naked but for a serape over her back and around her shoulders, was on her knees in front of Ol's fat blond companion, who now clutched a blue velvet robe to herself. Next to her, dark lips pulled back tight from stained teeth, eyes wide, stood a tall mulatto girl in a white nightgown. She held a carving knife out in front of her and the clean steel glinted yellow in the lamplight. Then Jesse looked down again at the woman on her knees. She had one hand to her face and another to her belly. A prodigal flow of crimson seeped between her fingers. As the blood ran down, it drained from Jesse all his rage over his money and the little bitch who had stolen it. He might have shaken her, got his goddamn money back, might even have beat her. But cut her?

–They Lord, Jesse said. What the hell you done, Wood?

XXIV

THE THICK ELMS AND COTTONWOODS OF THE BLUFF STILL BORE the scars of a battle that had raged in this place four long years before. The trunks of the trees had been stripped of bark and splintered by cannon shot. Branches had been torn away from the canopy of maple above him, and their loss gave the trees an aspect both unbalanced and misshapen. Six months previously, at Centralia, he had told himself, no, vowed, that he would never surrender. But that had been in some other reality, the reality of battle frenzy, where the world falls away and there is only the awful and exhilarating and terrifying present, which is like the face of God Himself, where His creation meets His destruction with man as

His instrument. To be conscious of this was to feel the power of God in his own veins, yet here he was now in front of Lexington's Union fortress, about to turn himself in close to home. The war was over. They had been down in the Burned Lands when they met a tinker who told them that Lee had indeed surrendered at Appomattox. With no cause to disbelieve it, they had skirted Neosho, Carthage, and Osceola and wound their way north toward Lexington, determined to surrender close to home. Anderson was dead. Quantrill was dead. The company had disintegrated.

Between the bluff and the broad Missouri River, the red brick Masonic College crowned a hill that rose above the flood plain. The two southernmost pillars of its portico — the only ones visible to Jesse from this angle in the woods — gleamed white in the bright June sunshine. The Stars and Stripes caught in the breeze off the river and floated, languid and massive, out in front of the building.

All around the college grounds, great long mounds of earthworks made of it a formidable redoubt. Just outside the earthworks, the ruins of a farmhouse stood, fire-blackened, the roof gone, brick walls crumbled. Beyond the fortress, the white spires of Lexington rose into the cloudless blue sky. Sterling Price had captured that stronghold for the Confederacy in 1861, but now, once more, only bluecoated soldiers marched within the perimeter. The sun shone bright on the victorious Union.

–Well, said Wood Hite. Are we going in?

–I reckon, Jesse said.

On the glinting Missouri, a white-and-blue-painted riverboat, chimney stacks belching out black smoke, paddled peaceably away from the Lexington shore and turned upriver toward Independence and Kansas City. If Jesse could follow that river all the way up to Rulo, Nebraska, he would find his family again and bring them home to Missouri. Just as soon as he received parole.

Wood spat a brown squirt over the shoulder of his bay. His plug of chaw made a pouch below his lip. The thin cheeks above the fair beard were so sunburned that his face appeared to be cut from burgundy leather. He kept his Sharp's carbine resting across the pommel of his saddle and behind the saddle holsters for his pistols. Two more dragoon pistols were wedged into a wide red sash wound about his waist. Wood looked as if he hadn't made his peace with anyone. And he was ragged. A hole was worn in his hat where the crown was pinched at the front, and the left sleeve of his duster was frayed away from the shoulder and connected now by not more than three inches of stitching.

It made Jesse mindful of the filthy, threadbare rag on his own back that passed for a shirt and the split in the crotch of his twill pants that he had found no will to mend on their long ride from Texas. No doubt the Union soldiers in the town would be wearing decent uniforms. The fruits of victory. Peace.

–Why don't we just scoot down behind this bluff and take off for the Sni country again, said Wood. Before it's too late.

Jim Anderson slowly shook his head. His hat brim was so limp it hung to the shoulders of his Confederate tunic. The tunic itself, once gray, had been faded and bleached to a pale yellowy-brown. He leaned on his pommel.

–I ain't doing this no more, he said. I'm tired of it. I cain't run no more. If they paroled George and Ol Shepherd a month ago, they sure as hell can parole me. I ain't done no worse.

–You reckon we can get as far as the provost-marshal's office, asked Wood, without some son of a bitch takes a shot at us?

–I ain't putting up my guns, said Jesse, till I'm sure they're going to parole us.

–We'd better put up a white flag, then, said Jim.

–I brought a piece of sheet, said Jesse.

His cheeks colored up and his ears burned under the brim of his hat at being the one who had thought of such a thing.

–You save it from that little whore's bed? Wood asked.

The grin on his face above the tobacco plug exposed his long brown teeth and his ragged gums.

–Keeps it under his blanket to sniff at night, Jim said.

He guffawed and shook in his saddle. If he could have elbowed Wood in the ribs, he would have done so, for his arms flapped at his sides like the wings of a chicken.

Jesse reached behind him into his saddlebag and pulled out the white sheet. He did not wish to think about Bonham and the whorehouse. It was embarrassing to have been robbed by a harlot.

–You sure that ain't stained? asked Jim.

–The hell with you, Jesse said.

He drew the shotgun from his saddleboot and a coil of string from his saddlebag. He cut two lengths of string off the coil and with one lashed a corner of the sheet to the muzzle; with the second length, he lashed another corner of the white cloth to the trigger guard.

–Well, he said, if we're going in, let's do it.

–I'm ready, Wood said.

Jesse put the chestnut stallion forward and the horse left the cover of the trees. The bare hillside sloped down to a wagon track that ran directly north-south beneath the walls of the redoubt. He propped the butt of the shotgun on his thigh and the white sheet fluttered out at his shoulder. Wood and Jim rode together behind him. The white of the flag would surely stand out against the green of the hillside. Someone on the walls of the fortress was bound to see them. The garrison was made up of regular soldiers. Of that, he was sure. They would respect a white flag. Not like the militia. He touched the stallion's flanks with his heels and the horse went forward at a trot down the slope. The horse was sure-footed on the bunch grass and quickly approached the wagon road.

The kepis of the sentries and the barrels of their sloped muskets moved along the top of the wall. He could hear their voices but not the words that they called out to him, for the white flag fluttered noisily in his ear. The stallion jumped a drainage ditch and Jesse had reached the road. He turned the horse south toward the town. The big earthworks of the fortress sloped up steeply on his right. The flag would hide his face from them. A troop of thirteen cavalrymen swung onto the road south of them. Their officer called his troop to a halt. Jesse judged them to be forty yards away.

–Shee-it, said Wood.

–Ain't nothin', Jim said. Ride for town.

Jesse let the stallion maintain a trot.

The troopers dismounted and formed two lines across the road, and Jesse thought of Bill Anderson and the last battle he had fought with him. Two troopers held the horses behind the line and the officer stood to one side. A line of Sharp's carbines pointed up the road toward them. Jesse drew the white flag behind his shoulder, and above him the parapets of the redoubt bristled with musket barrels whose muzzles followed them as they rode. He pulled the stallion to a halt some twenty yards in front of the troopers who blocked their way.

–Surrender your weapons, called the officer.

He was not a young man. His muttonchop whiskers almost seemed like a chin strap for his kepi. His eyes were narrow and his mouth a hard line. He was vested in the field uniform of the Second Colorado Cavalry, one of the outfits that had chased them and Bill Anderson all over eastern Missouri.

–I aim to surrender to the district provost marshal, Jesse said. This here is a flag of truce. We are soldiers of the Confederate States of America and we come to parley terms.

–You look like three goddamn bushwhackers to me, said the officer. Now toss down your weapons or I'll have you blown out of your saddle.

–I ain't surrendering my guns to no one but the provost marshall, Wood said.

–Hold up, Wood, Jim said.

–We ain't prisoners of war yet, said Jesse. This is a flag of truce.

–You ain't a soldier, boy, said the officer. You're a goddamn murdering bandit.

Jesse slid his finger onto the trigger of the shotgun. The stallion sensed the tension in his body, for it snorted and tossed its head. One hoof lifted and tapped the ground. Wood came up on one side of Jesse and Jim on the other.

–Move aside, Jesse said. The provost marshall's office is in town.

–Put your goddamn weapons down, the officer said.

–Kiss my ass, Wood said.

Jesse put spur to the stallion and the horse leapt across the drainage ditch and back into the field.

–Halt, there! the officer yelled.

Jesse twisted in his saddle to look back and a shot cracked on the wall of the fortress above and a bullet smacked into his chest and drove him hard against the neck of the stallion. He lost his grasp on the shotgun. The grip of his feet in the stirrups kept him in the saddle as the stallion galloped across the open slope. Blood soaked into his ragged shirt. He gripped the pommel of his saddle.

–Oh Lord, he gasped.

Wood and Jim were out on the slope to his right and left, bent down over the necks of their horses and riding hard for the cover of the woods. Muskets crackled behind him. He sucked in breath and pressed his thumb to the hole in his chest that was not an inch from the wound he had taken at Wakenda. He coughed as he bounced in the saddle and bloody sputum spilled out over his chin.

–Oh Lord.

Hooves hammered upon the slope behind him. He glanced back over his shoulder and saw two troopers rapidly gaining on him. He reached for a pistol in a saddle holster. The trees were not twenty yards ahead. He swung the Colt down to his right, leaned his head down hard upon the racing stallion's mane, lifted the pistol, and fired at the trooper who came up on his right. The ball knocked the trooper clean out of his saddle, and his horse veered away in panic.

Jesse's stallion reached the woods and raced among the trunks and branches that whipped around him, so that all he could do was moan and hold tight to the pommel with his free left hand and to the pistol pressed against it with his right, from which the nauseating stink of cordite rose to his nostrils. He pulled the stallion to a halt. He tried to straighten up in the saddle, but the pain in his chest kept him bent double. He listened for sign of pursuit. Not a twig cracked. Neither Wood nor Jim was near, nor was the other Union trooper.

Blood had soaked Jesse's shirt and it trickled down into his pants. He was not afraid any more. He put his heels to the stallion and the horse walked off through the woods. Jesse had no care where the horse led him as long as it was away from the fort. He had vowed that if he was given no parole, he would raise a company that would terrorize every Yankee in Missouri and states adjacent. And he vowed now that he would live to keep it. The leafy canopy began to spin above him and he was sucked into a whirlpool of green and gold and then the grass hammered against his back. A stream tinkled beside his head and darkness came pulsing up from some hidden well beneath him. It engulfed him.

BOOK THREE

XXV

JESSE EASED HIS CHAIR BACK OFF THE PORCH WALL, AND THE DECK boards creaked beneath him. He had ploughed the field behind the barn and had a work-ache upon him that made him feel the connection of every ligament and muscle and bone of his tall frame and awoke the old pain in his twice-wounded ribs. The bright afternoon sunshine fell upon the legs of his blue pants, and he leaned forward, clutching his blanket around him, to bring head and shoulders into the warmth. On the wind, he picked up the sound of hoofbeats, and he glanced toward the shotgun that was propped beneath the window sill. The newspaper had reported a bank robbery down in Lexington, so the militia would be looking for old bushwhackers to string up, innocent or guilty. No names had been named, but he was sure that the bandits were old comrades of his, and that made the law doubly likely to pay him a visit. Clay, his home county, was a country occupied by an enemy army. He wasn't going to run from any militia patrol. He leaned back for the shotgun and laid it across his knees. He didn't have any parole papers to show, so it was best to be cautious. Back in sixty-five, when he had tried to surrender, neither he nor the Union provost marshal at Lexington had cared a damn about any papers for they had both thought he was going to die from the bullet in his chest. The Unions had shipped him home to die. And since he had no papers, the militia might come for him any time just to settle an old score. He spat over the edge of the porch. Let them come. After three years of peaceable farming and living under the threat of arrest for no other reason than his guerrilla past, his aching and turbulent soul craved some release from the frustration and humiliation of living with defeat.

The hoofbeats grew louder. The wind caught at Jesse's long hair and flicked it into his narrow face. The same wind whipped at the budding trees that arched over the trail leading to the yard, driving seven ravens cawing into the cloudless blue and snatching them away like rags in the pluck of unseen fingers. Under the bare-branched arch, the riders appeared, but it was no Union patrol. All four of the riders wore gray linen dusters, as if to recreate a military company of that shattered Southern nation of which he still felt himself a part, as if the riders were an apparition arisen out of a time forfeited, and the joy of seeing them lifted him to his feet and the blanket fell from his shoulders and dropped behind his heels as if the weight of three long years might drop away as easily. His brother Frank was accompanied by one-eyed George Shepherd and his brother, Ol, and beside Frank was a horseman whom Jesse did not know.

–You expecting company? Frank called.

Jesse grinned and set the shotgun down beneath the window.

–By God, look what a ill wind blew in! he yelled back.

–Goddamn, Jesse, Ol Shepherd said.

–Long time, Jesse said.

–Too goddamn long, George said.

The Shepherds bared their brown-stained teeth and swung down off their mounts. Ol Shepherd's big spade beard hung down to his expansive chest. The hair of his head hung long past his shoulders. When Jesse reached for his hand, the old bushwhacker gripped it and hugged him hard until Jesse winced and had to turn his cheek away from the rasping beard.

–Ain't you sick of sitting on your ass for a living? Ol said.

–I been busting it farming, Jesse said.

–We done that a while, but we found something pays better, George said.

He brayed like a sick donkey, grabbed Jesse's hand, and pumped it hard. George looked as gaunt as ever he had in the bush, the one eye unnaturally wide as if to make up for lack of its partner that was but a weeping slit above the heavily stubbled cheek.

–You wouldn't have been down Lexington way, would you? Jesse said.

–Don't you be asking, George said. Better you don't know.

Jesse laughed. Frank came up onto the porch with the stranger.

–I don't suppose you was there, too, Jesse said.

–Missed out on it, but I come across all these boys down in the Cracker Neck, Frank said. I thought I'd bring 'em home. This is Cole Younger. Me and him was with Quantrill at Lawrence and Olathe.

Jesse gripped Cole Younger's hand. Quantrill had burned Lawrence to the ground back in 'sixty-three.

–Time we got us a drink here, Jesse said. All these old soldiers.

Cole Younger nodded and slid a quart bottle of bourbon from the pocket of his duster. He uncorked it and handed it untouched to Frank.

–Drink up, Cole said.

His voice was deep and resonant. He was dressed beneath his duster in a suit and a bow-ribbon necktie, and he held his hat down by his side as if he craved the touch of the spring sun on his slightly balding skull. Long sideburns grew to the line of his chin, and he had a thick mustache and a long goatee. There was an air of quiet confidence and easy violence about him that made him immediately likable.

Frank took a good swallow from the neck of the bourbon bottle and passed it back to Cole. Cole Younger took a small mouthful.

–That ain't sipping whiskey, Ol Shepherd said. Get ye a mouthful.

Frank leaned back against the porch rail. Cole waved the bottle to indicate the bench under the kitchen window. Cole sat down next to Jesse, and the Shepherds settled themselves on the bench. George leaned forward, his hands clutched between his knees. The one eye swiveled up under the bushy eyebrow to regard Jesse.

–You fit to ride?

–Race you round the county.

George bent his head and let a long brown gob of tobacco juice drop between his feet. He looked up, lower lip glistening.

–This ain't a social call, George said. We got a proposition.

–I thought you all come for a little reunion, Jesse said.

–Well, this is, of sorts, George said. The first time we had a reunion like this was with your cousins Bud and Donny Pence. And we took sixty thousand dollars from the bank at Liberty.

Sixty thousand dollars. Jesse's belly fluttered as if a pretty girl had sat next to him and he could feel the press of her thighs. He took the whiskey from Cole, ran the heel of his palm over the mouth of the bottle, and took a long, burning swallow.

–The next time, Ol said, down in Lexington, we got naught but two thousand dollars. But we all can do better than that.

Jesse nodded. He passed the bottle to George, glad that he had drunk from it before those foul lips could close upon it. George upended the bottle, squinched up his one good eye, and passed the bottle on to Ol.

–The militia's looking to lynch bushwhackers all over the state, Jesse said. They'll come looking for us sooner or later, whether we do something or not.

–That's right, Ol Shepherd said. We best not do nothing more in Missouri.

–Donny Pence got word to us, said George, that a Yankee opened a bank down in Russellville, Kentucky.

–Donny's sheriff of Nelson County, now, Ol said.

–Goddamn, Jesse said.

–The bank will be full of cash on the day of the town fair, Cole Younger said. And it's far enough from Missouri that ain't no one like to think we rode more'n a hundred miles to do it.

Ol opened his clasp knife and carved at a wad of chaw.

–Well, what about it? he said. Are you in?

Jesse glanced at the shotgun and then at Frank and then he stared straight into George Shepherd's one good eye.

–Count me in, he said.

The simplicity of it. Everything fades away to a blur but the foresight and the notch above the cocked hammer. And the target. At this moment, the pale space between the bushy eyebrows of the bank manager. In his hands, the means to dispense life or death. Jesse allowed his focus to relax so that he saw the whole face. The banker's heavy jowls and baggy eye pouches gave him the look of a habitual drinker, but the blue eyes that flickered from the pistol to the open safe were sharp and clear. Jesse felt Cole Younger like a shadow at his shoulder. There were no customers and no clerks. Just the three of them in the silence of the bank. A silence made all the more acute by the presence of Death in attendance. Something holy about it. Jesse tossed the rolled-up wheat sack and it hit the banker in the chest and fell to the polished oak floor.

–Pick that up and untie it, Jesse said, or I'll take your head clean off.

The banker's fat lips pursed. His shoulders shook and his fists were clenched.

–I'll do no such thing.

His voice was hoarse.

–Pick up the goddamn bag and fill it, Jesse said.

–Go to hell, the banker said.

Jesse squeezed the trigger and the Colt roared. The Yankee tumbled back over his desk, knocking over pens and inkwells, and rolled up groaning against the safe. A pall of smoke hung white and sulphurous over the counter.

–Jesus Christ, Jesse, Cole said, you'll have the whole goddamn town in here.

The banker pushed himself up on his hands and knees and turned his head. A bead of blood trickled down over his forehead from his now unruly hair and then the blood was more copious and suddenly it was a mask upon his face. He clutched the top of his head.

–Almost scalped the son of a bitch, Jesse said. Did you see that?

Cole Younger snatched up the wheat sack, unfolded it, and slid to his knees beside the open safe. He scooped bundles of federal currency from the green-and-gold iron box and dropped the money into the depths of the sack.

The banker made a mewling noise. Jesse leaned over him, the better to see the furrow that had peeled back the hair and skin from the skull. Everything so sharp and clear. Copious gouts of blood spilled up as if from the skull itself. Where did it well from? Not out of bone. The eyes were tight shut against the red flow over the brow and nose and cheeks. Moans still issued from the downturned lips.

–Almost scalped the son of a bitch, Jesse said again.

Jesse pressed the foresight of the Navy Colt into the creased whorls of the man's ear, the dark and hairy hole that led down into the hidden brain. He could finish it now.

The window shattered, and he ducked instinctively. The banker scuttled behind his desk. Outside, four shots rang out. Jesse glanced up at Cole. Cole scooped the last of the cash into the sack and clutched the mouth of it shut, then he was up and spinning away from the safe. He dodged through the gap in the counter and was out the door. The banker was curled up on the floor with blood spilling through his fingers. Let him lie. Jesse drew his second pistol and ran for the door.

The air was damp on the porch boardwalk. Cold. Mist clung to the dark pines on the hillside behind the square-fronted buildings. Two farmers stood on the opposite boardwalk with their hands held high. And in the middle of the street Cole was in the saddle, pulling his horse around, the wheat sack gripped tight. Frank was mounted, too, with the reins of his sorrel in one hand and a pistol in the other. Shots popped down the street close to the sheriff's office.

Jesse unhitched his reins from the post and swung up onto the chestnut. Cole and Frank galloped by him. George and Ol spun their horses directly in front of the sheriff's office, fired off three rounds each at the office door, and then raced their horses down Main Street. Jesse put spur to the chestnut and the stale must of horse sweat was in his nostrils and the coarse mane close to his eye and in his ears a tattoo of hoofbeat and mud-splash, the shrieks of the women on the boardwalks making descant to the hum and zing of bullets that cut the air around him and in his heart a sweet joy that filled his lungs more with every breath. War's wild music, oh yes, war's wild music reprised.

XXVI

A BLACK HOUND LIFTED ITS HEAD FROM THE TRENCH BESIDE the railroad tracks. The dog's black-fringed lips pulled back from pure white teeth and a pink slaver dripped from its chops. It snarled. Jesse feinted a slash at it with the bowie knife. The handle of the knife was slick and slippery in Jesse's bloody hands. The dog snapped its teeth at the air and hunkered back on its haunches. It leapt for him. Jesse swung up the knife. The door latch snapped, and he started from sleep.

He lifted his head from the pillow. In the half-light of his curtained room, his cousin Zee Mimms appeared in the doorway. Her white cotton dress flared out from her waist and fell to her ankles. She gave him a coy look through the steam from the ewer that she held in her two hands, one on the handle, the other under the lip of the spout; over her right arm was draped another white and flowing garment. Chestnut ringlets played around her face. Around her neck she wore a string of pearls that he had bought for her from the spoils of the Russellville raid. Zee set down the ewer and laid the white robe over the straight-backed chair next to the wash-basin stand.

Jesse rolled onto his side.

–Is it time? he asked.

–It's time.

She opened the curtains and a hard shaft of morning light cut the gloom and lit her face. Water splashed into the china basin that matched the ewer in her hand.

–You be quick, now, she said. I can't wait to see you all clean and dressed.

She turned toward the door, then her hand came up to her cheek and she turned toward the bed, the white flow of her above him, and her palm cupped his stubbled chin and her soft lips brushed against his dry lips and she was back to the door before he could lay even a finger upon her, drifting from the room like a holy apparition, her feet tapping down the passageway to the kitchen.

He pushed back the quilt. His pecker pressed hard against the pants of his long underwear. A ray of sunlight lit up the whitewashed walls of the room, and hundreds of dust motes danced about the room where Zee had stood not a minute before. He stripped off his underwear and stood naked and laved himself. Taking his razor from the drawer, he stropped it on the leather that hung next to the oval mirror and shaved his thin face smooth. He took clean long underwear from the drawer and pulled it on. He crossed the room to where Zee had left his baptismal robe. The linen was crisp under his fingers as he bunched up the cloth. He slid his arms into the sleeves and raised them to let the starched folds and creases fall down over his body. He looked down at himself. The pure white of the robe fell to his gnarled toes.

Her tap at the door made him start.

–Come in, he said. I'm decent.

She stood in the doorway like a female mirror image of him.

–You look beautiful, she said.

–I feel a mite abashed.

–Shall we pray together? she said. Let's pray.

She knelt down. He had prayed together with her in church and at home after she had read him passages from the Bible. He couldn't refuse. He got down on his knees. His tongue was dry. He joined his palms and glanced across at her. She had a sly smile on her face. She began the Lord's Prayer. He mouthed the words. He was aware that his face burned like a beacon, but kneeling beside her like this in these vestments, it was as if they were preparing to go to a marriage ceremony, not a baptism, and if he had ever prayed at all, he prayed then in the silence behind the words of the prayer that he would see such a day, when they would be married in the sight of man and God and she would bear his children so that his name would live on. And it made his face all the hotter that he felt that way.

She stood up then and reached her hand down to him. He curled his fingers over her palm and came to his feet. The scent of her close to him was like apple blossom. He reached for her, but already she had turned away toward the door. He followed her out of his room and along the passageway to the kitchen and caught up with her at the threshold. Mama was all got up in her green velvet dress that bulged from under her breasts over her gravid belly. She and Pa Samuels sat at the table along with his sister Susan, brother Frank, and all three of his young half-brother and sisters, John, Sallie, and Fannie, all lined up like an audience in a tent show revival. He had expected them to make some comment on his heavenly attire, but all of them remained solemn.

–Why the long faces? Jesse said.

–Ain't nothing, Frank said.

His hard, square face had a dour look upon it. The creases of his frock coat were powdered with pale trail dust.

–It's something. So say it.

Frank glanced at Zee, then looked back at Jesse.

–I just got word that the laws shot Ol Shepherd to death on his daddy's porch.

Like the pictures on a deck of cards falling through his mind, he remembered every skirmish and battle that he had fought with Ol Shepherd next to him. Jesse saw the river where he had first met the guerrilla company, and the homesteader George had killed, and Ol easing his mind over Jesse's first shocked reaction to war. He remembered him at Rocheport and Fayette and Centralia. And at the bank raid in Russelville.

–In front of his family? Jesse said.

Frank nodded. His hard face betrayed nothing of fear or regret or surprise.

–What about George? Jesse said.

–Caught him, Frank said. He's awaiting trial.

–Cole?

–He's on the dodge.

–They coming for us?

Frank shrugged.

–Ain't no one mentioned us yet. Unless George want to do hisself a deal.

–George won't do no deal, Jesse said.

Zee turned her face up to him, her complexion smooth and creamy, her green eyes bright upon his.

–If the Yankees killed Ol Shepherd, Zee said, you should make them pay in kind.

–Best lie low a while, Frank said.

Jesse put his arm around Zee. Mama and Pa Samuels and the children all looked up at him from around the table as if waiting for his decision. But it had already been made on their family porch when George and Ol had invited him on the Russellville bank raid.

–This ain't complicated, Jesse said. We just have to take a eye for an eye.

XXVII

THE WAGON RUTS OF GALLATIN'S MAIN STREET WERE SO FROZEN that the hooves of Jesse's chestnut mare skittered against the pocked and crystalline ridges. A sharp north wind cut down between the low buildings on either side of Jesse and Jim Anderson. Cold penetrated at the neck of Jesse's sheepskin jacket and through every gap between the buttons, froze his wrists above his buckskin gloves, and made his clean-shaven cheeks and the tips of his ears sting. He pulled his hat down low, but still his eyes filled and he blinked away the liquid and warm tears ran down over his cheeks. Jim Anderson sat up straight in the saddle, ramrod stiff. He had a heavy homespun scarf wound around his bearded face and tucked under the lapels of his linen duster. He squinted against the wind that gave his face a hard and pinched aspect.

This was the first time that Jesse had ever set out with the express intention of doing a killing. He had killed without regret in a world that was made for killing. He had killed in battle. He had executed prisoners. This, he thought, would be like executing a prisoner. But he had not yet captured him. He could afford no extraneous thoughts. The entire town was hostile. He needed all his senses open: what he saw, what he heard, and, above all, what he felt in the air with some finely honed sense other than the usual five. The cold was keeping the citizens off the boardwalks, and those few who were out hurried about their business from store to store. This was perfect. If they acted quickly and as coldly as the weather, they could finish their work and be gone before the town could react.

Clouds that were shadowed and heavy with the threat of snow hung down over the flat roofs and square facades of the stores. Just beyond the Daviess County Savings Bank, a bare-leafed rock maple clattered its branches with every gust of wind. The boardwalk in front of the building was empty. Jesse pulled the chestnut to a halt at the bank's hitching rail. In front of a feed store about twenty yards away, two bundled-up store boys loaded a buckboard with grain sacks. Three horses were tied up close to the loading bay. The sheriff's office was on the same side of the street as the bank, some thirty yards up. Jesse dismounted. He hitched his mare to the rail and Jim Anderson did likewise. No one looked at them. Jim followed him up the steps to the bank. Jesse unbuttoned the lower half of his sheepskin jacket and laid his hand on the grip of his pistol. He did not draw it. Not one citizen was closer than the feed store. The bank door rattled under Jesse's grip and he entered. Jim waited on the porch.

A clerk in a dark brown vest sat behind the counter next to the cashier's cage. The young man's sandy hair was trimmed up above his protruding ears. The sleeves of his white shirt were held up by arm bands. Behind the clerk, the bank manager sat at a desk, close by the window on the north side of the room. A cavalry saber leaned against the black steel safe that sat squat against the windowless west wall behind him. The manager had a military aspect, despite the three-piece, pinstriped suit. A thick mustache curved down from his red-lipped mouth and continued up to his muttonchop whiskers.

Must be Cox, Jesse thought. But he was unsure. He had seen Major S. P. Cox but once, across a melee of fighting men when Bill Anderson had been struck down. He had imagined that his entire body would shake with fury upon the sight of Bill's killer, but he felt strangely calm.

–Can you change a hundred-dollar bill? Jesse asked the clerk.

An eager-to-please grin spread across the clerk's lightly freckled face. He reached over for the bill in Jesse's hand. The bank manager stood up then. He resembled the man who had led the Union militia on the day Bill was killed, but still Jesse was unsure. The banker came over to stand at the clerk's shoulder. The clerk took the bill and the banker reached over and took it from him. Then he turned toward the safe at the back of the small room. Behind

Jesse, the door of the bank swung open. Jesse glanced over his shoulder. Jim Anderson strode toward the counter with his pistol down against his thigh.

Here it come.

–If you will write a receipt, I will pay you that bill, called Anderson.

The banker turned back from the safe without opening it. He looked from Jim to Jesse and back again.

Yes, you son of a bitch, Jesse thought. We come for you.

–A hundred dollars? asked the banker.

–A hundred dollars. Jim nodded.

–That's acceptable, said the banker.

The banker sat down in his swivel chair and picked up a pen. Jim Anderson quietly pushed through the swing gate beside the counter and walked toward the banker's curved back. Jesse drew his pistol and pointed it over the counter at the clerk. The clerk lifted a limp hand, but not a sound came from his mouth. The nib of the banker's pen came down on the paper just as Jim swung up his pistol. The gun barked flame and smoke. Bone and brain spattered across the white paper and the desk. The muzzle roared again before the banker hit the board floor.

–Don't shoot me, the clerk whimpered.

–That son of a bitch killed my brother, Jim said.

–Oh, Captain Sheets, the clerk said.

Jesse pushed through the swing gate at the counter, the better to see the body, but the head was such a bloody mess that he could hardly recognize it as human.

–That's Cox, Jim said. I swear to God.

Then the clerk's chair clattered to the floor.

Jesse swiveled on the balls of his feet into a low crouch. The young clerk was through the swing gate to the door. Jesse swung up his pistol. The first shot hit close to the band on the clerk's right arm and drove him hard into the doorjamb. The boy screamed a high, thin screech like a rabbit being torn by a pair of dogs. Jesse's second shot splintered wood, and the clerk was through the door and out on the street yelling robbery and bloody murder.

Acrid and greasy white smoke hung in the air behind the counter.

–He didn't even open the goddamn safe, Jesse said.

–This son of a bitch killed Bill, Jim said.

Jesse entered the cashier's cage and flung up the lid of the cash box. He saw but a few bills and coins.

–They ain't but three hundred dollars in here, Jesse snapped. I walked in here with more goddamn money.

He stuffed the bills into the pocket of his sheepskin jacket, came out of the cage, and made for the door. He stepped out into the cold air. Shots cracked up the street and clapboard splintered to his left. He ducked instinctively at the flat report of a shotgun. A hail of lead pellets rattled against the wall of the bank. Jim pushed by, ran down the steps, and swung up onto his gray. Jesse heard the clerk's high voice.

–They killed Captain Sheets.

Sheets, he thought. Shit. Where the hell was Cox? The tip must have been a mistake. He did not care a damn about the dead Yankee, but he had come for Cox.

Jesse leveled his pistol, fired three shots across the street, and ran down the steps to his mount. He grabbed the chestnut's reins and jammed his foot in the stirrup. Jim's gray swung away in front of the chestnut and galloped southward. The horse shied sideways, and Jesse's right foot slithered across a patch of ice. He clutched the pommel.

–Hold up, girl.

Another shotgun blast shattered the top of the hitching rail into matchwood, and the chestnut bolted. Jesse lost hold of the pommel and the signs on the sides of the buildings tilted at the sky and his shoulders slammed down onto the frozen ground and his foot was above him, still tangled in the stirrup. He jerked forward, and his hip almost tore from its socket. The sheepskin rode up his back and his flesh burned as the icy ground scraped away his skin. Hind hooves smacked the ground beside his head and sent ice chips and hard divots flying into his face. The back of his head cracked down against a hard rut, and the cord of his hat dug into the flesh beneath his chin. He kept his pistol tightly gripped as he bounced down the street with his foot in the stirrup above him. His foot came free, but he slid on another five yards before he skidded to a halt and the hooves and haunches of the mare disappeared from sight. His hip ached dully as if ball and socket still held together but only loosely. He turned over onto his belly, pushed himself to his feet, and limped down the street against the sharp pain in his hip. He heard more shots and the zing of bullets through the cold air. He would hang for sure. He was in the open in the middle of the street. He aimed and fired at the crowd of citizens outside the bank. They scattered off the boardwalk. Jim's horse whirled around in front of him. Jesse grabbed Jim's forearm and swung up behind him onto the dappled rump of the gray, clutching Jim's duster, and Jim put spur to the horse.

–Goddamn it, Jim shouted. I was sure that was Cox.

–We ain't never going get him now, Jesse said.

They reached the woods beyond the town, and Jim forced the double-mounted horse among the scaly trunks of slippery elm and shagbark hickory whose long bare branches plucked at them. The heavy sky sifted spindrift down through the net of branches, and the gusting wind set the twigs tapping and cracking above them. His hip still ached, but that was the least of his problems.

–We got to get you a horse, Jim said. We ain't gonna outrun no posse like this.

–Looks like we gonna be on the dodge a while, Jesse said.

–Reckon that woman of yours going to have wait on marriage, ain't she?

Jim pushed their mount across a ditch and through a broken stone wall. As the horse faltered in its balance, Jesse twisted over his pained hip and groaned.

–You be able to ride if we get a horse? Jim said.

–I don't mean to get hung, Jesse said.

The path ran beside a small stream, and they followed it downhill to the east. Big, bare-branched sycamores formed an avenue over their heads. Up ahead through the trees rose a large red barn with multicolored star designs that some Dutchman must have painted on it in order to ward off evil.

–I'll find me a horse in there, I know it, Jesse said.

Jesse slid from the haunches of Jim's mount and drew his pistol. He limped through the soft snow toward the barn, his breath rising in clouds before him. Smoke from the farmhouse smudged the gray sky.

Jim drew his own pistol and followed Jesse along the road.

–We best be splitting up once I get mounted, Jesse said. You get on back to Carrollton.

–The laws are gonna find that chestnut mare, Jim said.

–And ever' damn horse trader in the state will know that she belong to the Jameses, Jesse said.

A calm came over him then. All those years when the militia could have picked him up and tried him as an outlaw for his depredations with Bill Anderson because he had never been paroled. All those years of being halfway hidden were over. He would have a price on his head now. The wind whipped the powder snow into flurries, gyres within gyres, that coiled down the trail and over them and made yet smaller spirals around him as he stamped through the drifts toward the barn.

Mist obscured the hillsides all around the white clapboard farm buildings, and the ghostly shapes of the cottonwoods etched lines in the fog. It was uncannily warm, and a light misty drizzle began to settle on the dry ditch grasses and on the matted coat of the hack and on Jesse's sheepskin. What snow there was in the farmyard had turned gray and wet. A lantern was alight in the kitchen window. Outside on the porch, Frank leaned against the four-by-four pillar and smoked a cigarette. Jesse pulled up the plough horse in the open yard.

–I don't recall you left on that horse, Frank said.

–I lost the mare.

–You lose Jim Anderson?

–Heading for Carrollton.

–Let's go inside, Frank said.

–I've got to get a decent horse and get out of here, Jesse said.

–Come on inside, Frank said. You got time.

Jesse tied the hack to a porch pillar and followed Frank into the kitchen.

It was warm inside and smelled of coffee and woodsmoke and frying lard. Frank straddled a chair next to the stove. Mama was hunched at the table that was set with empty plates and forks awaiting his stepbrothers and sisters, who were not yet awake at this hour. She plained and purled at a heavy wool sweater that was bunched in her lap. Her fingers worked automatically, and her hard eyes looked directly at Jesse.

–What happened? Mama said.

–Jim Anderson shot a man he thought was Major Cox.

Her mouth pouted briefly and then dropped to signal her contempt for the dead man.

–Man's name was Sheets, not Cox, Jesse said.

–If he was from Gallatin, Mama said, like as not he was a Yankee just the same. Let him pay for Ol Shepherd.

–Well, Jim might of waited for the banker to open the darn safe first, and they would have paid a lot more.

–Family comes first, Mama said. If he thought that was the man who killed Bill, what would you expect him to do?

–I don't know what he got to do, but there's going to be a posse here soon 'cause I lost the mare. Won't take 'em long to find it and who it belong to.

Mama's eyes narrowed and she stopped her knitting.

Zee appeared in the doorway. She hadn't combed her hair, and it straggled over her shoulders. The shawl she had wrapped about her did not stop her from shivering. Her face was still slack with sleep.

–What happened, honey? Are you hurt?

–I lost the horse, he said.

–Is there some coffee? she asked. You should have some coffee to warm you up. You'll catch your death.

–I ain't got time for no coffee, Jesse said.

–Mama, what's the matter? Zee asked. He ain't telling me.

–Jim Anderson shot the Yankee he thought killed his brother, Mama said.

–I was with him, Jesse said, and I lost the chestnut mare. When they find the mare, they'll come looking for me. I don't aim to get hung.

Zee's eyes were glassy and liquid of a sudden, but not a tear fell. She tugged at her hair as if she could force it into place. Her small lips pressed together for a moment. She gripped Jesse's sleeve.

–You ain't gonna hang, she said.

Jesse touched her cheek.

–I'll send for you when I get somewheres safe.

–I won't cry for no dead Yankee, Zee said.

–It was a Yankee. But it wasn't Cox.

–It was for Ol, she said.

–I'll saddle the sorrel, Frank said. If they catch that horse, they'll use it as proof against either one or both of us. They wouldn't think twice to string me up if they got me as far as Gallatin.

–I got you into this mess, Jesse said.

Frank shrugged. He took his cartridge belt off the sideboard shelf and buckled it on. He lifted his Winchester that leaned against the back of the sideboard and levered a shell into the breech.

–Let's go.

Mama stood up and laid her knitting on the seat of her chair. She put her arm around Zee. Then she motioned with her chin for them to get out.

–Zee, Jesse said.

–Don't worry about me, she said. And don't git caught, neither.

–I won't.

Behind him, Frank opened the kitchen door. Jesse nodded once and turned to follow his brother onto the porch. Frank had his duster over his left arm and the Winchester in the crook of his right elbow. The young Negro, Ambrose, came out onto the porch from the slave quarters. He was alert and awake but flecks of lint still clung to his hair.

–What the matter, Mister Frank?

With every word, vapor rose in front of his lean face.

–Keep an eye on the road, Frank said. We'll get the horses saddled.

Ambrose nodded and went back inside for a moment. When he reappeared, he had a woolen blanket draped around his shoulders. He leaned against the second porch pillar.

Jesse untied the hack and led it across the yard. The barn door creaked open under his hand. Jesse unsaddled the plough horse and led it into the stall where previously he had kept the chestnut mare. Then he went along the stalls and chose a bay stallion that had been broken in just the last summer. The horse snorted as Jesse slipped the bridle over its nose and fed it the bit. Frank was in the next stall with his sorrel.

Jesse cinched his saddle girth and swung aboard.

One barn door banged, then swung outward.

–They's two mens coming up the trail, Ambrose called.

Frank backed the sorrel from the stall.

–Let her go, Jesse called.

Ambrose swung the door wide.

Jesse brought the protesting bay around, its eyes rolling. He drew his Navy Colt.

Frank jammed the Winchester into his saddle boot and pulled a dragoon pistol from the holster on his cartridge belt.

Jesse put spur to the bay and galloped him out through the barn door, swung him around in the middle of the yard, glimpsed the men at the gate. He hooked the stallion and drove him hard at the meadow fence, and the stallion soared over it, hooves drumming down beyond it, and the hooves of the sorrel rumbled on the ground behind him. Two shots cracked out from the line of cottonwoods at the edge of the meadow, and Jesse leaned down over the bay's neck and fired back where the smoke rose white. He forced the horse to leap the ditch at the meadow's edge where the trail led up a steep rise. The bay's hooves kicked up dirt and small stones as they dug for purchase on the hardly thawed track. Frank's pistol cracked, and Jesse glanced back over his shoulder. Only one of their pursuers had jumped his horse over the fence into the meadow. Now he had dismounted, holding his horse by the reins. The posseman raised his pistol. Jesse heard the crack and a simultaneous hum. A whinny. The posseman's sorrel, riderless, raced forward across the meadow after Jesse and Frank. Jesse drove the bay hard up the slope of the road between two meadows. Frank was right behind him on the sorrel. Jesse glanced back again, and the riderless sorrel leaped the ditch and raced up the track behind them. With no weight to carry, it caught up with them easily. Frank leaned toward it. He brought the muzzle of his pistol level with its eye. And fired. The riderless horse tumbled over its front hooves, then lay still and useless behind them in the road.

XXVIII

ON THE DODGE NOW. HE COULD HAVE RUN TO TEXAS OR GONE west and disappeared, but he had no intention of spending his life drifting from town to town, a broken and hunted vagrant. He was going to stay in Missouri. The state was full of old bushwhacker families and unrepentant Confederates who would give Jesse refuge and could be trusted never to open their mouths to the law. That web of safe houses was like a shadow state wherein he might move freely, but there was always the chance that in a moment of ill luck, the Unions might take him, and if he or Frank were caught, he knew that they might hang before they even came to trial. The laws had captured his horse from the Gallatin raid, had pursued him to his mama's house, and he and Frank had involved them in a shooting scrape. Still, he was now sure that with help, powerful help, he might yet be able to get the parole papers that were due to him and to cast enough doubt on his presence at Gallatin that he might get the better of a trial if he ever was caught and got that far.

Jesse combed his fingers through his bay's dark mane and patted the animal's neck. Under the clear blue sky, the four Doric columns of a portico and triangular tympanum gleamed white in the cold sunshine. Woodsmoke curled from the stone chimneys at each end of the single-story wings built out from the house's central pavilion and gave the house a mirror-like aspect.

–Shelby's house, Frank said.

–Big, ain't it? Jesse said.

Frank nodded. His square face was set like granite, with its wide thick lips and broad nose, the heavy brow lowered over the eyes, and the lug ears that stuck out beneath his hat. Frank had ridden with Shelby in the war, and it was Frank who had sent the letter to the general when Jesse wanted to arrange the meeting. That such a mansion belonged to the only Confederate general never to have surrendered to the Union signified to Jesse that there was yet some bastion against Yankee power if Shelby still was loyal to the Cause that was lost. The general had agreed to meet with them, at least, and Frank had been certain that Shelby would not use the occasion to turn the James boys over to the laws. He was at least too much of a Confederate for that.

Jesse dismounted and dusted down his frock coat, adjusted his hat, and tightened his cartridge belt a notch. A young stable boy dressed smartly in a white shirt, yellow vest, tan jodhpurs, and riding boots ran down the steps of the house and took the reins of Jesse's bay and Frank's sorrel. A portly Negro in a butler's suit appeared from under the portico's shadow as if some prescience had alerted him to their arrival.

–General Shelby is expecting you, gentlemen.

The butler led them through the portal and into the hall, where a double staircase swept up to a high, balustraded landing. It was as if the mansion re-created the world before the war and its servants drifted into being as in a dream. Unicorn tapestries hung on either side of the paneled double doors that the butler opened for them. Jesse stepped into a wood-paneled room that had well-stocked bookcases on the west wall. A blaze flickered in the black marble fireplace, and the morning light shafted through the high bay windows. Jo Shelby rose from behind the long mahogany desk. The Battle of New Orleans raged in oils behind him. Another man, in tweeds, sat in a leather armchair close to the fire. Jesse was uneasy at the unknown presence.

–Frank, Shelby greeted. And Jesse, I presume.

Shelby's widely spaced dark eyes beheld Jesse with a look of mock irritation, one eyebrow lifted. He had combed back flat the jet black hair from the sharp peak on the broad brow. The cheeks were shaved clean, but he had a perfectly trimmed heavy mustache and a thick, dark beard that fell to his wide chest. His double-breasted frock coat was fastened tight with brass military buttons. A slim cigar smoldered in a silver dish close to his right hand, which lay flat on the green leather blotter.

–I always wanted to meet you, Jesse said.

–You were with Bill Anderson's company.

–From 'sixty-four.

Jesse gripped Shelby's hand. Even those who sided with the Union respected Shelby. He had led his regiment into Mexico rather than surrender to the Yankees. Now he used other means to fight the Union. The general funded ex-Confederate Democratic politicians who were trying to regain the state legislature from the Radical Republicans, but Shelby was no outlaw. This mansion and plantation meant that he would have too much to lose.

–I want you to meet John Newman Edwards, Shelby said. Mr. Edwards is the editor of the *Kansas City Times*. Frank already knows him.

Dear God, Jesse thought, the general has brought in a newspaperman.

–Edwards was with us at Prairie Grove, Frank said.

Edwards rose from his chair. He was tall and heavy-set, his eyes bright and intense in the lined and craggy face. He held a large cigar between the first two fingers of his left hand and a glass of brandy in the other. Jesse knew of him. A good Confederate. But a goddamn newspaperman and a bookwriter just the same. It seemed that upon seeing Jesse and Frank, he could hardly suppress a broad grin that made a lopsided bend in the unruly bar of his iron-gray mustache.

–I am delighted to meet you, sir, Edwards said.

He set down his brandy glass, gripped Jesse's hand and shook it vigorously.

–I was adjutant to General Shelby for most of the war, Edwards said. In the thick of it with him. Followed him down to Mexico, too.

–So I heard, Jesse said.

–Wrote a book about it, Shelby said.

–Frank read it, Jesse said.

Edwards puffed at his cigar. He returned to the armchair. He lifted the snifter from the small table beside his chair, took a good slug at his brandy, and sucked what liquid remained from the ends of his mustache.

–Sit down, gentlemen, Shelby said.

Two leather armchairs stood next to the bookshelves. Jesse sat down on the one closest to Shelby. He leaned forward, hands clasped between his knees. The general unstoppered a crystal decanter that stood next to the blotter on his desk, poured an amber liquid into two glass balloons, and handed one to Jesse and the other to Frank. Jesse leaned his nose over the rim of the glass and the perfume of brandy rose into his nose, bringing back memory of Texas in the last days of the war and the memory of a whorehouse. Shelby returned to his armchair behind the desk. He steepled his fingers, the tips touching just below his lower lip.

–I could get into trouble having you boys sitting here, Shelby said.

Jesse glanced at Frank. His brother's block-shaped face remained set and the lips tight. Frank was a follower, not a leader, and he seemed to be in awe of the general as an enlisted man in front of a very high level officer.

–Yessir, Jesse said. That you could. We been accused of a certain crime. They say we robbed a Yankee bank and killed the manager.

–And it's not true? asked Shelby.

–I was nowhere near that bank, Frank said. There's plenty willing to testify to it.

Shelby glanced at Jesse.

–I know the shootist, Jesse said. He thought that the manager's name was Cox. The selfsame Major Cox as killed Bill Anderson. There's plenty ex-bushwhackers that wanted him dead, but the posse from Gallatin came for us.

The words in his head sounded lame, but Jesse had no intention of admitting involvement in a killing to anyone, friend or foe, especially not in front of a newspaperman.

–Can't say it would break my heart to see Cox dead, Shelby said. I always admired Bill Anderson.

He took a long pull on his cigar.

That was good to hear. Jesse slid back into the leather armchair and from its depths glanced across at the journalist to see his reaction, but Edwards had his nose in the snifter. Jesse took a good slug at his own drink. It was a fine and heady liquor.

–They got no proof on us, Jesse said.

Shelby said nothing, just watched him, indifferent. Maybe that was what made him a general. He seemed to like to sit there like a chess player, observing for weakness and awaiting Jesse's next move, but it was Edwards who spoke.

–The Gallatin papers mentioned a horse that belonged to the James family.

Edwards's voice was coarse and gravelly with the smoke and liquor.

–My mama sold that horse three days before the robbery to a trader from Kansas, Jesse said. She'll swear to it.

–With all due respect, Shelby said, your mama's word would appear to the world as being somewhat partial to your cause.

–There's a lot more in Clay County would swear to our being at home on the day of the robbery, Frank said. Including the sheriff. He seen me.

–But he didn't see your brother, Edwards said.

–They accused the two of us, Jesse said. They don't prove Frank was there, they cain't say I was there. Union vigilantes have been stringing up old bushwhackers all over the state, innocent or guilty.

–And you're saying it's your turn? Edwards said.

–That's just about the drift of it, Jesse said. And the Republicans have blamed us for every robbery committed since, in the state or out of it.

Shelby smoked. Edwards drank.

–I never surrendered at the end of the war, Jesse said. I was wounded. Now I just want parole. Plenty bushwhackers got parole papers after they turned themselves in. Frank for one. You know people in the House, General Shelby. They respect you. I want my papers.

Shelby rolled the ash off the end of his cigar. His head tilted slightly. The fact that Jesse had never surrendered seemed to strike a sympathetic chord within him, but he was enough of a general still to know that Jesse was trying to maneuver him into that position. He would not be impressed.

–To get you parole with a price on your head, Shelby said, Democrats would have to have control of the state legislature. Or at least some influence over the governor, and we're a long way from that. The Radical Republicans control the entire state and half of them commanded militia regiments during the war. They have no sympathy for former guerrillas. Your chances are slim to none.

That was blunt. Jesse could respect the man. He glanced across at Frank. They had been wasting their time with these fine, upstanding citizens.

–I'm sorry to have bothered you, General, Jesse said. I appreciate you seeing us and all.

Jesse stood up. He did not turn toward the door, for Shelby still sat at his desk and regarded him as if the interview could only be concluded on his, Shelby's time, not Jesse's.

–Frank? Jesse said.

Frank nodded, rotated the brim of his hat beneath his fingertips, eased forward to the edge of his seat but did not stand, as if held down by Shelby's gaze.

The newspaperman now slid out of his armchair and despite his bulk came nimbly to his feet, balancing brandy and cigar.

–Let me be blunt, gentlemen, Edwards said. I sniff a story here.

Edwards was irksome. Jesse wanted to get out of the room, but Frank sat as if transfixed.

–We already been in the newspaper, Jesse said.

–A story that does not endear you to either the law or the public, Edwards said.

–I thought we might be able to get help here.

–There's all kinds of help, Edwards said.

–I thought you could help with parole.

–Not in this political climate, Shelby said. The war's over. It's at the ballot that we have to win the state. But if we can get control, you'll get your parole. Even a full pardon.

–It'll be a long campaign for Democrats to get a majority, Edwards said.

–I ain't a politician, Jesse said.

–True enough, Shelby said. That's why when I got your letter, I telegraphed Edwards to come here. He and I have been thinking. Your story of victimization by the militia would get a lot of sympathy out there in the farmlands. The story could be quite a rallying point for the political campaign.

The newspaperman stood up again, spread one hand, and made a chopping motion as he declaimed each syllable:

–The depredations of the government militia and the draconian punishments meted out by the Radical Republicans in the House and Senate and the disenfranchisement of those who fought for the Confederacy have driven innocent young men like the James boys into the bush — unjustly accused of crimes they did not commit. A fine story. Inspiring to those who would strike back at injustice.

Jesse could not suppress a smile at the newspaperman's bluster.

He knew that he was being maneuvered by Shelby and Edwards. They saw him as a tool to use in their bigger game.

–All that a newspaper article is gonna do is to draw more attention to us, Jesse said. Make it easier to get caught.

–It's a risk, Shelby said, but have you not stated your firm conviction that you are the victims of injustice? We need to rally ex-Confederates to push for change in the legislature. This is where we have to fight the war now. Do you understand, Jesse? We need to motivate people to get control of the state. Get the Republicans out. That's the only way you'll get parole. You can be part of a broader campaign, just as Bill Anderson was a part of the Confederate campaign. And at the end of it, you get your parole.

Jesse suppressed a smile. Bill Anderson was a mad dog who had fought his own war against the Union, no matter what the Confederate high command had thought he was doing. Edwards and Shelby wanted something from him. He needed to find out how much and how far they would go with him.

–Until the Democrats get control of the state, I got to stay on the dodge, Jesse said. How am I supposed to live?

Edwards drained his brandy and a satisfied smile bent up his mustache.

–Well, I don't know, he said. When a man is on the dodge, forced into the bush by injustice, a lot of folks, Confederate folks, might find it understandable if he has to resort to extreme measures to survive. Very extreme. And it seems to me that when some bushwhacker hits a Yankee bank, it puts heart in the old Confederates throughout the state that someone is striking back against the victors who oppress them.

Jesse was beginning to like Edwards. He had picked up on the meaning of Jesse's question immediately. Seen a way to turn Jesse's plight to the advantage of both of them. Edwards was a man who wanted stories. Bank robberies in the name of the Lost Cause were good stories. And Edwards was Confederate to the marrow.

–There are plenty old guerrillas out there in the bush that would be glad to hit Yankee banks, Jesse said.

–Every blow struck against the Yankees will get full coverage in my newspaper, and I will see to it that the innocent are never held to blame.

Jesse nodded. Shelby and Edwards seemed to believe that he would lead a guerrilla arm of ex-Confederate resistance against the Radical Republicans, which could only help the Democrats' political campaign.

–What happens if I get caught?

–If you and Frank are ever brought to trial, Shelby said, the Yankees have to convince twelve good men and true to find you guilty beyond a reasonable doubt, and if the newspapers spread the word that Jesse and Frank James fled to escape a militia lynch mob, there would be plenty willing to believe it. And yet more who would be troubled by confusion. And there are counties in Missouri where no one would return a guilty verdict on an ex-Confederate if that man had John Edwards and Jo Shelby's backing. If you are ever caught, I will do everything I can to see you are tried in such a county. That I can do.

Jesse nodded.

–In the meantime, Edwards said, I will gather sworn affidavits of your innocence of the Gallatin raid from every prominent citizen in Clay County and publish them in the *Times.*

Shelby blew out a thin stream of smoke. A crease appeared between his eyebrows.

–If ever you gentlemen should need a roof for the night, Shelby said, you can count on my family's hospitality and complete discretion.

Shelby was a gentleman.

–I appreciate your offer, sir, Jesse said. I'd be honored to take you up on it.

–One thing we should do immediately, Edwards said.

–That being? Jesse said.

–I want you to write a letter declaring your innocence of the Gallatin robbery. As far as I'm concerned, and I speak for a great many others, you were no fools to run from a bloodthirsty mob of poltroons intent on lynching those who fought for the Confederacy. Even those who fought under the black flag are entitled to live peaceably under United States law since the war ended. I'll publish your letter and an editorial to go with it.

Jesse nodded, raised his glass, and took a sip of the fine liquor. He had no reason to doubt these men. In exchange for his cooperation over a few newspaper stories, he was certain that they would do everything in their power to get him parole if the Democrats did get control of the legislature and that they would provide him with the best lawyers if ever he was caught. Shelby's political campaign and Edwards's newspaper reports would be a buffer for the new company that he would form to hit the Yankee banks. It was worth the risk, even if his name would be known all over the state.

–Well, Mr. Edwards, Jesse said, all I need is a desk and chair and I'll commence writing that letter.

XXIX

WHEN HE HAD SLEPT BETWEEN THE CRISP SHEETS OF A FOUR-poster bed in Shelby's mansion, his spirit was fortified and he trusted in the Lord's blessings, but more often than not he lay in rooms such as this one — crumbling plaster, a narrow cot, lumpy ticking, and suspect sheets — and this was discouraging. The smell of damp and dust mixed with the sweet fetor of manure that penetrated the room from the stables at the back of the hotel. He awoke from an afternoon nap wanting a woman. And the only kind of woman he could bring to a room such as this was a sporting woman. On more than one occasion he had woken with a fur-covered tongue and a splitting headache in the arms of one. Back in Clay, Zee Mimms was waiting for him faithfully, despite the months that passed between one visit to her and the next. Everyone in Clay and Kearney knew that she was Jesse James's fiancée, so who else was going to come courting? But if he was going to settle down with a woman, he had to get away to a place where even friendly folks would not recognize him. Clay County and his mama's farm were having constant visits from the militia and the detectives that the governor had hired. In those counties that had been loyal to the Union, he never set foot. In those counties that had supported the Confederacy, not one local lawman even acknowledged his presence when he was among them, and they resented the militia patrols that turned over farms that belonged to their relatives. But the governor had ordered every sheriff of every county to step up their efforts to find him. He was twenty-five years old, famous all over Missouri and beyond, but until Shelby got him parole, he could not fully enjoy the fruits of his fame. It was too risky to stay in Missouri, for one loose word would finish him. If he was to stay in one place, he had to get away for a while, and it had to be to another state. To buy a house for him and Zee to live in would require a big stake. And today, the whole city and half the people from surrounding counties would be at the Kansas City Exposition Grounds, all having paid good money at the gate. No laws would expect him to strike in the middle of all those people. And every newspaper in the country would feature the story. It would be fine operation on which to leave Missouri.

The bedsprings creaked as Jesse swung his feet off the bed and leaned toward the rickety chest of drawers that listed beneath the sill of the splintered casement. He waggled the top drawer so that it racked open at angle enough to ease out his letter to Zee. Jesse lay back on the bed, unfolded the vellum, and with one hand behind his head and stared at his scratchy penmanship.

Thursday, September 26th 1872

My dearest Josie,
I think about you always and can only hope that you are patient with me. So far, this life has not permitted me to give you what it is that most women want and expect from a man. One day, Lord willing, we will settle to have home and family. The tide is turning and already good Confederates have been voted into the State Senate but JNE and the General say that they is still not enough votes to carry legislation. I cannot wait, as I know you cannot, so I am going down Kentucky where they are many friends to help us. JNE will meet me there and we will try to find a place where you and I might settle down as man and wife. For the present take heart with the tract I have copied out here. It have brought me succor in hard times. This is it.

Deliver me from mine enemies, O my God: defend me from them that rise up against me. Deliver me from the workers of iniquity, and save me from bloody men. For, lo, they lie in wait for my soul: the mighty are gathered against me; not for my transgression, not for my sin, O Lord. They run and prepare themselves without my fault.

Consume them in wrath. Let them make a noise like a dog, and go round about the city. Let them wander up and down for meat. Unto thee O my strength, will I sing: for God is my defense and the God of my mercy.

Trust me and be patient. Josie, I love you always.

Yours,
J. T. Howard

Jesse folded the letter and stood up. He tucked the vellum into the inside pocket of his jacket that hung on the back of the door. The low ceiling seemed to squeeze the light back out of the room. From outside, the sound of iron shoes struck against stone, and brass harness rang bit upon buckle. He peered through the dusty windowpane into the courtyard below. A stable boy was brushing down Frank's dark quarter horse in preparation for the saddle while Frank smoked a cigarette at the arched gateway to the cobbled street. Cole already had the saddle on his roan and was at the cinch. A second stable boy led out Jesse's bay mare. Jesse turned away from the window and holstered the Colt. He took a red-and-white-checked cloth from his trouser pocket and tied it around his head. He picked his hat up off the bed and settled it on his head and over the mask. He shrugged on his jacket, then locked the door behind him and cautiously made for the stairs along the dark passage. He kept a hand on the wainscoting as he descended in the darkness. He came out into the pale light of the courtyard. Cole and Frank were in the saddle already, stiff and elegant in their business suits and hard-brimmed hats. Steam from the damp cobbles and yellow balls of manure lifted around the hoofs of the horses in the afternoon warmth.

–We should be going, Cole said.

Jesse took the reins of his horse from the skinny stable boy. He checked the cinch for himself and swung into the saddle.

–Let's go, he said.

He touched heel to the bay's flanks and followed Cole and Frank onto the cobbles of Twelfth Street. The street was lined with dingy brick stockmen's hotels and tobacco shops and rope merchants. A dray wagon pulled up on the other side of the street, and four Negroes unloaded the barrels that rumbled down a ramp into the cellar of the Texas Hotel. The painted trollops in the doorway glanced up at him and made lascivious mime with their tongues and hips.

–We'll make 'em squeal tonight, Cole said.

–Not in this town, Jesse said.

A wagon piled with scrap metal clattered over the cobbles and blocked their way down the street. Jesse kept the bay on a tight rein and she tossed her head, both horse and rider made uneasy by the bobbing oblongs of tin and the jutting pipes and rusted railings that all but spilled over the wagon's sideboards. The hour was late. He had calculated that he should hit the main ticket booth before five o'clock, when they would be counting the day's takings, ready to carry the money to the county offices. Each time he guided the bay toward the tailgate of the cart, she shied away. They were stuck behind the cart until the buildings of Twelfth Street abruptly ended.

–Goddammit, let's get there.

Jesse swung the bay away from the rear of the rattling scrap wagon, out onto the open swath of weed-choked flat that was cut and crossed by the glinting steel of the railroad tracks just south of Union Station. He danced her over the iron rails and between the tarred ties half hidden by unrecognizable dry stalks that once were living plants. He guided her past a string of empty freight cars, with their painted logos readable still, though they had been blasted and faded by the dust-laden winds of the prairies. A train whistle pierced the air to the north of them, and a black steel behemoth crept out toward them.

The hooves of the bay clattered on the boards of the crossing, and once more Jesse rode up onto the cobbled thoroughfare where Twelfth Street recommenced.

–Goddammit, we'll be late, Jesse said.

–You called the time, Cole said.

Saws whined in the trackside workshops. He fought to keep the bay steady. Pumps and boilers and hoists stood piled on the cobbles amid coils of chain and hanging pulleys in the yard of the Keystone Ironworks. Brass pipes glinted where they were bent into eccentric configurations to couple with cast-iron blocks from which extended rows of valves and pistons, and each obscene and mysterious machine was steepled with a long and shining chimney. A steam hammer rose upon its gantry and clattered and smashed down upon a steel plate. They traveled down a cacophonous brick-lined corridor until they crossed Broadway. Now merchants and hostlers and fishmongers lined either side of the street, and the movement of the citizenry along the streetsides seemed to him soporific and sheep-like, gulled as they were by the victory of industrial capital and the mirage of empty promise that had followed the South's defeat. He put the bay into a trot as they rode across Troost Avenue. Buggies and horses and foot traffic came at them in a living tide down Twelfth Street. They could go no faster, and his sense of timing began to fracture. Prospect Avenue was just ahead. The gates of the Exposition were open, and a great crowd spilled out into the road from between the high stone walls. The ticket booth was a brightly painted timber-and-board structure to the right of the gate, a garish red, white, and blue affront. Jesse dismounted and handed the reins of the bay to Frank. He lifted his hat and pulled down his cloth mask. He was Death's clown. He turned to the counter. The clerk in his cage stared up at him, eyes wide in the thin face. A lock of hair dropped over the man's forehead. Jesse jabbed the muzzle of the Colt over the counter and into the clerk's cheek and the head jerked back. He grabbed the cash box from the small desk and set it on the counter. The clerk disappeared out the back of the booth. Jesse flipped up the lid. A feeble scattering of bills lay in the bottom of the box. He stuffed the greenbacks into his jacket pocket, a handful at a time, and the cash box was empty but for a few coins. He had drastically miscalculated. The day's takings were gone. Even had the scrap cart not held them up, they would not have been in time.

A screech came from his left, and two clawed hands raked down Jesse's face and knocked him sideways.

–Stand off there, called Cole.

Jesse swung the Colt up, but the swinging head of Cole's roan rose up between him and the mad clerk, whose hair was awry, the face contorted, devoid of reason. Jesse brought the foresight in line with the clerk's head to kill the son of a bitch, but now the rump of the roan swung in front of him.

–Let me get him! Jesse yelled.

Every nerve in his body quivered. He wanted that wiry son of a bitch. He wanted to put a bullet into the goddamn clerk's head.

Scratched at him like a woman. Had dared to touch him. The son of a bitch was as good as dead. He would fill the bastard with lead and leave him bleeding. Take a knife and cut the little bastard's throat.

–Get out of here! Frank called.

Jesse smashed the butt of the pistol against the empty cash box and it clattered away into the ticket booth. The little clerk's hands scraped and clutched at Cole's thigh. Jesse had a clear shot. His pistol roared as the clerk twisted away from Cole. Missed the son of a bitch. He squirmed off into the crowd.

–My child, my child.

A woman's voice.

He had missed the goddamn clerk and missed a decent haul. Jesse dodged behind the rump of Cole's roan and gripped the pommel of the bay's saddle. He swung onto her. A sea of faces and bodies surged around the gates as if Hell itself had let out all the lost souls within it. All staring up at him.

–Robbery!

–Stop them!

A girlchild's high whine cut across the shouts of the crowd. Frank fired in the air, and the crowd pushed back, still in a half-circle around them, and the clerk came racing out of the crowd and clawed at Cole's jacket until Cole pummeled his head with the butt of his pistol and the clerk fell bleeding. This time the son of a bitch was done for. Jesse pointed his pistol again but the hooves of Cole's roan danced around the clerk's head.

–Stand back, goddammit, Jesse yelled.

But Cole's horse was in the way again. No time to stop now. The laws would be filling the streets.

–Ride out! Jesse called.

He forced the bay to rear and spin and the crowd rolled away from him like an ebbing wave and left exposed the caterwauling child with the mother leaning over her, the woman screeching in incessant counterpoint to the child's wail. A pool of blood reddened the gravel around the girl's left leg. Jesse's shot had taken away the best part of the child's calf. Didn't the goddamn mother have the sense to keep a child away from a holdup? Was this another sideshow in the county fair?

–Get on out of here! Frank called.

Jesse spurred the bay and raced her east down Twelfth Street toward the woods along the banks of the Blue River. Not right. Nothing right. The whole world became an appalling circus wherein he was trapped in a whirl of faces and colors and senseless sounds and spilled blood. Iron-shod hooves rattled on cobblestone. Above the iron railings of Elmwood Cemetery, the branches of the trees stretched out to him as if the angels of that dark world sought to be his succubi. He could hear the pounding of hooves behind the galloping bay. He fled them. He fled.

XXX

AN UNBEARABLE SCREECH SET JESSE'S TEETH ON EDGE, AND HE pressed his fingernails into his palms as Edwards opened the chimney gate of a lantern and glass scraped against metal. Edwards struck a match that flared in his long, tapered fingers and lit up his face with quasi-demonic shadows as if he were a bogeyman slipped out from the attics and basements of Jesse's childhood. Edwards was a caped shadow in the dark of the barn where Jesse had been in hiding for four days, fitfully dreaming of pursuit and gunshot and clinging trees, dreams no less outrageous for having slipped away upon his waking. It was Edwards who had arranged this hideout for him, and Jesse half-blamed him for the hideous night visions. The wick caught light, and a whiff of kerosene staled the damp air as light banished the biblical blackness. A conical beam funneled through the domed lens of Edwards's lantern and formed a flickering circle upon the nearest stall, where a line-backed dun swung its pale head over the half-door.

–Look here, Edwards said.

He held up the folded newspaper as if it were bait to draw a fish from its hole.

Jesse unfolded his thin and hungry body and emerged from an empty stall. He brushed dust and flecks of chaff from his stale and rumpled frock coat and his faded pants. Beneath his soles, the herringboned brick of the barn floor was slick with watery green manure.

–What? Jesse said.

The iron-gray mustache was curved upward in a malicious grin.

–The editorial, he said. I wrote it after the fair robbery.

Jesse took the paper and leaned forward with it so that the light from Edwards's lantern pooled upon the page.

THE CHIVALRY OF CRIME, Jesse read.

He followed the lines of print with his forefinger.

There is a dash of tiger blood in the veins of all men; a latent disposition even in the bosom that is a stranger to nerve and daring, to admire those qualities in other men. And this penchant *is always keener if there is a dash of sin in the deed to spice the enjoyment of its contemplation. There are men in Jackson, Cass and Clay — few there are left — who learned to dare when there was no such word as quarter on the Border. Men who ride at midday into the county-seat, while court is sitting, take the cash out of the vault and put the cashier in and ride out of town to the music of cracking pistols. These men are bad citizens; but they are bad because they live out of their time. The nineteenth century with its Sybaric civilization is not the social soil for men who might have sat with ARTHUR at the Round Table, ridden at tourney with Sir LAUNCELOT, or worn the colors of GUINEVERE; men who might have shattered the casque of BRIAN DE BOIS GUIBERT. Such as these are they who awed the multitude on Thursday while they robbed the till at the gate and got away. What they did we condemn. But the way they did it we cannot help admiring. It was as though three bandits had come to us from the storied Odenwald, with the halo of medieval chivalry upon their garments and shown us how things were done that poets sing of. Nowhere else in the United States or in the civilized world, probably, could this thing have been done. It was done here, not because the law is weaker but because the men were bolder, not because the protectors of person and property were less efficient but because the bandits were more dashing and skillful; not because honest Missourians have less nerve but because freebooting Missourians have more.*

The words of Edwards were a medicine to him, but it was as if the words in the newspaper were written about someone else.

Every other newspaper in the state would recognize the work of the James Gang, but Edwards never mentioned his name nor any other, except to declare his innocence. This fame of his had taken on a life of its own. It was as if each group of citizens who read of him conspired to create a different Jesse James, each one according to his own imagination and prejudices. When he had first met Edwards, he had no idea that his actions and thoughts would be so distorted into the stuff of fantasy. And there were indeed those in the State House who were now actively lobbying to grant him parole while at the same time reading about his robberies with glee, as if every strike he made was a blow to the Republican majority. And neither would these Democrats admit his guilt.

–You are a Satan, Mr. Edwards, Jesse said.

–Every word of that article is true, Edwards said. Missouri people are behind you, Jesse. When we get enough members in the House, we'll go for full amnesty, not just parole. Whatever you did in the war and after, all pardoned by the state.

–You ain't gonna get full amnesty.

Edwards believed it. Did he, Jesse, believe it? That people saw him as this Launcelot all across the State and beyond? But what about these unquiet dreams and memories that caused him to start from sleep? As if something was eating him from the inside out: all that time with Bill Anderson, riding through the burnt and devastated country, the killings they did on the back trails, the soldiers in battle, the Negroes they strung up, Sheets with his head blown off in Gallatin, that child in Kansas City with her leg shot away. His memory was like a butcher's shop. All those wounds and faces. Well, damn them to Hell and Edwards, too. All he needed was a brief respite, a safe house in a county or a state wherein he was unknown and could lie up for a while, then he could find his balance again. Get these infernal dreams and visions that both revolted and excited him, out of his head. And if Edwards and Shelby got amnesty, all the better. He would put his fame to work for him. Maybe a seat in the House, himself.

–Now, Edwards said, I want you to meet some friends and neighbors.

–I'll saddle up.

–No need, we can walk.

Walk. Edwards nodded toward the barn door. Jesse led the way,

Edwards behind him like a malevolent shadow. They stepped out into the cold mountain air. Cedar and fir rose up the sides of the narrow valley. Heavy clouds drifted across the lower slopes, and the dark trees were blacker than the darkness of night. A squall of wind blew down the valley and whipped up the underbelly of the cloud bank and stripped away from it rags of vapor. Jesse pulled up the collar of his duster. A fine misty rain settled on the heavy cloth.

–Nasty night to be out, Jesse said.

–We aren't going far, Edwards said.

Jesse kept pace with the journalist. Edwards was a big man. He was made bigger by a worsted caped topcoat and a tall beaver hat that he wore against the fall chill. They set off down the farm's driveway to a wagon road that led up the valley. The valley made a steep curve to the west, and it seemed as if they ascended into thicker darkness with every step. The pathetic beam of the miner's lantern would serve only to indicate to unseen eyes where they were, rather than where they were going. They came around the bend in the valley. The road was about fifty feet higher than the river. Down to their left, there appeared to be a bonfire flickering through the trees. Behind it, Jesse made out the lines of a long, low house.

–That's the spread, Edwards said.

–Someone's fixing a hog roast, Jesse said.

They turned down a pathway through the pines that led toward the twisting orange flames. It seemed as if there were torches all around the clearing but he couldn't quite see, for the trunks of the evergreens were too close together. Where they came out of the trees, about forty men — Jesse assumed they were all men — stood in a circle around the fire. The sheets, the hoods, the red crosses stitched above the heart of each man — of course, Jesse had heard of them, and the burnings and lynchings done to shore up the damage done to the old order. But he had never seen such a sight before this night. Half of the robed congregation held flaming torches in their hands, along with Sharp's carbines and Winchester rifles and some shotguns. Orange light flickered upon Jesse's pale duster. As the flames lit him up, a cheer arose from the faceless crowd, and they waved their torches and guns in the air.

Everyone in the goddamn county must know I'm here, he thought.

Edwards's vulpine grin betrayed no sense of apology. The hooded forms closed around Jesse and hands reached out to shake his. He gripped each hand briefly. Pushed forward toward the porch of the low log cabin, where the leader stood above the jostling white-robed crowd like a mad wizard. Although he, too, was hooded, his mask was rolled up to his forehead, and his bearded face the only one visible of all the men present.

–They is the law of God! the Wizard shouted. And the law of man! And when man's law is turned to corruption, they is the law of the invisible empire!

Jesse mounted the porch steps and the Wizard clapped him on the back and then draped an arm over his shoulders.

–We are proud to have you among us, the Wizard said.

Hope for any hideout in these hills was gone. For tongues were loose and the Pinkerton detectives were not governed by the laws of this empire. But such madness was contagious. Exhilarating.

–You see, Edwards said. You have to believe. We can do it.

Firelight flickered upon the exultant face of John Newman Edwards, the genius behind the fame of Jesse James, Edwards the would-be orchestrator of the rebirth of the Southern Nation. Jesse waved and the crowd cheered. These men read the *Kansas City Times* editorials and believed them more than he did. But the adulation thrilled him. The fame that was his and not his. The fame that Edwards had brought him. He had cast his lot with Edwards and Shelby. If he had any hope of escape from this madness, it was through the parole, the amnesty, that dangled before him, ever out of his reach, ever out of theirs. The hope that drove him on to new extremes of action that inspired men like these, hooded and robed in the firelight, to go out and vote for men who would seek his pardon. But if he had hoped to find respite in these hills, all hope of that was gone.

XXXI

THE SUN HAD LONG SINCE GONE DOWN AND NO MOON RISEN BUT only stars. The trunks of ash and maple and sycamore in the woods below the railroad embankment glowed faintly as if they held within their bark a supernatural light or a trace of day. The Milky Way laid its pale path through the high blue darkness and Scorpio had appeared over the canyon's rim. A perfect night for the operation. He had never robbed a train before, but he remembered how Bill Anderson had brought a train to a halt at Centralia. Bob Younger and Frank had levered the pins out of the ties and loosened a pair of rails. A resinous scent borne on a balmy wind wafted under Jesse's hood. He held his bay horse within a juniper grove beside the tracks. The white of his long Klan robes gave him the aspect of a mounted priest and the company that surrounded him, his five acolytes. He took a perverse and childlike pleasure in the ghost robes and more pleasure yet that Cole Younger and his two brothers had gravely agreed to habit themselves so. Six months had passed since the Klan meeting. He had left Kentucky to winter in Texas and met up with the Younger brothers down in Bonham. Whether it was the whiskey or the nostalgia for the guerrilla days of yore, they had decided that with their next operation they would show the world that Dixie was still alive and dancing. There was something ridiculous about the costumes, as if they were a troop of actors about to put on a play. A show that would assure them a review in all the newspapers. And for it, they would be paid in gold being shipped from mines in the West.

In the distance, the shuff and clatter of a train echoed quiet warning of its approach down the wide canyon of Council Bluffs and the sparks from its smokestack sent tiny red fireflies scintillating above the inky blur of the trees. The company eased their horses forward, and he halted them beside the track. Jim Younger swung a red lantern and the light of it turned his robe a deep red. A plume of steam and smoke uncoiled into the sky and obscured a swath of stars, while the walls of the bluffs echoed with the noise of the wheels that rattled upon the rails ever louder. The screech of brake, steel on steel, split the still air as the train took the curve around a cliff buttress and emerged from the trees, shadow from shadow, two lanterns down low casting a dim light over the rattling grid of the cowcatcher. The black bulk of the engine was but fifty yards away, and he was going to stop that huge machine. The train's brakes squealed and the steel wheels slid on the tracks and white sparks cascaded across the gravel. The engineer must have seen them. Jim's red lantern. The loco skidded toward the gap torn in the mutilated track. It was not going to stop. He swung his horse toward the bluffs as the front bogie wheels of the engine gouged gravel and the lurching tonnage slowly toppled. The engineer screamed as he fell from the cab. He disappeared beneath the black metal boiler as the engine clanged down the embankment, and Jesse whooped as it ripped through juniper, cracking trunk and branch, until it came to a stop on its side, hissing steam from every vermicular pipe and twisted valve and ruptured plate, wheels locked still and upturned to the face of the bluff like some overthrown metal dragon.

A night breeze rippled the folds of Jesse's long robe and flattened the mask to his face. He spurred his horse past the inverted locomotive and along the gravel of the embankment toward the front express car. The coupling of the tender was bent and misshapen where the engine had torn free. He drew the Navy Colt from its holster. Behind the tender, the carriages in the gold and green of the Chicago and Rock Island Railroad Company stood still and silent. Jesse dismounted directly onto the platform steps of the express car and tied the bay's reins to its steel handrail. He tried the handle of the carriage door and it would not move. He hammered against the paneled door with the butt of his pistol.

–Open the goddamn door or I'll burn this carriage to Hell with you inside it.

He hammered once more and heard the rattle of bolt within and a key clicking as it tipped the tumblers of the lock. The handle dipped and the door opened a crack. Jesse slammed his shoulder against the door and the body behind it took the full brunt of the blow and was hurled to the floor of the carriage. He stepped through the opening with his pistol raised and leaned over the dazed messenger. He knelt and pressed the muzzle of the Colt into the middle of the man's mustache. Two rat-like eyes stared up at him from a sharp-featured face. The foresight pressed against the tip of the narrow nose. Fear. There was a scent to fear, gross and intoxicating. He could make this man sweat, scream, turn pale, blubber like a child, even make him shit in his pants if he had the time.

–If you don't want me to blow your goddamn head off, Jesse said, you will open the safe. Do you understand me?

The messenger made a sound of assent somewhere between a grunt and a whine. Jesse stood up and stepped back. The messenger scuttled backward into a pool of lantern light that cast a yellow pallor on him. His right arm flailed against a desk chair, and he used the seat of it to help himself get to his feet, totally uncoordinated by fear. Fear made a man lose his dignity. Made him malleable. Jesse had learned that from Bill. At the back end of the carriage, a mesh door was padlocked in the center of the makeshift wall. Behind the meshing were sacks and trunks and in the corner a black safe with gilded lock and hinges. He had no time to waste.

–Come on, goddammit, open up, Jesse snapped.

Cole came into the carriage. He was gigantic in the white robe. The hood added a good six inches to his already tall frame. He came forward to the mesh door. The rat eyes darted glances from one hooded figure to the other. The messenger picked up the keys off the desk. His hands shook as he separated one from the bunch and opened the padlock.

–That's it, Jesse said. Help us out, now.

The messenger pulled the door open and entered the cage. Jesse stepped in behind him. The messenger fumbled and rattled the keys again and fitted one into the safe. The heavy door swung open. Cole was in the cage now.

–Stay on your knees but move aside, Jesse said.

The messenger shuffled to his left and Jesse placed the muzzle of the Colt to the bony forehead. A little vein pulsed at the temple.

Cole's white bulk knelt beside the safe. He stuffed the wads of bills into his sack.

–Goddammit, Cole said. They ain't but two thousand dollars in here and nothing else.

The messenger's eyes were closed under the muzzle of the pistol.

–Where's the shipment? Jesse said. The goddamn mine shipment.

The grease with which the man had plastered down his ratty hair began to trickle past his ear. Jesse jabbed the messenger's forehead with the pistol muzzle, and the man squealed.

–I'm talking to you, boy.

The eyes were wide open now. He would make him shut his eyes for good.

–Not this train, he said. The express. Seven o'clock. What you see in the safe, that's all we carrying, I swear to God.

The eyeholes of the mask weren't wide enough. The cloth of it was damp in front of his nose and mouth, stuck to his cheeks and chin. Sucking into his mouth. Suffocating him. He tore at the hood and flung it away. He swung the Colt and his arm jolted as the butt cracked across the messenger's skull. A great gout of blood ran down over the whorled ear, and the messenger crawled on the sawdust-covered floor. A flap of skin had separated from the scalp. His squeals were intolerable. Jesse kicked at the squirming body but the robe impeded his swing.

–Goddammit, I'll kill you, you son of a bitch.

He pointed the muzzle and Cole grabbed his arm.

–They ain't no gold, you hear me?

He heard him. He heard him as if from a great distance.

–Sneaky little son of a bitch.

–He don't know nothing, Cole said. Nothing, you hear me?

Cole's eyes stared out of the hood and mask. He lifted the sack in front of Jesse's face.

–That's it.

The light in the car was garish. He could have killed the son of a bitch. One dead messenger. It was suffocating in the car. He spun around and was out the door and down the steps to the gravel. The juniper-scented air wafted cool across his bare face. Frank, still mounted, was up ahead beside the first passenger car with Bob and Jim Younger. Jesse rushed alongside the baggage car to the steps of the front passenger car and grabbed the handrail. He turned to Frank and Bob.

–Get on the train, Jesse said. Have the passengers give up all they got.

–Hey! Cole yelled from behind him. Hey!

His voice was muffled by the white mask. Cole would not call his name, but what did it matter if he did?

–The mask! Cole yelled. The goddamn mask!

–I don't need no goddamn mask, Jesse called back.

What did he care if the messenger saw his face? Or if anyone saw his face? The newspapers would blame him for the robbery, anyway. It would make no difference to his parole or amnesty, for if Democrats controlled the House they would be sure to grant it. Same for a trial. If he was tried in a Confederate county, he would be acquitted; and enough men feared him in other counties that they would be loath to declare him guilty.

–You looking to get us all hung? Cole called. You got a death-wish, boy?

Jesse shook his head. He was not looking for Death. Neither was he afraid of Death. Death would come to him unseen, unknown, as the Good Book said, like a thief in the night. And as long as he kept Death present in front of his face, he knew he would have nothing to fear. He was untouchable. And Edwards and Shelby would get him amnesty for all his crimes. Barefaced, he stepped through the door of the carriage.

XXXII

IT WOULD TAKE THE PASSENGERS A GOOD THREE HOURS TO GET into a town and the laws a few hours more to raise a posse, and by the time the possemen worked out which direction he had gone, he might be halfway back to Clay County. The dawn sun laid a dappled hand upon his duster, and the leaves of the aspens shimmered above, the patterns on trees taking on the shapes and shadows of deformed faces and fantastic animals, for he had not slept in twenty-four hours and he rode in the twilight world between dream and waking. If he had been carrying the gold shipment, he might have enjoyed the ride but four hundred dollars a head was not enough to make him a rich man. He would need to make another raise soon. And not encumbered by those robes, either. The others rode in silence. Jesse kept them to the back trails of the woods and then drifted south and by late morning picked up a trail along the Missouri River. In two or three days, he would be with Zee. Lie low. He had agreed to meet her at her sister Annabelle's house. It was more than six months since he had seen her. Too long. He had a letter from her in his pocket that he had collected from the Hudspeth farm in the Cracker Neck when he was on his way north. She was as ardent as ever. Still talking about marriage, even though she never knew where he was from one day to the next. He had promised her a house and a quiet place to live where she could have their babies. The gold shipment he had missed would have bought them a spread down in Texas where they could have started a new life, with new names. Now he had to go see her empty-handed. But his hungry senses could almost smell her perfume, feel the rich tresses of her hair in his hands, and his imagination had him warm and swollen against his pommel when he heard the hum and the crack and saw the bark of the poplar splinter all at the same time and he twisted and ducked in his saddle ready for the next shot. His hand was at the Colt, and he saw the drift of smoke on the bluffs above the river but he didn't waste a return shot. He spurred the bay and galloped hard for a thick stand of cottonwoods where the road afforded some cover. He bent over, head back over his shoulder ready for the next round, Frank and the Youngers galloping in a bunch just behind him. If the shootist risked another shot and missed, Jesse would get him one way or another but the horse made the trees and he pulled it around. He scanned the boulders and the sparse trees along the riverside behind and above them. Cole slid a Sharp's rifle from his saddleboot.

–They ain't many more'n one, Jim Younger said. Else they'd all a-been taking a pop at us.

–Got to be more'n one, Frank said. Else he wouldn't have fired at all.

–They follered us over the goddamn state line, Bob Younger said.

His voice was high with surprise, almost as if he was insulted.

Jesse pursed his lips. Neither Frank nor any one of the Youngers was going to mention Jesse's barefaced robbery, though they would be thinking about it, and for the first time since he had taken to the bush after the war, he considered that he had miscalculated badly. And if someone had decided that the raid was made by the James Gang, the posse would have made toward Missouri right away.

–Should we try'n take 'em, Cole? Jim said.

–Waste a time.

–First chance we get, Jesse said, we'll cut east over the bluffs and head for the Platte. Give 'em some rough country to trail us through.

–Those sons a bitches ain't gonna show theirselves, Frank said, and they gonna keep any posse posted no matter which way we go.

–They ain't gonna leave no main trail to foller us and lose them boys that's follering them, Bob said.

–Let's go, Jesse said.

He had to get back to Clay County. That territory was his. But he would have to stay away from his mama's. She had more detectives for visitors these days than family.

Jesse turned his bay horse through the gate and into the yard of Annabelle Mimms's farmhouse, and Zee came out through the kitchen door, raced down the porch steps, and stopped suddenly in the middle of the yard to look at him. In that midday heat, her skin looked fresh and smooth, framed by her auburn ringlets. Almost virginal, dressed in white, a blouse with flounces upon her breast, a brown leather belt cinched tight above a pleated cotton skirt that fell to her ankles. Jesse pulled the bay horse to a halt beside her, and before his foot was out of the second stirrup, she was upon him. She rubbed her cheeks against the raw cotton of his dark blue shirt as if the smell of his sweat mixed with the musty scent of horse and straw and leather was some balmy form of attar. Since he had split up with Frank and the Youngers, he had been sleeping in the woods.

–I thought you'd never come, she said.

–Been south, he said. I missed you.

–Newspaper said you was in Iowa.

–Iowa, too.

That one foolish action in Iowa had unhinged his normal calm.

He slid his hands into Zee's ringlets, and the feel of her drove away his discomfort. If his hat had not been pulled down tight against the sun, he would have laid his sweaty forehead upon her pale and smooth one. He felt a hard, pleasurable warmth swell at his groin again.

–Let's go inside, she said.

She slid her arm around his waist. He squeezed her shoulder and pulled her to him as he led the bay toward the barn. Her head lay upon his chest. This was a woman that cared about him. Who went for months on end without seeing him and grabbed him tight as soon as he reappeared. He sensed that she was waiting for the news of where, finally, they were going to live together. This was supposed to be what he had come to tell her. The warm idea of just seeing her again fell away, and he was left with the realization that he had not brought her news of what he had promised her. No house in Kentucky to retreat to. To lie low in. A hideout that he would have been glad to have now that his face might be recognized in a court of law.

He slipped from her grip.

At the barn door, he lifted his saddlebags from the horse's rump, slung them over his shoulder, and let Annabelle's stable boy lead the horse away. Zee had sensed something amiss. He could tell from the puzzled expression on her face, the slight frown and the mouth a little slack, but she guided him to the doorway on the east side of the clapboard house and he kissed her in the cool of the hallway and she pressed herself to him until he drew back to look at her, his lean face above her, and he kissed her again and pulled back. She grabbed him by the shoulder and led him down the shady passage toward the kitchen.

–Did you go to Kentucky? she asked.

–And Texas, too, he said.

–Texas?

She opened the kitchen door.

–I was there most of the winter with Frank and Cole, he said.

–Frank and Cole?

She looked disappointed as if by some clairvoyance she divined that such an answer was of evil augury. He guided her into the kitchen, where Annabelle Mimms sat at the table. She held a cup of coffee cradled in her puffy pink hands. Her chestnut hair was pulled back behind her ears and tied with a piece of string. Her oval face was flushed and full and smooth except for a fine web of lines at the corner of her eyes. She had opened the collar of her dress that hung like a great russet tent over her gravid body. Her hand moved languidly in the heat as if even to raise the cup to her lips was a burden. It was as though Annabelle was a swollen monument to his failure. He had to make light of it.

–Whoa, Mama's grown some, Jesse said.

He slid away from Zee and leaned his saddlebags against the table leg. He hooked his hat on the finial of a chair and shook out his long dark hair. Zee's teeth worried her bottom lip.

–Be due in a month, Annabelle said.

–I'm so jealous, Zee said.

Jesse flushed. His face and ears were hot and his tongue was wooden.

–I could eat, he said.

–Why don't you all go ahead, Annabelle said. I need to rest some. Take a nap.

–But I hardly seen you, Jesse said.

Annabelle pushed against the flat of the table to come to her feet. She swung from side to side like a great bell in motion and moved toward the kitchen door.

–We can talk later, Annabelle said. You two got a lot to catch up on.

He was suddenly awkward, alone in the kitchen with Zee.

–I thought we might have a picnic, Zee said, down by the river.

He was relieved by the suggestion.

–I can't wait, he said.

His words sounded awfully hollow.

Zee, nervous, dashed across the kitchen to the pantry cupboard and opened the perforated door. The smell of cinnamon and clove wafted out. She lifted out a tiered cake on a board and brought it to the table. Some of the fruit filling had oozed over the sides of each layer.

–I baked us a Kentucky stack cake, she said. In honor of our new home state.

He avoided her eyes.

–Here, he said, let's get down to the river.

* * *

Not a breath of breeze cooled the heavy air. A white haze of clouds sat like a lid on the world and seemed to force the sun's hard glare through the leaves of the cottonwoods. The incessant chirp of crickets grated in the stillness. Zee brushed by the Queen Anne's lace that grew over each side of the footpath. She was beautiful. If all went well, he would slip his arm around her down by the riverside and carefully, ever so carefully, help her take off her dress. The two baskets over his arms and his saddlebags over his shoulder encumbered him. Bright orange-and-black monarchs fluttered up off the purple clover to either side of them. It should have been idyllic, but there was a weight and an awkwardness between them.

At the riverbank, Zee entered a grove of cherry trees and unfolded a blanket. The scant shadow offered no relief from the stifling heat. Jesse could hardly breathe with it, and he felt sweat trickle down his ribs when he sat down next to Zee. He set down the baskets between them. He pulled the Navy Colt from his cartridge belt and laid that down next to him on his left side and unbuckled the cartridge belt and wrapped it around the holster for the Remington and set that down on the blanket close to his right hand for safety, even if he was sure that he had shaken the posse.

The river, low and slow-moving, reflected a harsh white light that was hard to gaze upon. Downstream, where the water pooled, a gray heron swiveled its long beaked head on the serpentine neck, one leg raised, the long clawed toes dangling as if in indecision as to the safety of its next step. The cloudy anvil of a thunderhead loomed over the trees on the opposite bank, and Jesse thought that if the storm did break, it just might freshen the air. Somehow make it easier between them.

–You was baptized in this river, she said.

–That was upstream a ways, he said.

–I guess you didn't find a place, she said.

–I met Edwards down in Kentucky like we planned, but he managed to let the whole of Nelson County know I was planning on living there. Even had a welcome party laid on for me.

–So you went to Texas? she said.

–Yeah, met up with Frank. . . . I thought maybe I could find a spread down there. I seen a place we could go, but I ain't got nary a nickel to set up house for you.

She looked puzzled.

–But the train in Iowa, she said. We already heard. The newspapers.

–We didn't clear but two thousand dollars between the five of us.

–That ain't what the papers said.

–The papers lie, he said.

–But Mr. Edwards?

–Well, Mr. Edwards.

He shrugged. He looked down at the veins and bones on the backs of her hands. The crickets to her right ceased chirping so that the river rill filled the silence. Lightning flickered across the water. The heron flapped its wings like giant sails and rose into the air, legs trailing, and then it was away over the trees and out of sight. The thunderclap was short and sharp as if a door banged shut. This was not how he planned it at all. On the ride down here, he had imagined them falling into each other's arms, kissing, catching up on all they had done for seven long months.

–Well, what we got in these baskets? he said.

Jesse pulled back the muslin covering-cloth. Three maps lay folded next to two china plates, two cups, a gingham tablecloth, two forks, two knives. He took out the maps and read the legends: Wright's New Map and Guide to the State of Missouri; another for the State of Kentucky; and yet another for the State of Tennessee.

–I thought you could show me where we was going to live, she said.

Her eyes were brimful.

He made as if to unfold the map of Kentucky, changed his mind, and set down on the blanket all three of those useless pieces of paper upon which she had wasted a dollar and five cents. Two fat flies buzzed around the second basket, and he waved them away before he lifted out the Kentucky stack cake and laid it on the blanket next to the three maps. The cake had sagged on one side; apple and sugar and spice filling dripped down and stained the cloth wrap. The flies whirled around his batting palm and settled again on the sticky muslin.

–How was Frank and Cole? she said.

–You know them, he said.

He looked up at her finally. His hand drifted toward the muslin, then across to his armpit and then he rubbed the back of his neck.

–You know, Zee, he said, this ain't no life for you.

–What you mean?

–The way things turned out, he said, I ain't got nothing to offer you.

That sounded wrong.

–Right now, I mean.

Both her hands fell in her lap and she clasped her fingers together.

–Is that what you come to say?

She raised her chin and sucked in breath, her mouth puckered up. Her thumbs were pressed down hard down on the backs of her hands. She looked him in the eye.

–What do you fear about marrying me? she said. That you'll drag me into your war or that I'll drag you out of it? Because I tell you one thing, I don't want no man as can't stand up for what he believe in. And what I believe in.

–This ain't a game, he said.

He regretted the words as soon as they left his mouth.

–You think it's a game for a woman to wait six years on a man? You think I don't have any desire in my body? You promised me before God. You promised me when my papa died that you would take care of me. I don't care if we ain't got a brass cent. But, you know, I cain't hold you to no promise if you're unwilling.

–I seen a place, he said. Don't think I didn't look.

Thunder rolled long and loud across the river.

–That ain't what I said, Zee said.

Shit, he thought. All I meant to say was that we'd just have to wait a while longer. The leaves in the cherry trees began to whisper. She reached across and picked up the pistol that lay closest to her. It was the Colt Navy, heavy and black, with a long octagonal barrel. She stood up, legs apart and feet planted firmly. She lifted the pistol with both hands, cocked it, and pointed at the river. Jesse came up on one knee. She squeezed the trigger. The gun roared and twisted in her fingers, the white ball of smoke rolled back toward her, and she screwed up her eyes against it. She cocked the pistol, the hammer coming back easily into place because it was worn and well oiled.

–What you doing Zee? he said.

–I thought I saw a cottonmouth swimming this way.

Jesse laughed.

–They ain't many I know could hit a cottonmouth twenty yards away. Not with a Navy Colt.

The branches of the cherry trees bent and rustled in the rising wind. She lifted the pistol and fired again, the flat report mingling with a rumble of thunder. A shower of rain hissed down over the river and rattled into the grove. He was on his feet.

–I don't see no cottonmouth, he said.

She brought the hammer back. Click. Cocked. She squeezed the trigger. The gun roared in her hands.

If a goddamn posse was about . . .

–Stop that! he yelled. You'll bring down half the county on us.

–Look what the Yankees have done to you, she said. Done to us. To me.

She bent her thumb over the hammer again. He twisted the gun from her hand, held it down by his side. The rain dropped a hissing wet curtain upon them, soaking her, soaking him, soaking the blanket and the baskets and the cake on the blanket and the useless maps.

–You could be dead tomorrow, she said. And me a widow. But I would rather live with the loss than only to have lived halfway.

She turned from him, scrabbled over the blanket, lifted the ruined cake, and dumped it back into its basket.

–I'll get the money, Jesse said. You just have to be patient. We'll get married when I can buy us a spread.

–You don't want to, she said.

She picked up the basket containing the sodden mess and ran into the downpour, back toward Annabelle's house.

–Zee, come back here!

That wasn't right at all. One big haul, that's all it would take. He would marry her and take her to Texas. And with what he had done in Iowa, he had to get away, now. Clay County would be crawling with detectives and lawmen for months to come. One big haul before he left Missouri was all it would take. He was sure that he could pull it off and they could get married and disappear.

XXXIII

A DARK HALO LAY AT THE PERIPHERY OF HIS VISION, WHILE ALL in front of him was lit up as if he regarded an underwater world through a glass-bottomed bucket. Between the steel gleam of the rails and the creosoted ties, each single nut of gravel rose off the earth so clearly that he felt as if he could count each one. This was the way that everything had looked when the clerk raked his face at the Kansas City Fair and when his rage exploded against the messenger on the train at Council Bluffs. But now the rage he felt was cold, silent, insinuating itself through his nerves, magnificently thrilling, beyond his control, and, as such, it revealed to him that he was a mystery to himself. He had once believed that each decision he had made had come through some volition of his own, but now it seemed that he had been guided by something unknown. This was a blissful rage, like the hand of God that had guided him on the battlefield. Everything was part of this greater power: the war, the killing in Gallatin, the meeting with Shelby and Edwards, his fame, and this act that he was about to perform in a tiny railroad stop in Missouri that would be trumpeted in the press by friend and foe alike across the nation. And so certain was he of the outcome of this raid, that in the manner of a prophet — upon the folded vellum in his pocket — he had written his version of what was about to happen. It was prophecy and divination both, for if all turned out as he had written it, would it not prove that he was but working God's Will?

Jesse reached the decking of the station building, soft and mildewed boards, lichens bright blue-gray in their fissures, that absorbed the sound of his footfalls. He walked as if in a silent dream toward the one-roomed flag station. The others who followed him were like ghosts. Each trunk and branch of the bare trees that rose above the building was purple in the dusk. The sign hanging from the paint-flaked timbers of the porch's batten board read Gad's Hill, black on white. The letters stood out sharp, each line stark. Change but two letters and would it not read God's Will?

The wind gusted and buffeted and slapped at the folds of Jesse's pale duster. The door of the depot was shut tight against the winter's chill. He — and each man of the company who followed him — raised a heavy bandanna to mask the lower part of his face.

Jesse leaned an ear to the door, and from within came the sound of men at cards, a so-called game of chance, but each fall of a card upon all those tables in the world now seemed to belong to some greater, preordained order.

–He raised again, by God.

–Damn your eyes, Sheldon, I ain't about to fold.

Jesse reached for the black metal latch. It clicked up and he stepped inside the room. Five men sat around a table close to a potbellied stove. They fell into silence when they saw him, their faces crestfallen as if each man had drawn a losing hand. And he, Jesse James, was the winner.

–I believe there's a train due, Jesse said.

His voice was muffled behind the mask.

–I'm the stationmaster here.

The man who had spoken pushed back his chair and came to his feet. He was not much taller than he had looked sitting. He was graying and corpulent and the nose on his round red face was bulbous from long years in the company of the bottle, but his bright dark eyes and well-trimmed mustache and whiskers gave him an air of authority. At least over this small domain. All the other card players sat hunched over the table. One man fumbled his cards: two pairs — tens and sixes — and an ace fell upon the green baize. Two of the others held their fans of cards in front of them like dowagers at an opera. The last of them — the one with his back to Jesse, the neck shaved and raw and pimpled — had his fingers clawed on the edge of the table, his cards folded in front of him.

At Jesse's shoulder, his brother raised a coil of thin rope.

–We'll have to inconvenience you gentlemen at the table by tying your hands and feet.

One man at the table nodded and Frank uncoiled the rope.

–I'd appreciate if you'd kindly flag the train, Jesse said to the stationmaster.

The stationmaster nodded. He reached for his uniform frock coat on the bench that ran along the far wall and pulled it on. He took his shiny-peaked hat from the bench and settled it on his head. Jesse motioned with the pistol and stepped aside to allow the stationmaster to pass by. The Colt followed his back as a divining rod follows water. A rusty tin pail stood behind the door, and within it was a set of flags furled tight and tied about their handstaffs, each color a simple cipher in the railroad man's code. The stationmaster reached down and selected the rolled red cloth, tucked the flag under his arm, and waddled out through the door and onto the platform.

A whisper of dry yellow oak leaves swirled and skittered past Jesse's boots and tumbled along the mildewed planks of the decking. The stationmaster was down on the track, his short legs stretching to reach each successive tie. A tall signal post stood at the top of a steep grade that emerged from a deep cutting. Bare sycamores crowded the cutting that in summer would have made a leafy tunnel. Red cloth fluttered in the wind as the station master unfurled the flag and reached up to plant the staff in the signal pole at the edge of the tracks. The stationmaster pulled his fob watch from the pocket of his vest.

–Won't be but five minutes.

–Get back on the platform, Jesse said.

Jesse let the stationmaster lead the way back to the building and sat down beside him on the damp bench that was formed of the same rotten lumber as the deck of the depot shack. He rested the Colt on his knee. Between his boots, the blue-gray lichens had eaten away the wood of the deck to form miniature caves that had spread like a diminutive forest through crack and hole, each clustered growth branched like coral testament to the wonder of God's creation. It was only in action that he felt this way. Was anything else worth living for?

–Two minutes, said the stationmaster.

He had his fob watch in the palm of his hand.

A labored shuffing and the clack of wheels and the hiss of valves rose out of the cutting. The high whistle screeched. The engine emerged. Great slow gouts of black smoke belched from the stack. Steam rolled and rose between the spokes of the steel wheels and around the boiler. The black bulk of the locomotive strained by and brought tender and carriages to a halt directly in front of the depot shack. In all that long assembly of wheel and truck and valve and piston, with its temporary population of passengers and crew, all that concerned Jesse was the contents of one small steel box.

Bob Younger and Arthur McCoy dashed out from the shack and ran toward the engine. Jesse got up from the bench and followed behind them. He stopped at the coupling between engine and tender. In the cab's twilight interior, orange light from the open firebox flickered on the sooty overalls of the fireman and the engineer and on Bob Younger and Arthur McCoy. Bob waved his pistols before the faces of the crewmen. Arthur was at the blackened rack of tools. He drew a heavy sledgehammer from among the sooty shovels and tongs and pokers and swung it down to Jesse. Jesse tucked the Colt in his belt, gripped the handle of the sledge, and ran back along the tender. He mounted the steps of the express car, swung up the heavy sledge, and slammed it down against the door. A great dent appeared in the woodwork, but the door held. He swung up the sledge and slammed it down again. The iron head bounced off the panel and dropped onto the car's platform and a muffled voice came from behind the door.

–I'll open up.

Jesse drew the Colt. The lock rattled and the door swung inward. The messenger had stepped well back into the car. He was a tall man and young. He sported a thin mustache that reached his chin and met the sideburns that followed the entire line of his jaw and disappeared under his peaked cap.

Jesse aligned the foresight with the bridge of the man's nose.

–I have a family, the messenger said.

Jesse looked into the blue eyes, but he could no more imagine the faces of this man's children than he could his own as yet unborn.

–Let's get to it, Jesse said.

He scanned the carriage for the safe. There was a rolltop desk and a wooden armchair and next to them a rack fixed to the wall from which hung a shiny black slicker. A shotgun rested on a different sort of rack on the other side of the desk. A small stove stood midway down the carriage. It was unlit, certainly, for the air smelled of damp and had a chill to it more than did the air outside. The safe was in shadow, butted up against the rolltop desk. Jesse waved the Colt.

–Open the safe, he said.

Cole came into the carriage. He had in his clutch a Smith & Wesson revolver. The barrel was shorter than the Colt's, and it gave the gun an ugly look. The messenger's face was a blank. He folded himself down in front of the steel box and unlocked it with a key that he took from a string around his neck. The door came open slowly. Jesse shook out a wheat sack and handed it to the messenger.

–Fill it, he said.

Jesse glanced inside the safe. Both levels of the safe were stacked with sheaves of new bills. Finally. He could keep his promise to Zee. Get out of Missouri to where he was unknown. Jesse saw Texas. Saw Mexico. He saw Zee in a bridal dress. And Mama beside her. He saw the sun a great white and blinding ball in the sky. The sound in his ears was like the sea.

–Praise the Lord, Jesse said. They's money in there.

The messenger scooped piles of bills into the sack. It bulged under the weight and bulk of the oblong packets. When the safe was empty, Jesse grabbed the sack.

–Let's go, Jesse said.

Cole followed Jesse out of the door and down the steps of the express car, and Jesse was running now, his boots grinding the gravel, the heavy sack swinging in his fist. They came up onto the deck in front of the depot.

–Hey you, Jesse called.

The stationmaster looked up. Jesse tucked the Colt into his belt, pulled back his duster, and took a folded piece of heavy-gauge paper from the inside pocket of his jacket. He handed the paper to the bleary-eyed stationmaster. It was as if the act of writing had ensured the success of the operation.

–You can give this to the first newspaperman comes around asking about the robbery, Jesse said. I left a space for you to fill in the exact amount we stole 'cause I don't have time to count it.

XXXIV

JESSE WAS AT THE ROUGH END OF A FIVE-DAY DRUNK AND IT WAS no time to stop, for the kitchen was full of friends and family in celebration of his setting a date for the wedding. Mama was flushed at the hearth, where a fire roared against a cold and damp March evening. She had the oven door open, and with a long meat fork she poked at a stuffed hog maw. All her family around her for the first time in years: Jesse and Frank and Susan and the brood of half brothers and half sisters that she had had with Samuels after Pa had died: John, Sallie, Fannie, and Archie. He could see that she was happy despite the risk they were running. The laws were now making regular stops at the Samuels farm.

Little Archie was behind Mama, leaning on her back, in seven-year-old heaven, for the grown-ups had been fussing around him for hours and even singing him songs. Jesse braced himself against the hearth mantel and looked into the mirror. His eyes had sunk into his head, and the five days of growth on his face gave him a seedy and haggard aspect. His long hair was lank and dirty and fell to the shoulders of his blue plaid shirt.

–Get ye a drink, he said to his reflection.

There was a whiskey bottle on the table in front of Jim Anderson, who sat at the table with Pa Samuels and John Newman Edwards. Jim had come over from Carrollton County; Jesse hadn't seen him since the Gallatin disaster, the operation that had begun his life on the dodge.

All the men were drunk or half drunk. Jim, bloodshot eyes peering up at him, poured a drink for Jesse and handed it up to him. Jesse sipped at it, eager for the warm glow to spread through his blood and take away his discomfort. Even Zee had been sipping at the bourbon, and she sat next to Frank near the kitchen door. She was searching through the family Bible for a passage to read out loud. The Good Book slipped off her knees, and she twisted her whole body to keep it from falling on the floor and not spill her glass over its pages.

–Go easy there, Miss Zee, called Edwards.

She smiled drunkenly back at him, then pointed at the window where the children stood.

–Oh Jesse, she said. The children.

–Whoa there, Jesse called. Let me do that.

Young Sallie, who was already eight, was at the lantern, and Fannie, who was ten, had the kerosene. And John, being the eldest at twelve, had the matches. Jesse downed his burning bourbon and set the glass back on the table next to the bottle at Edwards's elbow, and then he shooed the children away from the lantern and over toward Zee and Frank. Jesse took the glass chimney off the lantern, unscrewed the lamp fitting, and filled the glass reservoir. He looked out through the kitchen window.

Arthur McCoy came racing across the yard, his Winchester held across his chest, duster flapping. Then he was at the door and into the kitchen.

–We got a uninvited guest, Arthur said.

–Just one?

–Far as I can tell.

The whole kitchen was transformed into a silent waltz of impending violence. Frank picked up the shotgun that stood beside the sideboard and brought Jesse his Colt. Jesse stepped behind the kitchen door, the pistol barrel raised upright at his shoulder. Pa Samuels picked up little Archie to let Mama get up from the oven. Arthur twisted around to face the door, the Winchester cradled nonchalantly in the crook of his arm. Next to Frank's empty chair, young Fannie and Sallie held one another's hands and looked down at the floor. Jim Anderson crossed to the sideboard, where he had left his sidearms. Edwards poured himself another drink but remained uncharacteristically silent. Zee put her arm around John Samuels, and he made a pistol of his fingers, pointed at the door, dropped his thumb like a hammer.

–Bang! John said.

–Answer the door, Mama, Jesse said.

He was stone cold sober now. Every sinew and tendon in his body was taut.

In Pa Samuels's arms, Archie began to whimper and then to wail and, as if Archie's fear was contagious, John began to cry and Sallie and Fannie wrapped their arms around each other.

The stranger hailed the house.

–Get these kids out of here, Jesse said.

Zee opened the door to the passageway, and Pa Samuels shepherded his flock of children down it and toward the bedroom. Edwards sipped at his bourbon, keeping his eye on the door where Mama stood. Mama still had the long meat fork clutched in her grip. She lifted the latch when the drop of boots sounded on the porch steps.

–Mrs. Samuels?

The voice was a deep bass, but young.

–What can I do for ye? Mama said.

–I come looking for work.

–What kinda work?

–Just to hire on. Ploughing and planting time. Thought you might need a extra pair a hands and a strong back.

Jesse motioned with the pistol to bring him inside.

–Might be we do, Mama said. Come on in.

She stepped back from the door, and the stranger came into the room sideways. Jesse pushed Mama aside and pressed the pistol to the stranger's head below the battered brim of his hat. He had a narrow nose and a small mustache and the thin-lipped mouth was a tight, nervous line. The heavy eyebrows stayed slightly raised, and the stranger stared straight into the muzzles of two pistols, a Winchester, and a twelve-gauge shotgun. He was a big man and looked as if he was capable of hard work. His jacket was worn, but under it he had a set of new overalls with a bulge in the bib pocket.

–Do you know where you are, boy? Jesse said.

–Samuels farm, the stranger said.

–This farm been mentioned in every newspaper in the state of Missouri and far beyond and you decide to come here to look for work?

The stranger nodded.

–Empty your pockets, Jesse said.

–I don't see . . .

Jesse smacked the long barrel of the Colt across the top of the man's ear and the tattered hat tumbled from his head and his canvas knapsack slumped to the floor. The man's hand came up and blood seeped between the fingers. Jesse bent at the waist and swung the butt of the pistol against the side of the stranger's left kneecap. The man screamed and fell heavily on his side.

–Lord's sake, Jesse, you'll frighten the children, Mama said.

The children weren't in the room.

–Get up, you son of a bitch, Jesse said.

The stranger writhed on the floor, clutching the damaged knee. Jesse grabbed him by his collar and yanked him upright.

–Empty your pockets, Jesse said.

The man's hands fluttered around, and he pulled a handkerchief from his jacket pocket, then a wallet and two pencils and a tobacco pouch from the bib pocket of the overalls. He held the possessions in front of him on open palms. Blood trickled down onto the collar of his homespun shirt.

–That's it, the stranger said.

–Take your jacket off, Jesse said. Let the rest drop.

Wallet, pouch, and pencils fell from his hands and clattered to the floor. He pulled off his jacket and Jesse took it and turned every pocket inside out. He found nothing but lint.

–You got a gun? Frank said.

–No.

–Look in his poke, Frank, Jesse said.

–Listen . . . the stranger began.

Jesse banged the muzzle under the man's cheekbone and left a round welt on the skin. Zee giggled and her hand went up to her mouth.

–Mama, why don't you and Josie see how the children are doing? Jesse said.

–Come on, Josie, Mama said to Zee.

Zee looked across at Jesse and gave him a small nervous smile before she closed the door behind her. Jesse turned back to the stranger.

–Strip, you son of a bitch, Jesse said.

The stranger glanced from Frank to Jim Anderson and back to Jesse again. He unhooked the suspenders of his overalls and let them hang down by his sides. He pulled off his shirt. He wore a white undershirt and there was a chain around his neck. Jesse yanked at the chain and the clasp snapped. A round gold locket dangled from the chain. Jesse popped it open and saw that it was engraved with two names inside a heart, John and Molly. Jesse pocketed the locket. The man had the singlet off. He had a finely muscled body. He unbuttoned the sides of the overalls and they dropped to bunch around his ankles.

At the table, Edwards sipped at his bourbon as if he were watching a floor show in a Kansas City saloon bar. Jesse was sure as hell that he would not be printing this story.

–Take your goddamn shoes off, Jesse said.

The stranger struggled with the laces of his new brogans and pulled them off. Then he stepped out of his overalls. Arthur McCoy lifted them off the floor and turned out the pockets. He came up with six dollars and change. Frank was at the canvas knapsack. He pulled out a towel, four shirts, two sets of long underwear, and then he lifted a Smith & Wesson revolver out of the bottom of the bag. He turned it over in his hands.

–Well, what have we here? Frank said. P. G. G.

–You wouldn't happen to be a Pinkerton would you? Jesse said.

–May as well take off the socks and drawers too, Jim Anderson said.

Jim had a wide grin. The Pinkerton bent over, favoring his bruised left knee, and divested himself completely. His manhood had shriveled. It sat like a pale nubbin in the copious brown bush.

–If this man's a Pinkerton, Jim said, they come pretty ill-equipped.

–You come alone? Jesse asked.

The man nodded.

–If you come with others, Jesse said, you better tell us now how many.

–I'm alone, the Pinkerton said.

–You lying to me? Jesse said.

The Pinkerton shook his head.

Jesse tucked the pistol into his belt and reached into the back pocket of his pants and slid out his long-handled clasp knife. He opened it and turned the long thin blade sharp side up. At the table, Edwards stiffened.

–Arthur and Jim are going to look outside now, Jesse said. And if you are lying to me, I will cut that off and gut you. Do you understand?

The Pinkerton nodded.

–You have one more chance to tell me the truth. Is there anyone outside?

The Pinkerton shook his head.

–Put your clothes on, Jesse said. I ain't gonna harm you, I just want you to take a message to your brethren in Chicago.

Edwards stood up as the Pinkerton pulled on his overalls and his shirt. The journalist nervously smoothed at his heavy mustache as if he was anxious to ask a question but for once was unable or unwilling to open his mouth. Frank and Jim took the Pinkerton by the arms and led him out the door.

Edwards touched Jesse's elbow. Jesse had never seen him so uncomfortable, his eyes darting around and a slight twitch above the right side of his mustache.

–He's seen me here, Jesse, Edwards said.

–It don't matter, Jesse said.

As clear as daylight, he could already see the ditch in the woods in Jackson County where the Pinkerton's body would lie.

XXXV

HE RAN HIS FINGERTIPS OVER HIS SMOOTH AND ANGULAR FACE to trace for the prickle of a missed whisker. He was shaved clean and his hair washed and combed out long to the shoulders of his crisp cotton shirt. He pulled the bow tight on his black tie and smoothed down the long ends of it. His brother, Frank, helped him on with his frock coat and handed him his hat, which he settled solemnly upon his head as he regarded himself in the mirror of Press Webb's bedroom. It was neighborly of Press to loan his house for the wedding preparations. Jesse had been with sporting women and he had been with backwoods farm girls eager to please Missouri's most famous outlaw, but Zee Mimms had always been the woman he had come back to. The woman — a girl then — who had nursed him back to health after the war. Who had taken him to church to pray. Been at his side when he went to get baptized. Who had waited for this day, seven long years.

–Time to go, Frank said.

Frank had a twisted smirk on his square face. He had trimmed his mustache and oiled his hair. It wouldn't be long before Frank was married himself. When both of them had hidden out at the Ralston farm, Annie Ralston had made her intentions very clear to his brother. Frank was going to be his best man. Just as in any other operation. Jesse left the bedroom and descended the rickety stairs. Whoever had built them had had little skill as carpenter, for each tread seemed to be of a different width and distance from the next, and they creaked and moaned under the weight of a man's boot. Jesse came out onto the porch. The Younger brothers were already mounted, each one dressed in his black Sunday-best three-piece suit and armed with a Winchester rifle and two side arms. These men had stood by his side and would all risk their lives for him as he would for them. There was no stronger bond. His coming marriage could not interfere with that.

Cole Younger, broad-shouldered and bearded like the Devil himself, sat upon a liver-chestnut quarter horse. Beside him, his brother Jim leaned forward and caressed the neck of his grullo. Jim was somewhat slighter than Cole, though balding just like him where he had tilted his hat back to reveal the paler skin above his forehead. He had a scrubby beard but no mustache. And Bob, the youngest Younger, was with them, too. The boy had no meat on his bones and a little fuzz on his upper lip, but he belonged with the company as much as any of his older brothers. Jesse was going south after the wedding, and he did not know when he would see these men again. To this sadness was added the death of John Younger. All three of the Younger brothers wore black armbands in memory of John, who had been killed not a month before in a Pinkerton ambush. No vengeance could repair that loss. Jim Younger had done for the detectives who had shot John, but that was no consolation to the family. John's death had cast a pall upon Jesse's wedding day. Jesse trusted in the Lord's goodwill that the Pinkertons would not show up at Annabelle Mimms's house. Jesse mounted up and they all set off for the house of Zee's sister. He was riding with his pistols in saddle holsters, for he had no wish to take his marriage vows encumbered by his cartridge belt and weapons, though he already missed the weight of them upon his hips. A few white clouds drifted across the blue spring sky below which they rode through the woods of Clay County until they came upon the Mimms farmhouse from the rear. Beyond the split-log fence the lawn was freshly scythed and narcissus was in full bloom in the borders, the white and yellow trumpets at sway and purple and white crocuses in a line below them. Tent canvas lifted and fell in the garden as if it were a great white lung breathing the morning breeze. A vision of peace and tranquillity that he did not wish to be disturbed by any Pinkerton or lawman or any other unforeseen intrusion.

Zee's uncle, Sam Ralston, had a blaze going at the fire pit between the fence and the tent. A young hog was spitted and set between two sawhorses. The pig was pallid and forlorn-looking, with the slit in its pink skin hanging open and red where it had been gutted. Clell Miller and Arthur McCoy, both dressed in suits and hard-brimmed hats, sat on the fence rail. Clell Miller held a new Winchester rifle propped up on his thigh, and his jacket bulged at the waist on right and left where his pistols were holstered in his cartridge belts. He was a big-boned farm boy with a ring of whiskers around his smooth face. Trustworthy. He had been with them on a bank raid in Corydon, Iowa, and had acquitted himself admirably, showed no sign of fear or nerves. Next to Clell, Arthur McCoy looked a good deal more dangerous. A veteran of the war, he was grizzled and bearded and longhaired. It was a comfort to see him and the shotgun laid across his knees, though Jesse expected no trouble, for he had kept the wedding secret to all but their guests and they were all sworn to silence. Jesse dismounted, and Annabelle's stable boy, Quentin, came over to take the reins. Frank and the Younger boys climbed down and the James's own Negro, Ambrose, helped Quentin with the horses.

Close to the tent entrance, John Edwards bellowed a greeting and waved. This year, Edwards had said. The day was imminent when he would get amnesty. They had enough Democratic members in the House now to push hard for it. And Jesse's popularity among ex-Confederates had helped to put them there and would ensure the resolution's success. Edwards and Shelby would not let those members forget it. Edwards had already published a special supplement about the James and Younger families in his newspaper and entitled it *The Terrible Quintette.* Edwards had lavishly described their exploits in the war and reminded their supporters of the depredations of the Union militia during and after the war. Edwards would be writing a report on the wedding, and he would announce to the world that Jesse and Zee had left Missouri and gone to live in Mexico, adding a love story to Jesse's living legend. Edwards was certain it would build yet more sympathy for the James Gang. Zee had been thrilled by Edwards's articles, and she and Jesse had decided to name their firstborn son after him. A son that he was sure would not be long in coming.

Jesse raised a hand to the journalist. Edwards strode into the tent to take his place among the congregation next to General Jo Shelby, who sat ramrod straight on his chair, eyes front, the big beard combed out upon the chest of his uniform which lent a dignified and martial air to the coming ceremony.

From the road came voices and the clop of hooves and the rattle of buggy wheels as the last few stragglers arrived for the wedding. Under the tent a fiddler tuned up and sawed out a few bars of a reel. Jesse was surprised at how shaky he felt, and he wondered if it showed to his brother and to those around him. He thought of Zee and the night that they would spend together with unreasonable trepidation. This day and coming night, more than any other, were loaded with portent for his future. Jesse ran a finger inside the rim of his collar as if to loosen it.

–Let's go on in, Frank said.

Jesse nodded and walked shoulder to shoulder with his brother down the aisle between the wooden chairs. Jesse did not look to left or right but he was conscious of the eyes upon him, his family's and those of neighbors who had stood by him in wartime and since. Zee's Uncle William stood behind a wooden podium. He was bareheaded, and the skin of his clean-shaven face and his broad brow and the crown of his bald head was colored a deep red from the sun. Thick strands of silver hair were slicked back over the small ears that lay tight against his head. His eyes were round and wide as if he would read every face in his flock and miss not a wrinkle — of which he had few himself running down over his round cheeks almost to the pleasantly upturned mouth. Just as a preacher ought, he wore a dark suit and had a small brass collar button on his shirt. A black Bible was clamped to his side by his left elbow.

The piano began the introduction to the hymn. Fiddle and a strummed guitar joined in before the congregation's voices.

–The Lord's my-y shep-he-rd, I'll . . .

Jesse commenced to mouth the words, but he stopped and smiled awkwardly when he found a lump in his throat. He and Frank stopped in front of the preacher just as they had done in the rehearsal. But now this was real and all seemed to be happening so fast.

. . . and my cup overflows.

The preacher nodded up the aisle.

The band struck up the "Wedding March" and Frank stood at Jesse's shoulder and his big square head nodded. Jesse looked back down the aisle as the music played and Zee Mimms smiled through her veil at him. From her waist fell layer upon layer of white organza and white satin flowers all around the borders and a lace collar lay upon her shoulders and a tulle veil and a long satin train that Jesse's eight-year-old half-brother, Archie, held up off the grass. Archie's hair was slicked down and his freckled face was solemn. Jesse caught a glimpse of Cole Younger out of the corner of his eye and a sudden sense of dread trickled through his nerves about the Pinkertons. Then Zee was at his side. Praise the Lord. The music stopped. Uncle William opened his prayer book.

–Hey!

The sound came from the road, and Jesse glanced back over his shoulder and out of the tent. Beyond the fence, Clell Miller stood in the road. In front of him was no lawman or spy or Pinkerton. He had his shotgun pointed at a raggedy Negro who sat upon a motheaten mule. The Negro must have stopped on the road to watch the wedding ceremony.

–Git outta here, nigger! Clell shouted.

The mule turned, and all that Jesse could see was the Negro's back, the jacket ripped, head bowed under his battered hat, the bony shanks of his tired mount rising and falling, poking the air like sticks in sacking. The dark head nodded. The black man lifted a hand, the two middle fingers bent over as if in a gesture of contempt or to ward off some evil spirit or, worse yet, to curse them. Jesse prayed silently.

–Lord, Thou art my refuge and my strength, thwart Thou the devil's hand that snatches at my soul, for today is the day of my matrimony in Thy sight, and not yet the Day of Judgment. Hold at bay the forces of evil that clamor all around me.

And he turned once more to the radiant woman by his side.

XXXVI

JESSE SPUN THE CAST-IRON BLACK BAR ON ITS PIVOT AND PULLED back the stout oak shutters to hook them in place on the whitewashed wall. A draft bellied out the homespun curtains, its chill ethereal fingers pushing from the ill-fitting casement. He peered through the frigid gap between the curtains and out through the soot-streaked panes. Rain slanted and whirled between the townhouses of Twelfth Street and darkened the gray light of the afternoon. Across the street, a hearse drawn by two tired plug horses, knob-kneed and heavy in the hoof, clopped and rattled its way over the wet cobbles, east toward Elmwood Cemetery. The hearse driver leaned his stovepipe hat into the watery squalls that lashed against his black slicker and made of him a sodden Charon. Behind the hearse a cortege of the mourners sat in hackneys bedecked with drabbled black ribbons and wet rosettes, death's festoons. Outside, as the funeral procession passed, a streetcar slowly eclipsed it, the carriage drawn by animals equally as sepulchral as any hearse horses, the bones of the nags' shoulders resignedly rising and falling against the monstrous imposition of the worn leather collars that hung upon their bent necks as the horses plodded toward Union Depot. His first wedding anniversary was but twelve days away, and he and Zee would spend it in Kansas City. Jesse pulled the curtains closed against the draft. He scratched at the underside of his thick dark beard and picked off a fleck of pale fluff that originated on the blankets of his marriage bed. Zee, still in her white nightdress, drew a log from a cast-iron hod and laid it on the blaze that she had started in the hearth. She, as much as the fire, warmed the living room, a room that he had taken pride in furnishing with a table and six chairs and a glass-fronted sideboard, and two rocking chairs that stood on either side of the hearth, all turned in the strong and spindly Shaker style, a home ready for him and his wife to settle in once the amnesty vote had been resolved in his favor. The parlor was dark with the curtains closed. Jesse took down the lantern from the beam above the table and raised the glass. He lit the wick and a warmer glow spread throughout the room as he hung it up again. A false warmth, for his hopes to settle in Kansas City had been thwarted and once again he would be on the move. He had to leave this house behind.

And he could still imagine Edwards and Shelby as they had stood — where Jesse stood at this moment — in the middle of the room to bring him the news of the vote. He could still hear their voices, clearly hear every word they had said as if that sound and scene had been trapped in this space beneath the lantern to be relived every time he passed through it: Edwards with his collar still turned up, rain dripping off the brim of his hat, his big features twisted as if against the violence of some inner storm; Shelby, tall and straight beside him, equally grim-faced behind his huge beard; and neither one had made a move to unbutton his topcoat or remove his hat.

–The vote was fifty-eight to thirty-nine in our favor, Edwards had said.

But his demeanor had remained as dismal as the weather.

–We won, Jesse had said.

–A majority, Shelby had said. But not enough.

Edwards had avoided his eyes.

–They decided that such a resolution would need a two-thirds majority. We needed sixty-four to thirty-two to get it.

Zee's hand had fluttered at her mouth.

–But the Democrats, Jesse had said. You said we had enough.

Edwards and Shelby had failed him. The vote had gone awry.

–The House had enough Democrats all right, Shelby had said. But those from southwestern Missouri voted nay.

Edwards had butted in as if he wished to silence Jesse's reaction.

–They claimed the resolution was too Confederate in its tone.

–Too Confederate? Goddamn! They voted against its tone?

–Dear Lord, Zee had said.

It had turned his gut to gall. *Democrats* had voted against a Confederate resolution? Democrats had betrayed him and all that he stood for: the Cause those same Democrats had once espoused so fervently; the refusal to accept defeat; the fight back to gain control of the State House.

–You mean Hutchings and Jones couldn't keep the party together, Jesse had said.

–All of ours were right behind the vote, Shelby had said. But there were ten men who are out of our district that wouldn't listen to reason.

–Democrats?

–Democrats, Edwards had said.

–The gutless scum, Zee had said.

–I was counting on you, John.

–I know, Edwards had said.

–General? What the hell we gonna do?

Shelby had simply shaken his head. Jesse had never seen either man at such a loss. They had shuffled about the middle of the room like broken puppets, mortally embarrassed to look at him.

–I ought to gut those goddamn sycophants, Jesse had said.

But it was useless, he knew.

–Do it, Zee had said.

–I helped to put the sons of bitches in there, Jesse had said.

–This isn't what we worked for, Jesse, Shelby had said.

–I held back my hand when the Pinkertons maimed my mama and killed my little half-brother and them gutless bastards could not cast a vote in my favor? Leave me alone now, General. Go on home, John. I got to study this out.

But the vote was as unchangeable as a corpse. There was nothing to study. He had to leave Missouri. They would go to Nashville, where no one knew them. But first he had some affairs to put in order.

–I got to go out, Zee, he said.

–This weather's awful, Zee said.

–I'm meeting Frank and we're going to see Mama.

–Can I come?

–We got a message to deliver after we seen her.

Her head drooped and she poked at the fire.

–You take care now, she said.

He nodded but she didn't see it.

–Be sure to ask Frank how Annie's doing, she said.

–She'll be at her pappy's house.

–I'm sure glad Annie and her pappy reconciled. I thought he'd never forgive her for running off like that.

–I'll ask Frank how she's doing.

Light from the lantern glinted on the whorls and leaves and flowers of his tooled leather cartridge belt that was coiled about the holstered Remington. He lifted it from the sideboard. The belt unwound under his hand and he buckled it onto his hips, where it hung snug and a comfort. The sideboard drawer rumbled as he drew it open. From among the three pistols that lay within, he chose his Colt Navy, ready loaded and capped since the previous day. It was old and worn and almost ugly. Jesse tucked the pistol crosswise into the cartridge belt.

–When you coming back? she asked.

–Directly. Before noon tomorrow anyways.

Zee got up from the rocking chair. Soon the slender body under the nightdress would start to grow and he would have another mouth to provide for.

He reached out and laid his palms on her smooth cheeks, the ridged bones beneath his thumbs, his fingers resting on her temples and the strangely cold lobes of her ears. Her eyes were cast down. He tilted her head up and in her eyes two bearded faces resembling him but not him stared back like a pair of matching demons who mocked him from the depths of her pupils.

–You ain't worried 'bout *me*, are you? Zee said.

He bent to kiss her. Soft lips. A hint of yesterday's perfume and the smell of their bed. A lock of hair against his eyelid.

–I got to go, he said. Don't open the door to strangers.

* * *

Jesse picked up his bay horse from the stable on Commercial Street and rode east along the wharves down toward the Randolph ferry. Crane hoists rose like gibbets from the docks, their tackles tapping a melancholy beat, slow and irregular, against the leaning arms of the rigs. Negroes, cowled by pointed sacks, their faces shadowed, slouched in the shelter of the warehouses. Behind the warehouses, the city rose, roof upon roof. The space between the buildings grew greater as he rode eastward. The reluctant spring had kept the yarrow and the ragweed brown and stick-like to clatter and chatter in the wind as he passed. A sagging underbelly of wet clouds dipped down between the bluffs on either side of the boiling river, the waters bloated by the heavy rains that ceaselessly fell and soaked him through from hat to boot tips. Upon reaching the ferry, he guided the bay onto the listing deck and paid the ferryman his obol and an extra dollar to brave the tumbling trunks and the broken planks and knots of rope that had been torn from some collapsed jetty upstream and carried along in the foaming flood. He was the only passenger. All the while during the crossing, Jesse held the bay by the bridle as its eyes rolled with every shift of the craft in the current.

On the other side, he mounted the bluffs and rode out into Clay County. He kept to the back trails. It seemed the Missouri air that Jesse breathed had changed as if the once-accommodating hills and valleys and farmsteads that had for years given him shelter had turned implacably hostile to him. At every farm wherein he took shelter between operations, he had left largesse of hundreds of dollars and a promise to return. And a tacit understanding that any report of his presence to the law would be paid in coin of a baser metal. But there were few people he could trust anymore outside his family and the company. And the company was irrevocably outlawed.

The bay's hooves kicked up the mulch of last fall's leaves as he rode her through woods of dripping oak and elm and black ash in the endless dusk, the light of day sapped away by the still-storming clouds. About an hour after dark noon, he reached a burned-out chapel surrounded by rotten and mildewed graveboards and wonky crosses erected by the Negroes. They had long since been driven away by white men to whom emancipation heralded the heavenly turmoil foreshadowed by Revelation and whose prophecy had driven those old Confederates to arson and execution in the name of the Lord and the Lost Cause.

Frank's dark form drifted out from the shadow of a grove of yew trees, horse and rider blurred by the slanting rain that caused the ground to suck at the horse's hooves as if the souls below would draw the rider down to a loamy and suffocating revenge.

–How you been? Frank said.

–Lowly, Jesse said.

Frank nodded and guided his big roan onto the road.

–Mama ain't too good? Jesse asked.

–'Bout what you'd expect.

Frank spurred his roan on ahead and Jesse followed. They cantered hard against the slashing rain and again took to the woods; when they approached the house, they came across the back meadow and around the big white barn. The yard had become a lake whereon drops of rain merged circle into liquid circle; the branches of the barely budded elm next to the house were twisted by the relentless gusts and those branches lashed back at each lull in the tormenting storm. The barn doors creaked and strained against the buffeting wind.

Jesse and Frank dismounted and led their horses into the calm damp interior of the barn, with its sweet stink of wet hay and warm manure. When they had each horse in a stall, they unsaddled it and rubbed it down with dry sacks and poured oats into buckets and set the feed beneath the horse's nose and left it with its withers steaming.

They ran the last few yards of their journey, splashing through the ankle-deep water of the yard and onto the damaged porch. The parlor window had been replaced, but all around it the once-white clapboard was smoke-stained and blistered brown from the firebomb that the Pinkertons had left as calling card at the end of last January. Pa Samuels greeted them at the door, the eyes behind his glasses flicking this way and that; the cheeks were deeply lined and a twitch played at the corner of his upper lip.

–Worst April, I ever seen, he said.

Inside the narrow hallway, Jesse lifted his sopping hat and hung it on the back of the door. He stripped off his dripping slicker and hung it next to Frank's. He drew the Navy Colt and checked that the powder in the charges could not have taken damp. The metal of the cylinder was dry and the grease on the chambers intact. He did not unhitch his cartridge belt but tucked the Colt back crosswise above the buckle.

Frank led the way into the parlor. The walls were still bare, though they had been freshly painted. No pictures had replaced those damaged by smoke and flame. Mama was in an armchair beside the newly built hearth. She had a shawl wrapped around her legs and her right arm was tucked beneath it in her lap, her left hand clawed on top of it. She was pallid, and her eyes were sunken into their sockets, where they gleamed, baleful. Her cheeks were drawn and every muscle in her face quivered.

–How are you, Mama? Jesse said.

She drew her right arm from under the shawl and held up the tightly-bandaged stump. The absence of her hand was appalling. It brought a coldness to his skin chiller than any outer cold.

–And this ain't the worse loss, she said. That poor boy, I can still see him doing all those things he used to do. Helping round the kitchen, riding a horse with Ambrose leading it, or at your wedding holding up the train of Zee's wedding dress. And ever' thought ends with him lying dead and broken on the floor 'bout where you're standing.

Jesse looked down. He felt that Mama's eyes gazed upon a world other than the parlor around her. One that spilled out black and smoky from a rupture in time.

–Mama, don't torture yourself like that, Frank said.

–We know who led the Pinkertons here, Jesse said. He told them Frank was here.

–It *was* Askew, wasn't it? she said.

–Him and a few others we aim to talk to, Jesse said.

–Can't get a closer neighbor than the farm adjoining, Pa Samuels said.

–This world has turned upside down, Mama said. I don't know what to make of it.

–Me and Frank, we'll deal with it, Jesse said. You understand me?

Her head tilted up toward him. Her dark eyes were unblinking. The stump moved with a nervous sawing motion against the wooden arm of her chair.

–Make sure that son of a bitch knows why he's dying, she said.

* * *

The rain fell upon them steady and dark as they rode into Askew's yard and the dusk had all but ceded to night. In their soaked hats and long slickers they might have been any two travelers.

–Goddammit, Jesse said. We do this and we got to get outta Missouri again, you know that?

–I know it, Frank said.

–Ever' goddamn Pinkerton in Chicago be down here.

Frank was silent.

–Soon as I get to stop in one place, Jesse said, something come around to ruin it.

–I'd like to get a look at this Mr. Pinkerton, Frank said. He ruin't Mama.

–Well, Askew helped in it.

Lantern light made a glow in the windows at one end of the farmhouse. They walked their horses through the mud and pools of the yard and dismounted below the covered porch.

–Hallo the house! Jesse called.

He ascended the steps, his heels making a dead sound on the decking in front of the door. Frank leaned against the hinge side of the doorjamb. Water ticked around their boots and pooled there as it dripped down from the wet slickers. From behind the door came a voice.

–Who's there?

Jesse leaned his chin down on his chest to muffle his voice.

–Got caught out, he said.

–We use your barn? Frank said.

–Hold up, the voice said.

A sigh in it.

There came the sound of a bar scraping against the back of the door as it was lifted. The latch rattled and the door swung inwards. Jesse grabbed Askew by the hair and yanked him forward onto the porch. Frank kicked at the flailing man's ankles, and Askew dropped to the deck and lay framed by the rhomboid pool of light that fell from the doorway. Askew's arms crossed over his gray-bearded face as if he feared a blow, and Jesse stamped down through them and jammed his boot against Askew's throat. A rasping, choking sound came out of the open mouth and the face mottled. Askew's hands closed on the ankle of Jesse's boot, but Jesse would not be budged and he bore down with his full weight to keep Askew pinned. A heavy gust of wind drove a scattering of rain across the deck, and Askew squeezed his eyes shut against the lash of water.

–Foul night, Jesse said.

–Let it all come down, Frank said.

Frank pulled his slicker to one side and drew out his Colt. Askew was kicking now, the hanging suspenders flapping around his denim work pants. Frank leaned over Askew and brought the muzzle of the Colt to about a foot from the man's chest. The pale undershirt was spotted with raindrops.

–You know who I am? Frank said.

The eyes bulged in the spluttering face.

–And why I'm here? Frank said.

Askew squirmed under Jesse's sole.

–He knows who we are, Jesse said. Just be careful where you point that thing.

The roar of Frank's pistol caused Jesse to flinch, and his sole slipped off Askew's throat. But Askew didn't move. A deep stain spread across the chest of the pale undershirt. He wasn't dead. His breathing was shallow and labored. All struggle had gone out of him. The eyes were resigned.

–Daniel!

A woman's voice from within the house.

Jesse drew his own Colt. He brought the muzzle six inches away from the gap between Askew's eyebrows. The head rose up as if to meet the bullet. The pistol roared out, and the head slammed back to the deck with a neat hole in the powder-blackened forehead and lay like a ruptured melon in a bloody pool upon the boards, the eyes now wide and glassy. Devoid of sight.

–As a snail which melteth, Jesse said. *Let ever'one of them pass away.*

XXXVII

A LOUD MOAN SUDDENLY STARTED HIM FROM SLEEP. HIS BEARDED chin bounced upon his chest and the hearth swam into vision where, among the crumbling ashes, the red embers glowed at him like the myriad eyes of the Great Deceiver himself, in contempt for his lack of watchfulness. The moan filled the unfamiliar kitchen. Hummed in the air. Replaced half-sleep with a sudden panic. He twisted out of the armchair, still disorientated by the layout of the new house. A new house far from Missouri.

–Zee, he called. Are you all right?

No answer. His hair was awry, his shirt half out of his trousers, the odor from his whiskey sweat pungent and sour in his nostrils. The lantern guttered where it hung from the beam above the table, its fuel all but spent, and it sent the shadows of chair backs and empty bottle and empty glasses and a cold coffeepot flickering onto the whitewashed walls in a madcap ghost dance around the black hole of the bedroom doorway. He stumbled against a chair, his limbs still under the spell of sleep and the cling of whiskey. Should he call Frank's wife, Annie? This was woman's work. Mama would have loved to be present with him at this moment, but that was impossible. It seemed that everyone in Clay County had turned against him and his since the laws had found Askew's body on his porch. Even Sheriff Groom. Mama couldn't even sell the farm to move away. It was as if, when the bid for parole had finally failed, everyone had abandoned his family. Everyone in Clay. And too many people in Clay had known that he was in the whereabouts of Kansas City. He had Zee pregnant and he could trust no one to help them. At least down here in Nashville, he and Zee and Frank and Annie were simply Mr. and Mrs. Howard and Mr. and Mrs. Woods.

Zee's voice rasped out of the darkness.

–The light.

Then another moan from her that would raise the dead. He fumbled in his pants pockets as he crossed the room and struck a match at the bedroom threshold. In the flare, the mound of her shifted under the covers, her flushed and puffy face raised from the pillow, the eyes darkly ringed and squinting against the glare of intrusion, her lips pallid and dry even in that meager light.

–It must be time, she said.

She licked her cracked lips.

The flame moved down the match stem and the blackened spillikin curved toward his thumb and fingertip. He shook the match out and in the darkness scratched blindly in the box for another.

–I'll get the lantern, he said.

–It's on the commode.

He struck another flame, and by its light he found the lamp and raised its glass and set match to wick. Zee moaned again and her shoulders pressed back against the mattress. Beneath the red and white triangles of the quilt, the mound of her belly rose up as if the child inside her had stretched its limbs in preparation for its journey into the unforgiving world where they awaited it.

–What can I get you? Jesse said.

She breathed short and sharp. Her arms came back over her shoulders and she gripped the brass bed rail.

–The midwife, she said.

–You need some water?

–I need the midwife.

–I'll get Frank, he said.

He was more terrorized by the advent of his firstborn than he had ever been in the presence of Death, which he was well used to; and suddenly more exhilarated, too. Jesse darted out of the room and up the passageway past the parlor door to the back bedroom.

–Frank, wake up, he called.

He rapped against the panels. The bed creaked behind the door, the latch clicked, and Frank's wife, her blond hair disheveled and hanging down to the shoulders of her white nightdress, looked up at him out of eyes more alert than his own. Her full, wide mouth was turned up on one side as she framed the question.

–It's time, ain't it?

–Is Frank awake? he said. It's coming.

–Goddammit, Frank groaned in the dark.

–Get in the buggy and fetch that midwife, Annie said.

She pushed past Jesse on her way down the passage, and he followed the flowing white form of her, back to Zee, leaving Frank to gather himself and dress.

When Jesse reached the bedroom, the quilt was like the back of a giant red-and-white turtle where she raised herself off the bed. Zee tossed her head against the pillow, lowed a long low like a cow on its way to milking, her fingers twisting the quilt. She gasped when the pain that racked her had passed. Her voice squeaked out.

–Any minute, Zee said. It's gonna happen any minute.

–No it ain't, Annie said. You got a while yet.

–The water's broke. It's broke already.

–Frank's going to get the midwife, Jesse said.

–The baby'll be here before she is, Zee whispered.

–She'll be here, honey, Annie said.

Annie sat on the straight-backed chair next to the bed and took Zee's hand into both of her own. She leaned over and kissed Zee on the cheek. It was a marvel to Jesse how women could be so tender to one another, such a gesture forbidden among men.

–I'll be back directly, Frank called from the kitchen.

–Hurry, Zee whispered, though only Annie and Jesse could hear her.

–You must be all wet under there, Jesse said.

–Uuuuungh, Zee howled.

–By God! Jesse said.

–I'm with you, honey, Annie said.

Zee's face was flushed a deep red. He feared she would die with the pain of it. He saw knives and blood and heads shaking and condolences. A grave doctor. He willed away the horrid vision.

–When my sister Junie had hers, Annie said, even when the water's broke, it didn't come till nigh on two days later.

Zee's grip tightened on Annie's hands and Jesse gripped the brass bed rail at the foot of the bed. Zee let out another loud groan and panted short, sharp gasps, and he panted too. Her eyes squeezed tight shut so that they wrinkled up like an old woman's.

–Goddamn, Jesse said.

–Don't you push yet, Annie said.

–Don't cuss, Zee said.

She lay back again. The spasm seemed to have subsided, leaving her tossed up on the beach of the bed like some spent victim of shipwreck.

–What can I do? Jesse said.

–You cain't have it for her, that's for sure, Annie said.

–It's gonna get worse, ain't it? Zee said. I cain't do it.

–Oh you can, honey, Annie said. And you will.

Jesse stepped away from the bed, pushed his hands in his pockets, and looked toward the door. The whiskey bottle in the kitchen was empty. He wasn't a doctor. Annie had never helped a baby out before. Frank wouldn't be long, he knew, but what if the baby started to come before the midwife got here? Zee could bleed to death or the baby strangle on its cord. He'd heard that. That old witch better get here soon. He'd see to her if she didn't.

–Let's get you off of them wet sheets, Annie said, before the pains all start again.

–I don't mind the wet, Zee said.

–Come on, honey, Annie said.

Annie was so calm, as if this was natural. She pulled the quilt back and Zee pushed herself up with her elbows and blew, her chin on the neck of her nightdress that stretched over the great white expanse of her swollen breasts and belly. From the small of her back to her knees, a grayish-pink patch of fluid glistened on the sheet. The back of her nightdress was soaked with it, too. She slid on her behind toward the edge of the bed. Jesse came forward and took Zee by the elbow. She glanced up at him and smiled a broken smile.

–I love you, she said.

His eyes filled suddenly and his throat tightened. He looked at the floorboards so she wouldn't see him so unmanly. She was having his baby.

–My boy is coming, he said.

It was going to be a boy, he knew, for not a month ago the midwife had dangled a long, thin lodestone over her belly and it had turned clockwise upon its string. Zee's fingers tightened on his palm.

–Ready? Annie said.

Zee blew again. She leaned against him heavily and came to her feet. He and Annie guided her toward the chair where Annie had been sitting.

–Let me stand, Zee said.

She gripped the back of the chair.

–I'll get some water to wash you up, Jesse said.

–Let's get you some clean sheets and a nightdress, Annie said. Then your big, strong man can bring the mattress from the back room.

Jesse took the china ewer from the washstand and went into the kitchen. He was happy to be doing something. Some action. The lantern still guttered upon the beam, its wick sucking fumes from its glass reservoir.

A cast-iron pot sat deep in its hole on the hob. He lifted the heavy lid and steam rose into his face. He touched a fingertip to the still surface and whipped back his hand, nearly scalded. He took the tin dipper off its hook on the wall and filled the ewer three-quarters full and added cold water to it from the bucket next to the sink. He hurried back to the bedroom.

Zee was naked, her soiled nightdress in a heap at her feet. She gripped the back of the chair still. The taut and blue-veined drum of her belly pushed up her breasts. Everything about her was full to bursting. He had never seen her nipples so wide and brown and her hips so plump. Her big buttocks and thighs were stained a reddish brown from the birth waters.

–Don't look, she said. I'm so ugly.

Her dark-rimmed eyes glanced over at him and away in despair. Her face blotched with red as her eyes welled up. Her hair straggled in her face.

–You never looked more beautiful, he said.

She shook her head and the tears started.

–That's a lie, she said.

–There's truth in it, he said.

–Can you bring the mattress, Jesse? Annie said.

He turned to go for it.

–Oh, I wish Momma could be here, Zee said behind him.

He hurried down the passageway. His son was coming. A moan followed behind him down the passage. He didn't know whether to run back to the bedroom or rush forward for the mattress. He rushed for the mattress. The door to the empty third bedroom was opposite the parlor. When he entered, the room smelled musty from underuse and the damp of a cold December night. He dragged the mattress from the iron bedstead. She howled on the other side of the house and he wondered if she was still on her feet.

His fingers twisted in the ticking, and he half slid, half carried the mattress back down the passage to the bedroom as it tried to fold under its own weight.

Zee was kneeling with her forearms on the floor and her buttocks in the air. Annie was down beside her with an arm over Zee's back. The ewer and the china basin were on the floor beside them. Zee's behind was clean now.

–Breathe, honey, breathe, Annie said.

–Get her on the bed, Jesse said.

–No. No. I'm fine, Zee panted.

He let down the mattress at the foot of the bed and hauled the soiled one off the bedstead. Zee was grunting. When Annie tried to put a blanket over her shoulders, she shrugged it off. Jesse had the new mattress on the bed. Annie got up from beside Zee, took a clean white sheet off the top of the linen chest, shook it out, whirled it over the bed, and let it settle. Zee reached for the edge of the bed and upset the ewer with a clatter.

–Oh no, she moaned.

–Don't worry none, Jesse said.

He squatted beside her and stroked her hair. Water pooled around his boots. Her hands came up and her fingers crinkled his beard.

–I never knowed nothing like this, he said.

–Me either, she said. Let me get up on my own now.

Jesse stepped back from her. Annie tucked the sides and corners of the sheet under the mattress and flopped the pillows onto the bed. Zee gripped the bedrail and pulled herself up. She crawled onto the clean sheet like a wounded bear in its last agony.

–I need to shit, she said.

He had never heard her use that word before.

–Do we have a bedpan? Annie said.

–We got a big skillet, Jesse said.

Annie grimaced.

–I can squat and use the chamber pot, Zee said.

–I'll take out that old mattress, Jesse said.

–At least the quilt ain't soiled, Zee said.

Jesse dragged the wet mattress through the kitchen just as the lantern guttered out. Chairs scraped against the floor as he pushed by them in the darkness. An earthy odor rose to his nostrils from the damp patch on the mattress at chest height. Outside, the rattle of wheels and chink of harness and the drop of hooves heralded the arrival of a buckboard. It had to be Frank. He pulled at the mattress, aware that every step toward the back bedroom took him further from the Remington that lay beside his chair in front of the hearth. It couldn't be the laws on a night like this. He heard Frank and the midwife behind him in the kitchen, and he let the mattress drop on the floor of the bedroom and rushed back down the passageway.

–The goddamn lantern's empty, Frank said.

–Where's the lady, Mr. Woods? the midwife said.

–Go right on through, Frank said. I'll get the kerosene here.

–It's coming, Jesse said.

–Ah, Mr. Howard, the midwife said.

She stood in the square of light that spilled from the bedroom doorway. The bonnet was tied tight around her face and cut into her double chin. Her cheeks, glowing with the winter cold, had the deep red color of a dairy farmer's wife who ate too much cheese and drank too much milk, spidery lines stretching toward eyes and ears. A long woolen scarf hung from her neck and down over her heavy coat. She was all buttoned up tight over her big bosom and hips and belly, a short, round woman in her late fifties. Dangling from her pudgy little hand was a leather-handled canvas bag within which he assumed were the tools of her trade, should she need tools, which he hoped she didn't.

–Am I glad to see you! Jesse said.

–Whyn't you fill the goddamn lantern? Frank said.

–Go to Mrs. Howard, Jesse said. She's about to have it.

The midwife gave him a condescending smile.

–We'll see about that, she said. Now, you boys leave us alone for a while. You have that lantern ready, Mr. Woods?

–Just about, Frank said.

The stink of kerosene filled the kitchen. Frank rummaged in the sideboard drawer and then snipped at the ruined top of the wick with a shiny scissors. When he lit a match to it, the midwife crossed the threshold and closed the bedroom door behind her.

–Goddamn, Jesse said.

–Get you a chair, Frank said.

Jesse slumped down at the table. He rested his chin in his hands and scratched his fingers through his hair and beard. A full whiskey bottle appeared on the table right next to the empty.

–Where'd you get that? Jesse said.

Frank pulled off his hat and overcoat and hung them behind the door. A dark growth shadowed his hard, square face. The collar of his frock coat was turned up and twisted. He wore no shirt but his undershirt. He unbuckled his cartridge belt, wrapped it around the holster of his pistol, and slid the coffeepot aside to make room for it on the table.

–Walther give it to me. Her husband. Said we might have some time to kill.

Jesse uncorked the bottle. He pointed the muzzle of it at a glass. Another loud howl came muffled from behind the door. Frank nodded at the glass.

–That'll do it, Frank said.

–Should I go in there? Jesse said.

–Scares the shit out of me, Frank said.

–I can't wait.

Frank shrugged. Jesse gulped at the whiskey. Another howl from behind the door. Frank poured. Between them they listened to the yelling fits come quicker and quicker between quiet spells, and the level in the bottle lowered and the windowpane behind Frank paled with the dawn and turned lapis, then blue, until from behind the door came the whoop of Zee's voice.

–Oh my Lord, oh my Lord! Look at him.

And Jesse was stone sober and he rushed to the door and the fat little midwife with her sleeves rolled up and hands bloody sat at the foot of the bed and she had a long piece of offal in a kidney-shaped basin in her lap and Annie was on the bedside chair crying with the joy of it and a small creature, red-skinned and streaked with a creamy tallow, scrunched up his old-man's face as if he would cry, the tiny limbs waving like the feelers of an insect as he searched for his mama's breasts that were as mountains on either side of him and Zee's face like a sun beamed over this child new to the world.

–Oh my boy! Jesse said.

–Look at him, Zee said. Just look at him. He's so beautiful.

She was right. His son was beautiful. All the while she had been pregnant, the growth of this child in her body had been a mystery to him. Something that he had kept at a distance while he went about his business. Something in which he took a quiet pride. Zee had wanted this child so desperately, and now here he was in all his reality and making the world around him as vivid as if lit from within by that inner light that Jesse had only known in the midst of action, in the midst of rage. And here was another mystery, for he had always thought that preternatural light appeared only with the closeness of death.

XXXVIII

BEYOND THE COTTONWOODS, THE CANNON RIVER SPARKLED IN the late morning sunlight. Jesse hiked a gold watch out of his vest pocket. A little before noon. Right this minute Zee was probably mashing up little Jesse Edwards's dinner. Nine months old now, and it seemed but yesterday that Zee had told Jesse she was pregnant and Jesse was taken with the awe of it all. Nothing like a child to make you account for the passing of time and make you account that time itself had you on a rail and no matter how much you twisted and turned, the end of the track was the same for all: a box in the ground, your unseeing face to its lid, and six feet of dirt on top. He had produced his offspring, and nature now would only expect him to die.

Steam rose from the spout of the coffeepot, and the water made a little pinging noise as it roiled against the lid. He gyred his cup in his hands. Looked into the empty depth of it, where a black whorl showed through the cracked enamel. He was further north than he had ever been in his life or ever wanted to be. The distance from Northfield to Nashville would be measured in weeks rather than days. He had good property down there in Tennessee and a fine little sideline going in crop sales. With that and the money from the Rocky Cut train job, he could have stayed comfortably at home watching his little boy struggle across the carpet. There was no real need to ride all the way to Minnesota to do a bank job not two months after Rocky Cut, but the thought of a big raid on a Yankee bank had drawn Jesse like a lodestone draws iron. And what did he have to lose now? Certainly not amnesty.

–Too good a opportunity to pass up, Frank had said.

Frank was right, of course. Northfield was populated by a bunch of German wheat farmers, hardworking and prosperous, with hardly a thought that they might be robbed. It would be just like the old days. And, by God, those days seemed a long way off.

And Cole's friend Bill Stiles urged them on to it, too. Stiles was a Minnesota man. Solid in a pinch even if he was an ugly son of a bitch, with those slitty eyes and his narrow nose — features that looked too small on his broad face — but he had performed just fine at Rocky Cut. And he had guaranteed he could guide them out of Minnesota through lake and cottonwood country.

–You ready? Frank said.

His brother stood with his reins in his hand. With his broad-brimmed hat and long frock coat, he looked every inch the cattle baron.

–Soon as I've had me some coffee, Jesse said.

Charlie Pitts, the other new man, walked his horse up beside Frank's, thumbed back his hat, and winked at Jesse — if that's what you could call it when one of Charlie's half-hooded eyes closed slowly and opened up again. There was a hint of a grin in the thick brown beard. Pitts flipped back the flap of his saddlebag and slid a quart bottle of whiskey into sight.

–How about a little nip of this before we break camp, Mr. Howard? he said.

–We'll have a taste on the way into town, Jesse said.

Pitts mounted up and guided his dark quarter horse onto the trail. Bob Younger followed him and leaned over toward Jesse as he passed.

–Need a little Dutch courage now, Jess? the youngster said.

–Nope, just a little taste to lift the morale.

Cole Younger swung up on a wild-eyed bay that lifted its off-side front hoof as if to tear up the earth. The horse swung its dark head this way and that, shook the reins at its chops, and champed down around the bit, a stringy foam falling from its bared and discolored teeth, its nostrils flaring open and shut as if it would breathe contagion and blight the very soil it stood upon. Jesse could see why Cole liked the beast.

–By God, Cole, Jesse said, that horse is big enough to haul your fat ass, but he's a mean son of a bitch.

Mounted beside Cole, Clell Miller grinned and rubbed at the small mustache and sparse sideburns that reached his jaw. Clell was a little slow-witted, but good-natured and a reliable man in a shooting scrape.

–Let's be on our way, gentlemen, Cole said.

Jesse poured his cup full and took two sips of the hot and acrid coffee.

–Come on, Jess, Frank said. We got work to do.

Frank was in the saddle on his roan now. Jesse sipped once more at the bitter liquid and flung the rest into the fire, where it hissed and spat and steamed around the coffeepot. Jesse scratched his beard and stood up leisurely. Behind him, his own frock coat lay over a fallen trunk. He pulled it on, caught up the reins of his bay, and swung into the saddle and put spur to her, leaving Frank and Clell and Cole and Jim and Bill Stiles all behind him.

When Jesse caught up to Bob Younger and Charlie Pitts, he saw that Pitts had already broken the seal on the whiskey and he and Bob looked to have emptied the bottle by a third.

–Gimme a tetch of that, Jesse said.

The whiskey was hot and pungent in his mouth and burned its way down his throat and bloomed hot in his belly. He licked his lips and the ends of his mustaches and took another hard swallow before he handed the bottle back to Bob. A cloud of gnats suddenly rose around Jesse's head, and they stayed about him as he rode. He flailed at them, but the winged mites bobbed and bounced through the sunlight shafts and dipped and dangled before him as if hanging from invisible threads bent upon crazy and erratic orbits with Jesse's head as their gravity's center. When he came out of the trees, just as suddenly the gnat cloud was gone.

The three riders were between two wheat fields. A carrion stink arose from beside the split-rail fence to their right, where the body of a coyote lay flayed open, the darkened cage of its ribs curving skyward, the hind legs gone, the head twisted and matted where it had taken a farmer's bullet. The turkey vultures had completely gutted it. Two of them circled high above the golden crops that waved gently in the breeze and stretched away as far as the eye could see to east and west and the north, where the buildings of Northfield arose in the near distance.

The bottle came back to Jesse from Pitts, and he downed another hard swallow and another and then they were close to the bridge that led into town. They passed the bottle among them one last time, and before they reached the other side of the bridge, Jesse flung it away, glass flashing in the sunlight. It hit the rail of the bridge with a musical thunk and tumbled off the rail and blooped down unseen in the river below.

They were between the buildings of Division Street, and Jesse rode with Pitts and Bob Younger on each side of him. No other saddle horses were in sight, but the streets were busy with folk afoot. The riders passed a tack store that was built crudely of creosoted planks and roofed with shingles set upon a steep rake. At the corner of Division and Main stood an elegant two-story brick building with arched windows and doors. Above one set of doors the sign read SCRIVER'S and above the next, LEE AND HITCHCOCK'S. A barrel and some crates of dry goods were piled on the boardwalk outside.

Jesse dismounted and hitched his horse to a post among three at the corner. The building's south wall continued down Main Street. The bank was a few yards past the long set of steps that led to the upper floors of Scriver's Hotel. Jesse scanned Main and Division as he mounted the boardwalk and seated himself on a crate outside the dry goods store to wait for Cole and Clell. The whiskey had given the town a soft edge, as if all the buildings were blurring out of focus and preparing to disappear. Pitts sat down next to Jesse, and young Bob leaned against the wall of the store. The sun slanted into the right side of Jesse's face and warmed his numbed cheeks. Whiskey lingered on his tongue and his teeth. Under their heavy lids, Pitts's eyes had reddened. He dug at something in his beard as if to dislodge a crust or discourage vermin. To Jesse's left, Bob pressed his fingertips to his face and stretched his mouth open as if to yawn. No sign of Cole and the others.

A gray cat, its fur matted and mange-ridden, slunk out of the alleyway beyond Scriver's. It kept its ragged flanks close to the boards, inching forward toward Pitts, its bony shoulders rising above its torn ears. Pitts dipped a hand to the ground and feigned hurling a stone. The cat's eyes flared, its teeth bared, and it hissed, spat hard, and backed away to disappear into the alley again.

–Durn cat, Pitts said.

–There's Cole, Bob said.

Bob pushed his lanky form off the wall and marched off toward the bank. Pitts got off the crate and followed him. Jesse stared back up the street. His mouth was dry and the buzz in his head was slowing to a dull throb. Cole and Clell had only just come over the bridge. They moved as if through molasses. On Main Street, Pitts and Bob, a mite unsteady, marched past the hotel stairs. Jesse hurried down the boardwalk. God's clock was all wrong — someone had bent the hands and misaligned the cogs and ratchets. They should wait for Cole and Clell to cover the door. The street was in movement, folk on the walks. Too busy. Jesse unbuttoned his frock coat. Bob and Pitts were already at the door of the bank.

–Let's go, Bob said.

The kid was too eager. Jesse should have slowed him down, but it was too late. Bob stepped through the bank's entrance and Pitts was after him and there was nothing to do but follow them in. Jesse drew his new Remington #3 and stepped inside the bank. An L-shaped counter ran around the lobby, and the teller sat at the curved angle of it. He was a tall and gangly youth with red hair and a freckled face, and if his eyes could have opened any wider they might have dropped from the sockets. Pitts jumped up onto the counter and over it. The teller moaned like a frightened girl-child and stepped back to the wall of the vault.

–Shit, Bob said.

He followed Pitts over the barrier and pointed his pistol toward the bookkeeper's desk. The bookkeeper threw his hands in the air, where they quivered close to the long ears that were like handles on a smooth half-gallon egg. The big baby head moved from side to side as if he would will away the sight of bandits so close to his ledger and his desk.

The door of the vault was open, and the cashier started out of his cage toward it. Jesse missed the timing of his jump, bumped the edge of the counter, slid across it, and landed off balance. But the cashier hesitated long enough for Pitts to get between him and the vault door. Jesse leveled his pistol at the cashier. The man's hair was plastered into perfect place as if he had but an hour before come from the barber, though his thin face was red with barely controlled fury, his pale eyes hate-filled, the mouth a hard, straight line. Jesse grinned at the man's impotence.

–Are you the cashier? Jesse said.

The man shook his head.

–Are you the cashier? Bob echoed behind Jesse.

Jesse glanced back. Fool boy. The damn cashier was right in front of Jesse.

–No sir, the freckled teller said.

Bob swung his pistol towards the bookkeeper.

–Are you the cashier?

Jesse shook his head and pointed the muzzle of the Remington between the cashier's hard-staring eyes.

–You are the cashier, Jesse said. Open that safe damn quick or I'll blow your head off.

The entrance door rattled behind him. Jesse spun. The door was still closed. Outside it, Clell Miller had his pistol in some citizen's face. A shot went off and a cloud of powder smoke drifted past the window where Cole stood. Jesse turned back just as Pitts stepped inside the vault. The cashier lurched forward. The vault door. Jesse swung the Remington in a flat arc. The butt made a sickening crack against the cashier's head. The blow lifted the man from his feet, and he dropped in a heap on the floor.

–Oh! he said.

Nothing else. Just sat there. Jesse placed the muzzle of the Remington on the bridge of the cashier's nose. There was a little too much spunk and fire in this bean-counting son of a bitch.

–Open that safe damn quick or you haven't but a minute to live.

More shots in the street now. All was wrong, radically wrong.

The cashier shook his head. Blood trickled down his nose.

–There's a time lock on it, he said. It can't be opened now.

A time lock? Didn't Stiles check on that? Not if the safe was in the vault. The whiskey taste was stale in Jesse's mouth. The bars of the cashier's cage cut stark, bright lines across Pitts's body and the vault door. Bullets smacked against the outside wall of the bank. They had to get out.

–This safe ain't going to open, Pitts said inside the vault.

The dark walnut swivel chair tilted as the cashier tried to use it to pull himself up.

–You son of a bitch, Jesse said.

He holstered the Remington. He dug into the pocket of his frock coat and slipped out his long-handled jackknife. He pulled against the hard sprung blade till the boss snapped into the lock beneath the short steel guard. The last two inches of the straight-honed edge curved up to a point. The cashier glanced up and the fury drained from his eyes as Jesse swept the blade down backhand and cut a deep slash on the left side of his throat. The skin and flesh peeled open, red and raw, and a great well of blood gouted up over the white collar.

–Oh! the cashier said again.

He looked up into Jesse's eyes. Jesse saw disbelief in the glance. The damn Yankee had better believe it. Time was running out of him, red and copious.

–Dear God, Pitts said. Now how we gonna open the goddamn safe?

Jesse wiped the blade on the dry side of the cashier's vest. The eyes that looked down at the blade were now numb with shock.

Time lock. Time clock. Sands running out.

Jesse closed the blade and pocketed it. He drew the Remington again. It was all over. The operation botched. He placed the Remington's muzzle between the cashier's eyes. Fired. The head cracked back against the wainscoting, blood and brain and bone fragments spattering over the varnished wood and the leather seat of the swivel chair beside.

Jesse swung himself over the counter and ran to the window. Shots cracked out and puffs of white smoke filled the street. Cole and Clell were on the boardwalk yelling.

–Get off the street!

–Get off the goddamn street!

Frank, Stiles, and Jim Younger whirled their horses out front. They fired at anything that moved. A citizen was down on the boardwalk opposite. Cole saw Jesse at the window.

–Come on out of there! Cole yelled.

A splatter of blood erupted from Cole's thigh and he fell back against the wall.

Jesse yanked the door open to the humming street, and he felt a burn in the flesh just above his hipbone. Blood seeped into his vest and trickled warm down his groin. The glass door panel shattered behind him. He leaned back against the doorjamb, his pistol by his side. On the street in front of him, Clell Miller's frightened horse danced and jerked at its reins that were tied to the bank's hitching post. Clell ran to her and grabbed the reins. He pulled her head down and unhitched her. Just as he grabbed his pommel to mount, a crazy old man in a battered slouch hat ran from the cover of the hotel stairs. Jesse swung up his pistol, but before he could draw a bead, the shotgun blast punched Clell backward from the saddle. Jesse looked on numb. Failed to fire. And the old boy with the shotgun was gone again. Clell writhed on his back beneath the horse's hooves, his breath coming in hard, panicked whoops. His face was pocked with birdshot.

Angry hornets buzzed around Jesse's head, zinged and spat against the brick of the building. Jesse gingerly touched his side. It was bleeding, but he was sure there was no serious damage.

Down on the corner, Pitts's horse suddenly whinnied and crumpled as if poleaxed. The horse was a dead bundle of flesh and bone. Everywhere the flat pop and crack of ordnance. A rifle bullet hit Clell full in the chest and he whooped in one last breath and then lay as still as Pitts's horse.

Stiles was in the way of Jesse getting a shot at the rifleman who had appeared in the alley opposite. Then Stiles pitched clean out of his saddle. Stiles's horse pranced around the fallen body. Stiles wasn't moving.

Slow clouds of white smoke drifted and swirled. As if in a mad equestrian ballet, Jim whirled past Frank in the street, then shuddered suddenly and slumped over the neck of his mount, his pistol still dangling from his hand. Dust roiled from beneath the hooves of the maddened horses. A punch slammed into Jesse's upper arm and he staggered backward. The sleeve of his frock coat was torn. He was numb with disbelief. Nothing had ever been this wrong before. He stepped back inside the door of the bank. Jesse turned toward the counter.

–Where's the money outside the safe? Bob Younger said.

No time, Jesse thought.

The gangly teller laid a box on the counter. Bob began filling the wheat sack with the small change. The boy bolted for the back office. Bob swung up his pistol and fired and a great divot of wood sprang from the door jamb. The bookkeeper ducked down behind his chair.

–Goddammit, Bob said. He got out the goddamn window.

Bob returned to the small-change box as Charlie Pitts labored over the counter, his eyes glazed.

–Cain't get no safe open, Charlie said.

–Come on, Jesse said. Get outta here.

Behind Charlie the remains of the cashier were propped against the wainscoting. A pool of darkening blood had spread from the man's seat to his knees.

–Just get out of here, Jesse said.

Jesse drew his second pistol, the muscle of his left arm burning, aching. He could still lift it. He stepped out through the door. His bay horse was at the corner. He ran for her, firing both pistols to clear the street in front of him. He reached the post unhit and unhitched her reins. Pitts and Cole tried to lift Clell's lifeless body. Then they let it drop back into the bloody dirt.

Frank rode up to the corner and fired down Division Street just as Jesse mounted.

–My goddamn horse is dead, Pitts called.

Jesse was in the saddle. A shot cracked out.

–Goddammit! Frank yelled.

The left knee of Frank's pants leg was holed and the material began to darken and blood welled out over his boot. Red droplets cascaded from his stirrup. Jesse leaned over to grab Frank's bridle, but Frank waved him away.

–Look after your own self! he shouted.

Blood had run down Jesse's sleeve and made slippery his grip on the Colt. His whole crotch was stained dark from the wound above his hip. Frank spurred his horse and galloped down Division Street. Pitts, afoot, ran past Jesse and raced after Frank toward the bridge. Cole backed his snorting fiend of a mount toward the corner, firing all the while to cover Bob, who had finally come out of the bank. Bob dangled the pathetic empty wheat sack, a gun in his other hand, and ran toward his horse at the corner. More shots cracked out. Jesse forced the bay forward and up next to Cole and Jim Younger. A window was open on the second floor of the hotel. Jesse fired four rounds at it. Across the street, a rifle barked. Bob screamed. Jesse wheeled to see Bob pitch sideways. Bob's arm hung limp and useless as the rest of him writhed. The pistol was on the boardwalk beside him. Jesse fired off three fast shots at the rifleman in the alley. Bob raised himself slowly, left the pistol, clutched the wheat sack to his ruined arm, and stumbled toward his horse at the corner of Main and Division. Somehow he pulled himself into the saddle. Jim Younger turned his horse and rode back toward his brother.

Cole spun his horse and raced off after Pitts. Jim, his face drained from hurt, leaned down and took Bob's bridle and led the horse off down Division. Jesse had two rounds left in the Remington, one in the Colt. In each blurred building was a man with a gun. He brought the bay up to the corner. Down Division Street, Pitts swung up behind Cole onto the big powerful stallion, and they were off toward the bridge. Cole could pick a good horse. Jesse put spur to his bay and raced after them. He saw no end to this nightmare.

They had left the trail and were deep in the woods, but any tracker with the least of skills would run them down for certain. Jesse breathed hard as he slid from the saddle. He had no time to reload the Navy Colt, but he commenced right away on the Remington, ejecting the spent cases.

All three of the Youngers lay propped against a fallen tree trunk, Cole and Jim on either side of young Bob. Their horses were tied to the branches where Charlie Pitts, unscathed, was reloading his pistol. It reminded Jesse of a daguerreotype that he had once seen of three dead horse thieves cut down after a hanging. Bob Younger's arm was bloody and shattered at the elbow. A low wheeze came out of his equally bloody chest.

Frank leaned his shoulder against the earth-filled roots that had been torn up when the tree fell. He bent over to tie a bandanna around his leg to stanch the blood flow. Jesse's arm ached and he had lost blood from the wound above his hip, but neither wound had gone through more than flesh. Clell was dead. And so was Stiles. And Stiles was supposed to have been the one to guide them through the woods to make their escape.

–We can't rest up long, Jesse said.

–I can't ride, Cole, Bob whimpered.

The boy was in a bad way. He was probably telling the truth. His forearm was all but hanging off, and his blood had soaked the whole of his right side.

–You can't ride, boy, we leave you behind, Jesse said.

–We ain't leaving this boy behind nowhere, Cole snapped.

Cole's face was drained, his lips pursed under the mustache. He blew. He had taken a bullet through the thigh. Jim had been hit in the back, but the bullet couldn't have gone through a lung or he would be wheezing, too.

–They'll be onto us in less than a hour, Jesse said.

–We ain't leaving Bob, Jim said.

–I ain't staying around here to wait for no posse, Jesse said.

–Then get on your goddamn horse and go, Cole said.

–Come on, Cole, Frank said. Let's get Bob into the saddle.

–I cain't, Bob said. I cain't, Cole.

–Mount up, Frank, Jesse said.

–Mount up, Frank, Cole said. Best we can do is split up. More chance that way.

Frank nodded and untied the reins of his roan.

–You coming, Charlie? Jesse said.

Charlie Pitts holstered his pistol. He bowed his head, eyes half hooded. He raised a hand to stroke his thick brown beard.

–I reckon I'll stay here with Cole and the boys, Pitts said.

Jesse shook his head. Charlie was committing suicide, he reckoned. All of them. They would be shot or hanged or put away forever in a penitentiary. Jesse swung up onto the bay again. He looked down at the bleeding Younger brothers: Cole, Jim, and Bob. The three of them lying on the ground in front of him was a sight that his senses had no wish to accept. The Youngers had stood by him and he by them for nigh on ten years, and now he was about to ride out on them. Without amnesty he had thought that he, and they, had nothing to lose. He had never believed that an operation could go so badly awry. Yet he had lost the entire company. All that was left was family.

–Let's go, Frank.

The grimness of his decision to leave the others outweighed his sense of shame. The war was finally over, and there was no parole and no amnesty and no room for pity. Or loyalty. They had all come into the world alone, and so they would quit it.

–We'll try and lead 'em away, Jesse said.

Cole allowed him a wry and pained smile. His face was pale, a little jowly.

–Take care, boys, Cole said.

Jesse nodded to him and turned the bay south.

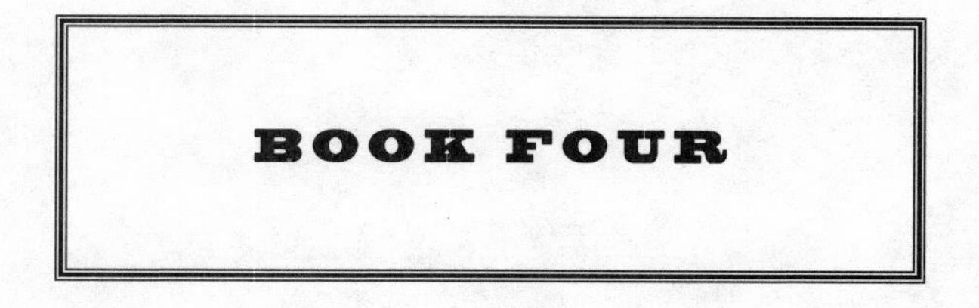

BOOK FOUR

XXXIX

LEAVES, DENSE AND RUSSET, CROWDED IN ALL AROUND THE LOW log-cabin home and over the split-log fence of the small yard and across the trail so close to the front fence that there was hardly any trail at all. The cabin belonged to Ben Morrow, old-time bushwhacker and friend of the family, who now stayed straight but would always provide a hideout in a pinch. Morrow wasn't home, but Jesse hadn't come to visit Morrow.

The wind stirred, and dry leaves swirled down into the yard like a suffocating waterfall of russet. Old, dry blood. Beneath a dry-leafed tree limb, Jesse dipped a tin cup into the water barrel and tasted it. It was metallic and cold. The barn door was still shut. The man he wanted to talk to was still inside. Morrow's hired help, Dick Liddil, was a good man with horses who had once tried his hand at highway robbery. Jesse could wait for Liddil to come out into the yard. It was three years since he had wanted to do another operation; living quietly in Nashville with Zee, he watched his boy grow, and bought and sold feed so that he had built up a prosperous merchandising concern. It was a false life. Upstanding Mr. Howard. He was sick of the charade. All the while, the nagging shame that he had abandoned the Youngers worked upon him. Since he was sixteen, he had built his life around loyalty. To the Cause. To the company, to the men around him of whom he had expected the same loyalty in return. Cole and his surviving brothers were behind bars. He would never know what would have happened had he stayed with them and tried to help them fight their way out of Minnesota. The Lord had always been a constant presence in his life, and he felt as if His eye stared down upon him in silent accusation. He had been living a life that was empty and false and shameful. He would build a new company and he had to do it without Frank, for since Cole Younger had been sent to the penitentiary his brother had refused to do another operation. Cole had been Frank's partner since the Quantrill days, and Frank counted on Cole more than he did on Jesse. That was a fact he couldn't fight against. And in truth, Jesse was not certain that any choice left to them was a righteous one. All he knew was that in action, he might feel clean again. Feel that mysterious presence that lit up the world around him that was the Lord's way of showing him that his path was the straight and narrow one, the presence that had been lost to him for three long years while he was like a dog wandering in the wilderness. He had already recruited his cousin Wood Hite from Kentucky. He needed at least one old bushwhacker, for the rest of the men on his list of possibles were all only up-and-coming troublemakers. New blood with no experience in the war. Wild boys who had all heard of Jesse James and held him in awe. That reputation would keep them in line.

Across the yard, the barn door creaked open, and a short, wiry man with a blond cavalier mustache and long blond hair appeared from within. He brushed dust and flecks of chaff from his blue plaid work shirt and his faded pants. He was built like a jockey.

–I heard you was out of the penitentiary, Jesse said.

Dick Liddil sucked in air when he heard the voice. Jesse liked to surprise a man.

–Ain't expected you, Liddil said.

Jesse sipped at the water, keeping his eyes on Liddil over the rim of the cup. Liddil had earned himself a reputation for highway robbery and horse-racing and betting swindles. Before he had been caught.

–You working? Jesse said.

–Two years now, Liddil said. Been working for Morrow. And Hudspeth.

–Pay much?

–I get by.

–Can I trust you, Dick?

Dick Liddil's shoulders went stiff and his fists tight. Jesse tossed what water remained in his cup into the dirt. Liddil's eyes dipped to Jesse's waist, where the Navy Colt was tucked crosswise in his waist behind the square brass buckle.

–More than most, I reckon.

–I'm broke, Jesse said.

Dick's lip curled in a half smile.

–Well, you ain't looking for a loan from *me*, that's for sure.

–You want to make a raise? I need some help.

–Need help?

–Good help. I'm kind of shorthanded right now. You interested?

–Maybe so, Dick said.

Dick's eyes were sharp now. He was thinking fast, but greed and the implications of it were no doubt firing off myriad considerations through his quick brain. He could calculate odds and the likely return upon them like a Chinese bookie with an abacus. Jesse had no time for Dick's calculations.

–Maybe or yes? Jesse said.

A wan light lit up the clouds and woods as if the world itself had opened upon Dick Liddil an unseen eye under whose scrutiny he beamed like a child chosen for a prize at a country gala.

–I'll do it, Dick said.

–You sure I can trust you, Dick?

Liddil nodded and grinned.

–Meet me here on Wednesday night. And we'll talk about the details.

The sky reddened toward the west, and bands of purple clouds shrouded the dying day. The blue of the sky's dome deepened at the zenith as daylight drained from it. As if the woods wished to reclaim the land upon which stood the Glendale Schoolhouse, thick ivy gripped the red brick walls and hung down over the lightless windows. Branches overhung the dry stone wall that marked the school's perimeter. Close to the northeast corner of the building stood a riven oak. The blasted tree was white-scarred where the bark had ripped open and blackened where the lightning's heat had smoked it. The leaves left on it were a pale yellow and hissed in the light breeze. All around the tree lay the limbs that had been sawed away from the listing trunk. One heavy branch was left.

And they should have cut that, too, Jesse thought. It could bring the whole damn tree down on some schoolchild one day.

He sat his white-faced bay between the stone pillars of the school's gate. Beside Jesse, his cousin Wood Hite, now known as Father Grimes for the operation, leaned over the neck of a skewbald paint as broad as a Hereford, and Grimes spat a brown stream into the dead leaves. A gnarled and freckled hand wiped at bushy whiskers that were streaked with gray. His hair hung to the shoulders of his duster in the fashion of an old bushwhacker. Grimes was the one man Jesse was sure that he could trust in a scrape and to keep his mouth shut, even if he was not too bright. He was a veteran of Bill Anderson's band, surly of demeanor, with a curl to his lip and one eye that closed in a squint each time he spoke to anyone he considered his inferior. And there were few that Grimes considered to be his equal. But with Jesse, he was deferential.

–Here they be, Grimes said.

Four riders approached along the leaf-strewn trail, beneath the sparsely foliaged branches. They were a passable crew, Jesse was sure, but not one of them of the caliber of the Younger brothers. Or Frank.

Goddamn, he missed Frank. But at least Grimes was kin.

–That Liddil knows horses, Jesse said.

Grimes gave a curt nod.

–Showy son of a bitch, though.

Dick Liddil kept his tight-muscled sorrel quarter horse on a short rein, and it pranced with a high gait. He wore his duster open and pulled back behind his hips. The handles of a pair of Smith & Wesson .44 pistols jutted from the holsters of his cartridge belts. Liddil was flanked on his right by Ed Miller. Ed was the brother of Clell Miller, who had been shot to death during the Northfield raid. He had just about begged to ride with Jesse. He was a soft-faced boy but tall and heavy from farm work around the chest and shoulders. He had turned up the collar of his duster, and a heavy green bandanna was bunched up under his double chin.

He was armed with a Navy Colt tucked in his belt — imitating me, Jesse thought — and he had a breech-loading shotgun in his saddle boot and a pair of Smith & Wesson .44's in his holsters, identical to Liddil's.

On the other side of Dick Liddil was Bill Ryan, a dark-haired, handsome Irishman with a strong, square jaw under his well-trimmed beard. His frock coat was dusty and well worn. He had no use for an alias, since he was known to all in the Cracker Neck and in the sporting houses of Kansas City and Independence. It was a risk to bring him along in case he was recognized, but Ryan was crazy enough. And Jesse needed someone besides Grimes with that kind of easy snap into violence.

Behind the other three rode the last of the company, Tucker Bassham — whom Jesse had named Arkansas. It was Grimes who had recruited Arkansas. Grimes reckoned he knew the boy's family. All bushwhackers. But Arkansas worried Jesse. He had a soft slouch hat jammed down around his round, red face. There was a glazed look in his pale-lashed pig eyes, and a plug of chaw bulged beneath his soft lower lip. He seemed none too bright, and fat and sluggish, too. A green-and-white blanket overcoat, patched at shoulder and elbow, stretched over his wide back and belly. But as much as he looked the poor dumb farmhand, he could obviously pick a horse, for he sat a fine-lined sorrel that looked as if it might have been foaled from the selfsame stock as Liddil's.

And this was Jesse's company, his own company, in the way that the old band had never been. Not with Cole and Frank being so much under their own control. Or even with the Shepherd brothers just after the war. And Jesse had tied his fate to that of all of these unknown and untried men. Or boys. They were boys. All except Grimes. Well, all these boys had to do was to follow the plan and they would be richer. Nobody hurt. They would be masked. Nobody would recognize them. Nothing go wrong. He looked into the faces of these strangers. Trust. He needed to trust them. He was trying them out.

–Get to it, Jesse said.

With Grimes and Ed Miller flanking him, Jesse led the way down the trail through the trees. Liddil, Arkansas, and Ryan followed. Their first time out. Everything needed to be perfect. They approached Moit's Trade Store — a long log cabin on a small lot cut back into the woods — and just beyond the store was the Glendale depot of the Chicago and Alton Railroad. Ryan, Liddil, and Arkansas reined in in front of Moit's and dismounted. Ryan would take care of Moit and his customers. He could trust Ryan. Jesse led Grimes and Miller on to the depot. A cold north wind ripped the tree branches on the other side of the steel railroad tracks, and a blizzard of yellow leaves swirled around him as he tied up his horse to a fence rail beside the depot building.

–Just stay by the door, Ed, Jesse said.

He had to look after the boy. Jesse had failed the boy's brother at Northfield. He remembered the shotgun blast that lifted Clell out of his stirrups. No time for memory now. Jesse pulled up a bandanna mask over the lower half of his face. Grimes and Miller did likewise. Jesse drew his Navy Colt and pushed open the door to the ticket agent's office. He stepped inside and leveled the pistol. Only one man in the office. Behind his desk. The frog-eyed railroad agent froze. He was a willowy, balding man with long sideburns, and his mouth was in a tight and nervous pout.

–Keep your hands still! Jesse called.

The agent sat in the chair and kept his hands on the blotter in front of him. A watch chain hung across the front of his vest. A big clock, roman-numeraled, tick-tocked high on the wall behind him. But time was frozen. All was just the perfect present. Jesse was sure of himself now. His crew behind him. Just like clockwork. A perfect operation, he was certain. The agent's desk was neat, with a writing set arranged along the top right edge of his blotter. A good sign. Jesse leaned over the desk. The agent's eyes were fixed on the muzzle of the pistol.

–What time is the next train? Jesse said.

–Eight o'clock.

The agent's voice was a croak.

–At a quarter to eight, Jesse said, you will go outside and lower the green flag so that next train stops.

The agent shook his head. The hair combed over the bald patch slipped over his left ear.

–I ain't helping you.

Dear God, this had to be perfect. Jesse smacked the palm of his left hand against the agent's forehead and jammed the muzzle of his pistol into the man's mouth. He had cut the agent's lip, and blood trickled onto steel. The gun barrel tapped against teeth. Was slippery on the tongue. The agent's eyes were wide now.

–I will blow the goddamn brains out of your head at the next wrong answer, Jesse said.

Yes, he would.

–Are you going to lower the flag? Jesse asked.

The agent's head dipped in a half nod, the best he could do given the amount of metal in his mouth. A long string of saliva stretched from foresight to lower lip and broke as Jesse drew the gun away.

–Just sit quiet now, Jesse said.

He was not agitated. He was calm. Miller was at the open door. The eyes above the bandanna were wide with fright.

–Don't worry none, Jesse said.

–Here come the boys from Moit's store, Miller said.

Ed stood away from the door, and the masked Bill Ryan appeared. He led man after man into the office: the long and the short and the lean and the fat. A good twenty of them. It was all part of the plan. Good man, Ryan. Arkansas's bulk came in behind the prisoners. The room was as crowded as a bar on a Saturday night, but the men were all slouched and frightened. Dick Liddil followed Arkansas into the office.

–Sit on the floor with your hands clasped at the back of your necks, Jesse said.

Each prisoner knelt and then dropped onto his haunches, not one of them lowering a hand. Ryan and Liddil kept them covered. Like the ticking of a clock, everything synchronized and running smoothly. They were frightened enough, but a little violence would bring the fear in them to a fine, high pitch. Jesse crossed the room and pushed Arkansas out of his way. A telegraph machine stood beneath the window on the east wall of the room. Jesse raised his pistol over his head. He hammered the butt down on the key tap and it skewed across the table. He smashed at the wire banks, shattering the insulators, which showered the floor with white porcelain. All of the prisoners winced and shied away from the flying wreckage.

–Hold up! Hold up there! Arkansas yelled.

Between the floppy brim of his hat and the line of his mask, his little pig eyes were agog.

–Ain't no call to wreck no sewing machine, he said. What's the pointa that?

The dumb hick. A dumb hick on his new crew. Grimes had recruited the son of a bitch, let him look after him. Jesse turned to his cousin.

–Take our friend outside, and you and him get some rocks and ties piled onto the track. We'll have ourselves a train wreck if the engineer decides he'd rather not stop.

–Come on, Grimes said.

None of the prisoners would look up. They darted little glances at their feet, the floorboards, the broken pieces of porcelain, but they would not look up. Jesse went back to the desk and brought his face close to the agent's. The frog eyes bulged. They couldn't turn away. His upper lip was swollen and the blood had formed a dark scab.

–Let's go lower the flag, Jesse said.

The agent nodded his bald head and stood.

Jesse turned to the prisoners from the store.

–Not one of you men show a whisker outside, you understand?

Jesse pushed past Ed Miller in the doorway and out onto the platform. The air was chiller now, and the wind still gusted leaves over the track and piled them between the rails. Ryan pushed the agent out behind Jesse. East of the platform, Arkansas and Grimes stood beside a pile of ties, tossing them on the track. Jesse led the way to the western flag station, where a green flag fluttered. He gestured with his pistol. The agent lifted it out of its socket. A small action, Jesse thought, to refuse which it was not worth taking a bullet through the roof of the mouth.

A whistle sounded in the twilight.

–He'll stop when he don't see no flag? Dick Liddil asked.

Jesse nodded.

The great black loco rounded the bend in the woods, slowed, screeched, its iron bulk drawing abreast of them, then the coal black tender and the express car and the passenger cars all rolled to a halt in the station. Dick Liddil left the agent on the platform next to Jesse and raced down toward the engine. Ed Miller ran behind him. Grimes and Arkansas passed them as they ran back along the tracks to cover the passenger cars. Dick's metal-plated heels clanged up the steps of the engine. Ryan was between the express car and the first passenger car.

–I can't get the goddamn coupling loose, he called. I ain't seen nothing like it before.

They didn't need to uncouple the carriages.

–Leave it, Jesse yelled.

From here on in it would all be routine. Just like the old days with the Younger Brothers: the express car, the sledgehammer, another frightened messenger to open the door and disgorge the contents of the safe. Jesse pushed the agent in front of him toward the express car. At the loco, Miller reached up to take a sledgehammer from Dick Liddil in the engine cab. It was something you could count on, a loco always had the same tools of his trade; no need to bring anything with them. Miller came running down with the hammer and mounted the steps to the platform of the express car. He tried the door handle. It was locked. A customary inconvenience. Miller drew back the sledge and slammed it against the lockset. The door didn't break. They never did. The sledge just made an impressive noise. Jesse fired a shot in the air. That was a more impressive noise. The agent covered his ears, a lank shock of hair in the fingers of his left hand, the bald dome glistening.

–Open the goddamn door, Jesse yelled.

Miller hammered the lockset again. The door splintered but didn't spring open.

Jesse fired off another round into the air. He climbed up beside Miller on the platform of the express car. He bawled out.

–Open the goddamn door or when I do get in, you're a dead man!

The lock rattled and the door swung inward. Miller pushed inside. The slightly built messenger squirmed by Miller through the door, and Jesse swung the Colt and fetched him a blow across the cheekbone that dropped him onto his ass, back inside the carriage. The messenger's eyes had a blank, stunned look about them. One hand clutched at his face, the other held on to a bunch of keys.

–Open the safe now, Jesse said.

The messenger glanced up out of one eye, then Miller grabbed him by the collar and dragged him backward to the squat green safe. A choking noise escaped the man's throat. The keys rattled.

–Get it done, Jesse shouted.

The messenger got up on his knees and selected a key from the ring. He turned it in the lock and then pulled open the thick metal door.

–Stay on your knees, Jesse said.

–Look at that, Miller said.

Piles of new bills were stacked on the shelves of the safe.

Miller tossed the sledge to one side and pulled a grain sack from the deep inside pocket of his duster. He scooped the piles of bills and papers and envelopes into the sack.

–There's a goddamn fortune in here, he said.

A goddamn fortune. First time out with a new crew and a goddamn fortune. Like clockwork.

–Come on, Jesse said. Fill it up.

With the safe empty, Miller closed the mouth of the sack and tied it with piggin string. Jesse gestured to the messenger with the barrel of his gun.

–You can stay where you are.

Miller swung the sack up and cradled it in his arms.

–Let's go, Jesse said.

He was out of the door and onto the platform, down the steps and running for his horse. He heard Dick Liddil clanking down the iron steps from the engine cab. Shots cracked from the windows of the passenger cars. Bullets hummed by him. He was a rich man. He knew it. And he could stand to be richer yet. This was his crew. The first operation of a scratch gang. A perfect start. No need for another operation for a while now. Time to see Zee and the children back in Nashville. He swung up onto the bay. Ed Miller mounted the horse beside him. Then Arkansas, Liddil, Ryan, and Grimes all took to the saddle. These sons of bitches had to keep their mouths shut. That was all. Grimes he trusted. The others? Young boys. He had warned them. They swung their horses around and galloped off down the trail toward the schoolhouse. Jesse put heel to the bay. Short of killing them all, there was no guarantee of silence.

XL.

JESSE LEANED OVER THE LONG OAK TABLE THAT WAS COVERED WITH twigs and leaves and dried flowers. The wreath that Zee was weaving made him nervous. She wound a sprig of blue vervain into the circle of dried marigolds, pearly sweet everlasting, and six red roses. Six roses: one for her, one for him, one for each child alive, and one for each of the twins, dead. Such a wreath, a mixture of the living and the dead, had a funereal quality to it. The last rays of the evening sun slanted through the chenille drapes and lit up the tulle veil over the boat-like crib wherein lay Jesse's daughter. Dick Liddil and Grimes stood next to it, a violent intrusion into the domesticity of this dark house. They were his good soldiers. In the fallow months, he let them go their own way. Liddil, he heard, had bought himself an outfit and a team and had gone into the hauling business. When he sent word to them, they showed up and worked with him. They had taken a good haul when they robbed a stage down at Mammoth Caves, and the best they had done was to rob a government paymaster in Alabama. A good haul and they could hold out for months. An easy life. But something was wrong. The usual self-satisfied smirk on Grimes's face was absent and had been replaced by a bovine melancholy, the eyes dead and flat, hard creases beside the curved nose, and the mouth all but invisible in the gray-flecked beard. The big bushwhacker, in his tight and dusty buckskin shirt, dwarfed the dapper and diminutive Dick Liddil. Grimes stood square and still with his thumbs tucked into his cartridge belt. Liddil looked as if he had just come from the racetrack. He was dressed in a dark frock coat with a Stetson to match. His blond mustache curled up on each side, and the cavalier beard under the middle of his lower lip had been meticulously trimmed. He fidgeted with a short leather quirt, twisting it and bending it between his fingers.

–Sit down, Jesse said.

Neither man moved toward a chair.

–They got Bill Ryan, Grimes said.

The voice gravelly, deadpan.

–Down in Johnsonville, Liddil said.

He looked down at the crib, glanced at Jesse, looked away.

–What happened? Jesse said.

–You know Ryan, Grimes said. A girl on each arm and drinks all around.

Liddil chimed in.

–He give one a necklace and the other a watch right out of his pocket. Watch was inscribed to that judge on the Mammoth Caves stage.

–Ever'body read 'bout that judge in the newspaper, Grimes said.

–The son of a bitch was drunk, Jesse said. I know it.

–Watch your language, Zee said.

–Ever' man that walked into that bar, Grimes said, he bought a round for 'em.

A wail arose from the crib where Mary lay. Little Jesse Edwards tugged at Zee's dark skirt. Her hand, a reflex, slid back to caress his soft fair hair. She set down the wreath and took their son's hand. There was a darkness to her since the twins had died, and over the house, and that shadow was in his soul, too. The babies had turned yellow as if the very milk from her breasts had poisoned them.

–Let's see what Mary wants, Zee said.

–Take the babies upstairs, Zee, Jesse said.

–I'm not a baby, Jesse Edwards said.

–No, you ain't, Jesse said. You're nigh on five year old, now. So you look after Mama, upstairs.

Behind Liddil and Grimes, Zee pulled up the crib veil and lifted their squalling daughter into her arms. The small fingers clutched at Zee's blouse. The voice howled. He would be patient. He would not rage in front of his children. Zee leaned to pick up a woolen shawl off the straight-backed chair beside the empty hearth. She wrapped it around Mary so that it helped support the baby's weight. Then she took Jesse Edwards's hand again and guided him in front of her to the stair door. Jesse Edwards's small fingers slid into the gap between the ill-fitting door and the casement, and he pried it open. He climbed up the stairs in front of Zee, his legs stretching up to each carpeted tread. Mary still cried in Zee's arms. The howls receded up the stairs.

Jesse turned back to Liddil and Grimes.

–Did I not say? Did I not say? No conspicuous spending? Did I not say that? And to keep your damn mouths shut?

Liddil twisted the quirt in both hands. He turned a bright red, but Grimes kept the same dull expression on his face.

–Sheriff put a gun to the back of his head, Grimes said. Deputy disarmed him. Got him to empty his pockets.

–Watches, rings, necklaces, Liddil said.

–Me and Liddil was playing cards. We left out by the back door. No one even knew we was with him.

–You think Ryan'll talk? Jesse said.

–Bill Ryan won't talk, Grimes said.

Liddil laid a hand on the crib and it tilted and creaked. The veil was pulled back. The emptiness of it reminded Jesse of the dead twins. This damned house. Ryan had been coming and going for months. Some lawman might know of the connection, even if Ryan didn't talk. Zee had wanted to leave Nashville ever since the twins died. He had to trust that Ryan had said nothing. Would say nothing. Not right away.

–You two get on to Kentucky, Jesse said. I'll follow on up when I get Zee and the kids organized.

–One more thing, Grimes said.

Jesse stood up from the table. He knew that this one more thing was not what he would want to hear. He lifted his chin.

–My brother Clarence telegraphed me from Nelson County, Grimes said. The laws went into the Cracker Neck. They arrested Tucker Bassham, too.

Two men gone and in the hands of the law. He had to get out of this house that had turned bleak. The house where his first child had been born. There was something off-kilter about it now that confused his good judgment. He would go back to Kansas City and recruit more new men. He had never had to think twice about the Youngers or Clell Miller or the Shepherds mouthing off in the wrong places or backing him up in a scrape. He had men around him, but he was more alone than ever. Grimes was his one link with the past. Liddil was of the same ilk as Bill Ryan. Or Bassham. A young upstart. With Frank by his side, everything would be in balance again. He had to plan another operation, as soon as he moved and got Zee and the kids settled, just a month or two. An operation that would persuade Frank to rejoin him.

XLI

FROM CLAY PIPES AND BRIARS ROSE REDDISH-BROWN SPIRALS; curls of blue wafted up from fat stogies and thin cigarillos; gray plumes bloomed over the hats and heads and seat backs of the passengers. The fog folded back upon itself and formed intangible and fantastic landscapes that floated by him in which he imagined places of torment for those who had wronged him and continued to wrong him. The lateral rocking of the carriage lulled Jesse into a sense of ease, a satisfaction, a sense that each small cog in God's greater clockwork was inexorably meshed and driving along his plan with preternatural precision.

Jesse pulled back the lapel of his linen duster and reached inside his jacket pocket for his embossed silver cigar case. He eased off the top and drew out a slim Havana that he had bought at Maude LaRue's, on the corner of Fifth and Broadway in Kansas City. Such a luxury was one of the advantages of renting a house in Kansas City. Once more, he and Zee were hidden in the heart of a densely populated city. Close to their Missouri families, too. He placed the cigar between his lips, let it dangle onto the full beard that curled over his chin. He snapped a match alight and pressed his lips together to bring up the cigar and puffed and twirled to bring it to life.

The conductor entered through the front door of the smoking car. He tugged at his shiny peaked cap as if in greeting to all the passengers bound for Gallatin and points beyond. He was a broad-shouldered man with a waxed mustache, around forty years old. Jesse knew him. Even his name. Westfall. A trusted employee of the Chicago and Alton Railroad Company. Five and a half years earlier, he had brought a special train from Chicago on January 26, 1875. That special train had carried a team of Pinkertons down to Kearney: the men who had maimed Mama. Some slights and blows a man might forget, or time heal, but for such an outrage upon his own mother, the desire for vengeance had remained smoldering, awaiting only the occasion that nature's balance might be tilted a little closer toward the true again. And did not the Lord provide the means for dispensing justice? For this train was tipped to be carrying five thousand dollars in the express car. Jesse puffed on the cigar. Already he could celebrate. Westfall had been the bait to bring Frank back to the company. How could Frank have refused a chance for revenge on one of those who had maimed Mama? Especially with an easy five thousand dollars coinciding with it. As if they were being paid to exact revenge. It was not Pinkerton of course, or one of his agents, but if he could not get close to the detectives themselves, then he could still deal with their lackeys.

Oh Mr. Pinkerton, he prayed, I hope that our Heavenly Father may deliver you, yourself, into my hands. And I believe He will, for His merciful and protecting arm has ever been with me and shielded me. And during my persecution, He has watched over me and protected me from workers of blood money who are trying to seek my life, and I have hope and faith in Him and believe He will ever protect me as long as I serve Him.

For now, Westfall was in his hands. His execution would send a message to all those who would consider helping the detectives to capture Jesse James. Or Frank. And that was why Frank had agreed to the mission. Jesse needed Frank. Especially since the laws had captured Tucker Bassham and Bill Ryan. And he was worried about Dick Liddil and Ed Miller. This robbery would provide another means to ensure the loyalty of the new gang members. Jesse intended to tie them in tight with his own fate.

The conductor leaned over the first seat with his book of tickets and his pencil and shiny clippers, where sat Frank and their cousin, old Father Grimes. Frank and Grimes paid their fare, and Westfall moved closer, leaning over the passengers, quickly pocketing the coins that were dropped in his hand.

–Ticket, sir? Westfall said.

–Gallatin, Jesse said.

He dropped a quarter into the conductor's hand. The hand was pink and smooth. A hand never given to manual labor. The shiny clippers clicked on Jesse's ticket. Westfall moved on. Jesse crumpled the ticket and let it fall to the floor among the crushed stubs of old stogies and the spent black ash knocked from pipes and the mashed ends of dead cigarettes. He pulled his fob watch from his vest pocket. Seven minutes past six. Ed Miller, Dick Liddil, and Grimes's brother, Clarence, should be on their way to the engine cab. Jesse dropped his cigar and crushed it under the sole of his boot. Brakes squealed and the train slowed. From his waistband, Jesse drew the Navy Colt. Stood up. A silence fell upon the passengers around him. It was as if each one of them was frozen in the moment of the pistol's appearance.

–Put your hands up! Jesse called to Westfall.

Did Westfall not hear him? The conductor still leaned over a passenger as if clipping a ticket.

–Put your hands up! Jesse called.

Westfall's back commenced to straighten.

Jesse fired.

Book and clippers clattered to the floor. Westfall staggered sideways, clutched his back close to his kidneys, blood oozing through his fingers. He moaned. He reached for the rear door of the car. Jesse raised the pistol, drew the foresight in line with the spine, just below the shoulder blades, squeezed the trigger and his ears rang with the shot that knocked Westfall clear through the door and dropped him onto the car's platform.

That will make Mama happy.

Passengers yelled behind Jesse. A shot. Another. Jesse spun and fired. Bangs, powder smoke, and flashes through the tobacco fog. Passengers crawling in the aisles among the ash and filthy detritus. Jesse waded through the panicked mass that squirmed about his knees like a living stream. He beat against the heads that rose to his waist. Frank and Grimes blocked the front door of the car so that no passenger could escape. A blood-stained corpse lay in the aisle, its arms twisted around the metal bracket that fastened a seat to the strewn floor as if the man had been drowning and sought to pull himself to shore. The suit was streaked with dirt and ash. Two dead. A hanging matter. Now if Liddil and Miller got caught, the laws would be loath to parlay a deal with a pair of accessories to murder. Murder in the first degree.

XLII

HE PUSHED THEM HARD THROUGH THE WOODS DEEP INTO RAY County. He had kept the gang on the move since the Winston killings, for the Republican newspapers had been howling for James Gang blood. Some of the Democrats, too. He wanted Liddil and Ed Miller close by him all the time so that he could keep an eye on them. These new boys had grown up wild and cocky on stories of old bushwhackers and the exploits of the James and Younger Gang and had thought to try their own luck at raiding and living in the bush. But they had not been forged in the war, as he had, as Frank had, as Grimes had, and as the Youngers had been. Liddil and Miller had waved their pistols around at unarmed passengers, but they had never done or even seen a killing. Liddil had turned white when Jesse broke the news that he had executed Westfall. Ed Miller hopped from foot to foot like a boy in need of a piss. The killing was irrevocable. If they considered making a deal with the law, they would have to find some way to deny any knowledge of Westfall, of who he was, that Jesse didn't know him, that it was all an unfortunate mistake. That might bring the charge down to second-degree murder. Murder in commission of a robbery. It could still get them hanged. He was convinced that his hold over them depended only upon the money that he put in their pockets, their fear of the law, and their fear of him. Mostly upon their fear of him. A whisper worked within him, a wordless voice of suspicion that grated away his confidence like a needle against bone. He would be glad to have Frank with him again. He hadn't been able to stop him from taking off to see Annie Ralston, but Frank was due to meet up with Jesse again at Blue Cut, where he planned to hit another train. Everything had become so complicated, now. Even Edwards had warned him that fewer and fewer people had sympathy for his raids, no matter how daring they seemed. But in action, everything was simple: his thought was on one object; the men around him were committed to working together, each one with a specific act to undertake, and every move was under his order, his control. Liddil and Ed Miller and even Grimes were expendable extensions of his own mind and limbs, a living shield around him. Jesse, along with Edwards and Shelby, had tried to orchestrate a massive political campaign and he had lost control of it. He had not been able to stand with a gun at the head of every Democratic member of the House or the Senate to vote for his amnesty, but he did stand with a gun behind the back of every man who worked for him. He knew it and they knew it. Above all, he had to keep control of those around him or he was a dead man, or worse, an incarcerated man. Like the Younger brothers were now.

Jesse eased the roan forward and he descended the hill toward the farm. A stark Missouri beauty. His home country. Clouds bellied from horizon to horizon, lit up the color of a pale peach where the sun struggled to make its presence felt among the leafy branches of the western trees. A desultory chorus of unseen birds piped out of the woods. Bare meadows, black and yellow with loam and corn trash lay to the north and west of Mattie Bolton's box-like house that nestled in the stubbled hollow. Mattie Bolton's place was on the way to Blue Cut, and it was Liddil who had suggested holing up there. Jesse went along with it. Ray County was right next to Clay, where Jesse grew up. One time it had been Confederate country, but now the war seemed to be a long way in the past. Dick had used the farm as a rendezvous point for a girl he was poking. Another Mattie: Mattie Collins. And Jesse knew it was safe. Mattie Bolton was the widowed daughter of the Ford family; and the Reverend and Mrs. Ford had been solid Southerners back when it still counted. They had always given Jesse a bed to lie in. The Fords had a wild bunch of boys, too: Capline and Charley and Bob. Their mama and papa had brought them up with a healthy respect for Southern heroes. And Jesse had kept them amused since they were little, with stories about the war, every time he had hidden out on the Ford farm. The Ford boys, too, fancied themselves as outlaws. Charley had robbed a stage with Dick Liddil. Charley and Dick had gone whoring together. And Charley, Dick said, liked to take the morphine that the sporting women gave him before he poked them. Word was that the three brothers had maybe robbed a store or two up near Gallatin. Nobody knew for sure because they didn't brag about it. He liked that about them. Might be he could use them on the next train job. In case anything happened to Liddil or Miller.

All of their horses were breathing hard. On Jesse's left side, Dick Liddil sat a stolen roan. Dick's sallow cheeks were sunken, eyes bloodshot, the blond mustache drooping. On Liddil's left, Ed Miller slumped over his sorrel's neck, his fat farm boy's face flushed, the eyelids crusted from sleeping rough in the woods and barns of Ray County. Not like Grimes. Grimes was of the old school. Used to long campaigns, riding day after day, week after week, dodging soldiers and militia patrols. He sat up straight in the saddle, his chest and shoulders stretching his buckskin shirt taut. The sunset light brought out the hardness in his face, wrinkles tight around the narrow eyes, mouth downturned in his gray-whiskered beard, face framed by the lank and matted long hair. A cruel face. And a face he trusted. He couldn't afford to lose Grimes.

Down the slope, he recognized the gangly form of Charley Ford ambling across the yard from porch to coldhouse that was in a small grove of aspen. A smaller figure, that Jesse took to be Bob Ford, climbed onto the five-bar gate and sat and watched them as they came down the trail. Jesse put his horse forward in a canter. He pulled up in front of the gate where Bob Ford sat on the top bar. The boy made no move to open the gate. His only sign of nervousness was that the heel of his right boot jiggled on the third bar down. His smooth-shaved face had a wicked smirk. A defiance. Jesse considered the boy a dandy. He was overdressed for country living: a gray three-piece suit and a matching hat. He had a shiny new gun belt with a holster on his hip. The boy was trouble. Potential trouble even if he had never been in any serious scrape yet. He must be at least nineteen by now.

–I'm looking for the widow Bolton, Jesse said.

The palest of gray eyes regarded Jesse.

–I know, Bob said. That's my sister.

–I didn't ask what kin she was, boy.

Grimes guffawed and leaned forward over the pommel of his saddle. He spat in the dirt.

–She's inside, Bob said.

–I believe we're expected.

Bob nodded and grinned and got down off the gate.

Jesse dismounted. Bob Ford unlatched the gate and swung it open. The smirk irked Jesse of a sudden. He needed to bring this boy down to earth. Teach him some respect. The muscles of Jesse's jaw tensed. He stared hard into the boy's gray eyes.

–Put these horses in the barn, Jesse said. And give them a good rubdown before you give them any feed.

Let him be a gray-suited stable boy. And it was as if Bob Ford's feet were controlled by nerves other than his own. A marionette under invisible fingers. Bob Ford approached him now and meekly took the reins of the bay from his hand. He could mold the boy in his own image as he, Jesse, had been molded by Bill Anderson. Jesse strode up to the kitchen door without a glance backward. He would wind the boy up and let his clockwork run down, and then he would put him to work for him.

Jesse pushed into the kitchen and nodded to Mattie Bolton, who was at the hearth, where she stirred a blackened pot over the fire. Her blond hair was pulled back from her face and tied with a green ribbon. Her small bowed lips pursed as she looked at him out of big blue eyes that always seemed to have dark shadows beneath them since her husband, Bill Bolton, had died.

–Come on in, Jesse, she said.

–Evening, Mattie.

–How many are ye?

–Four.

She lifted her chin to indicate the table. Mattie Collins was already seated there. Waiting for Liddil, no doubt. Jesse had heard rumors that Liddil had been with both of these women, but Mattie C. had claimed him. Despite the heat of the kitchen, Liddil's woman had a dark green woolen cape draped over her shoulders. Her brown hair fell long and framed a wide face with a scattering of freckles over her turned-up nose. Liddil did well with women.

Jesse took his seat at the head of the table. He pushed his hat back, scratched at the underside of his thick beard, and laid a pistol laid next to the bourbon bottle that Mattie B. had thoughtfully provided.

–Hidy, Grimes said.

–Set down, Mattie Bolton said.

–Ed outside? Jesse said.

–At the gate, Grimes said.

Jesse nodded. Mattie set a plate of succotash in front of him and then served Grimes. She set another steaming plate upon the table and one plate in the warmer. Then Bob Ford came into the kitchen with Dick Liddil. Mattie Collins smiled broadly enough to show her uneven white teeth.

–You want a plate, Bob? Mattie Bolton asked.

–Sure, he said.

–The one that's out is for your friend, Mattie said.

–That's Dick Liddil, Bob said.

–I know him well enough, Mattie said, and she gave Liddil a saucy smirk.

Liddil went to sit close to Mattie Collins. Her hand came up and rested on the shoulder of his dusty frock coat. Bob Ford sat down at the opposite end of the table beside Liddil. A few flecks of chaff and flakes of oat clung to the sleeve of his fine suit. Jesse nodded and smiled at him. He detected a trace of resentment in the boy.

A plate full of biscuits stood in the center of the table, and Jesse reached for one. Bob did likewise.

–Well, Bob, what's in the holster? Jesse said.

Bob Ford smiled. It seemed as if he was trying not to by the way only half his lips curled.

–S. and W. number three, he said.

He was grinning all over his damn face, but he obviously couldn't stop himself.

–You know how to shoot it? Jesse said.

–I can shoot it.

–How old are you now?

Bob's smile faded. Grimes just kept shoveling food into his mouth, washing it down with bourbon and staring at Mattie Bolton, who was at the hearth, scraping the ladle around the bottom of a pan.

–Nineteen, Bob said.

–I took you for younger

Jesse figured that would needle him.

Bob Ford flushed.

–Yeah, Bob said. A lotta people do.

–Should we try him out, Dick? Jesse said.

Dick Liddil moved away from Mattie Collins, took off his hat, and hung it on the back of his chair. He smoothed down his long blond hair. He shrugged at Jesse and raised his eyebrows at Bob.

–You want to make a raise, Bob? Dick said.

Mattie came over from the hearth and sat beside Bob. Her face had suddenly turned wan and drawn. She didn't look at Bob. Or anyone at the table. A worried older sister. A grin split Bob Ford's cheeks again. The boy would make an awful poker player. His face just shone right out whatever was going through his head. Right now, he was thinking about riding with Jesse James.

–Bob can handle hisself, Charley said.

–You name the time and place, Bob Ford said. I can do it.

Why not try him out on a small job?

–You, Dick, and Charley can go with Grimes while I take Ed to meet Frank at Blue Cut. The Short Line stage runs from Gallatin to Lexington. Passes through the woods just north of the river. Let's see how you operate.

Bob Ford was beaming. He had always liked the kid. He had seen him grow up from a spindly little boy to a spindly young man. He had balls, but Jesse would tell Grimes to ride Bob Ford hard just to see how he stood up to pressure. He wanted more men that he could trust. More men between him and the law.

XLIII

HE HAD IDOLIZED JESSE JAMES EVER SINCE HE WAS TEN YEARS OLD and sitting in his mama's kitchen with Jesse by the hearth telling stories of Bill Anderson's guerrillas. Stories of revenge and reprisal. It seemed that Jesse had told of a time of giants, when each man of his company seemed to be a storied hero who could boast of great acts of violence against those who had burned Confederate farms and imprisoned Confederate women. And now, he, Bob Ford, was riding with the outlaw gang that was famous all over the known world, though not yet with Jesse James himself. He had stepped into a world that was infinitely greater than life around the farm trails of Ray County or any small robbery that he had previously been capable of imagining. There was a sense of vertigo about it. As if he had stepped outside a cage that had been oppressive to him but had also protected him from greater forces of violence and retribution that could be called up by the law as well as by the men he rode with.

In the deepening dusk of the woods, his brother Charley and Dick Liddil guided their horses off the main trail and onto the narrow wagon track, where Bob sat Mattie's chestnut mare, next to the gray-bearded outlaw Jesse had called Father Grimes. Jesse had entrusted Grimes with leadership of the holdup that they, he, Bob Ford, were about to stage.

Grimes fished a gold watch from his vest pocket and sprung the lid of it. Bob had no watch of his own. He reckoned that it was around nine o'clock, but there was no way to tell from the sky, for the close-set trunks shut out what light there might have been post-sunset, and as if to mock his impatience, the pulse of peepers and the crickets' trill in the still air marked the passing of the seconds like the forest's own handless chronometer. The Short Line stagecoach was due to come through the wood close to nine o'clock. He willed it to be nine o'clock. Grimes made a show of studying the watch face, tilting his head this way and that before snapping the contraption shut and nodding. He did not favor the company with the time. Early starlight glinted through the leafy canopy. Bob's duster felt tight across his back and restricted the movement of his shoulders and elbows. He shifted his shoulders to loosen it up, a nervous action that caught the eye of Grimes.

–You never done a holdup, Grimes said.

–I done one, Bob said.

He had only robbed one store. Him and Charley and Capline. Up close to Gallatin, where Jesse had done one of his first raids after the war. But he had felt invincible. Such a charge of joy when they had grabbed the small amount of cash in the storekeeper's drawer, mounted up, and ridden off south into the woods unfollowed, but the act itself was more thrilling than the paltry reward their action had rendered to him and his brothers. Paltry beside Grimes's experience. Grimes had robbed trains and banks. Still, he didn't want to seem green in front of Grimes.

–Don't seem like there's much to it, Bob said.

–They ain't, Dick said.

–Not if you can hold your sand, Grimes said.

–Me and Dick robbed the Excelsior Springs stage, Charley said.

–That's you and Dick, but I'm talking to the boy here. He looks like he's about to shit.

–Quit riding him, Dick said.

–What do you say, boy?

What Bob wanted to say was, kiss my ass, but Grimes scared him more than the thought of the robbery. The sheer brute presence of him made a dwarf of Dick Liddil and a ghost of Charley's already shadowy self, and the violence in Grimes's muscled form seemed ready to erupt at the least provocation. They were about to rob a stage together, so why was Grimes needling him?

–I ain't scared, Bob said.

–I'll be watching you.

Grimes spat over the neck of his horse. Contempt in it.

You can watch, you son of a bitch.

–That your sister at the farm? Grimes said.

–You know it, Bob said.

–I'd like to poke her. Think she'd let me poke her?

Just the idea of this bear of a man with his sister disgusted him.

–I don't know as she's your type, Bob said.

–What's my type? Grimes said. You insinuating something?

–I ain't insinuating nothing. I just don't rightly know.

–She's my type. You think I'm her type?

–Leave him be, Grimes, Dick said.

–I ain't asked you, Dick. Did I ask you?

Only the narrowing of Liddil's eyes betrayed a tightly caulked resentment, but he didn't open his mouth.

–Your sister like a poke, Bob? Grimes said.

–She got two kids, Bob said, so she must have done it some time.

–What about with me?

–You're too goddamn ugly, Dick said.

Bob's laugh came out high and strangled. Grimes turned on Liddil.

–Listen, pretty boy, Grimes said. I bet you ten dollars I get to poke the widow Bolton, and for another ten, I'll let you boys watch. You might learn something.

There was a venom in Grimes toward Liddil and Liddil gave it right back.

–You couldn't learn me nothing, you ugly son of a bitch.

–You think you're the ladies' man, Grimes said. But let me tell you: Mattie Bolton ain't the only one round here go for old bushwhacker meat.

Down the trail, the rumble of wheels and the creak of wagon springs made a welcome sound. Grimes turned his horse away from Liddil. Bob pulled the cloth mask up close to the bridge of his nose and drew his revolver.

–Easy, Grimes said. Don't no one give us away here.

But Grimes, too, pulled up his mask and slid a breech-loading shotgun from his saddle boot. Bob cocked his pistol, and with the click Grimes glanced at Bob.

–No shooting for nothing, Grimes said. Just cover the guard.

Six cantering horses dragged the big stagecoach around the bend, and it rumbled and slewed over the trail. Dick and Charley pulled up their masks and drew pistols. Bob, along with the others, eased his mount forward into plain view of the oncoming driver and his guard.

–Stand up there! Grimes bellowed.

As if the sound of Grimes's voice had erected a wall, the front horses tossed their heads and came to a stop with short, low whinnies of alarm. The fat driver sawed at the reins and yanked up the brake. His hat was tilted back on his head, a dark halo around the face, with its thick, scrubby whiskers and slack mouth. By his side, a guard held a shotgun propped up on his thigh. Behind the crew, the coach was piled with trunks and mail sacks on its roof.

–What you fellas all up to here? the driver said.

–Stand fast! Grimes called.

Bob drew a bead on the guard just as Grimes had said to do, the foresight aligned with the center of his chest. The shotgun stayed at an angle, propped up on the man's left thigh. The guard's right hand was held in the air, palm out. His face was hidden under the brim of his hat. Bob stared at the chest. If the shotgun swung down, he would squeeze the trigger on the pistol, slow and easy.

–Lord Jesus, the guard said, as if there was a telegraph line along the possible trajectory of Bob's bullet through which they communicated the gravity of their intentions.

–Throw down the ordnance, Bob said.

The guard held up his shotgun by the twin barrels and let it drop from the box. He took a pistol from his belt and tossed it down beside the shotgun. He raised both hands, but Bob kept the man's chest under the sight. Beside the guard, the driver unholstered his pistol and tossed it onto the trail.

Dick Liddil and Charley pushed their horses by the coach's team and dismounted. Grimes had his shotgun at his shoulder, masked cheek on the stock.

–Everybody out, nice and easy, Dick said. We ain't here to keep you long.

Charley ran to the back of the coach and trained his pistol on the door. The hats and masks and long dusters made of his brother and Dick featureless revenants in the thickening dark who glided about their thievery. The door of the stagecoach swung outward.

–The ladies can remain seated, Dick said. Just the gentlemen out here.

Six men in well-cut suits stepped down next to the coach.

–Is this Jesse James?

Bob grinned under the mask. The man who spoke looked to be in his sixties. He had a fine handlebar mustache that curved under his narrow cheeks. He held himself like a preacher or a politician: shoulders back, chest out, chin up. There was a comic air to him. As if he was pleased to be in such a living tableau from a storybook or lurid newspaper account.

–This is a holdup, Dick said. We don't do no introductions. Line up along the coach now.

–Don't shoot nobody, now, the driver said. No heroes here.

Bob's gun sight drifted toward the driver, then he drew his aim back upon the unarmed guard. Grimes still had his shotgun trained on the driver.

–Hands in sight, please, gentlemen, Dick said.

All the passengers had their hands held high. Charley holstered his piece and pulled a grain sack from the inside flap pocket of his duster.

–Disgorge, gentlemen, he said.

He held the mouth of the bag in front of the first passenger, and the man dropped in a wallet and a watch and chain. Charley went along the line. There wasn't going to be any shooting, and for that he was glad. It was one thing to rob these folks' belongings, quite another to drop one dead. He had played his part. Grimes could fault Bob for nothing. Time to start counting the money. Somewhere to his right, the high screaming buzz of a cicada rose and fell among the trees. Dick and Charley were back in the saddle. Grimes glanced over at the wagon driver but kept the shotgun pointed at the coachmen.

–You wait a half hour and then you move out, Grimes said. If we see any of you again tonight, none of you will see the morning.

Dick and Charley guided their horses between Bob and Grimes. Then Grimes slid his shotgun back into the saddle boot. Bob uncocked his pistol and holstered it. He turned Mattie's horse after his brother and Dick, put heel to the mare, and she raced off after them down the trail. The hooves of Grimes's horse rumbled behind him. Dick and Charley turned down a side trail and he followed them into the darkness. He yanked down his mask to breathe in the heavy forest air. Having Grimes behind him made the skin of his back crawl. The mare stumbled but kept her feet and raced on.

He slowed her to a walk as they came out of the woods and he was on a low hillside above North Lexington. Dick and Charley were silhouetted against the sparkling sky. The lights of the city below were a serene reflection of the stars above them. Not a breath of wind stirred on the bluff. The peepers and crickets still marked time in the forest behind them. He stroked the neck of Mattie's mare. The mare nodded her head toward Dick and Charley's mounts. Grimes pulled up his horse next to Bob.

–What we got, Charley? Grimes said.

Charley had the sack open between his thighs.

–Two hundred sixteen dollars, a gold watch and chain, silver watch with no chain, nickel-plated watch and gold chain and one pocket knife. Ain't bad.

–How do we divide it? Bob said.

–I divide it, Grimes said. Fifty bucks a head to start. Give Liddil the gold watch and chain. I'll take the silver one, Charley the extra sixteen bucks, and Bob gets the nickel watch and gold chain. I'll take the pocket knife.

Fifty dollars and a goddamn watch and chain. Grimes even seemed fair. Charley handed Bob the watch and a handful of bills. After he had stuffed the money into the pocket of his jacket, he polished the watch against his vest and he pried open the lid. It was nine forty-three. In Roman numerals. The second hand kept beat with the peepers. He grinned at Grimes and looked back at the watch face and clicked it shut.

–Nice watch, Bob said.

He fastened the gold chain in a buttonhole of his vest and dropped the watch into his vest pocket. The chain dangled almost to his cartridge belt. He winked at Charley. They were going to do a train job with Jesse James. Now that was money. Big money. Dick had said they got a thousand dollars a man on the Glendale train, and they were going to Glendale again.

–Now what? Bob said.

–Me and Dick are going to old man Ralston's to meet Jesse and Frank, Grimes said. Charley, you head on down to Doc Reed's at Glendale. And you, Bob, you go on back to your sister's house and tell her that old Father Grimes will be over in a couple days to poke her.

–Mattie ain't gonna poke you, Grimes, Bob said.

–Then me and you got a bet, Grimes said. If I poke your sister, I take that watch off of you. Now get along.

–When do I meet up with you all? Bob said.

–When we come looking for you, Grimes said.

–What about the train?

–I don't want you on no train.

–There's money on that goddamn train. Big money.

–Mr. Howard ain't said nothing about you on no goddamn train, Grimes said.

–Hey, Charley, Bob said.

Charley shrugged.

Not even his brother was going to back him.

–Dick?

–Get on to Mattie's, Dick said. We'll be back soon enough.

–And I'll be wanting that watch, Grimes said. You can count on it.

XLIV

JESSE JAMES WAS IN MATTIE'S KITCHEN AGAIN, AND EVEN FROM the yard Bob could hear the laughter and shouts and the clink of glass against glass. His sister screeched, and some of the men roared with laughter. It sounded like quite a celebration, considering that all they had gained from the train robbery at Blue Cut was a hundred and sixty dollars apiece and a few watches and stick pins. Charley had given him fifty dollars, but that wasn't the point. Bob strode into the kitchen. They were all of them drunk.

Jesse James, hat pushed back, thick-bearded, with a pistol laid next to the bourbon bottle, sat at the head of the table like a king at a banquet, but there was only booze. He glanced at Bob as he came in, and Bob stopped as if he had walked into an invisible wall. The scrutiny was like being filleted. When Jesse's eyes dropped to the bottle, Bob felt free to move again, and he hesitated, not knowing where to sit at the table. Charley was by Jesse's side, chair turned outward. Jesse raised the bottle and poured a heavy shot of whiskey into Charley's glass, but Charley didn't need any whiskey. He was on the medicine again, head nodding in time to a slow beat that only he could hear. That was his way of celebrating his first train robbery with the James Gang, and nobody seemed to mind. On Jesse's right hand, Bob's sister, Mattie, sat in Grimes's lap. He had a hand cupped around her left breast and it seemed that she suffered his pawing rather than welcomed it. One eye half closed, he leered at her. He pushed his whiskey glass at her small bowed lips, trying to get her to sip at it, but she turned her head away, her blond hair coming loose from the bun at the back of her head and falling down to the shoulder of her white blouse. Bob blushed when Mattie let herself go slack and lay back against the brute.

Frank James was at the far end of the table. He had a big, square face and brown mustache and low-slung ears that stuck out from his head. He was just as alert as Jesse, but something about his demeanor suggested a man under a shadow. Dick Liddil and Dick's girl, Mattie Collins, cuddled up on the chair to the right of Frank. Mattie Collins's brown hair fell to her shoulders and framed a wide face with a scattering of freckles over her turned-up nose. Despite the heat of the kitchen, she had a dark green woolen cape draped over her shoulders. Ed Miller sat on Frank's left. In front of the group at that end of the table, there was a bottle of bourbon about two-thirds empty. There were three empty seats next to Ed Miller. Bob slid into one of them and clasped his hands in front of his face, elbows on the table.

–Get ye a drink, boy, Jesse said.

–I'll have the bourbon, Bob said.

–They ain't nothing else, Jesse said and laughed at him.

–Let me get him a glass, Mattie Bolton said.

She pushed herself up out of Grimes's lap and moved her shoulders in order to settle her wrinkled blouse straight again.

–Aw, come on, Grimes said.

She pulled the hair back out of her face and stumbled at the sideboard. Bob reached out to her over the back of his chair but she batted his hand away. She took a glass from the cupboard and pressed it into Bob's hand, the small lips in a smile, the blue eyes bleary. Grimes started to rise but Jesse James reached across and pulled him back into his seat. Grimes squinted at Bob's sister. Then at Bob. Then at Jesse. He leaned forward, forearms flat on the table, his glass cupped in his two massive hands, and Jesse poured it full. Mattie B. picked up the bottle at Dick's end of the table and poured a stiff measure into Bob's glass. She sat down between Bob and Ed Miller and draped her left arm over Bob's shoulder. Her breast pressed against his upper arm. Her breath was volatile and sweet, stronger than the French perfume on her long neck or the sweat from her full blouse. Bob leaned his head against his sister's. He could see why Grimes was so hot for her.

–Come back here, honey, Grimes slurred. I want to toast with you.

Mattie raised her head off Bob's.

–Go to hell, she said.

Bob didn't want his sister in Grimes's lap. It had nothing to do with the bet he had made.

–Everybody got a drink? Jesse called. I got a toast.

He raised his glass.

–A toast, Grimes said.

Grimes raised his glass and squinted at it through one eye,

Mattie Bolton momentarily forgotten. All around the table, Dick, Mattie Collins, Frank James, Ed Miller, Jesse James, and even Charley, raised their glasses. Mattie B. poured herself another drink and raised her glass. Her hand waved close to Bob's.

–To the new James Gang, Jesse said.

–Yeah, Grimes growled and sank his full shot in one gulp.

Bob sipped at the strong, sweet liquor.

–Damn, we lost a good man when the laws got Bill Ryan, Dick Liddil said.

He twirled the ends of his blond mustache. Mattie Collins rubbed her face against his cheek.

–To Bill Ryan, Jesse said.

–To Bill Ryan, Dick Liddil said. But Tucker Bassham wasn't worth a shit.

–Not a shit, Grimes said.

–Don't forget, Jesse said. Bill Ryan ain't convicted yet.

–He will be, Frank said.

Frank wiped down his mustache with thumb and forefinger.

–Why are *you* so sure? Jesse said. What evidence they got?

–They got a witness, Frank said.

–Who? Jesse said. Ryan was masked.

–Mr. Tucker Bassham made himself a deal, Frank said.

The room was quiet. Bob took another tentative sip on the bourbon, wished he hadn't, almost coughed, ran a nervous hand through his oily hair and worried that he had mussed it.

–Why am I the last to hear about this? Jesse said.

–You ain't, Grimes said.

–I just heard this morning, Frank said. Don't want to spoil the celebration, but Tucker Bassham gets a full pardon if he testifies against Bill Ryan.

–Tucker Bassham is bushwhacker stock, Jesse said. He will not testify.

–Tucker Bassham will testify, Frank said.

–If Tucker Bassham makes this deal, they ain't nowhere in the state of Missouri where that man could lay his head safe.

–That, said Frank, I reckon he knows.

–You cain't blame him, Ed Miller said.

Bob turned his head to look at Ed. Mattie slid her arm off Bob's shoulder. Everybody turned to look at Ed. The fat farm boy's red cheeks glowed redder under his sparse sideburns. He raised his glass to them, grinned, put it down, reached for it again. Jesse pulled at the hair of his beard. Bob looked into his glass as if the warm golden liquid could reveal the secrets of the future.

–You know what I mean, Ed said.

Nobody moved or said a word. Ed cleared his throat, a dry sound.

–Look, Ed said. Tucker Bassham's facing twenty-three years' hard time in the pen. Long years. Along comes Bill Ryan. The governor offers a deal. Tucker can get out.

Ed smiled. His hands fluttered like a pair of awkward birds in flight. Then his voice got high and loud.

–A free man! Ed said. Boom!

He punched the air.

–Come here, honey, Grimes said.

A cold sound. Mattie's fingers tightened on Bob's forearm. Bob turned to look at her. Her sharp white teeth worried for a second at her small lower lip. To Bob's horror, she stood up, walked over to Grimes, and let him pull her into his lap. Grimes fished his watch from his vest pocket and swung it like a pendulum, all the time looking at Bob. He smirked as if the bet was won. The room was still silent.

–Boom, Jesse said.

Real quiet.

XLV

THE TREES ON THE TRAIL FROM BOB HUDSPETH'S TO BEN MORROW'S were leafless, but a low gray sky that refused to rain pressed down around them and made twilight of the afternoon, a wintry darkness lying amongst trunk and branch. Jesse hummed a hymn to himself. Grimes rode to his left and Ed Miller to his right. Their horses walked with a strong jouncing gait along the tree-lined trail. So young Ed Miller thought that Tucker Bassham had done right to make a deal with the laws. Yes, it was understandable. A young man with his whole life ahead of him, and why would he want to spend it in jail if he could make a deal and bring to justice a bigger felon?

–You reckon I can trust Dick Liddil, Ed? Jesse asked.

–Just as much as anyone, I reckon, Ed said.

Grimes shook his shaggy head.

–I don't reckon you can, he said.

Yes, Grimes understood, too. Even suggested how they might deal with this unfortunate situation in which one of their number had shown a certain understanding, no, a sympathy even, for poor Tucker Bassham up there in the state penitentiary with nothing but a cold, piss-stinking room with bars on the windows wherein to spend the rest of his born days. And for what? Just that he happened to fall in with the wrong sort of company. Jesse's company.

–How come you cain't trust Dick? Ed said.

–We heard he's gone into a partnership, Jesse said.

–Partnership?

–With a nigger, Grimes said. Name of Silas Strickland.

–Oh, that ain't nothing, Ed said. Ever'one knows Strickland. He's a prizefighter. Liddil knowed him since the penitentiary. They worked the fall fairs together, Strickland fighting and Liddil horse racing.

Jesse nodded. Times had certainly changed. He could not imagine one of Bill's old company going into business with a black man. He had fought for the Confederacy so that it would not be so. And what was worse, he could not imagine this boy's brother, Clell Miller, who had died at Northfield, ever expressing the remotest understanding for a goddamn deal-maker like Tucker Bassham.

–They bought a outfit and a team, Grimes said. Gone into the hauling business.

–Strickland's good people, Ed said.

–He's a goddamn nigger, Grimes said.

–I cain't argue with that, Ed said.

The boy had started to look a mite nervous. His glance flitted from Grimes to Jesse and down to his hands. He knew that they were not funning with him. Grimes's eyes had narrowed as if he were looking at the boy through smoke.

–Old Father Grimes, here, Jesse said. He reckons that Dick palmed an extra hundred from the Blue Cut job.

Ed screwed up his soft-featured face.

–I don't believe he'd do no such thing.

–You contradicting me? Grimes said.

Grimes was easy to read. There was an evil about him like an extra shadow. Jesse was pleased at the alias he had given his cousin. It suited him. Like an old judge and preacher and executioner all in one name.

–I'm just saying, is all, Ed said.

–What about you, Ed? Grimes said. You palm anything?

Grimes spat over the neck of his horse. Ed turned on him, indignant.

–I ain't never palmed a cent, Ed said.

Jesse believed that. The boy was ingenuous. All the more dangerous for it. He could see him blabbing away to the first lawman that offered him a hot cup of coffee if ever he was caught and tried. It was a shame.

–You see, Ed, Jesse said, a man works with me, I'm straight with him. We make a raise, we always share it out equal. A man palms more than his share, he's stealing my money, our money, you understand.

–I understand.

The boy looked uncomfortable now. He needed to calm him down.

–Can I trust you, Ed? Jesse said.

Ed swiveled in the saddle.

–You trusted Clell, Ed said. He was family.

Jesse smiled. He nodded.

–You still got that bourbon in your saddlebags?

–Sure do.

–Let's get us a drink here, Jesse said. Drink a little toast to Clell.

The boy grinned. Still nervous, but maybe he felt he was off the hook. Ed turned in the saddle and reached for the offside flap of his saddlebags. In one fluid movement, synchronized with Ed's turning body, Jesse's right hand dropped a slack rein, glided back to his belt and swung the Colt Navy out from his body, muzzle pointed at the back of Ed's head, and bang — the pistol bucked —

and Ed dropped from his horse beneath a wreath of smoke and a spray of blood drops.

If Jesse could not be sure of a man, he had better be rid of him. And it would put the fear of God in the others.

–I figured I could trust Tucker Bassham, too, Jesse said.

–Cain't risk nothing, Grimes said. Let me deal with Liddil.

XLVI

HIS SISTER MATTIE'S HOUSE WAS A WELCOME SIGHT AFTER LONG hours of hard riding and a steadily creeping hangover that left Bob's mouth dry, his guts knotted, his throat closed against an acidic nausea, and the tight band of his hat seeming the only restraint to his skull splitting in shards. Bob could hardly feel his feet in the stirrups, and what he could feel was chafed and icy. By his side, Dick Liddil sat a stolen roan. Dick's sallow cheeks were sunken and his eyes bloodshot. Bob and Dick were at the end of a four-day drunk that had taken them across half of Clay and Jackson Counties, transported by train, stolen horses, ferry boats and stolen skiffs. They had chased the ladies — with some success — drunk moonshine in the kitchen of Lamartine Hudspeth and bourbon in the kitchen of Bob Hudspeth and washed it down with beer when the bourbon ran out. There were various black holes in Bob's memory that Dick could probably not fill for him either. Given half a chance, Bob knew that he would do the same thing all over again.

–Mattie'll be up soon, Dick said. Get us some breakfast.

–I don't know if I need a shave, a shoeshine, or a plate of short ribs, Bob said, but I do need a smoke and a cup of coffee and a quarter pint of bourbon if it would take away this pain in my head.

He dismounted at the barn.

–Let's get these animals rubbed down, Dick said.

Bob led his horse into the barn.

Next to Mattie's four horses, Charley's liver-colored quarter horse was in one of the stalls and beside it an unknown grullo.

–Got company, Bob said.

Dick nodded and led his horse to an empty stall.

Bob unsaddled his new mount — a fine new saddle and fine new mare — and rubbed down the horse's steaming flanks with a sack that hung on the door of the stall. He brought a bucket of oats into which the animal buried its nose.

–Let's get straightened out, Dick said.

–I'm with you, Bob said.

He stiff-legged his way across the yard, Dick beside him. There was something about the long drunk together that had brought him close to Liddil. He appreciated the way Liddil had stood up for him. Bob pushed through the door into the warm kitchen, and Mattie twisted around in her chair. The left side of her face was blue and red and swollen around her eye, the blond hair hanging over it, the small lips quivering. She had been weeping. Her white nightgown was buttoned up tight to her throat.

–Goddamn, what happened to you? Bob said.

–Grimes is here, she said.

Bob flushed. He bent over to peer at the bruise. Rage fed the splitting pain in his head, and the pain fed his rage. Every bourbon-raw nerve quivered in his body.

–What about Charley? he said.

–Charley was asleep and . . . I don't know, Mattie said.

–Didn't you yell for him?

She mimed the action of injecting herself with a hypodermic syringe.

–I'll kill that son of a bitch, Bob said, Grimes and Charley both.

–Bob, I'm afraid, Mattie said.

He reached for his gun, but Dick grabbed his arm and pulled it off the handle before he drew it.

–Hold on, Bob, Liddil said.

–I'll goddamn . . .

–He's looking for Dick, Mattie said.

–Who, Grimes? Dick said.

His hand fell away. Bob did not draw his gun.

–He says you palmed a hundred dollars of the Blue Cut train money, Mattie said.

–Lying son of a . . .

–What the hell is going on? Bob said. Is Jesse here?

–I reckon it was Jesse that sent him looking for Dick, Mattie said.

A chill spread across Bob's shoulders and down his arms and back and his thighs.

–What about me? Bob said.

Mattie shook her head, bit her lower lip. Shook her head.

–Just Dick.

Dick blew, turned away, and slowly walked to the hearth.

–Well, I ain't going nowhere . . .

He raised the lid of the coffeepot.

. . . I need a cup of coffee is what I need.

Everything was off kilter. Dick palmed a hundred? Jesse sent Grimes. Nothing was right. And Mattie's face was all out of proportion.

–Where's Grimes? Bob said.

–In the attic with Charley, she said.

Dick lifted the coffeepot off the hearth.

–You want some coffee? Dick said.

–Coffee! Bob said. What about goddamn Grimes?

–Leave him be, Dick said. He'll be down for breakfast.

–What you saying?

–Have some coffee, Liddil said.

–I don't want no coffee, Bob said.

Liddil's hand shook as he poured three steaming cups.

–I reckon you do, Dick said.

It was a threat.

–I ain't got no beef with you, Dick, Bob said.

–Take the goddamn coffee, Liddil said.

Liddil's eyes shifted from door to Mattie to Bob to the coffeepot.

–Gimme the damn coffee, Bob said.

Liddil nodded. He blew. His shoulders relaxed a little.

–That son of a bitch, Bob said.

The whole room had a flat brightness to it: the green-painted sideboard opposite him. The boards creaked upstairs.

–Here comes a hungry man, Dick said.

–I don't want no goddamn coffee, Bob said.

–Jesse sent him, Dick said.

Bob stood up and paced across to the sideboard. Liddil paid him no mind now.

–I'm scared of him, Mattie said.

Dick set down his coffee cup and leaned back against the kitchen counter.

–Liddil Dick, Grimes said.

He stood in the doorway. The buckskin shirt was open over the broad and hairy chest. His long gray hair was uncombed. He wore his sidearms in their holsters. His black pants were rolled up above the ankles of his boots. He glanced at Bob, then fixed his stare on Liddil.

–How are you, Bob? Grimes said.

But he kept his eyes fixed on Liddil.

–Fair to middlin', Bob said.

The son of a bitch did not turn. He had beaten and poked his goddamn sister and now he did not even have the respect to look his way.

–Don't say a goddamn word to me, Liddil said.

–I got a message for you, Grimes said.

Mattie had both hands up beside her mouth. Her face was all twisted and mottled.

–I said, don't talk to me, Liddil said.

Grimes grinned and stepped over the threshold into the kitchen. Mattie whimpered.

–Come here, honey, Grimes said. Let me show you how they do it in the penitentiary.

–You son of a bitch, Bob said.

–Keep out of this, little boy.

–I said, don't say a word! Liddil yelled.

Grimes reached for his gun and Liddil reached and Mattie screamed and the kitchen was all flash and bang and smoke and Bob pulled the Remington and pointed and fired and the gun bucked and he whipped back the hammer and fired again and cocked and fired through his own smoke and cocked and fired until the hammer clicked on an empty chamber, and through the ringing in his ears he heard Mattie sobbing and Dick groaning and not a sound from Grimes.

Greasy white powder smoke hung in the heat of the kitchen,

floating slowly toward the ceiling. The caustic bite of cordite tingled on Bob's tongue and in his nostrils and stung his eyes. Dick sat on the floor of the kitchen clutching one pistol, the other beside him. With the heel of his left palm, he pressed against his thigh where a dark stain spread over his pants. Mattie bent over with her fists pressed against her mouth, the mottled eye shut and the other wide open. Somewhere down the passage her daughter Ida screamed, kept on screaming in terror, the sound muffled by the walls and doors. Grimes lay quiet on the floor. He was still breathing, the chest under the buckskin shirt heaving up and falling. Bob let the Remington hang in his hand and crossed to look at Grimes. There was a small dark hole from which blood trickled two inches above Grimes's sandy right eyebrow, and a small pool of blood was spreading out from under the left side of his head. His eyes, expressionless, were fixed on the ceiling as if by their stillness he might yet slyly cheat death. Bob leaned over him. The exit hole, not so neat, was just above his left ear. Blood and a pinky gray substance dripped onto the floor.

–I reckon I got him, Bob said.

–Mama, Mama, Ida called from behind a wall.

–Ida, stay there, honey! Mattie yelled.

–For chrissakes, Dick said. Help me up here.

Bob holstered the empty Remington. Dick's face was chalk white.

–You reckon I got him or you got him? Bob said.

–Help me up here, Dick said.

–Open the goddamn door, Mattie, Bob said. I cain't breathe in here.

Mattie yanked the door open, and a cold wind filled the kitchen. Bob took Dick under his armpits and helped him up onto one foot so that he could lean back against the counter.

–Went right through the muscle, Dick said.

Up the passageway, he heard Charley on the stairs, then shuffling along to the kitchen. He was still in his red flannel underwear, hair tousled, unshaven, bootless but with a revolver in his fist. The supine Grimes blocked his way into the room.

–Who shot Grimes? Charley said.

–Either me or Dick, Bob said.

–Well, one of you sons of bitches just killed Jesse James's favorite cousin.

–He ain't dead yet, Mattie said.

–Grimes, can you hear me? Charley said.

Bob left Dick propped against the counter and walked over to look at Grimes again. The head didn't move. His eyes stared up at Bob. Fixed on him. The pool of blood still spread slowly. The head still dripped. Grimes didn't utter word one.

–I reckon it was me who got him, Bob said.

–I reckon I'll help you bury him, Charley said. Just as soon as he's dead.

XLVII

THE REVEREND FORD HAD BEEN STANDING AT THE KITCHEN WINdow since sunset, for which Jesse was pleased, since he had ridden to the Ford home unaccompanied and he had no one to set as sentry.

–Snow's getting worse, the reverend said.

Jesse sat in the rocking chair on the left side of the hearth. Mrs. Ford had trimmed his hair and beard, and he sat content in the cozy warmth of the fire. He reached into the pocket of his frock coat that was draped over the back of the chair and took out his cigar case. The Colt in his belt pressed into his belly. He snapped a match and lit the cigar evenly. He blew smoke toward the chimney.

–The boys are here, the reverend said. Liddil's with them.

–'Bout time, too, said Mrs. Ford.

Mrs. Ford was at the kitchen table working on a piece of crochet that looked big enough to be a tablecloth. Her hair was pulled back from her emaciated face and bobbed behind her birdlike skull. The dark eyes were like glass marbles staring down at hook and stitch. There was a rigidity in her hands and her spare frame as if with fierce indifference she held at bay a constant pain. The hardness in her soul that showed upon her face was the result of bitter deprivation caused by Yankee requisition during the war years, reprisals for her known Confederate sympathies. She still held a hatred for the Union, and that was why Jesse was always welcome in her house.

The reverend pulled open the kitchen door, and an icy gust of wind freshened the air in the hot room. His round face crinkled up around his small eyes. He rubbed at the rolled-up sleeves of his white shirt and then pulled closed his brown worsted vest that hung over his ample belly.

–So many visitors, Mrs. Ford said. Makes it feel like a holiday season.

Dick Liddil supported himself on the doorjamb a second and hobbled into the kitchen. He had his arm draped over Bob Ford's shoulders. Dick leaned on his uncocked Winchester as a cane. Bob laid his hand on his pappy's shoulder, and Charley followed them in. The reverend blocked their sight of Jesse at the hearth.

–Evening, boys, Jesse said.

Liddil's lips pressed tight and white under the blond mustache. Young Bob Ford's mouth opened and his eyes widened in surprise. Charley looked as languid as ever, probably because of the medicine that he had been taking every day since the Blue Cut raid.

–Howdy, Jesse, Bob Ford said. Hi, Momma.

–Jesse. Liddil nodded.

–Good to be home, Charley drawled.

Bob unbuttoned his sheepskin coat and hung it on one of the pegs on the kitchen door. He hooked his hat over it and smoothed back his oiled hair. It seemed that Bob was scared of something. He had a malicious grin on his face as if to brazen out some sense of guilt. What was he feeling so guilty about? Something to do with Liddil surely. Liddil looked terrified. But Charley just had a glassy look in his eyes. Something was amiss among them. Jesse could sense it. Maybe Liddil had caught wind of being under suspicion. And maybe he had talked to the others.

–Come on inside and get warm by the fire, Mrs. Ford said.

–How are you, Momma? Bob said.

–Same as ever.

Jesse drew on the cigar, leaned forward, and rolled his ash against the brazier.

The Reverend Ford resumed his seat opposite Jesse. Jesse smiled at him, then looked Dick over and examined him like a piece of livestock. Damaged goods.

–What happened to the leg, Dick? Jesse said.

Dick leaned to his left over the barrel of the Winchester. Snow melted on his blanket coat and glistened wetly upon it and dripped around him onto the floor. His hand lay on his injured thigh. He was an ashen gray.

–Come off a horse, Dick said. Slid on the ice. But I didn't want to impose on Mattie no more. I been there long enough, I guess.

–I'm sure she would have been more than hospitable on a day like this one, Mrs. Ford said.

Bob's voice cracked as he put in his contribution, the last two words a rising squeak.

–It wasn't so bad when we started out.

They were hiding something, all right.

–Fact is, ma'am, Dick said, there was a posse out beating the woods and they were set on beating on Mattie's door.

Jesse held the cigar away from his mouth. Was that what they were hiding? Maybe the posse had followed them through the snow.

–We just got out in time, Charley said. Managed to lose them close to the Clay County line, then we doubled back into Ray. Figured they gone on that way. Back towards Lexington, anyways.

Bob walked over to the sideboard. There was a sharp crack. He held a wooden nutcracker in his palm. The hull of the filbert tinkled in the glass dish beside the basket. Bob seemed to be trying to regain his composure, but he was breathing shallowly and his hand shook ever so slightly. Maybe the posse had spooked him. Maybe something else. Jesse fixed his eyes on Dick. None of them had mentioned Grimes. But that could be because he had taught them never to talk needlessly in front of anyone, neither friend nor family. It was possible that Liddil had taken Grimes out, but it would be hard to believe. Grimes was one of the old company. One of Bill Anderson's boys.

–Dick don't look too good, Jesse said.

–I didn't think it would hurt so much riding, Dick said.

–Fact is, Jesse said, you being here, Dick, saves me a journey. I come all the way down here from Nebraska looking for you. And

Grimes. I was hoping you two could give me a hand moving house.

–Dang, Dick said. I cain't move till this leg heals up. Then I be glad to help out.

Dick leaned the Winchester up against the doorjamb. He winced as he tugged at his coat, supporting himself on one leg with a hand upon the wall.

–If that posse comes back this way, Jesse said, our being here might embarrass everyone. I think we better go.

–They ain't coming this way, Bob said in a hurry.

–I cain't ride no more, Jesse, Dick said. I'll take my chances here. That is if you don't mind, Mr. and Mrs. Ford?

–You're more'n welcome, son, Reverend Ford said. You know that.

Liddil's face was so pale that his veins showed blue beneath the translucent skin. He wasn't faking injury at least. He limped over to the table and took a seat opposite Mrs. Ford.

–Jesse, you all should stay, Mrs. Ford said.

He had no intention whatsoever of staying. If that posse picked up Liddil and the Ford boys' trail in the snow, he was bound for slaughter or worse. The laws had nothing on the Ford boys, so the only one to go down would be Liddil. Liddil was known well enough as one of the James Gang. The only problem was he might look to do a deal, but until they caught Jesse James, Liddil had nothing to deal with. Liddil would be back in the penitentiary.

–Thank you, Mrs. Ford, Jesse said. But I'd best be on my way. Best if we split up.

–I'll come with you, Charley said.

–You ain't seen your folks in a while, Jesse said.

–I wouldn't have you go alone, the reverend said. Go on, Charley. Go on with him.

Charley wouldn't be much good in a shooting scrape, but he was better than nothing. And he was an extra pair of eyes should they put up for the night somewhere.

–Come on with me, Charley, Jesse said.

–Maybe Bob should go with you, too, the reverend said. We can look after Dick.

–I think Bob should stay with Dick, Jesse said. Till he gets better. Eh, Bob?

He didn't want Dick disappearing on him. He could always find one or the other, Bob or Dick.

–I'll keep a eye on him, Bob said.

There was a forced grin on the boy's smooth face. He probably suspected why Jesse wanted Liddil under scrutiny. Bob was sharp and intelligent. It was time to put him to good use. Maybe on the Platte City bank job. Jesse settled his hat upon his head and pulled on his frock coat, always facing outward into the room with everyone in front of him.

–Dick, have you seen Grimes? Jesse said.

Liddil licked his lips. Nervous.

–Last I heard, Liddil said, he was headed for Kentucky.

–Who'd you hear it from?

–Mattie.

–Strange, Jesse said. Last time I seen him he reckoned he was going to look for Mattie and then come back to Kansas City.

–He must of changed his mind, Bob said.

Jesse turned his scrutiny upon Bob then. Bob's pale eyes flicked away. The boy breathed slow and turned back to face Jesse.

–You ain't seen him at Mattie's? Jesse said.

Bob Ford shook his head.

–I been in Kansas City, Bob said. He'd already gone by the time I got there.

Charley brought Jesse's duster for him and he slid his arms into it. Liddil, seated at the table, would not meet Jesse's eyes.

–When did you see Grimes last, Charley? Jesse said.

–Ain't seen hide nor hair of him since the Blue Cut job. Ed Miller neither.

–I reckon I'm going to have to come back for you, Dick, Jesse said.

–He ain't going far, Bob said.

Jesse nodded. The boy had a look of resolve on his face, as if he had made his mind up then and there to carry out what Jesse expected of him. Face set like a mask in front of Liddil. Or he was damn good at hiding something.

–You take care of him for me, boy, Jesse said. And I'll be much obliged.

Bob nodded.

–I'll look after him.

Jesse crossed to the door. Charley was at his heels like a faithful hound.

–You're always welcome here, Jesse, Mrs. Ford said.

–Bye, Momma, bye Pa, Charley said.

–Come back soon, now, Reverend Ford said.

Dick Liddil kept his gaze down on the crochet work that was spread over the table in front of him up to Mrs. Ford's gnarled and busy hands.

–You can count on it, Jesse said. That you can.

XLVIII

BOB KEPT WATCH OVER THE TAILGATE OF THE COVERED WAGON while behind him Dick Liddil shivered, one leg out straight on the wagon floor, his back against a pile of hessian sacking. Neither one of them was going to forget this day, January 24, 1882, a cold and icy day, with the streets of Liberty piled with rotten snow, stained yellow with horse piss and flecks of fibrous manure. Bob was about to deliver Dick Liddil to the law, and from this moment forward there was no turning back from his plan to save his own life and Charley's and Dick Liddil's. The wheels rattled over the cobbles.

–I ain't ever wanted to do something like this, Dick, Bob said.

–Well, you're in it now.

–I just wanted . . . I looked up to him. Shit. Jesse James. Since I was a kid.

–Who he is, is different than what you think, Dick said.

–Shit. It's Grimes's fault.

–Ain't a question of fault. Grimes is family to him. Grimes is dead and even God Almighty can't change that back.

Bob recalled what Charley had said to him as they were burying Grimes's body. It made terribly sickening sense.

–It don't matter that you love the guy, you killed his cousin.

When Charley had said that, all the glee and excitement about shooting Grimes had drained out of Bob, and as he calmed down he became aware that this was now a family matter. He had shot one of Jesse James's family. And just as bad as that, one of Bill Anderson's old company. Some things were simple with Jesse. Jesse lived by Bible law, an eye for an eye, and if Jesse James found out that Bob and Dick had killed Grimes, it would require that the balance for family outrage should be redressed, and the only way to redress that balance was to shoot the shootists. In this case, Bob Ford and Dick Liddil. And Charley for helping them. If they could get Jesse into the hands of the law, they would be safe. And they wouldn't have to try and kill him their own selves.

–You think he knows yet? Bob said.

–Who? Dick said. What?

–Jesse. About Grimes.

–Well, I didn't tell him.

–That ain't what I said.

–He's wondering where the hell Grimes is, and I know he suspects I got something to do with it.

–You think he suspect *me* of being in with the laws?

–He don't trust no one, so he want you under his eye, I know that.

–Hell, I don't want to end up like Ed Miller.

–Jesse reckoned Ed died of consumption, Dick said.

–It took him awful fast, didn't it?

Dick chuckled.

–Right after he opened his big mouth about how good a deal Tucker Bassham done with the law. Well, Jesse ain't one to take no risks.

All the mirth drained out of him then, and his face was pale and drawn. Dick looked down at his leg as if puzzled about something. Dick's sudden change of humor and his looking down like that at his wounded leg made Bob uneasy and aware that the link between soul and body was a tentative one and depended on so many organs and muscles working right and together and in harmony and how a piece of lead, shot from a .44, could disrupt those organs and muscles abominably, could separate soul from body in a matter of minutes, even seconds. Such a thought suddenly generated a terrible fear within him, and he had to put it aside, push it away from his mind.

–You think about the reward? Bob said.

Dick looked up.

–What?

–The reward.

–I'd take it.

–There's big money there, Dick. More than any holdup.

–Shit, I just want to get out of this alive and not do no time, Dick said.

Bob nodded.

Yeah, the reward could wait. Just one step after another. Everything was set up. What choice did he have? What else could they do to make sure that Jesse James would not shoot them both dead and leave them in a ditch somewhere, just as Bob and Dick had done to Grimes? They just needed to stay alive. And Bob's plan was a good one. He had thought it for all of them. He had sent Mattie to Police Commissioner Craig, and Craig had arranged the meeting with the governor; then Mattie had negotiated the deal in the governor's mansion just before Christmas. Bob Ford had offered Jesse James to the law. What other way was there to stop him from killing them? For Jesse would find out. He would. And the governor had promised Mattie that he would give a full pardon to Liddil and Bob and Charley if they brought in Jesse. A pardon even for murder. And if Jesse could be brought to trial, Liddil would be the state's major witness. Liddil had been at every James Gang robbery since Glendale. But the success of the whole venture depended on Bob. He was about to pit his own wits against a killer who had evaded the law for thirteen years. A man he had looked up to ever since he had been old enough to understand his momma's and his papa's stories.

The wagon came to a halt. The pins of the tailgate rattled and Silas Strickland let the board drop flat. His wide black face had an expression of regret, the eyes half-hooded. Bob slid out of the wagon and onto the street. He kept one hand on the Remington. He glanced around at the citizenry on the sidewalks, but it was all but impossible that Jesse James should have learned of their plan. Dick grimaced as he slid his wounded leg out of the wagon and set his good foot down on the cobbles. Bob slid his arm under Dick's armpit and helped him to lower himself gently to the ground.

–Look after the wagon, Strick, Dick said. Mattie Collins, too.

–Look after your own self, Dick, Strickland said.

–I won't have you in there to watch my back, Dick said.

–You be out soon enough.

–You ready, Dick? Bob said.

Dick had a sickly look on his stubbled face, but he twirled up the ends of his blond mustache.

–Maybe they'll get me a doctor for this leg now.

–They'll treat you right, Bob said.

–Everything's about to change now, ain't it? Dick said.

–Let's get inside, Bob said. Too many peepers about.

–Don't stay in too long, Strickland said.

He clasped Dick's hand and with his rolling fighter's gait, he walked back toward the driver's seat of the wagon and didn't look back.

Wide stone steps led up to the quoined main entrance, where a young deputy with a ten-gauge breech-loading shotgun cradled in his arms pushed off from the wall of the portico and stood at the top of the steps. The support straps for the deputy's cartridge belt came over the shoulders of his brown vest so that he had a military aspect despite the wide-brimmed slouch hat that hung down over his smooth-shaven face and flattened the tops of his ears so that the deputy had to tilt his head back the better to observe their arrival. Bob gripped Dick's elbow. The steps were wet where they had been salted against the ice. Dick took them one by one, lifting his good leg up first and drawing the bad after, leaning his weight hard on Bob. A sharp wind cut at them. Below the steps the windows in the walls of the foundation were all barred.

–We was told to expect you, the deputy said.

They reached the top of the steps and the deputy stepped aside for them. The shadowy portico was in the lee of the wind. The door rattled under Bob's hand and they were into the main office. A deputy with a heavy dark mustache looked up from the desk. He had a pile of papers on the blotter in front of him and an inkstand that was encrusted with dry ink. The nib of the pen next to it had not been dipped in liquid for a long time.

–We're looking for Timberlake, Bob said.

–You're the parties he's expecting, I guess.

–That's right.

–What's wrong with his leg?

–Nothing a doctor cain't fix, Dick said.

–Unhitch your firearms, boys.

Bob unbuckled his cartridge belt and swung belt and holster onto the deputy's desk. The deputy wrapped the belt around the holster and put all into a steel cabinet behind him. The distance between Bob and the cabinet was but six feet, though Bob felt as if he were in a heavy river current that was already dragging him away and it was too late to stop it now. Dick had his lips pressed together in a tight bud. A slight twitch tremored under his right eye and lifted one corner of the blond mustache. He handed over both his belts ready rolled up, and when the deputy had locked them safely in the cabinet, the lawman came out from behind his desk.

–Come on through, the deputy said. The commissioner's here, too.

The deputy led the way down a narrow corridor that was ill-lit by a barred square of light from the window at the opposite end. A Negro woman on her knees rubbing a duster against the wainscot stopped her motion to watch Bob pass and then Dick, who shuffled along behind him. Their heels clacked on the dark oak floor. At a recessed door, all shadows, the deputy stopped and knocked. Sheriff Timberlake opened the door himself, the pale light behind him giving his skin a sallow cast, a complexion that seemed to know no sun. A broad grin lifted his mustache into the hollow of his cheeks. He looked from Dick to Bob.

–Where's Charley? Timberlake said.

–With Jesse, Bob said.

–Come on in, boys.

Bob let Dick go by him. Dick's eyes flitted a swift glance into Bob's. Bob was going to leave Dick behind and walk back down that echoing corridor and out onto the street, but in his mind even the streets of the town were but an extension of this prison world whose threshold they had already passed. Dick shook his head, giving him a wry smile. Bob followed him into the office. The room was sparsely furnished: a chained rack of long-barreled rifles and shotguns upon the right-hand wall, a set of wooden filing cabinets beneath it, a desk arranged kitty-corner with a green leather-covered swivel chair behind it, two cheap pine armchairs in front. The desk was neat, a wooden tray on each corner of the desk top. Neither tray was full; the papers inside lay flat and orderly. The writing set on the blotter was clean, and fresh ink glistened in the polished brass pot. The air in the room was frigid, the round stove in the corner obviously unlit, but Timberlake showed no sign of any discomfort, although he wore his frock coat over his vest.

Timberlake closed the door on the deputy. Police Commissioner Craig stood to the left of the barred window. He had a woolen muffler knotted around his neck and tucked into the front of his handsome brown suit jacket. His nose was tipped with a cheerless red shine, and the thick mustache glistened with a bead of mucus that had escaped his handkerchief. His hands were thrust deep into his jacket pockets. He cleared his phlegmy throat and his voice was thick and nasal with his head cold.

–Dick Liddil, he said. You are under arrest for the robbery of the Chicago and Alton Line train at Glendale on October 8, 1879.

A cold tingling wave spread up Bob's back and over his scalp. Dick frowned.

–And for the robbery of the Chicago and Alton Line train at Winston, Daviess County, and for the murder of William Westfall and Frank MacMillan on July 11, 1881, and for the robbery of the Chicago and Alton Line train at Blue Cut on September 7, 1881. Anything you may say after this point may be taken down and used in evidence against you. You have the right to remain silent and to seek legal representation.

Dick's eyes were glazed and his mouth slack as if he had ridden hard into an overhanging tree branch.

–Before you can be pardoned, you have to be tried and condemned, Craig said.

Dick nodded. They all knew the terms of the agreement.

–Mr. Ford, Timberlake said, right now all we got is Dick Liddil. You don't bring in Jesse James, your partner here is looking at long penitentiary time.

Timberlake had an ugly sneer on his face; this was the goddamn lawman who had botched every attempt he had ever made to catch Jesse James: all those useless raids on farmhouses that did nothing but antagonize the people of Clay County. Timberlake had never once seen Jesse James face-to-face.

–I'm going to get the son of a bitch. And just so we get this clear, there's some serious reward money gonna be due to me and Charley and Dick, here.

–Let's see you bring him in, Timberlake said.

–I can guarantee you all a share in the reward money, Mr. Ford, Craig said. It will be a matter for the courts to decide how any such monies should be divided up among you and the law enforcement officers involved in any arrest.

These lawmen were out to swindle him already. He knew it and they knew it.

–Get me out of here, Bob, Dick said.

Bob nodded. He wanted Dick out of there all right, but more than that, he didn't want to be hunted down and shot like a dog when Jesse James found out what they had done. This could only be kept quiet for so long. Someone would get wind of Liddil's arrest either inside or outside the jail, and then word would get to Jesse that Bob was involved in a deal with the law. He could run, but he would never be safe for the rest of his life. He would end up as he knew Ed Miller had ended up. As Dick Liddil would have ended up if Bob hadn't shot Grimes.

–I'd best be going, Bob said.

One step at a time.

XLIX

OUT OF THE DAWN MIST THAT LAY OVER THE BLUFFS ON THE other side of the Platte River, the sun's pale orb appeared like a veiled eye, and the sky above it was lit up bright blue with the feathery mares' tails of the clouds, a stark white, a sky that pretended to fair weather but promised foul, April's opening. Jesse was out to make a fool of Platte City's bank manager, and to that end he had dressed in a smart frock coat and suede leather vest and white shirt and a burgundy four-in-hand tie; his beard was neatly trimmed close to his face and he had shaved his neck. He would pass for a prosperous commission agent in front of any bank manager. Beside him, Bob Ford was in his Sunday-best suit, and like a pair of mountebanks they had taken to the road intent on deceit in ever more intricate patterns. Jesse felt deceit in the air, as if something awaited him hidden behind the curtain of the world's outward appearance. Beside the road, the swollen river rushed and roared and combined with the trilling of myriad birds in dawn's chorus to make bedlam in Jesse's ears as they rode south. Bob Ford was quiet. Too quiet. He had denied knowing anything at all about Grimes or Liddil, and Jesse suspected he was keeping some creeping secret. Could be he was just scared. The boy had been close to Liddil, and he must have known that Jesse had lost his trust in Dick. If he didn't want to reveal Dick's whereabouts out of some loyalty, he could respect that up to a point; but Bob was also a boy with good sense and must know that his future was safer by being loyal to Jesse James than ever it would be with Dick Liddil. Then there was Grimes. If Grimes was at large, he should have been in contact. But if the laws had got him, Jesse should have heard about it. They would have written about it in the newspapers, surely. Now the only men Jesse had between himself and the law were the Ford boys. Charley Ford was so doped up on morphine that all he was good for was driving Zee to town in the buggy. That left Bob. Grimes had said that Bob Ford had done well on the Short Line job.

–You scared? Jesse said.

–Wha'?

–A stagecoach in the woods is one thing. A bank in a town might not be so easy.

–Oh, Bob said. No.

–So you're scared?

–No. I ain't scared, Bob said.

–It's just me and you.

Bob nodded.

–To do the bank operation, Jesse said.

Bob's mouth twisted like a piece of rubber toward the semblance of a smile.

–Just the two of us can do it? Bob said.

–I reckon. We'll look it over today.

–Why don't I try to wire Mattie Collins, so she can let Dick know?

–Wire?

–She'll know where he is.

–I don't trust Dick.

–Well, Grimes then.

Grimes couldn't have heard that Jesse had moved up to Saint Joe, but he might have contacted Mama. Jesse leaned close to Bob to whisper as if someone within earshot might be hidden in the trees. Bob's whole body went rigid from stirrups to hat crown. The boy was too nervous.

–You go to the telegraph office and wire my half-brother. If Grimes is about the county, he'll know and get word to him.

–I'll do that.

Bob Ford smiled. He relaxed in the saddle. He was so easy to read. He was pleased that he was going to the telegraph office. Who else did Bob want to wire? Liddil? Some woman? The law? Not the law. He had been living with Jesse for two months and he couldn't possibly have kept that kind of secret from him. Unless the boy was a born actor. Bob had seemed enthusiastic about the reconnaissance for the bank raid. Jesse would watch every move and twitch he made. They rode in silence and came around a turn in the road where great swaths of stump and slash lay upon the low and ravaged hillsides and the bluffs echoed with a mechanical racket. Waste fires crackled and burned and sent red sparks and smoke rising skyward where the sun had burned away the fog of early morning. Three teams of docile oxen hauled cut trunks down toward the riverside sawmill, whose waterwheel still turned, but smoke rose, too, from the chimneys of the steam engine that drove the blades that whined within.

–Goddamn, they are burning this country to the ground.

–They just logging, Bob said.

–This was good country, Jesse said.

The boy had no appreciation of how Missouri had been. Great expanses of woods where the old guerrilla company could ride for days and see no sign of human beings. These newcomers were turning the bush into meadow. Jesse urged his horse into a canter as if he would escape the sight, but most of the low hills that rose away from the riverbank were pasture where herds of dairy cows grazed on the gentle slopes. Every mile or so they came across a new clapboard house or a foundation where another was under construction. He could not imagine Bill Anderson in this tamed landscape. He, Jesse Woodson James, was thirty-five years old, with a wife and two children and a reputation that was worldwide; a reputation that he had grown on this soil and no other. But now this country, which had made him what he was, was becoming alien to him. Bill Anderson had seen this pacific world emerging as the war drew to its inexorable end, and for that reason Bill had ridden into storms of ever greater violence in search of extinction, for he knew that he could have no place in what he saw coming. It had become impossible to maintain the world where action was all, where they had raged and rampaged between vibrant life and bloody destruction. Theirs was a war that had raged on the border of Kansas and Missouri before the Great War between the States had ever begun. Family business. Bob Ford, riding beside him, had no inkling of what had gone before. It was not imprinted within his blood and bones as it was within Jesse's. Bob Ford was part of a world where men in the smoky committee rooms of the State House decided the course of the lives of farmers and city dwellers alike under the influence of industrialists and railroad companies. This very world that they rode through. Perhaps Bill Anderson's choice had been the sane one and Jesse's the one of a fool.

At around ten-thirty, they reached the bridge that would take them into Platte City.

–Don't look so nervous, Jesse said.

–I ain't, Bob said.

But the boy's eyes flitted this way and that as if he feared the discovery of some clandestine guilt before he had even set foot in the bank. The buildings of Main Street rose on either side of them. A high scaffolding was lashed to a tower that stood half formed. Upon the scaffold's topmost deck, a mason leaned out over the gantry of the hoist and called out for more stone, while a white dog, tiny at such an elevation, yipped around his heels and gave Jesse a sense of vertigo as he sat in his saddle only fourteen hands from the solid earth. And on the street itself, a great pile of cobbles stood ready to be set where a crew of roadworkers raked out a smooth bed of fine gravel on the right side of the road. Hooves and wagon wheels had churned up the narrow space left for traffic, and he halted his horse to allow passage to a wide furniture wagon drawn by a massive pair of gray Percherons. A prosperous town of the new Missouri.

–Let's make us a deposit in the bank, Jesse said.

–Ready, Bob said.

–Just keep your eyes open.

Jesse urged his horse through the thick mud. At the corner of Main and Fifth, they dismounted, tied up the horses, and walked up the boardwalk and into the bank. In action, now. His mind calm and without thought but all his senses raw and alert to fix in his mind the bank's layout ready for the operation. Two men stood in front of the teller's station. The counter was arranged in a U shape around the vault, with the bookkeeper off to the right and the cashier's cage to the left. Jesse did not wait in line but went directly to the cashier's cage. Bob Ford stood at his shoulder. He did not seem so nervous now. All Bob had to do was observe. This was not the operation. The cashier was counting a sheaf of bills. He made a mark on the paper band with his pencil, then he looked up through thick round spectacles. His upper lip pulled back from his yellow teeth as he squinted at Jesse.

–Yes, sir?

–I want to change this bill, Jesse said.

He handed the cashier a fifty. The cashier made a show of raising it to the light to check its authenticity, turning it this way and that, and then he winked at Jesse.

–Wouldn't want to be taking any wooden nickels, he said. Not today.

–I'll take twenty ones, two tens, and four fives, Jesse said.

The cashier wagged his finger.

–Not today, he said.

Jesse nodded and smiled affably.

The cashier got down off his stool and walked into the vault. He took a key from the wall and opened a squat steel safe that was painted green, deposited the bill, and locked the door again. There was no time lock. Back at the counter, the teller opened his drawer and counted out twenty ones, two tens, and two fives.

–How would I open an account? Jesse said.

–Mr. Hargrave, the manager, will help you, the cashier said. He's out at an appointment but he should be back within fifteen minutes.

–I'll call back, Jesse said.

–Who should I tell him to expect?

–J. T. Howard, Jesse said.

–That your son? the cashier said.

He turned his ugly smile on Bob.

–No, I'm his nephew, Bob said.

–Do come back, the cashier said.

Bob turned toward the door. The two other customers had already left. He held the door open for Jesse and they stepped onto the boardwalk.

–What you see? Jesse asked.

The smooth face looked confused. A puzzled frown.

–Where was the safe?

Bob shook his head.

–I didn't see no safe.

–You see the vault?

–Yessir.

Jesse nodded. It didn't matter. Bob would be there to cover the door. Two people would be enough, if he worked fast.

–You go on down to the telegraph office, Jesse said. It's a block down on the left. You send a wire to John Samuels, Kearney, Missouri. You write: Have Grimes meet me in Saint Joe, April 3rd at the latest. Sign it Joe Mimms.

–Yessir.

–I'll go buy the papers across the street.

Bob nodded and set off down Main Street. Jesse watched him go as he bumped and wound his way through the citizens on the boardwalk. A tram creaked by and after it passed, Jesse stepped out into the street. Something was not right. Why was he letting the boy go alone to the telegraph office? What would it take to wire the law? Arrange an ambush? Why did he not turn now and rush down to the telegraph office? Time enough. The boy was straight up. Jesse balanced his way over four slippery boards that had been laid across the street, and he came onto the boardwalk in front of the newsstand. He nodded to the seller. He reached for the *Kansas City Evening Star* and his hand stopped. No April Fool's trick this headline: DICK LIDDIL SURRENDERS. He slipped the paper out of the pile and paid for it. He scanned the column. The son of a bitch had surrendered back in January, and only now had the papers got wind of it. Jesse glanced across the street. One block down, the telegraph office was a small storefront with a plate-glass window. As if in a picture frame, Bob Ford was leaning across the counter. Bob had been Liddil's constant companion around Christmas and New Year's and well into January. He must have known about Liddil. Grimes was probably in a ditch somewhere. Jesse was being set up. The whole of the goddamn State of Missouri knew about it and he didn't. That little son of a bitch was wiring the law. A dray wagon blocked his way across the street. A confusion of citizens milled around him, and above them the half-built vertiginous tower seemed to sway as he pushed his way into the mud of the street. It sucked at his boots. Weighed them with clay. He reached the opposite boardwalk, his newspaper clutched in his hand. He rattled through the door of the telegraph office just as Bob turned away from the counter.

–Who'd you wire?

–Samuels. Like you said.

The boy looked surprised. Worried.

–Where's the goddamn slip?

–Right here, Bob said.

Jesse pushed past him to the counter. Behind it was a desk, a telegraph machine and wizened old telegraph operator hunched over the tap key, the wrinkled face made doubly so by the way he peered at something in front of him.

–Where's his goddamn slip?

The desiccated old doll did not even raise its face. He waved a bony finger at the pile in a tray. Jesse grabbed the topmost.

TO: *John Samuels, Kearney, Mo.*
FROM: *Joe Mimms*
MESSAGE: *Have Grimes meet me in St Joe April 3rd at latest stop*

So he had wired for Grimes. Jesse spun around. He slapped the newspaper into Bob's chest and it fell at his feet, the headline clear upon the floor.

–Son of a bitch, Bob said.

He leaned down and picked up the paper and made a show of reading it.

–That's a pal of yours, ain't it?

–He ain't no pal of mine, Bob said. Not after this. Dear God.

–You know about this?

–First I heard, I swear to God.

An icy calm came over Jesse. The boy could not have lived in the house of Jesse James for two long months and kept such a secret from him. It was impossible. The boy could be read like a book. He was hiding something but he could not have hidden something of such magnitude as this. Or the Lord had blinded Jesse and His hand was about to eradicate him. What did Bob Ford have to gain from a deal with the law? A few dollars' reward money? It wasn't enough. But if Bob Ford was lying to him, it would be revealed, and he would butcher the son of a bitch like a hog.

L

THE LIGHT IN THE BEDROOM WINDOW PALED TO GRAY. SHADOWS cast a bluish tinge over the chairs and the walls and on the pictures upon them. Zee was curled up on the other side of the bed. He had slept fitfully. Outside the window, dawn's birds were in erratic song. All night he had felt that this small house wherein he lay with his family was exposed to some malevolent eye that had watched him for months but had only just now revealed itself. The eye of the law. The eye of the Great Deceiver. Bob Ford was the instrument of that eye. Jesse lay on his back, half paralyzed. Had he lost all of his old instincts that had kept him and his family safe for thirteen years? Had he been hiding the truth from himself? He had been utterly deceived. In the parlor, Bob Ford lay abed, supposedly as a sentry. All night Jesse had thought of Liddil's surrender. The news had shaken him at first. Not so much that Liddil had surrendered, he had half expected him to do so, but that it had taken two months for the word to come out. No word from inside or outside the jail. And in the same two months, he had had the Fords living with him. The timing was too perfect for there not to be a connection. But if the Fords had made a deal with the law, why hadn't the law come raiding the house? He could see but one reason. Liddil would be a star witness for the prosecution, but he was compromised by the fact that he was doing a deal to get himself a pardon. The law needed unconnected witnesses, too, and for that they had to catch Jesse James in the act of robbery. Like the bank job on the morrow. And in order to know when he would strike next, they had succeeded in putting two spies into his very own house.

He slid his legs out from under the warm blankets. He rested his elbows on his knees and rubbed his palms over his face to chafe some life into it. Every time he had his family settled, he had to move them to safety again. Frank had tried to persuade him to get out of Missouri altogether and leave behind the life of Jesse James. Try to live straight with his wife and kids under a new name. Disappear. And in a few years he would be forgotten. But what would he have to live for? Become some kind of commission agent? If he wanted to escape, he could take Bill Anderson's way and ride right into the ambush that was set for him in Platte City on the next day. But neither was that his way. He could never give up and allow that the Yankee laws had beaten him. He had not done so in 1864, when Bill was killed, nor in 1865, when the war was lost, nor in 1876, when the old James and Younger Gang had been destroyed. He would just take the Fords out to the woods and shoot the sons of bitches. Then he would rebuild all over again. With Frank or without him.

His day clothes were draped over a chair back. He reached for his pants, pulled them on, and belted them. Gooseflesh stippled the skin of his body. He rubbed at his upper arms. In an hour or so, the heat from the kitchen stove would have warmed up the house, but now the air was chill and damp. He pulled on his shirt, buttoned it, and tucked it in. He buckled on both cartridge belts and slipped the Navy Colt in behind his buckle. Then he pulled on his jacket. Charley Ford was a walking dead man. It was only Bob that might put up a fight. The bedroom door opened a crack.

–Mama.

Timmy appeared in the gap, his head tilted to one side, the homunculus of his father in striped flannel pajamas, one hand reaching up to the door latch, the other on the jamb. From the bedroom next door came his sister's sudden high whine like an early morning alarm that gained steadily in pitch and volume. Zee came awake. Her blond hair was tousled, the eyes puffy from sleep; the flesh of her face was slack and her lips were pale. She slid out of bed and pulled on her robe, clutched it about her.

He had let those two sons of bitches into his own home. Allowed them even to touch his children.

–Come on, Timmy, Zee said. Mary's crying.

Jesse followed his wife and son into the parlor. Bob Ford was already awake and fully dressed and was checking the chambers of his Schofield.

–Morning, Bob.

Bob nodded. Glanced down at the gun and back to Jesse. The boy had a pistol in his hands right now. He had a chance to try and take Jesse James. But he wouldn't. He would wait for the ambush. Two months of deceit that was set to culminate in a bank in Platte City. All Bob had to do was to survive until the next day, and Jesse James would be in the hands of the law, Liddil would be free, and Bob Ford would take his cut of the reward money.

–Quiet night?

–Yessir.

–Let's get some breakfast, Jesse said.

–Yessir.

He waited for Bob to get up and lead the way to the dining room. Bob tucked the pistol into his belt, and his hands swung freely by his side. Jesse could not execute him now in front of Zee and the children. He would be patient. Bob would not see it coming. It would be just like when he'd done Ed Miller. He adjusted the Colt at his waist and sat down at the head of the table. Bob sat at the opposite end. Zee, with more life in her face now, came in with Mary on one arm and trailing Timmy by the other. She sat down next to Jesse, kept Mary on her lap, and lifted Timmy onto the seat next to her. She darted a glance at him, aware in some feminine way that he was unquiet.

–How's my young man Timmy? Jesse said.

–Hungry, Timmy said.

Timmy fisted the fork that he had found in front of him. He whacked the end of it down on the table. Bob winced. He glared at Timmy, then stared down at his plate. His eyes were sunken. He had a few bristles on his smooth face. He moved as if even lifting a fork was an effort. All his muscles tight.

–Ain't you slept? Jesse said.

–Oh, I slept, Bob said.

–You look like . . .

–Ain't nothing wrong with me.

Coffee cups clattered upon the table and against one another. In the kitchen the skillet spat fat. Charley came into the dining room and scooped out fried eggs onto each plate. Bob kept his head bent to his plate. Jesse forked up a mouthful of egg white that was rubbery and greasy as he chewed at it. He washed away the taste with the acrid coffee. Knives and forks scraped against plates. Bob Ford forked up tiny mouthfuls and chewed as if he was ready to vomit.

–What's the matter, Bob? Jesse asked. No appetite?

Bob looked up. On the wall behind his head was Zee's wreath of dried flowers: a dozen marigolds, a twining of vervain and sweet everlasting, and six dried roses arranged over the top of it. It framed Bob's head like a halo, a hideous parody of sainthood. Or some kind of flowered pervert, a queen of the May.

–Ain't hungry, I guess.

–If ever'one's done, I'll clear up, Zee said.

Jesse got up from the table and led the way into the parlor. In that moment of distraction, the boy had a clear shot at his broad back if he took the chance. Jesse glanced over his shoulder. Bob was brushing crumbs from the skirt of his jacket. He didn't have the instinct for seizing such a God-given moment that could make him a killer. Jesse walked into the shaft of light that came straight through the parlor window. The sun was well risen, and it lit up the house and warmed him through the glass. Upon the windowsill, Zee had left a feather duster. He twisted the handle of it as he looked out across the flat flax fields that stretched off and ended at a small woods. He would take the Ford brothers out there this afternoon and do it. It would be easy to kill Charley. But Bob. It saddened him. In the same way that killing Ed Miller had saddened him. Such a waste. These boys were from a good family. But they had never been formed as their mama and papa had been formed in those bloody fights on the border, never remembered having their stock and crops stolen by the Union militia. Jesse turned back to the room. His shadow fell forward toward Charley. Charley had that glassy look in his eyes that showed he had already been at his morphine. Bob stood close to his cot. He avoided Jesse's gaze.

–You nervous, Bob?

–No, I ain't.

Bob took a deep breath then and stood up straight as if he had resolved himself. That defiance. It was what he had always liked about the boy. As if Bob could put behind himself whatever weakness he had and take on the world. It was what Jesse had hoped to develop in him. Bring him along. Make him one of the company.

–Still just you and me.

–I ain't worried.

–Let's see if Grimes shows up today, Jesse said.

–You'll see him soon enough, Charley said.

Charley was being wise with him. Jesse felt a coldness coming over him. A silent rage. Everything bright. Every nerve in his body singing. He would put them at their ease. As you might soothe a pair of useless coon hounds before putting them down.

–These guns are heavy, Charley, Jesse said. All the time this weight on me. A man gets tired. You boys wouldn't believe it.

–I believe it, Bob said.

Jesse drew the Colt from his waist. It was old and worn. He tossed the pistol onto Bob's cot and the gun bounced, the blanket indented, raised, settled, the gun lay still. Cat and mouse. A little game with them. The leather of his cartridge belt creaked as he pulled it loose from the brass buckle and unwound it from his waist. He wrapped the belt around the holster and regarded the wooden grip.

–This is a Schofield, Bob. You like the Schofield?

–Truth to tell, I prefer the forty-four.

Jesse set the belt, gun, and holster down next to the Colt on the brown blanket. He pointed at Bob's waist. Bob's hands began to tremble.

–That's a Schofield, ain't it? Jesse said.

–You give it to me, Bob said.

Jesse unhitched the buckle of his second belt. He wrapped the belt around the Remington in its holster and set that on the bed. There now. No weight on his hips anymore. Bob's mouth gaped. The boy was puzzled. Confused. Yes. No guns. Completely unarmed. Trust me, Bob. You wait. The angle of sunlight shifted slightly and the planes of the room seemed suddenly off square as the shadows of the sofa and the armchairs became skewed upon the walls and each picture seemed tilted out of square. A renewed sense of vertigo. Just as he had had looking up at that half-formed tower in Platte City two days before. Jesse turned back to the warm window and the stable horizon. The sun was up over the treetops in the distance. Between the window and the front door Mama's picture was tilted. Was really tilted. And dusty. He looked at Bob. His smooth jaw was clenched tight.

–That won't do, boys, will it? Jesse said.

He indicated the picture.

–I don't guess, Bob said.

Jesse picked up the duster off the sill. Dark feathers. Black and green. An iridescent sheen in the sunlight. A feather duster in his hand in front of Bob Ford. His guns upon the bed. He suddenly felt foolish and naked under the boy's gaze. Hard gray eyes with that defiance and determination. Mouth set in a tight line. Hands down by his side. A clatter of plates came from the dining room. Zee clearing the table. The voices of Timmy and Mary in some kind of childish dispute. Charley Ford glanced back toward the dining room door, but Bob Ford kept his eyes fixed upon Jesse. For two months these two malevolent presences had lived undetected in his house. But they had been revealed now. Only a matter of time.

He picked up a straight-backed chair from beside Bob's bed. His guns lay stark and abandoned, one next to the other. He was going to turn his back on the boy. It was his will against Bob Ford's, and it was the boy who would buckle. Everything was in the will. That was why men obeyed him. Even unto death. The legs of the chair scraped across the pine floor as Jesse set it against the wall. Leg bent, one foot upon the seat, he stepped up. That sense of vertigo as if the chair and the floor were falling away from under him. Three boot steps sounded upon the pine boards behind him and stopped. He steadied himself with a hand against the wall. All the planes and angles of the room were still off-kilter. His mama's face swayed in front of his. He ran the soft feathers over the glass. Motes of dust still clung to it, and he couldn't get them off. His mama's hard eyes stared into his. This had all slipped out of control. His own face reflected darkly in the glass. He had to set the picture straight. He reached up to adjust the frame, the duster's absurd plumage clutched in his right hand. There. Was that it? Everything steady again. All square and plumb. He turned slowly. Glimpsed the black muzzle of Bob Ford's Schofield. Then a blinding flash of light.

BOOK FIVE

LI

THE RED LIGHT OF THE SUN'S DYING RAYS CAST BLACK SHADOWS of iron bars across the cell so that all was striped and broken and divided by the insubstantial lines of darkness. So similar was the cell on each of the two nights that Mr. Ford had come to tell his story that it seemed as if time had not passed from one telling to another and the night and subsequent day's anguish and grief had faded as if it were a dream though the evidence of Joshua's misery was present in the twisted blanket that was bunched up between pillow and cell wall and in the increase of wrinkles and creases in his borrowed brown suit. The story was temporary respite for Joshua knew that the images of his father's death that so tormented him would not stop, not until Joshua was cut down dead from the scaffold. The next day would be the day of Da's funeral. He couldn't stand to think about it any more. The constriction in his throat eased when he listened to Mr. Ford. The hissing in Joshua's ears that tortured him by day abated. The burning in his eyes was salved as Mr. Ford's words became pictures in his head.

–You see, I didn't shoot him in the back, like they say I done. I shot him right behind the left ear. Boom! You're dead, and don't get up. Noise was so loud in the room. Smell of powder and his singed hair. He commenced to turn around from the picture on the wall and — boom! — right behind the ear. I got him. Blood spout out like a fountain.

Mr. Ford sat at the foot of Joshua's cot. His lank frame was bent over as he rolled a cigarette. His smooth-skinned face was drawn. When he had licked the paper and rolled it up, he let the cigarette dangle from his lips as he brushed crumbs of tobacco from the trousers of his gray suit and off the ticking of the mattress. He snapped a match alight. His face glowed in the flare. He blew out a plume of smoke. It curled upward and formed a small cloud — gray tinted red by the dying sun's light — that gathered beneath the low ceiling of the cell.

Speak now, Joshua thought, don't stop.

–And in she come screaming, Mr. Ford said. And I stand there with the gun in my hand and not knowed what to do next and Jesse James down there on the floor, blood still spurting from the hole in his head. But not so strong now. There warn't much of a charge behind the slug, because it didn't blow his brains right out. I'da thought it would of. Come out the other side, that is. Killed him stone dead, though. One shot, by God. That was the only chance I had or ever would have. Found out later the bullet was lodged behind the other ear. Did a autopsy, I guess. Sawed the top of his head clean off. You see what it was like? Jesse James tossed his Colt on the cot. He unhitched his gun belts, all stiff and shiny and black leather and heavy with the Remington in one and the Schofield in the other and he lays them cool as you please next to the Colt. Them pistols not five feet away from him. On the bed that I slept in. In the parlor. Next to the door. Because I was the sentry. Him pretending that nothing was wrong. Like he didn't read in the paper the day before that Dick Liddil give hisself up. Turned state's evidence against the James Gang. And Jesse knew that I knew Dick was in custody, though I'd told him different; so he knew what I said was a lie. It was only a matter of time before he had me kilt, or done it his own self. And by God he would of shot me in the back just the same as I done him. Just like I know he done others. Ed Miller for one. *Do unto others*, you know what I mean? Son of a bitch. I went right into Jesse James's own house and shot the son of a bitch. Who else would of done that?

– –Get the sheriff, Charley, I says.

–But now Charley was holding Zee James back. I swear to God I didn't feel nothing. Just numb. I'm standing over the body. Charley's holding her away from me. And my ears ringing from the shot still. I didn't know if I should run in case they wanted me to swing for it. People is quick to lynch a man. But I had a deal with the governor and the sheriff and I thought, By God, now I done it, why shouldn't I get the reward? Then there was all that ruckus. A crowd of neighbors come in right through the front door. They must of heard the shot.

– –Get him. Get him. He shot Mr. Howard.

– –That there's Jesse James, I said.

–That stopped them for a second.

– –Call the doctor! Call the doctor! she yells.

– –Call the coroner, I said.

–And I couldn't help but laugh, and they all whack at me and punch me in the head, but I could hardly feel it. Then the sheriff come and he took my gun and Charley give him his, too. They had me by the arms. I was laughing so hard like I couldn't control it all of a sudden but old Charley looked like he was ready to cry. I wanted to say something to him.

– –Hey Charley, it's fine.

–But it seemed like there was a million miles between us. The laughing all echo in my head and the ringing still ringing in my ears. And the house was real crowded now.

– –That's Jesse James, I said. And I had a deal to bring him in.

–She wouldn't say it right off, denied it even, but then the bitch admitted it. Couldn't see much point doing otherwise, I suppose. He was dead. Why keep up the show? Then everybody starts grabbing for souvenirs. Cartridge box. Pistol. But then the sheriff and his deputies dragged us down the street like we was two murderers and that bitch following behind with the kids screaming.

– –Hang them! Hang them! They killed my husband!

–I thought, That dead bastard killed many a woman's husband, lady. Same way as *I* killed *him*.

–Well, they put us in the cell all right, but I had them telegraph the governor to say that we had done it. We had got our man. Me, I got him. They say the governor didn't believe it at first, but we had the body to show. They couldn't deny that. Hard evidence of the death of Jesse James. We was acting on the governor's orders, but they still tried me and Charley for murder. Convicted us, too. And sentenced us to hang. But then the governor pardoned us just like he said he would. And I tell you what. We never got much of that reward money. Sheriff Timberlake and Police Commissioner

Craig got the most of it. And they done nothing. I was the one that went into his house and killed him. Gave them a corpse to put on show for folks. I seen it before the inquest. Jesse's corpse. They'd put mortician's paste on his face and rouged up the cheeks and the lips like a doll, like a woman. Like that actor we got to play his part in the show. Armstrong, his name was.

Mr. Ford seemed agitated now. He puffed a few times on his cigarette as if to stop it from going out.

–We done a show, did you know that? Me and Charley, on Broadway, New York. Bunnell's Theatre. And one in Brooklyn, too. And Albany, the state capital. Every night I saw that corpse turn around to face me, and I killed the bastard one more time. By Christ, he didn't stay down for long, did he? Next night the same. Boom! You're dead. And don't get up. And the night after. That's all I know. All the time. And I did it over and over and over again. But it was rough on Charley, by God. We showed them the true story. It was a good show. Genuine reenactment. Me and Charley. How we shot Jesse James. Wasn't Charley done it, though. It was me. Charley just stood there and held back that screaming bitch after I done it. And the kids crying, too. But we didn't show that. We didn't need to show that part, Bunnell said.

– –It ain't part of the dramatization, Bunnell said. Just Jesse. That's what they come to see.

–We had a actor by the name of Armstrong to play the part of Jesse James. Armstrong was from St. Louis, but he pretended he was a Englishman.

– –All the best thespians are Englishmen, Armstrong said.

–Armstrong could pretend to be anything or anyone he wanted, though why he wanted to pretend to be an Englishman when he wasn't on the stage was beyond me. So now me and Charley were thespians too. But we just acted as ourselves. I don't know if that counts as real acting or not. Whatever it was, it drew a crowd back there in the East.

– –They all come to see *me*. I was the star of the show. The killer. And Charley. I guess they come to see him, too. He didn't kill anyone, of course, but he was there. Armstrong looked just like Jesse James. Red lips. False beard. Kohl-rimmed eyes. A walking corpse. Bunnell's wife done the makeup from the photograph of Jesse dead. She done the makeup for all three of us. We would sit in front of a mirror. In the dressing room. Cheap goddamn mirror, too. It was all veins. I hated the stink of greasepaint when it mixed with the kerosene of the lanterns. But we had to have the makeup for the show. And I tell you what, you never knew what you was going to find in Bunnell's dressing room. On Broadway, like I said. One time, I seen this woman with the skin of her shoulders, her neck, her chest, her arms, even her tits, all tattooed with snakes and flowers and snow-capped volcanoes, and fountains and fruits, swallows and crows and song birds swirling around a broad-branched tree with roots that must of started at her cunny, though I couldn't say for certain because I never did get into her bloomers, though not for want of trying. Anyway, she leaned toward her mirror and to put on her lipstick. And cross her shoulder blades and down the V of her back, there was a three-masted ship that was caught in a storm and a raging tidal wave with whales and mermaids, rocks, coral flames, anemones that all spiraled around a sun and a moon. And by God, behind that tattooed woman, if there wasn't four midgets at a big trunk flinging out miniature cowboy hats, vests, plaid shirts, gun belts, and cowboy boots. Then there was a big blond woman dressed for burlesque — off-the-shoulder flouncy blouse, waist cinched in a black bustier, flared skirt. She was stroking a real python that hung down from neck to waist, the snake head in her open palm.

– –He eats mice, she told me.

–Charley laughed when he seen it.

– –By Christ, Charley, I said. We come a long ways, ain't we?

–Then you'd hear the whistles and stomps when the dancing girls were on the stage. Bunnell had their costumes designed from drawings that came from the Folies Bergères in Paris. The girls liked that. Bunnell even had a small orchestra to play for them. The dancers would finish, and seven beautiful girls crowded into that room full of midgets and freaks. The dressing room rumbled with the noise of the audience stamping their feet. The girls had three lacquered screens set up on the wall opposite the door. There was so little room that they had just draped their street clothes over the screens and undressed in front of them. The girls didn't even care to hide themselves. I'd pretend to fix my eye makeup and ogle them in the mirror. All them bare titties. Charley didn't give a good goddamn about any of it. Because of the morphine. Not the women dancers nor Bunnell's wife, who was rouging his cheeks.

–Just before our turn on stage, they'd have an Irish tenor. And the audience was quiet for him. I liked his voice. Everyone did. The applause and cheers filled the house. The dressing room shook again as the men in the audience stamped their feet. Bunnell signaled for the curtain. Stagehands ran on with furniture for the Jesse James set. I lifted my gun belt off the dressing table. Buckled it on. Slid the Schofield from the holster. Checked to see it was loaded with stage blanks.

– –You two ready? I'd say.

–Then Armstrong slid his arm under Charley's elbow. Mrs. Bunnell stepped back. Charley did a little shuffle, his elbows and forearms raised like a chicken. Armstrong nodded, face painted and bearded like the real Jesse James. It was always a moment that I felt complete. The moment before I shot him. We took the stage. Cheers and whistles. Armstrong under that beard. Mortician's paste on his face. Cheeks all rouged and kohl on the eyes. He unhitches his gun belt, all stiff and shiny and black leather and heavy with the Remington, and he lays it cool as you please on the bed. His pistol not five feet away from him on the bed. He takes the feather duster and gets up on the chair to dust the picture on the wall. Him pretending and all that nothing was wrong. I don't shoot him in the back, like they say I done. Shoot him right behind the left ear. Boom! You're dead, and don't get up. Noise was so loud on the stage. Armstrong wore ear plugs. He commenced to turn around from the picture on the wall and — boom! — right behind the ear, I got him. Armstrong claps his hand to his head and bursts a balloon of stage blood. Morticians' paste on his face and rouged up the cheeks and the lips like a doll, like a woman. He falls off the chair and onto the stage.

– –We killed him, Charley, I say. That murdering desperado is dead.

–Cheers and stamps then. That's what they come to see. Two convicted murderers up on the stage. Me and Charley. We were supposed to hang. We done murder and got away with it. There ain't man nor woman in that crowd who don't want to know what it feels like to pull the trigger. To see how someone else can die right there in front of you. And you get away with it. And I done it. And this is how close *they* come to it. That feeling. Me on the stage. A man who's done it. Had the guts to pull the trigger. And not just on any man, but on the one they been reading about these past ten years in every newspaper and penny storybook. And I got away with it. A damned man. Me and Charley. And Jesse James. Damned for murder, by God.

Mr. Ford got up off the bed and walked to the corner of the cell and back. He was frowning as if he was trying to solve some problem, like trying to balance two columns of figures and not getting a zero at the bottom. He coughed dryly.

–When you kill someone, you unleash a force in nature that turns the world agin you. It ain't like killing an animal. It is as if something has tilted off-kilter and nature seeks to put it to rights, no matter what the cause of the killing. You know about that right enough.

Joshua remembered the pumping of his father's blood, the hopping dance, the gray face turned up toward him again. Remembered the sheriff's face as he locked the cell door.

–I killed one man that half the world wanted dead, and the whole world turned agin *me*. Jesse was so deep in blood that it was only a matter of time before nature destroyed him. I was only the instrument of that destruction, but I still had to pay my price. And you, Joshua, you know what I mean. You already begun to pay, ain't you? It's obvious. What I say is true. Jesse James waited a long time to pay for what he done, because he began his killing in times of war. And in times of war, nature is in turmoil. Destruction unleashed upon the earth. Some men survive that and they get to feel immortal. But more than that. You have never been so alive in all your life. If you see that kind of power in war or nature, or in the act of killing a man, you can only feel awe. Like when I shot Jesse James. I felt terror but just as much joy. I felt so alive. I had sucked the power out of him. There is power in blood and the spilling of blood. You feed off the sight of it. You always want more. I know that right enough.

Mr. Ford took a drag on his cigarette. His eyes looked out into the cloud of smoke that swirled beneath the ceiling.

–But what happens when the war comes to an end? Mr. Ford said. The survivors are not punished. So some folks come home and they are torn apart by guilt over what they done. Others feel justified by the cause they fought for, win or lose. And still others know that never again will they feel so alive, have such intense and thrilling pleasure as they felt during wartime.

–Some people in Missouri would have you believe that the Radical Republicans in the State House made life hell for former guerrillas and Confederate families after the war. But that is a lot of eyewash, boy. I lived there. Half the guerrillas became lawmen and turned a blind eye to their former comrades who robbed and plundered still. The James family had a farm and ran it with niggers that didn't want no emancipation. What did the James and Samuels family want for? None of those old rebel families gave a damn for the Union winning the war, and they carried on as if the war had never ended. And the women was as bad as the men. Egged men on to retribution for the Lost Cause. Old Ma Samuels, Jesse's mama, was one of the worst of them. And Jesse's wife, Zee. They lived to see more Yankees dead. You tell me if Jesse and Frank didn't think to get back in the saddle when the war was done.

The glowing end of Mr. Ford's cigarette fell from his fingers, and his heel swiveled and his toe crushed it out.

–And I killed Jesse James.

Mr. Ford fell silent. He looked at the cell door as if he wished to escape. But Joshua didn't want Mr. Ford to leave him alone in the cell. Not yet. Mr. Ford sat down again at the end of the bed. He pulled out his tobacco pouch. At least one more cigarette before Joshua was left alone.

–What about Frank James? Joshua said.

Mr. Ford looked up.

–Frank? Frank turned hisself in. He was tired of it all. They tried him in Gallatin, and Dick Liddil testified agin him just like Dick promised Timberlake and Crittenden. John Newman Edwards hired Frank the best lawyer in the state and General Jo Shelby testified for the defense. The jury was packed with Democrats and Confederates. And they acquitted him. Frank James is a free man. And a drunk. And Crittenden gave Dick Liddil his pardon like he said he would. Crittenden was an honorable man. And I ain't never had no bother with Frank James.

–What about your brother? Joshua said. Charley.

Mr. Ford's face creased around the eyes as if he had a sudden headache.

–Charley done fell apart on me. He couldn't stand it. Everywhere we went, some folks called us cowards and traitors. And you know that song. The dirty little coward. You know it. Hist'ry does record, That Bob and Charley Ford, They laid Jesse James in his grave. What with the morphine and all. And he had the goddamn syphilis, too. He was a mess. Claimed he had consumption, but I don't know if he had *that* or not. One day, he laid hisself down on a hotel bed and shot hisself with a .44. Clean through the heart. I seen the body.

Mr. Ford shook his head. He had his elbows on his knees and his hands came up and covered his face. Joshua thought that he might be covering tears, but there was no sound behind the hands. Mr. Ford lowered his hands. He had not been crying, but there was a darkness in his face that had not been there before.

–I got away with it, you see, said Mr. Ford. Charley didn't. And Jesse didn't. But Frank did. And I did. But I couldn't stand to live in Missouri no more. Not with Charley dead. And I had too many enemies. That's why I come up here. To Weaver. Start fresh. That's how we got to meet, ain't it?

Mr. Ford stood up.

–I got to go now, he said. You just . . . But I'll have you out of this jail. Don't worry none. Mr. Pearl, the lawyer, will be here to see you just after your daddy's funeral tomorrow.

–Thank you, Joshua said. I can't thank you enough.

Mr. Ford pulled open the cell door.

–I'll see you in the morning, Mr. Ford said.

–Yessir, Joshua said.

And then Mr. Ford was gone and Joshua's mind began to race again.

Why was Mr. Ford so intent on helping him escape the noose? Why was it that Mr. Ford had come these two nights to talk to him? Or was it that Mr. Ford's telling of the story was some form of exorcism? It was as if the act of murder had given Mr. Ford possession of the soul of Jesse James so that all his mannerisms and gestures and words while he told his stories became those of someone else, of the dead outlaw, of Jesse James.

Would his da live on inside him in the same way? The sobs erupted like vomit from Joshua's throat. Dear God, such a haunting would be worse than death on the gallows.

LII

JOSHUA SAT ON THE EDGE OF THE BED WITH HIS BLANKET OVER his head and pulled tight around his shoulders and chest to block out the morning light. The darkness made a poor simulation of the oblivion of sleep. Joshua was exhausted by the constant thoughts that sought to undo time and memory's torment: the bloody dance of his father's final moments that played over and over again in his imagination. He had passed two nights in the cell and one full day, with his only waking respite coming from his immersion in the words of Mr. Robert Ford and his story of Jesse James. It was Wednesday, the day his father was to be buried. Sheriff Gardner had promised him that he could go to the funeral. Mr. Ford had said he would come by with a wagon. The muffled scrape of a key in the jailhouse door penetrated the warm darkness beneath the blanket. The latch clacked and hinges squeaked and feet scuffled on the floor in front of his cell.

–Come on out, boy.

It was the voice of Fat Wallace.

Joshua loosed his clutch on the blanket and let it slip off his head. He blinked behind his glasses. Morning light suffused his cell with the sick color of soapy water and turned the walls gray and the steel bars gray and overwhelmed him in renewed anguish. On the other side of the cell bars, Deputy Wallace held a bunch of keys in one hand and a steaming bowl in the other. Wallace rattled the key ring and deftly selected the long iron key to the cell door and unlocked it. Over his right forearm dangled a pair of chains with shackles fastened to each end of them. Wallace's round red face was unshaven, the eyes bleary, the mouth slack, and his double chin hung over his twisted ribbon tie. A few white flecks of corn mush stuck to his black waistcoat and to the cuff of his black frock coat. Joshua pushed his glasses back up onto the bridge of his nose. He was surprised that he was suddenly hungry. He remained seated on the edge of the bed as Wallace handed him the loaded, steaming plate. On top of the white grits wobbled the bright yellow eye of an egg yolk, and beside it a fork lay half buried in the pale and sticky mush.

Joshua extricated the slimed fork and scooped up a hot mouthful of grits that scalded the roof of his mouth. But he didn't care about such discomfort. With the tines of his fork, he burst the yolk of the egg, and the deep yellow of it ran down over the rubbery white of the egg and the grits and pooled at the edge of his plate. He blew upon the next forkful to cool it and shoveled it into his mouth and continued shoveling as Wallace knelt on the floor in front of him as if in supplication. Puzzled, Joshua regarded him over the rim of his plate.

–Might as well do this now, Wallace said.

The deputy clapped a shackle around Joshua's left ankle and fastened it with a small padlock. The weight of the iron dug into skin and bone above his boot. Joshua pulled his right foot back when Wallace tried to encircle it with the next iron cuff.

–What are you doing? Joshua said.

–Sheriff Gardner won't let you go to your daddy's burial if you ain't chained up right.

Joshua saw no point in fighting anything anymore, so he slid his foot forward again and allowed the deputy to fasten his other ankle while he continued to scoop down his breakfast. The shackles were heavy on both legs. With the edge of the fork, he scraped up the last of the grits and the congealed yolk. Wallace relieved Joshua of his empty plate and laid it on the floor. Then the deputy took the second chain and set of locks and shackled Joshua's wrists. Wallace nodded, satisfied, and stood up just as Mr. Ford came in through the jailhouse door.

Mr. Ford was accompanied by a clean-shaven man who wore a white Stetson hat. His long silvery hair flowed down to the shoulders of a fringed white buckskin jacket. Even the skin of the stranger's face seemed to glow. It stretched over his knife-edged nose and cheekbones with hardly a wrinkle except around the sparkling green eyes. A large turquoise-and-silver tie clasp hung at the throat of his cream shirt. Mr. Ford was as immaculately dressed as ever in his gray suit and homburg, but the attire of the man who accompanied him was far more striking. Mr. Ford did not introduce the stranger. His eyes bored into the back of Wallace's head.

–What the hell you doing, Wallace? Mr. Ford said.

–Gardner's orders.

The sight of Mr. Ford had brought a smile to Joshua's face.

–You think the boy's going to run away from his own daddy's funeral? Mr. Ford said.

–Cain't risk it.

–Where could he run to, anyways?

–He's going on trial for murder. It's a hanging offense so he might just risk it.

–Anything you can do, Counselor Pearl? Mr. Ford said.

Pearl shook his head.

–I'd rather not antagonize the sheriff quite so quickly, he answered.

So this primped-up oldster was the lawyer that Mr. Ford had hired to defend him. Wallace turned to Joshua.

–Stand up, boy, he said.

Joshua came to his feet and shuffled forward. The chain clanked along the floor. It was too long to keep taut by widening his gait and too short to reach down and hold it up in his hands. He wondered how he would walk and how far he would have to walk with the chain dragging between his legs through the inevitable mud in the street and on the road to the cemetery. Counselor Pearl gave Joshua a glowing smile, and Joshua felt a momentary confusion.

If Mr. Ford trusts him, why shouldn't I? Joshua thought.

–The undertaker's outside, Mr. Ford said.

That meant that his da's body was outside too. Joshua wanted to see his father's face one last time, but Mort Gardner had said that it was too late, for the coffin lid had already been screwed down tight. Joshua did not believe him, but he had no way to escape his cell and find out the truth of it. He thought of asking

Pearl to do something, but then decided against it, for if the undertaker was outside, then the funeral was about to start. He had no wish to expose his father's body to every passing stranger on the street, and he knew they would not turn back to the undertaker's mortuary just to please an accused murderer.

Wallace swung open the barred door of the cell.

Joshua held his arms stiffly out in front of him, and the chain between his wrists dangled almost to his knees. He moved each foot deliberately, one after the other, afraid that his feet might tangle and the dragging chain trip him. Mr. Ford momentarily laid a hand on his shoulder as Joshua passed by. Joshua felt his throat constrict at the tenderness of the gesture, but he feared that he would shed enough tears in grief to be wasting them unduly on Mr. Ford's kindness. Counselor Pearl's sharp-angled face turned grave suddenly, as if he could produce emotion on cue.

–We'll talk about your defense after the funeral, Pearl said.

Joshua nodded and shuffled past him and entered into the sheriff's office from the jailhouse. The room was heated by a potbellied stove, and the cloying warmth brought a flush to Joshua's face after the chill of his cell. He wished that Pearl could have arrived after the funeral. He did not wish to be distracted from his father's last rites.

Sheriff Gardner stood in front of his cluttered desk. His habitual black suit was ideal for funeral or trial or wedding. Joshua wished that he was wearing some easily acknowledged sign of mourning, such as a black crepe armband or a black tie. The fact that he had no such token to display his grief shamed him worse than the irons at wrist and ankle.

Gardner settled his hat on his head and lifted a shotgun off the edge of the desk. He tucked the shotgun into the crook of his arm, opened the office door, and stepped outside in front of Joshua. Joshua shuffled onto the boardwalk. The undertaker's wagon was drawn up directly in front of the office. The undertaker was a skinny and unshaven old man in an old black suit and hat, both of which had a greenish tinge. He leaned over his reins and did not look at Gardner or Joshua or Mr. Ford or Wallace, but he did sneak a glance at Pearl as he emerged from the office in his white buckskins. Rain, carried by a gust of wind, spat down upon the plain pine box on the wagon and speckled it with droplets. His father could not hear the rattling of the rain's insult, locked as he was in the darkness of that wooden box and the deeper darkness of death. Joshua recalled how his father's face had relaxed into peace as life drained out of him while he had lain in Joshua's arms. It was one of the few occasions in his recent memory that his father had visibly displayed his love. At least his da would carry that look with him as they laid him in the earth. It would have been a comfort to Joshua to see that expression once more, but the world seemed more intent on Joshua's punishment than on his quietude. The world stared upon him with loathing. The boardwalks on either side of the sheriff's office were packed with wide-beamed women and unkempt loafers and strangely silent children. Had their mothers told them of his crime? A crime that to them would be unspeakable? None of the crowd would meet his gaze, but turned their heads. He was already beyond childhood. Now he was beyond humanity. What jury would fail to convict him? To rid the world of him. Up the street, north of the wagon, stood Soapy Smith, surrounded by his band of henchmen, Ed O'Kelley, Mickey James, and Clarence Thompson. Behind them were a group of bearded Mormons with round-brimmed hats. They all stared at him in silence. All of these bystanders had come not to show their respects to Aaron Beynon but only to ogle a parricide.

–Come up here, Honeyjosh.

Mrs. Ford's voice was warmth and sweetness. He thought of his mother. And his father about to join her.

Mrs. Ford was seated on a wagon behind the undertaker's. She had squeezed herself into a tight-bodiced green dress that was trimmed with black ribbon. Her hair was coiled on each side of her chubby face, and it seemed that she disdained to wear a hat despite the overcast sky and the squalls of storm that blew between the high redrock walls of the canyon. Beside her, Silas Strickland held the reins of the two-horse team. He had perched a stovepipe hat on top of his thick white curls. He grinned at Joshua all across his wide and battered fighter's face. Behind him, Dick Liddil, his blond mustache and beard waxed into three points, sat with two long-queued Chinamen on the sideboards of the wagon. Joshua was puzzled by their alien presence but had no thought to ask why they had been invited along.

Sheriff Gardner lifted his chin in the direction of Strickland

and Dot Ford. Joshua, with his chains scraping the ground, shuffled toward the wagon. Mr. Ford descended the steps of the boardwalk behind him. The chains restricted the stretching of Joshua's legs so that he could not lift his foot high enough to climb aboard. Mr. Ford ignominiously boosted him upward by the seat of his pants, and Silas Strickland gripped him by the scruff of the neck and hauled him up beside him like a drowned kitten. Dot Ford reached across Strickland's lap and squeezed Joshua's hand. Tears welled hotly in Joshua's eyes and he bit his lower lip to hold them back. Fat Wallace, toting a shotgun, climbed over the tailgate of the Fords' wagon and sat down on a wooden crate directly behind Joshua. Sheriff Gardner, Mr. Ford, and Counselor Pearl all mounted saddlehorses that were tied to the rail outside the sheriff's office.

–Let's go, Gardner called.

Gardner, Ford, and Pearl guided their horses into the middle of the muddy street. Gardner kept his shotgun propped up on his thigh. The undertaker flicked his long whip and his team plodded forward, dragging the wagon through the mud of the street toward the cemetery that was up past the livery in the direction of Mr. Ford's cabin. Silas popped his own team into motion and the small cortege was underway. The bystanders on the boardwalks followed them in silence, and Joshua feared that they would stare at him all the way to the cemetery and at the graveside as his father was lowered into the earth.

–Murderer!

It was a woman's voice.

Joshua searched the crowd for the source of it.

–Pay no mind, Strickland said.

His gravelly voice was a comfort. The wagon creaked and listed as it rolled down the uneven street behind the undertaker and his father's bare coffin. As the team picked up speed, the crowd upon the boardwalks kept pace with them, flanking the cortege between the ramshackle buildings and flapping tent stores of Main Street.

Then a shower of grit rattled against the side of the Fords' wagon.

–Goddammit, Dot cursed.

–Parricide!

The voice of a Mormon, Joshua thought.

The wagons cleared the last of the town's buildings, but still the crowd surged along beside them, closer to the wagons now that there was no boardwalk to keep them off the road. A bearded prospector thrust his face upward, eyes wide and angry.

–We'll see ye hang, he cried.

–Get back! yelled Sheriff Gardner.

Joshua gripped the seat of the wagon. The mob swarmed around it like a pack of predatory animals. A clump of turf shattered on the footboard. The tails of the team flicked up nervously and the mules tossed their heads. Strickland jockeyed the reins to steady them.

–What's wrong with you, Gardner? Dot called.

Mr. Ford spun his horse in the road and drew his pistol, and Counselor Pearl urged his horse ahead past the undertaker's wagon. Beside Mr. Ford, Sheriff Gardner cocked his shotgun.

–I want no trouble here! the sheriff called.

Gardner halted his horse and the Fords' wagon was by him. Mr. Ford rode up alongside the wagon, close to Joshua's side.

If the mob should hate his father's murderer, Joshua could understand, but they were showing no respect for his father's last passage. He wanted to cry out against these people, but his fear of provoking them to greater sacrilege kept him tongue-tied and frustrated. He yanked at the chain between his wrists and twisted the links. He wished the townspeople to disappear, but they continued to follow like mindless creatures out of a nightmare. Up ahead, the undertaker's wagon took the westward fork in the road that led up to the graveyard. Strickland swung his team behind it. Joshua looked back over his shoulder.

Next to Joshua, Dick Liddil had drawn his pistol and laid it flat upon his lap. He nervously twirled one end of his blond mustache. The Chinamen hunched over in their padded jackets, both of them staring at their feet as if they inhabited a world entirely other than the frenzied mob that thronged around the wagon. The crowd, which Joshua numbered in scores, surged into the road and continued to follow. Sheriff Gardner, the shotgun raised above his head, drifted like a cork on the crowd's current.

Mr. Ford raised his pistol and fired a shot in the air. The leaders of the crowd momentarily balked.

–No shooting! Gardner yelled. I don't want no shooting.

The undertaker's wagon was through the three-poled gate and the white-clad Pearl drew his horse off among the headstones to let it pass. Strickland drove the team up to the graveside, where a mound of freshly dug loamy earth marked the location of Aaron Beynon's final resting place.

–Stay back! called Mr. Ford.

–That's right! Gardner shouted.

Dick Liddil, pistol in hand, jumped down off the wagon, and the two Chinamen and Fat Wallace followed him. The crowd had halted some twenty yards away from the grave. Out in front, five or six scruffy prospectors passed a jug among themselves. A knot of Polish women clustered under a yew tree, and a group of adolescent boys swarmed through the oak planks and slate headstones to form a line, up the slope from the freshly dug grave. They all had handfuls of stones and divots of earth that dangled from their fingers like miniature heads under grassy hair.

–Hang him now! called one of the drunks.

–Leave him be! Dot called. Show some respect!

–He ain't showed none to his daddy.

Joshua laid his palms to his face and impotently wished them all away. The chains hung down heavy. He pressed the heel of his palms to his eyes to stop the tears. He had no wish to display his grief in front of these monsters. He let his hands drop.

–Oh, Da, he murmured.

And then he couldn't stop himself. His body was racked with sobs that seemed like huge hiccups that heaved up out of his chest into his throat and shook his shoulders so that the chain swung between his wrists. He felt Dot Ford's arm around the small of his back and the pressure of her soft breast against his own arm, the scent of her cologne. She laid her palm on his wet cheek for a second and he shook his head to show his disbelief.

–Get down off the wagon, now, she said.

Joshua jumped down off the footboard of the wagon. His chains rattled as his feet hit the ground. Mr. Ford dismounted and tied the reins of his horse to a stanchion behind the seat. Joshua stumbled to the graveside.

The two Chinamen, Dick Liddil, Silas Strickland, and Fat Wallace stood at the tailboard of the undertaker's wagon. Mr. Ford joined them and they slid the coffin out and onto their shoulders.

Da had not been a big man, and the six pallbearers had little trouble carrying the coffin and laying it down on the three red velvet-covered ropes beside the hole.

The old undertaker shuffled forward. He removed his black hat and stood at the head of the grave. He cleared his throat and looked directly at Joshua.

Not without kindness, Joshua thought.

–Aaron Beynon was a friend of mine . . .

The undertaker raised his voice for all to hear.

. . . I often raised a glass with him. He seen his wife and two of his kids precede him into death, and he fell by the hand of his own son. I don't believe that this boy meant to kill his own father. There's no sense to it. Neither did Aaron see much sense to why his wife and two youngest was taken, all three of 'em. I heard the preachers tell it that God works in mysterious ways. Sometimes it seems nought but cruel, and there ain't much sense to it. Aaron couldn't fathom it and I don't know as I can or if anyone can. That's why there ain't no minister present to perform an oration here, since Aaron refused to go to chapel for the last year of his life. I don't know as Aaron had much belief left in him anyways. Looking upon the folks around his final resting place, I don't see much that would have changed his mind. Well, I say God have mercy on the soul of Aaron Beynon. And God have mercy on us all.

One of the Polish women raised a furled umbrella.

–You are all blasphemers and parricides and thieves and murderers!

A hail of small stones and divots sailed through the air and a stone stung Joshua upon the cheek and a clod of earth broke against his ear and dirt infiltrated the collar of his shirt. At his feet, the coffin rattled under the bombardment that continued to rain down. The pallbearers all bent over with their arms flung up to protect themselves.

The flat report of a shotgun split the air and echoed off the canyon walls, and Joshua ducked lower with everyone else. Silence followed.

Mort Gardner rode his horse up the slope and halted in front of the line of youths.

–The next one to disturb the peace of this gravesite will take a load of buckshot, and I ain't jesting.

The two Chinamen, Fat Wallace, Dick Liddil, Silas Strickland, and Bob Ford took hold of the red velvet-covered rope and swung the earth-spattered coffin over the hole in the ground. Joshua would only remember his father's face at the moment he had died in his arms. He wondered if he would see his father again soon in some region beyond death, for if his jury was to be chosen from among the mob present, he had little hope of life and little will to live it.

LIII

THE GRIEF CAME UPON HIM IN WAVES. ONE MINUTE HE WAS SITTING numbly on the edge of the prison cot and staring blankly at the bars, and the next he was howling at the aching loss of his whole family — father, mother, brother, and sister — all of whom this canyon had swallowed into its maw as if in forfeit for the minerals ripped from its soil and the timber stripped from its slopes and the poisonous tailings disgorged into its waters. Such explanation would at least give meaning to their deaths. But why was it that *his* family had to pay the price of such despoil that had turned nature — or was it God — malevolent? Why had such powers not taken Soapy Smith the whoremaster or Bob Ford the assassin or Ella Mae Waterson the whore and addict? He could not accept the injustice of his family's sacrifice. He ached with every breath he drew into the inconsolable and unfillable void within him. No sunlight penetrated his tomb. The overcast sky and the desultory rain of the day had conspired to fill the cell with a creeping dampness upon which his breath condensed as he exhaled. The barred and paneless window framed oblongs of dark gray. The cell around him was but a visible manifestation of the loneliness and desolation he felt in muscle and nerve and tissue. He shivered and wiped away the tears that had stained his face and emptied him once more of emotion to leave him newly numb.

Beyond the jailhouse door a lantern was lit and laid a barred yellow rhomboid of light on the west wall of the cell, the color of piss. He heard voices, and the jailhouse door opened. Sheriff Gardner, carrying lamp and keys came into the jailhouse. He was followed by Mr. Ford and the effeminate lawyer in his white Stetson and buckskins. Both of his visitors carried straight-backed chairs from the office, and the lawyer in addition dangled a leather briefcase that had been tooled with flowers like a pretty belt. Gardner turned the key in the lock of his cell door and the bars swung open.

–Evening, Josh, Mr. Ford said.

Joshua didn't answer. The lawyer and Mr. Ford set their chairs down between the bed and the south wall. Gardner hung his lantern from a beam in the cell.

–Goddamn, it's cold in here, Mort, Mr. Ford said.

Gardner shrugged.

–It's a jailhouse.

Gardner swung the cell door closed behind him but didn't lock it, and he returned to his office, leaving lawyer and prisoner and Mr. Ford to begin their deliberations.

Seated now, Counselor Pearl opened the flap of the fancy leather briefcase and pulled out a sheaf of papers, a bound notebook, an ink bottle, and a new pen with a shiny brass nib. He arranged them on his lap, the notebook serving as his desk. Mr. Ford leaned forward and rested his forearms on his knees. He still had his hat on and the brim of the homburg threw a shadow over his eyes.

–Well, Josh, Mr. Ford said, Counselor Pearl here is the best lawyer in Colorado.

–So you said, Joshua said.

–Thing is, Mr. Ford said, we have to straighten out a few things before we start because he don't work for free. As you might expect.

Joshua couldn't read Mr. Ford's expression. He imagined that Mr. Ford was a good poker player. Whatever was coming, Joshua knew that he was about to find himself indebted to one or both of these men. The thought of it disquieted his already fragile disposition so that he interlocked his fingers to stop his hands from shaking. He shivered again. He could blame the cold. His blanket was behind him on the bed, but his nervousness prevented him from pulling it up over his shoulders.

–Now, Mr. Ford said, we're going to have to be straight with you about certain matters that you might find upsetting, but the way I see it, we have to face the facts.

Joshua adjusted his glasses and glanced at Pearl. The lawyer's face was equally composed as Mr. Ford's but all sharp angles framed by the brim of the Stetson and his long white hair. Joshua did not trust Pearl. Mr. Ford had paid Joshua well, invited him into his home, protected him from the law, and arranged his father's funeral, but now something was amiss. Somehow Mr. Ford had allied himself with this man.

–You see, Joshua, Pearl said, Mr. Ford has paid me a small retainer that just about covered my traveling expenses from Denver. Now if I am to prepare your case, we have to discuss where the rest of my fee is going to come from. And we can't expect Mr. Ford to pay for it, now, can we?

Joshua shook his head.

–I've got no money, he said.

–We can come to an arrangement, Counselor Pearl said. I've studied on it and I see that you have some equity.

–Equity?

–Your daddy owned a house. Now that he is deceased, that house belongs to you as the sole living heir. But you have a problem in realizing that equity, for you are incarcerated.

–I don't understand, Joshua said.

–If you were to make me executor of your father's estate, the lawyer said, I would be happy to put your house on the market and you could make a handsome profit that would enable you to pay any and all legal fees due to me for closing the property deal and the administration of your father's will and all defense fees for your upcoming trial; and you will be able to reimburse Mr. Ford for his outlay of the retainer and the cost of the funeral to the undertaker.

So that was it. Pearl would sell the house and gouge him for as much as he could possibly get. Joshua looked from Pearl to Mr. Ford. Mr. Ford's part in this was still puzzling. Joshua assumed that the house was worth a lot of money and that he had to face the fact that Mr. Pearl wanted paying and it was unfair that Mr. Ford should foot the bill. As far as Joshua could tell, there was little choice.

–What do I have to do? he said.

Pearl opened a sunny, beaming smile upon him. The teeth were extraordinarily white in the tanned face.

–Before I left Denver, Pearl said, one of my clients asked me to look into acquiring some property for him up here in Weaver. Fortune has smiled upon us, at least in regard to a buyer. Of course, we don't have time to sell the house before the trial, so we have a number of steps to take in order to solve our financial problems. Firstly, I need you to sign a paper making me executor of your father's estate. Then I can contact my client in Denver. Should I be successful in getting you acquitted before the court, we have plenty of time to sell the house, you will pay my fees and your debt to Mr. Ford, and you will have a sizable sum of money left in the bank.

The plan sounded fair. He would have to pay Pearl top dollar, but he had no choice in that. Joshua nodded. He reached behind him for the blanket and pulled it up over his wide shoulders. He tucked in his elbows so that he didn't resemble an overgrown chicken.

–And Mr. Ford has a further proposition for you, Pearl said.

Mr. Ford sat up straight and gripped the lapels of his jacket.

–What I got to offer is this. When you get out of jail, I want you to be my partner in the saloon business. Equal shares. What money you got left over from the house sale, you can invest the equal amount that I paid for my property, so that we can build a frame-and-clapboard saloon where there is but a tent at the moment. What do you think?

Joshua beamed. It was more than he could ever have hoped for. Partnership with the famous Robert Ford. The offer seemed genuine enough. It was as if the sun had risen above the depths of his despair. Where he had been mired in the grief of the present, now a future had opened before him.

–There's just one problem, Counselor Pearl said.

–I'll do it, Joshua said. I'll sign the paper.

–Just a minute, Pearl said.

–What is it?

–We have to get through the trial. And though I'm confident, I can't guarantee complete acquittal.

The joy drained out of Joshua, and suddenly the enormity of the trial and the shadow of the gallows filled him with terror. He wished to cling to Counselor Pearl like a shipwreck victim to the gunwale of a lifeboat.

–Well, I . . . What do you mean, then? Joshua said. The house? The partnership?

–We have a plan, said Pearl. First of all, let's get all these papers in order. I need you to sign a declaration making me the executor of your father's estate. Then, I have drawn up a partnership agreement between you and Mr. Ford. Lastly, and I hate to bring this up, Joshua, we should have you draw up a will in case — and I want to say that this is unlikely — the trial goes badly for you.

–A will? Joshua said.

–It's just a precaution, said Pearl. That way your property will be disposed of as you wish it.

–Do I have to name a relative? Joshua said. I don't want to leave the house to my uncle's family. They abandoned us.

–Anyone you want, Pearl said. You can name your new partner if you want to; that way you won't be beholden to him if the worse comes to the worst. But it won't come to that. I have a sure plan that is guaranteed to save your life.

–A plan? Joshua said.

–This might be hard to accept, but it's a sure way to escape the gallows, Pearl said. I want you to plead guilty to second-degree murder so that I can make a deal with the judge for you to do penitentiary time. I think I could get a sentence as low as ten years. And you might not serve all of it, for you would have possibility of parole. All being well, you could be out and free again before your twenty-second birthday.

Joshua turned toward Mr. Ford. The gray eyes in the smoothly shaved face were unreadable. Mr. Ford just nodded.

–What about this partnership with Mr. Ford? Joshua said.

–Mr. Ford, Pearl said, will still be your partner, even though you might be in the penitentiary. You would still share in any profit he might make, and he would hold that profit in trust for you until you were released.

It dawned on him then.

–This is just a way to get the house money, Joshua said. Isn't it?

Mr. Ford reached up and resettled the homburg on his head and glanced at Pearl. Maybe he wasn't such a great poker player after all.

–I am simply trying to prevent you hanging, Joshua, Pearl said.

–I didn't murder my father, Joshua said. It was an accident.

–If you plead not guilty and the jury condemns you, we have no deal with the judge. That's a hanging matter.

–I'm not guilty, Joshua said.

Pearl suddenly turned indignant.

–You saw those folks out there today. They were but a hair from lynching you.

–Well, you better save me if you want to be paid.

–I could walk out of here right now and let you hang.

–Are you in on this? Joshua said to Mr. Ford.

Mr. Ford raised his hands, palms up.

–Hold up, Josh, he said. Let's come to some agreement here.

–Get out of here! Joshua yelled.

Tears were in his eyes and his cheek quivered. He felt ashamed to be betrayed so. He knotted his fingers in the blanket and drew it taut over his back. He bit down hard on his lip. Pressed his forearms down on his thighs as if the tension of his body would be enough to drive them away.

–Listen, Mr. Ford said, this is hard for you, I know. But Counselor Pearl and myself, we both want to see you go free. Point is, this is a legal matter and we have to go by legal rules. The easiest way to keep you alive is a plea bargain. The other side of it is, you got to pay your own way. You're a man now. Your pappy's dead and you got to fend for yourself. Painful though it is, there are facts to face here. And we got to work them out. You understand me?

Joshua reached up and pulled off his glasses. With the heel of his hand, he pressed away the tears. This pair of bastards had come to fleece him, but they were his only hope of life. He wanted to live long enough at least to see that they were paid back for what they were doing to him. He was in a cold, hard rage.

–All right, Joshua said. Firstly, I will sign the paper making Counselor Pearl executor of my father's estate and authorizing him to sell the house and agreeing to pay him his legal fees for such duties. Secondly, I will sign a partnership agreement with Mr. Ford as long as the clause is added that the agreement depends on my being declared innocent at my trial; and that way you two have some reason for keeping me out of the penitentiary. I am not signing any will naming anybody my heir, because if I do, it's in your interest to see me hang. Draw up the papers, Mr. Pearl.

Pearl carefully unscrewed the top of his ink bottle. His smile bared his eyeteeth and crinkled his eyes into slits.

–You are making my life difficult, Joshua Beynon, Pearl said.

And I'll revenge myself on both of you, Joshua thought, if only you can get me acquitted.

LIV

A HIGH-BACKED CHAIR STOOD EMPTY ON THE LOW STAGE WHERE usually dancing girls and traveling players plied their lugubrious trade. The plush velvet curtains had been drawn aside to accommodate the judge's bench and tables for prosecution and defense. A low-backed armchair that was to serve as the witness stand stood next to the judge's chair. Two of Soapy Smith's barmen carried an oak table from the wings, stage left, and set it in front of the judge's seat. Joshua sat stage right with Counselor Pearl beside him. The lawyer was in no way out of place in front of the footlights, for he might have passed for a sideshow cowboy, dressed as he was in white buckskins. The white Stetson rested on the table beside the tooled leather briefcase, and Pearl, limp-wristed, ran his long, soft fingers through his shoulder-length silvery hair.

Joshua rested his shackled hands on the tabletop and pulled the loose links of his chains consecutively into patterns circular, triangular, figures-of-eight, and four-square, crossing his wrists when it was necessary for the design he sought to conjure as he waited for the makeshift courtroom to fill up. His arraignment had been a swift formality in Mort Gardner's office, but the trial itself was to take place in the barroom of the Orleans Club in order to accommodate the great number of spectators who everyone knew would show up, seeking corroboration for their solidly formed opinions as to Joshua's innocence or guilt. The stares of the already seated bored into him as if to fix upon him the fate that they deemed provident. Counselor Pearl had told him not to be afraid, that he had a strong case for acquittal, but as the same prospectors, matrons, and Mormons who had abused him at the cemetery took their seats, Joshua felt little hope and saw the life before him, at best, as a decade-long continuation of the mere three days he had passed in the jailhouse, which had felt to him like an eternity of sorrow and shame. At worst, he could expect the gallows in a matter of days. Perhaps the rope would be a blessing, but he feared death's unknown, whether it should be salvation, damnation, or oblivion, or some state of being unimaginable to those yet living. Every cell in Joshua's body wanted to cleave to life. And Counselor Pearl was his only hope, a thief who hoped to rob him.

Opposite Joshua's table, the state prosecutor, James Whitmarsh, a corpulent and balding individual with oiled hair slicked back behind his ears, peered down through half-moon spectacles onto a sheet of paper that he tilted toward him with fingers so stained by nicotine that their yellow-and-brown complexion was visible even from twenty feet across the stage, despite the dimness of the barroom. His cheeks were sallow and the hanging jowls hardly masked by the curls of his beard. From under that dense growth, his underlip glistened red. Sheriff Gardner had informed them that Counselor Pearl's adversary was known to be both meticulous and tenacious in search of a conviction.

Mr. Ford sat in the front row of the auditorium along with Dot Ford, Dick Liddil, and Ella Mae Waterson, who looked calm and composed and elegant in a striped red-and-black dress. The copper coils of her hair had been drawn into a cascade behind the crown of her head, and she looked both coquettish and childlike, animated even, so that Joshua was certain she had dosed herself carefully with opium. Mrs. Ford wore the same clothes that she had for his father's funeral, a green dress with black ribbons, which Joshua thought was ill-omened. On the far end of the front row, Soapy Smith sat among his bodyguards. Frazee the grocer sat in the middle of the same row next to Sheriff Gardner and Deputy Fat Wallace.

Joshua scanned the room for Silas Strickland, who, being a Negro, had to stand at the back of the hall. Silas was leaning up against the doorjamb to allow the still arriving spectators to get by him. The two Chinamen who had been pallbearers stood next to him; and dressed in a finely tailored black pin-striped suit, Chang Jen Wa himself stood with his arms folded and surveyed the gathering crowd, his expression revealing a certain disdain. The bar itself was in use as a high seat, and a row of scruffy drunks and adolescent boys swung their dangling feet as they waited for the proceedings to begin. The whores from Soapy's cribs stood in clusters of crinoline and boa feathers just behind and below the prosecutor's table. Along the wall next to them was a row of twelve empty straight-backed chairs that awaited selection of the jury. The two windows behind the seatbacks cast a pale light under the chestnut beams of the low-ceilinged room.

Mort Gardner stood up suddenly and turned to face the crowd.

–All rise for Justice Willard P. Owens.

Joshua raised himself from his seat, and the cramped hall was a cacophony of scraping chair legs and coughs and murmurs. Justice Owens entered stage right close to the defense table. He was a tall and dour man with deep wrinkles that scored his cheeks, so shadowy as to appear dirt-filled. Heavy bags hung beneath eyes that were at once piercing and shifty. His thick white hair receded from his forehead like a badger's brush. Justice Willard's suit was black and cut long in the jacket, and he wore a white shirt with a black tie. A man like this, Joshua thought, would take a dim view of Pearl and would sympathize more with the dull-looking prosecutor, Whitmarsh.

–Be seated, Owens said.

He had a deep and dour voice to go with his demeanor.

–District Court of the State of Colorado is now in session, Gardner announced, Justice Willard P. Owens presiding.

The judge turned to Gardner.

–Let's find us a jury here.

It took but an hour and a half to find twelve men both sides deemed suitable. The prosecution objected to no one, but Pearl ousted two of the most dissipated-looking individuals, who declared themselves to be prospectors and admitted to having been in the cemetery on the day of Joshua's father's funeral. The panel seemed to Joshua to be made up of men at least halfway respectable: Ernest Stevens, a short and stocky mason, the only man unbearded and rosy-cheeked among the twelve; Bob Starks, the owner of the mining supply store on Amethyst Street; George Tilly, who ran the hard goods store near the Orleans Club; Jim Shaw, the liveryman; Bill McCall, the mule skinner; Charles Harmon, a Mormon sawmill owner; Jeremiah Smith, another Mormon and a raiser of horses; Colum Reilly, a big and dark-haired Irish miner; Josef Sidleski, a Polish miner who could have been Reilly's pale and blond twin; Edwin Hunt, the narrow-backed clerk from Greene's Assay Office; Harvey Scott, a stooped and consumptive-looking man who ran the Silver Dollar Hotel; and Joseph Simms, railroad engineer; men, Joshua thought, who might weigh evidence rather than be swayed by the hysteria that had swept the town not two days before. But there was no certainty in that.

The judge was a fearsome man, the wrinkled face dark and humorless throughout the proceedings. At least Owens was a Welsh name, Joshua thought, but he saw little evidence of sympathy in the man. The judge turned to face Joshua, the eyes searching and steady.

–Joshua Beynon, you stand accused of murder in the second degree of one Aaron Beynon. How do you plead?

Pearl answered for him.

–Not guilty, Your Honor, Pearl said.

–Counselor Whitmarsh, the judge said, proceed, if you please.

Whitmarsh came out from behind his desk and approached the judge's bench. He turned his wide back on the defense table so that he faced both judge and jury. Joshua drew his hands off the table, and the chains cascaded into his lap. He lowered his head to listen. He could not look at the faces of the jurymen.

–Your Honor, gentlemen of the jury, the State of Colorado will prove beyond the shadow of a doubt that the accused, Joshua Beynon, murdered his own father while in the callous undertaking of a robbery in the act of which he was discovered. We will prove that such an act was in keeping with the boy's character and ambition; that he had become altogether wayward, hateful, and out of control; and that this act was the culmination of the boy's chosen road of rebellion. The state will present material evidence that places the accused at the scene of this brutal murder and which will clearly illustrate the motive for this shocking crime. You will hear the testimony of witnesses who had contact with the accused both immediately before and after the act who will testify as to the boy's guilt and to the animosity displayed by the murderer to the victim, who had struggled all his life to provide for a son who turned around and, in an explosion of rage, slew his own father for a handful of coin. The enormity of this act finally opened the boy's eyes to his own evil. He sought help among certain citizens of this town who were wise enough to turn him in. The law does not distinguish or provide for a greater punishment for those guilty of parricide as opposed to homicide, so the State of Colorado will prove that the boy who stands before you committed murder in the second degree. This does not mean that such an act was premeditated. But one of the definitions, under law, of murder in the second degree, is any killing carried out in the commission of a robbery. The state will prove that just such a murder was committed and will seek the punishment for this crime to the fullest extent of the law.

It was as if Whitmarsh had been pouring poison directly into Joshua's ear. At each sentence and pause Joshua shook his head. The malleability of fact astonished him. He was certain that Whitmarsh had not told one word of a lie. This trial was to be a nightmare reliving the way Da had died at his own son's hands. The only way that Joshua could imagine enduring it was to detach himself from the proceedings as if he gazed through a glass darkly. He saw himself as already dead, his father waiting for him on the other side of oblivion.

–Counselor Pearl, the judge said.

Pearl stood up and moved behind him. He laid his hands on Joshua's shoulders. Joshua tensed his muscles at such violation of his person but there was nothing he could do but suffer the unwelcome touch of the manicured fingers and bow his head under the honeyed tones of Pearl's oration.

–Your Honor, gentlemen of the jury, do you see a heinous murderer sitting before you? No. You see a young boy caught up in the direst circumstances, misunderstood, persecuted by those who would wreak fearful retribution for a terrible accident blown up by hearsay and innuendo until the actual events of Monday, the sixteenth of May, have become so distorted that they no longer bear any resemblance to reality but have become our own feverish nightmares that we now seek to obliterate. No one was in that room but the deceased and his son when the gun went off that killed Aaron Beynon. The only evidence that will be presented to you by the prosecution will be circumstantial. Nothing but speculation and interpretation. And I am here to remind you, members of the jury, that the law requires a conviction only if you are certain beyond all reasonable doubt that this boy is guilty of murder. If you, gentlemen, harbor one uncertainty in your minds as to the guilt of this child, you must declare him innocent. That Aaron Beynon is dead, no one can dispute. That Joshua Beynon was in the room when the gun went off, no one will dispute, but that Joshua Beynon pulled the trigger in the commission of a robbery, no one can prove because no one else was in the room to see what transpired between Joshua and his father. The only person who can tell us that is the defendant himself: the only witness to Aaron Beynon's decease. A boy who is left alone in the world, who is devastated by the loss of his father. If this boy was a robber and a murderer, why did he not try to escape from the law? This orphaned boy went for help to the only people in the town that he felt he could trust. And he was right. Those people advised their young charge as to the correct way to behave now that this terrible accident had occurred, and the boy concurred with that advice. He did not try to hide anything but waited for the sheriff's arrival with his trust in the law and justice. He trusts you, twelve good men and true, to vindicate him in the face of this misplaced accusation. The onus of this case is upon the prosecution to prove beyond all reasonable doubt that Joshua Beynon shot his father while committing a robbery. There is not one jot of material or verbal evidence that will be presented to this court that will stand up to the scrutiny with which we shall examine it. I have no doubt that you, gentlemen of the jury, will send Joshua Beynon out of this court as free and innocent as he deserves to be, albeit to carry the burden of his loss and grief for the rest of his days, but vindicated of any crime.

Pearl released his shoulders, and Joshua looked up at the jury for the first time. The bearded mule skinner, one leg folded over the other knee, leaned back in his chair and nodded his head, while all the others sat upright, severe of expression, hands on their thighs.

–Counselor Whitmarsh, the judge said. Call your first witness.

–I'd like to call Sheriff Mort Gardner.

Gardner stood up from the front row, mounted the podium, and took the low-backed chair next to the judge. He laid his hand on the heavy black Bible that rested on the corner of the judge's table and swore himself in with the air of a man performing a habitual prayer.

–Sheriff Gardner, Whitmarsh said, were you called to the house of Aaron Beynon on May sixteenth, 1892?

–I was.

–Would you tell the court what you found there?

Joshua closed his eyes. In the half-dark, the vision formed as vividly as if he stood once more in that room with his father's dead body.

–I found the corpse of Aaron Beynon in his upstairs bedroom. He was lying in a pool of blood with one wound in his thigh from which he had bled to death. Next to him was an open cash box that contained but a few coins.

–Sheriff Gardner, how was Aaron Beynon's wound made? Whitmarsh said.

–With a forty-five-caliber bullet from a Colt Peacemaker.

–Was there anyone with you when you made the discovery of the deceased?

–Yes. Deputy Henry Wallace and Mr. Robert Ford.

–What were the circumstances that brought you into Aaron Beynon's house?

–Robert Ford came down to the office and told me that Aaron Beynon had been shot by his son, Joshua, and that he feared Aaron was already dead.

–And where was Joshua Beynon at this time?

–He was at Mr. Ford's house.

–Did you proceed to Mr. Ford's house?

–I did.

–And did you find Joshua Beynon there?

–I did.

–Could you describe Joshua Beynon's appearance when you found him?

–He was covered in blood from head to toe.

–Deputy Wallace, would you bring in the clothes that will be our first exhibit that we wish to submit as material evidence.

Joshua looked up. Whitmarsh curled his stained index finger over his mouth. His other three fingers stroked at the beard beneath his chin. Wallace crossed left to a table below the stage and in front of Soapy's bevy of sporting women. A number of them squealed when Wallace lifted up the blood-encrusted shirt and pants and underwear that Joshua had worn on the day of the killing. Wallace mounted the stage and laid the clothes down on the judge's table. Judge Owens peered at the stained rags and back at Counselor Whitmarsh.

–Proceed, he said.

–Sheriff Gardner, do you recognize these clothes? Whitmarsh said.

–We took them off of Joshua Beynon.

–Was Joshua Beynon wounded?

–Nary a scratch.

–The blood on the clothes was from Aaron Beynon?

–Yes, sir.

–I request that these clothes be entered into evidence as exhibit number one.

–So approved, the judge said.

Wallace took the clothes back to the table by his seat.

–Did Joshua Beynon have any money upon his person? Whitmarsh said.

–Five dollars and fourteen cents, Gardner said.

–A lot of money for a young boy.

–Yes, sir.

–Did Joshua Beynon have a weapon? Whitmarsh said.

–There was a Colt's Peacemaker on the Fords' kitchen table that belonged to him.

–Did he admit to owning the gun?

–He did.

–Did he say where he obtained this gun?

–He bought it at Frazee's store.

–He bought it?

–Yes, sir.

–Deputy Wallace, Whitmarsh said, would you bring the gun up here, please?

Wallace brought the Colt onto the stage.

–Is that the gun that belonged to Joshua Beynon? Whitmarsh said.

–It is, Gardner said.

–Has it been fired?

–Yes. There's powder residue in the barrel and one empty chamber.

–What are those stains on the metal and the wooden handle?

–Blood.

–Is that Aaron Beynon's blood?

–Yes.

–I request that this Colt's Peacemaker revolver be entered into evidence as exhibit number two.

–So approved, the judge said.

Wallace took the gun away.

–So, said Whitmarsh, we have Aaron Beynon dead in a pool of blood, an empty cash box in the room with him, his son, Joshua Beynon, pockets full of money, covered in his father's blood, with a gun that had been fired, likewise stained with Aaron Beynon's lifeblood. What did you do next, Sheriff Gardner?

–I arrested the boy for murder and took him into custody.

–Thank you, Sheriff Gardner. No more questions for now.

Whitmarsh sat down. He adjusted his half-moon glasses and reached for a pen. He dipped it in his ink bottle and began writing, scratching away with an exaggerated look of concentration on his face as if he were entirely alone in the world.

Judge Owens turned to Counselor Pearl.

–Counselor?

Pearl stood up and smiled toward the jury. He approached Gardner across the stage.

–Sheriff Gardner, did Joshua Beynon offer any explanation as to where the money came from that was in his pocket?

–Yes, sir, he did.

–What was that explanation?

–That he had won it in a bet with Jefferson Smith.

–So that is verifiable?

–That he won a bet is verifiable.

–Did you verify it?

–There was some disagreement as to whether the boy was entitled to the money. Jefferson Smith and Mr. Frazee, the storekeeper, said the boy just grabbed the money from Frazee's store.

–Oh . . . Not from the cash box?

–Not the money from Frazee's store.

–How much money did Joshua Beynon take from Frazee's store?

–Five dollars and fifty cents.

–And how much did he have in his pocket at his arrest?

–Five dollars and fourteen cents.

–Did you see the incident at which Aaron Beynon met his death?

–No, sir, I didn't.

–Did Joshua Beynon admit to killing his father?

–No, sir.

–Did he offer any explanation of the incident?

–He said it was a accident.

–Was there any money left in Aaron Beynon's cash box?

–Yes, sir.

–Thank you, Sheriff Gardner. No further questions.

The judge turned to Whitmarsh.

–Redirect?

Whitmarsh stood behind his desk.

–Sheriff Gardner, how much money was left in Aaron Beynon's cash box?

–Just sixty six-cents.

–Is there any way to verify that the money in Joshua Beynon's pocket was the same coin with which he left Frazee's store?

Gardner looked puzzled.

–No, sir.

–Thank you, Sheriff Gardner. No further questions.

Judge Owens banged his gavel.

–Call Tobias Frazee, Whitmarsh said.

Frazee came up out of the audience and was sworn in. He bent his long body forward and his thick hair fell down around his face. Without his glasses, his eyes seemed to be deeply sunken in the hollows under his brows and behind the mounds of his cheeks. He stroked down his heavy mustache with thumb and index finger. He glanced quickly toward Joshua and then away again, afraid to meet his gaze. He looked down to the front row toward Soapy Smith as if waiting for a cue.

–Mr. Frazee, Whitmarsh said, do you remember Joshua Beynon coming into your store on Monday, May sixteenth?

–Yes, sir. He looked awful peaky.

–Ill?

–Pale, he looked, and not altogether the full sixteen ounces. Drunk maybe. He said that he come for the Colt. He put what money he had on the counter and said that the rest was in the pig. That is, in a porcelain piggy bank that he had left in my store on Saturday, May fourteenth.

–As a deposit on the gun.

–That's right.

–So it seemed that the boy had raised the money.

–I asked him if he stole it, and he got awful mad. He picked up a mallet and smashed that pig to smithereens. The boy may be but fifteen, but he's as big as I am and a mite heavier too, I'd say. Looking all deranged like that and with the hammer, I feared him.

–So you gave him the gun?

–No. I just put it on the counter and he took it and then swept all but a quarter piece back into his hand.

–You didn't bring the sheriff in on this?

–I figured that I could work it out with the boy's daddy, Aaron, but the next thing I heard was that Aaron was dead and the boy had shot him.

–Thank you, Mr. Frazee. No further questions.

Pearl stood up next to Joshua but didn't move out onto the stage this time.

–Mr. Frazee, Pearl said, did not Joshua Beynon and Jefferson Smith enter into a wager over this gun?

–There warn't no wager.

–Was Jefferson Smith in your store when Joshua Beynon made a deposit on the gun?

–Soapy, that is, Jefferson, was going to buy the gun, and then the kid come in and said he wanted it. Jefferson told the kid that if he could get the money by Saturday, he'd let him buy the gun instead. Jefferson figured the kid couldn't get that kind of money, so he paid me for it in advance.

–Was this not the stake for a wager?

–That gun was as good as stole.

–Answer the question, Mr. Frazee.

Mr. Pearl had Frazee squirming. He had turned a bright red.

–I never seen it as such.

Joshua pulled the chains tight between his wrists. Frazee was lying under oath. Before God he was perjuring his immortal soul and was damning himself to Hell. He was more afraid of Soapy Smith than he was of God Almighty.

–But the boy saw it as a wager, Pearl said.

–Well, I guess he might of.

–When Sheriff Gardner brought Joshua Beynon to your store upon his arrest, was Jefferson Smith present?

–Yessir, he was.

–And did Jefferson Smith deny to Sheriff Gardner any wager with the boy?

–He did deny it.

–And you backed up his word.

–Yes, sir. I did.

–Did Mr. Jefferson Smith ask you for his money back?

Frazee looked toward Soapy and his eyes flicked toward the judge and back to Pearl.

–Well, no. He let me keep the money when all this brouhaha come about.

–He paid his debt on the wager.

–That ain't what I said.

–No, that's what I said. Thank you, Mr. Frazee.

Joshua looked across at the jurymen. They all sat dour and unreadable. They couldn't have believed Frazee.

–Redirect? the judge said.

Whitmarsh stood up then, and Joshua felt a chill in his body. Whitmarsh seemed to be able to twist the truth into any form he chose and all of it damning to Joshua.

–Mr. Frazee, would you consider Mr. Jefferson Smith a friend of yours? Whitmarsh said.

Frazee looked puzzled.

–Yessir, I guess I do.

–A generous friend?

–Well, yes, I guess so.

–Did Mr. Smith consider this exchange with the boy a prank?

–Yes. Yes, he did.

–It was not a wager but a prank that got out of hand.

–Yes, sir. That's it precisely.

–In your opinion he had no intention of taking money from the boy?

–No, sir. No money.

–Thank you, Mr. Frazee. No further questions.

–Stand down, Mr. Frazee, the judge said.

Frazee kept his head bowed and his long body stooped as he resumed his seat in the barroom auditorium. Frazee was willing to see him hang. Just to please Soapy Smith. Joshua wished that his father was still alive to see what Frazee and Soapy were doing. He would kill them both.

–Counselor Whitmarsh, the judge said.

–Call Edward O'Kelley, Whitmarsh said.

Joshua turned to look at Pearl. They had expected Whitmarsh to call Soapy Smith. Pearl shrugged, nonchalant. O'Kelley took the stand and Gardner swore him in. The normally scruffy Irishman had shaved his gaunt cheeks and combed out his drooping mustache. His hair was freshly barbered, and Soapy must have bought him a new suit. Joshua didn't see that his new visage would impress the jury, for all of them must have seen O'Kelley in his normal squalid state.

–Mr. O'Kelley, Whitmarsh said, were you acquainted with the deceased, Aaron Beynon?

–We had a drink together.

–How often?

–Most every Friday and Saturday night.

–Did Aaron Beynon ever discuss his son with you?

–From time to time. He said the boy was wild. Getting out of hand and that he didn't know how to put a stop to it.

–How did he say that the boy was out of hand?

–Staying out late at night. Consorting with known thieves, murderers, and whores.

–Do you know Joshua Beynon?

–I do.

–When was the last time you had a conversation with Joshua Beynon?

–Sunday, May fifteenth.

Joshua sat back in the chair. That was the day that he had unloaded the wagon for Mr. Ford. When O'Kelley had threatened to shoot Mr. Ford.

–Do you remember that conversation?

–Every bit of it.

–Did Joshua Beynon refer to his father in that conversation?

–Yessir, he did.

–How did Aaron Beynon come up in the conversation?

–I told Joshua that his pa would take a strap to him because Aaron knew that the boy had been hanging around Bob Ford and his loose women.

–What was Joshua Beynon's reply to that?

–He said to me these exact words, "If that drunken son of a bitch takes a strap to me, I swear to God I'll kill him this time."

–Ooo! sounded in chorus from all of Soapy's sporting women and half the matrons in the audience.

Joshua felt the blood drain from his face, his skin grow chill, his bowels loosen, his bones shrink to sticks in his clothes. He raised a hand to his eyebrow and the chains rattled against the table. Pearl glanced at him and lifted a blank sheet of paper and studied it as if it was filled with tiny script.

–Exactly those words? Whitmarsh said.

–Exactly.

–No further questions.

–Counselor Pearl, the judge said.

Pearl rose. Joshua was certain that he had been unprepared for O'Kelley's statement.

–To your knowledge, Mr. O'Kelley, did Aaron Beynon ever beat his son Joshua?

–He should have.

–But did he?

–Far as I know, yes.

–Often?

–Often enough, I'd think. The boy was going off the rails.

–Do you think Joshua feared his father's beating?

–Aaron could lay on a lick or two, if he had a mind. Boy ought to be afraid.

–When Joshua came out with the statement that you testify he made, do you think he could have been exaggerating as boys will and that he was not in fact telling the literal truth?

–Aaron Beynon is dead. Ain't much more literal than that.

–Do you drink, Mr. O'Kelley?

The wags in the courtroom guffawed.

–I take a dram or two.

–Alcohol affects the memory, doesn't it?

–So they say.

–How much did you drink on the night of Saturday, May fourteenth?

–I don't recall exactly.

–Did you drink on into Sunday morning past midnight?

–I reckon.

–What time did you get to sleep?

–I don't rightly know.

–Where did you sleep?

–On the boardwalk outside the Orleans Club.

Judge Owens banged his gavel against the laughter of the boys on the bar. Counselor Pearl had O'Kelley on the defense now. Joshua smiled.

–Did you make a bed there or did you pass out in a drunken stupor?

The boys on the bar snickered. Counselor Pearl had turned the tide against O'Kelley. Silently, Joshua urged him to make a complete fool of the Irishman.

–I didn't make no bed.

–What time did you meet Joshua Beynon on Sunday morning?

–It was early.

–But what time?

–Must have been around eight o'clock.

–What time exactly?

–I can't rightly say.

–So you don't know how many drinks you had. You don't know

what time you passed out in a drunken stupor in the gutter outside the Orleans Club, and you don't know the exact time that you met Joshua Beynon on Sunday morning, May fifteenth. Am I correct?

–Well, I guess.

–Would you say that alcohol had affected your memory in any way, Mr. O'Kelley? Just answer yes or no without any "I guess" or excuses or qualifications. Just yes or no?

–Yes.

–You don't remember those simple facts, but you can recall word for word a conversation that was held early Sunday morning while you were still in a state of drunkenness?

–I was not drunk.

–You had passed out in the gutter but you were not drunk?

–No, sir.

–Thank you, Mr. O'Kelley. No further questions, Your Honor.

Counselor Pearl swaggered across the stage toward Joshua like a knight in shining armor. Joshua was close to tears. Pearl glanced across at the jury as if to make sure that they were looking and gave Joshua a sharp nod and his bright white smile.

–Redirect, Counselor Whitmarsh, the judge said.

Whitmarsh stood. He looked at the jury over his glasses. He took off his glasses and looked at Pearl with a scowl of disdain. Then he turned to O'Kelley.

–Just answer this question yes or no, Mr. O'Kelley. Did Joshua Beynon say these words to you on Sunday morning, May fifteenth, and I quote, "If that drunken son of a bitch takes a strap to me, I swear to God I'll kill him this time." End quote. Just answer yes or no, Mr. O'Kelley.

–Yes.

–No further questions.

–You may stand down, Mr. O'Kelley, the judge said.

LV

COUNSELOR PEARL UNPACKED HIS PEN, INK BOTTLE, AND NOTEBOOK from the tooled leather briefcase. This morning, the counselor's tanned face appeared drawn, with a few sparse white whiskers on the end of his chin. Joshua bent in a big-boned slump over the defense table beside him. The chains at Joshua's wrists seemed to have become part of his long arms. The links dangled as he reached up to adjust his heavy-lensed glasses. He could not shuffle his feet without the chains fastened to his ankles scraping upon the floorboards. The sound of them grated on his exhausted nerves. The night before, Pearl had told him that he would have to testify on his own behalf. The sight of the bloody clothes and the gun, Pearl had said, would have affected the jurors unfavorably. And Ed O'Kelley's testimony had been too damaging to leave unanswered.

Every seat in the Orleans Club was taken, and the back of the barroom was filled with spectators standing shoulder to shoulder. The crowd of onlookers was even greater than on the previous day. Mr. Ford and his women were once more at one end of the front row, and Ed O'Kelley, Soapy Smith, and his cronies at the other end, with Sheriff Gardner and Fat Wallace between the two groups. It was Mr. Ford who had arranged for Joshua's defense — but what was behind it? Mr. Ford's extravagant payment of wages, his invitation into his house, the hiring of Pearl, all those visits to his cell and his long recounting of the story of Jesse James and his outlaw band might have been naught but the laying of a sweetly baited trap for the covert sake of lucre. Mr. Ford was a con man. Perhaps his con man's nature could only out.

–All rise for Judge Willard P. Owens, Sheriff Gardner called.

The long-shanked judge took his high-backed chair and the spectators resumed their seats. Owens looked to be in a foul mood. His dark and wrinkled countenance seemed puckered around his brooding brows that were bent down over the glittering brown eyes, eyes that seemed to lack pupils.

–Counselor Pearl, are you ready? he snapped.

Pearl stood up.

–I would like to call Mrs. Dorothy Ford to the stand.

Plump and blond, still in her green-and-black dress, Mrs. Ford mounted the podium, and one of the wags seated upon the bar whistled. The judge's gavel whacked the bench, and Mrs. Ford jumped back from in front of the witness stand. The crack brought Joshua to a sharp clarity. Owens was livid.

–Get that man out of here! he yelled.

Fat Wallace, his face full of consternation, stood and nervously pulled at the lapels of his black frock coat.

–Who was that man? Wallace croaked.

No one would admit to the whistle. Every one of the disheveled men seated on the bar gazed in deep concentration at the floor in front of them, their faces distorted with barely suppressed mirth like a distorted reflection of the twelve men opposite them, an anti-jury, set upon their high bench as a clownish parody from some madcap or carnival court.

–I know who it was, Owens said. And if that man does not leave this room at once, he will spend thirty days in a jail cell for contempt of court.

A red-haired youth with a sparse growth of sidewhiskers slid from the bar, placed a battered derby upon his head, and shuffled his way alongside the rows of seats and through the standing crowd at the rear of the Orleans Club. Silas Strickland grinned and nodded to him as he pushed by him and the two Chinamen beside him.

–If I hear a sound from that side of the room, Owens said, every man of you will be held in contempt. Proceed, Sheriff Gardner.

Gardner swore in Mrs. Ford, who declared her oath to tell the truth as a little girl might recite an earnest prayer at Sunday School. She laid her hands in her lap and glanced across at Joshua. Her kohled eyes flicked away when he smiled at her, and he judged it prudent that she not return it for fear that the jury might see her as too partial to his cause. She looked intently at Counselor Pearl.

–Mrs. Ford, you were the first person to see Joshua Beynon after Aaron Beynon's demise?

–I believe so, yes.

–Would you describe the circumstances to us?

–I heard a knock on the door and I went to open it. The poor boy was standing there like a broken heart. He was crying and he said his father was dead.

The judge turned into a bleary shadow in front of Joshua's eyes as they welled with tears at the memory. Mrs. Ford he counted on more than her husband.

Pearl's buckskin fringes waved as he leaned toward Mrs. Ford to ask her a question. The eyes of the audience were all on her. Joshua felt utterly alone at the table. He had an urge to get up from his seat and to slip behind the curtain on his side of the stage and to stumble out into the fresh air through the stage door and escape the town, whose streets would be empty, for every idle body was crammed into the Orleans Club. He could almost taste the clear air. He shifted his feet and his chains rattled to bring him back to reality.

–Did Joshua Beynon give any indication as to how Aaron Beynon had died? Pearl said.

–He said that his father tried to take the gun from him, and it just went off and killed him.

–Did Joshua Beynon indicate that he wished to run away from the town?

–No, sir.

–Did he ask for your assistance to conceal him from the law?

–Not at all, Mrs. Ford said. Bob, that's Robert Ford, my husband, came in from the bedroom at that point and the story come out in bits and bobs. Aaron was shot in the leg.

–Joshua was covered in blood?

–Yes, sir.

–Did Joshua Beynon indicate how he had come to be covered in blood?

–He said that he tried to stanch his father's wound but it didn't work. He bled to death.

Joshua gazed down at the tight grain under the varnish of the oak table. He remembered how she had made the men wait outside while she stripped him of his blood-encrusted clothes until he stood naked and how she had ladled hot water from a caldron on the stove into a pan and washed his body with tallow soap and a rag as if he were a baby. But he wasn't a baby even if he cried like one. He remembered that as she had laved him, his prick had suddenly stood up straight. He had not felt ashamed, and she had ignored his hard manhood and told him that everything would be all right and not to worry. So tender she had been. Then she had given him Mr. Ford's clothes to dress in.

–How did Sheriff Gardner become involved? Pearl said.

–Bob, my husband, after he heard what happened, said that we should call the sheriff.

–Did Joshua object in any way to calling the sheriff?

–No, sir.

–Did he try to run off when Mr. Ford went for the sheriff?

–No, sir.

–What did he do?

–He just sat quiet most of the time. Cried some of the time.

–What did you do?

–I waited with him.

–Then Sheriff Gardner arrived?

–Yes, sir.

–Did Sheriff Gardner ask Joshua any questions about the circumstances of Aaron Beynon's death?

–Not directly.

–What did he ask about?

–He asked about the cash box.

–But not about how the gun went off?

–No, sir.

The voices came across the stage to him as if echoing out of some cave mouth, oracular voices from some distant dimension.

–So all that Sheriff Gardner was concerned about was the money in the cash box?

–That's all he talked about.

–Did that surprise you?

–Objection, said Whitmarsh.

–Sustained, said the judge.

And the whack of the gavel brought him sharply awake once more.

–So, Mrs. Ford, Pearl said, Joshua Beynon made no attempt to escape, did not solicit help to make an escape, and declared that Aaron Beynon was the victim of an accident?

–That's correct.

–Thank you, Mrs. Ford. No further questions.

Pearl sauntered as he returned to the defense table, the languid movement of his limbs driving into Joshua's mind that Pearl belonged to the world of the unconfined, the unshackled. Then Whitmarsh approached Mrs. Ford. He made an elaborate show of cleaning his half-moon spectacles with a paisley silk kerchief. The little lower lip jutted out red and glistening in his dense beard.

–Mrs. Ford, how did you come to know Joshua Beynon?

–He did a job of work for my husband.

Whitmarsh tucked the kerchief into the breast pocket of his suit jacket that lay open, falling to each side of his expansive belly.

–What kind of work?

–He unloaded a wagon.

–Do you work, Mrs. Ford?

–I don't.

Whitmarsh replaced his spectacles and tilted his head back to look at Mrs. Ford through the lenses as a surgeon might view a body before making his incision. Joshua interlocked his fingers and willed away Whitmarsh's questions.

–Have you ever been involved in any profession?

–Some, I guess.

–What profession would that be?

–They call it a sporting woman.

–You were a prostitute?

–Yes, sir.

Joshua looked toward the bar-bench, but the smirking wags stayed silent. On the other side of the room the real jury sat dour-faced behind their beards. They would all have known Mrs. Ford's profession by reputation.

–Mrs. Ford, Whitmarsh said, did you ever have carnal relations with Joshua Beynon?

Pearl was on his feet beside him.

–Objection, Pearl said. Such innuendo.

Joshua looked up at Mrs. Ford and flushed. He thought of her brief touch as she washed him, the tenderness, the pleasure, the confusion of feeling such a thing while his father lay dead.

–Overruled, Counselor Pearl, Judge Owens said. It seems to me that Counselor Whitmarsh is merely seeking to establish the relationship of the witness to the defendant, which has direct bearing on the witness's character and her reliability. Ask your question, Counselor Whitmarsh.

Pearl pressed together his thin lips. He was visibly angry. It seemed that now Pearl was in the courtroom, even if he had no personal allegiance to Joshua and his motives beforehand were entirely mercenary, he was determined to win this case for its own sake, as a matter of personal satisfaction.

–Mrs. Ford, Whitmarsh said, did you ever have carnal relations with Joshua Beynon?

–No sir, I never, Mrs. Ford said.

–Has Joshua Beynon ever been naked in your cabin?

Fat Wallace coughed nervously and colored up. He stared down between his feet under Joshua's gaze. Wallace must have told Whitmarsh about Mrs. Ford cleaning him up that day.

–Well, yes but . . .

–Why was he naked?

–He needed to wash the blood off of hisself.

–And you were present in the room?

–Yes, but . . .

–Did you touch him when he was naked?

–No, I did not.

Joshua blushed. Darted a glance at Mrs. Ford that Whitmarsh noted. She had lied under oath. Perjured herself for him. Why didn't she tell the truth? It would have been better for him.

–What were you doing in the room?

–I brought water for him to wash himself.

–You did not touch Joshua Beynon?

–No, sir.

–Do you drink, Mrs. Ford?

–Yes, sir.

–Have you ever taken any other kind of intoxicant?

–Some.

–Morphia, opium?

–Opium, some.

Joshua was panicked. He looked across at the Mormons on the jury but their gazes remained fixed, their expressions belying whatever prejudice they might have had toward such a one as would poison herself so. Had they believed her about the carnal relations?

–Had you taken any kind of intoxicant on the day that Joshua Beynon came to your home seeking help?

–No, sir.

–How about the night before?

–Yes, sir.

–What intoxicant?

–A little whisky.

–No opium?

–No, sir.

She had lied again. A web of lies coming out of her mouth that Joshua knew would entangle him if he had to testify himself.

–Were you drunk the night before Aaron Beynon's death?

–No, sir.

–So drink or morphia or opium could not have affected your memory of what Joshua Beynon said to you concerning his father's death?

Mrs. Ford's eyes widened with her ferocity.

–He said it was a accident.

–Yes, Mrs. Ford. Thank you. No further questions.

–Redirect? said the judge.

–Mrs. Ford can stand down, Pearl said.

Joshua hung his head between his hands. She *had* touched him when he was naked and she *had* taken opium and she had lied to protect him. Trying to make it seem as if her testimony could be trusted. If Whitmarsh asked him all the same questions, Joshua would reveal Mrs. Ford to be a liar. And if he showed her to be a liar, then the jury would think that she was hiding something about him. Maybe that he admitted to murdering his father. Was there anyone else to testify that could prove Mrs. Ford was lying? Could Whitmarsh call another witness? What would Mr. Ford say?

–The defense will call Mr. Robert Ford, Pearl said.

Mr. Ford took the stand. As he composed himself in his seat, every angle of his body looked to have been drafted by a geometer's set square: feet planted firmly, shins straight, thighs flat, hands on thighs, trunk erect, head and chin held stiffly. Even his mouth was set in a line. His short fair hair was parted straight and sharp on the left side of his head. He looked every inch the gentleman in his gray suit but not a man or woman in that courtroom was ignorant of the fact that they were looking at the Slayer of Jesse James, a man reviled in both ballad and story. Pearl's willowy form swayed in front of Ford.

–Mr. Ford, you brought Sheriff Gardner to the Beynon residence. What did you find there?

–Well, Aaron was dead all right. He was laying on the floor in the bedroom in a pool of blood. There was a towel wrapped around his leg, but that was soaked through, too.

–A towel?

–As if someone had tried to stanch the wound.

–It was a leg wound?

–We pulled the towel away and saw the hole in the pants. It was blackened at the edges where the muzzle blast had burned it.

–So the gun that fired the bullet was fired at close range.

–Damn close, I'd say.

–Close enough to have gone off in a physical struggle between two people?

–Yes, sir.

–Do you have some expertise concerning firearms, Mr. Ford?

–Everybody knows that.

–In your expert opinion, judging from the nature of the wound, would you say it was more likely that the gun was fired deliberately to cause such a wound or that it went off by accident?

–Objection, said Whitmarsh. Mr. Ford was not in the room, this is mere conjecture.

–Sustained, said the judge.

–Sheriff Gardner mentioned a cash box, Pearl said. Where was that?

–On the floor, near the wardrobe.

–Was there any money in it?

–Yes, sir.

–How much?

–I didn't count it.

–But there was some money in the box.

–Yes, sir.

–Mr. Ford, did Joshua Beynon object in any way to you going to get Sheriff Gardner to investigate his father's death?

–Not at all.

–How did Joshua Beynon describe his father's demise to you?

–It was a terrible accident. And from what I seen, I believe him.

–Thank you, Mr. Ford. No further questions.

Joshua was convinced that Mr. Ford genuinely wanted to see

him acquitted. He did not understand how a man who would testify for him in a court of law in order to save his life could at the same time have concocted such an elaborate con game to swindle him out of his father's money. Angels good and evil did not seem to vie for Mr. Ford's soul but politely took turn and turn about in their wielding of influence over him. And he was just as at ease with the Lord's or the Devil's party.

–I have no questions for Mr. Ford, Whitmarsh said.

–You may stand down, Mr. Ford, the judge said.

Joshua's every nerve began to tremble. He knew that he was supposed to testify after Mr. Ford, but he had expected Whitmarsh to ask at least some questions. He was not ready to stand up there. Mr. Ford made his way back to his seat in the front row. Pearl was on his feet.

–I wish to call Joshua Beynon.

Joshua touched his fingertips to his face and they were cold. The skin of his cheeks was cold. His lips parted and his tongue was large and dry in his mouth. He touched his glasses out of habit, a nervous gesture to reassure himself that something in his world was yet familiar. The chair scraped back from behind his knees. He could not feel the support of his legs, and his head and shoulders and chest seemed so heavy that they swayed over the nothingness below them. The judge's beady glint peeped at him from out of gnarls and wrinkles, his nose and mouth rat-like, his gray-and-black brush crowning his animal aspect. Joshua stepped a short step toward the center of the stage, and between his ankles the chain rattled like the cracked bell of a leper. In front of him dangled the chain from his wrists. Asleep or awake, Joshua had been living in the same clothes for a week — Mr. Ford's underwear and shirt and old brown suit — and only now did they feel stale and chafing and creased and misfitting. The room tilted, a sea of lined and whiskered and painted faces swam before him, hideous and predatory. He wanted to moan out his fear, but he choked back his anguish for fear that his voice might lose all cogent arrangement of his senses and he would be flooded by sound and color that would form no more pattern recognizable or sane and he would be lost in some otherworld. His gangling body jutted and bent as if in the power of a drunken puppeteer as he focused all his attention toward the low-backed chair wherein he was required to sit. Pearl, in the garish white buckskins, drifted by him toward the front of the stage, where the half-shelled footlights were mercifully unlit.

Joshua lowered himself and balanced on the edge of the witness chair.

Sheriff Gardner approached him in his black frock coat. The hard-angled face and the iron-gray mustache gave him the aspect of an undertaker come to measure a corpse. Joshua set his chained hand down on the black cover of the Bible and swore to tell the truth. And even if truth were to be told, he feared that he would be condemned regardless.

The lanky Pearl, old-womanish with that smooth tanned face and long silver hair, swayed in front of him.

–Joshua, I know this is going to be hard for you, but just tell His Honor the judge and the gentlemen of the jury what happened on May sixteenth, after you bought the gun at Frazee's store.

Joshua wished that he could ask for water to drink, for all moisture had drained from his mouth. He drove his tongue against his palate in an effort to produce saliva, and the little that came allowed him to begin speaking but all memory of the rehearsed speech of the previous evening was gone. He was afraid he would start sobbing. Then he knew that he just had to keep speaking. As long as he kept speaking, the grief was choked down. Couldn't come out of him. Was caged up in his chest. He panted.

–I went home. I had the money that had been in the porcelain pig. And the gun. And a box of shells. When I got home, I loaded the gun. I wanted to shoot it. I thought that I might go up on Campbell Mountain. I owed my da thirty six-cents. I went into Da's room and the cash box was still on the floor where I left it. Then I heard Da downstairs. He should have been at work, but he had been out all night drinking. He came upstairs and saw me kneeling down by the cash box. In front of the wardrobe. I was putting the money back in, but he must have thought that I was stealing his money. He didn't have but sixty-six cents in there. He drank it all away. I had a silver dollar to give him, too. But he just commenced to beat me. I told him I was putting the money back.

–I *said*. I told him. But he didn't believe me. He tried to grab the gun off me. But I wouldn't let him take it. I sort of folded down over it. As he beat me. Then he wrenched my hand out and tried to pull the gun away from me. It went off. It was funny for a minute. Hopping around like that. Then I saw the blood. It just poured out like a fountain. It wouldn't stop. And he fell down. I told him to wait. I went to look for a bandage. But we had no bandages. There was a towel in the bottom of the wardrobe. I tried to tie it round his leg. He wanted to get up. But he couldn't. Then all of a sudden he was dead.

As if a darkness welled up from deep in his body, suddenly sobs wracked him and he howled. He howled without control. He dug at the skin of his face with the steel of the shackles on his wrists. His glasses twisted from his face and he heard them hit the floor. He felt other hands pulling his own hands back from the damage he was doing to his cheeks. An arm around his back. He heard the crack of the judge's gavel. Half-shouted words. The noise of chairs. A rumble in the auditorium. He pushed upward, and whoever held him fell back. He raised his arms and the chain pulled taut. The light of the room refracted in the blur of his tears. He took two steps forward, and the chain between his legs hooked on something, possibly a foot, and he fell, twisting sideways, and dropped heavily to the boards of the stage. He whooped for breath. Bright unreal lights flashed. Great circles before his eyes. His limbs were stiff. Trembling. Fingers dug into his armpits and half-raised him from the floor. His right arm felt crippled by a sharp pain. He was stunned by the power of his own grief. The world took shape again, and once more he was present before the silent faces of the prurient who wished to watch him as he rode the precarious balance between freedom and the gallows.

There had been a recess ordered. He sat in the wings of the Orleans Club's stage. Pearl was nowhere to be seen. Or Mr. Ford. Fat Wallace brought Joshua a plate of lumpy mashed potatoes and a curled and greasy pork chop from Dave's Place. Sheriff Gardner had found Joshua's glasses and returned them to him before he went off for his lunch. One sidearm was twisted and so one lens rested slightly higher than the other in front of his eyes. No other damage.

Joshua scooped up the potatoes on his fork and pressed them

into his mouth, where gradually the mush dissolved. He swallowed it little by little. He left three-quarters of the potatoes on the plate, and he had trouble even looking at the meat without being visited by nausea. He had regained his composure somewhat. He still had a sharp pain in his right arm that seemed to originate near his collarbone. His face burned where he had torn at it. He did not touch his fingertips to his scratched cheek, nor did he care to look in a mirror. He had ceased to care whether he lived or died.

Not long after Wallace lifted the plate out of Joshua's hands, the spectators began returning to the auditorium. Mr. Ford ascended the steps, and Fat Wallace stepped in front of him. The big, black-suited deputy eclipsed the slender Mr. Ford entirely.

–You cain't talk to the prisoner, he said.

–Move aside, Wallace, Ford said.

–Court orders, Wallace said.

–Joshua, Mr. Ford called.

He stepped to one side of Wallace like a bantam-weight fighter looking for an opening. His eyes narrowed and he feinted to go one way, which Wallace fell for, and Mr. Ford stepped by him, dapper as you please.

–Listen, Joshua, he said. This might not mean shit to you right now, but I want you to know that me and Dot and Ella and Liddil and Strickland, too, we all just want you to win.

Wallace drew his gun.

–I'm going to have to arrest you, he said.

–No you ain't, said Mr. Ford.

He turned smartly on his brightly polished boots, skipped past Wallace, and ran down the steps of the stage to his seat in the front row. Wallace turned his gun one way, then the other, and reholstered it. Joshua shook his head and let the chains dangle between his clenched fists. He was tired of Mr. Ford, too.

The jury filed in, led by Bill McCall, the mule skinner. Counselor Pearl came in through the stage door. He laid a hand on Joshua's shoulder, and for the first time, Joshua didn't feel as if he'd been caressed by a leper.

–Can you get back up there? Pearl said.

–No choice, Joshua said.

–Just signal if you want me to ask for a recess.

–I'll be fine.

The judge reappeared through the stage door, and he showed no sign of anything being amiss. As usual, he did not even glance at Joshua or Pearl; as Mort Gardner called the court to order, the judge drifted like a shadow into his high-backed chair.

–Recall Joshua Beynon, Gardner said.

Joshua shuffled across to the witness chair.

–You are still under oath, Gardner said.

Joshua nodded.

Pearl came across the stage.

–I have only very few questions, Pearl said. After your father died, what did you do?

–I went to Mr. Ford's house.

–Why did you go to Mr. Ford's house?

–I thought he might know what I should do.

–Did you plan on running away?

–No.

–What did you plan on doing?

–I didn't plan on doing anything. My da was dead. I didn't know what to do at all.

–You had never planned on killing your father?

–No, sir.

–You have never robbed your father's money?

–No, sir.

–You are innocent of the crime of which you are being accused?

–Yes, sir.

–I have no further questions, Pearl said.

Whitmarsh approached him now. The prosecutor had taken off his glasses, and he stared at Joshua out of bright brown eyes, the lips pursed within the beard.

–Mr. Beynon, how old are you?

That was an easy question to answer.

–Fifteen.

–Have you ever drunk whiskey?

–Yes, sir.

–Have you ever been drunk on whiskey?

–Yes, sir.

–When was the last time you were drunk?

–I was only ever drunk once, Joshua said. And that was the night before my father died.

–Have you ever taken morphia or opium?

Joshua couldn't help but glance toward the Mormons. Twelve pairs of eyes upon him. Dour faces. Pitiless, it seemed. Whitmarsh was a dark and hostile presence not a yard from him.

–Yes, sir.

–When was the last time you took either one?

Joshua knew that Whitmarsh was going to ask him soon about Mrs. Ford. His stomach gurgled and he felt a loosening in his bowels. He pressed his hand to his belly as if he could stop the noise.

–I only ever took opium.

–When?

–The night before my father died.

–Were you still under the influence of whiskey or opium on the day that your father died?

Whitmarsh was staring at him, and it made him blush.

–I felt strange when I woke up.

–Drunk or ill?

He didn't know what to answer. He had told him, hadn't he, he had only ever been drunk once.

–Not ill. No. I don't know. Just strange.

–Could that have been due to the opium?

–I don't know.

–Where did you obtain the whiskey and the opium?

He had no time to think before Whitmarsh asked him the question.

–I was at Mr. Ford's house.

–The night before your father died.

–Yes, sir.

–What time did you leave Mr. Ford's house?

–Some time in the morning. I'm not sure.

–So you stayed at Mr. Ford's house all night imbibing whiskey and opium and you left some time the next morning.

His cheeks and ears were burning. He felt that he must look like some kind of beacon of guilt to the jurors.

–Yes, sir.

–Did you also have carnal relations with Mrs. Ford or Ella Mae Waterson during that night?

Joshua focused through his skewed glasses on Whitmarsh's hard brown-eyed stare.

–No, sir. I didn't.

–Did Mrs. Ford imbibe opium that night?

Joshua's palms were cold and damp. He kept his gaze on Whitmarsh's face, for he had no desire to look toward the front-row seats where Mr. and Mrs. Ford sat side by side.

–Yes, sir, she did.

Whitmarsh's little lower lip overlapped the upper and disappeared into the curly mustache. His frown creased his forehead almost to his bald crown.

–Were you ever naked in the presence of Mrs. Ford?

He didn't want this question. It was unfair. All this was unfair. He didn't kill his father. All those wags on the bar would start howling again.

–Answer the question, Whitmarsh said.

–Yes, sir.

It came out in a croak.

–Did she touch you in any way?

He couldn't lie.

–Yes, sir.

Every spectator in that room made some form of noise, and the judge's gavel banged. Whitmarsh wheeled away from in front of Joshua, and the prosecutor faced the jury with a broad smile of triumph. Joshua kept his eyes on the boards of the stage. He had no wish to see either Mr. or Mrs. Ford's reaction. Or Pearl's for that matter. Joshua was burning. He leaned forward and dangled his chains between his knees. When he breathed, the sharp pain in his arm stabbed through muscle and bone.

–She had physical contact with you?

–Yes, sir.

She had touched him. It had a warm feeling. Just after his father had died.

–When did this occur?

–It was when she washed me. When Sheriff Gardner and Mr. Ford had gone outside.

–When she washed your father's lifeblood from your body?

–Yes, sir.

Joshua had lost all friends, he was sure. Mr. Ford had been right to try to con him out of his father's money. Had Joshua not betrayed and humiliated him and his wife in front of the entire town?

–Let us return to the day of your father's death, Whitmarsh said. You went to Frazee's store in order to buy a gun?

Joshua kept his head down.

–Yes, sir.

–You entered into an agreement with Frazee to buy a Colt Peacemaker on May fourteenth?

–Yes, sir.

–We have heard testimony from Mr. Frazee concerning the unusual nature of the purchase, but for the moment we don't need to concern ourselves with that. Were you still under the influence of opium, Mr. Beynon?

–I don't know.

–Did you then return to your home?

–Yes, sir.

–And at that point you went to your father's cash box?

–First I went to my room, and I loaded the gun.

–Then you went to the cash box?

–Yes.

– And your father returned unexpectedly?

–Yes.

–Your father saw you stealing money from the cash box and he challenged you?

Joshua looked up at Whitmarsh. The prosecutor had his thumbs tucked in the pockets of his waistcoat, the nicotine-stained fingers curling and uncurling upon his wide belly. He wished that the questions would just stop.

–He thought I was stealing the money, but I wasn't.

–You weren't?

–No.

–You did take money from the cash box?

–Yes, before I went to Frazee's. To buy the gun.

–When Sheriff Gardner and Mr. Ford saw the cash box, it contained but a few pennies. Did you hide any of the money that you took from the cash box?

–No, I didn't. That's all was in it. What they saw.

–Your father thought that you were stealing his money and he challenged you?

–Yes.

–Then you turned the gun on him?

–No.

–You struggled with him and the gun went off?

–Yes.

–And your father met his death?

–Yes.

–And afterward you went to Mr. and Mrs. Ford's residence?

–Yes.

–And it was there that you were naked in a room with Mrs. Ford, a known prostitute, and she *washed* you while you were naked.

–Yes.

–I have one more question. On the morning of May fifteenth, did you in reference to your father say to Edward O'Kelley, quote "If that drunken son of a bitch takes a strap to me, I swear to God I'll kill him this time"? End quote.

–Yes, I did.

The judge banged his gavel against the murmurs that filled the low-ceilinged room.

–Thank you, Mr. Beynon. No further questions.

Whitmarsh returned to his table and left Joshua in the witness chair with nothing between him and the eyes of the spectators. Joshua became aware of how twisted and uncomfortable his position was, but he was afraid to move. It was as if the eyes of all those spectators had pinned him like a butterfly to a board. The judge turned his sepulchral gaze upon Pearl.

–Redirect?

Pearl rose slowly from his seat and came out from behind the table. He stood center stage, directly in front of Judge Owens. He regarded Joshua calmly.

–Did your father beat you?

–Yes, sir.

Counselor Pearl was like a buckskin curtain between Joshua and the audience. Joshua sat up straight in the chair and breathed out a long breath. Pearl nodded.

–Often?

–When he thought I'd done something wrong.

–Was he drunk when he beat you?

–I suppose so.

He would let Counselor Pearl lead him wherever the lawyer wanted him to go.

–It was more likely to happen when he was drunk? Pearl said.

–Yes, sir.

–When you said those words to Mr. O'Kelley, did you mean to tell him that you intended to kill your father?

–I was angry.

Pearl's thin eyebrows drew together above the dark eyes, the pointy nose seemed aimed at Joshua like a long beak, and the narrow lips were tight.

–But did you mean those words literally?

–I never wanted to kill my father, Joshua said. I wish I'd never said it.

Pearl nodded and the muscles in his face softened again. He paused and looked toward the jury for a moment.

–Joshua, we need to examine another incident now. Did Mrs. Ford have carnal knowledge of you?

Joshua's face turned as hot as a signal fire again.

–No, sir.

–But she touched you when you were naked?

–It was when she was washing me.

–You did not instigate the encounter?

–No, sir.

–And after she touched you, did you then go to another room?

–No, sir.

–Did she raise her skirts to consummate a carnal act?

–Sir?

To Joshua's undying humiliation, the wags on the bar could contain themselves no longer. They hooted and thigh-slapped and elbowed each other like a breed of half-monkeys, beings such as would have given credence to the claims of the notorious captain of Her Majesty's Ship *Beagle.* The gavel banged and the noise receded to chortles and snorts. The judge remained dour and silent. The taut clench of Pearl's jaw softened and a slight lift appeared at the edges of his lips.

–Did she raise her skirts to consummate a carnal act?

–No, sir.

–What then?

–She just touched me.

–With her hand?

–Yes.

–No other part of her body?

–No, sir.

–While she was washing you?

–Yes, sir.

–Joshua, he said. Has every word of your testimony under oath been the truth?

–Yes, sir.

He was ready to cry again. It was coming to an end. All these questions.

–Do you maintain that the gun you bought from Frazee went off by accident?

–Yes, sir.

–Did you steal anything from your father's cash box?

–No, sir.

–I have no further questions, Your Honor, and the defense rests its case.

–You may stand down, Mr. Beynon, the judge said.

Joshua raised himself from the witness chair. Blood pumped in his ears and his breath was short. The deep hot flush in his face caused the scratches from his manacles to burn upon his cheeks. Through the tilted lenses of his glasses, he looked down into the front row of the audience and saw there first the furious face of Mrs. Ford. Her kohl-rimmed eyes glared. Her lower lip was drawn in under her front teeth, and her chin was tucked back so that her soft flesh beneath it doubled. She shook her head slowly as if in disbelief at his folly, his betrayal.

Joshua shuffled across to the defense table. Pearl's face was unreadable. Joshua sat next to him.

–Counselor Whitmarsh, do you wish to recall Mrs. Ford? the judge said.

Whitmarsh steepled his yellow fingers in front of his hairy chin. He looked over his half-moon lenses at the jury.

–I don't think that will be necessary, he said.

Owens banged his gavel.

–Court will adjourn until three-thirty, and then you gentlemen can sum up.

Down in the front row, Mr. Ford ran a hand through his short fair hair, settled his homburg upon his head, and tipped the brim to Joshua, a gesture that was difficult to interpret, for once more he wore that poker player's straight face. He laid a hand on Mrs. Ford's shoulder. She had a fierce and grim look upon her plump face. She turned and led the way toward the aisle between the seats and the bar. The whole auditorium was thankfully emptying. Dick Liddil guided Ella Mae Waterson after the Fords and none of them so much as glanced back at him.

–Why didn't Whitmarsh recall Mrs. Ford? Joshua asked.

–She's done so much damage to our cause already, Pearl said, he doesn't want to give her the chance to squirm out of it.

LVI

COUNSELOR PEARL GATHERED HIS SILVER HAIR IN BOTH HANDS and pulled it back behind his shoulders. He was about to play out his final act on Joshua's behalf. The shock of the imminent end of the trial numbed and nauseated Joshua. While the trial yet endured, he did not have to face death. But as soon as this summing up was over, twelve men would sit in judgment upon him, and the thirteenth would sentence him. He willed Counselor Pearl all the force and conviction within his own mind and body to make the truth real. Each lawyer had sought to compose reality into convincing fictions to sway the thoughts of the twelve dour men of the jury, and Joshua's own voice and integrity counted for little in this garish and fatal theater.

Pearl swayed like a great white heron, his hands limp-wristed at the level of his chest, the fringes on his buckskins swinging with every dip and bob of his head. He approached center stage, where Judge Owens sat in his high-backed chair, a dark Solomon, the wrinkles and folds of his long face composed into an expression of somber patience, the wooden gavel like a mystic weapon of his restrained wrath resting close to his right hand upon the table in front of him. As for Pearl, the buckskins, the hair, the angles of his face, his sharp dark eyes, and his carefully groomed persona were all as if sculpted to make him seem larger than life in front of the ordinary men of the jury, so that they would see him as giving voice to a greater truth that had little do with earthly events. He was Joshua's champion. Joshua found it hard to believe the revulsion he had felt for him when the lawyer had touched him in the cell.

Both Judge Owens and Counselor Pearl were lit up by the hot-burning lime lamps that had been set in the half shells, stage front, against the gloom of the low-ceilinged room grown murky, window light obscured by a mountain storm that spat hailstones rattling against the dusty glass.

–Gentlemen of the jury, Pearl began.

The voice was calm and measured.

–Sitting shackled hand and foot in that chair is a young man who was caught up in a whirl of circumstance and ill luck that resulted in the death of his own father. A death that leaves him without one living member of his close family to rely upon. His mother, his sister, and his brother all died in the pneumonia epidemic just over a year ago. And now his father in a terrible accident. I do not say that Joshua Beynon has never once strayed in his life. What boy hasn't at his age? But Joshua Beynon is not a murderer. He drank whiskey. Once. That is no crime. He smoked opium. Once. That is no crime. He has just crossed the threshold of manhood. He bought a gun. That is certainly no crime. What man among you does not own a gun? To buy that gun, he worked hard. He worked for Mr. Frazee in his store. He worked for Mr. Robert Ford.

And Joshua remembered the wagon and Strickland and for a moment he felt once again the happiness of that day when he had met the famous shootist.

–But he was a few cents short of his target, Pearl said. Foolishly, he thought of a scheme to raise the last few cents that would bring that coveted Colt Peacemaker into his hands. Yes, he admits, he did take thirty-six cents from his father's cash box, knowing that he could return that money before his father came home from work. Joshua Beynon had made a wager with Jefferson Smith, and he had won that wager.

The wager that they lied about, Joshua thought. Both Frazee and Soapy.

–We have heard Mr. Frazee deny that any wager was made, but Mr. Frazee did not report any theft to the sheriff, and neither did Jefferson Smith take back the money he had left on Frazee's shelf. Why would Mr. Frazee lie? He lied to support the lie he told to Sheriff Gardner when the boy was arrested.

Joshua inclined his head. The jury wouldn't see any real reason for Frazee to lie. They had no idea of Soapy Smith's devilment: the desire to see Joshua hang in order to spite Mr. Ford. They would not even suspect it. Pearl's argument was lame.

–In Joshua Beynon's mind, Pearl said, all he had to do was to collect his winnings and return a fraction of them to his father's cash box before his father came home from work. But his father had not gone to work. Aaron Beynon, Joshua's father, had been on a drinking binge. So, in a state of drunkenness, Aaron Beynon, Joshua's father, came into the room at the precise moment when his son was returning the money to the cash box. Aaron Beynon jumped to the drunken conclusion that his son was stealing money.

The chains rattled on the table in front of him. He ought to object to Pearl speaking so ill of his father, but he could only let the lawyer speak for him. His voice was frozen in his throat. He would never want such words to be his. It was a betrayal of the way he wanted to remember his father.

–But at this point, Pearl said, Joshua Beynon had no need of any money. He had already bought the gun he wanted. He had a pocket full of money from the bet he won with Jefferson Smith. Aaron Beynon didn't know that. Drunk, and unfortunately prone to violence, Aaron attacked his son, beat him, and foolishly, as every man here who owns a gun will attest, he tried to wrest a loaded weapon from his son's grip. And the gun went off.

Mr. Pearl paused. He moved to the edge of the stage and placed himself between Whitmarsh and the jury. He pointed at Joshua. Joshua felt the eyes of the jurors turn upon him. He kept his gaze on the tight grain of the oak table. He didn't want to see them or them to see him.

–That boy, Counselor Pearl said, that young man saw that his father was wounded. At first, he thought, not seriously. A leg wound. But by some terrible aberration of circumstance, the bullet had hit the artery in Aaron Beynon's leg, and Aaron Beynon had no chance of survival. Joshua ran to aid his father. He brought a towel — the best he could do — and tried to stanch the flow of blood. He was covered in his own father's blood as he ministered to him.

Joshua could see it all again: his father's hopping dance, the fall, the blood pumping out, the draining of life from his face, the eyes turning to dead glass.

–But all of Joshua Beynon's efforts were in vain.

Pearl's voice had suddenly turned to honey.

–Such a wound could only be fatal. And Aaron Beynon died in the arms of his son. The poor boy was in a state of grief and shock. So he went to where he could find help. The Ford family took him in. Mr. Robert Ford did his duty and reported the incident to Sheriff Mort Gardner. Joshua Beynon made no attempt to run. No attempt to hide. He had nothing *to* hide. His father had died in a firearm accident. A tragic occurrence. But not uncommon. Then Sheriff Gardner came on the scene.

Pearl's voice hardened. He stalked the stage, staring down at the sheriff in the front row. All the jurymen were looking at him, too. And Joshua could believe that Counselor Pearl would win the case. The sheriff squirmed under his gaze like an insect beneath a magnifying glass.

–His interpretation of what he found — without Joshua Beynon even present to explain what happened — led Sheriff Gardner to jump to the conclusion that Joshua Beynon had murdered his father. Sheriff Gardner did not ask the boy what had happened. He arrested him. No doubt, Sheriff Gardner considered that he was doing his duty. But he was amiss in the way he carried it out. He had no evidence of murder. He found a cash box that was open next to Aaron Beynon's body. A cash box with money still in it. He found money on Joshua Beynon, every cent of which can be accounted for as having come to the boy by legal means. He found a gun with one chamber that had been fired. A gun that went off through Aaron Beynon's drunken folly. He found the boy covered in blood. Why wouldn't he be so ensanguined if he had tried to save his wounded father?

Counselor Pearl's voice ranged high and loud.

–And that's *all* the so-called evidence that Sheriff Gardner had and that the prosecution now has. And so we find ourselves in this court of law to determine the innocence or guilt of Joshua Beynon. Mr. and Mrs. Ford have both testified as to the veracity of Joshua Beynon's innocence. Joshua Beynon himself has testified before this court, holding to the truth even when he must have considered that some of the answers that he gave might weaken his case and cast him in a *terribly* poor light. He has admitted his shortcomings: imbibing whisky and opium. Even that he took without permission some thirty-six cents from his father's cash box. That money that he was returning to the cash box less than an hour after having taken it. But shortcomings and indiscretions do not a murderer make. If there is doubt, any reasonable doubt in your minds, that murder was committed, and there are reasons aplenty to doubt that murder was committed, you must acquit Joshua Beynon. This boy has told the truth, the whole truth, and nothing but the truth. You gentlemen hold Joshua Beynon's fate in your hands. And it could mean his life. You cannot send an innocent young man to the gallows.

Pearl fixed his heron's gaze on each one of the jury, turned away from them, and strode back toward Joshua. Joshua smiled up at him, but the lawyer was grim-faced and seated himself beside Joshua without a glance. Was this an evil augury? Pearl sat upright, his gaze fixed on Whitmarsh, who rose, as if wearily, from his table, stage left, Pearl's nemesis who could twist the most innocent reality into damning condemnation.

Whitmarsh took out his paisley kerchief, dabbed at his bald crown, and replaced the kerchief in a perfect three-point tuck in his breast pocket. He nodded to the somber judge, adjusted his half-moons a fraction, and turned to face the jury. Joshua both wanted and didn't want to see the prosecutor's face. To see how he would work on the jury like a conjurer to spirit away any thought of innocence.

–It is a sad day when the people of the State of Colorado bring a charge of murder against a son for the killing of his own father. Murder itself is abhorrent. But parricide creates in us a revulsion that is instinctive. At fifteen years old, Joshua Beynon is long since past the age of reason. Not only his family but society expects him to be able to tell right from wrong. To respect the law. We make allowances for lack of experience at that age, certainly, but we do not make allowances for acts that are in wanton disregard for life itself. Acts perpetrated and driven by base appetites. Joshua Beynon is a man. Not a child. He has the appetites of a man, which he has not learned need to be tempered. He wanted to act like a man. But he wanted only to follow a path of vice. His appetites were out of control. After a night of debauchery, of drunkenness, of opium smoking in the company of an admitted prostitute and convicted murderer, he set out to buy a gun.

A cold prickling spread over Joshua's skin. Every word of Whitmarsh's increased his sense of shame and guilt. All of Pearl's arguments upon which he relied as a foundation for his innocence began to crumble, and he was left vertiginous, as if the chair beneath him was suspended in empty air.

–At Frazee's General Store, Whitmarsh said, he behaved in a manner both deranged and violent. He was still under the influence of drink and opiates and driven to steal money from his own father. He was discovered in that act of robbery which resulted in a struggle with his father. And in that struggle his father was shot dead. There was a robbery by Joshua Beynon's own admission. He claims that it occurred before he bought the gun. There is no evidence to corroborate that. He has even admitted that he threatened to kill his father should his father beat him again. And his father was seeking righteously to punish Joshua for theft. He has admitted that his father was shot as they fought over the cash box.

Whitmarsh paused and turned to face him. He pointed a stained finger at Joshua. The hard dark eyes and the lines and creases of Whitmarsh's face were transformed into a mask of utter revulsion. As if it was Whitmarsh's father who had been killed. And rage took Joshua now that this mountebank should so unjustly seek to damn him to the gallows. And he could do nothing. He could not rave at his accuser, but only sit mute and chained in front of him and listen to the allegations.

–At that point, it seems that he realized the enormity of his crime, and he returned to the house of Mr. and Mrs. Ford. It is true that he waited for the arrival of Sheriff Gardner. He did not resist arrest. What happened between Joshua Beynon and Mrs. Ford at this point is unclear because of the contradictory testimony of Mrs. Ford and Joshua Beynon himself. We are not here to determine what was the nature of the physical encounter of Joshua Beynon and Mrs. Ford. But such testimony calls into question the veracity and reliability of the witnesses for the defense.

I told the truth, Joshua thought. They have to believe me. That has to be on my side.

Even-toned, Whitmarsh continued.

–If you, gentlemen of the jury, consider that a robbery was taking place in the bedroom of Aaron Beynon, that a struggle occurred to prevent that robbery, and that Aaron Beynon was shot during the course of that struggle causing his death, there is no doubt that murder took place, and you have no alternative but to declare Joshua Beynon guilty of murder in the second degree.

Not one word out of Whitmarsh's mouth was fair to him or just plain fair. Or just. Or was justice being served and Joshua a fool to believe otherwise? He had killed his own father in a fight. And he was to hang for it.

–I have a few words to say, Judge Owens began.

Joshua turned to look at the saturnine magistrate. He would be a fool to look for succor in that dark presence.

–You men must make your decision based on the evidence and the reliability of the testimony of witnesses. The fact is that no one saw the actual death of the victim but the defendant. There was a cash box in the room, and what you must decide is if that cash box was being robbed. If it was, and Aaron Beynon was shot during the robbery, that constitutes murder in the second degree whether that gun went off by accident or not. That is an important point to consider. You have heard all the evidence. I trust you all to come back here with a decision based on that evidence. Do we have a foreman of the jury?

–Yes, Your Honor, Gardner said. Ernest Stevens has been so chosen.

Stevens, the plump little man with the red face. A kindly man at home no doubt, but one who would seek to act on the evidence as it was presented and without the least equivocation. Joshua knew that Stevens would declare him guilty if Whitmarsh had succeeded in convincing him, would be sad to see Joshua hang, but would watch the execution with a clear conscience and then go home and eat dinner with his family.

–There is yet some time this afternoon, said the judge. Mr. Stevens, you will inform Deputy Wallace when you have come to your decision, however long it takes you. We can come back tomorrow, or Monday, if necessary. Court is in recess.

The barroom of the Orleans Club was still full, and a cloud of tobacco smoke hung under the dark chestnut beams of the ceiling. Joshua sat beside Pearl at the defense table. The judge's high-backed chair, stage center, stood empty.

The lawyer pulled back a hanging hank of his silver hair in the crook of thumb and forefinger and tucked the long locks behind his right ear.

–Mr. Pearl, Joshua said. What do you think they'll say?

His voice was tremulous.

Pearl pressed his lips together and tilted his head, the eyes unfocused as he considered his answer.

–I don't know. I've seen men convicted on less and acquitted on a darn sight more.

–What about the sentence? Joshua said.

–You ain't guilty yet, Pearl said. Put your mind on acquittal and pray to the Lord. He might just be listening.

Joshua thought that the Lord had done scant listening to his prayers since he had crossed the ocean to the Americas. All his family lay in the cold graveyard beneath the canyon's rock walls, and within the time it took to build a scaffold, he, Joshua, the last of the Beynon line, might join their dried and rotting corpses, their names forgotten in this desolate place, less than a whisper on the winds of the high Rocky Mountains. Death, ever present and invisible, inhuman and tantalizing, was in the air that he breathed, behind every sight he looked upon, and fell behind him like a shadow upon his back.

A scant hour had passed when Fat Wallace came out of the back office.

–They come to a verdict, he announced.

So soon. It was almost over now. This whole charade wherein he was chained, an actor who was muted while Counselor Pearl was his voice.

–All rise for Justice Willard P. Owens, called Sheriff Gardner.

Joshua stood and let the chains dangle low. The judge took his judgment seat, and the auditorium was a shuffle and rattle of chairs and a buzz of murmurs.

–Call in the jury.

Stevens led the jurymen like a file of Old Testament prophets back to their places. Joshua fixed his eyes on Stevens. The round little man did not meet his gaze. Stevens rocked nervously from side to side, running the edge of a sheet of paper around and around between the fingers of both hands. His face was flushed, the little eyes flicking down to the paper, up to the judge, and back to the paper in his hands again.

–Come to order, Judge Owens said.

–Order, called Gardner.

–Mr. Stevens, the judge said. Has the jury come to a decision?

–Yes, Your Honor.

Stevens's voice was a quaver.

–The defendant will rise, intoned the judge.

Joshua came to his feet. He was aware that Pearl had risen beside him. The grim faces of the bearded jury were all upon him.

–The defendant Joshua Beynon stands accused of murder in the second degree. How do you find the defendant?

Stevens lifted the paper and it shook in his hand as if he needed to read what was written there.

–Not guilty, Your Honor.

Joshua wept. But he stood up straight. Now the manacles on his wrists and feet seemed an outrage. He reached up to brush away the hot tears from his scratched and burning cheeks. Counselor Pearl put an arm around Joshua's shoulder, and Joshua turned on him a crooked smile, unafraid of the man's touch. Welcomed it, even. The lawyer seemed a grotesque parody of a buffalo hunter in the ludicrous buckskins, the sharp eyes and pointed nose that of a predator, while the silver hair and tanned skin betrayed a pretension toward the softer qualities of womanhood. Pearl was a living contradiction to Joshua, a man who had saved his life even as he prepared to rob him. And Mr. Ford was of the same ilk. Down in the front row, Mr. Ford had his arms wrapped around his wife's plump shoulders. Dot Ford's small and pouty lips were twisted into a grin of joy. The judge banged down his gavel to quell the exclamations of the spectators, each one of whom expressed an opinion of approval or disapproval through screech or grunt or nervous laugh. Gardner, red-faced behind the iron gray of his thick mustache, sheepishly mounted the steps to the stage while the gavel yet rapped.

–Come to order, called Gardner.

The noise in the room lowered to a murmur.

–The State of Colorado, Judge Owens dryly stated, finds Joshua Beynon not guilty of murder in the second degree.

He wanted to howl for joy, but the theatrical solemnity of that stage-turned-courtroom gagged him.

–All rise, yelled Gardner.

It was a redundant order, for every able body in the Orleans Club was already standing as the judge rose from his seat, and without a glance at free man or counsel or at the wags who now yelled for drink and stood facing the bar where once they sat, Judge Owens strode off the stage.

Mr. Ford bustled up to the defense table then. He had his homburg tilted back on his head. His smooth face beamed. He thrust out a hand, and when Joshua gripped it, he was squeezed and pumped until the chains rattled. He felt as if he were flying, but he could only stumble out from behind the table, his ankles trailing chains. Mr. Ford had saved his life. Counselor Pearl had saved his life. Now he, Joshua Beynon, was under contract to sell off his father's house, pay off Counselor Pearl, and invest money and soul in partnership with the famous Robert Ford.

–We'll have us a drink tonight, Mr. Ford said.

Joshua shook his head.

–I'm sorry, he said.

Mr. Ford looked askance.

–Why not?

–No, not that. About Mrs. Ford, Joshua said. That business. On the witness stand.

He blushed deeply. Mr. Ford leaned forward, his mouth so close to Joshua's ear that he could smell on the shoulder of the jacket old smoke and some kind of lavender scent that Mr. Ford must have splashed upon himself.

–Mrs. Ford has had a peter in her hand more often than a

rolling pin. It's kind of her line of business. She's madder'n hell about you making her out to be a liar up there, but her reputation cain't get much lower in this town.

Mr. Ford leaned back and grinned at Joshua, a white-toothed grin, mighty pleased, it seemed, with his own sense of magnanimity. With his father, mother, brother, and sister all dead and gone, Joshua had a new family within which he was both partner and prey to the patriarch. Along with Liddil and Strickland and Ella and Dot, he was part of a clan comprised of whores and drug fiends and former members of the James Gang; the only friends he had left in the world.

–Gardner, called Mr. Ford, get these goddamn irons off the boy.

LVII

BRIGHT SUNLIGHT SHONE UPON THE PROSPECTORS' PANS AND THE jaws of traps and the tin bathtubs that hung from the rough-sawn boards of Bob Starks's mining supply store. It made the nails glisten in the barrels on the porch of Tilly's Hard Goods. It suffused the steam that rose above Chang Jen Wa's laundry, where the third wash of the day was boiling. It silvered the water that lay in the red-mud wagon ruts of Amethyst Street, where Carys, Joshua's coon hound, lapped and sent shimmering waves across its surface. The day that marked the grand opening of Mr. Ford's tent saloon would have been perfect had not Soapy Smith, Ed O'Kelley, Mickey James, and Clarence Thompson not emerged from the front door of the Orleans Club at the very moment of Joshua's passage and the four bodies blocked the boardwalk in front of him.

–What have we here? Soapy said.

Soapy tilted back his head to give the semblance of looking down his nose, but he was at least two inches shorter than Joshua and the posture gave him a frightened look. Thompson and

James, his simian bodyguards, instinctively took a step forward, one on each side of him, while O'Kelley, slovenly and disheveled as usual, slouched forward and reached out to finger the lapel of Joshua's new suit. Instinctively, Joshua batted away the offending hand, and O'Kelley crouched into a fighter's stance, bared his mottled teeth under his mustache, and feinted a blow with his open palm. Carys raced toward the boardwalk. She growled and snapped the air.

–Get that dog away, yelled Clarence Thompson.

–Leave me be, Joshua said.

–Done up like a show monkey, Soapy said.

Carys, still snarling, crouched near Joshua's feet.

O'Kelley straightened up.

Joshua brushed at his lapel as if to free it of contamination. The charcoal pinstripe suit had become Joshua's daily wear since Mr. Ford had taken him to a Chinese tailor in Jimtown. A fine suit: the pants cut narrow to fit into English-style riding boots, the vest with four pockets, two up, two down, and the frock coat cut to his knees. Joshua had the outfit topped off with a round-brimmed black hat, the unfortunate choice of which gave him the aspect of an apprentice preacher — not an image he cared to present to the world — but having spent so much money on the outfit, he felt obliged to wear it.

Smith hooked his thumbs in the pockets of his yellow brocade waistcoat, one finger plucking at the dangling gold watch chain as if at the loose string of a banjo.

–We're off to the horse race, boy, Smith said. Up at Bob Ford's. Care to accompany us?

–I'll be there after I've eaten, Joshua said. Come on, Carys.

He stepped off the boardwalk and into the red mud of the street, and the dog followed at his heel. He did not look back at his tormentors, and he did not look forward to encountering them again at Mr. Ford's tent saloon, either, but Weaver was a small town in a narrow canyon that cast its shadow over few streets, and there was little or no possibility of avoiding them, especially if Soapy Smith was determined to aggravate him more.

Across the street, Joshua's haven was a restaurant of sorts, Dave's Place.

The structure was made of rough pine salvage crudely nailed

onto a crooked frame that some called the Lean-to. It actually leaned against nothing at all, but it did lean downhill and to the east.

–Stay, girl, Joshua said.

Carys hunkered down outside the unpainted door that bore the smell and the scorch marks inflicted by an old house fire and Joshua entered.

Dave himself, stripped to the stained shirt of his long underwear, squatted in front of a flat-topped iron stove, its firebox open as he fed the blaze with split dry oak. Blue smoke twisted up from the griddle and fouled the air above the counter, where three prospectors turned to look at Joshua as he entered. Their faces were stubbled and worn. Not one of them acknowledged him, and they turned back to the plates in front of them and fell to once more.

At least some folks in the town know how to mind their own business, he thought.

–You're becoming a regular, boy, Dave said.

Dave's bearded grin revealed a row of dark-gapped, stained, and crooked ivories set in carious gums.

–Have to eat, Joshua said.

Dave prepared a plate of food for him, and Joshua ate his fatback and eggs and fried bread at the only table in the room. It stood next to the small window that looked out over the boardwalk, its position not accidental, since there was no other space for it. Joshua ate at Dave's Place every day now, for he had no more kitchen of his own where he might prepare his own breakfast. Mr. Ford had not yet forced him into the partnership deal made in the jail cell, but Counselor Pearl had insisted on Joshua honoring their pretrial agreement. Two weeks earlier, the lawyer had sold the Beynon residence and land to his client in Denver and had taken a twenty-five percent cut of the money as his fee for executing Joshua's father's will and for defending Joshua at the trial. Joshua was not unhappy to lose the house. He had no wish to see again the blood-stained boards whereon his father had died. After the lawyer's cut was taken out of the sale money, there was still nearly eleven hundred and twenty-five dollars left for Joshua, and he had deposited it in the Colorado Cattleman's Bank in Jimtown. Since then, Joshua had created for himself a clean and Spartan sanctuary in the dark warren of the Silver Dollar Hotel. The room was not large; on the day he moved in, he had bought new bedding and hired a Polish domestic to scrub the room clean and disinfect it with lye. The room was a temporary camp, certainly, while he awaited the sign that would reveal to him the direction of his fate. A sign that he knew he would recognize when it appeared. He hoped it would not be an ugly portent. Every day he awaited Mr. Ford's request for the promised partnership money. But so far Mr. Ford had not even mentioned it. It was as if Mr. Ford held an ace in his hand that he could play whenever it was to his greatest advantage. Mr. Ford seemed to enjoy having Joshua in that position. And in the small town of Weaver, Joshua could no more avoid Mr. Ford than he could Soapy Smith.

Joshua mopped up the last of the grease with a crumbly finger of corn pone, paid Dave, and set off for the races.

–Come back some time, Dave called after him.

Carys followed Joshua down Amethyst, turned up Main, and kept pace with a mule team under harness that hauled a heavy wagon on which sat a festive squad of racegoers dressed up in battered hats and tattered suits, the women in gingham dresses and straw sunbonnets, jostling and tugging at the children who squirmed and tumbled between their knees. Word of the horse race — and the boxing match — must have traveled all the way down the canyon to Jimtown, and every shrewd man with buckboard or wagon had recognized a way to earn a few dollars carrying would-be wagerers up into the high canyon.

At Jim Shaw's livery, the driver pulled the team to a halt to let the passengers off. As many wagons and buggies as would equip a supply train for a small army were ranked in the field next to the livery and all the way down to the creek. The horses were still harnessed, some motionless and asleep in the traces, others with their heads deep in buckets or draped with feed bags. A number of Negro hostlers moved among the conveyances with sacks of grain and oats, while yet others lounged upon the wagon beds to wait for their customers' return.

The race track had been plotted by Dick Liddil. It ran from the livery uphill to the cemetery gates and curved back down the knoll and across the meadow to the finish line outside Bob Ford's tent saloon. The course was marked by a series of varicolored guidons planted on the slopes and flats, and they fluttered noisily in the cool breeze that blew down off Bulldog Mountain. The course would pass close by the mounded grave of Joshua's father. His da would have been the first to lay a bet at the track, though not on the prizefight — men were far more devious than horses in arranging a profitable outcome — but he would have been tight up to the ringside rope to watch the pugilists' battering match.

A crowd had gathered outside the tent saloon, where a schoolteacher's blackboard was set up. On it were written the names of various horses and jockeys and the odds on their chance of victory. Dick Liddil, who would be riding his own thoroughbred in the race, was in front of the board. He called out odds, yelled the virtue of every mount, invented stories for the jockeys. He had waxed up the ends of his blond mustache. His short and wiry body twisted to left and right as he reached for dollar bills and half-dollar pieces and handed out a slip to every eager wagerer.

Mr. Ford was visible above the heads of the crowd at the entrance to the tent saloon. He had a wide grin on his smooth-shaven face. A white carnation was fastened in the buttonhole of his gray suit. From within the long marquee behind him arose the chatter and laughter as from an overcrowded aviary, while a fiddle and squeezebox played a hornpipe above the din. The cloud of tobacco smoke that was trapped beneath the canvas roof seeped out in wisps and spirals through the apex of the triangular entrance, and the smoke curled around Mr. Ford's homburg like a devilish nimbus.

–Joshua, he said, how would you like to do a little job for me?

Mr. Ford came down the steps to meet him. Joshua shook the proffered slender hand. He was not sure that he did want to do a little job, but it was hard to refuse Mr. Ford.

–What do you need doing? Joshua said.

–Come on up, Mr. Ford said.

Immediately, Mr. Ford skirted the crowd and set off up the grassy slope toward his cabin. He entered the cabin and left the door open behind him. Joshua hadn't been in the Ford home since the day his father died, and he remembered the drink and the opium and the dreams and awaking from the dreams and the nightmare that followed. He hesitated at the threshold of the door. Joshua feared to face Mrs. Ford, for he had not seen her since the trial, when he had exposed her as a perjurer. He left the dog outside.

Seated at the long table where Joshua had been drinking with all of the Ford clan on the night before his father's death was Silas Strickland, stripped to the waist, the big ebony muscles of his chest and shoulders and arms still defined, though he had obviously run to weight. His dark banana-thick fingers protruded from bandages tightly wound around his palms and down to his wrists.

–Joshua. Get you a drink, boy, Strickland growled.

He nodded his big prizefighter's head, with its bush of curls gone white too early. Joshua feared for Strickland, going into the ring with Colum Reilly, the big Irish miner.

–Hey! Joshua! Mrs. Ford fairly shrieked, come on in.

It was as if she had forgotten the entire matter of her perjury, and he was sure that she had and that perjury meant as little to her as plying her trade as a sporting woman. Something frowned upon by others but resorted to when necessary. She had a hairbrush in one hand and a spiked wooden roller in the other that she must have just taken out of Ella's red ringlets. Both of the women were in the same dresses that they were wearing when first he had seen them: Ella in purple satin and Mrs. Ford in blue, but the dresses had been laundered and ironed and they belled out over layers of crinoline. Mrs. Ford's full face — its slight double chin that took away her jaw's definition, and the small red lips, and the button nose and the lively kohled blue eyes — was like a full moon, a halo above Ella's dark Hecate.

–Ah . . . Joshua, Ella drawled. Back from the dead, are we?

The glassy eyes, half visible under the shadowed lids, regarded him as if he were a shade or a dream figment arisen in her opiate dominion. Framed by the ringlets, her face was more gaunt than ever, the cheeks sunken. No amount of powder could disguise the deep crescents beneath the hooded eyes. Her wide red mouth was slack. She had gone beyond any dosage of opiate administered merely to keep herself functional.

–Hey, Ella, Joshua said. Hi, Mrs. Ford. Hi, Strick.

–Are you ready, Ella? Mr. Ford said.

–For what? Ella said.

–The apple, Mr. Ford said.

–The apple, ah yes, Ella said. Am I ready, Dot?

–You're ready, honey, Mrs. Ford said.

Ella got up off the chair by the cold stove and glided across to where Strickland sat. He pulled out a chair for her beside him.

–Sit down there, Joshua, barked Strickland, waving one big hand at a chair opposite him. My, aren't you the fine young man in that suit!

Joshua took off his round-brimmed hat and sat where he was told. On the table between him and the other two was a slim mahogany oblong box like a cigar case, a dark bottle about the size of an ink bottle, and a plate with an apple on it. Ella opened the box and plucked out a glass cylinder with brass fittings at either end. She screwed a long brass needle on one end of it. Strickland uncorked the bottle for her, and she dipped the needle in and pulled up on the plunger so that the cylinder filled with liquid. She picked up the apple, slid the needle into it, and pushed down the plunger. A little liquid oozed out of the puncture hole, but most must have stayed inside. Joshua had a moment of dread. They were planning on poisoning someone.

–You think that's enough? Mr. Ford asked.

–More than I'd use on me, Ella said.

–Well, that should slow him down then, Mr. Ford said.

–I don't know, Ella said. I ain't a horse.

–Well, put some more in, then, Mr. Ford said.

–As you like, Ella said.

Ella repeated the process with the needle. Then she passed the apple, shiny and rosy, to Mr. Ford. Mrs. Ford set a shot glass down in front of Joshua. He sipped at it and without grimacing let the whiskey burn down his throat to his belly.

–Joshua, Mr. Ford said. Wayne Stacker's got a dun quarter horse down in the livery. Soapy and O'Kelley have bet hard on that horse, and that's making others wager the same way. If that horse wins, not only do we not make a cent on the day, but I'll have to go into hock to pay off Soapy and everybody else from Weaver to Jimtown. I cain't afford to risk that. I want you to take this apple and feed it to Stacker's dun horse. You go down there with Dick Liddil when he saddles up the thoroughbred and just toss it in the stall if you can't feed it to the dun by hand.

Joshua's insides turned liquid and his feet to clods. If he went through with this, he was helping to swindle hundreds or even thousands of dollars out of Soapy Smith, Ed O'Kelley, and any one of a hundred small-stakes gamblers who had laid their bets on this dun quarter horse in Dick Liddil's horse race. But he couldn't refuse. He wanted to. But the words wouldn't come out of his mouth. Numbly, he took the apple in his hand and let it drop heavily into the right-hand pocket of his frock coat. He got up from the table.

–Don't look so worried, Honeyjosh, Mrs. Ford said. No one ain't gonna see you.

–Where's Dick? Joshua said.

But he knew where Dick was. He just wanted this to be done and over with. But it would never be done and over with. He was being pulled into a world of which he was not sure that he wanted to be a part: the world of shootists and gamblers and con men and thieves. Not now. Not after his da. No good would come of it. And still he couldn't refuse.

–Drink up, Honeyjosh, Mrs. Ford said.

And he drank the whiskey down, too, while they all grinned in approval.

–Come on, Josh, Mr. Ford said. I'll take over from Dick.

Outside the door, between the red rock walls of the canyon, the tent and the buggies and all the horses and the guidons and the festive crowd seemed to have but a tawdry glamour. Carys had run off somewhere in all the confusion of people and animals. She could look after herself.

Joshua waited at the edge of the crowd of bettors while Mr. Ford pushed through them to Dick Liddil, and Joshua heard Mr. Ford's voice begin with the bookie's banter. Then Liddil emerged from the throng. He seemed a little heavy for a jockey. No doubt his weight had increased apace with the gray in his hair and mustache.

–Let's give that dun a treat, Dick said. You put a bet on?

Joshua shook his head.

–I reckon my thoroughbred would beat him anyway, but the course is a tad short and it ain't worth taking the risk.

The apple bulged in the pocket of Joshua's frock coat. He was afraid that someone would ask him what he had in that pocket, afraid that someone might see him give the apple to the horse, afraid that he wouldn't get close enough to the horse to give it the apple and that Mr. Ford would blame him for being ruined if the dun horse beat Dick Liddil's thoroughbred. They approached the livery now, and Joshua moaned to himself when he saw Soapy Smith. Soapy was leaning back against the corral fence. He held a silver hip flask in one hand and a cigar in the other. Mickey James and Clarence Thompson flanked him as usual, but there was no sign of Ed O'Kelley.

–I got bad news for you, Liddil, Soapy called.

Joshua did not want to stop to talk to him. He wanted to finish his mission and be gone from there, but Dick Liddil, with his splayed gait, ambled over to the half-drunk owner of the Orleans Club. Joshua suddenly feared for Dick's horse.

–What's the matter? Liddil asked.

–Colum Reilly, Soapy said. Your nigger's would-be sparring partner, he just took sick. Ed O'Kelley's with him now.

–What the hell you mean? Liddil snapped.

–Took sick, Soapy said. Bad fever. Maybe got the dysentery.

–Goddamn you, Smith, Liddil said.

–Ain't nothing to do with me, Soapy said. But I might could help you out.

–Help?

Soapy waved his cigar at Mickey James.

–Another Irishman, Soapy said. Mickey'll take on your nigger.

Mickey's small eyes glinted under a heavybrow ridge. The twist in his rubbery lips below the broad flattened nose might have been a smile. Joshua thought Mickey James at least fifteen years younger than Strickland, and if Reilly had a glass jaw, Mickey's resembled a squared-off piece of four-by-four rough oak.

Liddil didn't balk.

–Strick'll whip him, Liddil said. Now I got a race to ride. Come on, Joshua.

Soapy laughed like a drunken burro. He gestured with the silver flask.

–You like a little nip, Josh?

Joshua shook his head. He was about to do to Soapy what Soapy would do to Liddil and Mr. Ford. Soapy had taken Colum Reilly out of the fight as sure as Joshua hoped to take the dun out of the horse race. Not to mention the beating that Strickland would take. But Soapy had just made it easier for Joshua to feed the apple to the horse, even if he was making of himself another of Soapy's ilk.

–Goddamn him, Liddil said. That Mickey James is more ape than man.

–Do you think Strick can whip him? Joshua said.

Liddil didn't answer, but turned into the stable, and Joshua thought that boded mighty ill for Silas Strickland.

The space between the two rows of stalls was already crowded with jockeys and horse owners and stable boys. Some riders were saddling their mounts. Joshua searched along the row of stalls for the dun. If the horse were being saddled, it would be impossible to feed it the apple. He didn't know what he would tell Mr. Ford if he failed. He stepped around piles of manure that littered the brick herringboned floor. Halfway along the stable, Liddil lifted his chin in the direction of the dun and went on toward the thoroughbred's stall. Joshua slid his hand into his pocket, and his fingers closed on the poisoned apple.

The dun's stall door, both halves, was open, and the horse was tethered by a rope halter to a ring on the wall. A long-haired stable boy dropped a curry into a tin bucket and left the stall.

–Hey, boy, Dick Liddil called. Come and take care of this thoroughbred. I want to saddle him.

–Yessir, the boy replied.

Joshua looked around for anyone who might be the owner. He had no idea what Wayne Stacker might look like. He just had to risk going into the stall. He drew the apple from his pocket. The stable boy disappeared into Liddil's stall, and Joshua, furtive, was in beside the dun. The horse twitched its ears nervously back and forth as Joshua laid a hand on its haunch and approached the horse's head along the same side the stable boy had left. The horse flung its head toward him and snorted, and Joshua instinctively reached up to calm it with a hand upon its curved neck. He had the apple out of his pocket and lifted it to the horse's mouth. The horse's pink lips pulled back, it shied its head away, and then swung back and knocked the apple from his palm. Joshua reached down to pick it up, but the horse's head dipped and the apple was gone and crushed in its teeth. Joshua straightened up, stroked the dun's muzzle, and at that moment a lean-faced wrangler with a hard chin and swarthy skin appeared at the entrance to the stall. Joshua assumed it was Wayne Stacker, for he carried a saddle on the shoulder of his blue overall jacket and a halter dangling from his hand. The tall body looked as if it was born on a horse, the long legs bowed a little to the scuffed high-heeled boots.

–What you doing in there, boy? the wrangler said.

The voice was quiet and inquisitive without a trace of meanness or suspicion. Joshua did not know if the wrangler had seen him feed the apple to the horse.

–Beautiful horse, Joshua said. I was going to put some money on it.

The wrangler gave a slight smile.

–You do that, boy, he said. It's a sound investment.

–I'll get out of your way, Joshua said.

–No trouble, the wrangler said.

–Really, I'll be going.

Joshua hurried out of the stall and toward the high and open barn doors. Whatever happened to the horse, the wrangler would remember that Joshua had been in the stall. Such a deed as he had done would not have been amiss on the pages of the *Police Gazette*. And the villain would pay. Out in the air once more, Joshua frantically brushed away at his pants and frock coat, trying to free himself of the clinging chaff.

The race was about to start. Mr. Ford had given him a pair of binoculars, and Joshua stood on the tent platform so that he had a clear view of the whole course, from the starting line at the livery all the way up the canyon past the cemetery and across the meadow to the finishing post. Mr. Ford was still at the blackboard below, taking last minute bets, though the racehorses were all mounted. Shaw's stable boys were acting as stewards and led the horses by the bridles in an attempt to bring them into line. Dick Liddil's sorrel thoroughbred kept prancing away from the starting post. The dun quarter horse seemed none the worse for whatever was in the apple and stood in the middle of the line, the wrangler in the blue overalls even having to fight the dun to keep its head pointing uphill toward the cemetery and the first curve in the track. Dick Liddil finally managed to get the sorrel pulled into one end of the line, and the gun went off. The field was away. Jim Shaw's big roan was the first to show, closely followed by a white-faced bay from Jeremiah Smith's horse farm, and the nobbled dun ridden by Wayne Stacker, was hard on the bay's heels. Dick's sorrel was driven to the outside by a bunch in the middle of the field, but Dick, whip working already, drove hard after Stacker on the dun. The horses rounded the curve and raced along the flat toward the cemetery gate, where they would turn for home. The dun had pulled past the bay now, and finally Dick's thoroughbred raced up shoulder-to-shoulder with the third-place horse. He was two lengths behind the dun.

Maybe the damned horse liked what Ella put in the apple, Joshua thought.

Shaw's roan began to falter as the horses passed the cemetery gate and made the meadow turn, and then the dun was ahead and Dick raced by the roan, too. Into the final straight they came, and Joshua feared that Mr. Ford would not believe that he had in fact given the dun the apple, though Dick's sorrel was gaining fast and was only a half a length behind Stacker's dun with fifty yards to go. Dick worked the whip hard.

Fifteen yards out, the thoroughbred put a neck in front of the dun, then half a length, and Dick sped past the finishing post, the clear winner by a length. Jim Shaw's roan came in third, and the rest of the field thundered past the finish line behind it.

Joshua dropped the binoculars and let out his breath that he had held since the horses came around the final turn. Down at the bookie's blackboard, Mr. Ford was beaming, arms raised above his head in triumph, and Wayne Stacker would need have no suspicion, because the dun had performed so well. The jockeys all brought their horses to a walk somewhere past Mr. Ford's log cabin. Stacker leaned over to shake Dick Liddil's hand, and then he turned the dun to come back down toward the tent saloon. Suddenly the big quarter horse stopped as if it had breasted a fence. The dun shook its head. Then its whole body trembled from shoulder to hind hoof and its legs buckled and Stacker leapt from its back as the dun dropped to the earth like a poleaxed steer. Immediately a crowd of onlookers swirled around the fallen dun and hid it from Joshua's sight.

Joshua pressed the binoculars to his vest and jumped down off the tent platform. He feared that the horse was dead, and dead by his hand. Mr. Ford grabbed Joshua by the arm as he passed by the bookie's blackboard.

–Take it easy, Josh, he said. We made us a little money here and I'll take care of you, don't worry.

–I want to see what happened to the horse, Joshua said.

–Keep away from there, Mr. Ford said.

But Joshua elbowed his way into the crowd, and Mr. Ford was right behind him. Wayne Stacker knelt next to the dun and had the horse's head cradled in his arms. He seemed to be trying to divine the horse's ailment by peering into its rolling eye.

At least the animal isn't dead, Joshua thought.

Then he thought that it would have been better if it were dead, for that might throw less suspicion on him.

Dick Liddil had dismounted from the thoroughbred and held it by the reins, leaning over the felled animal.

–I ain't see nothing like this, Stacker said.

–By God, that horse gave its all, Liddil said. I thought it must have burst its heart.

–He ain't burst nothing, Stacker said. I run him round that course yester'eve and he hardly broke a sweat.

–He must have caught the colic, Dick said. I had a horse like that once down in Neosho. Run him in two races, and in the second he collapsed not a hundred yards from the starting post.

–I ain't seen a colic like this, Stacker said.

The horse raised its shoulders and shook its head free of Stacker's grip. It came up on its forelegs like a newborn foal, swayed a little, and regained its hind legs, but it seemed to have no coordination among its four hooves, and it sidled toward Stacker and pushed him back at the crowd. Stacker grabbed the halter and the dun steadied. It was then that Stacker saw Joshua. Stacker's eye's narrowed slightly as if he was trying to place him.

–You was the boy was in the stall, Stacker said.

Joshua nodded.

–He seemed fine then, Joshua said.

Soapy Smith came through the crowd.

–Why'd the horse give out, Stacker?

–It ain't right, Stacker said. I'm going to get the vet up here. See if he can't tell what's wrong with him.

–It's the colic, Dick Liddil said. I'd lay odds on it.

–I don't know as it's safe to bet with you, Liddil, Soapy said.

–You making an accusation, Soapy? Liddil said.

Stacker shot a hard glance at Liddil and back to Joshua, and then he led the dun on its wobbly legs down the trail toward the livery. The horse seemed to regain its balance, though it shook its head every few steps as if to rid itself of a swarm of invisible flies.

–What were you doing at the livery with Liddil, boy? Soapy said.

–I just went to look at the horses, Joshua said. Same as you, Mr. Smith. You didn't have anything to do with this, I suppose?

–Me! After I bet on the dun, Soapy said. Who did you bet on, boy?

–I didn't bet a cent, Mr. Smith.

The mood of the crowd was sullen, and Mr. Ford was nowhere to be seen among them.

Then the fiddler and the squeezebox player were out in front of the tent and they struck up with a lively jig. Mr. Ford appeared from the tent and ran down the steps to the bookie's table. He called out over the music.

–Collect your winnings, now, and place your bets. The boxing match starts in half an hour.

The women of the crowd, at least, refound their merriment, while the men who had bet on Liddil's horse waved their slips in the air and made for the bookie's blackboard.

–I'll put two thousand dollars on Mickey James, Soapy yelled out. That's a sure way to get my money back.

Some of the crowd cheered and followed Soapy toward the bookie's table. Joshua was all shoulders and elbows as he pushed his way among them, eliciting curses and complaints, but he fought his way past Soapy at the head of the crowd and was the first to reach Mr. Ford.

–Ten dollars on Strickland, Joshua called.

He turned to Soapy.

–Now I'm betting, Mr. Smith.

As if laying the first bet was a prayer or a charm to ward away evil from the old black prizefighter.

JOSHUA LICKED HIS LIPS AND SHIFTED IN HIS CHAIR ON THE EDGE of the tent saloon's platform. He overlooked the ring as if he were a Caesar at the Coliseum. His heel tapped against the boards as the drunken crowd gathered around the rope circle where Mickey James was to fight Silas Strickland in a boxing match on which almost every man in Weaver had laid a bet. The ten dollars that Joshua had wagered added spice to his desire to see Strickland a winner, but James looked like a formidable opponent. Diagonally opposite Joshua, not fifteen yards away, on the southeast corner of the ring, an awning had been set up. Under it on a low stool sat Mickey James, stripped to the waist, a white-skinned giant, with his gloved fists resting on the thighs of his dark pants. His dark red hair had been cropped up above his ears. One of those ears was puffed and gnarled like a vegetable, but not any one known to be grown on this earth. Between his thick eyebrows, a knot of flesh — or bone — gave him the look of being constantly puzzled, but he sat with a quiet malevolence, staring intently at the empty corner where Strickland would soon take his place. Soapy Smith and Ed O'Kelley, Mickey's seconds, stood one on each side of him, exchanging banter with those closest to them in the still-gathering crowd. They looked too confident. If Mickey James won the fight, then Mr. Ford was going to be ruined with all the money he would have to pay out to the gamblers. And if Mr. Ford was ruined, so was Joshua, for he had yet to sink his money into the partnership agreed with Mr. Ford in the jail cell. All that money that Mr. Ford could demand of him Joshua would see go to pay off Mr. Ford's gambling debts. Strickland had to win.

A few in the crowd — a very few — cheered, and Joshua turned in his chair to see Mr. Ford came out of the tent saloon followed by Silas Strickland, with Dick Liddil bringing up the rear. The slight Mr. Ford was dwarfed by the hulking Negro behind him. Strickland had a blanket draped over his oiled body and grease had been smeared thickly over his heavy eyebrows. His shock of white hair gave him a fearfully ancient aspect, but there was no trace of weakness or fear in his demeanor: his knotted arms were raised in a loose guard at the level of his massive shoulders and his hands were exaggerated by heavy hide gloves and he scowled down at the hostile crowd below him. But big as he was and mean-looking, he did not appear equal to being in a ring with Mickey James.

–Don't say a word about the damned apple, Mr. Ford said.

Joshua nodded. He had had no intention of mentioning any apple, but the memory of it added to his disquiet, for was that not a fraudulent and criminal act for which justice would seek some rebalance?

Beads of sweat glistened between the brim of Mr. Ford's homburg and above his pale eyebrows. His carnation had wilted somewhat, the edges of the white petals turning brown. He was nervous, and to see him so when he was normally so calm augured ill.

The air between the red rock walls of the canyon was hot and dry, and not a breath of wind bent blade of grass or stirred the still-standing guidons that marked the now empty race course. It was but three o'clock, and the afternoon sun was dipping toward the thunderheads that had begun to bank up thick and high over the ramshackle buildings and the cableway tower of the Amethyst Mine. The unquiet crowd that was gathered around three sides of a small rope enclosure, many of the men reeling and drunk, was a potential storm of another ilk that might sweep away Mr. Ford, the tent saloon, and Joshua, too.

–Let's get this done, Strickland said.

He jumped down off the platform into his corner of the small ring, and Dick Liddil jumped down after him. There was a surge that sent a rippling wave through the crowd as those in the rear tried to get closer to see the impending violence. An unseen jeerer close to Mickey James's corner yelled out.

–You're in for a beating, nigger.

And a great cheer went up among the blood-hungry on that side of the ring.

–You won't fix this one, Ford, called Soapy Smith.

The crowd cheered again.

–Good luck, Strick, Mrs. Ford called.

Mrs. Ford waved as she came up the steps of the tent saloon. Her high woman's voice seemed a paltry confrontation to the sea of hostility that seethed beneath the tent platform, but her ingenuous good cheer brought a smile to Joshua's face. Ella was leaning on Mrs. Ford's arm, and the two women fairly floated down to their reserved seats like great bell-shaped hot air balloons, the one purple, the other pale blue.

–I'm gonna sit by you, Honeyjosh.

Joshua got up to let Mrs. Ford and Ella pass him by. They were all crimped and crinolined and perfumed and pasted. The warmth that he felt from Mrs. Ford and this intimate company doubled his sense of terrible exposure up there on the platform above the crowd of onlookers.

Down in the corner, Dick Liddil pulled the blanket from Strickland's shoulders, and Strickland danced forward in a shuffle like an awkward bear. Sheriff Mort Gardner came under the rope and out into the middle of the small ring. At last, the fight was about to start, and it would take the minds of the townsfolk off the horse race, at least for the battle's duration. Now Mickey James left his corner. He was taller than Strickland by a head, and his great long arms hung beside his pale and heavily muscled body. Intelligent he might not be, but for such a big man Mickey was surprisingly nimble on his feet, and he shadow-boxed all the way to where Mort Gardner stood. Joshua bit back a yell of encouragement for Strickland, for the crowd suddenly quieted and he had no wish to draw attention to himself.

Mickey looked eager for the fight, while Strickland kept up his slow shuffle until he joined Mickey and Gardner at the center of the ring. Mr. Ford, in an effort to present himself as fair and aboveboard, had persuaded the sheriff to referee the contest. Gardner was the only man that Joshua thought physically capable of pulling the two heavyweights apart if they got into too tight a clinch.

Dick Liddil pulled himself up onto the platform and seated himself on the edge of it, close to Joshua's feet.

–What do you think, Dick? Joshua asked.

–If Strick was ten years younger, I think he might could do it.

That wasn't the answer that Joshua wanted to hear, but it was close to what he expected. In the center of the ring, Gardner examined the boxers' gloves, stepped back, and waved them together. And the fight was on. And would go on until one of those giants, the black or the white, could no longer stand. Joshua concentrated all his will into the muscles and brain of the black fighter.

Mickey James circled around Strick's solid stance. He danced in toward the broad black man and flicked out a long left. Strick took it on his shoulders and came forward, guard high in front of his face. Mickey tried to force him back with some straight left jabs, but Strick caught them all on his gloves. Strick feinted, and Mickey dropped back. Joshua and the rest of the crowd yelled their disapproval that the white man wouldn't stand and fight.

Mickey was too canny to be goaded into a slugging match. He feinted with his shoulders, he moved around Strick and came in fast and caught him in the ribs with a right hook and danced away again without Strickland laying a glove on him.

–Nail him, Strick, Joshua yelled.

Mickey closed in. He must have hurt Strickland and he let loose a combination, once, twice, that Strickland caught on his elbows and Strick got in his first jab to the chest that rocked Mickey back.

–Yes, Joshua called.

But Strick's follow-up roundhouse right was all air and Mickey leaned away and counterjabbed and caught Strick on the left side of the head.

–Goddamn.

It must have stung for Strick bulled forward as if in a rage and his shorter body smacked into Mickey. Strick tried to get him toward the rope with short body punches but Mickey draped his weight over Strickland and held Strick's arms close so that he couldn't get in a good punch.

–Get off him, you son of a bitch, Joshua yelled.

Gardner came forward then and separated them. It didn't look good. Strickland, it seemed, could do little but keep moving forward and force Mickey to dance and jab, but the jabs were striking home around Strick's head and shoulders. Strick's guard lowered as if the blows around his arms and the effort to keep his fists up were already taking its toll in the afternoon heat. All that money that Mr. Ford was going to lose. The ten dollars that Joshua bet now seemed so paltry. And all his money in the Cattleman's Bank seemed to be dissolving into thin air. Mickey closed in again to work on Strick's body, fast combinations to the ribs, but he had left himself open. Strickland swung a big right hook that crashed in the side of Mickey's face and the sweat flew from Mickey's head as it snapped back. Mickey was off-balance and Joshua roared with the crowd as Strickland shuffled forward and fired off a right and a left to the ribs. He'd hurt Mickey. And now Mickey was back-pedaling and the fighters came close under the tent platform right below Joshua's feet. The thuds of the blows that the two fighters traded he heard loud and clear. He could see the fighters' bobbing head movements and the hate and concentration in their eyes as they looked for openings in each other's guard. Mickey jabbed straight and hard at Strickland, and Strick's white-haired head bobbed back under each blow. He was swollen around the left eye. His body ran with sweat. Where Mickey had taken Strick's blows, he had great red patches on his lily-white skin. They stood toe-to-toe and now Mickey seemed content to slug it out under the plat-form.

–Go for him, Strick, Joshua called.

Short hooks and hard uppercuts pounded into Mickey's body and the white man fell back against the platform. Joshua could have touched the top of the sweaty, carrot-topped head. Strickland drove into him with his whole body and Mickey twisted away from under the rushed onslaught and Strickland fell against the side of the platform. He turned again to face Mickey, and a huge haymaking left thudded into the side of Strickland's head. Joshua moaned. Strick dropped onto one knee and Mickey came forward and kneed him in the shoulder. Strickland dropped and his chin ran as a plough through the dry grass.

–You son of a bitch! Joshua yelled.

Gardner tried to push Mickey away as Strickland raised himself from the ground but the Irishman fought Gardner aside and jabbed at Strickland's head before he regained his balance. Strick-land was back against the platform and Mickey hammered at his ribs.

–Oh dear God, Liddil moaned.

–Get up, Strick, called Joshua.

The swelling over Strickland's eye had burst and blood ran in rivulets down his face. Strick surged forward again and Mickey skipped aside, catching Strick with a glancing blow to his ruined eye. Strick staggered sideways and Mickey moved in close and hammered down on Strickland with two rights that sent the Negro sprawling. The crowd howled.

Mrs. Ford squealed. Joshua held his head in his hands. Money or no money, that was Strickland down there getting a beating, and he wished it would stop. Just be over with, and he would face up to whatever loss of money he had to take, but he just wanted Strickland out of the ring.

Mickey James danced around the fallen boxer. He was breathing hard and his steps seemed less bouncy than when he began the contest, but at least he was standing. Gardner got his body between Mickey and Strickland this time, and the white man didn't try to wrestle the referee aside but just stood panting. Strickland came to his feet but stayed bent over at the waist. Gardner stepped away. Mickey danced forward. Strickland rushed him low and bumped Mickey off-balance. Strick's wicked right cross caught Mickey on the left side of the face and jarred his head back. Mickey swung back toward the crouched black man, and Strick stepped inside his guard again and unloosed a straight left to the jaw that had all of his weight behind it. It lifted Mickey off his feet, and the Irishman thudded against the ground and raised dust.

–Dear God, Strick, Joshua said.

He shook his head.

The great black chest heaved as Strickland took gulps of air while Gardner held him back. His gloves were planted on his hips as he waited for Mickey to raise himself. Blood dripped copiously from his forehead to the ground as he leaned over. Swelling had left one eye but a puffy slit smeared with greasy crimson. The white man came to his feet, and Joshua spat.

–He got up, Joshua said to no one.

Mickey raised his guard. There was no spring in his step now and no dance. He walked flat-footed toward Gardner and Strickland. Gardner stepped aside. Strickland brought his fists up again to shoulder height. His head was turned slightly so that he could use his good eye. Mickey jabbed again and Strickland blocked two but the third jarred his head back. He staggered backward as Mickey closed in. Mickey feinted to the head and unloaded a right cross and Strickland crashed back against the tent platform right at Joshua's feet.

–Get up, Strick, Joshua murmured.

But he was sure that the black man could hear nothing. Strick leaned back against the platform. Then, as Mickey came in the for the kill, Strickland spread his arms and he took Mickey's right and left hooks on them, pushed off from the platform and used his whole body to knock Mickey off-balance. The Irishman's legs wobbled. Strick pummeled him with a heavy left hook and Mickey wheeled away, bent over. Strickland pounded down on him with a ferocious left hammer that caught Mickey above the right ear and the Irishman shuffled sideways to keep his feet. Mickey spun and swung at the advancing Strickland. Strick stepped back and Mickey's blow was all wind and Strick caught Mickey with an uppercut to the sternum that half folded him. Like a bear gone mad, Strickland pounded at Mickey's bent head — hook and cross — and the Irishman dropped his useless guard as if to swing his body away again. Would they never stop pounding each other? How could either one of them stand it?

Strick stepped in, feet planted solid, and caught Mickey with a savage uppercut to the body that dropped the Irishman to his knees. Mickey, guard down, swayed back. The bloody hole of his mouth gaped for air, his face lifted as if in supplication and Strick hit him with a pummeling right hook that unhinged Mickey's joints and the Irishman collapsed in the dirt like a pile of loose lumber that had fallen off a wagon. Strick bent over with his gloves on his knees and gasped for air. He stared down at the stricken Irishman. Mickey's limbs scraped fitfully over the grass but an unseen weight seemed to pin down his body. Joshua added the weight of his will to keep the Irishman down. Gardner stood by Strickland's side. The referee's white shirt was damp with sweat and spattered with crimson. Voices in the crowd were howling for Mickey to get up, but when Strickland turned away from his fallen foe and wobbled back toward his corner, the crowd fell silent. Mrs. Ford squealed with delight. All of a sudden Joshua was scraped by crinoline and smothered by the soft flesh beneath it. A kiss squashed into his lips and a powdered cheek brushed against his smooth one. Mrs. Ford had his jaw between her plump palms and she gazed into eyes. A faint scent of whiskey lingered where she had kissed him.

–He done it, Honeyjosh. Strick whipped the son of a bitch.

And Joshua grinned at her

–By God, he did, didn't he?

And he got up and jigged with her on the spot till he realized that they were jigging in silence, and he sensed the ugly menace of the crowd. Liddil jumped down off the platform and ran to Strickland. The big black man waved Liddil away. Beyond Mrs. Ford, a pistol clicked. Mr. Ford had the Remington down by his side. Joshua jumped down into the ring when he saw Soapy Smith and Ed O'Kelley rush from their corner toward Mickey.

–That goddamn nigger! O'Kelley shouted. Are you going to let him whip a white man?

A yell went up from the crowd. At the far side of the ring, a wave surged forward and the rope fell and the ring was swamped. Joshua stepped between Strickland and the crowd. A shot cracked out, and the crowd ebbed to a halt in the middle of the ring next to Mickey's sprawled body. Up on the platform, Mr. Ford had his pistol raised above his head.

–It was a fair fight! Mr. Ford called out. You all seen it. Mickey got whipped fair and square. Now, for the next hour there's free drinks at the bar.

Mrs. Ford and Ella hurried away around the corner of the tent. Joshua backed away from the middle of the ring toward the tent platform, keeping himself between Strickland and the still and silent mob. The rage stirred by the blood and the violence of the prizefight and the chicanery of the con man who stood, pistol in hand, was dammed up for the moment. Mr. Ford held them all at bay, a slim figure in a gray suit in front of the four empty chairs and the white canvas backdrop standing above a seething mob. Joshua's partner in perdition seemed dreadfully alone.

LIX

JOSHUA PUSHED THROUGH THE ENTRANCE TO THE TENT SALOON and into the throng of burly backs, tweed-clad and leather-clad and homespun and buckskin.

–Make way! Make way! he called.

Strickland was bent over and gasping behind him, and Dick Liddil had his arm around the fighter's back, holding a blanket in place. The miners and the prospectors and the wranglers and trappers pressed back, one against the other, hands protecting mugs of beer or shot glasses of whiskey as Joshua forced a passage toward the bar at the far end of the tent. At the left end of the bar was a podium whereon a fiddler and a squeezebox player scratched and wheezed out a reel. Four sporting women that Joshua had never seen before danced in the arms of four drunken miners. Tobacco smoke lay like a fog under the canvas roof. His eyes began to smart behind his glasses. The tent was a good forty feet long, and every face turned to view their arrival, Joshua the herald, Liddil the trainer, and Strickland battered and lumbering, his white-haired head swaying like a wounded bear's.

A lean and stubbled prospector in torn buckskins, Ike Picket, an enforcer for the town's Vigilance Committee, followed them to the bar. His eyes were bloodshot and glazed, his thin, cracked lips pulled back from his chaw-stained teeth.

–What's the nigger doing in here? Picket said.

–He's getting a drink, Joshua said.

Joshua moved in close to Strickland, who slumped onto the bar and supported himself on his elbows. The fighter gasped for air. Blood still dripped — slower now — from his swollen eye. Around his temples, dried blood encrusted his white curls. The left side of his face was swollen like a balloon filled with water. Strickland lifted his gloved hands up to chest height, and Joshua reached between his forearms and shoulders and unknotted the laces at the wrists. He loosened the gloves and drew them off Strick's bandaged hands. Mickey James's blood and maybe Strickland's own had soaked into the rough leather and stained it a deeper brown. Joshua had never seen such a brutal fistfight. It made him conscious of the weakness of his own gangly body. He would have lasted scant seconds in a ring with either boxer.

–Give me a bucket of water and a couple of clean rags, Liddil called to the barman.

A hand fell on Joshua's shoulder and turned him around. Ike Picket's hard, angled face was scarred above the right cheek; there was a viciousness in the narrow eyes that marked him as a devotee of easy violence and veteran of a hundred barroom fights.

–You brought a nigger in here? Picket said.

Above their heads the tent canvas rattled in the wind, and the tobacco smoke shifted like a storm cloud. The crowd of drinkers formed a tight half-circle around them. The heavy gloves dangled in Joshua's hand. The faint trembling that had begun as he faced the mob in the boxing ring outside now shook his whole body. He was amazed at the sheer stupidity of his rage and how he could not stand down. The brightness of it. He glanced at the big handle of the bowie knife at the prospector's waist.

–You don't like it, drink elsewhere, Joshua said.

The prospector's eyes widened and his mouth dropped open. Strickland pushed himself up off the bar and turned his head as if to look out of his good right eye.

–I come in here under my steam, Strickland said.

But Picket ignored him.

–Who the hell are you to tell me drink elsewhere, little boy?

Everything about this confrontation now seemed suddenly absurd. So absurd that it paralyzed him and turned his tongue to wood. But then Mr. Ford pushed through the semicircle of onlookers.

–He works for me, Mr. Ford said.

He said it quietly. He still held the Remington down by his side. The carnation on his lapel was positively dead now. There was an angry menace about him as if he was at odds with the entire world, and Joshua was glad of it, for Picket stepped away with his arms spread away from his sides as though to show that he presented no threat.

–The boy ain't got no manners, Mr. Ford, Picket said. And I ain't never seen a nigger in a white man's bar before. I don't know that the Vigilance Committee would allow it.

–This is my bar, Mr. Ford said. And the boy knows who I let drink in it.

Picket opened his mouth as if to say something and then settled for silence. Joshua nodded to Picket, who stared hard back at him. He had made another sure enemy, along with Soapy Smith, Ed O'Kelley, and Mr. Frazee.

–Give this man a drink on the house, Mr. Ford said. We had enough fighting for today.

–I need a beer, Strickland said.

–Get a drink, Josh, Mr. Ford said.

The barman poured the drinks, and the prospector drifted toward the bandstand. The fiddler and the squeezebox player struck up a two-step. Joshua took a sip of his beer. It was yeasty and bitter in his mouth. He was not sure that he liked it. Warily, he eyed Picket over the rim of the mug, then one of the dance girls took Picket as a partner and whirled him around the floor. The barman set a tin bucket on the counter in front of Dick Liddil, and Joshua wanted to know how he would deal with Strickland's woes. Liddil reached in and wrung out a white rag. There was little to it. He pressed the rag to Strickland's open eye wound, and Strickland reached up to hold it in place. With a second rag, Liddil began to clean the gore from Strickland's cheeks while Strickland ignored his ministrations and lifted his own mug of beer. He downed it in one draft, the thick neck working to swallow, and he slammed the mug back onto the bar.

–It's time you retired, Strick, Liddil said.

–It was your goddamn idea I should fight in the first place, Strickland said.

Joshua turned to see where Ike Picket was, and suddenly a thin-faced girl was standing in front of his face. Joshua backed up against the bar and leaned away from her. Her brown hair was piled upon her head and a red satin flower had been woven into the tresses on one side. Her large dark eyes looked up at him, and then her thin-fingered hand rested on his shoulder. Visible at the open neck of her blouse, her collarbones were sparrow-like, frail, and the green satin of the blouse made scant swell at her bosom.

–Are you shy? she said.

–Shy? Joshua said.

–You want to dance? she said.

–Dance?

–Come on.

Mr. Ford nodded, and Joshua drifted with the girl in his arms, one hand in the curve of her thin back, and they were afloat on a semisolid sea of humanity, befogged by tobacco smoke, following the siren sound of fiddle and squeezebox toward which she guided him — despite his clod-like dance steps, his rhythmless sway, and his embarrassed delight — with her small right hand in his left, her left arm around his ribs, her perfume rising to his nostrils, the frailty of her in his arms belying her will that brought them through the crowds and past Ike Picket and his partner and once more through the crowd and back to the bar. Then the music stopped.

–You like that? she said.

Her deep eyes looked up into his once more. Her small mouth was open in a smile that showed her front teeth slightly overlapped by those on each side of them. He still had his arm around her tiny back. She was about his own age, he thought.

–I liked it, he said.

–You got fifty cents? she said.

–Yes, he said.

–Gimme fifty cents.

Joshua hunched his shoulders as he pulled back his frock coat and dug into his pocket. He had change. He had plenty of change. He even had a half-dollar piece. She took it from him and tucked it into a drawstring velvet purse that was a darker color green than her blouse.

–Do you want another? she said.

He wasn't sure that he could refuse even if he wanted to, and he was not sure that he did want to refuse even if she was hustling him and therefore making of him a mark for her con, which he had no wish to be, but he had enjoyed the feel of her close to his body, and the fact that she was hustling *him* and not some ugly drunk miner made him feel that he was somehow special to her, a chosen one, or at least someone she would prefer to be with more than anyone else and he knew that that was exactly how she planned he should think in order to have him pay her for that dance and maybe another dance until he tired of being hustled and she would move on to the next mark. Unless she should proposition him for something else, which he began to hope for, though he was too shy to ask outright.

–I'll pay for it, called Mr. Ford.

The duo struck up a waltz, and he tried to follow her long-one, short-two-three, long-one, short-two-three stepping, but he lost all coordination, and she stopped and started him again and they stagger-stepped all the way back to the bar, where Strickland was still being ministered to by Dick Liddil. Mr. Ford nodded his head in time to the waltz and he had a glass in one hand and the Remington still in the other, hanging down by his side as if he had forgotten to holster it. And Joshua didn't want to let go of the Sparrow. She eased herself out of his arms.

–Set 'em up, called Mr. Ford. You two have a drink with me.

The barman was short and jaunty in his movements. A dark curl of hair bobbed at his forehead. He winked at Joshua, grabbed two shot glasses off a white cloth behind the counter, flipped them into the air, caught them, and banged their thick bottoms onto the bar. He filled the glasses by pouring from two bottles simultaneously as if part of the same juggling trick. He made a show of rushing over to them, deposited the glasses in front of them, and swirled the glasses under his hand as if a sharper playing at Find the Lady. The dance girl downed her shot as if it was water — and it might have been — and before Joshua could say another word to her, she had drifted into the crowd and he leaned after her as if drawn by some magnetic current. At least, her hand fluttered at him over the shoulders of the crowd before she was gone behind the closing bodies.

–You like that one? Mr. Ford asked.

–She's pretty, Joshua said.

–Got her to come up from Jimtown.

–Is she . . . ?

–Yep. I'll introduce you closer tonight.

Joshua felt his face tingle and heat. Mr. Ford was the devil himself. He was a trafficker in souls. Did Mr. Ford own the girl's soul already that he could give her to Joshua whether she wanted to go with him or not? Joshua did not even know her name, nor she his. And she *would* go with him, he knew, and she wouldn't care if she knew his name or not. Joshua sipped at the burning whiskey, the tiny glass a barrier to hide behind for a second while he tried to collect his thoughts, which would not collect. Everything was moving so fast: the apple that he hadn't wanted to deliver, the fallen dun, the prizefight, near riot, the bowie knife beneath the torn buckskins, the girl's hand upon his shoulder, the flower in her hair, the scent of her, her frail body so close to him. He wanted her and he would take her if Mr. Ford offered her. Another kindness from Mr. Ford. Another willing act on Joshua's part. Joshua gulped down the whiskey. He grimaced as it burned down his throat and into his belly. He looked back over the crowd and he saw her near the entrance. She was holding Ed O'Kelley in the same way that she had been holding him. Mr. Ford hadn't noticed. The Sparrow was in Ed O'Kelley's vile claws and he couldn't stand to see it.

–Mr. Ford. Mr. Ford, Joshua said. She's with Ed O'Kelley.

Why was he telling Mr. Ford? Shouldn't he deal with it himself?

–That bother you?

Joshua nodded. It was a cowardly way to act, but it was too late now.

–You know what? Mr. Ford said. It bothers me, too.

Mr. Ford's lips pressed hard together. The pale eyes were cold and wide, and if his smooth face had a color, it was ashen. The slight frame of his body in his elegant suit was all violence, like a taut violin string vibrating in a high wind, as if the entire day's tension that he had kept under control was now about to find its release. He launched himself into the crowd, and the Remington was at the height of his hat brim. Joshua followed behind him as if in the grip of a whirlwind, and the drinkers fell back away from them and Mr. Ford was in front of O'Kelley, who had the Sparrow gripped by her thin wrists now, and he held her as a shield between himself and Mr. Ford. Her head was twisted back over her right shoulder, and her dark eyes were wide with fear. The musicians abruptly stopped. Mr. Ford was between Joshua and the Sparrow and Joshua was acutely aware of being weaponless and without the wherewithal of the scores of gouges and head butts and glass slashings with which O'Kelley was doubtless familiar.

–Take your hands off her, Kelley, Mr. Ford said. And get out of my bar.

She tried to disentangle herself from O'Kelley's clutch, but he held her tight. His face was mottled and leery.

–She asked me to dance, O'Kelley said. I aim to dance.

The Sparrow was still between Mr. Ford and O'Kelley and Joshua was terrorized by the idea that she might be hurt or marred in a fight. Ike Picket pushed through the crowd to get a better look at the action, and he shook his head at Joshua, an expression of contempt. Then Mr. Ford's gun arm came back and the pistol swung in a great arc over the girl's head and the butt of the gun caught O'Kelley high up on the side of his derby so that it softened the blow but the hat tumbled from his head. The Sparrow screamed. O'Kelley still held her as he staggered to his right in front of the tent entrance and she lost her footing and the small weight of her dragged his arms down away from his body. Mr. Ford's arm swung up backhand and the butt of the gun caught O'Kelley in the throat. He squawked. The Sparrow fell to the floor as O'Kelley lost his grip on her, and he tottered backward but still kept his feet. Mr. Ford nailed him with a straight left, and blood gouted from O'Kelley's nose and over the brushy mustache. But he still stood. His hand moved toward his gun. Then stopped.

–I'll leave, Ford, O'Kelley said. But no one wants you in this town. And I'll be happy to help them get rid of you.

Mr. Ford holstered the Remington.

–Try now, O'Kelley.

The disheveled drunk shook his head. The Sparrow lay on the floor between O'Kelley and Mr. Ford. She was curled up, one arm over her face, and Joshua wanted to go to her and help her up, but that might distract Mr. Ford and give O'Kelley a chance to reach for his gun in that moment. And Joshua was ashamed of his lack of courage. With his grimy hand, O'Kelley wiped away the blood from his mustache and it smeared over his cheek.

–Not now, he said. I'll come back when I'm sober.

–I'll be here, Mr. Ford said.

O'Kelley backed out of the tent saloon, and as he stood beyond the threshold, framed by the triangular entrance, the last rays of the descending sun caught him slantwise and his face and hair were lit up red and garish, as if he was by Hell itself aspersed.

LX

THE SPARROW — HE STILL DID NOT KNOW HER NAME AND FELT shy to ask her — held on to Joshua's arm, and she guided him out of the tent saloon and down the steps of the platform and up the grassy slope to Mr. Ford's cabin with just as much will and skill as she had shown in whirling him around the dance floor. The sky had deepened above the canyon, and the thunderheads that had gathered above the canyon's rim began to drift in a mass and tumble forward toward Campbell Mountain but with no sign yet of unleashing lightning or lashing rain, though Joshua could see that it was coming. He held himself with his shoulders wide and his chin high as if he was used to accompanying a sporting woman to her crib. There was nothing to it. He had read all about it in *My Secret Life*. And she was about his own age. No old woman like Mrs. Ford or Ella, past their prime. Maybe the Sparrow was just starting out much as he was, new to the sporting game, a career — sporting that is — that seemed nebulous in definition but included for men, gambling, boxing, horse racing, the fixing of the results of such events, and the sale and imbibing of liquor; and for women, the sale of dances and gambling and what the Sparrow was about to do now, with him, Joshua Beynon. And he felt easy about it, and it wasn't just the relaxation he felt from the whiskey, but this was a moment he had been waiting for since . . . He couldn't remember the first time he thought about it, but it was around three years previously that he had begun to become acutely aware of such a thing as what he was about to do now, when his body began to sprout little spirals of hair and his peter demanded more attention.

Carys the coon hound lay at the threshold of the cabin with her head between her paws. She looked up and sniffed as the Sparrow lifted the latch on the cabin door, stepped around her, and drew Joshua inside.

Ella stood next to the long table. She was buttoning up a maroon double-breasted overcoat. Her eyes darted from Joshua to the well-stuffed carpet bag that was on the table, and her wide mouth opened as if in shock. As if she had been caught in a shameful act.

A theft perhaps. Her red hair was pulled back in a chignon, and she quickly covered it with her bonnet and began to tie the ribbon under her chin.

–Where are *you* going? the Sparrow said.

Ella's white hands fluttered away from the bow at her chin and settled on the handle of the carpetbag. The hard-angled face now looked prim and old and wasted.

–I have to go away from here, she said. For a few days.

Why is she being so furtive? Joshua thought.

–Denver? the Sparrow asked.

–With Chang Jen Wa, Ella said.

–The Chinaman?

–To San Francisco.

–*San Francisco!* the Sparrow exclaimed.

–He's taking me with him, Ella said. Chang Jen Wa.

–With a goddamn Chinaman? the Sparrow said.

That's a few months at least, Joshua thought. San Francisco. She's leaving for good. She's leaving Mr. Ford.

And Joshua somehow felt betrayed himself. As if he should run and warn Mr. Ford. Was it his job to warn Mr. Ford? Ella *must* have told him. He *must* know. She wouldn't leave without telling him.

–What are you two doing here? Ella asked. You got work to do?

She had a hard edge to her voice, now. As if she had remembered herself, who and what she was, and her eyes had turned predatory and the Sparrow clutched Joshua's arm and leaned against him. He could feel the fear in her as if her touch transmitted it through his bones. She was the new girl. Ella could make her suffer if she had a mind. Even if the girl told Mr. Ford. Made Ella stay. And Joshua feared Ella, too. And he feared Mr. Ford. He knew that. Mr. Ford must know that Ella was going. He shouldn't meddle in their business.

The Sparrow looked up at him.

–Let's go into this room, she said. I'll make you feel good.

Ella nodded.

–You paying? she asked him.

Joshua blushed.

–Mr. Ford said to . . .

–He sent me up here, the Sparrow said. With him.

–Show him a good time, Ella said.

–Crib's in here, the Sparrow said.

She guided him past Ella and opened the door of the room next to the one in which he had smoked opium. He glanced back at Ella but she was on her way to the front door and she did not look back at them. He followed the Sparrow into the crib room and closed the door behind them.

Whatever confidence or bravado he had mustered on their short walk from tent saloon to cabin had evaporated. The room that he was in horrified him. Four tarpaulins, two to the right, two to the left, hung like rough curtains from ropes strung across the room from each side of the doorjambs to above the window casings opposite. The remaining daylight that entered through the window seemed to be swallowed up by the short and shadowy canvas corridor.

–Ain't our business, the Sparrow said. We never seen her, you hear?

Joshua nodded.

She lifted the nearer of the right-hand tarpaulins.

–My crib's in here, she said.

A narrow cot and a bedside table made up the furnishing of the canvas chamber. Upon the table were a ewer and a china bowl and a bottle of Prescott's Malt Vinegar. A scuffed and rusted tin trunk lay under the bed. At the foot of the bed hung another tarpaulin, so he judged that the one large room of the cabin had been divided into four cribs. He breathed deeper to calm himself down.

My Secret Life, he thought. *My Secret Life*.

Half or more of the miners in Weaver had done what he was about to do and he knew that his da had done it too. So why shouldn't he — Joshua? But he didn't want to think about his da right now or Ella or Mr. Ford and the Sparrow helped him away from his thoughts by unbuttoning her green satin blouse. She stood before him in her bodice and picked at the white lace tie. When she opened it, the breasts beneath were but scant folds of flesh with the nipple on each one about the size and color of a filbert. He reached out and touched one and she didn't stop him.

–Don't you want to undress? she said.

He took off his round-brimmed hat and laid it beneath the bedside table. He saw nowhere that he might hang his frock coat but he slid out of it and the Sparrow took it from his hands and draped it over the end of her cot. He could not take his eyes away from her bare breasts. She unhitched her skirt and stepped out of it and she was less Sparrow and more frail angel in her white bloomers and her open white bodice and her white skin. Joshua was all buttons and buckles and fumbling fingertips and falling clothes and elbows flapping against the canvas wall. She wriggled out of her bloomers and knelt on the straw-mattressed cot. Her thighs were pressed together so he couldn't see what was between them. Then he sat on the quilt next to her to pull off his knee-high boots and the sight and scent of her made him flush, made him hard. He stood up to step out of his trousers. His prick sprang up when he pulled his long underpants down to his thigh. And then his underwear was down and off. He did not know if he should take off his glasses. The Sparrow pulled back the quilt and there was a red sheet beneath, which he was glad to see was clean. He would leave the glasses on.

–Oh, you're so handsome, she said.

He hoped that would be the last lie that she said, for heaping falsehood upon falsehood unnerved him. He wanted no pretense. He needed no lies for encouragement. He desired her as she was. The dark eyes and the overlapped teeth, the half-mocking smile. He lay down next to her and a thin smooth arm slid around his ribs.

–You can touch me, she said.

The red satin flower in her hair was crushed against the pillow. He slid his palm across the pillow, cradled her head, and brought it forward. He liked the weight of it. Like a full cup. With his other hand he cautiously explored the indentations of her ribs and then the fold of her small breast. Her hand came up and she laid her fingers upon his lips, his chin.

–I like you, she said.

And he knew that that was not a lie, and it pleased him so that he smiled beneath her fingertips. Her right hand ran down over the bumps in his spine and over one smooth dome of his behind. He quivered. Her one hand was still on his chin, and the other came around his ribs and onto his chest and she squeezed his nipple. He rolled over on top of her and her legs opened to let him between.

–You're so beautiful, he said.

And he meant it, and he was afraid that she would lie right back at him.

–Do you want to go in there? she said.

He was aching to go in there. He pushed his hips forward — his pretense at experience — and the head of his prick bumped against maybe bone. He reached down and tried to guide it where he thought it ought to go but it rubbed against her scratchy curls and folded flesh and he couldn't see down there even with his glasses on but then there was a slippery feel and he blushed and her eyes were on his face — her lips in a half-smile — and oh that place was hot and he sank all down the whole hot length of it and he was joined to her and pressed right up to the bone, yes, the bone.

She rolled his body over to one side of the narrow cot and he became aware again of the tarpaulin walls. He wanted to do it again but she slid from the bed and poured water from the ewer into the bowl and added vinegar to it from the Prescott's bottle. She took a cloth from the bedside table and washed herself between. Then she stepped into her bloomers. Joshua felt a tenderness toward her and a desire to hold her in his arms and have her hold him and talk to him and tell him about her life as he would tell her his. But she pulled on her bodice and began to lace it up.

–Won't you come back in the cot with me? he said. Just for a minute.

–I have to get back to the tent, she said. Mr. Ford told me not to be too long.

Mr. Ford gave and Mr. Ford took away. He controlled the Sparrow and he controlled Joshua but he did not control Ella any more. She had slipped out of Mr. Ford's grip. A desertion from the clan. Joshua should tell him before it was too late and Mr. Ford would bring Ella back. Maybe give her a beating. The hell he would tell him. Goddamn Mr. Ford and all his unholy family. He could find out for himself in the morning.

LXI

THE AIR BENEATH THE CANVAS ROOF STANK OF STALE BEER AND tobacco, and the floor of the tent saloon was littered with crushed butts like flattened tarry spiders. Joshua sat on the low podium on which the musicians had played the night before. His elbows were balanced on his folded knees and his face cupped upon palms and long fingers. The far end of the mahogany bar was piled with empty shot glasses and rancid beer glasses and a few spent clear glass bottles. No one was behind the bar to clear them away or wash them. No one was in front of the bar to demand a drink. No one was even present to guard the cases of liquor and the barrels of beer and no one was there to pilfer it, either. Joshua had come just after dawn from the Silver Dollar Hotel to look for the Sparrow, but he knew that she would be asleep in her crib, for she had worked her trade deep into the night while there were yet revelers to drink and not yet drunk enough to pass out or to give up waiting their turn with her. Did all the men who had been with her feel as he did? He doubted it.

The tent roof rattled in the wind and the front flap lifted. Ike Picket, dressed in the same rancid buckskins he had worn the night before and armed with the same long-bladed bowie knife, stood within the threshold of the door. As if pulled by strings, Joshua was on his feet to face him. Weaponless. Ike Picket's scarred and hard-angled face creased with what passed for a smile. He tapped a long piece of white paper or an envelope against the palm of his left hand.

–Just you and me now, boy, Picket said.

Like frost on a glass pane, an unpleasant chill spread along the paths of Joshua's nerves. He clenched his teeth against it to stop it making him shake. His hand came up to push his glasses tight to the bridge of his nose.

–Are you looking for Mr. Ford? Joshua said.

It was a cowardly thing to say.

–Mr. Ford? Picket said.

–He's at the house. Asleep, I would think.

Picket nodded.

–I got a letter for him, Picket said. From the Vigilance Committee. You can give it to him.

He *had* come for Mr. Ford.

Joshua's legs swung as if made of badly jointed wood. Picket's pale eyes did not move from Joshua's face as he approached him. Joshua held out his hand palm up for the letter, and Picket dropped the hand with the letter and swung it up, backhand. The blow exploded against Joshua's cheekbone and his head snapped back and the tent roof and the bar and the floor spun around each other. His arms flung out and his feet twisted around each other and he staggered away from Picket and hunkered into a crouch. His cheek throbbed. It was not an entirely unpleasant sensation. He pressed his fingers against it.

–Next time you tell me to drink elsewhere, little boy, you better be able to back it up with something. Now come and get the letter.

Joshua tensed his arms and approached Picket again. But this time Picket held the letter at arm's length and Joshua reached out to take it from him. Picket turned and was gone through the flap of the tent. Joshua followed him outside. At the bottom of the steps stood Soapy Smith and Ed O'Kelley and Wayne Stacker, the owner of the dun quarter horse. They stared beyond Picket toward Joshua. When Picket reached them, all four men turned and went down the canyon toward town.

The envelope in Joshua's hand fair made his fingers itch. Mr. Ford's name had been stamped there, but the top of the *M* and the *R* and the *F* were faded, as if the typewriter had had a worn ribbon.

Joshua ran up the slope to Mr. Ford's cabin. Dick Liddil's thoroughbred and Strickland's broad-backed sorrel quarter horse were tied to a sawhorse close by the door. Both mounts were saddled and fresh as if they had just come from the livery. They tossed their heads as Joshua banged on the door with the meat of his fist.

–Come on in, called a gravelly voice.

Joshua snapped up the latch. Carys raise her head from between her paws when she saw him but made no move to rise from the mat outside the crib room behind whose door the Sparrow was probably still asleep.

Strickland was seated next to the cold stove. His face was still swollen from the beating that Mickey James had meted out to him the day before. The big fighter was fully dressed in his overalls and plaid shirt and even hatted with a passable brown homburg perched on top of his white wool. But his head was bent to his chest. He had a woolen jacket draped around his shoulders. Between his boots was a canvas carryall. Mr. Ford paced the rag carpet in front of him.

Joshua held up the letter, but Mr. Ford ignored him. Mr. Ford had an unlit cigarette between fingers and thumb and he rattled a box of lucifers in the other hand. His face was pasty and drawn as if he had not slept all night, and his shirt and suit had a seedy and unpressed look about them.

–You cutting out on me, you son of a bitch, Mr. Ford said.

Dick Liddil was at the larder cupboard. He laid a strip of jerky onto the pile he had made upon the sideboard. He folded a piece of muslin round the dried meat and tucked the long pack into one of his leather saddlebags that was open on the floor in front of him. He, too, had his hat and heavy jacket on. The light caught the blond stubble between his mustache and his sideburns.

–We come here to run a race and stage a fight, Liddil said. We done it. It's over. We're gone. I ain't come here to work no bar, you know that.

–And you ain't seen Ella? Mr. Ford said.

Joshua looked down at the envelope. He hadn't told Mr. Ford where Ella had gone. She might already be on the way to San Francisco.

–No, I ain't, Liddil said.

–She ain't come back last night, Mr. Ford said.

–She prob'ly at the Chinaman's, smoking opium, Strickland said.

–Mr. Ford, Joshua said.

–You got plans to leave town, boy? Mr. Ford said. Like every other son of a bitch?

Joshua shook his head, lowered the envelope. He had never thought of that. Leave town? Could he? With Dick Liddil? With the Sparrow? He would happily get away from this place where his father had died. To get away from con artists and crooked lawmen. If there was such a place in the world. Maybe San Francisco. Where Ella was going with Chang Jen Wa. What would it take to leave? Pack his bags, buy a horse. But he had no plan.

–No, sir, I haven't, Joshua said.

–Dick and Strickland are cutting out on me.

Joshua looked across at Liddil, who fastened the flaps of his saddlebags and slung them over his shoulder.

–Why don't you cut out with us, Bob? Liddil said. Ain't no one in this town wants you around.

–Cut out? I just built a goddamn saloon.

–It's a goddamn tent, Liddil said. And you got four Jimtown, two-dollar whores to work your cribs. That ain't big money, Bob.

–I ain't cutting out.

–Come and work the Kansas racetracks for the summer. We'll do fine. Bring the boy along.

Liddil waved his hand at Joshua and Joshua beamed. He would leave in a second. He hoped Mr. Ford would say yes. At least they would be out of Weaver. Away from the graveyard and the memory of his dead family and the trial he had gone through. Joshua held the envelope down by the side of his leg. He should ask him.

–What about it, Mr. Ford? Joshua said.

Mr. Ford's lips pressed together and his pale eyes hardened. Anger behind them.

–I ain't going and you ain't going, Mr. Ford said.

Mr. Ford treated him as if he owned him, and Joshua blushed. Somehow Joshua was allowing this to happen to him just like the Sparrow allowed everything to happen to her.

–Suit yourselves, Liddil said.

–What you got there, boy? Strickland growled.

Strickland pointed at the envelope. Joshua held it up again.

–It's for Mr. Ford, Joshua said. From the Vigilance Committee.

Mr. Ford pocketed the dry cigarette and the lucifers.

–Shit. Now what?

Mr. Ford looked tired. He beckoned with two fingers, palm up. There was no respect in that gesture. Joshua gave up the envelope.

–Who give you this?

–Ike Picket.

–Just Ike?

–Soapy was with him and Ed O'Kelley. And Wayne Stacker.

Dick Liddil shook his head.

–There, you see? he said.

–See what? said Mr. Ford.

He tore up the flap of the envelope.

–What's it say? Liddil said.

–It says that the Vigilance Committee wants to meet me on the morning of June eighth. In the tent saloon.

–It say why?

–Nope.

–There you go, Liddil said.

–There you go what? Mr. Ford said.

–Just leave town with us. Then they can't run you out.

It was a logical enough argument, and Joshua was certain that Mr. Ford ought to acknowledge that. Without Strickland and Liddil, Mr. Ford had no one to back him up in front of Soapy Smith and his gang. They evened the odds.

–I ain't leavin'.

–Son of a bitch! Liddil said. Come on. They'll forget about you in two months, then you can open up the saloon again. They might throw you out for good this time, and then you got nothing. Or they might look for a way to jail you.

And me, Joshua thought.

–For what?

–For what? Liddil said. For the goddamn race we rigged.

–You're cutting out.

–Just let this all blow over. Two months. They'll forget all about it.

–I ain't leavin'.

–Shit, said Liddil.

Liddil turned to Strickland.

–Come on, Strick.

Strickland stood up and lifted his canvas carryall.

–That letter's trouble, Strickland said.

–I got the boy here, Mr. Ford said. The boy'll stay with me. He's going to be my partner. Invest in the saloon.

A pit opened in Joshua's stomach. Mr. Ford was calling in his debt. Joshua wanted to go. He wanted Mr. Ford to go. Weaver was not a good place to do business in. Liddil shook his head and pushed past Mr. Ford. Strickland followed Liddil to the door.

–I hate to leave this way, Bob, Liddil said. I didn't know about no letter.

–Then stay.

–I ain't staying.

–And I ain't leaving.

They shook hands then, and Liddil opened the door and Strickland shook hands with Mr. Ford. Joshua followed them all outside to where the horses were tied.

–Fine day for travel, Liddil said.

Mr. Ford stayed silent, but what Dick Liddil said was true, for a light breeze blew down off Campbell Mountain and tempered the heat of the early June sun that lit up the town of Weaver and all the canyon below. Dick Liddil flung his saddlebags over the thoroughbred's rump and untied the horse. He grabbed the pommel of his saddle, leather creaked, and he swung up onto the horse.

–Come here, boy, Strickland said.

Strick's big black hand crushed Joshua's in its grip, the dark head nodded a few times, and then he turned to the sorrel quarter horse. He tied the carryall to the cantle, then took his reins. Strickland grimaced as he lifted his foot into the stirrup and hauled himself aboard his mount.

–Hey, Joshua, Liddil said. Look out for this son of a bitch, he ain't got a lick of sense.

Joshua grinned at him and nodded.

Mr. Ford retrieved the cigarette from his pocket and lit it. Phosphorous and tobacco sullied the morning air.

–We'll be back in the fall, Bob, Liddil said.

Mr. Ford blew out smoke.

–No you won't, he said.

–Mr. Bob, Strickland said. You'd best do what's wise.

–I'm staying here, Mr. Ford said.

Strickland shook his head.

–That ain't wise, Strickland said.

Liddil turned the thoroughbred and Strickland the sorrel, and they kicked the horses into a canter. Joshua shifted his weight from foot to foot and fidgeted with the lint in the side pocket of his frock coat. Watched in silence as the mounted forms of Liddil and Strickland got smaller on their way down toward the buildings and tents down the canyon, and when the riders passed the livery they disappeared from sight.

–Well, Joshua, Mr. Ford said. We should discuss this partnership money.

He turned then and went back inside. Joshua pulled off his round-brimmed hat and followed Mr. Ford into the cabin. Mr. Ford sat at the table. His complexion looked as gray as his rumpled suit. His eyes had dulled. Joshua sat down opposite him. The time had come. They would make their partnership formal. He had nowhere else to go.

–I ain't going to take advantage, Mr. Ford said. I arranged to meet Counselor Pearl down in Jimtown on the ninth. You can get the money from the Cattleman's Bank and Mr. Pearl will have all the papers ready. We just got to deal with the Vigilance Committee the day before. I want you to be there with me.

Joshua nodded. If the Vigilance Committee ran Mr. Ford out of town, then maybe they could yet go to San Francisico.

–I'll be there. But I reckon we both should have left with Dick and Strick, Joshua said.

–I'm glad you're being straight with me, Josh. I need a partner who's straight.

Well then, he should have mentioned Ella, too, but it was far too late for that.

LXII

MR. FORD'S LONG PALE HANDS RESTED ON THE TABLE, ONE ON EACH side of the cartridge belt with its holstered Remington. The fingers were so clean. The cuffs of his white shirt were pristine and starched where they showed below his pressed gray jacket. He would be hard put to maintain his suave appearance now that Chang Jen Wa's laundry had closed and Chang Jen Wa was gone and his laundry workers were gone, along with his road crew, and Ella gone with them, too. Joshua thought him more upset by Ella's desertion than by Dick's and Strickland's. But at least this morning, June eighth, Mr. Ford was suave and clean-shaven, the narrow face calm despite the anticipation of his meeting with the Vigilance Committee.

–It's the horse race, isn't it? Joshua said.

–It's the horse race and the fight and the nigger drinking in my bar. It's Soapy Smith not wanting anyone cutting in on his turf. Anything the law can't prove or legislate against.

–You think they'll run you out again? Joshua said.

–Good chance.

–Where will you go?

–Close by. Jimtown again. After me and you sign the partnership agreement with Pearl, tomorrow, you can come up here and look after things with Dot.

Joshua nodded. If Mr. Ford was down in Jimtown, at least he couldn't keep Joshua at his immediate beck and call. But Joshua's future was tied to Weaver and to Mr. Ford and Counselor Pearl. Joshua's round-brimmed hat was on the table in front of him and he rotated it through his fingers. He had no wish to see Counselor Pearl again. Joshua remembered the cell. And the judge. And his father's funeral.

–Here, Mr. Ford said. This is for you.

He pushed the cartridge belt and the Remington across the table.

Joshua tilted his head, thought: It's his gun.

–What's wrong with you? Mr. Ford asked. Take it.

–You're giving me your gun?

–For you.

Joshua had not even reclaimed his Colt from Sheriff Gardner after the trial was over.

–I don't know, Joshua said. Not after what happened with Da.

–If you get thrown by a horse, Mr. Ford said, what do you do?

–But this is your gun, Joshua said.

–You don't want it? Mr. Ford said.

Joshua did want the gun and he didn't want it. Mr. Ford's gun. Joshua could own a gun that belonged to the Slayer of Jesse James. Maybe not the weapon itself that had done the deed. But a weapon of the doer. Joshua stood up and grabbed the belt by the buckle. It was heavy. Held a full load of shells in the bullet loops. It unwound from around the tooled leather holster. Mr. Ford nodded.

–Put it on, he said.

Joshua buckled the belt around his waist and felt the weight of it on his hips and — this frightened him — there was a joy in wearing it. He thought of his father beneath the ground, but the wrenching grief that inhabited his whole body had slackened its grip. That confused him.

–What about you? Joshua said. This is your gun.

–I got other guns, Mr. Ford said. But I can't go into that meeting armed. I got my saloon here. I got to reason with them. Show respect.

–But this is your gun.

–Well, that gun will be there, won't it? If I need it.

Joshua flushed. His body tremored ever so slightly.

–You think there'll be trouble?

–Nothing you can't take care of.

Why is he putting me here? Joshua thought.

–Oh no, Joshua said. I never . . .

–You just point it at a broad target and squeeze the trigger.

–I can't . . .

–There won't be no trouble. Mr. Ford grinned. The gun's yours.

Yes, the gun was his. He would take it. Joshua drew the gun and checked the chambers. It was loaded. Mr. Ford had made him a shootist. His bodyguard. Just point at a broad target and squeeze the trigger. Ike Picket would be there. Joshua could not hide behind Mr. Ford's jacket skirts any longer. If he was to be a partner to Mr. Ford, then he had to show Weaver and Soapy Smith that he was not afraid to face up to any trouble, would even welcome a chance to prove himself. He would have to prove himself sooner or later. But the Vigilance Committee were respectable townsfolk. There wouldn't be any trouble today.

–Let's go down, Mr. Ford said. They should be there by now.

He stood up. As if in a mirror, Joshua and Mr. Ford reached for their hats and settled them upon their heads. But it was Joshua who led the way to the door.

Carys yipped when he came out, and Joshua reached down to stroke her chops.

–Stay here, girl, he said.

Her breath was rancid as she panted and tongue-lolled. He pulled her long ear, made her sit, and then he started down the slope.

A fog lay on the upper slopes of the mountains. Not yet burned away by the morning sun. The damp air chilled him. His frock coat hung down over the gun. Bulged at his thigh. Not fifteen yards away was the tent saloon. And the Vigilance Committee. Joshua Beynon was the shootist. It embarrassed him. At his shoulder, the dapper Mr. Ford seemed so vulnerable without the cartridge belt and the Remington that he always wore when he was outside. Joshua led Mr. Ford up the tent platform's steps. He lifted the tent flap and they entered.

Ike Picket, Soapy Smith, Wayne Stacker, Jim Shaw, the livery owner, Ben Greene from the Realty Office, and Bob Starks from the mining supply store were all in a line with their backs against the bar. None of them was armed. Mrs. Ford and the Sparrow stood behind the bar. A full bottle of whiskey was set next to six shot glasses. All empty. All clean.

–Morning, Bob, said Ben Greene.

Greene might have been the only one among the Vigilance Committee who had not lost money on the betting scam. He was tall and well dressed, with a green satin vest and a black frock coat that fell to his knees. His dark beard was trimmed close to his jawline. The eyes were lively and sharp.

–Morning, Ben, Mr. Ford said.

Ike Picket and Wayne Stacker the wrangler stared at Joshua. Every man there must have noticed the bulge at his hip, the heavy buckle at his waist. He crossed to the end of the bar and leaned his elbows upon it so that the weapon was out of sight. He tried to catch the Sparrow's eye, but she was too intent on the Vigilance Committee.

–I been asked to present a complaint to you, Mr. Ford, Greene said.

Mr. Ford nodded.

–You see, Greene said, Mr. Stacker's dun quarter horse was poisoned in some way.

Joshua's face burned. Mr. Ford might have been the mind behind the deed, but it was Joshua who had fed the apple to the horse. He wished that Liddil and Strickland were standing next to him, but they would be halfway to Denver by now.

–Poisoned? Mr. Ford said.

–In the horse race, Greene said.

–By you, Soapy said.

And me, Joshua thought. And Soapy Smith has never been part of the Vigilance Committee.

But all the others were respectable citizens. Except Ike maybe. If Joshua and Mr. Ford were going to be arrested, it was Mort Gardner who would have done the arresting. All the Vigilance Committee could do was to run them out of town, and Joshua would even be glad of it.

–I was at the tent all day, Mr. Ford said.

Stacker jerked forward his hands as if to bring his cuffs beyond the frayed sleeves of his denim wrangler's jacket. His hands were as sunburned as his gaunt face. He pointed at Joshua.

–I seen your boy in the stall, Stacker said. Before the race.

Joshua's face flushed hotter.

–The boy was with Dick Liddil, Mr. Ford said.

–And Dick Liddil was your partner, Stacker said.

–And you made a lot of money on that horse race, Mr. Ford, Greene said.

–Stacker's horse lost. Ain't my fault.

–You poisoned my horse, Stacker said.

–That is slanderous, Mr. Stacker, Mr. Ford said.

Mr. Ford was without his gun. Joshua was his gun.

–It's the truth, Stacker said.

–The people of this town want justice, Greene said. The law can't give it, so they come to the Committee.

–What does that mean? Mr. Ford said.

–It means we have to come to some arrangement, Greene said.

–Arrangement?

The least they would want was that Mr. Ford should give back the money he had won on the wagers, but Dick Liddil and Strickland had already made off with their shares of the pot. If Mr. Ford agreed to pay them back, Joshua could see him insisting on using the money in the Cattleman's Bank. His money, ill-gotten or not, Joshua would rather that they were thrown out of town than have to pay back the wager money.

–People had enough of your scams, Ford, Soapy said.

Outside the tent, Carys started barking. Someone was coming.

–A lot of people lost a lot of money, Stacker said.

–We are here to protect the people of this town, Mr. Ford, Greene said.

Mr. Ford nodded sharply.

–And I'm one of them.

–Not for long you ain't, Soapy said.

A breeze passed over Joshua's hot cheek and he turned around and Ed O'Kelley came in through the tent flap. O'Kelley held a double-barreled breech-loading twelve-gauge across his body.

Beyond the canvas, Carys howled.

–Hey, Bob, O'Kelley called.

He swung up the twelve-gauge and sighted down it. Mr. Ford half-turned in the middle of the floor. Joshua's hand dropped to where the butt of the gun pushed out the skirt of his frock coat. He should draw. Aim at the broad target. And squeeze the trigger. Mr. Ford glanced across at Joshua. His mouth opened as if he would shout. Time moved so slow. Mr. Ford's empty hand dropped to where his gun ought to be. His gray eyes on Joshua. He trusted Joshua to pull the gun. Pull the gun. Joshua was not going to pull the gun. Mr. Ford shook his head and the shotgun roared and a fountain of blood sprayed sideways from Mr. Ford's neck and the two women screamed and Mr. Ford's arms lifted and wobbled in the air and again the shotgun roared and Mr. Ford's head twisted at a bizarre angle above his shoulders and he toppled hard to the floor. An enormous pool of blood silently spread around his shoulders and chest and the pocked and spattered face. Mr. Ford's head was attached to the neck by a few ligaments and ruined shreds of flesh. Blood pumping from the neck stump. Ridiculous. Hideous. Mrs. Ford was screaming behind Joshua. And no one held her back. She pushed by him and then she was kneeling over the body, wailing. Her blue dress soaked up the blood in which she knelt. Wisps of blond hair fallen down around her fat cheeks. Her hands fluttering up and down. Bloody.

O'Kelley bent over to look at Mr. Ford's body.

No, Joshua thought. They won't shoot me.

–Goddammit, O'Kelley! Greene yelled. Goddammit!

Greene, eyes wide in disbelief, stood over Mrs. Ford and the nearly decapitated body.

–You killed him! she screamed. You killed him!

Yes, Joshua thought. I killed him.

O'Kelley cradled the empty shotgun and walked toward Joshua at the bar. The Irishman's thick mustache curled up in a smile. The skin around the eyes crinkled. Bright eyes boring into Joshua's. Something in that gaze perversely paternal.

–Well, boy, O'Kelley said. Ain't that exactly what your daddy would of wanted?

LXIII

April 17, 1906

For thirteen years, I have haunted the morgues of newspapers and dug up every article that I could find on Jesse James and his Slayer, Robert Ford. I have tracked down their survivors. I have stood with guerrilla veterans over the grave of William Clarke Quantrill, where they gather every year, and I have recorded their reminiscences of Jesse James. I have spoken with Martha Bolton, Bob Ford's sister. And his surviving brother, Capline. My journey has taken me to Kansas City, Clay County, Jackson County, New York, Bonham, Texas, and has finally brought me to San Francisco.

Where are those others of Weaver whose lives crossed mine? Ed O'Kelley is dead. Shot by a lawman after his release from prison in 1905. Soapy Smith is dead. Shot by one Henry Reed in Skagway, Alaska, in 1898. Ella Mae Waterson is dead. Drowned on her own vomit after inhaling chloroform obtained from a trail dentist. She did not make it to San Francisco with Chang Jen Wa. Dot Ford went to work as a crib girl for Dave Sponsilier in Jimtown. I don't know what became of her. Chang Jen Wa is here in San Francisco: my benefactor, who introduced me to Ming Shu Yi, the master puppeteer.

When I finished the writing of the saga that began for me on May 13, 1892, I thought that my commitment to Robert Ford and his victim Jesse James would be over. What folly. These stories continue to obsess me. And Ming Shu Yi gave me a new way to present them. First he taught me how to prepare the wax plates for the hero sheng *and the heroine* dan, *the painted-faced* jing *and the* chou *clowns for* Havoc in Heaven *from* The Journey to the West *and for* The White Snake *and* The Double Dragon Mountain. *Then I cut the shapes of the puppets from cured horse skin. And when I had learned his art, I made my own shadow shows called* Jesse James in the Civil War *and* Jesse James the Master Outlaw *and* The Slayer of Jesse James, Robert Ford. *Ming Shu Yi helped me to put them on despite their break with tradition.*

And tonight, while Ming Shu Yi the ganjiao *works the wires of the Jesse James puppet, I will work those of Mr. Robert Ford, showing once more the tales of my obsession. Jesse James will rise upon the screen, balancing on the shadow chair, and as the horrified audience looks on, Mr. Ford will raise his pistol. The pigtailed patrons will yell out warnings and cries of despair, but Jesse James will not hear. The reed of Shu Yat Shi's* shawm *will squeal and Sun Wang Chun will furiously bow the strings of his* erhu. *Mr. Ford will pull the trigger. And I will hammer on my drum for the sound of the shot.*

ACKNOWLEDGMENTS

The title for *The Chivalry of Crime* comes from an editorial by John Newman Edwards that was published in the *Kansas City Times* on September 29th, 1872. The idea for the book was inspired by hearing the Pogues version of *The Ballad of Jesse James* recorded on *Rum, Sodomy and the Lash* and my wondering how "the dirty little coward who shot Mr. Howard" would tell the story. Stephen Koch was a solid source of advice and encouragement from the first one-paragraph outline of the novel. Thanks to the staff of Columbia University Library's Special Collections Department and the reference librarians for obtaining so much source material for me. *The Story of Cole Younger by Himself* was invaluable, especially for details of the Northfield raid, and John McCorkle's memoir of his service with Quantrill provided background for the Civil War years. Of the secondary sources, the most scholarly of biographies of Jesse James is *Jesse James Was His Name* by William Settle, University of Missouri Press. Carl Breihan's book *The Man Who Shot Jesse James* provided some material on Robert Ford but seems less reliable historically, especially when comparing quoted sources with the originals. Luc Sante's *Low Life* was a priceless source of information on nineteenth-century drug use, prostitution, and gambling.

Special thanks to Peter Carey for his generosity, warmth, honesty, and patience and to the Mellon Foundation for a grant which enabled me to work with him on *Jack Maggs* and to get his editorial notes on the early drafts of the book. Thanks to Peter Saidel, who did an enormous job of reading and line-editing various drafts. To Patricia O'Toole, Raul Correa, Jill Bossert, Mark Kurdizel, Clark and Lotti Sanders, and Pierre Crosby.

Thanks to Chogyal Namkhai Norbu and his advice: "Just write the story."

Thanks to Michael Pietsch for his eagle editorial eye. To Amanda Urban for all her care and attention. And to my wife, Paula, for her encouragement, patience, and love during the making of this book.